CW00666208

Quicksilver

Also by Callie Hart

Fae and Alchemy series
Quicksilver

Requiem

Crooked Sinners series
Riot House
Riot Rules
Riot Act

Raleigh Rebels
The Rebel of Raleigh High
Revenge at Raleigh High
Reckless at Raleigh High

Dirty Nasty Freaks series
Dirty
Nasty
Freaks

Roma Royals Duet
Roma King
Roma Queen

Chaos & Ruin series
Violent Things
Savage Things
Wicked Things

Rooke

Between Here and the Horizon

Calico

Vice

Blood and Roses series
Deviant
Fracture
Burn
Fallen
Twisted
Collateral

Dead Man's Ink series
Rebel
Rogue
Ransom

CALLIE HART

HODDERSCAPE

First published in Great Britain in 2024 by Hodderscape
An imprint of Hodder & Stoughton Limited
An Hachette UK company

1

Copyright © Callie Hart 2024

The right of Callie Hart to be identified as the Author of the Work has been asserted
by her in accordance with the Copyright, Designs and Patents Act 1988.

All rights reserved. No part of this publication may be reproduced, stored in a
retrieval system, or transmitted, in any form or by any means without the prior
written permission of the publisher, nor be otherwise circulated in any form of
binding or cover other than that in which it is published and without a
similar condition being imposed on the subsequent purchaser.

All characters in this publication are fictitious and any resemblance to real persons,
living or dead, is purely coincidental.

A CIP catalogue record for this title is available from the British Library

Hardback ISBN 978 1 399 74541 3
Trade Paperback ISBN 978 1 399 74542 0
ebook ISBN 978 1 399 74543 7

Typeset in Crimson Text

Printed and bound in Great Britain by Clays Ltd, Elcograf S.p.A.

Hodder & Stoughton policy is to use papers that are natural, renewable and
recyclable products and made from wood grown in sustainable forests.
The logging and manufacturing processes are expected to conform
to the environmental regulations of the country of origin.

Hodder & Stoughton Limited
Carmelite House
50 Victoria Embankment
London EC4Y 0DZ

The authorised representative in the EEA is Hachette Ireland, 8 Castlecourt Centre,
Castleknock Road, Castleknock, Dublin 15, D15 YF6A, Ireland

www.hodderscape.co.uk

For those who live their nightmares,
so that others may have their dreams.

N
W
E
S
AJUN SKY
THE MIDNIGHT EYE
WICKE
WOOD
THE WINTER PALACE
YVELIA
CAHLISH
TARRAN ROSS ISLAND
OMNAMERRIN
WESTERN
DOW
IRRIN
AMMONTRIETH
SANASROTH

THE BREACH

BALQUHIDDER
CLAN LANDS

GILARIA

THE SHALLOW MOUNTAINS

THE DARN

GILLETHRYE

BALLARD

INISHTAR

THE SHIELD

LÌSSIA

NEVER FORGET...
MONSTERS THRIVE
BEST IN THE
DARK.

COMMIT ALL YOU
READ HERE TO
MEMORY.

PREPARE FOR WAR!!

PRONUNCIATION GUIDE

PEOPLE

Saeris – Sair-iss

Rusarius — Roo-sar-ee-us

Omnamshacry — Om-nam-sha-cry

Iseabail — Ee-sha-bahl

Belikon —Bell-eh-con

Oshellith — Oh-shay-lith

Taladaius — Tal-ah-day-us

Daianthus — Day-an-thus

Lorreth — Lor-uth

Balquhidder Clan — Bal-kid-er (clan)

Te Léna —Tay Len-ah

Danya — Dan-yah

PLACES

Zilvaren — Zil-var-en
Yvelia — Ee-vel-ee-ah
Cahlish — Call-ish
Sanasroth — San-az-roth
Gilarian — Gil-ah-ree-en
Lìssian — Liss-ee-an
Ammontraieth — Ah-mon-tray-eth
Omnamerrin — Om-na-mer-in

Quicksilver

1

THE CLIMB

"Y'know, there's really no need for all this *violence*."

It was common knowledge in Zilvaren City that to lie to a guardian meant death. I knew this in a firsthand, painful way that most other Zilvarens did not. Almost a year ago to the day, I'd watched one of the queen's men clad in beaten golden armor gut my neighbor for lying about his age. And before that, and far worse, I'd stood silently in the street while my mother's throat had been split wide open, spilling jets of hot, peasant blood into the sunbaked sand.

As the handsome guardian's hand closed around my neck now, his beautifully engraved gauntlet reflecting the glare of the twin suns overhead like a golden mirror, it was a miracle I didn't crack open and yield my secrets like a piece of overripe fruit. His metal-tipped fingers gouged deeper into the hollow of my throat. "Name. Age. Ward. Spit it out. Low-tier citizens aren't permitted in the Hub," he snarled.

Like most cities, Zilvaren, the Great and Shining Banner of the North, was fashioned after the shape of a wheel. Around the city's outer limits, the different spokes—walls designed to keep people contained in their wards—towered fifty meters high above the shanty towns and overflowing sewers.

The guardian gave me an impatient shake. "Answer quick, girl, or I'll have you dispatched through the fifth gate of hell directly."

I groped loosely at his gauntlet, nowhere near strong enough to break his grip, and smirked, rolling my eyes up toward the bone-white sky. "How am I s'posed to tell you...anything if I...can't... fucking...breathe?"

The guardian's dark eyes simmered with rage. If anything, the pressure he applied to my windpipe intensified. "You have any idea how hot it is down in the palace cells during reckoning, thief? No water? No clean air? The reek of rotting corpses is enough to make the high executioner vomit. You'll be dead within three hours, mark my words."

The palace cells *were* a sobering thought. I'd been caught stealing once before and had been sent down there for a grand total of eight minutes. Eight minutes had been enough. During reckoning, when the suns, Balea and Min, were at their closest and the afternoon air shivered with heat, being trapped belowground in the festering sore that passed as a prison beneath the immortal queen's palace would not be fun. And besides, I was badly needed *above* ground. If I didn't make it back to the forge before dusk, the deal I'd spent hours brokering last night would fall through. No deal meant no water. No water meant the people I cared about would suffer.

Much as it irked me, I submitted. "Lissa Fossick. Twenty-four. *Single.*" I winked at him, and the bastard squeezed harder. Dark hair and blue eyes weren't common in the Silver City; he *would* remember me. The age I'd given him was real, as was my pathetic romantic status, but the name I'd provided wasn't. My *real* name? No way I was handing that over without a fight. This bastard would shit himself if he realized he had *the* Saeris Fane in his grasp.

"Ward?" the guardian demanded.

Gods alive. So insistent. He was about to wish he'd never asked. "The Third."

"The Thi—" The guardian shoved me down onto the blistering sand, and super-heated particles scorched the back of my throat as I accidentally breathed them in. I sucked my next breath in through the sleeve of my shirt, but filtering out the sand that way only did so much; a couple of grains always worked their way through the fabric. The guardian staggered back. "Residents of Third Ward are quarantined. Punishment for leaving the ward is...is..."

There *was* no punishment for leaving the Third; no one had ever done it before. Those unlucky enough to find themselves scraping out a living in the dirty back alleys and stinking side streets of my home usually died before they could even *think* about escape.

Standing over me, the guardian's anger shifted into something closer to fear. It was then that I noticed the small plague bag hanging from his belt and realized that he, like thousands of others in Zilvaren, was a Believer. With a panicked lurch, he raised his foot and brought the sole of his boot crashing down onto my side. Pain stole my breath as he brought up his boot to kick me again. This was far from my first beating. I could take a shit-kicking as well as the next downtrodden scammer, but I didn't have time to accommodate Madra's fanatical followers this afternoon. I had somewhere to be, and I was running out of time.

With a quick twist and a forward lunge, I grabbed the guardian just below his knee—one of the only places he was unprotected by his heavy golden armor. The tears came in quick and hot. Believable. I gave a solid performance, but then again, I'd had a lot of practice. "Please, Brother! Don't send me back there. I'll die if you do. My whole family has the rattles." I coughed for effect—a dry hack that sounded nothing like the wet, congested cough of the almost dead. But the guardian had probably never even seen someone with the rattles before. He stared down at the point where my hand closed around the material of his pants, mouth gaping open in horror.

A second later, the tip of his sword punctured my shirt, right between my breasts. A little weight on the hilt of his weapon and I'd be just another dead thief bleeding out on the streets of Zilvaren. I figured he'd do it—but then I watched as he processed the situation and realized what he'd have to do next if he killed me. The dead were left to rot in the streets of the other wards, but things were different in the tree-lined, leafy walkways of the Hub. Zilvaren's well-heeled elite might not have been able to keep the sands borne on the hot westerly winds out, but they wouldn't tolerate a diseased plague rat rudely decaying on one of *their* streets. If this guardian killed me, he'd have to dispose of my body right away. And from the look on his face, that hazardous task was one he didn't wish to undertake. See, if I was from the Third, then I was far more dangerous than any normal, run-of-the-mill everyday pickpocket. No, I was *contagious*.

The guardian ripped the gauntlet and glove from his hand—the hand he'd used to half-choke me—and dropped them to the sand. The burnished metal released a sustained hum as it hit the ground. It sang in my ears, and just like that, all of my plans went up in smoke. I'd been caught lifting a tiny scrap of twisted iron from a market stall. I'd weighed the odds and considered the risk worth it, knowing the small ingot would earn me a tidy profit. But this? So much precious metal, tossed to the ground like it meant nothing? This, I couldn't resist.

I moved with a speed the guardian wasn't expecting. In a lithe, explosive maneuver, I sprawled forward and grabbed the gauntlet, targeting the larger of the two pieces of metal. The glove was stunning, skillfully made by a true master. The tiny circlets of gold looped together to form a chainmail that was notoriously impenetrable by blade or magic. But the weight of the gauntlet, the solid amount of gold that comprised the piece of armor—it was unimaginable that I'd ever hold that amount of gold in my hands again.

"Stop!" The guardian lunged for me, but too late. I'd already snatched up the gauntlet. I'd already shoved it over my hand and jammed it onto my wrist. I was already sprinting toward the Hub wall as fast as my legs could carry me. "Stop that girl!" The guardian's bellow bounced around the cobbled courtyard, his command echoing loudly, but no one obeyed. The crowd that had gathered to watch the spectacle when he had first captured me had dispersed like frightened children the moment I'd uttered the word "Third."

A recruit underwent formidable training before being accepted into Queen Madra's guard. Those who were selected for the grueling eighteen-month program were repeatedly half-drowned and had the tar beaten out of them via every martial arts system recorded in the city's dusty libraries. By the time they graduated, they could tolerate unimaginable amounts of pain and had mastered their weapons to the point that they were unbeatable in a fight. They were machines. In the barracks, on the training floor, I wouldn't last four seconds against a fully trained guardian. Queen Madra's pride demanded that her guard be the best of the very best. But Madra's pride was a hungry thing and quite insatiable. Her men not only had to be the best. They had to *look* the best, and a guardian's armor was no light thing. Yes, on the training floor, the asshole who'd caught me stealing the iron would have bested me in short order. But we weren't on the training floor. We were out in the Hub, and it was reckoning, and this poor bastard was trussed up like a feast day turkey in all that ceremonial armor.

He couldn't run, weighed down with all of that metal.

He couldn't even *jog*.

He sure as hell couldn't fucking *climb*.

I took off toward the eastern wall, pumping my arms and legs as fast as my aching body would allow. Launching myself into the air, I hit the crumbling sandstone hard, the oxygen wheezing out of my lungs from the impact.

"Ow, ow, *ow*." It felt like Elroy had taken a mallet from the forge and swung it right into my solar plexus. I didn't dare think about the bruises I'd wake up to in the morning—provided I *did* actually wake up. There wasn't time. I jammed my fingers into a narrow gap between the hefty sandstone blocks, bared my teeth, and hauled myself up. My feet scrambled for purchase. Found it. But my right hand...

The gods-cursed gauntlet.

Such a *terrible* design.

The gold clanged, the resonance of the metal a siren's song as I slammed it against the wall, attempting to catch hold of something to help pull myself up. My fingers—deft, slim, made for picking locks, unlatching windows, tousling Hayden's thick hair—wouldn't be enough if I couldn't bend my wrist. And I couldn't.

Fuck.

If I wanted to live, there was nothing left for it. I'd have to drop the gauntlet. But that was a preposterous thought. The gauntlet weighed at least four pounds. Four *pounds* of metal. I couldn't just walk away from that. This gauntlet was more than a piece of stolen armor. It was my brother's education. Three years' worth of food. Tickets out of Zilvaren, south, to where the reckoning winds that buffeted the dry-boned hills were twenty degrees cooler than here in the Silver City. We'd have enough money left over to buy a small house if we wanted to. Nothing fancy. Just something weatherproof. Something I could leave to Hayden when, not *if*, the guardians finally caught up with me.

No, dropping this gauntlet would cost me something far more valuable than my life; it would cost me hope, and I wouldn't surrender that. I'd rip my arm out of its socket first.

So, I went to work.

"Don't be ridiculous, girl!" the guardian hollered. "You'll fall before you even make it halfway!"

If the guardian went back to the barracks without his gauntlet, there would be consequences. I had no idea what those consequences would be, but they wouldn't be pretty. They could cut off the asshole's hands and bury him up to his neck in the sand to bake in the reckoning's heat for all I cared. I was going home.

Pain sang from my fingertips, up my arm like a rope of fire, blazing in my shoulder as I pulled myself up, kicking with my feet, leaping up the wall. I aimed for a section of the stone that looked worn but stable. Or as stable as I could hope for. If you gave it enough time, the wind ate everything in this city, and it had been grinding its teeth against Zilvaren for thousands of years. The sandstone was deceptive. The city's structures and walls looked sound but were far from it. One hard kick had been known to bring down an entire building in the past. It wasn't as if I was overly heavy, but that was neither here nor there. I was risking life and limb by slamming myself into the brickwork.

My stomach bottomed out as I sailed through the air...and then clenched tight as a fist when I impacted with the wall. Adrenaline soaked my blood as three miracles happened in concert.

First: The wall held.

Second: I grabbed a stellar handhold with my left hand.

Third: My shoulder *didn't* come out of its socket.

Footing. Footing. Foot—

FUCK!

My heart wedged itself in my throat as the sole of my left boot slipped against the wall, setting my whole body swinging.

Below me, a genteel, feminine gasp parted the silence. Guess I *did* have some spectators after all.

I didn't look down.

It took a moment to still myself and a handful of strained curses before I felt confident enough to breathe again.

"Girl! You're going to kill yourself!" the guardian shouted.

"Maybe. But what if I don't?" I shouted back.

"Then you'll have wasted your time anyway! There isn't a fence in this entire city stupid enough to buy a stolen piece of armor."

"Ah, c'mon now. I think *I* might know a couple!"

I didn't. No matter how tight things were, no matter how many families starved and died, not one resident of Zilvaren would dare to deal in something as dangerous as the gauntlet I had wedged onto my forearm. But that didn't matter. I wasn't going to try and sell it.

"I won't pursue you any further. You have my word. Drop the gauntlet, and I'll let you go!"

A bark of laughter ripped out of me. And they said guardians had no sense of humor. This one was a fucking comedian.

Another jump. Another staggering jolt of pain. I calculated the trajectory as best I could, making sure to aim for the least pitted section of rock each time. At last high enough above the streets of the Hub, I allowed myself the luxury of a moment to collect myself. If I moved the armor to the other wrist, would I drop it? More importantly, would I be able to hold on to the wall with my weaker arm while I performed a swap? There were too many variables to calculate and not enough time to do so in.

"How do you think you're getting down the other side, child?"

Child? Hah! The gall of the bastard. His shouting was quieter now. I was fifty feet up—close enough to see the top of the wall. Far enough from the street for a bristle of cold sweat to break out across the back of my neck when I looked down.

The guardian raised a good point. Descending from the wall would be just as perilous as the ascent, but the Undying Queen's whipping boy down there had been born into a good home. He grew up in the Hub. His parents didn't lock their door at night. That man had never even *considered* trying to climb the walls that protected him from the ungrateful, infectious rabble on the other side of it. I'd spent half my life running the tops of these walls, slipping from one ward to the next, finding ways into places I had no business being.

I was good at it.

Moreover, it was *fun*.

I completed the rest of the climb in under two minutes. The gauntlet slammed into the tiny dune of sand shored up along the top of the wall. As I heaved myself over the ledge, particles of quartz in the sand began to vibrate, jittering in the air a millimeter above the sandstone as the gold came alive.

I froze, the breath trapped in my lungs, caught off guard by the peculiarity of the sight.

No. Not here. Not now…

The gauntlet whispered, rocking rapidly as I brought myself up to straddle the wall. The particles of quartz rose up, up, up.

She sees us.

She feels us.

She sees us.

She feels us.

She—

I slammed my hand down on top of the gauntlet, and the piece of stolen armor stilled. The glinting specks of quartz fell back into the sand.

"I'll find you, girl! I swear it! Drop that gauntlet or make an enemy for life!"

At last, there it was—a tinge of panic riding the guardian's plea. The truth of the situation had caught up with him. I wasn't going to fall to my death. Neither was I going to accidentally drop the armor he threw to the ground in disgust once he'd realized he'd touched a plague rat.

I'd slipped through his bare fingers, and there was nothing he could do about it beyond shouting threats up at a ghost in the sky. Because I was already gone. The idiot below wouldn't be the first enemy I'd made out of one of Madra's men, but I wouldn't be giving him another thought. I was far more concerned with all of the incredible things I was going to forge with his impressive gauntlet.

But first, I was going to melt the glorious thing down to slag.

GLASSMAKER

"No. Absolutely not. Not here. Not in my furnace."

Elroy glared at me like I was a four-headed serpent, and he didn't know which one of my heads would strike him first. I'd upset the old man a million different times, a million different ways, but this disapproving look was new. His expression was one of equal parts disappointment and fear, and for the briefest of moments, I questioned my decision to bring the gold into the workshop.

Where else would I have taken it, though? The loft over the tavern where Hayden and I had been sleeping these past six weeks was infested with cockroaches and stank worse than a sand badger set. We'd found a way into The Mirage through a damaged section in the cracked slate roof. We were quiet when we crept in there to sleep amongst the rotten, long-forgotten wine crates and moth-eaten stacks of heavy, folded canvas, and so far, we hadn't been discovered. But my brother and I weren't stupid. It was only a matter of time before we *were* found out, and the proprietors of the public house evicted us from their attic space at the end of a blade. There'd be no time to collect our belongings. We didn't *have* any belongings aside from the clothes on our backs. Hiding the gauntlet there would be folly. Elroy's workshop was the only place I could take it. No matter what, I needed to use the furnaces. I didn't have a choice. If I didn't melt down the metal and make something else out of it (*very* gods-cursed quickly), the gauntlet was a millstone around my neck that would wind up getting me tortured and killed.

"It's bad enough that I had to tell Jarris Wade that you weren't here an hour ago. He was furious. Said you'd broken some trade agreement with him. But then you show up here with *that* thing. What the hell were you thinking?" The despair lacing Elroy's voice made me regret showing it to him. "Why did you take it in the first place? We'll have Madra's vipers scouring this place with a fine-toothed comb, searching for it. When they find you, they'll flay the skin from your bones in the square for everybody to see. Hayden will be right there next to you. And me? *Me?* Even if they *do* believe I had nothing to do with this, they'll take my hands for even allowing that thing under my roof. How am I supposed to make a living with no hands, you stupid, *stupid* girl?"

Elroy's business was glass. With an abundance of sand at his fingertips, he'd made it his life's work to become the best glassmaker and glazier in all of Zilvaren. Only those living in the Hub were rich enough to afford windows, though. And there were people who lived in the Third who sought other items that could be forged in a hearth. Once upon a time, Elroy used to make illicit weapons for the rebel gangs who fought to overthrow Madra. Rough-edged swords made from scraps of iron, but mostly knives. The blades were shorter and required less steel. Even though the pig iron was of the worst quality, it could still be honed into an edge sharp enough to send a man to the makers. But as the years had passed, life as an insurgent within had grown untenable.

Fresh food was impossible to find. In the streets, children clawed each other's eyes out over a heel of stale bread. The only way to survive the Third now was by barter and trade...or by whispering secrets about your neighbors into a guardian's ear. As a resident of the Third, if you weren't dead or dying, then you were hungry, and there wasn't much a starving person wouldn't say to quell the ache of an empty belly. After too many close calls to count, Elroy had declared he wouldn't be hammering out any more of his vicious, needle-like knives and told me I wasn't welcome to forge them in his fires anymore, either. We were to be glassmakers and nothing more.

"I'm stunned. *Stunned.* I just…I can't even comprehend—" The old man shook his head in disbelief. "I can't even *begin* to fathom what you were thinking. Do you have any idea what kind of doom you've brought down on our heads?"

When I was little, Elroy had been a giant of a man. A legend amongst even the most dangerous criminals that ran the Third. Taller than most, broad, his back muscles straining beneath his sweat-stained shirt. He'd been a force of nature. A pillar of rock hewn out of a mountain. Immovable. Indestructible. It was only recently that I'd begun to understand that he was in love with my mother. After she was killed, little by little, piece by piece, I'd watched him wither away, becoming less of himself. Becoming a shadow. The man that stood before me now was barely recognizable.

His calloused hand shook as he pointed at the polished metal glittering like sin on the table between us. "You're taking it back is what you're gonna do, Saeris."

A huff of laughter escaped me. "The forgotten gods and all four fucking winds know that I'm *not*. Not after everything I went through to get it. I nearly broke my damned neck—"

"*I'll* break your neck if that thing isn't out of here in the next fifteen minutes."

"You think I'm just going to walk up to the sentry post and *hand it over—*"

"Don't be ridiculous. Gods, *why* do you have to be so ridiculous? Scale the wall again and toss it back into the Hub once the Twins dip. One of those inbred bastards will find it and return it to the guardians without a second thought. They won't even realize how much the damn thing's worth."

Gritting my teeth, I folded my arms over my chest, trying to ignore how prominent my ribs felt beneath the fabric of my shirt. My skin prickled with sweat. I was losing moisture I couldn't afford to part with. I'd left my water ration hidden inside a wall in the attic back at The Mirage—hadn't been able to risk someone trying to jump *me* for it while *I* was picking pockets—and the workshop was hellishly hot, as per usual.

I couldn't count how many times I'd passed out at the bellows here. I had no idea how Elroy survived it. For a moment, I gave the man the respect he deserved and considered his demand. And then I fantasized about what a cool breeze from the south might feel like, and the delirious weight of a full stomach, and how blissful a feather bed might be, and what a future for Hayden might look like, and my affection for the man who once loved my mother dwindled into insignificance. "I can't do what you're asking me to do."

"Saeris!"

"I can't. I just can't. You *know* we can't go on like this—"

"I know that struggling to scratch out a life here is better than bleeding out in the fucking sand! Is that what you want? To die in the street in front of Hayden? For your body to rot in the gutter like your mother's, stinking and picked over by the crows?"

"*YES!* Yes, of *course* that's what I want!" I brought my fist crashing down on the table, and the gauntlet jumped, a cascade of rainbows leaping up the walls. "Yes, I want to die and ruin Hayden's life. *Your* life. I want to be made a spectacle of. I want everyone in the ward to know me as the glassmaker's apprentice who was stupid enough to steal from Madra's guard and got herself killed for it. That's *exactly* what I want!"

I'd never spoken to Elroy like this before. Ever. But the man had experienced loss after loss at the hands of the city's guardians. People he'd loved, dragged from their beds and executed without trial. His own brother had died just before I was born, starved to death during a particularly hard year because Madra wouldn't divert any food from the Hub to the other parts of the city. The richest of the queen's people had continued to throw lavish parties, had dined on exotic imports sourced from pastures well beyond Haeland, had drunk their fill of expensive rare wines and whiskeys, and all the while the people of Zilvaren had starved in the streets or shit themselves to death. Elroy had borne witness to all of this. Even now, he barely survived from week to week himself. If the guardians weren't pounding on his door, checking to make sure he wasn't making weapons, then they were kicking it down, hunting for mythical magic users who didn't even exist. And he allowed it all to happen. Just sat there and did nothing.

He'd given up. And there wasn't a single part of me that could accept that.

Elroy's heavy brows, shot through with gray, bunched together, his eyes darkening. He was about to launch into another one of his rants about staying out of the guardians' way, avoiding drawing attention to ourselves, about how cheating death here was a daily miracle that he thanked the makers for each night before he passed out in his shitty cot. But he saw the fire simmering inside me, ready to burn out of control, and for once, it gave him pause.

"You know I fought. I did, I fought the same way you want to fight now. I gave everything I had, sacrificed every last thing I held dear, but this city is a beast that feeds on misery, and pain, and death, and it's *never* full. We can throw ourselves down its throat until there's none of us left, and we won't have made the slightest lick of difference, Saeris. The people will suffer. The people will die. Madra's reigned over this city for a thousand years. She will live as she has ever lived, and the beast will still feed and demand more. The cycle will go on forever until the sand swallows this cursed place and there's nothing left of us but ghosts and dust. And then what?"

"And then there will have been the people who fought for something better and the people who lay down and took it," I spat.

Snatching up the gauntlet, I made to tear out of the workshop, but Elroy still had a little speed left in him yet. He grabbed my arm, holding me back long enough to look me in the eyes. Pleadingly, he said, "What if they track you down and realize what you can do? The way you can affect metal—"

"It's a parlor trick, Elroy. Nothing more. It doesn't *mean* anything." Even as I spoke, I knew I was lying. It did mean something. Sometimes, objects shook around me. Objects made of iron, tin, or gold. Once, I'd been able to move one of Elroy's daggers without touching it so that it had spun around and around on my mother's dining table, balancing on its cross guard. But so what? I met his exasperated gaze. "If they track me down, they'll kill me for a slew of other reasons before they kill me for that."

He huffed. "I'm not asking for you. I'm not asking for me, either. I'm asking for Hayden. He's not like us yet. The lad still laughs. I only want him to keep that innocence a little longer. And how's he gonna do that if he watches his sister hang?"

I tore my arm free, my jaw working, a thousand cold, hard insults clambering over one another, competing to be first out of my mouth. But my anger had fled me by the time I spoke. "He's twenty years old, El. He has to face reality at some point. And I *am* doing this for him. Everything I do is for him."

Elroy didn't try and stop me again.

There were ways in which Hayden and I were similar. His height, for instance. We were both tall, lanky creatures. We shared the same sense of humor and were both champions at holding a grudge. We both adored the briny, sour tang of the pickled minnows the skiff merchants occasionally returned from the coast with. But apart from our shared personality quirks and the fact that the two of us loomed over most people in a crowded room, there wasn't much about us that was alike. Where I was dark-haired, he was light. His hair was curly to the point of chaos, and there was so *much* of it. His eyes were a rich, liquid brown and bore a gentleness to them that my blue eyes did not. The cleft in his chin came courtesy of our dead father, his proud, straight nose from our dead mother. She used to call him her summer child. She'd never seen snow, but that's what *I* had been to her: her ice storm. Distant. Cold. Sharp.

It didn't take long to find Hayden. Trouble had a way of following him, and I was an expert at seeking it out, so it was no real surprise I almost tripped over him, sprawled out and bleeding into the sand in front of The House of Kala. Kala's, as it was known by most, was one of the only places in the ward that would trade food and drink for goods instead of money. A chancer with empty pockets and an empty belly could also gamble for goods with some of the tavern's more disreputable types if they were brave or stupid enough. And, since we never had any money or items for trade, and Hayden was an outrageously proficient cheat at cards (second only to me in Zilvaren, perhaps), then it made perfect sense that he would be here, trying to swindle a pitcher of beer out of someone.

Blazing-hot gusts of sand blew over Hayden; they gathered in little pools in the bunched-up material of his shirt, which still bore the handprints of whoever had grabbed him and tossed him out of Kala's onto his ass. A bawdy group of revelers passed by, their scarves pulled up over their faces against the Twins and the sand, stepping over him without sparing him a glance. A young man with a split lip and the beginnings of a black eye lying in the gutter was nothing out of the ordinary in this part of the world.

I stood at my brother's feet, folding my arms across my chest, careful to keep the satchel containing the gauntlet pinned against the side of my body. Pickpockets and cutpurses weren't unusual here, either. A crew of hungry street rats wouldn't think twice about performing a snatch-and-grab if they suspected the prize would be worth it. I kicked Hayden's dusty boot. "Carrion again?"

He cracked an eyelid, groaning when he saw me. "Again! You'd think...the bastard would...have better things to do than beat the shit out of me." The way he gingerly clutched his ribs suggested a few of them might be broken.

I nudged him with the toe of my boot, considerably harder this time. "You'd think *you* might have learned your lesson and would steer clear of him by now."

"Agh! Saeris! What the hell? Where's your sympathy?"

"In Carrion's back pocket, right alongside the money I gave you to buy *water*." I considered bruising the other side of his ribs, but the sheepish smile he sent my way doused my anger. He had that way about him. He was foolish and careless more often than he wasn't, but it was impossible to stay mad at him for very long. Offering him my hand, I helped him to his feet. After much grumbling and complaining, Hayden dusted off his shirt and pants and adopted a wolfish grin that implied he'd discarded the ache in his ribs and felt brand spanking new. "Y'know, if you have a chit, I bet I could win back the water money *and* the red scarf Elroy gave me."

"Hah! Keep dreaming, buddy." I skirted around him and jogged up the steps to the tavern. As always, Kala's was packed to the rafters, and stank of stale sweat and roasting goat meat. A dozen heads swung in my direction as I entered, a dozen pairs of eyes going wide when they observed who had just walked in. Hayden was a daily visitor here, but *I* only ventured across the tavern's threshold when I'd had a bad day. I came here to blow off steam. To fuck. To fight. A wild array of outrageous things was whispered about me behind the backs of sunburned hands here: that a man might either get lucky or be beaten unconscious depending on my mood when I sat my ass down at the bar.

I didn't sit at the bar today. Peering over the drunken rabble before me, I craned my neck, searching for a flash of color amongst all of the dirty whites, grays, and browns. And there it was. There *he* was, sitting at a table on the far side of the tavern with three of his dim-witted friends, his back to the corner so he could keep a weather eye on the crowd. Carrion Swift: the most notorious gambler, cheat, and smuggler in the entire city. He was also uncommonly good in bed—the only man in Zilvaren who'd ever made me scream his name out of pleasure rather than frustration. His bright auburn hair was a signal flare in the dimly lit tavern.

I beelined right for him, but my pathway was quickly blocked by a beleaguered-looking woman in her early forties brandishing a giant wooden ladle.

"*No*," she said.

"Sorry, Brynn, but he swore he'd leave him be. What am I supposed to do, just let him get away with it?"

Brynn had a surname, but no one knew it. When asked, she'd say she'd lost it as a child and had never bothered to locate it again. She said family names made you easier to find, and she was right. As proprietor of The House of Kala, folks who didn't know any better tried to call *her* Kala, presuming she'd named the place after herself, but she'd glower at them and show them her teeth. Where she was from, Kala meant *funeral,* and Brynn didn't appreciate being likened to death.

"Doesn't matter to me whether he gets away with it or not." She cast a baleful sidelong glance at Hayden, who had skulked back into the tavern on my heels, looking rather sheepish. "*He* knows Carrion cheats, and I don't need another full-blown brawl breaking out in here. Not tonight. I've already had to toss two chairs out the back for mending, thanks to that swine and your idiot brother—"

"I'm not an idiot!" Hayden objected.

"You *are* an idiot," Brynn insisted. "You're also on a twenty-fourhour ban. Back outside with you. If your sister pays, I'll have someone bring you a cup of ale on the steps."

"I'm not paying for anything."

Hayden had the nerve to look disappointed. "Well, I'm not leaving without that scarf," he said. "My lungs will be flayed raw by the time I get home."

"Best hold your breath, then. Go on. Out with you." Brynn waved the ladle menacingly in Hayden's direction, and my brother paled. He eyed the over-large spoon as though he'd already been introduced to it once today and was well aware of what it could do. I wouldn't have been surprised if *Brynn* had given him the black eye rather than Carrion.

"I'll get the scarf for you. Go and wait for me outside," I told him.

"You'll not be taking it by force," Brynn warned. She swung the ladle in my direction, but it didn't have the same effect on me, and she knew it. A weapon had to be considerably shinier and a whole lot sharper to make *me* blink. She lowered the ladle, opting for a gentler approach. "I mean it, Saeris. Please. Keep the peace, if only for my sake. I'm at my wit's end already and it's not even eight."

"You have my word. I won't break any more furniture. I'll get what I came for and be gone before you know it."

"I'm holding you to that." Clearly, Brynn didn't think I was going to honor my word, but she sighed, stepping aside anyway. Hayden gave me a look that begged for me to vouch for him—he *always* had to push—but I knew better than to give in to those pleading eyes.

"Outside. *Now.* Hold on to this. Do *not* let it out of your sight." I thrust my bag into his chest and was wracked with a spasm of panic as he took it. It was one thing wandering around the ward with a giant piece of gold just sitting in the bottom of a bag. It was another thing entirely to stand in front of Carrion Swift with such a valuable piece of contraband on your person. The man was capable of anything. His fingers were lighter than the dawn breeze. He'd talked me out of my underwear—perhaps the greatest heist ever performed in Zilvaren—and people hadn't stopped talking about *that* for months. I wasn't willing to risk that he wouldn't catch a whiff of something interesting in the bag and endeavor to relieve me of it.

"I'll be ten minutes," I told Hayden. He pulled a face as he left the tavern.

Kala's patrons paused their games of bones, their rowdy conversations faltering as I made my way to Carrion. Everyone followed me out of the corners of their eyes, half-watching as I arrived at the grifter's table. Sparkling blue eyes danced with amusement as Carrion met my gaze. His hair was copper and gold and burnished umber, as if each strand were a fine thread of the metals that were so precious to Queen Madra. He was always the tallest person in a room by at least a foot, broad across the shoulders, and held himself with a confidence that made girls all over Zilvaren swoon. I hated to admit it, but it was that confidence that had lured me into his bed. I'd wanted to disprove it, to show him that his self-assuredness was nothing more than a façade. I'd planned on crushing that ego of his once I'd finished with him, but then he'd done the unthinkable and proven that his swagger was well-earned. *More* than well-earned. It made my blood boil just thinking about it. The man was a thief and a liar, and he loved himself far too much. I mean, who in their right mind wore this kind of finery? To a tavern full of savages who'd cut your throat and steal the dirty boots off your feet as soon as look at you? He was *mad*.

"Asshole," I said stiffly by way of greeting.

He grinned, and my stomach rolled in a weightless way that made me curse under my breath. "Bitch," he replied. "Nice to see you. I didn't think we were...*spending time together* anymore." His friends guffawed like morons, elbowing each other. Even they knew that this was a prod from Carrion. A poke. The last time I'd seen him, I'd been scrambling out of his bed, clutching hold of my bundled clothes, swearing on the forgotten gods and all four winds that I'd rather die than stick around for a repeat performance of the show he'd just put on for me. He knew he'd won. The supercilious prick hadn't been shy about it. He'd told me I'd be back for more, and I'd told him in very colorful language that I'd snap his cursed cock right off his body if he ever tried to come near me with it again. Or something to that effect, anyway.

I got straight to the point, ignoring his friends *and* his suggestive barb. "You promised you wouldn't gamble with Hayden again."

Carrion angled his head, eyes drifting upward as he pretended to think about this. "Did I?" he asked incredulously. "That doesn't sound like me at all."

"*Carrion.*"

The bastard sucked in a sharp breath, his attention snapping back to me. "She said my name." He pretended to swoon. "You all heard it. She said my name." Again, this earned a round of snickering from his infantile accomplices.

"Not only did you break your word, but you beat the living shit out of him, Carrion."

"Ahh, come on. Don't be so sour." He held out his hands, palms up, fingers splayed. "He begged me to play with him. Who am I to say no? And if I'd beaten the living shit out of him, I wouldn't have seen your little brother sulking around by the bar just now, would I? He'd still be out on the street, spitting blood into the sand. I hit him..." He thought about it. "Once. Maybe twice. That only qualifies as a light beating. And what's a light beating between friends?"

"Hayden isn't your friend. He's my brother. Messing with him is against the rules."

Carrion leaned forward, propping his elbows against the table. He bounced his eyebrows in the most infuriating way. "I never met a rule I didn't wanna break, Sunshine."

"We had a deal. I specifically remember saying I wouldn't interfere with your supply lines to and from the Hub, and you said you wouldn't mess with Hayden anymore."

He frowned. "Yeah, I suppose that does ring a bell."

The gall. The nerve. The out-and-out *audacity.* "So then why are you gambling with him?"

"Maybe my memory's patchy these days," Carrion mused.

"You *do* get hit in the head a lot."

"Or maybe," he said, swirling the ale around in his glass, "I knew if I messed with Hayden, I'd get to see you. And maybe that was an opportunity too good to pass up."

"You broke my brother's ribs just so you'd get to see me?" I couldn't have heard him correctly. There's no way he'd be insane enough to hurt Hayden for such a ridiculous reason.

Carrion's tone was suddenly sharp when he fired back, "No, Saeris. I broke them because he tried to stab me with one of your knives when I wouldn't play another round. Even *your* brother doesn't get away with that."

My shock was a cold, dead weight in the pit of my stomach. "He wouldn—"

"He *did*." Carrion drained his ale. When he set his empty glass down, his charming smile had returned. "Now that you're here, you might as well join me for a drink. No hard feelings and all that."

It was amazing how quickly Carrion could flit from one emotion to another. Also impressive was his ability to delude himself completely and utterly whenever it suited him. "I am not drinking with you. It makes no difference if Hayden deserved what you did to him. He probably pulled the knife on you because he was trying to get his mask back. He wouldn't have needed to do that if you hadn't encouraged him to gamble!"

"You like whiskey, right? Double sound good?" He was getting to his feet.

"Carrion! I am *not* drinking with you!"

The handsome snake attempted to slide an arm around my waist, but I'd dealt with predators far quicker than him. Ducking back, I put three feet of space between us, hands itching to move to my knives— the ones Hayden hadn't "borrowed"—but I'd given Brynn my word there'd be no fighting. Carrion's eyes traveled down my body, his smile broadening when they skimmed over my hips, and the memory of his *tongue* skimming over my hips slammed into me out of nowhere, drawing a wave of heat to my cheeks.

"You're pretty when you blush, y'know." The gods-cursed thief didn't miss a thing. "I tell you what. Sit down and have a drink with me, and I'll give you Hayden's mask."

"No deal."

"No deal?" He seemed genuinely surprised.

"Enduring fifteen minutes at a table with you is worth more than a ratty mask, you vulture."

"Who said anything about fifteen minutes? You know I like to take my time when I'm enjoying myself."

Holy martyrs. I did my level best to block the other memories that were trying to shove their way to the forefront of my mind. Carrion wanted his off-the-cuff comment to remind me of how long he spent working with his tongue between my thighs. He wanted me to recall just how long he held back his own pleasure—like it was his gods-cursed *job*—while he teased out mine. I wouldn't give him the satisfaction.

"One drink. Fifteen minutes. And I want the chits back that you took from him, too. Plus another five on top for the inconvenience of having to breathe the same air as you."

Carrion arched an eyebrow, considering me. I already knew I wouldn't like what was about to come out of his mouth. "Saeris, if I knew I could *buy* your time, I'd be bankrupt, and you would be a very rich woman. You'd have spent the past three months on your back, begging for me to ride you harder, and—"

"One more word and I'll relieve you of your fucking balls, thief," I snarled.

What he lacked in manners, Carrion Swift made up for in common sense. He knew when he was about to cross a line that would cost blood to *uncross*. His hair glinted red, then gold, then deepest, richest brown as he held his hands in the air, bowing his head in surrender. "All right, all right. The scarf, the chits, and five extra because you're greedy. Sit. Please. I'll get you that drink." He gestured to his table as if he intended for me to squeeze in between him and his cronies, but there were things I would do for my brother and a clean glass of water and things I would not. I picked out an empty booth three tables away and went and sat there instead.

I was going to kill Hayden. Kill him dead. What was he playing at? He'd tried to *stab* Carrion? The boy was only three and a half years younger than me but he acted like he was still waiting for his balls to drop. At some point, he was going to have to stop acting so recklessly and start considering the consequences of his actions. Even as I thought this to myself, Elroy's words echoed around inside my head, shockingly similar to my own.

"I can't even begin to fathom what you were thinking. Do you know what kind of doom you've brought down on our heads?"

"Here." Carrion set a glass of amber liquid down in front of me; the damn thing was almost full to the brim.

"That is not one drink."

"It's in one glass," he countered. "Therefore, it's one drink."

I'd be staggering back to The Mirage if I drank all of that. I'd fall off the roof and break my neck trying to get back into the attic. Still, I picked up the glass and swallowed a healthy mouthful. I wouldn't make it through this if I wasn't a little buzzed. The whiskey burned all the way down my throat and set a fire in my stomach, but I refused to react. The very last thing I needed was Carrion Swift telling everyone who'd listen that I couldn't handle my liquor.

"Well?" I demanded. "What do you want?"

"What do you mean, what do I want? Your company, of course."

I knew a liar when I saw one, and the man sitting opposite me was a seasoned professional. "Spit it out, Carrion. You wouldn't have bullied me into staying if you weren't trying to work some kind of angle."

"Can I not just be enamored by your beauty? Can I not just want to sit and listen to the angelic tone of your voice?"

"I'm not beautiful. I'm filthy, and I'm tired, and my voice is full of sarcasm and annoyance, so let's just get on with this, shall we?"

Carrion huffed a silent breath of laughter. He raised his own (considerably smaller) glass of whiskey to his lips and took a sip. "You were more fun three months ago, you know that? You're so cruel. I haven't stopped thinking about you."

"Oh, please. How many women have you slept with since then?"

He narrowed his eyes, looking confused. "What's that got to do with anything?"

This was growing tedious. Shoving the glass toward him, I made to get up.

"All right! Martyrs, you are all business." He took a steadying breath. "I suppose now that you come to mention it, there *is* something I wanted to talk to you about."

"I'm shocked."

Ignoring my tone, Carrion plowed on. "I heard something very interesting earlier. I heard that a raven-haired rebel from the Third viciously attacked a guardian and stole a piece of his armor. A gauntlet. Can you believe that?"

Huh. The asshole sure did love to play. Every line of his face and the way every muscle in his body was *so* casually relaxed gave me all the information I needed. Of course he knew that I had taken the gauntlet. I wasn't going to admit to it, though. I wasn't that stupid. "Oh? Really? But...how? It's impossible for a resident of the Third to *leave* the Third." I took another pull on the whiskey.

For a moment, Carrion did nothing but stare at me. He was reading me. Naturally, he didn't buy my feigned ignorance for one second but wasn't about to start openly flinging accusations around in the middle of Kala's. "I know, right?" he said airily. "Crazy. Crazier still to think about that poor girl out there now, trying to find a place to hide such a massive piece of gold. Y'know, they're saying that she brought it back here, to the ward." He laughed quietly. "But of course...she wouldn't have done that. That would have been way too dangerous."

"Absolutely. Incredibly dangerous," I agreed.

"She would have made sure she put it somewhere safe. Somewhere the guardians wouldn't think to look."

"Without a doubt."

"Do you think a girl stupid enough to attack and steal from a guardian would have the sense to secret away her prize somewhere like that?"

I was gripped by the overwhelming urge to damage Carrion's

pretty face; it was only with a monumental force of effort that I refrained. "I don't think the girl's stupid. If anything, I think she's brave," I said through gritted teeth. "I think it was more likely that the guardian tried to arrest her, and he dropped his gods-cursed armor in the sand. I think—"

"But did she put it somewhere *safe?*" Carrion hissed. "We can debate this girl's actions forever and a day, but if there's a problem in the ward—"

I rocked back into my seat. "What do you care about the Third? You don't even live here anymore, Carrion. Everyone knows you've got yourself a cushy little apartment below the second spoke."

"I have a *warehouse* outside of the ward," he said in a low voice. "It's the safest way for me to get my wares from one ward to the other. I *live* here, so I can take care of my grandmother. You know that. Gracia, remember? You've met her. Gray hair? Wicked temper?"

"Yes, I know Gracia, Carrion."

He leaned closer, eyes sharpening. "Those golden fucks will rain almighty hellfire down on this place if they think we have something that belongs to them, Saeris. You know they will. There'll be a river of blood running through the streets by morning if *this girl* brought the armor here."

He had a point. The guardians were all-powerful. They didn't have much to be afraid of, but they were terrified of the queen. Her justice would be swift and brutal if she had any idea the gauntlet was here. The gauntlet *I* had brought here. Elroy's dismay didn't seem like such an overreaction anymore. If Carrion, of all people, was this panicked about the whole thing, then maybe I should spend some time rethinking my plan. Or come *up* with a plan, perhaps.

"You're thinking. I can see that you're thinking. That's good," Carrion said. He donned an arrogant smile, but it was for show. He wanted Kala's other patrons, along with his friends sitting in the corner, to think that he was shamelessly trying to antagonize me into bed again, but the spark of concern I saw in his eyes was real.

"That warehouse," he said. "It isn't far from the wall. It would only take half an hour to move an item from here to there."

Gods, he really was mad. "You think I'd give it to *you?*" Too late, I realized that I'd given myself away. But what did it matter? This game we were playing, tiptoeing around the truth, was only wasting time. "You don't have anywhere near the amount of money it would take to convince me to hand that gauntlet over to you, Carrion Swift."

"I don't want it for myself, idiot. I just want it out of the Third." He murmured as if he were whispering sweet nothings to me, but his words were laced with venom. "Our people suffer enough without a hundred guardians storming the ward, tearing the place apart and killing anyone who gets in their way. Take it to the warehouse. Take it anywhere. It doesn't matter where you take it, so long as it's far away from here. You hear me?"

There was something very galling about being lectured by the likes of Carrion. He was one of the most selfish, most arrogant men alive. He loved for the world to believe that he didn't care about anyone or anything. But it seemed that he did care, and *I* had done something so selfish that he couldn't stand by and watch it happen? Gods.

I threw back another manful gulp of whiskey and discarded the rest, pushing the glass away. "I have to go."

"You're going to fix it?" Carrion's pale blue eyes drilled into me as I stepped away from the booth.

"I'm going to fix it," I snarled back.

"Good. Oh, and, Saeris?"

The guy just didn't know when to quit. I spun around, scowling at him. "What!"

"Even filthy and tired, you're still beautiful."

"Gods and martyrs," I whispered. He was relentless. Carrion Swift's silver tongue didn't bother me for long, though. I had bigger things to worry about. When I stepped out into the brilliant evening, Hayden was gone. And so was the gauntlet.

3

THE KINDEST PURPOSE

HE *NEVER* LISTENED. Sure, he acted like he did. Repeated back the words you said to him. Nodded his head. But when it came down to it, Hayden refused to do what was asked of him, never paid attention, and then typically went and did the one thing you begged him not to.

Normally, the stakes were pretty low when he misbehaved, but today, the stakes were more than high. They were astronomical. They were *catastrophic*.

I did my best to walk calmly in the direction of The Mirage— there was every chance Hayden had grown bored of waiting for me and decided to make his way back to the other tavern with the bag. But the more I played out the various scenarios in my head and thought about which was more likely, a creeping panic began to tighten a handhold around my throat.

If he'd looked inside the bag...

If he'd gone rummaging around in there, martyrs only knew where he was now and what the hell he was up to. The Twins beat down on the top of my head, their punishing heat making my mind swim. When was the last time I drank any water? This morning?

No, I'd saved my ration for when I got back to the forge, but after the disagreement with Elroy, I'd forgotten to collect it. I should *not* have had that whiskey.

Once I was a respectable distance from The House of Kala, I broke into a nervous trot, and then a jog. I tried to look casual, but there was no such thing as a casual jog in Zilvaren. The people here conserved energy as best they could. There was only one reason a person might run here, and that was if they were being chased.

Suspicious eyes trailed after me as I darted through the streets, past crumbling sandstone houses and covered market stalls owned by vendors selling stringy roasted meats, swaths of cloth, and pungent herbal remedies from the north. Familiar, faded posters papered the alleyways, promising hefty rewards for any information leading to the capture of suspected magic users. I knew the side streets of my ward like the back of my hand. The left up ahead would take me by Rojana Breen's place—my mother used to send me by there when she'd heard the traders had come back with fruit. Unlike the rest of the Third's smugglers, Rojana only traded in food and water. Her illegal trade would still get her hands chopped off, but they wouldn't get her killed.

Ahead on the right, however, another trader had set up shop. Vorath Shah peddled snake oil: tiny fragments of metal that he claimed contained traces of arcane magic; the stuffed, stinking feet of sand rabbits that were said to ward off disease; glass vials full of cloudy liquids that were supposed to bestow gifts upon you if you drank them. Gifts that had long since been lost to us. Humans were no longer capable of reading each other's minds, or making the blood boil in their enemy's veins, or granting themselves eternal luck. Everybody knew that we'd been stripped of those heretical powers hundreds of years ago, but Shah still made a handsome living selling useless trinkets to the hopeful and the desperate. He had outlandish explanations for the eternal question that all Zilvarens asked in hushed whispers behind closed doors: How, after over a thousand years, did the queen still live? Madra was human, so why didn't she die? He claimed to have access to the fount of her eternal youth and peddled that in bottles, too.

Shah was also known to buy artifacts. If a thief found themselves in possession of a very niche item, Shah could theoretically connect you with an interested buyer. But there was also a chance he might gut you and pick your body clean before leaving you out for the drift crabs. Catch him on a bad day, and by the next morning, there'd be nothing left of you but sun-bleached bones.

"Tell me you didn't," I muttered under my breath, taking the right. "Hayden Fane, tell me you did *not* try to take that gold to Sh—"

A piercing cry tore the arid air apart. It was distant. Muted. But it came from the east and set my teeth on edge. The *Mirage* was to the east. And the only time anyone screamed like that in the Third was when a guardian was taking liberties or spilling blood. Instinctively, I knew. I felt it in the marrow of my bones: the cry had something to do with Hayden. My brother was in danger.

I was running before I had time to think. The streets blurred by in my peripherals. My heart thrummed out a chaotic rhythm. Fear pooled like acid in my gut.

Behind me, out of nowhere, came the sound of clanging metal.

"Stop her! Stop that girl!"

The shout came from behind. Guardians. Five of them? Ten? I risked a glance over my shoulder, but all I saw was a wall of brilliant, flashing gold. The thunder of their boots striking the ground flooded my ears.

Gods, Saeris, move. Fucking move!

I urged myself on, digging deep. I *had* to run faster. If they caught me, I was done for. Hayden was done for.

Another eerie, agonized cry stopped my heart for a moment, but I willed it to pump again, needing it to drive me forward. I would not be run down in the streets by these bastards. I fucking *refused*.

The residents of the Third shouted, leaping out of my way as I hurtled past them. The guardians bellowed orders, again commanding someone to stop me, but no one did. I was known here. The people I tore past loved me because they'd loved my mother. They also hated me because I was a troublemaker and a thorn in their side. But even so, they hated the guardians more.

My lungs burned. My muscles screamed, begging for mercy, but I ran faster, pushing myself to the brink of exhaustion. The Twins throbbed in the sky, washing the streets in a pale golden light, the larger of the two suns rimmed with a strange blue corona as I barreled toward The Mirage and the attic, and hopefully *not* my brother.

If he had any sense whatsoever, he'd have seen the guardians or overheard talk of Madra's guard flooding the Third. That was a lot to hope for. Hayden wasn't very observant at the best of times, and Carrion had rung his bell for trying to shank him. He was probably still lost in his own little world, griping bitterly about the money he lost and his stupid fucking scarf.

I dragged my own scarf from my face, gasping for air, only to receive a lungful of blistering sand particles as I sped around the dumpling stand on the corner of Lark Street—

"Halt! Stop right there!"

Terror made me skid to a stop. It closed around me like an iron fist, squeezing my ribs to the breaking point as I took in the scene playing out in front of The Mirage. I'd never seen so much gold in one place. A multitude of glittering suns reflected off vambraces, chest plates, and gauntlets, forming brilliant white-gold orbs bright enough to burn the retina. Spots and flares traced across my vision as I looked from one guardian to the next, trying to run off a count in my head. What use was counting, though? One guardian, I could outrun. I stood a fair chance of giving two of them the slip. But three guardians? No chance. And there were far more than three of Madra's city guards gathered in a phalanx formation outside The Mirage. There had to be thirty of them at least, and they'd come fitted out for a fight. The swords in their hands were held ready, a wall of polished, golden shields tessellated in front of them, building an impenetrable wall. Each of them wore glittering mail over their arms and legs. Their mouths were covered with loose white hessian cloth. The eyes visible above their masks were narrowed, full of a burning hatred that every one of them leveled at my brother.

"No. No, no, no..." This *wasn't* supposed to happen. I was supposed to process the gold at the forge and hide it somewhere inconspicuous. Hayden was never going to even know the gauntlet existed, let alone come into contact with it, the stupid bastard.

If he hadn't gambled with Carrion...

If he'd listened and stayed put...

If he hadn't looked inside the damn bag...

Even as I made the excuses and blamed him for this predicament, guilt choked me. I'd stolen the gauntlet. I'd been caught stealing. I'd decided that snatching the metal was worth the risk that came with it. And now Hayden was going to be killed by an entire unit of guardians, and it was all my fault.

Hayden staggered away from the men and their sharpened blades. He would have retreated farther than he managed, but his back hit the wall after three feet. In his hand, he held the gauntlet loosely by the wrist, the armor damning him from a mile away. Terror shone from his face like a beacon.

"Stay where you are, rat!" the guardian at the forefront of the phalanx roared. As one, the men crept forward an inch at a time, their polished boots sliding forward in the sand. Over the tops of their masks, they glared at Hayden with unbridled conviction, all drawing from that common well of hate. They despised him for his suns-bleached clothes, his dirty skin, and the hollows beneath his eyes. But mostly, they despised him because any one of them could have been him. Luck dictated where you ended up in this city. A stroke of good luck had allocated their grandparents lodgings in one of the higher-tiered wards closest to the Hub. They'd never have had the opportunity to become guardians otherwise. Ill luck had rolled the dice against our grandparents, which was why we found ourselves quarantined in a plague ward—a filthy corner of the city that Madra hoped to starve to death or else allow sickness to bite chunks out of us until we all had the common courtesy to die.

It was *all* luck. Good or bad. And luck could change at any moment.

"The armor in your hand is property of the queen!" the captain shouted. "Toss it over, or we'll kill you where you stand!"

Wide-eyed, Hayden looked down at the gauntlet, staring at it as if this was the first time he realized he was even holding it. He turned the metal over, the muscles in his throat working as he tried to swallow.

If he gave them the armor, they'd slap him in chains and drag him back to the palace. He'd never be seen again. If he didn't surrender the gauntlet, they'd rush him. All of that sharpened, honed metal would find flesh, and the sand would turn red, and I'd stand once again over the dying body of somebody that I loved. Neither option resulted in Hayden walking away from this...and that I couldn't bear.

The captain of the guardians stepped closer, his men following behind as one like some dazzling golden beast brought forth on a leash. Hayden's back pressed against the tavern door. At the filthy windows, faces appeared then quickly disappeared as the patrons, who had been enjoying an afternoon drink when Madra's men stormed the ward, realized that all hell was erupting in the street outside. Hayden's head whipped around, his wide eyes searching for an escape route that didn't exist. He found me, though, standing twenty feet away, and for a second, relief shuttered across his face.

I was here.

I would help him.

I would get him out of this.

I would fix it, the way I fixed everything.

My throat closed up as I watched his relief drain away again. This wasn't a back-alley brawl or some silly scrape he'd gotten himself into with Carrion. This was about as serious as it could get.

He was facing down an entire unit of guardians, and there was nothing I could do about that.

"Throw me the armor!" the captain ordered, his voice booming. From a narrow alleyway on the other side of the tavern, a rag-tag group of children darted out into the street and took off, screaming at the tops of their lungs, but the wall of guardians didn't even flinch. Their focus was trained on Hayden and the piece of gold I had stolen in his hand. Pale as sun-bleached bone, my brother gave me a long, miserable look, and I saw in his eyes what he was planning to do next: the idiot was going to *run.*

"Don't you *dare*, boy," the captain snarled. Obviously, he'd seen Hayden's look as well and knew what he was planning. If Hayden bolted, the guardians would put him down immediately. Madra wouldn't be happy if her men returned to the palace with a dead body in tow. She'd probably told them to bring her back a *living* thief—one she could torture and question for hours. A corpse would prove very dull entertainment.

"Saeris!" Hayden moaned. His fear had him by the throat.

"Stay right there!" The captain was almost within lunging distance now. His unit bristled with pointed steel, swords at the ready. It would all be over in seconds.

Hayden's eyes were brimming with tears. "Saeris! I'm sorry!"

"Wait." The word caught in my aching throat.

"That's it, boy. That's it." The guardians drew closer.

"Wait! STOP!" My challenge bounced off the buildings on either side of the street this time. The guardians heard my shout, but only the captain deigned to glance in my direction. His attention shifted for a split second, eyes skimming over me; then he quickly returned his focus to Hayden.

"This doesn't concern you, girl," he said coldly. "Get back inside and let us do our work."

"It *does* concern me." I approached, biting the inside of my cheek to steady myself. With a mouth full of copper, I spread my arms open wide. "He didn't do anything wrong. I asked him to hold my bag. The piece of armor he's holding is mine—"

The captain's sharp eyes snapped back toward me. "It is *not* yours. Only a member of the guard may own that armor. Wearing it is an honor that is earned, and not by the likes of *you*."

His hessian mask puffed outward with the force of his words; he spat each one of them, fury burning bright in his tone. This wasn't the guardian I'd taken the gauntlet from. No, this one was colder. Harder. Meaner. There were no lines framing his eyes, but his dark brown irises held a bottomless eternity within them that made a chill skitter down the backs of my legs.

"I'm the one who took the gauntlet," I said slowly. "I'm the one who scaled the wall and escaped with it. Not him." I jerked my chin toward Hayden. "He had no idea what he was carrying."

"She's lying," Hayden said in a shaky voice. "It was me. I took it."

Of all the dumb, half-thought-through ideas my brother had ever had, this was the most dim-witted. He wanted to protect me. I knew that. He was afraid—more afraid than I'd ever seen him—but beneath his fear, he was steeling himself, drawing together the courage to face what was about to come. To *save* me.

The gauntlet was my responsibility, though. Elroy had been right back at the workshop; taking the armor had been the most reckless thing I'd ever done. I should never have stolen it. I'd let my greed, my own *hope* get the better of me, though, and I'd be damned if I was going to let Hayden pay the price for something so foolish.

"Don't listen to him," I said, glowering at him.

"*I* took it," he insisted, glowering right back.

"Ask him where he got it, then," I demanded, facing the captain.

"Enough of this," the captain barked. "Restrain her."

An irritated flick of his wrist separated three of his men from the phalanx. They stalked forward, shoulders tucked up around their ears, swords at the ready, and the fire that had been simmering away inside of me since I was a child finally boiled over.

I wasn't going to be restrained. I wasn't going to be bullied, or pinned down, or told to be quiet by these bastards. Not anymore.

What I did next was pure madness. I reached down into my boot, and I pulled out the blade I kept there. The action couldn't be undone. There was no taking it back. I had drawn a weapon on the Undying Queen's guard. In short, I was dead. My body just didn't know it yet.

"Well, well. We got ourselves a feisty one, boys," the guardian on the right growled.

"Let's teach her a lesson, then," the one in the middle sneered.

I focused on the one on the left. The quiet one. The one who moved like a predator. The one with death in his eyes. *He* was the one I needed to worry about.

He let the mouthy guardian lunge first. I ducked beyond his reach, using the short end of my dagger to deflect his sword as he swung at me wildly. The one in the middle cursed, darting forward, trying to spear me in the chest with his weapon, but I sidestepped, avoiding his attack altogether. This put me squarely in the quiet guardian's path— which I was sure was his plan all along.

He winked at me over the top of his mask. And then he came.

The rebels my mother had helped before her death had done more than hide in our attic. They had trained me. Taught me how to steal. How to survive. How to fight.

And now I fought like hell's own fury made flesh.

He rained down blows with his blade, calculated and measured. Each of his moves was a question to which I had an answer. I watched his annoyance build as I batted away his sword for the fourth time, using only my short dagger to divert his killing blows.

The middle guardian, the shortest of the three, charged at me, letting out a mighty bellow of rage. I danced back, light on my feet, temporarily dodging beyond the skilled fighter's reach so that I could twist and bring my dagger down from above, cutting through the air. The angle of the strike was unwieldy, but it was one I had practiced more times than I could count. It was the angle a blade needed to be brought down to find that narrow opening in a guardian's armor. The slim gap between pauldron and neck brace, where a sliver of metal might find a jugular. I'd never had to use the maneuver in real life before. I did it without thinking. I didn't even pause to reflect on the arc of bright red arterial blood that jetted up from the guardian's neck as he dropped to his knees, clutching at his throat.

No guilt.

No mercy.

No time.

I snatched up the guardian's sword and left him to die in the sand.

The quiet guardian narrowed his eyes at me, as if reassessing the situation. The other guardian wasn't as smart. He howled, his anger claiming him as he ran at me, ripping his mask away to reveal a mouth full of shattered teeth. "Stupid bitch! You're gonna pay—" I pivoted, darting back, and flicked out the sword. It was heavier than the wooden practice swords I'd always trained with, but I *was* used to the length. I knew exactly where the sharpened tip of the steel would meet his skin: just below his right wrist. I timed it perfectly. With little more than an adjustment of my sword hand, I cut down, and then the guardian's hand, still holding his sword, hit the sand with a dull thud.

"My hand! She...she cut off my...hand!"

"I'm coming for your fucking head next," I seethed.

Rage washed my vision red.

They'd killed my mother.

My friends.

Elroy's entire family.

They'd caused the deaths of thousands, and now they were threatening Hayden. All of the pent-up rage stored inside my chest came rushing out in an unstoppable torrent. I prowled toward the guardian, dagger in one hand, sword in the other, ready to end his miserable existence...but came face-to-face with the quiet guardian instead.

Again, he didn't say anything. A spark of amusement flickered in his eyes, though. Slowly, he shook his head, his meaning clear as day. *If you're gonna fight any of us, you're gonna fight* me.

The air came alive with the sound of crashing steel. He was a whirlwind, his movements lithe and graceful. Every time his blade scythed toward my head, I expected the world to go black. But somehow it didn't. Somehow, I managed to bring the sword I'd taken up in time. Somehow, I held my own.

And just when he was getting comfortable, when this predator thought he'd finally gotten a read on my capabilities as a fighter...I stopped holding back.

His eyes went wide when he saw it happen. When I loosened in my stance and brought the blade up to guard my face. The second when I bared my teeth and came for *him.*

He spoke, then, at last. Just one word. *"Shit."*

He didn't retreat an inch. He held his ground. But he knew this wasn't going to be the kind of fight he'd thought it would be. Our weapons met, edge-to-edge, and we went for it, each knowing what it would cost to lose this fight.

He was good. Really good. My feet kicked up the sand as I spun around, working constantly to make sure he didn't get through my guard.

He lunged, trying to strike at my rib cage, but I brought the butt of my dagger crashing down on his forearm, shattering bone. Without even flinching, the fucker grabbed the hilt of his sword in his other hand and delivered a battery of blows that nearly sent me to my knees. A bright sting of pain flared across my chest as he slashed across my collarbone.

I saw the smile at the corners of his eyes. He thought he had me. And he nearly did. His sword sliced through the air—a backhanded stroke that took me off guard—but I'd trained for this. He wasn't the only one who could think fast. Definitely wasn't the only one who could *move* fast, either.

I dropped and tucked myself into a roll, slashing up with my dagger as I did so. The blade found its mark, and it was done. Just like that.

He didn't notice at first. Spinning, he rounded to meet me again. It was only when he tried to take a step forward and his legs went out from beneath him that he realized something was wrong.

I'd thought about leaving the dagger embedded in his leg. That would have given him a couple more moments to process his death. But in the end, the deep gash I'd carved inside his thigh was kinder. Quicker. Dark, ruby-red blood pumped out of the wound I'd inflicted in great waves, running down his leg. He glanced down at the sight of it, huffing out a breath of surprise. And then he toppled forward into the sand, dead.

My chest heaved. I fought for breath, trying to silence the maddening rushing in my ears. I—

"Foolish girl," a cold voice intoned. It was the captain who had ordered his men to restrain me. He had turned away from Hayden, his attention fully on me. "I admit, I didn't think you'd be capable of taking a gauntlet from a guardian. I see that I was wrong now."

The street came back into focus. The phalanx of guardians, all glowering at me, swords raised. And Hayden. My little brother. Tears streamed down his face as he stared at me, stricken dumb by what I'd just done.

"Saeris, run!" he hissed. *"Go!"*

But the captain laughed. "All four winds combined couldn't carry her far enough from my reach now, boy. She just killed two of the queen's guards and maimed another. Her death warrant's already signed."

"No! Stop! Take me! I'm the one who stole—" Hayden rushed forward, trying to block the captain's path, but the man shoved him roughly to the sand.

"For better or worse, she just saved your life, wretch. Don't waste your life by laying hands on a guardian, too."

The phalanx marched toward me, and I saw the captain was right. I couldn't outrun this now. They were going to take me. They were going to kill me for what I'd done. But there was still a chance for my brother. "It'll all be okay, Hayden," I called to him. "Go and see the old man. He'll let you stay with him now. Go on, go. I'll be back by dinner, I promise." It was a bald-faced lie, but any false hope I could give him was better than nothing. I needed him to believe that this might all blow over. If he didn't, he'd never do as I told him. He'd follow us all the way to the gates, screaming and shouting and demanding that I be set free. "Did you hear me? Find the old man, Hayden. It's important. Go to him. Tell him what's happened. He needs to know."

Hayden's face was streaked with tears. "I'm not leaving you."

"Just do as you're told for once in your life! Just fucking *go!* I don't need your help. I don't *want* you following after me, blubbering like a little brat who needs his hand held all of the time." It was harsh, but sometimes the cruel things we said served the kindest purpose.

Anger flared in Hayden's eyes, just as I'd hoped it would. He set his jaw, his arms falling to his sides, and my bag dropped to the sand. "I didn't realize I was such a burden," he whispered.

"Well, you are, Hayden. Your entire fucking life, that's all you've been. Now leave me alone. Don't follow. Do *not* come looking for me. *GO!*"

THE PRICE

I USED to dream about visiting the palace when I was a child. I'd fantasize that I'd be chosen somehow, stopped in the street and told that Queen Madra had noticed *me*, a common street rat from the Third, and had decided she wanted me as a lady's maid. I'd be given beautiful dresses to wear and exotic flowers for my hair, and I'd have hundreds of bottles of perfume to choose between. Every day, I would dine with the queen, and chefs from the north would treat us to feasts, our plates overflowing with mouthwatering food. Never once would we have to eat the same meal twice. I'd drink only the best wine from Madra's stores, because I would have been the queen's favorite, naturally, and she would want only the finest, nicest things for her favorite lady's maid.

As I'd grown older, the daydreaming had evolved. I was still chosen to be Madra's lady's maid, but I'd cared less about the dresses and the food. I'd wanted the position, *needed* to be Madra's favorite, but not so I'd be lifted out of poverty to be kept like a novel pet. I'd suffered too much by then. Known too much injustice. Seen such unspeakable acts of violence that all of my innocence had been washed away. I'd needed to be chosen by the queen so that I could get close enough to *kill* her. I fantasized about how I would do it each night when I closed my eyes. When my mother was slain in the streets and left to rot, those fantasies were all that kept me sane.

I'd plotted a million different ways to secure myself an audience with the eternal virgin, our lady of Zilvaren, most revered Queen on high. From applying for a job in the kitchens to learning how to perform in the traveling theater that visited the city during Evenlight to scaling the walls and breaking into the palace, I'd planned every minute possibility and eventuality and decided that it *could* be done, and it *would* be done. By *me*.

I never thought I'd find myself within the palace confines under these circumstances, with my hands bound tightly behind my back, ribs bruised and cracked, and a violet bruise blossoming like a death flower beneath my right eye. I wasn't supposed to be gasping for air in a tiny, windowless box, with a river of sweat running down my back for six hours straight. *This* had not been the plan at all.

Captain Harron—I'd learned this was the bastard's name—had tossed me unceremoniously into the tiny cell to await the queen, and I'd been pacing up and down the length of the six-foot-long cell ever since, counting the minutes that passed by until they turned into hours. I was counting for counting's sake now, purely so I could shut out the dark thoughts that had been assailing me since my arrival. I wouldn't be any use to anybody if I let fear take root and panic to set in.

The city bells were ringing, signaling day's end, when Captain Harron finally came back for me. My mouth felt like it was full of sand, and I was almost delirious from the heat, but I kept my back straight and my chin raised high as he entered the cell. His gleaming, beautiful armor was gone, replaced by a well-oiled leather chest plate, but the menacing sword with the cloth-wrapped grip still sat at his hip, his short sword sheathed at the other side. Adopting a casual lean up against the wall, he tucked his thumbs into his belt, and he looked me up and down; he didn't seem all that impressed by what he saw. "Where did you learn to fight like that?" he demanded.

"Just hang me already and be done with it," I snapped. "If you don't hurry up and get on with it, you're gonna miss your opportunity."

He arched an eyebrow. "I wouldn't bother trying to escape."

I rolled my eyes. "I meant that I was dying of *boredom* in here."

Captain Harron let out a mirthless laugh. "Apologies for the delay. Don't worry. The queen has plenty of ways of entertaining her *guests.* She just had some matters to attend to, and she wanted to make sure she could give you her full attention."

"Oooh, lucky me. I'm honored."

The Captain pouted, nodding. "You should be. Do you know how many people Queen Madra deigns to see in person these days?"

"Not many? I can't imagine she has that many friends."

Harron rubbed the pad of his thumb over the pommel of his sword. "Leave the sharp tongue at the door when we exit this cell. It won't serve you well where I'm taking you."

"You might be surprised, Captain. Most people think I'm pretty funny."

"Madra's sense of humor runs a little darker than even *you're* used to, Saeris Fane. You don't want to provoke her into using you for sport. But by all means, do as you wish. These are *your* last hours in the Silver City." He shrugged. "Are you ready to meet your Queen?"

"Ready as I'll ever be." It was a relief to hear that my voice didn't shake. My insides were a quivering, knotted mess as Harron took me by the arm and guided me through the lower levels of the palace, though. I breathed in through my nose and out through my mouth, the pull and push of air level and drawn out, but the normally steadying technique did nothing to quiet my nerves.

Twenty-four years.

That's all the time I'd been given in this cursed existence.

Despite how hard, and miserable, and hot, and frustrating it had all proven to be, I'd bizarrely hoped for more of it.

We hiked up endless staircases, Harron prodding me in the

small of my back when I stumbled or tripped on a step. Once we were aboveground, the palace proper sprawled out before us, all vaulted ceilings, arched alcoves, and disturbingly lifelike paintings depicting the dour faces of men and women whom I presumed were Madra's predecessors. I'd never seen anything so grandiose before, but my head was swimming, black spots dancing in my vision, and I couldn't muster up the energy to appreciate any of it. And I *was* being marched to my death. Funny how your own impending demise will rob a girl of her desire to take in the scenery.

Our trek through the palace seemed to take forever, but in truth, I was moving so slowly that Harron threatened to toss me over his shoulder and carry me three separate times. When I staggered, the cavernous hallway spinning around me in a blur of light and color, Harron dragged me roughly to my feet but then surprised me by shoving a water canteen into my stomach.

I took it, unscrewing the top as fast as my trembling fingers could manage. "I'm shocked. Wasting water on the dead?"

"You're right. Give it back," he growled.

But I was already drinking. I was so thirsty, so desperately dehydrated, that the water felt like liquid fire as it went down, but I paid no heed to the burn. I swallowed, swallowed, swallowed, panting down my nose as I fought to breathe around the flow.

"All right, all right. That's enough. You're gonna drown yourself," Harron warned. When I didn't return the canteen, he tried to rip it out of my hands, but I stepped back out of his reach. "You're gonna drink the damn thing dry," he groused.

This comment was the thing that finally made me lower the canteen. "Oh? Let me guess. You'll have to walk all the way to a tap somewhere to refill it now, will you, Harron? My heart bleeds for you. Tell me, have you ever had to try and survive a day on the water ration Madra issues?"

"*Queen* Madra's water allowances are more than generous—"

"I'm not talking about in the Hub or any of the fancy inner

wards. D'you even know how much she gives *us* to drink every day? In the Third?"

"I'm sure it's enough—"

"Six ounces." I shoved the water canteen into his stomach so hard that his breath made an *"ooof"* sound as it rushed out of his body. "*Six. Ounces.* And our water doesn't come from a tap. It comes from a standing reservoir that fills from your run-off. Do you understand what that means?"

"There's a filtration process—"

"There's a *grate*," I snarled. "It catches the solids."

Harron's features remained impassive, but I thought I caught a flicker of something close to disgust in his eyes. He rolled out his shoulders, then shook his head, looping the canteen's strap across his chest. "If the queen's advisors think that system works for the Third, then I'm sure it does. And look at you. You seem pretty healthy to me."

The confession was right there, on the tip of my tongue. *"If I seem healthy to you, then that's because I've been stealing from the Hub's water reservoirs my entire life."*

I caged the words behind my teeth. I was already neck-deep in shit, and I didn't need to add water theft to my charges. And there was Hayden and Elroy to think about. They'd still need to siphon water to survive, and they wouldn't be able to do that if the guardians suspected for even a second that such a crime was possible.

Harron shoved me forward again, but this time when I walked, the stone floor was a little steadier beneath the soles of my boots. "You people walk around with those plague bags hooked on your belts," I said. "You say our ward's locked down so tight because we're quarantined. You say we're afflicted with a sickness. That we're contagious. But we aren't, Captain. We're being slowly and methodically poisoned because we don't matter. Because we ask questions. Because we say no. Because Madra sees us as a burden on the city. She feeds us foul, dirty water, and we die in droves because of it.

Meanwhile, you and yours turn the handle, and fresh, clean water flows into your canisters. No one standing over you, looking over your shoulder, beating you and telling you enough. Have you ever asked yourself why—"

"I'm not paid to ask *anything*," Harron interrupted in a clipped tone.

"No, of course not. Like I said. Ask a question, and you'll get sent to the Third. It isn't disease that's contagious in my ward, Captain. It's *dissent*. Anarchy and rebellion spread like a wildfire. And what do you do with a fire? You blockade it. Trap it behind a wall. Give it nowhere else to go until it burns itself out and dies a quiet death. That's what Madra's doing with my people. Except our fire hasn't burned out the way she'd hoped it would. We've been reduced to embers, yes, but the coals that lie beneath the ash of my ward are still hot enough to burn. Do you know much about metalwork, Captain? I do. It's under the most unbearable conditions that the sharpest, most dangerous weapons are forged. And we *are* dangerous, Captain. She's turned us *all* into weapons. *That* is why she won't suffer my people to live."

Harron was silent for a long time. Then he said, "Just walk."

The air danced with heat as we crossed an internal courtyard. I breathed a sigh of relief when we reentered the building through a crenelated archway, glad to be back in the shade. Harron refused to speak again as he ushered me toward our destination. We passed endless alcoves and hallways, but he didn't stop driving the hilt of his sword into my back until we came upon a set of tall, dark wood doors, three times my height and at least eight times as wide. The captain produced a heavy, rusted iron key from his pocket and inserted it into the keyhole.

Why would a room within Madra's own fortress need such an

imposing door, and why would it need to be kept locked? I wanted to know but didn't ask. Harron was unlikely to give me an answer, and I'd find out soon enough, anyway. I was probably about to be fed to a pack of hell cats. An uneasy prickle bit at the tips of my ears as Harron shoved me through the doors. The air in the large, vaulted room beyond was no cooler than anywhere else in the palace, but there was a strange quality to it, as if it were thicker than normal and hadn't been disturbed in a very long time. My feet felt like they were wading through shifting sand as I proceeded through the darkness toward a lone burning torch that hung on the wall.

In rows, huge sandstone columns filled the cavernous space, at least thirty of them propping up the buttressed ceiling high above. Our footsteps echoed around the hall, Harron guiding me by the shoulder now. I thought the hall must be completely empty, but as we drew closer to the flickering flame throwing shadows up the wall, I saw that there was a series of stone steps that led up to a dusty, raised platform.

Something long and narrow protruded from the platform. From a distance, it looked like some sort of lever. I couldn't tear my eyes away from it. My attention seemed to be snared by the shadowy shape, and no matter how hard I tried, I couldn't rip my gaze away. The closer we drew, the more focused I became. It was as if the platform were drawing me to it, beckoning me forward...

"I wouldn't if I were you." Harron tugged me away from the platform, back toward the flaring torch; I hadn't even realized I'd altered course and was heading right for the stone steps. For a moment there, I'd lost myself, but the sound of the captain's low, quiet voice brought reality rushing back into sharp relief.

I was suddenly feeling rather nauseous. The water I'd drained from Harron's canteen rolled in my stomach, my mouth sweating unpleasantly, but I swallowed down the sensation, determined not to give the asshole the satisfaction of knowing he'd been right when he'd told me not to drink so fast. "What is this place?" I whispered.

"It used to be a hall of mirrors," the captain answered. "But that was a long time ago. Stand still. And don't think about trying to escape. This place is packed full of guards. You won't get five feet beyond that door now." He moved behind me and grabbed my wrists, binding them tight with rough hands. "There. Do *not* move." He took the torch from the wall and gave me a stern look, half of his proud features cast into darkness by the flame.

He went about lighting other torches along the wall then. Soon there were at least ten of them casting off circles of golden light that revealed the dour faces of long-forgotten gods chiseled into the stonework of the walls. Amongst them, the only two I recognized were Balea and Min, the physical embodiment of Zilvaren's suns— twin sisters, identical in appearance, beautiful and cruel. The sisters stared down at me with regal indifference as Harron finished his task. Even with the additional burning torches, the hall was so vast that the darkness still licked up the walls and crept close across stonework as if testing the boundaries of the light, trying to push it back.

I did my best not to look at the steps, the platform, or the lever. I tracked the edgeless, blurred shape that was Harron as he returned, but even so, my eyes kept drifting, drawn back to the steps.

The silence vibrated in my ears—an uncanny, unsettling feeling, like the moments after a scream, when the terrible sound tears the air in two, and for a split second afterward, the memory of it hangs there, determined to still be heard. I found myself straining, listening as hard as I could, searching for a voice that wasn't there.

Harron stood in front of me, his dark brown hair painted with strokes of copper beneath the torchlight. He opened his mouth to speak, and—

"I hear rumors," a cool voice said. It was rich and low, though undeniably feminine. I startled, casting around for its source. I hadn't heard the door open again, and there had been no echoing footfall against the stone, yet there was someone else in the hall with us now. Queen Madra emerged from the darkness as if she were made of it. People said she was young. Beautiful. Magnificent to look upon. I'd seen her from a distance, but never this close. It was hard to comprehend how someone who had ruled for so long could look like this.

Her skin was fair and flawless, her cheeks flushed pink. Her hair was the color of spun gold, thick and braided into complex knots. Bright, quick, intelligent blue eyes took me in as she approached. She was certainly beautiful. More beautiful than any woman I'd ever seen. Her gown was a deep, rich sapphire blue, made of a stunning, silken fabric that I'd never even laid eyes on before. She was a dainty, graceful thing, but just like everything else in this strange hall, there was something strange about her.

She gave me a coquettish smile as she came closer, absently twisting a golden bracelet around her wrist. Harron averted his eyes, bowing his head when the queen looked to him. His deference appeared to please her. She placed a familiar hand on his shoulder, having to reach up to do so, then turned around and faced me.

"Rumors are wicked things," she said. A moment ago, her voice sounded lower, full of reverberations, but it had altered somehow, and was now high and bright, as clear and pleasant as the ringing of one of Elroy's glass bells. There was no anger on Madra's face. If anything, her expression was one of curiosity mixed with mild amusement. The corners of her mouth tilted upward again, her eyes shining, bordering on kind. "I'm not fond of rumors, Saeris Fane. Rumors are next-door neighbors to gossip, and gossip *always* breaks bread with lies. It's just the way these things go."

She paced around me in a circle, those quick blue eyes drinking all of me in. "I apologize for the shackles, but I'm not overly fond of low-born rats from the Third, either. You never know where their hands have been. In the very least, they're always dirty, and it's so hard to get stains out of satin."

Low-born rats.

Her smile was welcoming, as was the softness of her gaze, but her words told the truth at least. She tipped her head back, exposing the column of her neck as she got a better look at me. Diamonds winked at her ears, and the choker that circled her throat dripped with glittering jewels that I didn't even have names for. She wore no crown, which seemed odd considering the other finery she was decked out in. "Harron here tells me that you stole from me today. He tells me that you *murdered* two of my guardians?"

I said nothing. I hadn't been invited to speak yet, and I knew how these things worked. I'd been dealt enough backhanded blows by the guardians to know that I shouldn't make a peep until told directly to open my mouth. Madra huffed down her nose, arching a sardonic eyebrow at me as her smile widened. I got the impression that she was disappointed and had wanted me to breach propriety. "Theft of crown property is a serious charge, Saeris, but we'll get to the armor you took shortly. First, you'll explain how you managed to best two of my men. You'll tell me who taught you to wield a sword. You'll give me details. Names. Meeting locations. Everything you know. And when you're done, if I feel that you've been honest, I will see about commuting a part of your sentence. Go ahead," she commanded.

Turning her back on me, she started pacing up and down along the length of the wall, looking up at the stonework, at the torches, at the ceiling, waiting for me to speak.

"Get on with it," Harron hissed between his teeth. "Delaying won't aid your case, I assure you."

"It's all right, Harron. Let her get her falsehoods in order. It doesn't matter. I'll untangle her web even as she spins it."

A bead of sweat streaked over my temple, rolling down my cheek, but I found myself shivering despite the stifling heat. I wanted to look at the raised platform. With every fiber of my being, I was desperate to look. It took every ounce of strength I possessed, but I managed to keep my eyes trained on Madra. "I taught myself," I said. "I made myself a wooden practice sword, and I trained by myself."

Queen Madra snorted.

I waited to see if she would say anything—she was clearly

thinking plenty—but she lifted her brows in a silent signal to continue.

"That's all there is to it," I said. "No one trained me."

"Liar," the queen purred. "My guardians are seasoned fighters. Second to none when it comes to swordplay. You have been shown how to use a weapon, and I want to know by who."

"I already told you—"

The queen's hand whipped out, fast as lightning. Striking my cheek as hard as she could, the resulting crack echoed around the empty hall as her palm met my skin. Pain exploded in my jaw, traveling up into my temple. Damn, that *hurt.*

"It was the Fae, wasn't it?" she hissed. "They've found a way through. They've come for me at last?"

She'd struck me hard, but not *that* hard. I shouldn't have been hearing things. It seemed that I was, though, because for the life of me, it sounded like she'd just said, *the Fae.* "I don't know what you mean." I glanced at Harron, trying to decipher from the look on his face if she was playing some kind of game with me, but his expression was blank. Unreadable.

"What isn't there to understand?" The queen's sharp words dripping with ice.

"I've heard stories. But..." I wasn't quite sure what to say. Was she mad? Did she believe in unicorns, too? Lost lands that existed millennia ago, swallowed by the desert? Ghosts, and the forgotten gods? None of it was real.

As if reading my mind, the queen adopted a slow smirk. "The Fae were warmongers. Cannibals. Beastly creatures with no temperance, sense of morality, nor any notion of mercy. The eldest Immortals visited their wrath upon the land with an iron fist, leaving a path of chaos and destruction in their wake. The seven cities rejoiced when I cast them out. And now they have sent you to try and kill me?"

"I assure you, no one has sent me to do anything of the sort."

Madra dismissed me with a bored tut. "They want this land, I assume. Tell me, what will they do if I don't return these arid, worthless, barren sand dunes to them?" she asked skeptically.

"I've already told you—"

"STOP...*lying,*" the queen barked. "Just answer the question. The Fae wish to come and take these lands from me. What do you think they will have to do in order to seize my throne from me?"

This felt like a leading question. One I knew better than to answer. But I had to tell her something. She was clearly unhinged, and choosing to protest my innocence on this front clearly wouldn't get me anywhere. "Kill you," I said.

"And how do they plan on doing that?" She seemed genuinely interested in how I'd answer *this* question.

"I...I don't know. I'm not sure."

"Hmm." Madra nodded, still pacing, appearing to think very deeply. "It strikes me that the Fae haven't really thought about how they might destroy an immortal, Saeris. It seems that the Fae are foolhardy and are ill-prepared to deal with the likes of me." Her vivid skirts rustled as she approached. "I will say that the ruckus you caused today *was* a little exciting. I felt a frisson of..." She looked up at the crenelated archways above, frowning. It was as though she were grasping for a word that eluded her. She shrugged, lowering her gaze. "I suppose I'm just *bored,*" she said. "So long in power. No real threat to the throne. Nothing to do but drink wine and slaughter peasants for fun. For one second, you had me wondering..." Even the broad, cold smirk she wore didn't mar her beauty. Maybe if the women of the Third were given the same luxuries Madra had enjoyed, they'd look just as pretty as her, but as it stood, even spiteful and cold, she was still the loveliest creature I'd ever laid eyes on.

She spun around suddenly, opening up her arms and laughing dryly as she gestured to the room about her. "That's why we met here, of course. I had to see for myself if this place remained untouched. The banished Fae can't return so long as all remains the same here, you see. I *knew* nothing would have changed, but I do have a nasty habit of letting paranoia get the better of me."

She sobered. A fine young thing in a fancy gown, spoiled and over-indulged—but something ancient and malicious lurked behind her bright blue eyes. "I should know better by now than to indulge the riffraff, Harron." She addressed the captain, but her eyes drilled into *me.*

"Riffraff indeed, Majesty," Harron said stiffly. "It is a queen's duty to protect her people, though. It's only right that you investigate threats against Zilvaren."

Boot-licking, flattering, fawning sycophant. The Harron I met in the streets of the Third was nowhere to be seen, nor was the man who dragged me up from the dungeons, kicking and screaming. This version of the captain was meek and diminished. Afraid for reasons I couldn't discern.

Madra didn't seem all that impressed by his simpering, either. Her mouth twitched at either corner, lifting just a fraction. "Deal with her, Harron. When you're done, head back to where you found her and root out the rest of her people."

My people.

She didn't mean...

A wave of panic took me. "No. My brother...I told you. He had nothing to do with the gauntlet. I swear—"

The queen's face was blank as she reached out and ran an index finger down my cheek. I was slick with sweat. The air stank with my fear, yet the woman before me was impervious. Her skin, perfect and so very pale, bore no perspiration whatsoever. "You are a rat," she said simply. "Rats are an eternal bane upon a city, it's true. You can kill one, but it will already be too late. It will have spawned ten more before it found its way to you. Ten more grotesque, fat rats, gnawing away on grain that does not belong to them, tainting water that they have no right to drink. The only way to deal with a rat's nest is to hunt it down and smoke out its occupants. Even if there are no Fae in the

Silver City, somebody trained you. Somebody showed you how to hurt and kill my men. Do you think we'd leave a form of rebellion that insidious to fester? Oh no." She bared her teeth, gripping hold of my jaw, her nails suddenly too sharp, too long, gouging into my skin.

"You *took* something of mine, girl, and I am not in the business of letting theft slide. So, I will take from you. First, your life. Then, I'll make a column of greasy smoke out of those who matter to you, and when they're gone, I will tear the Third Ward to the ground. For the next one hundred years, anyone foolish enough to think twice about stealing from me will remember the black day Saeris Fane offended the Zilvaren crown and a hundred thousand people paid the price."

5

HERETIC

An entire ward put to the torch because of me. A hundred thousand people turned to ash and bones. She wasn't serious. Elroy told me how they slaughtered cows once. They hit them in the forehead with a piercing bolt, taking them by surprise. That's how my guilt came at me on the heels of the queen's promise: out of nowhere. Right between the eyes.

Queen Madra spun around, her dress rustling, the color shifting like the sheen atop an oil slick, and began to walk across the vast hall, her feet silent as she went. "Make her sing, Harron. I want to hear her music echoing from the dungeons to the towers. It's been too long since we heard something sweet."

Sick. Twisted. That's what she was. Madra's fair face had fooled many, but a dark, ugly pit roiled away behind the mask she wore. I saw it. I felt it in her words. The countless horrors this woman had commanded in that sweet, lilting voice...

Harron's eyes were glassy as he reached for his sword. The sound of the blade scraping against its sheath filled the air as he drew the weapon free. He wore no remorse. No regret. Whatever sympathy he might have felt for me as he dragged me up here from the cells was gone now, replaced with...*nothing.*

When he came for me, he came quick and quiet.

It would be over the same way, then. My life, gone in a heartbeat, my cry severed in my throat before it could meet the air. But Madra *wanted* my screams to flood the palace. She'd said so, and Harron was her creature to the end. I was helpless to stop him when he grabbed me. With my wrists still bound, I had no way of fending him off. I aimed a kick at his stomach, throwing my weight behind it, but he deflected the blow, twisting away, wearing a look of bored contempt.

"This is nothing to you, is it? Taking an innocent life."

A flicker of something passed over his features. Not empathy. More...exhaustion. "You aren't innocent. You're a thief," he replied flatly. His hand clamped around the top of my arm, his grip an iron vise. I attempted to dig my heels in to slow his progress as he dragged me across the hall, but the stone underfoot was too slick.

"The Third is full of thieves," I spat. "It's the only option open to us. We take more than we're given, or we die. It's an easy decision. You'd do the same if it meant the difference between life and death."

"Don't presume to know which way my moral compass points, girl." He wrenched me forward, snarling when I tried to pull myself free. My shoulder throbbed, promising to dislocate if I strained the joint any further, but there were plenty of things I would do to survive and theft was the least of them. If ripping my shoulder out of its socket gave me an opportunity to run, then I'd endure the pain.

"Easy to judge...from a position of privilege," I ground out. "But when your family...is dying..."

"Death is an open doorway that's meant to be walked through. On the other side of it lies peace. Count yourself lucky that you get to make the journey at all." Shoving me forward, he threw me to the ground. I landed on my side, hard, my head smashing against the stone and sparks exploding behind my eyes. For a moment, all I could do was gasp through the skull-splitting pain. My vision cleared just in time for me to register Harron lifting his sword.

"For what it's worth, I *am* sorry," he said. And then he brought the blade swinging down.

Lightning tore a pathway through my side and up, into my brain. White hot, the sensation transcended pain. This was more. Raw agony, the likes of which I had never experienced, splintered my mind as the horror of it intensified. I didn't even know pain like this existed. A rush of wet heat spread over my stomach. I looked down and immediately wished I hadn't. Harron's blade was buried in my stomach, the metal plunged deep. The captain's brows drew together for the briefest second—the smallest flare of something he refused to give way to—and then his features smoothed out. "Ready, Saeris?" He closed both hands around the hilt of his sword. "This is the part where you scream." And then he twisted...

A wall of sound and panic tore out of me, too much, the fear and vicious burn in my gut overwhelming my senses. Like a feral animal caught in a snare, I bucked and writhed, desperate to escape, but the ties binding my hands behind my back grew tighter the more I pulled, and Harron had only twisted his gleaming silver blade. He hadn't pulled it out. I was skewered to the stone, and no amount of thrashing would fix that.

I gave Madra the music she requested. I screamed until I tasted blood and my throat was raw. It was only when I started choking on blood that I understood that I was coughing it up. It spilled out of my mouth in a hot stream that wouldn't stop flowing.

"I know it hurts," Harron murmurs. "But it's temporary. It'll be over soon enough."

As he stooped down over me, taking a beautiful, engraved dagger from a sheath at his thigh, I clung to those words. Soon, this would end. I would sink into oblivion. I didn't believe in an afterlife, but nothingness would do. I—

Fire erupted below my collarbone. I couldn't breathe. I thought for a moment that he'd punched me, but no. His dagger protruded from my shoulder. A ragged howl bounced around the hall, growing louder and louder with each repetition. It was an inhuman sound, chilling and pitiful.

Escape.

Escape.

Escape.

There was no room to think around the word.

I couldn't—

I had to—

I—

ESCAPE!

"You're lucky. This is faster than it will be for the others," Harron said softly. There was a hint of kindness to his tone; he took out another dagger and looked down at it, considering its edge. "They'll burn or choke to death. Stomach wounds are painful, yes, but I made this one quick for you. Now…" He shook his head, flipping over the blade in his hand. "One last, really good scream for the queen, and we'll have you on your way, all right?"

The dagger flashed, quick as lightning. Harron thrust down, aiming to drive it point-first into my other shoulder, but…something happened. The metal tip froze an inch away from my filthy, torn shirt, hovering above me. He…he stayed his hand?

I gagged on another mouthful of blood, struggling to swallow it back down, to breathe around it. When I looked up at Harron, his eyes were wide, more alert than they had been a moment ago. He stared at me, his disbelief plain as day. Shaking with the effort, he was using both hands now, struggling to drive the knife home.

"How…are you doing that?" he grunted. "That…isn't…possible."

I couldn't answer him. I was a burning wick, consumed by pain, but there was something inside of me, something cool, and calm, and made of iron, that rose up and *claimed* Harron's knife as its own.

The stillness wanted the blade, and so it took it. As if I had a third, invisible hand, I reached out toward the dagger, and I wrapped my will around it. The weapon trembled, its tip quivering.

"Stop," he whispered. "This is *heresy.*"

I couldn't stop. I had no control over what was happening. I desperately wanted the dagger away from me, and so I forced against it in my mind, commanding it to...

Harron gasped as the dagger glowed white hot. The metal screeched in my ears—a horrific, awful sound that cleaved me to my soul. The sound of madness. Gritting my teeth, I answered the voice inside of me, commanding me to *unmake* the dagger, like such a thing was even possible. And it was. Almost as stunned as Harron, I watched as the knife liquified in the captain's gloved hand and ran through his fingers in rivulets of rolling silver.

"Heretical...*magic!*" Harron gasped. He tried to lunge away but lost his balance, toppling backward onto his ass, his boots kicking against the stone as he struggled to get away. "Where did you learn how to—no. *No!*"

Terror claimed the captain. He cast about, wild-eyed, breathing heavily as the thin streams of metallic liquid that had once been his weapon rolled toward him, pooling and diverging, as if it were seeking him. As if it were *alive.*

"End this," Harron panted. "Even if it takes me, you won't escape the palace. You're bleeding out, anyway. You're already dead!"

A strange, rippling weight shifted in my stomach. I could barely feel it over the pain, but I could sense that calm, unknown something inside me was turning its focus back toward me. It was a question. Did I want to stop whatever course I had set the once-knife on? It would be easy. To call it back. Bring it to heel. Because it *was* dangerous. There were things it could *do.* I didn't know what, but...

I would find out.

Harron was right. I *was* already dead. No one could survive the injuries he'd inflicted upon me. But Hayden was still alive. Elroy. Maybe even Vorath, though the cry that came from his shop as I fled earlier suggested otherwise. So long as my friends still lived, I had every reason to hurt Harron. And if the flowing metal I had created from the dagger he had planned on stabbing me with might prevent him from hurting the people I cared about, then I'd use it to hurt him first.

I couldn't speak anymore. Couldn't move. I was so dizzy that the vast hall pitched up and down like I was drunk...but I wasn't done yet. I had enough strength to see *this* through.

Madra would have to find someone else to murder my people. She had an endless supply of guardians who were more than willing to do her bidding, but this man wouldn't be amongst them. Harron wouldn't be the one to spill Hayden's or Elroy's blood, the way that he had spilled mine. I knew that I could end him with this strange and hungry metal if I wanted to. And why shouldn't I? Life wasn't fair. I'd never expected it to be, but I did believe that you reaped what you sowed in this city, and that meant that Harron, Captain of Madra's guard, had a debt he needed to settle before I died.

"Saeris? Saeris! Call it off! You don't...you don't *understand*—"

"Oh, but I do," I croaked. "You expect me to die by your hand, but—" I held my stomach as I coughed, spluttering on another mouthful of blood. "You don't want to come with me through that doorway you mentioned, do you, Captain?"

"I can't go. She won't *let* me!" Harron had plenty of room to flee, but the man was frozen solid, muscles locked up, too petrified to move an inch. He whimpered as the humming threads of silver branched out like the tributaries of the rivers I'd marveled over in library books and began creeping up the toe of his leather boot.

What would happen to him?

It didn't really matter. He was going to suffer the same way he'd made me suffer. I was growing weaker by the second, my wounds losing blood at a phenomenal rate. The clock was ticking. I'd be gone soon, but...the stubborn part of me wanted him to die first. And I wanted to be standing on my own two feet when it happened. So, I got to work.

Saeris Fane was twenty-four years of age when she died. Honestly, she should have died a lot sooner, but the girl never did know when to give up.

My epitaph would be short and sweet. Elroy would see to something for me, provided that he survived any of this. In the meantime, I was going to drag my bleeding backside up off of this hard floor and watch whatever came next.

I was sweating, weak-legged, and nauseous when I finally managed to get up. Panting hard down my nose, I took one staggering step toward the captain and realized just how hard it was going to be to stay conscious. I was a (temporarily) living, breathing pin cushion. Harron's sword and his other dagger were still sticking out of me. It was a miracle the sword hadn't fallen out yet. The weight of it twisting inside me was excruciating, but I held back my screams as I stumbled, dragging myself on ice-cold feet toward Harron.

Frantically, he slapped his pant legs, brushing the fabric with a sweeping motion, though very careful not to touch the molten silver at the same time. "Monster," he hissed. "You'll end the world with this. D-don't let it take me. P-please!"

What did he expect? Had he listened to me when I was pleading for my life? Had he taken pity on me right before he drove his sword into my gut? He hadn't. I had no understanding of what it was I was doing, but if this was a world-ending gift, then good. Fuck this city and fuck this world. My family was already doomed, and what did I care for anyone else? If Harron was telling the truth, then I'd be doing the rest of the people in the Third a favor.

The torches resting in the sconces blazed, roaring as their flames danced and leaped, casting an eerie orange glow up the walls. On the ground, the silver threads persisted in climbing up Harron's legs, probing, ever moving upward, on a mission to find skin.

How I knew that, I couldn't comprehend, but I did know that Madra would be hearing Harron's music as soon as they achieved their goal.

"Please," Harron whispered.

"No." The word was as hard as granite. I looked down at the bastard's sword protruding out of my chest, wishing I could pull it out. What a dark and beautiful irony it would be to end this fucker's

life with his own sword, but I'd be dead the second I withdrew the thing, and I wanted to hang around long enough to see...

I needed something else. One of the torches, perhaps. If I could muster the energy to shuffle across the hall and reach one, I could use it to set him alight, the way he planned on torching the Third. I'd made it three bracing, agonizing steps before I noticed the *other* sword to my left. I'd seen it when Harron had dragged me in here, though I hadn't been able to make out what it was then. I'd thought it was some kind of lever. But this close, I could see that it was, in fact, a sword, buried halfway up to its hilt into the ground.

Gods only knew if I had the strength to free it, but I was going to try.

There were steps up to the raised platform where the ornate weapon had been buried. When I heaved myself up the first of these steps, groaning out loud in pain, Harron broke free from his hysteria. He got to his feet, his voice ringing out, loud and urgent.

"Saeris, no! Do *not* touch the sword. Do *not*...turn the key!" he panted. "Do *not* open the gate! You—you've no idea the hell you will unleash on this place!"

He thought I would *care*?

My vision flickered red, a lifetime of rage and injustice finally demanding retribution. Hell had already been unleashed upon this place centuries ago. What was a little more suffering?

The second step up toward the platform was slightly easier, but only because it was a step closer to death. A cold, numb feeling washed over me, dulling my senses and fogging my thoughts. I'd left a pool of blood on the floor behind me, along with a wide trail of it in my wake when I got up and limped up here, but now my heart was laboring, almost out of blood to pump.

I reached the top step of the platform, dizzy and exhausted. I immediately dropped to my knees and retched. I wanted to be sick so badly, but my body was shutting down. It couldn't remember how, or else my stomach couldn't contract properly with the blade of a sword slicing through it, so I spat out globs of congealed blood onto the smooth ground instead.

The sword was old. I felt its age on the air somehow—a prickle of energy that spoke of hidden, ancient places.

"Do *not* touch that sword!" Harron repeated. He panicked, rushing toward me, about to hit the steps. He'd given up swatting at the filaments of silver spreading out over his chest, slowly rising up toward his throat.

If he made it to the top of the steps, I was done for. Ignoring the pain and my darkening vision, I sank back onto my heels and turned my back to the blade, resting my wrists against the ancient weapon's edge. I expected it to be dull—I somehow *knew* that it hadn't been touched by another living creature in centuries—but I hissed in surprise when I lifted upward, and the thing cut through the ties at my wrists like a hot knife through butter.

"Saeris, *no!*"

Harron almost had me. I twisted, releasing an ungodly scream as *his* sword tipped forward and slid free from my stomach, clattering to the ground. I felt it then: the loosening at the very center of me, as if something fundamental had come undone. There was no putting me back together now. *"Let's be done with it, then,"* a small voice whispered in the back of my quieting mind. I grabbed the old sword by the hilt, a bolt of energy firing up both arms as I drew it from the stone and turned it on Harron.

I wheezed out eight words, knowing they'd be my last, enjoying the stupidity of them. "This is the part where...*you* scream...Captain." And then I swung with all my might.

The sword sliced into Harron's shoulder, cutting right through his oiled leather breastplate like it wasn't even there, leaving a bright red line of blood in its wake. Harron's bark of pain echoed around the vaulted ceiling. The wound wasn't enough to kill him, but I'd certainly hurt him. He came at me, pressing a hand to his chest to stem his own flow of blood. I assumed he would grab me again, but this time, he lunged for the blade, the whites of his eyes showing.

"Put it back! You've got to put it back!"

It was too late for that. A song couldn't be unsung. The sword was free, and every part of me knew that it wasn't going back into...

Into...

I was sinking.

The ground that I had assumed was solid stone beneath my feet was nothing of the sort. Harron's blade had melted into a respectable amount of liquid metal, but the ground at my feet...the *pool* at my feet...was more silver than I had ever seen in my life, and it was hissing and spitting like an angry cat. It hadn't been like this a moment ago. It had been solid. Now it was softening by the second. The roiling mass of it was already up to my ankles.

I couldn't pull my boots free. The surface of the silver pool shone in the dim light of the hall, emitting its own sort of light. With my feet stuck in place, Harron could have ended me once and for all, but the thin threads of silver that had been his dagger had now reached the collar of his breastplate and were greedily climbing up his throat.

His skin was white as ash. "Gods," he breathed. "It's so..." But he didn't finish his sentence. His eyes rolled back into his head, and he began to shake.

The pool of silver I stood in rose at an alarming rate. Or was it just getting deeper? I couldn't tell the difference. My thoughts were so scattered, none of them making sense. This was the blood loss. It had to be. I'd die soon enough, and then it would all be over.

Hayden. Hayden would be...

The queen would forget.

They would be safe.

All of them would be...

My eyelids were so heavy. Ten feet away, at the base of the steps, Harron cursed, thrashing against an invisible foe. I would leave him to his private war. It was time for me to sleep. I—

The liquid metal erupted underneath me, the silver slopping over the sides of what was now clearly a circular pool. Freed from its hold and with nothing to keep me up any longer, I toppled side-ways onto the stone steps, a snapping sensation jolting me, though I mercifully felt no pain.

My vision was going at last. Blackness crept in, rolling before my eyes like a midnight fog. Only it wasn't a fog. It was something else. It was...

Death.

The bastard had come to claim me in person.

Emerging from the silver, the huge figure rose up from the pool as if ascending from the very depths of hell itself. Broad shoulders. Wet, shoulder-length black hair. Tall. Taller than any other man I'd ever seen. His eyes shone an iridescent, shimmering green, the pupil of the right eye rimmed by the same shining metallic silver that ran in ribbons from the black leather armor that covered his chest and arms.

He towered over me, his lips pulled back into a snarl, revealing gleaming white teeth and sharp canines. In his hand, he held a monstrous sword forged out of a black metal that vibrated with a tempestuous energy that sang in the marrow of my bones. He raised the sword, about to bring it down and cleave me in two, but then his quick eyes landed on the ancient sword *I* was still holding and he froze, arm raised above his head.

"Graceless gods," he hissed. "What's this? A fucking joke?"

"Die!" Harron bellowed. "I will *not!* Take your lies and your serpent tongue. Choke on it! Die!"

Death snapped his head to Harron, forgetting that he'd come to end my suffering. His hair hung in damp waves about his face, though the silver that he had risen from wasn't coating his hair, his clothes, or his skin as it was Harron. The metallic fluid ran off of his boots and defied the laws of nature as it pooled back together, rolling *up* the steps and pouring back into the pool.

I didn't have the energy to raise my head and watch as Death descended the steps toward Harron. My eyes were flashing now. Flickering. My ears still worked, though.

"Obsidian. Ob-obsidian!" exclaimed Harron. "Broken. Every-where, everywhere, everywhere. Down in the ground. In the pas-sageways. In the walls. They move. In the ground. I can't...it won't *die!* It *has* to!" he screamed.

"Unfortunate." I had known Death's voice to be a howling hot wind across the parched desert. A wet, hacking cough in the night. The urgent cry of a starving baby. I had never for one moment imag-ined his voice might also be the stroke of velvet in the ever-encroaching darkness. "Where's Madra?" he demanded.

Harron didn't respond. A scurrying, scratching was the only sound that reached me where I lay on the steps.

"I can't pull it out of you," Death said wearily. "Your fate's sealed, Captain. You deserve far fucking worse."

The ground. The passages. They m—they move. In the ground. Obsid-ian. Ob...obsid...obsidian...

A scuffling. A scraping. A low, hard thud. Harron let out a pan-icked screech, but his cry was quickly shut off.

When Death climbed the steps again, his boots were the only part of him that I could see in my narrowing field of vision. My heart wanted to pound when he crouched down beside me, coming into view, but it could only manage a weak squeeze of fear.

Of course Death was beautiful. How else would anyone choose to go with him without putting up a fight? Even though he scowled at me, his dark brows tugging together to form a dark, unhappy line, he was still the most savagely beautiful thing I'd ever seen.

"Pathetic," he murmured. "Absolutely..." He couldn't seem to find the words. Shaking his head, he reached into the front of his chest plate, fishing around for something. A moment later, he withdrew his hand, a long silver chain hooked around his index finger. He unfastened it.

"If you die before you can give this back, I'm *not* going to be happy," he groused. The chain was warm against my skin as he looped it around my neck. Ever since I'd fallen against the steps, my body had been blissfully numb, but the reprieve proved temporary as the stranger in black lifted me roughly into his arms.

The pain shattered me this time, until there was nothing left.

My silent scream died on my lips as Death carried me into the pool.

The darkness took me before the silver could.

6

EVERLAYNE

ONCE, when I was eight, it rained in the Silver City. The heavens cracked open, and a deluge of water fell from the sky for a whole day. The streets flooded, and buildings that had stood for generations washed away. No one had ever seen such a blanket of clouds blotting out the suns. And for the first and only time in my life, I had known what it was to be cold.

I wasn't cold now. This was something else entirely, and it was *unbearable.* My bones were made of ice. They promised to shatter if I dared to move, but no matter how hard I tried, I couldn't stop shivering. Locked in darkness, I could see nothing at all. There were sounds in this icy prison, though. Voices. Sometimes many. Sometimes just one. I began to recognize them as time passed. I heard the female voice the most. She spoke to me, talking softly, telling me secrets. She sang to me as well. Her voice was soft and sweet and made me miss my mother in a way that caused me to ache inside. I couldn't understand the things she sang about. Her words were a mystery, the language she spoke unfamiliar and strange.

I lay in the darkness and shivered, wishing that she would fuck off. I didn't want to be haunted by these ghosts. I wanted to slip into the nothingness, until the cold froze me over, and the silence blocked my ears, and I became nothing and forgot that I had ever lived.

Instead, the tips of my fingers came back to me. Then my toes. My arms and legs followed. Gradually, over a span of time that could have been an hour but just as easily a week, my body returned bit by bit. The pain made me wish I'd been better in life. This had to be a punishment. My ribs threatened to crack with every breath I drew—and I *was* breathing somehow. My insides felt as if they had been torn out of my body, shredded to pieces, and then stuffed back inside me. Everything hurt, every second of every minute, of every hour...

I prayed for an oblivion that refused to come. And then, out of nowhere, I opened my eyes, and the darkness was gone.

The bed I was lying in didn't belong to me. The only feather mattress I'd ever slept on in my whole life was Carrion Swift's, and this bed didn't belong to that asshole, either. This bed was far bigger, for starters, and it didn't smell like muskrat. A set of immaculate white sheets covered my body, on top of which lay a thick, woolen blanket. High overhead, the ceiling was not the pale golden color of sandstone. It was mostly white, but...no. It wasn't white. It was a pale, washed-out blue, and there were streaks and dabs of dove-gray sporadically daubed here and there, forming clouds. It was beautifully done. The walls of the room were a darker shade of blue, bordering on violet.

As soon as I marked the color, along with not one but five different paintings, displayed in heavy gilt frames mounted on the walls, the plush-looking couch in the corner of the room, and the shelf opposite the bed, loaded up with more books than I'd ever seen in one place at any one time, a sinking dread sank its claws into me.

I was still in the palace. Where else could I be? No one in the Third could possibly have scrounged together the type of money it would cost to create the dye for violet paint. Not to mention the only artworks I'd ever seen were faded pictures in books, but these were real. Oil paint on canvas, with real wooden frames.

I let out a panicked breath, my alarm rising in magnitude when I saw the cloud of fog form on my breath. Where was I, and what the five hells was happening? Why could I *see* my breath?

I tried to move, but my body wouldn't comply. Not even the smallest twitch. I might as well have been paralyzed. If I could swing my legs out of—ah, ah, no. No, no. No. That wasn't going to work. I—

I froze as the door to the opulent room opened. My eyes were already open. It was pointless closing them now, when I'd already been caught awake. I was too anxious to look at whoever had entered the room, so I remained perfectly still, staring up at the clouds painted on the ceiling, holding my breath.

"Master Eskin said you'd wake up today," a female voice said. The same voice that had sung to me. That had reached out to me in the dark. "And here I was, doubting him. I should know better by now." The woman, whoever she was, laughed softly.

Was she one of Madra's lady's maids? Was she going to gut me the moment I stopped playing dead and looked at her? Common sense rejected both of these possibilities. A lady's maid wouldn't be so chatty. And why would they have gone to the effort of keeping me alive if they only planned on murdering me?

I slowly moved my head, turning to inspect this newcomer.

She leaned against the wall by the door, holding a stack of dusty books. Her hair was the lightest blond, so long it reached well past her waist, tamed into two elaborate braids, each as thick as my wrist. She could only be, what, twenty-four? Twenty-five? Around the same age as me. Her skin was pale, her eyes a vivid shade of green.

The hunter-green dress she wore was a work of art. Brocaded, the bodice was embroidered with golden thread that shimmered when it caught the light. The full skirt was decorated with embroidered leaves. The stranger grinned at me, still clutching hold of her books. "How are you feeling?" she asked.

The urge to cough hit me out of nowhere. I did my best to answer her question, but I couldn't help it. I started to sputter, a spiderweb of pain spreading up my sides as my body jerked.

"Oh no. Wait. Here, let me help you," the girl said. She rushed into the room, set her pile of books down on a small table by the window, then picked up a cup and brought it to the bed. Holding it out, she beamed, offering it to me. "There. Down in one. Eskin said you'd be parched when you came around."

I shrank back into the bed, tucking my arms in tight against my body, eyeing her warily. "What is that?"

"Nothing. Just water, I promise."

Nothing? I took the cup, peering over its rim, feeling lightheaded. She wasn't lying. The receptacle was full to the brim with water. Four days' worth. I'd spend a month trying to get out from underneath the debt this amount of water would put me in down in the Third. And she was just...*handing* it to me?

"Go on." She smiled uncertainly. "Drink. I'll refill it for you when you're done."

She was toying with me. Well, more fool her. I held the cup to my lips and started to drink, swallowing as quickly as I could. The water was cold—so cold that it made my throat ache. It hurt to drink it so quickly, but I wasn't giving her a moment to change her mind. By the time she realized that I wasn't entitled to a ration this big, the water would be gone, and there wouldn't be any way for her to get it back.

Gods, it was clean. Clean water. It almost tasted sweet.

"Whoa, now," the girl said. "Slowly does it. You'll make yourself sick if you're not...careful."

I'd already finished, though. I handed her back the cup, expecting her to hold out a hand for payment now that I'd drained it dry. But she just smiled and returned to the table by the window, where she refilled the cup from a tall copper pitcher. I eyed her suspiciously when she came back and gave me the full cup again, wondering if she was mad.

"I'm Everlayne. I've been visiting you," she said.

"I know."

She glanced down at the cup, nodding to it. "It's okay. You can drink that, too, if you're thirsty."

I sipped the water this time, watching, waiting for her to pull a dagger from her voluminous skirts and pounce.

"Since I told you my name, maybe you could tell me yours?" She canted her head to one side. "Gods, actually, do you mind if I pull up a chair? I've been climbing up and down the stairs all day, and I forgot to eat this morning."

"Sure?"

She—*Everlayne*—grinned as she snagged a simple wooden chair and dragged it to the bedside. As soon as she had the chair positioned to her liking, she sat down heavily in it, tucking rogue strands of hair behind her ears. "All right. There. I'm ready. What are you, then? A Marika? An Angelica?" Her eyes, bright as jade, flashed as she spoke. "I'm not a very patient person," she admitted in a confessional tone. "I've been calling you Liss for the past ten days. That seemed as good a name as any, but..." She slowed, the light in her eyes dimming as she took in the look on my face. "What is it? What's the matter?"

"Your *ears*," I whispered. I'd been staring at them ever since she'd tucked her loose strands of hair behind them. They were...

I swallowed hard.

Took a deep breath.

They were *pointed*.

Everlayne touched her finger to the tips of her ears, frowning softly. Her expression went blank when she realized what I was referring to. "Ahh. Right. They aren't the same as yours, no."

The Fae were warmongers. Cannibals. Beastly creatures with no temperance, sense of morality, nor any notion of mercy. The eldest Immortals visited their wrath upon the land with an iron fist, leaving a path of chaos and destruction in their wake. The seven cities rejoiced when—

"It's upset you. My appearance," Everlayne said quietly. She placed her hands in her lap, all of her effervescence quickly fallen flat. "You've heard of my kind?" she asked.

"Yes." Was this really happening, or was this some kind of sick joke? Was Hayden teasing me? Getting me back for being so cruel to him the last time I saw him? This would be a fine way of getting revenge, making me doubt my sanity, but...

I'd left my brother in the street outside The Mirage. I'd gone with Captain Harron. I'd met the queen, and she'd ordered my execution, along with the execution of my friends, family, and every other living soul in the Third.

Death had come for me, with wavy black hair and wicked green eyes.

He'd carried me away from that place.

He had brought me *here.*

A wave of heat swept over me, making my mouth sweat. I hadn't paid much attention, dying as I'd been at the time, but when the dark-haired stranger had picked me up, the tips of his ears had been strangely shaped, too. And his canines...

"Show me your teeth." The demand slipped out before I could reel it back.

The woman in the green gown clapped a hand over her mouth, her eyes widening. "What? No!" she exclaimed behind her palm. "Absolutely not! That's...that's so *rude!*"

"I'm sorry. But...you're *Fae?*"

The statement sounded like the punchline to a bad joke, but Everlayne wasn't laughing. "I am," she answered, still hiding her mouth.

"But...you're not real."

"I beg to differ," she fired back.

"Myths. Stories. The Fae are folklore. There's no such *thing* as the Fae."

"Don't I seem real to you?"

"I suppose so. But...the Fae had wings."

Everlayne snorted. "We haven't had *those* for thousands of years." She dropped her hand, huffing a little as she pointed to the cup of water I was still holding. "Look. You have a concussion. Finish that and see if you feel any better. Things might feel a little backward for a while."

My disbelief had nothing to do with the lump on the back of my head. You didn't just forget an entire race of people because you hit your head too hard. The Fae were *not* real. I squirmed, trying to prop myself up a little better, still scrutinizing Everlayne's ears. "My mother told me stories about the Fae when I was little," I said. "The Fae visited the shores of our land, bringing with them war, disease, and death—"

A look of indignation stole across Everlayne's pretty features. "Excuse me, but the Fae are not diseased. We haven't been afflicted by blight of any kind in a millennium. Humans, on the other hand, are riddled with all sorts of germs. You fall sick and die at the drop of a hat."

I'd offended her. Again. That was twice in the space of a minute. As far as first meetings went, I wasn't doing a stellar job of making a good impression here. Taking a steadying breath, I tried to formulate a question that wouldn't come across as rude, but Everlayne huffed, speaking before I could.

"You're telling me that the Fae have become a bedtime story meant to scare children in Zilvaren?"

"Yes!"

"What else do they say about us?"

"I...I don't know. I can't remember right now." I remembered plenty, but none of it was very flattering. I had no desire to offend her again by telling her that Zilvaren mothers warned their children that a Fae hag would come and eat them in the night if they didn't behave themselves.

Everlayne frowned, peering at the side of my head. "Hmm.

How's your short-term memory? What's the last thing you *can* remember?"

"Oh. I was in the palace. Madra's captain was trying to kill me. I... stopped his dagger somehow and grabbed hold of a sword. Then the floor turned to molten silver. A big pool of it. And...something came out of it."

"Something? Or some*one*?"

"A man," I whispered.

But Everlayne shook her head. "A *male*. He came because the sword called to him..." She trailed off, throwing her hands in the air. "Gods, I still don't know your name. Unless you don't *have* a name."

"Of course I have a name," I said. "It's Saeris." I could count on one hand the number of people I'd given my real name to when prompted. But for some reason, lying to her seemed wrong. I had no idea how long I'd been unconscious for, but Everlayne had visited me. Talked to me. Watched over me, and sung to me, and kept me company. Those weren't the actions of a being who wanted to cause me harm.

Everlayne's eyebrow arched knowingly. "Ahh. *Saeris.* A pretty name. A *Fae* name. How are you feeling? You're sore, I bet, but you must be feeling a lot better than when you first arrived."

"I feel..." How *did* I feel? The last time I'd checked, I had a monstrous hole in my stomach and a dagger sticking out of my shoulder, not to mention that I'd lost near every last drop of blood in my body. With stiff arms, I slowly lifted the blanket covering me and surveyed the damage beneath. There wasn't much to see. I was wearing some type of tunic—pale green and made of soft, buttery material. I patted my stomach, feeling for the gaping wound through the fabric, but there was nothing. My stomach felt smooth. There wasn't even any pain.

"Our healers are extremely talented. Though, it's been some time since they worked on a human with such catastrophic injuries," she admitted. "They decided to keep you sedated while your internal organs repaired. I argued to wake you up as soon as you were officially whole again, but Eskin said you needed another couple of days for your mind to calm after the trauma you'd experienced."

"Wait. So I'm *not* going to die?"

Everlayne chuckled, shaking her head. "No. Eskin's success rate is a point of pride for him these days. He hasn't lost a patient in nearly two centuries."

Two *centuries?* The songs our mother sang to Hayden and me when we were tiny always spoke of the Fae's unnatural life spans. I still couldn't wrap my head around the fact that Everlayne was Fae, though. Did I believe it? Was my mind even capable of accepting that as the truth? It just wasn't *possible.*

"I take it...we're not in the Silver City, then," I said slowly.

She smiled. "We're not."

My stomach rolled. "Then where are we?"

"Yvelia." She beamed, as though her one-word answer explained my entire situation.

"And...where is that?"

"*Yvelia!* More specifically, the Winter Palace. Didn't your mother's bedtime stories tell you anyth—"

The door crashed open.

Cold light flooded in from the hallway beyond, and a monster clad in leather armor prowled into the room, eliciting a gasp out of Everlayne. His eyes were the darkest brown, his fair skin splattered with what looked like mud. His sandy brown hair hung past his shoulders, the top part sectioned and tied back into a war braid. He was frighteningly tall, his bare, muscular forearms covered in intricate, interwoven tattoos that blurred as my eyes tried to focus on them. The murderous look on his face softened somewhat when he saw Everlayne.

Everlayne, however, had turned purple. "Renfis! What in all five hells! You nearly gave me a heart attack."

Chagrined, he hung his head. And there they were: another set of pointed ears. This time, they were tipped red with embarrassment. "Layne," the male said. His voice was lightly accented, the words lilting, though made harsh by his deep register. "Sorry. I didn't know you were in here."

"Clearly. You nearly ripped the damned door off its hinges. It's polite to knock *before* you hurl yourself into a room."

The male—Renfis—glanced briefly in my direction, eyes shifting over me where I lay in the bed, before returning his attention to Everlayne. "Right. Sorry. Manners have never been my strong suit. Irrin's destroyed what little etiquette I had to begin with."

Everlayne's mouth twitched. Was she trying not to smile? "Why *are* you bursting in here, anyway?" she asked.

"I came to find the human." Renfis's eyes darted to me again. "He needs his chain back."

"His chain? Oh!" Everlayne's frown mirrored my own, but hers disappeared a split second after it formed. She'd obviously worked out what Renfis was referring to while I was still in the dark. Turning to me, she looked at the hollow of my throat, her lips drawing into a small pout. "She might still need it," she said.

I raised my hand to my throat. The second my fingertips found the cool metal resting against my skin there, I remembered. Death, dressed in midnight, taking a chain from his neck and looping it around mine. Death, scooping me up into his arms. The look of disappointment in his eyes. Death—

"Believe me. He needs it more than she does right now," Renfis said darkly.

Suddenly, the chain felt like a noose around my neck. What the hell was it? And why had the male who had carried me away from Madra's palace put it on *me?*

Everlayne got to her feet. "It's only been ten days. He shouldn't be affected yet, surely?"

"He's *struggling*," the warrior said awkwardly. "He shouldn't have been without it at all. It gets worse every time he takes it off. If your father finds out he's even here—"

"I know, I know. Gods. I want to *see* him, Ren. This is getting ridiculous."

Renfis looked at his boots. "He wasn't in any fit state. Still isn't. The best thing you can do for him right now is help me get the pendant back to him."

The set of Everlayne's shoulders was stiff. The two of them traded a tense look, but she dipped her head and sighed. Turning to me, she said, "All right. Fine. Saeris, I hate to ask, but the chain you're wearing around your neck..."

I was already fumbling with the clasp, trying to get the damned thing off. If the savage who owned the necklace wanted it back, I wouldn't give him a reason to come and get it himself. A cold shiver shot through me as I finally managed to unfasten the chain and offered it out to Everlayne.

I hadn't noticed it before, but there was something dangling from the necklace—a small silver disc. A family crest, perhaps? The disc was engraved with tiny markings, but I'd be damned if I was going to study it up close. Now that it wasn't hanging around my neck anymore, the chain felt like it was humming. The strangest energy fired up and down my arm, not painful but certainly not a pleasant sensation. And it was cold. *So* cold. By the time Renfis strode across the room and stopped by the bed, holding out a small, black velvet pouch, the chain might as well have been made of ice.

"Drop it inside," Renfis said. He held the mouth of the pouch open, very careful not to let the chain touch his skin while I did as he'd bade me. As soon as the chain had disappeared inside, the warrior pulled a tie on either side of the pouch, cinching it shut. Without another word, he spun away and made for the door.

"I want to see him before he goes, at least," Everlayne called after Renfis. "There are things I need to ask him."

Renfis paused, his massive frame filling the doorway. "He has to leave, Layne. I've kept him hidden this long by luck alone. The guards are starting to get suspicious. If they find out he's here..."

Everlayne looked down at her feet. "Yes, you're right."

"He's needed back in Cahlish, anyway. Write to him if you have to. Visit in a month or two. But having him stay here a moment

longer than necessary would be"—he chose his last words carefully—
"*ill-advised.*"

Everlayne had gone pale, but she didn't fight him. "Okay, I'll write.
Tell him he'd better write back, or there'll be trouble."

Renfis bowed his head. "It was good to see you," he murmured.
And then he was gone. With him, he took the tension that had
flooded the room when I'd removed the necklace, and for that I was
eternally grateful. Everlayne didn't relax the way I did, though. Her
eyes shone bright with the beginnings of tears as she put her back
to the door and said in a forcefully cheery voice, "All right, then. I
expect *you'll* be wanting to have a bath."

"A *bath?*"

"Yes. It's been at least ten days since you've had a proper soak.
Come on. I'll draw some hot water for you. It'll make you feel a million times better, I swear."

Hot water? A whole tub full of it. For me to *wash* myself in. The
waste of so much water would have stricken me dumb on any other
day, but today there were far stranger things to concern myself with.
And besides, I was too focused on something both Renfis and Everlayne had said.

Ten days. That's how long I'd been unconscious for, lying in this
bed, recovering in peace, while my brother was back in Zilvaren,
potentially fighting for his life.

"I don't need a bath," I said. "I need to go home. My little brother
needs me."

Whatever Everlayne was about to say died on her lips. Slowly, in
increments, her smile faded. "I'm sorry, Saeris, but that isn't going to
happen."

"What do you mean? I have to go back. I don't have a choice.
Madra's planning on wiping out my entire ward. I have family back
there. Friends." I ignored the small voice in the back of my head,
whispering that it was already probably too late. Madra would have
been furious when she discovered what had happened in that hall.
Scratch that. Furious wouldn't have even come close. Not only did I

not die, but I'd somehow liquified Harron's dagger, it had attacked him, and I'd...I'd...fuck, I didn't even know *what* I'd done with that sword. I'd drawn it from somewhere I shouldn't have and summoned the devil himself. Harron was probably dead. Madra was not a merciful monarch. Her vengeance would have been swift and horrific. Odds were that the Third had already been reduced to a crater in the sand, but I still had to get back there. If there was even the slimmest chance that she'd temporarily stayed her hand, I had to try and stop her. It was the least I could do.

Everlayne did look sympathetic as she headed slowly toward the door. But she also looked resigned. "I'm not going to lie to you. Some of the tales your mother used to tell you were true. My people can be ruthless and cruel at times. There are those of us who endeavor to be different, but...occasionally there's simply no other option. We've been waiting to retrieve that sword you drew for a very long time. But to have found *you* along with it..." She shook her head. "You have no idea how important you are, Saeris. I'm afraid my father isn't liable to give you up any time soon. And he wants to see you in an hour, so unfortunately, the bath isn't up for debate."

"You can't keep me trapped here. This is kidnapping. It's inhumane behavior!"

Everlayne at least had the decency to look contrite. "It's in*human* behavior. But we aren't human, Saeris. We're Fae. We don't behave like you. Don't think like you. We don't operate by the same moral guidelines that *some* of your kind do, either. The faster you remember that, the easier this will be," she said a little more gently. "Now, please. Bathe before the water gets cold. When you speak to my father, you can ask him about returning to your Silver City."

"And who the hell is your father to tell me if I get to go home?" My anger echoed loudly up and down the hallway. Both guards, who stood in stern silence, flinched, looking deeply uncomfortable.

"He is Belikon De Barra," Everlayne said evenly. "King of the Yvelian Fae."

I sobbed while I soaked in the copper tub. I had an inconceivable resource at my disposal and no way to share it with the people I loved. If Hayden and Elroy were alive, then they were dizzy with their thirst, just as they had been every day of their lives. Meanwhile, I was luxuriating in so much water that I could *drown* in it. It was black with dirt, and a film of scum bobbed on its surface when I was done scrubbing my skin until it was pink—probably the cleanest I had ever been. I'd never washed my hair properly before, nor had access to shampoo, and I used way too much, not expecting the amount I scooped into my palm to produce so many suds. It took forever to first work it through all of my tangles and knots, and then another age to rinse out all of the soap. Everlayne was prowling back and forth outside the room like a caged hellcat by the time I told her that I was done.

She looked harried when she bustled back into the room. "We don't have time to deliberate over what you should wear now. We'll have to get you laced into the first thing that fits and worry about style another time."

"Laced? What are you talking about?"

"Your *dress!*" Everlayne made a beeline for the large, dark wood wardrobe, throwing open the doors. "With that dark hair and your eyes such a lovely shade of blue, I think we should stick to royal blue, or maybe..." The top half of her body disappeared into the wardrobe. When she emerged again, she clutched a staggering amount of cobalt fabric in her arms. I backed away as soon as I saw it.

"No. No, I'm not—I don't *do* dresses, Everlayne."

"What do you mean?" She looked genuinely confused.

"I wear pants. Shirts. Things I can move easily in. So I can run, and climb, and—" *Kill people.*

"You're not wearing a shirt and pants to meet the king, Saeris.

He'll see it as a slight. If you're not well turned out, he'll have you thrown into the cells."

Hah. Another day, another monarch throwing my ass in jail. Honestly, a cell was what I deserved. After stealing the gauntlet and landing my entire ward in such trouble, I didn't deserve to see the light of day again. I was numb as I let Everlayne shake me into the dress. *Gown* was a more appropriate name for it, really.

"You look like a dream," Everlayne announced when she was done jiggling and poking me, tugging on corset stays so hard that I thought I might pass out.

"And yet I feel like I'm trapped in a nightmare," I added dryly.

She tutted. "Turn around and sit down on that chair. I need to deal with your hair next."

"What's wrong with my hair?"

"Well, hmm. How do I put this delicately? It looks like it's had a family of field mice living in it for a couple of years. And I'm betting it's been a while since it's seen a brush. So…"

"It doesn't *need* brushing if I just tie it back into a braid." I wasn't stung by the criticism. Seriously, I wasn't.

Everlayne laughed quietly—did she think I couldn't hear her chuckling? I slumped down on the chair where she'd told me to sit, fuming under my breath as the female wrestled with my knots. She was loving this, wasn't she? A little prisoner of her own. A doll to play dress-up with. But I wasn't a toy or a pet. She'd learn that the hard way if she treated me like one.

"You have beautiful hair," she said, running a wide-toothed comb through the strands. I winced as she swept it back over my shoulders. "It'll grow well here. Long hair is a sign of high-born status for Fae women. Others will be jealous of your dark coloring, too. Dark hair is a royal trait amongst the Yvelian Fae."

I didn't give two shits about Fae fads or trends. I didn't care whether Fae women were jealous of how I looked or if they thought I was a hideous monster. Up until four hours ago, I didn't even know they existed. I sat very still as Everlayne braided my hair with nimble fingers, biting the tip of my tongue. Once she was finished, she ushered me in front of a full-length mirror hanging on the wall in a scrolled and gilded frame, glowing with pride as she showed me her handiwork.

I'd made plenty of mirrors in the workshop with Elroy, but I'd personally never had much use for them. I knew what I looked like well enough. Yes, I had a pretty face, but pretty faces were used as currency in the Third when a girl ran out of coin or water to trade with, and that was more of a curse than a blessing. Masks and scarves were my friends. No one knew what you looked like behind a piece of sand-blasted sacking and, therefore, had no reason to try and take your *goods* for themselves.

There were no masks or scarves to hide behind here.

While it was true that I paled in comparison next to Everlayne's beauty—the female was radiant. Perfect in every way—the color of the ridiculous dress she picked out for me *did* complement my complexion as she'd said it would. It drew attention to my eyes and made them pop. And the magic she'd worked on my hair? The elaborate braided crown she'd fashioned for me was stunning. My hair had never looked so healthy.

"You don't need any blush," Everlayne's reflection said in the mirror. "You're rosy enough. Though…here." She hurried away for a second and then returned holding a small pot. She removed the pot's lid and offered it to me. "Your lips were so cracked when you arrived. I've been applying this for you every few hours, but now that you're awake, you can do it for yourself. Here, like this." She swept her fingertip across the thick, waxy resin inside and rubbed it across her lips.

I stuck my finger in the pot and did the same, if only to shut her up.

She looked desperately pleased with the results. "Wonderful. All right, then. I'd say we were ready. Brace yourself. It's time to meet the king."

THE DOG

THE BEDROOM HAD BEEN a level of luxury I'd never known before, but it served as no indication of the world beyond its door. I gaped as Everlayne guided me through the halls of the Winter Palace; the place made Madra's royal seat in Zilvaren look like a run-down backwater hovel.

The walls were opalescent white marble, faceted with sections of shimmering metallic blues and greens, as were the floors. We had no stone like this back in Zilvaren, but Everlayne explained that it was a rare type of pale labradorite. High archways lined the corridors we moved through, giving view to stairways and other corridors on other levels. Plush tapestries and framed paintings hung from the walls, and gigantic sprays of real flowers overflowed from vases everywhere I looked. Sunlight poured in through wide windows, though the light itself was devoid of any warmth— nothing at all like the punishing glare of the Twins. Everlayne urged me past these windows quickly, the world beyond them a blur of white and gray.

Dipping, she pressed the tips of her index finger and middle finger to her forehead, bowing her head in reverence as we passed a series of statues. Down another hallway, she repeated the process when we passed another row of the same figures cast in stone, again set back in alcoves.

"Who are they?" I asked, eyeing the tall, menacing-looking crowned males and females as she touched her fingers between her brows.

"The gods, of course." She looked a little surprised. "Don't you worship the Corcoran in the Silver City anymore?"

I shook my head, staring up into the coldly handsome face of one of the male deities. "My mother told me once that the people used to pray to gods in Zilvaren, but their names and their temples were eaten by the desert a long time ago. We say 'gods' to curse our luck or emphasize emotion. Other than that, Madra's the closest thing we have to a god in Zilvaren. At least that's how she fashions herself. The Undying Herald of the Northern Banner. Believers carry strands of her hair in leather pouches on their belts. They scrape ash from the funeral pyres of the living sacrifices that are burned in her honor and put that in them, too. It's supposed to act as a ward against plague. They think doing that will give them never-ending life if they're worthy enough."

Everlayne scoffed. "Superstition and sacrilege. Your queen is human. And even though the sand and the wind swept away the names of the gods, I assure you Madra knows them. That she's chosen to let them vanish from her people's history speaks volumes of her corruption." Everlayne pointed up at the male I was still staring at. "Styx, god of shadows." She moved along the line, inclining her head and touching her brow to each of her gods before she named them. "Kurin, god of secrets. Nicinnai, goddess of masks. Maleus, god of dawn and new beginnings. These two are often counted as one god," Everlayne said, gesturing to the two beautiful females who stood arm in arm atop the same marble plinth. "Balmithin. Twin sisters. Goddesses of the sky. Legend says that they once were one god, but a mighty storm came, and Balmithin refused to take shelter as it raged across the land. The powerful spirit within the storm was furious that Balmithin didn't cower before him, and so he lashed her with forks of lightning. Again and again, the lightning struck Balmithin, but she didn't die. Instead, she cracked and split in two, becoming Bal and Mithin. Bal is the goddess of the sun, but goddess of the day in a looser sense. Mithin is the goddess of the moon, but again, she presides over all of the night."

Bal. Mithin.

Balea. Min.

The Twins.

As I studied their faces closer, I realized that these two women did bear a startling similarity to faces I'd seen carved into the walls in the Hall of Mirrors. This was an undeniable link between this place and my home. One that made me feel strange.

I could have told Everlayne of the similarity between these goddesses' names and the names of the suns that perpetually blazed over Zilvaren, but for some reason, the words stuck in the back of my throat. I had too many questions, chief amongst which was how did the Fae here know of Madra? Everlayne spoke as if she was familiar with the queen of the Silver City. She had said Madra was a human with undeniable certainty. I also had no idea what a moon was, but I set all of that aside for now.

The final statue was tucked much farther into its alcove than the others. Unlike the others, it had been arranged so that its back was to the hall, its face pointing at the wall. I nodded to the male god with the broad shoulders and asked, "And him? What is he the god of?"

Everlayne eyed the statue warily, then gave me a chagrined smile. "That's Zareth, god of chaos and change." She walked up to him and bowed, placing her fingers on her brow as she had done with all the others, but then she reached around and placed her hand on his foot. I saw that the stone was patinaed there, on Zareth's right boot, as if thousands of hands had touched the god there.

"We Fae can also be a little superstitious sometimes," Everlayne admitted. "To look upon Zareth's face is to draw his focus. And very few people enjoy Zareth's attention being focused on them. We respect and revere him, but we'd all rather he was paying attention to what other people were doing instead of us. We touch him on the foot to guide him away from us." She patted his boot, stepping back. "We pray to each member of the Corcoran that they'll return to Yvelia someday. But in secret, a lot of us pray that Zareth gets a little lost on his journey home."

As Everlayne set off walking again, I paused by the tall god's back, studying it. I don't know why I did it. It seemed like the right thing to do, though. Reaching out, I placed my hand against the statue's boot, then hurried away.

On we went, passing too many open doorways to count. Bedrooms and studies. Rooms full of maps. Rooms full of books. Rooms with benches and glass vials of bubbling liquids suspended over fires. I should have been terrified of these strange new sights, but my curiosity won out over my fear.

The people we passed were interesting, too. Scores and scores of Fae, their clothes and visages so strange that I had to remind myself not to stare. Their ears were sloped to points, but that was where many of their similarities ended. Their hair was a veritable rainbow of colors, their eyes every natural and unnatural shade. Some of them were willowy and tall, some short and squat. The Fae who occupied the palace were a fascinating bunch, to be sure. They glared at me with open hostility as I struggled to keep pace with Everlayne's graceful, long strides.

The cold was pervasive. Everlayne had given me a strange look when I'd requested another layer, but she'd provided me a silken shawl all the same. Not that it did much. The chill in the air crept into my bones and settled there, forming ice in my joints. My teeth chattered loudly as we hurried toward our destination.

"You're being dramatic," Everlayne said, giving me an arch look.

"There are fires in every grate. And even if there weren't, the palace is kept at a steady, comfortable temperature at all times."

"How?" It wasn't that I didn't believe her. But, well...I didn't. I could still see my breath clouding in the air.

"Magic, of course," Everlayne replied. "There are wards cast over all of Yvelia to keep the cold at bay."

My mind balked at this. Magic. She said it so easily, as if the existence of such a thing were plain fact instead of straight-up impossible. But my definition of impossible needed revising, it seemed. If Everlayne existed, then so could magic, and I was fairly sure Everlayne was real. There was a chance that I was hallucinating, but the odds of that being true decreased with every passing moment that she guided me through the Yvelian Court. Hallucinations ended. This nightmare wouldn't fucking quit.

Eventually, we turned down a hallway, taking a left. A long, straight walkway stretched ahead of us. At the end of the walkway stood a massive set of wooden doors, twenty feet high, looming and ostentatious. Armed sentries dressed for battle stood on either side of it. As we hurried down the walkway, tiny birds with bright, colorful feathers flitted and chirped above us, engaged in aerial acrobatics. They were breathtaking. Under any other circumstances, I would have stopped to watch their impressive game of tag, but my heart had set to hammering and my palms were sweating, my attention drawn toward those ominous doors and what waited beyond them.

Up close, the guards were far more formidable than the ones outside my room. Everlayne didn't even acknowledge the males. Her confident stride didn't slow as she marched up to the doors. Wordlessly, the males snapped to attention and moved in concert, taking hold of the carved handles and pushing the doors open for us.

"Lady Everlayne De Barra," a powerful voice announced as we entered the hall. I was not announced. Like a dog nipping at its master's heels, I rushed along behind Lady Everlayne, feeling like a complete idiot for ever thinking that she was some kind of maid.

If I'd thought the Hall of Mirrors back in Zilvaren was big, then the Grand Hall of the Yvelian Court was ridiculous. The abyssal space must have taken years to construct. To the left and the right, seating stretched back, fifty rows deep. Hundreds of Fae sat there, watching with silent judgment on their faces as we entered.

The corniced ceiling forty feet above us was adorned with sculptures, the stonework etched with figures and details too small for me to see. Lavish tapestries and embroidered banners hung from the walls. Ahead, a fire burned in a brazier at the foot of a dais made out of more labradorite, and *oh!* Oh, holy *fuck!* The skull of a giant beast loomed over the labradorite dais, the bone bleached white and ghostly. Its orbital sockets were six feet wide. Its horned brow plate jutted from the shadows like the mast of a sand skiff. And its teeth. Saints and martyrs, its teeth. They were stained and terrible, each one razor sharp and at least twelve feet long.

"What *is* it?" I breathed.

Everlayne responded quickly in a muted whisper. "A dragon. The *last* dragon," she said meaningfully. "Its name was Omnamshacry. A legend amongst my people."

"It must have been a hundred feet tall!" I craned my head back as we approached and still couldn't quite grasp the beast's size. "How did it die?"

"Later," Everlayne hissed.

I was so mesmerized by the sheer horror of the skull that I barely noticed the six stately chairs positioned atop the dais below until we were standing in front of the crackling brazier.

"Daughter," came a cold, rough voice.

The king was an imposing male. His hair was black as jet, tinged gray at either of his temples. His eyes were a deep, dark, murky brown, sharp, and unfriendly. Though he wasn't thin by any means, he clearly wasn't given to excess. He sat before us in state wearing a heavy green velvet cape with the heads of scaled, snarling beasts cast in gold affixed upon the crest of each shoulder. One hand rested on the arm of his ornate throne. The other, encased in a leather glove, clutched the grip of a sword, the point of which bit into the ground at his feet. It was the sword. The one I'd drawn in the Hall of Mirrors. The metal glinted, reflecting the firelight, as the king absentmindedly spun the blade.

Everlayne stooped into a low curtsey before the King. Her father. "Your Highness."

Belikon's cloudy eyes came down on me with the force of a sledgehammer. I tried my best to meet them, but the intensity of his gaze was weaponized and difficult to withstand. A male seated to his left spoke, his voice rasping. "Do you not bow before a king, Creature?"

He was gaunt. Sickly looking, his skin as pale and thin as parchment. A network of blue veins snaked out across his cheeks like lashes of forked lightning. Eyes the color of dull pewter assessed me, simmering with distaste. Unlike the king, the male's attire was simple—a plain black robe that swamped his thin frame.

"He isn't my king," I answered tartly.

Everlayne flinched, though her reaction was fleeting. "Forgive her, Majesty. Your guest is tired and unaccustomed to her new surroundings."

Damn right, I wasn't accustomed to my new surroundings. It would take a miracle from every single one of the gods Everlayne just introduced me to before I acclimatized myself to all of this, and from the way she'd spoken about them, Everlayne's gods weren't even around anymore.

"Ignorance is no excuse for disrespect," the male spat.

"Quiet, Orious," King Belikon rumbled. "I haven't witnessed such open contempt in a long time. It's refreshing. I'll tolerate it until it grows tiresome. Step forward, girl."

Only three of the six seats on the dais were occupied. An ancient woman with thick gray hair and gnarled hands, dressed in white, observed me with eyes like twin pits as I lifted my chin defiantly and did as the king bade me.

"You stand before me a guest of this court, girl. As such, you're entitled to a certain amount of political leniency," Belikon said. "When you leave this throne room, you'll no longer be my guest. You'll be my subject and, therefore, will no longer benefit from clemency."

I opened my mouth, ready to argue against this declaration, but a swift kick to the ankle from Everlayne warned me to hold my tongue.

"There are rules to this kingdom. Rules that will be obeyed. You're about to spend a great deal of time in the libraries, learning about our ways. Any willful infraction of our laws will be dealt with swiftly. Now. You were brought here to fulfill a specific task. You'll complete that task quickly and efficient—"

I couldn't hold my tongue any longer. "I'm sorry, but...what do you mean, *task?*"

A cry went up amongst the Fae sitting in the gallery. I didn't need to be told that interrupting a king was execution-worthy, but the question had slipped out before I could stop it. And anyway, if he wanted to behead me, then so be it. I'd had the snot kicked out of me by Harron. I'd come this close to dying, and yes, it had sucked, but I wasn't afraid of death anymore. I was angry, and I wanted answers.

The king tipped his head an inch to the left, regarding me with the cruel intrigue of a hunter studying his quarry. "What do I mean?" he repeated.

Beside me, Everlayne whispered under her breath. Was she actually praying? I lifted my chin and said in a strong, clear voice, "No one's said anything about a task. I was carried here against my will—"

"If you'd been left where you were found, it would have cost you your life." Belikon's voice rebounded around the hall so loudly that the walls themselves seemed to tremble. "Would you rather have been abandoned there to perish?"

"I need to get back to Zilvaren. My brother—"

"Is already dead." The finality in Belikon's words made my head spin. "The Bitch Queen put an end to your home and all who resided in it."

"You don't know that."

The king's mouth twisted sourly. "She declared that she would. At least that is what I was told. We know your queen. A power-hungry despot with a black and shriveled heart. Violence is her creed. If she swore to kill them, then everyone you once knew is now long dead, along with thousands more. You, on the other hand, are still alive and, as far as I am concerned, owe the Fae of Yvelia a debt of gratitude. Your task will ensure that you repay that debt. I've only just learned the details of how you came to find yourself in Yvelia. The individual who brought you to my court"—Belikon ran his tongue over his teeth like he was trying to sweep away a foul taste—"told my guards that you were the one who reopened the portal. It seems highly unlikely that a human woke the quicksilver." He grunted, displeased. "But after a thousand years of waiting, we can't afford to dismiss this as heresy without checking first. Believe me when I say that we're all praying such a holy position hasn't fallen to such unholy blood." He inhaled sharply. "But the fates are strange. And one way or another, I will have the portals restored."

"I—"

The king lifted the sword in his hand and brought it swiftly down. The tip of the weapon crashed against the dais, and a shower of bright blue sparks exploded into the air. "You will not interrupt me a second time!" he roared. In the space of a heartbeat, his expression had gone from consternation to bitter outrage. "You're charged with awakening the quicksilver and reopening the pathways between this world and others. Your cooperation in that task will dictate how you spend your time in Yvelia. Rail against your purpose and life within the walls of this palace will become infinitely more uncomfortable for you. I have spoken."

I waited for him to give *me* leave to speak; a litany of objections and choice curse words burned hot on the tip of my tongue, but Belikon didn't extend me the courtesy. With a bored flick of his wrist, he gestured me away, like I was of no further interest to him. Anger ate a hole in my stomach. Refusing to be dismissed so rudely, I stood my ground. I anchored my feet to the floor, but Everlayne took me by the top of the arm, pushing me off to the right. Apparently, my audience with the king was at an end.

"Go." Everlayne shoved me harder, forcing me to move. I complied numbly, letting her lead me away from the dais toward the unoccupied bench at the front of the gallery to our left. Once I was sitting, she hissed, "Is your life really worth so little to you?"

"If Hayden really is dead...then yes," I whispered. "It's worth nothing."

Everlayne observed me with pensive eyes, but I didn't look at her. My focus was locked onto the bastard up on the dais. The king already seemed to have forgotten about me. His cruel features had grown impassive again. "I have other matters to attend to," he called. "Bring in the dog and let's be done with this."

The dog?

A susurrus of chatter spread through the gathered Fae. On the other side of the dais, a tall Fae male with flowing red hair brought down the butt of a heavy, gilded staff, and the resulting *Boom! Boom! Boom!* made the crowd fall silent. The doors at the end of the throne room groaned loudly, and chaos erupted as a group of warriors dressed in full armor entered the hall. There were six or seven of them, maybe. Amongst them, thrashing like a rabid animal, they dragged a male up the walkway toward the dais.

The male kicked and raged. The guards did their best to keep a hold of him, but despite their best efforts, he took two of them down, sending them crashing to the floor. Eventually, the guards managed to wrangle the straining figure to the front of the throne room, where they forced him to his knees.

Dark waves tumbled into the Fae male's face.

Dressed all in black, his shoulders were drawn up around his pointed ears. His chest rose and fell with the sawing of his breath. Tattoos writhed and shifted like smoke across every patch of visible skin, creeping up the back of his neck and swirling over the backs of his hands.

It was Death.

In such a feral state, he bore little resemblance to the male that had scooped me off the floor in the Hall of Mirrors. It wasn't until he threw his head back, baring his teeth, that I allowed myself to believe that it was him.

Beside me, Everlayne sucked in a sharp breath, pushing forward to the edge of her seat. "Shit."

When the rest of the crowd got a clear view of the male's face, they began to swear, too.

"Living Curse."

"Bane of Gillethrye."

"Black knight."

"Kingfisher."

"Kingfisher."

"Kingfisher."

The name Kingfisher echoed throughout the hall, spoken with a mix of reverence and fear.

"He lives!"

"He's returned!"

Beside me, Everlayne's eyes bore down on this Kingfisher as he gnashed and snarled, straining against the guards. "It's worse," she whispered. "So much worse."

"What's wrong with him?" I hissed.

Everlayne didn't say a word. She stared at the male on his knees in front of Belikon, her fingers trembling as she held them to her lips.

"Behold!" Belikon stood. Pacing toward Kingfisher, he dragged the sword behind him rather than sheathing it, and the tip of the blade sent sparks flying in its wake. A terrible, multi-layered scream ignited inside my head as the metal scraped across the dais this time. The sound of it was deafening. It set my stomach churning, bile bubbling up the back of my throat. I clapped my hands over my ears, trying to block out the sound, but the nauseating pitch intensified as Belikon drew the weapon closer.

"This…is the price of folly!" Belikon boomed. "Madness. Madness and death!"

Kingfisher lunged, trying to free himself, desperate to reach the king, but the guards wrestled him down, pinning him to the floor. One of them laid a knee into the back of his neck, but Kingfisher bucked, trying to be free of his captors. King Belikon sucked on his teeth, shaking his head with disdain.

Throwing his arms wide in a theatrical gesture, he shouted, "The scourge of Yvelia! The male that stalks your children's nightmares. The male who torched a city on a whim. The male who'd cut your throat as soon as look at you. Does this pathetic creature strike such an imposing figure now?"

A rumble traveled across the hall, but it was impossible to decipher what the true consensus was amongst the Fae. Those who thought Kingfisher was a terrifying monster were scrambling over each other to put some distance between him and their families. Others wore stony, hard expressions and looked at each other with clenched jaws, nostrils flaring, obviously not enjoying the display one bit.

"His exile was not at an end, but he's returned anyway. Just over a century has passed since Gillethrye. Our losses have dulled. The pain stings a little less brightly. But does that mean we should forgive?"

A roar surged up around us, the wall of sound battering at my eardrums so loud that they felt as if they would burst.

"Mercy!"

"Kill him!"

"Banish him!"

"Protect Yvelia from the Scourge!"

"Kingfisher!"

"Kingfisher!"

"Kingfisher!"

"Send him to his grave!"

Anxiety radiated from Everlayne as she surveyed her father's subjects over her shoulder. Shaking, she clasped and unclasped her hands, wringing them fitfully. "He'll murder him," she whispered. "He'll work them into a frenzy until they demand his death." She seemed to consider a moment, whipping around to look back up at the dais—not to Belikon, who loomed over Kingfisher, but to the old female sitting on the dais with the gnarled hands and the milk-white eyes.

"Malwae." She spoke the name only a shade louder than a whisper, but the old woman slowly turned away from Belikon, who was gesticulating rudely over Kingfisher, to the beautiful female beside me.

"Do something. Please!" she begged.

Malwae went rigid in her seat. Sitting up a little straighter, she gave Everlayne a look that seemed to say, "*What do you expect me to do?*" Everlayne whimpered, letting out an even louder cry of alarm when King Belikon raised the sword he'd dragged over to Kingfisher and held it aloft over the dark-haired male's torso.

"What say you, Fae of Yvelia? Should we stab this bastard in the back, just as he drove his blade into our backs and stabbed us?"

"Mercy! Please! Mercy!"

"End him!"

"Protect Yvelia!"

It sounded like this Kingfisher had killed a lot of people. The king made out as though he'd done it on a whim, out of spite. If that was true, then it could be argued that the male deserved to be punished. But the pageantry of this felt off. Belikon's behavior was too showy and cavalier, and Everlayne's reaction was affecting me, too. I barely knew her, but she seemed, well...good. Would she be this concerned if her father was threatening to execute a cold-hearted murderer? Wouldn't she be demanding justice along with the rest of the mob?

My nerves got the better of me. "He isn't actually going to kill him, is he?"

The question fell on deaf ears. Staring up at the dais, Everlayne focused on the gray-haired woman, her eyes burning into her ferociously. "Malwae, now! If you bore my mother any love at all, you'll do something to save him," she hissed.

A look of resignation claimed Malwae's wrinkled features. She groaned as, reluctantly, she drew herself to her feet. The crowd's shouts grew frantic as King Belikon caught the stooped crone's approach in his peripherals.

"What's this? Support for the traitor?" Belikon laughed coldly. "Sit down, Malwae. Rest your old bones. We'll be done here soon enough, and you can return to your scrying."

"Alas, I wish I could, Highness," Malwae croaked. "But the sword calls to me. I feel it. The last vestiges of the weapon's power echo with prophecy. I'm half deaf with the blasted thing ringing in my ears."

"A prophecy?"

"The sword still retains some power?"

Questions rose up around us. Too many to count. The Fae sitting on the benches seemed perturbed by the crone's declaration.

"In order to hear the prophecy in full, I must hold the sword, Highness," Malwae said. She held out her hand expectantly.

"The Oracle Sees!" a young female cried a few rows back. "A blessing! It's a blessing!"

Belikon assessed the crowd, his murky eyes narrowing. Turning to Malwae, he said, "An audience in private, I think. An Oracle's prophecies are for a king alone to decipher. But don't worry, you may hold the sword once my work here is done."

Malwae's hand shot out and closed around Belikon's wrist. In an instant, her cloudy eyes burned brilliant white, light spilling out of them and illuminating the dais. "The gods must be obeyed!" Her voice was a rasp a moment ago, but now it was all thunder and judgment. Her words boomed over the great hall. "The gods must be obeyed, lest House De Barra fall!"

Belikon's mouth fell open, but before he could speak, Malwae grabbed the sword and closed her bony hand around its edge. A river of blood—bright blue—spilled down the steel.

A stunned silence fell over the crowd. Only the male in black, Kingfisher, broke it. He roared, scrambling, still trying to get loose.

"This Kingfisher does not die by your hand. Not today," Malwae droned. "The Kingfisher shall not die by your hand."

"What the hell is happening?" I whispered.

"Wait." Everlayne clutched hold of my hand. "Just...wait."

"What should a king who loves his people do, then?" Belikon bit out. "Allow mad criminals to walk amongst them?"

The light leaking from Malwae's eyes dimmed and then flared bright anew. "Return to him that which you have taken from him," she intoned.

"The sword is mine—"

"The pendant," Malwae interrupted. "It must be returned."

"That pendant contains powerful magic. It doesn't belong around the neck of a treacherous dog. It belongs to me. I'll be cold in the ground before I give it back to this...this..."

"The gods must be obeyed lest House De Barra fall!" Malwae cried. "The gods must be obeyed lest the Winter Palace fall!"

The king fought to master his obvious rage. "And who am I to argue with the gods?" He grinned at Malwae—a quick flash of brilliant white teeth, sharp as daggers—and then turned ruefully back to the crowd. The Fae in the gallery were up out of their seats, arguing with one another over Kingfisher's fate. "Peace. Peace, my friends. Malwae has reminded me that issues such as these must be handled correctly. The Bane will be granted his sanity for a time."

"Lock him away!" a woman screamed, her voice tinged with hysteria.

"Keep him in the dungeons!"

"Set him free!"

"SEND HIM BACK TO THE FRONT!" a deep voice boomed. "Make him fight! Make him finish what he started!" From wall to wall, floor to towering ceiling, the thunderous voice commanded silence from the other Fae, who all ceased their shouting.

I'd been staring at the male still pinned to the floor, watching him thrash. I tore my gaze from him, looking over my shoulder, trying to locate the owner of the ringing demand. Everlayne did the same; I could see her pulse fluttering frantically in the hollow of her throat.

Belikon smiled thinly as he, too, searched for the source of this disruption amongst his subjects. "It would be ill-advised, unleashing a dangerous threat upon a war camp. Come forward and defend your suggestion, speaker. Explain yourself."

A shock wave of tension rippled through the cavern. Malwae and Everlayne shared a cautious look, but both held their tongues as the Fae parted and the huge male who visited my room earlier came into view.

Seven feet tall and heavily tattooed, Renfis emerged from the crowd, making himself known. His sandy brown hair fell past his shoulders. Since I'd seen him last, he'd landed himself a black eye and a split lip. He had also developed a slight limp when he walked, which led me to believe the past few hours had not been fun for him. Whispers followed on his heels as he made his way toward Belikon and the restrained Kingfisher.

"General Renfis?" Belikon cast around, frowning as if confused. "You're supposed to be at the front. Didn't I charge you with winning my war? And here you are, entering my palace? And armed to the teeth no less? I have to say, this is very confusing."

Gods, this bastard lived to put on a show.

"Aye, Your Highness," Renfis answered. "I was at the front, but when I heard he had returned, I came here immediately."

He.

Kingfisher.

Even the general wouldn't speak his name.

"Against my orders, then?" Belikon's newly minted smile had a dangerous edge to it.

"I was following your orders directly, Highness."

"Oh? I don't recall telling you to abandon your post."

While others shied away from Belikon's wrath, the general was stoic, hands resting easily at his sides. "The situation at Cahlish is grave. Our men die in droves every day. The beasts that patrol the enemy's borders range farther afield, claiming our sentries and outposts. Supply routes are closed to us. We're surviving on what we can hunt and gather. Within six months, the war will be over, and Yvelia will find itself on the wrong side of victory. So yes, Your Highness. I'm doing what you commanded of me. You told me to win the war by any means necessary, so I came to claim the only tool that'll win us back our advantage. I came for him."

Belikon let out a bark of stunned laughter. He pointed down at Kingfisher's twitching form. "This? You came here for *this*? You're telling me that this traitorous, lying, ravening dog is the only thing standing between us and complete annihilation? You're as mad as he is, General."

Scattered, nervous laughter broke out amongst the Fae. Again, General Renfis maintained his composure. "As Malwae implied, Your Majesty, all he needs is the pendant, and he'll be fine. Either way, I'd rather have him fighting for us, a little off-kilter and unpredictable, than not."

"If things are as bad as you say they are, he'll be killed in a matter of days," Belikon said dismissively.

"Likely, yes, Majesty. But, with all due respect, wouldn't that likelihood save you the trouble of a trial for what occurred at Gillethrye?"

The King hesitated, on the verge of saying something, but then reconsidered. For all his pomp and show, he wasn't a very good actor. "Now that you mention it, yes. Perhaps you're right, Renfis. Maybe a return to the front would be a just punishment. Why shouldn't he aid the war effort?"

Mere seconds ago, Belikon had been readying to punish Renfis for showing up at the Winter Palace, but the beatific smile he turned on him now felt like forgiveness of a sort.

"A week, then," Belikon announced, his mind made up. "You can take him back with you in a week. Since he knows so much about the quicksilver, he'll stay here and help Rusarius deal with the girl first. The second she's capable of waking the pool by herself, Kingfisher will once again be banished from this court."

Renfis bent into a deep bow. His relief was palpable.

The king slid a hand inside his embroidered robes and took out the very same pendant Kingfisher had fastened around my neck back in Zilvaren. He didn't even look at the male when he tossed it down at Renfis's feet.

"Get him out of my sight, General. Before my benevolent nature takes its leave."

Renfis swooped to pick up the pendant from the floor; the shining silver chain looked fragile in his huge hands. He winced as he carried it quickly over to Kingfisher, snarling at the guards who were still fighting to hold him down. Belikon's men seemed relieved to let go of their ward. Kingfisher snapped his teeth at Renfis, an animal growl building in the back of his throat. It looked like he would attack, but behind the madness that lurked in his brilliant green eyes, there came the faintest flash of recognition.

"Please. Please. Gods, just. . ." Everlayne whispered. She caught her bottom lip between her teeth, eyes locked on the two males at the foot of the dais. I had no idea what she was begging for, but she was coiled like a spring, ready to leap to her feet. A ragged breath escaped her when Kingfisher stilled, lowering his head, his halo of black hair hiding his face.

Renfis acted fast, looping the chain around the other male's neck. He fastened it in a flash and stepped back, waiting. It took a moment, but...yes. There. On his hands and knees, Kingfisher began to shudder. He only shook a little at first, but soon his whole body was trembling. Renfis was there to catch him when his arms gave out.

"You have five seconds," Belikon warned.

"Go, go, go," Everlayne urged under her breath.

Renfis grabbed Kingfisher and hauled him to his feet. He threw the disheveled male's arm over his own shoulder and then began to walk. Kingfisher's head lolled a little, but he didn't put up a fight. With Renfis's help, he was able to put one foot in front of the other until they reached the doors at the end of the hall.

Everlayne watched with wide eyes as the males paused there. She covered her mouth with her hands, her anxiety eating her alive. "Go!" she hissed into her hands.

Renfis spoke to Kingfisher, his mouth moving close to his ear, and for the first time, Kingfisher seemed to understand his surroundings. He shook his head and then slowly turned to look back over his shoulder at the gathered court.

All was still.

All was silent.

My heart hammered in my throat when I saw the look on Kingfisher's face.

Gods, he looked so young. Way younger than he'd looked back in the Hall of Mirrors, when he had seemed made of shadow and smoke.

His haunted expression promised pain, and blood, and death.

And he was looking right at the king. Or perhaps it was the dead dragon's skull that elicited his hate. I couldn't tell.

"Come on. We need to get out of here." Everlayne grabbed me by the wrist and tugged me up from the bench. A second later, we were standing in front of the dais, and she was dragging me down into a low bow next to her. "We beg your leave, Highness," Everlayne said loudly. "Saeris is keen to get to work."

The only thing I was keen to do was escape, but I kept my mouth shut. The sooner we got out of this hall, the better.

"You may go," Belikon said. When we were halfway to the doors, the king called after her again. "Keep an eye on her, Everlayne. She's your responsibility now."

Everlayne's pace didn't falter. She hurried out of the throne room, dragging me along behind her. We found Renfis in the hallway beyond the doors, his face gray as ash. Six feet away, Kingfisher stood with his hands braced against the wall, bending forward as he spat on the floor. There was a pool of vomit at his feet.

Everlayne locked eyes with Renfis. "You're fucking insane!"

"What was I supposed to do? He was going to string him up, for fuck's sake."

"You were supposed to get the pendant back to him and get him the hell out of here hours ago!"

The bruise beneath Renfis's right eye was darkening right in front of us. The split in his lip had started bleeding. He gestured pointedly to his injuries. "Eight of the bastards jumped me right before I entered his room. They must have followed me. They knocked me out, Layne. By the time I regained consciousness—"

"Yes, all right. All right. It's done now. The die is cast. We'll just have to deal with the consequences—"

"Stop bickering."

A thrill of energy rocketed up my spine at these two words. Kingfisher's voice was rough and pained, but it was also electricity. It made every hair on my body stand to attention.

Renfis and Everlayne faced him, the first hanging his head, the second on the verge of tears. "You went through the pool? Of all the reckless, idiotic, stupid things you could have done..." Everlayne's voice cracked as she spoke. Kingfisher scrubbed a hand over his face, then swept his hair back out of his eyes. It had been dark in the Hall of Mirrors, not to mention the fact that I'd been bleeding out. He'd thrashed so much that I hadn't been able to make out much of him back in the throne room behind us. Now I saw him properly for the first time, and a wave of shock rippled through me, down to the roots of my soul.

His jaw was defined, marked with dark stubble, his cheekbones high, his nose arrow straight and proud. There was a dark freckle just below his right eye. And…those eyes. Gods. Eyes were not that color. I'd never seen that shade of green before—a jade so bright and vibrant that it didn't look real. I'd noticed the filaments of silver threaded through his right iris back in Madra's Hall of Mirrors, but I'd assumed I'd imagined them, being so close to death and all. The silver shone there, though, definitely real, forming a reflective, metallic corona around the black well of his pupil. The sight of it made me feel strange and off-balance.

Kingfisher spared me the briefest of glances and then addressed the female. "Hello, Layne."

Everlayne let out a strangled sob, tears chasing down her cheeks, but she scowled at the warrior dressed in black. "Don't 'hello, Layne' me after a hundred and ten years. Answer the question. Why the hell did you go into that pool?"

He sighed wearily. "I had two seconds to decide. The pathway was already closing. What was I supposed to do?"

"You should have just let it close!" Her voice was hard as stone.

Kingfisher groaned, then craned his head forward and spat again. "Chastise me tomorrow, please. Right now, I need two things. Whiskey and a bed."

Everlayne didn't seem inclined to allow him these things. She huffed, folding her arms across her chest. Renfis stepped in between them, shaking his head. "How about we all get some rest? We'll figure this out in the morning."

"You can sleep in my room. Both of you," Everlayne commanded. "You'll be safest there. Go now before he dismisses the whole court. I'll be along shortly."

I was invisible. Inconsequential. Neither Renfis nor Kingfisher said a word to me as they turned and left. Kingfisher stumbled a little as he went, batting away Renfis's hand when he tried to help.

"Come on. We need to get you back to your room, too." Everlayne tried to grab my wrist again, but I jerked back before she could get a hold of me. "If you want me to walk anywhere, then just ask me to go with you," I snapped. "I'm sick to death of being dragged around like an animal on a leash."

"You're not safe here, Saeris."

"You're right. It doesn't sound like I am. Don't you think you should have told me that your people are at war?"

She frowned. "I didn't mention that?"

"No!"

"Oh, well. We've been at war with Sanasroth for longer than I've been alive. It must have slipped my mind," she said impatiently. "Will you please come back to your rooms with me, Saeris? I'll answer all of your questions in due time, but not here and not now."

Elroy always said I was as stubborn as an ass. I wanted to dig my heels in and refuse to budge an inch, but I got the feeling that I'd regret it. And the promise of answers was enticing. I had too many questions to count, so many that my head was fit to split open, and no one else seemed likely to cough up any information about the hot water I'd found myself in.

I scowled as I set off walking.

Everlayne shot me a grateful smile. "There is one thing I can tell you right now," she said, striding out in front of me to guide the way. "Even in times of peace, the Fae are always at war. There are those among our ranks that might pretend to be your friend, but often they're hiding knives behind their smiles, ready to sink them into your back. You'd do well to remember that."

As I followed after her, rushing to keep up, I couldn't help but wonder if she counted herself among that number.

8

ALCHEMIST

THE MORNING BROUGHT with it a series of revelations. It was dark
when Everlayne came to fetch me, which wasn't out of the ordinary.
Even the poorest home in Zilvaren drew black-out curtains across
the windows when it was time to sleep. But I realized there were no
curtains at the windows in my room as Everlayne cajoled me into
yet another ostentatious dress. The *world* was black outside of the
window.

"The suns are always in the sky, then? And there are two of
them?" Everlayne asked, pulling my corset stays so tight that I'd
wheezed.

"Yes."

"Well, things are a little different here."

It took a monumental force of effort to grasp just *how* different
they were. Yvelia had only one sun. And it went down at night, disappearing beyond the rim of the horizon. The prospect made me feel
like I was hallucinating again—a concern that intensified when the
scene beyond the palace's windows began to lighten on our way to
the library, and I saw what was out there.

"What do you mean, what is it? It's snow!" Everlayne said, laughing.

I stood before the massive window in the hallway, my tongue stuck to the roof of my mouth, struck dumb. The view beyond the pane of glass wasn't real. It couldn't be. There were mountains in the distance, huge jagged-peaked monstrosities that made my legs wobble just to look at them. And there were trees. So many trees. I'd only seen the skinny-limbed ones with the jaundiced leaves that lined the walkways of the Hub. These trees were tall and green, pressed tightly together to form a canopy that stretched as far as the eye could see. Directly below the window, a sprawling city with buildings constructed out of dark stone swept down toward a shimmering blue-gray ribbon that I realized was a river only when I saw that its surface was rippling.

Everything was capped with a thick layer of white. Everything apart from the river. So much water, rushing and flowing and churning. I stared at it, unable to understand how such a large body of water could even exist.

"This is the *Winter* Palace," Everlayne reminded me, trying to coerce me away from the window. "It snows year-round here. At least once a day. Come on, we're going to be late."

I moved through the palace as if walking through a dream. The colors were garishly bright, the sights and sounds of the place too surreal for words.

Yvelia.

It still hadn't sunk in. Wherever I looked, beautiful Fae females regarded me with cold disdain. Males watched me pass, sneers on their mouths, eyes flashing with hate. I was *not* welcome here, that much was obvious, and yet they needed me for something. I was supposed to repeat whatever I'd done in the Hall of Mirrors to that silver pool. While I figured out how to do that, I enjoyed the king's protection. But protection did not mean kindness, and it certainly didn't mean respect.

The library was at the far end of the palace, up flight after flight of stairs that felt like they would never end. I was panting and had broken into a sweat by the time we arrived, even though the temperature seemed to plummet the higher we went. Through an enormous set of black, engraved doors, a huge space opened up with cathedral ceilings and twenty-foot-high stained-glass windows that would have made Elroy weep.

Before she'd died, my mother had worked in the library back in the Third for a while. The underground warren of tunnels and hollowed-out caves had resembled a tomb and had stunk worse than death. The tiny number of books it had boasted had been half-eaten by mold, but at least it had been cool down there. Fifteen to twenty degrees cooler on a good day. The residents of the Third had to petition to visit the stacks; they needed a token *and* a recommendation from their employer before they were granted entry. My mother's position as a clerk there meant that she could come and go as she pleased, and that boon had been extended to me. I hadn't appreciated the unfettered access to the library at first. But when Elroy had accepted me as his apprentice, I'd combed through the library's information not on glass working as he thought I should have, but on metalwork. Reeking of forge smoke and covered in grease, I'd pored over the written work of Zilvaren's old masters late into the night, daydreaming of what it would have been like to have access to so much metal.

Yvelia's library was staggering in comparison. So many books all in one place. Stacks upon stacks upon stacks. So accustomed to hunkering down, peering at crumbling, mildew-covered scrolls by candlelight, I was unprepared for how the sight of so many bound, hardback books would affect me. This was a treasure beyond Madra's hoard of gold. More precious than rubies and diamonds. The information inside a place like this was too vast to comprehend. And the light!

Thirty feet above our heads, a glass-domed ceiling showcased a crystalline, bright blue sky. Wisps of clouds, tinged pink, stretched from one side of the dome to the other as if placed there by an artist's paintbrush. The early morning light bore a sharp quality that washed the walls of the library in hues of blue, green, and white rather than the warm yellows, oranges, and golds I was used to.

It was beautiful.

So beautiful.

"You'll make yourself dizzy, gawping up at the sky like that," a cheery voice said. Bustling out from behind one of the far stacks, a portly male in a blue robe with wiry gray hair and warm, dark brown skin appeared. Hazel eyes dancing with mirth met mine as the male trundled across the library's main floor toward us, clutching a tattered tome to his chest, limping ever so slightly. He was old, though how old was tough to guess. His hair was thinning on top and looked like it hadn't seen a brush in a month.

"Rusarius." Everlayne's smile shone from her eyes. I realized how disingenuous she'd just been when interacting with other members of the court. She beamed at the old male, then squealed as he swept her up in a one-armed hug and spun her around, lifting her off of her slippered feet.

"Put me down, you fool. You'll throw your back out again!" she cried.

"Nonsense." Rusarius did set her down again, though. He held her at arm's length, looking her up and down with an unmistakable fondness. "Too long. Far too long. I can't tell you how surprised I was when I woke up in the night to those rough-handed bastards dragging me out of my bed. I assumed they'd come to do me in. I'd stabbed one of them in the buttock by the time they told me I was being called back to court."

Everlayne laughed. "The buttock? Hardly a fatal wound. Good thing you were brought back to your books. By the sounds of things, you need to brush up on your anatomy."

Rusarius wagged a finger at her. "If I'd wanted the bastard dead, he'd already be in the ground. I only wanted to punish him for his bad manners. He'll knock before battering down someone's bedroom door in the future. Now..." He trailed off, his attention slipping back to me. "*This* is a most fascinating turn of events. Yes, *most* fascinating. A human, walking the hallowed halls of the Winter Palace for the first time in an age. I never thought I'd live to see the day. I am Rusarius, librarian, newly reappointed master of this domain. Who are you, and what name do you go by? I wasn't told much before I was ordered back to work."

Since I'd woken up yesterday, I'd been stared at, whispered about, threatened, and treated like a performing monkey. All of the attention had begun to chafe a little. Rusarius's curiosity bore no malice, though. A childlike inquisitiveness radiated from him as he circled around a table and came to stand on the other side of it, his gaze roaming over me with what seemed to be a purely academic interest.

Having decided that I didn't mind these questions coming from him, I bowed deeply and laid it on thick. "I'm Saeris Fane, apprentice to the Undying Queen's master glass worker. I hail from the third spoke in the blessed wheel of the sacred Silver City."

Rusarius's mouth turned down at the corners as he nodded. "The Silver City? Zilvaren, then. Is *that* so?"

"It's true," Everlayne said quietly.

The light in Rusarius's twinkling eyes guttered out. "But...the quicksilver awoke? That's not..." He seemed struck by an epiphany, his head whipping back to me. "Oh! So...so, this one's an Alchemist, then?"

"Shh!" Everlayne flinched. "We don't know *what* she is just yet. Kingfisher felt Solace calling, and he answered. He found it in Saeris's hands."

His lips parted slightly. "She was *holding* Solace?"

"Yes."

"Sorry to interrupt, but what's an Alchemist? And what's Solace?" I wasn't used to being on the outside of conversations like this. It was zero fun. Neither of them bothered to answer me, though.

"Then I think it's safe to assume that she *is* an Alchemist, wouldn't you?" Rusarius said, raising his eyebrows at Everlayne.

"It's—no! Well, it's not that simple. The Alchemists were all *Fae*—"

"She must have a drop of Fae blood," a deep voice murmured. "Enough to stop Solace from burning off her hands. But not enough to matter." The owner of that voice was somewhere deep within the stacks. I'd only heard him speak briefly yesterday, but it was him all right. Kingfisher. Everlayne rolled her eyes, throwing her hands up in the air.

"You were supposed to wait for Ren to finish up in the bathhouse. You came up here by yourself?"

Through the glass dome overhead, the sky was still a bright, crisp blue, but the library somehow seemed darker as Kingfisher's tall frame emerged from the center of the stacks. Yesterday, he'd worn a simple black shirt and black pants. No armor. No weapons. Today, he was dressed as he had been when he came for me in the Hall of Mirrors. A leather protector that covered only half his chest and one shoulder, a strap fastening underneath his right arm and around his ribs. Black leather tassets over his thighs. Bracers over his forearms. A polished silver renegade's gorget gleamed at his throat. His hair was wet, the ends of his ink-black waves dripping beads of water onto the pages of the open book that he was reading.

Aghast, Rusarius leaped, snatching the tome out of Kingfisher's hands. "Give me that! What's *wrong* with you? That book is a first edition."

Kingfisher turned a blank gaze upon Rusarius. He towered over the librarian, but that didn't seem to matter to the older Fae. It couldn't have mattered to Kingfisher either because the warrior dipped his head and cast his eerie eyes briefly to the floor. "My apologies, Rusarius. I'll be more careful in the future."

"Where's Ren?" Everlayne demanded.

Kingfisher's expression hardened. "I assume he's still scrubbing his *balls*," he said dryly.

"If you're trying to shock me by mentioning random parts of male anatomy, then you're out of luck," the blond-haired female snapped. "I've seen Ren's balls. I've seen yours, too. I've seen *everything*," she said, pointedly glowering at Kingfisher's crotch, "so I know exactly where to aim my knee if you continue to test me. You don't seem to appreciate the level of danger you're in right now, Fisher."

The huge male glanced down at himself, then back up at Everlayne from beneath dark, drawn brows. "The amount of armor I strapped on this morning would indicate otherwise," he said, his low voice deep and smooth as silk.

"Belikon's assassins could be anywhere—"

"Sounds to me like *you're* the one I should be watching out for, darling Layne. You're the one who just threatened to knee me in the cock." A hint of a smile twitched at the corner of his mouth, though it never materialized. He was as serious as the grave when he said, "None of Belikon's men would be stupid enough to try and assault me within the walls of this court now. Not when I have a sword strapped to my back and my head screwed on straight."

Gods, he *did* have a sword strapped to his back. I hadn't noticed right away. Only the sleek black hilt was visible over Kingfisher's shoulder. Out of nowhere, his eyes flickered to me—the first time he'd even acknowledged that I was there—and again, the library grew yet another degree darker. Was *he* doing that?

"It's rude to stare at a male's hardware," he said stiffly.

What had he called me back in the Hall of Mirrors? Pathetic? A fucking joke? I felt like both of those things under the cold weight of his gaze. I didn't have it in me to look away, though. I wouldn't be cowed by the likes of him. He was the reason I was in Yvelia, trapped here against my will in the first place. If he'd just left me where he found me...

If he'd left you where he found you, you'd be dead.

Gods, even the little voice in the back of my mind was turning against me. Well, I wasn't thanking him. Not when he was being so openly hostile.

"Don't worry. I wasn't planning on stealing it. It isn't very impressive. Looks more like a *toothpick* to me."

Everlayne stifled a bark of laughter with the back of her hand.

"Oh, ho ho! I think that one might have drawn blood!" Renfis stood in the library's open doorway, shaking out his hair like a wet dog. His shirt was soaked through. By the looks of things, the male had barely bothered to dry himself off at all before he got dressed. He carried a bunch of leather armor under one arm and a sheathed sword bundled in a piece of black fabric under the other. Despite the wicked grin he wore (courtesy of my sharp tongue, it seemed), the general was pretty pissed; his annoyance burned in his eyes as he set his load down on the long clerk's table with a clatter.

Kingfisher didn't pay him a lick of attention. He was still glaring at *me*. "This sword has slain thousands," he seethed.

"I wouldn't have thought *that* was anything to brag about," I replied. "You should probably get it looked at."

"Hah!" Renfis stuffed his fist into his mouth, biting down on his knuckles as he tried to swallow down his laughter. Rusarius glanced at each of us, his warm hazel eyes bouncing from me to Kingfisher, to Ren, and then to Everlayne, who had turned crimson and was making a show of looking through a stack of books resting on the table.

"I don't understand," the librarian said. "Nimerelle *is* a formidable sword. Alchimeran. A much-lauded, storied weapon of the ancients. It's an honor to even look upon—"

"Let's get started, shall we?" Everlayne interrupted. "We're wasting time, and we have a lot of information to cover. Fisher, sit down and stop scowling. It doesn't suit you. Ren, you go down that end and make sure he stays in his seat. Saeris, you come and sit here." She pointed to the chair at the very end of the long table—the farthest away from the seat she told Kingfisher to sit in.

Rusarius frowned, still confused, but then Everlayne shoved a book into his hands, and his face lit up. "Ahh, yes, wonderful! *The Dawn Genesis of Yvelia*. One of my favorites."

I'd taken my seat, if only to end the staring contest Kingfisher was silently challenging me to, but I nearly leaped up out of it again in protest when I heard this title. "A *history* book?"

"One of the best," Rusarius said, beaming. "Not just history, though. There are a number of chapters on Fae etiquette and politics that I think will be very useful in this particular situation."

"I don't care about Yvelian history. I don't give a shit about etiquette, either."

"Clearly," Rusarius sputtered.

"Your politics and your courts are *your* business," I pressed. "I want to figure out how to open up these quicksilver portals again, and then I want to do it and get the hell out of here. You all keep insisting that my brother and my friends are dead?" Even speaking the words out loud was tough. My throat ached as I forced myself to continue. "If they *are* dead, then I want to see their bodies with my own two eyes. I want to bury what's left of them. They don't deserve to be left out in the burning heat to be picked clean by the rats and the vultures."

The library was silent. Ren hadn't sat down yet. He quickly began donning the armor he'd carried in with him under his arm like he might have need of it any moment.

"Saeris, it's been well over a week. I'm sure it's already too late for that," Everlayne said gently. "As hard as it may be, it's better for you if you just accept that—"

"Do you have a brother, Everlayne?" I spat.

"I—" She blinked rapidly, flustered. Her eyes darted to Kingfisher for some reason, who kept his eyes fixed on a point on the other side of the library, his gaze steady and even. "Yes, I do," she said.

"And do you love him?"

"Of course."

"And wouldn't you want to know for certain, one way or another, if he was dead or alive?"

She sat very still, her back straight, but it was as though a part of her was wilting inside. She glanced down at her hands clasped in her lap, saying in a small voice, "I'm sorry, Saeris, but it's more complicated than that."

"Is it?" Kingfisher asked abruptly. He was no longer staring into space. His eyes bored into Everlayne so intensely that I found myself thanking the gods that he wasn't looking at me like that. "Humans are usually weak, fickle creatures, but I'll admit, I admire this one's loyalty. She values her family over everything else. There's something to be said for that."

"*Fisher,*" Ren said.

I started when Fisher looked away from Everlayne and turned his attention to me. "They won't tell you this because they want you to behave. But there *is* a chance your people are still alive, human. A decent chance."

A spark of white-hot hope flared to life in my chest. "How? What do you know?"

"Fisher!" Everlayne cried.

"Graceless gods." Ren turned and walked away from the table, running his hands through the wet strands of his hair in frustration. Only Rusarius remained calm.

"Madra used Solace to seal the pathways a long time ago, but with the sword returned to us and an Alchemist in our midst, she knows she'll have a war on her doorstep any day now—"

"She *doesn't* know we have an Alchemist," Everlayne argued.

"The pathway couldn't have opened without one," Kingfisher fired back. Undeterred, he asked me, "How many soldiers does Madra train and keep these days?"

"I don't know. One, maybe two thousand."

"Two thousand?" Kingfisher snorted. "Without a fresh army at her fingertips, she knows she'll be swept away by a sea of Fae warriors thirty-thousand deep once Belikon wedges the door into her world open. She lied to him. Tricked him. Cut off his trade lines to the other realms. Not to mention the fact that there are still rumors floating around that the Daianthus heir is in Zilvaren somewhere. The King *will* want a war and a bloody one at that. He'll use it as an excuse to make sure there are none in the Silver City who might challenge him for the throne. Madra won't have torched ten percent of her people to exact revenge against one silly girl. She'll have conscripted them."

Conscripted?

Kingfisher thought Madra would have put a sword in Hayden's hand rather than kill him? Could that be true? There hadn't been any kind of war in Zilvaren for centuries. The desert took a hefty tithe when an armed force attempted to cross it. By the time an army reached Zilvaren, it was half as big as it had been when it had set out, and extremely dehydrated. They could never win against her without access to a water source, so eventually, they stopped coming. Madra no longer kept an army the way she had done centuries ago. She didn't need one. But if Kingfisher was right and she was worried about an army rising up out of the quicksilver, maybe she would conscript people from the wards. While I didn't relish the prospect of war between this realm and my own, the possibility did present me with some time. I was grasping at straws, but it was something.

"So only one of these Alchemists can open these pathways between Yvelia and Zilvaren, right?" I asked.

Everlayne paled. "It's a dangerous process, Saeris. And we don't even know if it was you who activated the quicksilver the last time."

"She was the one holding Solace," Kingfisher said flatly. "There was no one else in that hall. Harron didn't wake the quicksilver, and *I* sure as hell didn't do it. If I *were* capable of activating it, I would have razed that infernal city to the ground a long, long time ago."

He said it without any emotion at all. It was just a straight fact. He'd snuff out a million lives in the blink of an eye, just like that. I could see it now. He wouldn't feel a thing at all.

"You shouldn't have given her the pendant when you came through," Everlayne whispered.

Kingfisher held up his left hand, which he'd clenched tight into a fist. "I still had the ring." Sure enough, a plain silver ring flashed on his middle finger, catching at the light.

Everlayne shook her head, her eyes bright with unshed tears. "It wasn't enough. You took more in, didn't you?"

Kingfisher looked away, up at the sky, and the bank of thick clouds that were amassing overhead. "What does it even matter? I got the sword. I even got a new pet for you. One capable of performing fancy magic tricks that'll make all of our lives better. So let's just get on with this, shall we?"

I couldn't stop staring at the silver plate he wore at his neck. It was beautifully engraved with elaborate lines, but it was the snarling wolf head at its center that captured my attention. The insignia was fierce and eye-catching. Prudent that he'd worn it to the library this morning, seeing as how Everlayne looked like she wanted to slit his throat.

"We're going to fix this," she murmured under her breath.

The silver in Kingfisher's eye seemed to flare at her promise. "But there's nothing to fix," he said. "Only a human to teach and a queen to put in the ground. Once that's out of the way, we can all get on with our lives. The girl can go back to her city and what's left of her people, and Belikon can chew his way through yet another realm for all I care. My work will be done."

"Don't say that. Please."

"You forget we're already fighting a war." Ren leaned against the back of one of the wooden chairs, his knuckles turning white. "The real war with Sanasroth is killing members of our court, *your* court, every single day."

"The last time I fought in that war, a city burned to the ground. I think I've shed enough blood for Yvelia, Brother."

"Then shed it for your friends! Put all of this Madra business aside. Let Belikon deal with her and help *me!*"

It was as if there were a cord at the center of Kingfisher's soul, and I could see it tugging him backward, further away from these people who so clearly cared about him. He was beyond their reach, it seemed. Nothing would draw him back to them. He blinked, leaving Ren's plea unanswered. "I have two questions for you, human."

I was the only human in the room. Clearly, he was talking to me. "Okay," I said.

"Have you ever channeled a metal's energy before?"

I narrowed my eyes at him, insides twisting. "What do you mean?"

"If you'd done it, you wouldn't need to ask. You'd already know," he said flatly.

I thought about it. All of the times I'd made Elroy's tools hum. That spinning blade on my dead mother's dining table. The guardian's gauntlet, when I'd slammed it down on top of the wall—how its vibrations had made the grains of quartz in the sand dance. How I'd turned Harron's dagger into a river of molten silver and steel.

"All right, then." I met Kingfisher's steely gaze. I didn't blink. "Yes. I have."

"Good. And my second question. Do you have any experience working in a forge?"

Laughter burst up my throat and out of my mouth. "In a forge? Yeah. You could say that I know my way around a forge."

RIGHTEOUS PURPOSE

"THEY WON'T LET you in. There's no way. The bastards have been guarding that door since the dawn of time." Renfis hurried along after Kingfisher, but his limp was proving a hindrance.

"They don't have a choice," Kingfisher replied. He wasn't slowing his pace for anyone. Not for his injured friend. Not for the king's daughter. And certainly not for me, the only human in the group, whose legs were considerably shorter than everyone else's. I was on the verge of breaking into a jog just to keep the three of them in sight.

Now would be a perfect time to escape. I'd been looking for the right time to make a run for it, but Kingfisher had said the magic word. *Forge.* I couldn't help myself. What did a Fae forge look like? Did it work the same way as a human forge? Was there *magic* involved? Gods, I hoped there was magic involved. And anyway, escaping Everlayne and the two warriors at this point would have been foolhardy.

I had nowhere to go. I'd been unconscious when Kingfisher brought me back through that rippling pool of silver. I had no idea where it was located. Or if it was even in the palace. The probability of me finding it on my own was slim, and even if I did, what then? I'd drawn that sword out of Madra's pool the last time. Belikon had it now. Did I need it to activate the pool? Could I do it again? And how? I had no idea how I woke the quicksilver the last time, and by the sounds of things, the Fae didn't know how to do it, either. Plus, they kept saying pathways. *Plural.* How the fuck would I make my way back to Zilvaren, specifically, if there was more than one pathway?

My anxiety over Hayden was all-consuming. Come hell or high water, I was going to get back to my brother, but I couldn't rush into this. Rushing something so dangerous that I had no understanding of whatsoever would undoubtedly mean death or, at the very least, serious trouble.

So, for now, I was staying. Mind made up, I finally broke into that jog and caught up with the group. The three Fae were passing one of the many sets of alcoves occupied by statues of the gods. Everlayne bowed and touched her head to them as she hurried by. Ren grumbled, giving them a cursory nod. Kingfisher stuck out a hand and flipped all seven of them off as he stormed by.

Everlayne cried out, horrified, but Kingfisher only rolled his eyes, continuing whatever it was he'd been saying. "...then talk to Belikon. You heard him. He's the one who told me to help Rusarius with the human."

"This isn't helping. This is diving into something headfirst without considering the consequences!" Everlayne's frustration had become a permanent fixture since Renfis had fastened that pendant around Kingfisher's neck. "We have to cover the theory first."

Kingfisher huffed derisively. "*What* theory?"

"He's right on that, at least," Ren chimed in. "There *are* no written accounts of the Alchemist's processes. If there was, the elders might have had some luck understanding their abilities. How can we start at the beginning if there *is* no beginning?"

Everlayne's loose hair streamed out behind her in a golden banner as she rushed forward and prodded Kingfisher in the back.

Hard. "We start out slow, then. With the important things she needs to know about Yvelia. She won't survive here without—"

Kingfisher stopped dead in his tracks, turning. Everlayne ran straight into his chest, but the dark-haired warrior didn't flinch. He stepped around her and prowled toward me like a hell cat creeping up on its dinner. I was an accomplished fighter. I knew how to put a guardian on his ass in three seconds flat. I could scale forty-foot-high walls and sprint across rotting rooftops, but the sight of Kingfisher prowling toward me turned my insides to a double knot.

Stumbling back, I nearly tripped over my feet in my attempt to put some space between us, but the bastard kept coming.

"All right, *Oshellith.* Layne isn't going to let this go until you've been given the Cliff Notes, so listen close. I'm about to furnish you with the only information you really need to know. *You* have the distinct pleasure of being the only living human in all of Yvelia. You are *not* safe here." He bared his teeth, flashing long, sharp canines that lengthened right before my eyes. "There was a time when this place teemed with your kind—"

"Fisher, stop." Ren tried to grab him by the shoulder, but the warrior in black jerked away and kept coming.

"Our ancestors were cursed millennia ago. As a result, we ended up with these," he said, gesturing to his canines. "We used them to drink your kind dry. We drained you by the millions before the blood curse was lifted. This was long before *our* time, of course, but the Fae line still bears the marks of its past. We might not need blood to maintain our immortality anymore, but by the gods, do we still have the teeth for it. Our dirty little secret. Our awful, horrible shame—"

"Fisher!" Everlayne had reached her breaking point. Tears streamed down her face, leaving wet tracks over her cheeks. She moved in front of Kingfisher and slammed her hands into his chest. "Why are you being like this?" she cried.

Kingfisher shrugged. "I'm only telling her the truth."

"You're being an asshole!"

This elicited a scornful blast of laughter from the warrior. "You should be used to that by now, Layne. Or did you spend the last century forgetting what a shit I am? I'm the Bane of Gillethrye, remember? The Black Knight?"

"You're my *brother*," Everlayne hissed. "Though I sometimes wish you weren't!"

Kingfisher jerked back as if she'd struck him. Even Renfis took a step back, his jaw dropping a little, but the general regained himself quickly, glancing up and down the hallway. I got the feeling that he was checking to see if anyone might have heard Everlayne's little outburst. The long, open-aired hallway stretched off in both directions, though, completely deserted apart from our group.

"Careful, little sister," Kingfisher rumbled. "We don't want to spill *all* of our secrets in one go now."

Everlayne's sob filled the hallway. "Oh, fuck you, Fisher." She bolted, running back the way we'd come, as fast as her legs could carry her.

Well. It seemed that even the immortal Fae were still susceptible to family drama. I looked back over my shoulder, watching the poor female flee. "I...I should go and make sure she's okay..."

"I'll come, too," Renfis growled, casting Kingfisher a look of unmistakable disgust. "You can't wander the court without one of us to watch over you. And you? Everlayne's right. You *are* being an asshole. The Kingfisher we used to know cared about his family and his friends."

Even with the cruel smirk playing across his mouth, Kingfisher was savagely handsome. "What can I say?" he purred. "Being completely cut off from civilization and summarily forgotten about has a way of changing you after a while."

Renfis was already walking backward. "We didn't forget about you. You have no idea what we went through to try and get you back."

"Oh, yeah. I'm sure my suffering *paled* in comparison to yours."

A look of hurt flickered across Ren's face, but he said nothing more to the male at my back. "Let's go, Saeris. We'll find Layne and head back to the library."

"Oh, come on. She's not going with you," Kingfisher drawled. "She's coming with me, aren't you, Oshellith? She wants to know secrets, and I'm the only one willing to give them to her."

"Why are you calling me that? Oshellith?" I snapped. "What does it mean?"

He'd turned around. Was walking away. I listened to his boots striking the cold stone beneath his feet, each step ringing in my ears. "An Oshellith is a type of butterfly," he called as he went. "Osha for short. They hatch, live, and die all in one day. The cold kills them *very* fast. Isn't that right, Renfis?"

Ren scowled at Kingfisher's back, though he didn't answer him. "Ignore him. Will you come, Saeris?"

I was stuck between the two of them, being asked to make a decision I was in no way qualified to make. Everlayne had been kind to me. Taken care of me. Made sure I was comfortable here. Renfis was full of laughter and seemed solid and good. Kingfisher was a miserable, grouchy bastard without a kind word for anyone. The way he called me that—*Oshellith*—like it was a dirty word, made me want to smash my fist right through his gorgeous face. But he *was* offering me the truth, even if it was frightening. The quickest way out of this nightmare was through Kingfisher.

I winced at Ren. "Sorry. Can we do the library later? I...I just..."

"Told you so!" Kingfisher called out in a singsong voice.

Renfis just nodded, his mouth drawing into a flat line. "Of course. I understand. I'll come and get you in a couple of hours."

Unlike all of the other doors in the palace, this one was of a normal height. Plain. Simple. No ornate carvings or embellishments. It was just a wooden door. And it was locked.

I risked a sidelong glance at Kingfisher out of the corner of my eye. "Should we, uh…knock?"

An arrogant smile curled up at the corner of his mouth. "*Sure,*" he said, as if this was a charming suggestion made by a single-brain-celled idiot. A second later, he slammed the sole of his boot against the wood, and then the door was on the ground in pieces. "Knock knock." He stepped to one side, holding his hand out in a mockery of manners, gesturing for me to go ahead of him. "I don't think anyone's home."

"I'm not going first. What if it's warded by, I don't know…by *magic*, or something?"

Kingfisher waggled his fingers, his eyes going wide. "Oh no, not *magic!*"

"Ass."

"Coward," he volleyed back. "I knew it wasn't warded."

"How?"

"Because *I'm* magic."

"What about *you* is magic?"

"Everything," he said, entering the room. "My looks. My sword skills. My personality—"

"Your personality is trash." The quip was out before I had a chance to bite my tongue. Ever since I was little, I got mouthy when I was nervous, and I was really nervous right now. Literally nothing about this male screamed, *"Bait me and see what happens."* I clenched my jaw, cursing myself for my own stupidity as I followed behind Kingfisher, studiously staring at the ground.

Kingfisher said nothing.

I looked up and—

Holy hells.

Maybe this place had been a forge once, but now it was nothing of the sort. The rough stone walls were slick with frost. The workbenches were covered in vines that were such a dark green they were almost black. Pale blue, purple, and pink flowers dotted their stems like tiny, upturned daggers, their shape strange and unusual. A variety of other flowers, creeping vines, and plant life exploded up the wall on the far side of the cavernous space, crowding around a large window, hungry for a spot in the light.

The thickest of the vines actually climbed *out* of the window, the glass having been smashed out. The rest of the uneven stone floor was carpeted with broken glass. Vials, beakers, bulbs, and flasks. Shattered equipment lay strewn around the room, as if someone had flown into a rage and destroyed the place.

Rust had been busy eating away at all of the tongs, pliers, and hammers. Clearly, it hadn't satisfied its voracious appetite because the anvil next to the cracked enamel water bath was so pitted that the iron was sloughing off in great orange flakes. And the forge itself. Gods, the forge. The open-sided hearth was nice and large, there was no denying that. Big enough for a whole family of furry animals to have made a den in it, by the looks of things, though its occupants were either out and about their business or had bolted when Kingfisher kicked the door down. It was vented, too, thanks to the yawning hole in the roof directly above it.

Kingfisher sifted through a pile of decaying wood with the toe of his boot, scowling darkly. "I see why Clements has guarded this place so fiercely now."

"Who's Clements?"

"The king's royal archivist. He's been receiving a royal stipend for the past two hundred years or so, charged with figuring out how the Alchemists used to activate the quicksilver. A handsome stipend if I recall correctly. Looks to me like he pissed it all up a wall, though, 'cause this place is a fucking disaster."

He was right. This was no working forge. The hearth hadn't been fired here in a long time. The place smelled of dust, age, and animal musk.

"I'm going to kick his teeth down his throat," Kingfisher announced.

"How about you help me instead of threatening violence?" I countered.

His lip curled with distaste when I stooped down and started stacking some of the shattered pieces of wood by the now-empty doorway. "You're going to clear all of this by hand?"

"Unless you can utter some sort of spell and clear it all up with magic?"

"I don't do *spells*. I'm not a witch. Fae magic isn't some kind of cheap conjuring trick, human. Our abilities are sacred gifts to be used discerningly, for righteous purposes."

My cheeks colored hotly at that. Of course he wasn't just going to click his fingers and whisk all of this away. He had a real knack for making me feel stupid, though. He didn't need to do it. No, he did it because he *wanted* to.

Arrogant bastard.

He obviously thought I was worth less than the dirt beneath his feet. He didn't like humans. I doubted that, if the situation were different, he'd bother to put me out if I was on fire. But as it was, he needed me, which meant that I could get away with asking a few questions. Right?

I grabbed a rusty old bucket by the rim and began picking through the debris on the ground, looking for any tools that might be salvageable. "If there's a Winter Palace, then there are other royal residences, too, yes? An Autumn Palace? Spring? Summer?"

Kingfisher drew his sword.

"Whoa! Whoa, whoa, whoa! Sorry. Gods alive. I didn't—I'm not—"

His nostrils flared as he unfastened the leather strap at his chest and slid the scabbard from his back, re-sheathing the weapon and propping it against the wall. Running his hand through his hair, he looked askance in my direction, his fingers moving deftly over more leather straps and buckles as he began removing pieces of his armor. "Nervous?" he asked conversationally.

"No! I just...Well, I thought—"

"You can learn about the other courts in your library sessions with Layne and Rusarius. I offered you truths earlier. Don't squander the opportunity to ask more *interesting* questions." He reached around behind his neck with one hand and unfastened the silver plate with the snarling wolf's head engraved on it, letting it slip away from his throat. Tossing it down onto the pile of leather he'd made—chest protector, shoulder guards, wrist guards—he then unfastened the top buttons of his shirt. Once upon a time, not too long ago, I would have lunged for that neck plate and made a run for it. I didn't need the silver anymore, though. I had enough food and water to last me a lifetime here, and I hadn't been asked to pay for any of it. Not yet, anyway.

So, I ignored the plate and pointed to the chain hanging around his neck instead. "All right. What is that? What does it do? And why are you completely unhinged without it?"

Kingfisher smiled a cold smile, pressing the tip of his tongue into the point of one of his sharp canines. "Straight for the jugular then, Little Osha? Ruthless. I like it."

"You said to ask an interesting question. I want to know about the chain."

Kingfisher laughed silently. He bent double, scooping out a bunch of leaves and rotting wood from the hearth. Gods, he actually was going to help? That was why he removed all of the armor, then. I figured he was taking it off so he could sit down and make himself comfortable while he watched me do all of the work. "To explain the pendant, there are other things you need to know first. Things Layne probably hasn't told you."

"She hasn't told me much of anything yet."

"Well, let's start at the beginning, then. The quicksilver pools are pathways that connect different realms. I'm sure you've figured as much."

"Yes."

"The quicksilver itself is volatile. Some of our elders believe it possesses a low level of sentience. Whether this is true or not doesn't really matter. The stuff is dangerous. If the quicksilver comes into contact with bare skin..." Kingfisher trailed off.

"It was in Harron's dagger, wasn't it?" I asked.

Kingfisher nodded. "It was an ancient blade. Alchemists used to forge quicksilver into weaponry for Fae warriors. Harron had no business touching that weapon, let alone claiming it."

"It made him see things, I think. When it touched his skin, he started screaming." The sound of the captain's horrified wailing still haunted me when I closed my eyes. It was a chilling thing to hear such a powerful, strong fighter pleading for his life.

"Oh, he saw things all right. The quicksilver will push any living creature beyond the boundries of sanity."

I had done that to Harron. I'd panicked and unwittingly lashed out, and Harron's blade had responded and embarked on its mission to destroy him. But Harron had speared *me* through with his sword first. He had tried to kill me on Madra's orders. He would have succeeded, too, if Kingfisher hadn't brought me back here. I wouldn't feel guilty for defending myself.

If only it was as easy as telling myself that...

I changed the subject. "So, these Alchemists. They inherited their abilities? It's about blood?"

"*Everything* is about blood, human. Now, do you want to know about the pendant, or do you want to harry me by continually interrupting?"

I made a show of sealing my mouth shut.

"My mother gave me this pendant, this *relic*," he clarified, "when I was eleven. The night before we left for the Winter Palace. She knew I'd have need of it. Later, when I came of age and joined Belikon's army, I was called upon to travel between Yvelia and the other realms because my pendant was one of the most powerful. To cut a very long and boring story short, I was forced to travel a pathway without it once. The quicksilver took me, just as it takes everyone. A healer managed to draw most of it from me once I made it back to the Winter Palace, but I was left with a few...*lasting* reminders. Most Fae only wore their relics when they traveled from one realm to the next. But wearing mine is the only thing that calms the noise in my head. Without it, the line between what's real and what isn't blurs very quickly."

His eye. That was his lasting reminder? It had to be. The filaments that marked his jade iris were actually remnants of quicksilver. Gods. It was inside him, always there, always whispering in his ear, pushing him toward madness. The relic really *was* the only thing keeping him sane.

Nausea rolled in the hollow where my stomach used to be. I did my best to swallow it down as I collected another set of pitted tongs and dropped them into the bucket. The iron clanged loudly, sending up a puff of rust into the air. "Then...why did you give *me* the relic? Back in Zilvaren?"

He held up his hand. The thick signet ring flashed on his finger.

"Ah, right. Yes. You have a ring, too," I said.

"If I hadn't given you the relic, you'd have died."

"And why didn't you? Just let me die? You could have left me there."

Kingfisher dumped the armful of faded, dog-eared papers he was carrying onto the workbench, his expression blank. "You haven't been paying attention, human. Yvelia is at war, and war machines are hungry beasts. They require constant feeding. Food. Clothes. Gold. Building supplies. Weaponry. Before Madra drove that sword into her pool, stilling *every* pool in *every* realm, Belikon used the pathways for supplies. It was the only way to trade in many magical items. When the pathways closed, the door to our supply trains slammed closed, too. You shouldn't have been able to touch that sword, let alone draw it. And the silver responded to you. You activated it. You did what only an Alchemist can do. So, no. Human or not, I could *not* have just left you there to die."

"Great. So, you brought me back so you could save your people and win the war."

Kingfisher ran a hand through his ink-black waves again, his eyes cold as chips of ice. "You think very highly of me, human. In a way, I suppose what you say is true. But don't mistake me for some kind of saint. I don't give a shit about Yvelia, and I don't give a shit about Belikon's war. You are a bargaining chip. I saw my only avenue to freedom, and I took it. Ask me what I would have done had I found you in that condition under any other circumstances."

I stared at him, at the unfriendly set of his jaw, the tension in his shoulders, and the cruel lift to his mouth, and a body-wide shudder ripped through me, leaving panic in its wake. "I don't think I want to know," I whispered.

Kingfisher's suggestion of a smile grew wings and took flight. "Clever girl."

It took hours to finish clearing the forge, and we did so in silence. I didn't ask any more questions, too afraid to hear the answers, and Kingfisher kept his thoughts to himself.

Every so often, I found myself watching him. With his sleeves rolled up to his elbows and his cheek streaked with soot, he looked so normal. But then he'd snarl under his breath or meet my gaze with those silver-streaked eyes, and I'd be reminded that this male was not human. It was neither safe nor smart to let my gaze linger on him. The wisest thing I could do was figure out how I accidentally activated that pool and hightail it back to Zilvaren as quickly as possible.

The sky was darkening out of the window—*such* a bizarre sight—when Renfis came to find me. He looked tired, though the bruise beneath his eye and his split lip had miraculously healed themselves over the past few hours. Standing in the doorway, he surveyed the nearly cleared floor and the bucket of rusting tools I'd collected and sent a confused look Kingfisher's way. "What's this? You haven't even started working."

"The place was a disaster!" I cried. It was easy for him to come along and criticize. The forge looked so much better than it had. And he hadn't seen it before.

Kingfisher sighed. The chill in the air grew to icy degrees as shadows leaped up the walls, conjured out of nowhere. They spilled like wet paint across the floor, darting up the legs of the work-bench, blossoming in the air until everything went black. *Every-thing.* The forge itself became a pit of ink. It felt as though the shadows slipped down my throat and into my lungs when I drew in a gasp. This was true dark. Even deep in the underground tunnels that formed a network below the Silver City, the darkness wasn't this absolute.

"Oh, gods. What's happening?"

"Fisher," Renfis scolded. "Enough now."

The darkness snapped back like a rubber band. What was left of the day's light flooded back into the forge, and the forge was immac-ulate. The window was fixed, a fresh pane of glass glinting in the frame. The shattered vials and beakers that we'd swept into piles all over the place were gone. The hearth was brushed out, the bricks bright red and brand-new. The shelves were stocked with all kinds of fantastical pieces of equipment that I'd never even seen before. The plant life that had claimed the forge for its own was still there, though tamed back into pots and a small planter that sat beneath the window. And it was warm. All day, I'd been freezing, my teeth chattering while I'd cleaned and picked up with numb fingers, and *now it was warm?*

I spun, searching for something to hurl at Kingfisher. The closest thing that came to hand was a brightly shining, beautiful set of tongs. I snatched them up and stabbed them at the dark-haired warrior. "You! We broke our backs cleaning this place! What's *wrong* with you? What happened to, 'our abilities are sacred gifts to be used for righteous purposes,' or whatever the hell it was you said?"

"Him? Righteous purposes?" Renfis stifled a cough that sounded a lot like laughter. "The male standing before you isn't shy about using his gifts to complete mundane tasks."

I glowered at Kingfisher. "You *monster.*"

There wasn't a scrap of remorse to be found on the warrior's face. He scooped up his armor and his sword, then paused beside me on his way toward the brand-new door that now hung in the doorway.

"I just wanted to see if you knew what hard work was. I *told* you I was magic," he whispered.

And then he was gone.

10

CRUMBS

THE NEXT MORNING, Everlayne brought a breakfast of fresh fruits and yogurt—foreign delicacies I'd never tasted before. She sat with me and ate in my rooms, subdued and silent. I wanted to ask her about what she'd said back in the hallway yesterday. She'd called Kingfisher her brother, and not in the same way Kingfisher and Renfis called each other brother, like warriors who'd fought alongside each other. She'd meant it in a more literal sense, as if she and the evil bastard shared blood.

I didn't bring it up, though. I'd made a choice when I'd decided to go with Kingfisher to the forge rather than chase after her to see if she was okay, and by the way Everlayne kept sniffing indignantly as she spooned her yogurt into her mouth, I'd hurt her feelings in the process.

She forced me into yet another dress with voluminous skirts—shimmering purple this time—and fashioned my hair, winding the thick braids she'd plaited so that they trailed down the center of my back.

When it was time to leave my room, she smoothed her hands

down the lovely ivory gown she was wearing, then fiddled with the lace cuffs at her wrists, refusing to look at me. "If you want to come to the library with me, Rusarius and I collated all of the information we *do* have relating to the Alchemists and their processes yesterday. There isn't much, but I believe it's worth reading through—"

"I definitely want to join you," I said. "I'm sorry I didn't come yesterday. I know how badly you're trying to help me, and I do want to learn." How to get the hells out of here. How to find my way home. When I offered out my arm to her, she broke into a reluctant smile and slid her own through mine. And that, it seemed, was how long it took Everlayne De Barra to forgive a slight.

In the library, Rusarius was having a fit.

"Renfis, please! This is *not* a mess hall! There are precious works of art stored here, and…and…just…*look!* Look at all of that *grease!*"

I smelled Rusarius's issue before I saw it. Something meaty and smokey hung in the air, the scent so mouthwatering that my stomach audibly snarled. What *was* that? It smelled divine.

"Gods, Fisher," Everlayne muttered when she saw what he was doing.

The male sat at the head of the long clerk's table, a plate on the polished wood in front of him. He speared a piece of ambiguous meat onto a fork, then popped it into his mouth.

Renfis was propped against the wall by the far window, arms folded over his chest, watching the proceedings with an air of resignation. "Sorry, Rusarius. I don't know what you think I can do about it. The day I manage to make Kingfisher do anything is the day the Corcoran return."

"Well, there's no need for blasphemy!" the old librarian squawked.

"Where did your gods actually *go?*" I whispered to Everlayne. I'd been too overwhelmed to ask before.

"They set off on a pilgrimage thousands of—urgh! Another time. I'd better confiscate that food before Rusarius's head explodes."

Kingfisher remained focused on his breakfast. He didn't say a word when Everlayne approached and stood next to him at the head of the table. He just *growled.*

"And you wonder why Belikon calls you a dog," she said.

That got Kingfisher's attention. Slowly, his head rose, the silver flashing brightly in his right eye as he turned a baleful gaze on the female. "I don't wonder. I *know* why he calls me that."

"It's because of his deep loyalty to the crown," Renfis said, biting back a smile.

Kingfisher's eyes flashed, the quicksilver writhing amidst the green. He snapped his teeth at his sister. *"It's because I bite."* His hard expression could have made grown men turn tail and run scared into the night, but Everlayne arched an eyebrow at him and waited.

The male was once again dressed in black. He was armored up to the eyeballs this morning; the engraved chest piece he wore was black leather today instead of dark tan and bore a crest comprised of twin crossed swords wrapped in a tangle of vines, backed by the silhouette of a rearing stallion. He wore the same gorget at his throat, though—brilliantly polished silver with a snarling wolf etched into the metal. His thick dark hair was extra wavy, curling almost, not quite brushing the tops of his broad shoulders. When I realized how intensely I was studying the tips of the pointed ears poking through his hair, I quickly looked up at the glass-domed ceiling, clearing my throat, pretending to inspect the sky.

"Give me the plate." Everlayne's tone brooked no argument.

"Certainly." Kingfisher set down his fork, picked up the plate, and held it out to Everlayne. She took it. "By all means," he said. "Put my food on the fucking ground, outside, by the stables. I'll go eat with the other dogs presently."

Everlayne's shoulders sagged. *"Fisher."*

"Scratch that." His chair legs scraped loudly as he got up. Snatching his plate back, he strode away with it, heading for the door...and right for *me.* "I'll save you the trouble and take it there myself," he said. His eyes glittered as he passed me. "Enjoy your dusty books, human. I'll be waiting for you in the forge this afternoon. Don't make me come looking for you."

"Fisher, you're being ridiculous. Come back!" Everlayne called after him.

He ignored her, spine ramrod straight, the midnight sword strapped to his back leaving a trail of wispy shadows in its wake as he stalked out of the library.

"Well, I didn't mean for him to *leave* again," Rusarius grumbled. "But I've said it a thousand times, and I'll say it again. No cooked food in the library. I, myself, only eat dry crackers while working here. And I'm here for days sometimes. *And* I lean out of a window to avoid crumbs!"

"It's all right, Rusarius," Everlayne said softly. "He's not himself at the moment. It might be a while before he stops behaving like a spoiled brat."

"I'll go and train with him. Let him blow off some steam," Renfis said, pushing away from the wall. He paused by the seat Kingfisher had been sitting in a moment ago and rested his hand on its carved wooden back, frowning down at it. "He does deserve *some* grace, though. He has no rooms here. Nowhere to eat. Nowhere to sleep. No provisions. And a hundred and ten years, Layne. Can you imagine what a hundred and ten years would have been like in that place? Alone?" Sorrow dripped from each word. The princess and the soldier traded a long look. Eventually, the tension in Everlayne's ticking jaw muscle eased.

"I can, actually. I spent the first three decades imagining it in great detail every day. After that, I did my best not to think about it—or *him*—at all. My heart couldn't take it. And now he's back, and I don't have to wonder what kind of hell he's enduring. Now I get to *watch*."

Her voice was thick with emotion, but she didn't cry. She picked up a book from the table and set it on top of a stack, then moved on to fussing and fiddling with a sheaf of loose papers.

It was hard to see her in pain like this. And she *was* in pain. You'd have to be blind not to see that she was suffering. I stood on the peripherals of this group, which gave me an excellent view of the dynamics between them all. There was so much hurt between them. So much time, and history, and so many secrets. From the outside looking in, it was impossible to unravel all of the threads that connected them.

Renfis sighed. "There's a way to fix him. We just haven't found it yet. In the meantime, I'm not going to give up on him. Are you?"

A long pause filled the silence. Rusarius coughed uncomfortably; he gathered up a set of writing quills, carrying them into the stacks and disappearing off to gods only knew where. I didn't have a pile of quills to carry off, and this wasn't my library to go poking around in, so I had no choice but to hover at the end of the clerk's table and stare down at my feet. Or at the point where my feet should have been. I couldn't see them beneath my cursed dress's skirts.

"So that's it, then? You *have* given up on him?" Renfis demanded.

"No! No, I haven't. I just...I feel *hopeless.*"

"If I have enough hope for him, then I've enough for you, too." Renfis sighed out a long, steady breath, tapping the table with his fingertips. "I'll see you later. Good luck. And good luck to you, too, Saeris." He smiled warmly at me as he passed, which made me feel slightly less like I was eavesdropping on a private conversation.

Once he was gone, Everlayne bustled around the table, riffling through more pieces of parchment, organizing, and then reorganizing them. "All right." She sniffed. "Where should we begin? Hmm. I think, maybe, if you start by telling us what you know about alchemical practices and how they might be used—"

"Uh, I don't even know what alchemical *means.*" I didn't want to interrupt her, but I figured it was best to get that out of the way before she went any further.

"Oh! Right!" She smiled broadly, but it seemed as though there was a hint of hysteria to her. "Well. That's okay. I suppose that might even be for the best. No bad habits that way. We'll start from the beginning, just as soon as Rusarius—" She broke off, looking over her shoulder. "Rusarius? Where in the five hells did the man *go?*"

"Everlayne? Are you, uh, okay? You seem a little..."

"No, I'm fine. Fine. Really, I'm fine." She pressed her fingers into her forehead, screwing her eyes shut for a moment, completely *not* fine. "I. . ." She let her hand fall, all pretension dropped. "He was the very best thing in my entire life," she said. "The *only* good thing. And he's gone. I knew he would be, but it's hard...to see, and...to accept, and..."

"Speaking of crackers, I knew I had some somewhere. I found a whole tray of them on a shelf in the Seventh Era Land Records section. Must have left them there the other day." Rusarius emerged from the stacks again, carrying a small silver platter of what indeed looked to be very dry crackers. Oblivious to the fact that Everlayne was dashing tears away with the back of her hand, he placed the platter down on the table with a flourish. "Help yourselves, my darlings. But, uh...yes, please. Make sure to keep the crumbs to a minimum."

Alchemy, it turned out, was a form of magic. Forgotten, long-dead, old magic that was as much a myth to the Fae of Yvelia as *they* were to the people of Zilvaren. There had once been three branches of Alchemists—Fae who sought to discover the path to immortality, Fae who sought to create and invent by transmuting various metals and ores, and lastly, Fae who sought to cure illness and disease.

Everlayne and Rusarius thought I was somehow like the second type of Alchemist—the kind that transmuted metals. At the beginning of our first library session, I had no idea what the word "transmute" even meant, and by the end I still wasn't sure I understood.

Thousands of years ago, the Alchemists used their magical gifts to alter the state of compounds and transform them into precious metals. There was no record of which compounds were used, or what was done to them, but the Alchemists were successful. They found a way to transform elements into vast amounts of gold and silver, which was reportedly used to fill the royal coffers. At some point, the quicksilver was discovered along with the other realms its pathways connected, and all manner of chaos ensued afterward.

"None of this indicates how I'm replicating what the original Alchemists could do, though," I said, snapping the book I'd been scanning closed. "How did they actually control the quicksilver?"

Everlayne shrugged. "It's assumed that they activated and deactivated it—or opened and closed the pathways—by using their magic."

"It's hotly debated whether they controlled it at all," Rusarius said. "According to most documents from around that time, the second order of the Alchemists lived very short lives. They often went mad and killed themselves."

"Oh, well, that's just *great.*" Whatever the Alchemists of old had done to earn themselves that fate, I wanted to know so I could do the exact opposite. But...damn it. Burying my head in the sand wouldn't help me activate the quicksilver again, and I had to work out how to do that if I wanted to know what had happened to Hayden. The idea that Hayden might have been conscripted into Madra's army was preferable to imagining him dead, but I needed to *know*. If Hayden was gone, he needed to be buried, and I needed to stand the customary seventy-two-hour vigil over his grave. If he was trapped as a new recruit of Madra's army, then I needed to save him and get him out of there.

Either way, I had to figure this out, no matter *what* it cost me.

I rubbed at my temples, trying to ease the tension headache that was forming there. What with all of the thieving and black-market trading just to survive, life back in the Silver City hadn't left much room for reading. My eyes weren't used to it. I stared down at the book I'd been...

Huh.

Wait.

I held up the book, tilting my head, eyes narrowed at Rusarius. "How come I can read this?"

"What do you mean?" he asked.

"Well, I'm from another place. An entirely different realm. What are the chances that you and I even speak the same language? That we share a written language? It's just...it's impossible." It was wild that this hadn't occurred to me before.

"Hmm, no. Not impossible. Not even improbable, actually," said Rusarius. "You explain this one, sweet," he said to Everlayne. "There's one more book I want to find before you leave."

Everlayne seemed happy to be given the task. "Well," she said, leaning across the table to take the book out of my hand. "Right now, you're speaking Common Fae. This book was written in Common Fae, too. There are other languages in Yvelia. Other dialects. But Common Fae is spoken by all of the courts as a shared, well, *common* tongue. When the first Fae traveled to your realm, the humans there spoke a different language altogether. Over the years, our language and our written word became adopted by the humans. Even though we were cut off from the other realms, it seems as though our language has thrived. In Zilvaren, at least. Zilvaren had Madra, and your queen has always spoken Common Fae. She served as an anchor to our language. Perhaps in other realms, languages and alphabets have changed."

Madra.

As ancient as the stone halls at the center of the universe.

I had to ask. I had to *know.* "You seem to know a fair bit about her," I said.

"Madra?" Everlayne pursed her lips. "I suppose I know as much as anyone here. She was young when she ascended to the Zilvaren throne. Bloodthirsty and hungry for power."

"But how can she be so old if she's human? How has she managed to reign for over a thousand years? And how could she have closed all of the pathways with that sword if she wasn't an Alchemist?"

"We don't know how she did it, but yes, Madra should have died centuries ago. It must be some form of magic, but we have no clue who performed it for her or why. We don't know how she discovered that the quicksilver could be stilled with an Alchimeran sword, either. That information was closely guarded by our kind for generations. But you don't need to be Fae or possess any special gift in order to *close* the doors between our realms. The sword will do it for you. As far as we know, when one pool of quicksilver is activated, all quicksilver everywhere is activated. It's joined by some kind of..." She frowned, searching for a way to explain. "A ribbon of energy, I suppose. If you take a sword like Solace and plunge it into the quicksilver, it severs that energy in a way that paralyzes it. Until Solace was removed, every entrance to the pathway became frozen. There were members of this court on scouting parties, exploring new pathways that had only recently opened up when Madra cut the cord. Friends. Family members. They became trapped wherever they were. They haven't been seen since."

"Is it...I mean, is there a chance that any of them are still alive? I know very little about Fae life expectancy. How long do your people even live for? How old are *you?*"

Everlayne choked on a huff of laughter, covering her mouth with a hand. Was it me, or did she seem a little embarrassed? "That's... not something we really talk about. You'd know that, but we haven't really covered court etiquette yet."

"Sorry. Gods, I should mind my own business. I—"

"No, no, no, it's okay." She shook her head. "I know we've only known each other a few days, but I sat with you for a long time while you were recovering. I'd like to think that we're friends."

"Me too." It was the truth. I was starting to think of her as a friend, and I was glad she thought the same of me. Having a friend in a palace full of enemies could never be a bad thing.

"Right. Well, now that we've established that," she said, grinning. "Let me start out by asking you how old you *think* I am?"

"If you were a human, I'd say you were a little older than me. Twenty-seven? Twenty-eight, perhaps?"

"Gods." Her eyes went wide. "This will come as a bit of a shock, then." She took a deep breath. "I was born at the very beginning of the tenth age. I've been alive for one thousand four hundred and eighty-six years."

"One thou...?" I nearly swallowed my tongue. Everlayne was nearly *fifteen hundred* years old. I couldn't force my mind to make sense of that. She looked so young. Did I dare ask my next question? The one that burned on the tip of my tongue? I shouldn't even want to know, but I couldn't help it. "And Kingfisher? How old is *he?*"

Everlayne regarded me, a small smile playing over her lips. She took a long second to answer, during which time I internally berated myself for giving in to my infernal curiosity, but then she said, "I'd say that you needed to ask him. It's not really my place to share information like that. Often, we don't even know how old other members of our court are. But I do know how old Kingfisher is and telling you to ask him directly is just cruel. He'd never tell you, and he'd mock you for asking besides. Kingfisher was born at the end of the ninth age. Does that help you form some sort of a guess?"

"I don't know. I'm not sure. He looks like he's about thirty. So, maybe I'd say he was..." Gods, convincing the words to come out of my mouth was impossible. This was madness.

"Go on," Everlayne prompted.

"I don't know, eighteen hundred years old?"

"Not bad. He's one thousand seven hundred and thirty years old."

"One thousand seven hundred and thirty-*three*," came a deep voice. Adrenaline exploded through my veins, shocking my system so badly that I nearly toppled sideways out of my seat. I twisted around, and there stood Kingfisher in a recessed reading alcove, bathed in shadows. Half of his body was concealed by a pool of darkness that was very out of place in the well-lit library. He studied his fingernails, that metal wolf-head gorget glinting at his throat. "What's three years between family, though?" he said, shoving away from the wall and out into the light. "I'm sure it's hard to keep track of time when you're so distracted by the comings and goings of court life." He gave her a tight-lipped smile. "Glad to see you're finally sharing some truths with your new pet, Layne. I have to say, I'm a little scandalized to discover that they're *mine,* though."

"You wouldn't have discovered anything if you weren't eavesdropping."

"Forgive me. I was bored. I decided to come and fetch the human after all, and you two seemed to be having *such* an interesting conversation."

Everlayne rolled her eyes. She placed her hand on my forearm. "Never mind him. In answer to your other question, technically the Fae who found themselves trapped when the quicksilver was stilled could still be alive, yes. But the realm they were visiting was a volatile and dangerous place. It's unlikely that old age killed any of them. But the local clans probably did."

"Next time you're curious about me, feel free to ask me," Kingfisher said as he laid his hand on the forge's brand- new door. This was the first time he'd spoken since we left the library, preferring to march through the Winter Palace in stony silence.

The door swung open, and he went inside.

I hovered on the threshold, trying to decide if I wanted to go in after him or if I wanted to run in the opposite direction, back to my room, where he wouldn't be able to give me any grief. The palace was a winding nightmare of hallways, staircases, and corridors, but I thought I could find my way if I really tried.

My legs were as heavy as hewn stone as I followed him into the forge. "If I'd asked you something, you wouldn't have answered me. And if you had, it wouldn't have been the truth."

"Incorrect. If you asked me something worthy of a reply, then I'd answer. If I answered, then it would be the truth." Just as he'd done yesterday, he began stripping out of his armor, again starting by removing his sword. This time I was prepared and didn't flinch when he drew the weapon.

"Right. *Sure.*" Humans and Fae were different in many ways, but sarcasm was universal.

His hands worked deftly on the strap that went around his side, unfastening his chest protector. "Try me, human."

"All right. Fine." Thanks to Kingfisher's little clean-up trick last night, the forge was spotless today. The workbench was free of debris, the floor immaculate. All of the tools were good as new, hanging on hooks on the wall opposite the hearth. I maneuvered myself around the other side of the workbench, putting the biggest, heaviest obstacle that I could between us as he continued to remove his armor, just in case he didn't like my questioning and came for me. Because I planned on riling him. Annoying him. Baiting him the same way he baited me, with his constant *Osha* name calling, and his open derision.

Screw him.

Kingfisher dropped his chest protector to the floor.

I braced against the workbench and said, "Elroy swears that a man will lie about the size of his cock every time a woman asks him."

Kingfisher stilled. "Are you asking me how big my cock is, Osha?"

"I don't care how big it is. I care about the way you answer."

A slow, terrifying smirk spread across his face. "It's big enough to make *you* scream and then some."

"*See.*" I jabbed a finger at him. "You're not going to be honest."

He looked around the forge, feigning confusion. "I'm sorry, I'm not sure that I understand your meaning."

"Ask a man how big his dick is, and he'll show you that he's full of shit."

"Maybe. But I'm not a man. I'm a *Fae male*." He paused. "And maybe I'm just well-endowed."

"Or maybe you're just wasting my time, and we should get on with whatever you're going to attempt to teach me here," I snapped.

Kingfisher's hands moved to the back of his neck. It took him all of four seconds to unfasten his gorget and slide the silver plate free. "Maybe the issue is that you asked me a question about my *cock* like a hungry little bitch in heat and didn't ask me something that mattered."

Gods, but he kept surprising me. Every time I thought I'd reached the limit of how much one living being could detest another, he went and proved to me that I was capable of so much more. "All right. Okay. Fine. I will ask you something that matters. You were banished from the Yvelian Court because you did something bad. Belikon said you razed an entire city to the ground."

He crooked a dark eyebrow at me. "That was a question?"

"Did you do it?" I asked.

"Why do you want to know?"

"Because I'm sharing a very small space with you right now. Because we're alone. Because I want to know if I'm breathing the same air as a mass murderer. And don't dodge a question by asking *me* a question. *Did you do it?*"

He surveyed me intensely. Even from a distance, I could see the trapped quicksilver swirling in amongst that sea of vivid green. "Yes." The word came out abruptly. Defiantly. "I did."

"Why?"

"Because I didn't have a choice."

I slapped my hands against the workbench, my anger a clenched iron fist in my chest. *"Why?"*

"You're not ready for that information. You'll never be ready."

"Why?"

"Because you're human, and humans are weak," he snarled. "Because it's none of your business. Because it doesn't matter *why* I did it. Because no matter what reason I give to you, it won't be good enough. Now ask me something else."

My voice shook when I spoke. "Renfis said that you've been suffering for the past century because you were banished after you destroyed that city. Where did they send you?"

Kingfisher prowled toward the workbench. All of the armor was gone now. He was dressed in a simple loose black shirt and black pants again. At his throat, the silver chain hanging around his neck—the one he'd loaned to me when I was dying—glinted, catching my attention. I tried not to pull back as he drew closer, but he was huge. He towered over me, taking up so much room, invading my space, blotting out the damn light. He was all I could see. All I could smell. He was cold morning air, and smoke, and fresh-turned earth, and a thousand other complex scents I didn't even have names for.

Canines bared, he leaned in so close that barely an inch separated the tips of our noses. And he snarled, *"Hell."*

I couldn't breathe. Couldn't think. He was so close. So angry. It was as if he was on the verge of breaking and only being held back by the thinnest of threads.

Out of nowhere, his composure snapped back into place, his canines disappearing in a flash. "Pray you never have to experience it firsthand, human," he whispered. "Hold out your hand."

"Hold out my...?"

"Yes, hold out your hand."

Up this close, he could take my hand and the arm it was attached to if he wanted to. He could tear me limb from limb and there wouldn't be a thing I could do about it. Numb and trembling, I held out my hand, praying wholeheartedly that he wasn't about to start breaking my fingers for upsetting him. Something cool and smooth pressed into the center of my palm. Kingfisher closed my grip around it, then cupped his huge, tattooed hands tightly around mine. At first, I didn't feel it. I was too aware of his proximity and the wild array of different scents that kept rolling off of him and slamming into me.

Wood, and leather, and spices, and something green, and faint musk, and—

"Ow."

Kingfisher narrowed his eyes. "What is it?"

"Ow! That hurts!" I tried to pull my hand free, but Kingfisher's grip tightened. He held on, grasping my hand tighter and tighter in his, and the burning sensation in the center of my palm really started to sting. "Kingfisher," I said in a warning tone. He didn't release me, only stood there, staring down at me, watching me, the metallic threads of silver shifting wildly in his right eye. "Fisher, what are you doing?"

"Tell me what it is," he demanded.

"It's *hurting* me, is what it is!" I cried, really pulling on my hand now. I wrenched and yanked, putting my whole bodyweight behind the motion, desperate to free myself, but Kingfisher held fast.

"Is it hot? Cold? Sharp? Soft?"

"Cold! It's cold! It's *burning*, it's so cold!" That made no sense, but it was true. Ice crawled inside me, leeching into my bones. "It hurts! Let go, Fisher! Please! Make it stop!"

"You make it stop," he commanded.

"I can't! I can't!"

Resolve flickered in his eyes. "You can."

"Let go!"

"You want to prove me right, is that it? You're weak? You're a human, so you're weak and useless and pathetic? Is that it?"

"FISHER!"

He spun us around so that my back was to the workbench. I felt the edge of the wood digging into the small of my back, but the pressure was nothing compared to the awful ball of pain he had trapped between our hands. *"Listen* to it," he commanded.

"What?" He wasn't making any sense.

Kingfisher removed one hand, but it made no difference—he only needed one hand to hold both of mine. With the hand he now had free, he grabbed me firmly by the chin, forcing me to be still. To look at him. *"Listen,"* he repeated. "What is it saying?"

"It's saying that you're an...evil...piece of...shit," I ground out.

He didn't react to that. "The sooner you do as I say, the sooner this all ends, human."

My jaw was screaming, I was clenching my teeth so hard. "Fuck—*you*—"

"There you go again. Hungry, needy little bitch in heat, begging to be fucked..." he taunted.

"Let. Go!"

"LIIIIISTENNN!!" Kingfisher's roar snatched my breath away. It snatched the light, too. The whole forge went black as pitch in an instant, and the pain in my hand, traveling up my arm, turned into a rope of fire. "There is you, and there is the pain. Nothing else," he whispered. "Move past it. Move through it. Let it roll over you."

This was cruel. This was torture. I was burning alive. He was going to kill me. "I can't," I sobbed.

"You can. Show me that I'm wrong. Show me that you're tougher than I think you are."

Of all the things he'd said to me, it was this that somehow reached me. I sucked in a stuttering breath and tried to calm my mind. The thrumming, throbbing, panicking, desperate part of me calmed the tiniest fraction. An infinitesimal amount. It made the pain flicker for a second—not long enough to provide any real kind of relief—but it was long enough.

There was a voice.

A million voices.

Annorath mor!

Annorath mor!

Annorath mor!

Annorath mor!

The sound was deafening. I screamed around it, shaking my head, trying to get it out, but it blazed through every part of my mind, consuming me, eradicating every memory, every thought, every feeling...

"Annorath...*MOR!*" I screamed.

The pain blinked out.

The light rushed back in.

The voices fell silent, and the quiet they left behind was deafening.

Kingfisher stood frozen, still far too close for comfort, his hand loose around mine now. For once, that cold arrogance he always wore was nowhere to be found. With wide eyes, he looked down at our joined hands, his breath catching slightly in his throat.

I tensed when I saw the tiny ball of silver liquid rolling around in the well of my palm. Quicksilver. Not much. Little more than the size of a pinkie fingernail. But quicksilver all the same. And it was in a *liquid* state.

I panicked, trying to fling it away, but Fisher gripped hold of my wrist, shaking his head. "So long as I'm touching you, you're safe. I'm wearing the pendant. It won't harm us."

"What are you talking about? It'll definitely harm us! It just nearly froze me from the inside out!"

"That was nothing. A test. It's over now. You passed."

Incredulous, I gaped up at him. *"What would have happened if I hadn't?"*

"That's academic. You did."

"Get it *off* me, Fisher!"

"Make it still," he said.

"How the fuck—I don't know *how!*"

"Close your eyes. Feel it in your mind. Reach for it..."

I did as he said, closing my eyes, trying to remember how to breathe around the knowledge that this tiny bit of quicksilver pooling in my hand was enough to rip apart my mind. I'd seen what it had done to Harron. I was about to curse Kingfisher again, to tell him that I couldn't feel the cursed silver, but then...I *could* feel it.

It was a solid weight, resting there, right in the center of my mind. It was nothing. Not hot. Not cold. Not sharp. Not soft. It just was. And it was waiting.

"I feel it," I whispered.

"Okay. Now tell it what you want. Tell it to sleep."

I told it exactly that. In my mind, I willed it to still, to go to sleep. The solid little weight seemed to roll over restlessly.

"*No, not sleep. Not now. Slept for too long,*" it hissed, an innumerable number of voices all layering over one another.

"*Sleep,*" I ordered more firmly.

This time, it obeyed.

The weight lifted from my mind, disappearing until I felt almost back to normal. *Almost,* because Fisher was still holding my hands. When I opened my eyes, he was looking at the solid bead of matte, inert metal in my hands, a look of wry amusement on his irritatingly handsome face.

"I have to say, I was expecting that to go differently," he mused.

And then I punched him square in the mouth.

11

SWALLOW

"Too tight! Too tight! I can't breathe!"

To say Everlayne was angry would be an understatement. She yanked on the corset ribbons at the back of my dress with a strength I didn't know she possessed.

"If you keep on pulling like that, you're going to crack my ribs," I groused.

"Good! Maybe then, you'll…stop…complaining!"

"Broken ribs won't stop me from complaining," I muttered sullenly, tugging on the corset stays. They were digging into my skin, pinching me in places my clothes back home had never pinched me before. It sucked.

"Stop that!" Everlayne slapped my hand away, tsking. She faffed with my skirts, bustling around me, swatting at imaginary pieces of fluff that only she could see. As with the other dresses Everlayne had given me, this garment was absolutely stunning. A shimmering red affair made of raw silk. It was the kind of dress that would bring most men to their knees. I fucking hated it.

"What were you even *thinking?*" Everlayne growled, slapping down the folds of the skirt some more so that it hung properly.

"He's a Fae warrior, Saeris. You can *not* go around punching Fae warriors."

"Can I *please* wear some pants?" I observed myself glumly in the full-length mirror. "And don't tell me that pants are only for males. I've seen plenty of females wandering around the palace wearing pants."

"We've been over this. You're too *pretty* to wear pants. Are you listening to me? About Kingfisher?"

I gave her a hard look. *"No."*

"You could at least tell me what he did to make you punch him like that."

"Just trust me. He deserved it."

"Well, I don't doubt *that.*"

She'd asked me to explain what had happened seven times in the past hour, but her pleading hadn't broken me. It would do no good to tell her about the stunt Kingfisher had pulled with the quicksilver. I didn't want to make things any more tense between them. If Everlayne knew he'd thrown me into a situation that I was fairly sure could have killed me, then things wouldn't just get worse. They'd become catastrophic, and we *were* friends. I didn't want her to suffer any more than she already was. Having Kingfisher as a brother was burden enough, I was sure.

"You're lucky he didn't react any worse than he did," she said.

"Oh?" I scoffed. *"I* thought his reaction was a little over the top."

Everlayne had been waiting for me when I returned to my room yesterday. She hadn't banked on Kingfisher kicking in my bedroom door, me thrown over his shoulder like a sack of potatoes and wailing like a banshee. Nor had she expected his ultra-foul temper, his split bottom lip, or the thin line of blood trickling down his chin. She'd squawked when he'd thrown me unceremoniously down onto my bed and snarled, *"Bad* human," at me.

"He could have been far worse," she assured me. "Warriors like Fisher don't react kindly to violence."

"Are you saying that he's so feral that one small right hook is enough to send him on an explosive killing rampage?"

She thought about this while folding a blanket. It took her a while to make up her mind. "Yes," she decided.

"Then your brother isn't a warrior, Everlayne. He's a mindless savage with a shitty temper. But I think I could have already told you that."

"Please just call me Layne. And do *not* say that out loud!"

"It's hardly a secret. I think everyone knows Fisher's a savage—"

"Not that. The *brother* part," she said in a loud whisper.

"That's not common knowledge?"

"Well, yes. And no. It's just not spoken about. And it's very, *very* complicated."

"Let me guess. Your mother had an affair because the king's a vile monster, and she ended up pregnant by someone else?"

Everlayne—*Layne*—sighed. "No. My mother was married to a Southern lord before she married my father. She had Fisher with her first husband. When Fisher was ten, the king sent his father on a mission to Zilvaren. He never returned. That's when the gateways were stilled. The king said that Finran, Fisher's father, was responsible for the quicksilver stilling and declared him a traitor to the Fae—"

"Wait. Kingfisher said that Madra was responsible for stilling the quicksilver."

Everlayne's expression became troubled. "And that might be true. Fisher has certainly never believed his father was responsible. But without any proof to the contrary, Belikon announced that Finran was to blame. Less than a year later, Belikon announced his engagement to my mother. By all accounts, she was surprised, given that she'd never even *met* the king, but Belikon made it clear that marrying him was the only way for her to prove that she wasn't a traitor to the crown, too. Plus, Finran had been very wealthy, and Belikon needed money to pay for the conflict breaking out with Sanasroth. Belikon informed my mother via royal herald that she was to report to the Winter Palace, and she was to bring all of her assets and money with her. Rusarius still talks of how furious the king was when she arrived with Kingfisher in tow."

"He didn't consider a son from a previous marriage an asset?"

Layne's laughter sounded flat. "Not even a little. He wanted a son of his own, and as quickly as possible. He didn't want Kingfisher as his heir by marriage, but it took a long time for my mother to fall pregnant again. Fae children are a rare gift. Most couples are lucky if they have even one child. Belikon thought Fisher had 'used my mother up.' He actually said that once. He still insists that when our mother did fall pregnant with me a long time later, it was Fisher's fault that she wasn't strong enough to produce another male heir. His fault that she wasn't strong enough to survive the delivery, either. Her pregnancy with me was difficult. None of her healers were surprised when she passed shortly after I came into the world, but Belikon..." Everlayne shook her head sadly. "According to the king, everything's always Fisher's fault. But our mother's death wasn't because of him. It was because of me."

"It wasn't anyone's fault," I said. "Women have died in childbirth since the dawn of time. Human or Fae, it makes no difference. The child can never be held accountable."

Layne had probably heard all of this before. She just nodded, stroking her hands over the blanket she'd placed on the back of my reading chair. "How did you know Fisher wasn't Belikon's illegitimate son?" she asked. "He's had enough affairs over the years."

That one was easy. "Because, illegitimate or not, no father would hate their own blood the way Belikon hates Fisher."

"Yes, well..." Layne's jaw worked as she stared unseeingly down at the blanket. "You're right about that. Anyway!" She inhaled, straightening as she came back to herself, shedding the heavy topic like it was an oppressive robe. "I'm going to fetch us something for breakfast. When we're finished eating, we'll head up to the library."

She left, and I sat myself down on the edge of my bed, relieved that I was alone at last.

Annorath mor.

Annorath mor.

Annorath mor.

Kingfisher had told me to listen to the quicksilver, and I'd heard it. I couldn't *stop* hearing it. The voices in my head were gone. They'd vanished as soon as the quicksilver had stilled, but that *phrase*. I kept repeating it to myself, over and over again, as if it were the answer to a question I didn't know how to ask.

Annorath mor.

Annorath mor.

Annorath mor.

Kingfisher had responded when I'd said it out loud. He'd been wide-eyed. Shocked, even. He hadn't explained what it meant, though, and the not knowing was driving me crazy.

I dug my fingernails into my palm, applying pressure to the rhythm of those words as they cycled around in my head. It felt almost as if they had replaced the beating of my heart. My trance only ended when a loud knock at the door sundered the silence.

At some point, Layne would accept that I just didn't eat that much, and she'd stop loading up my plate with so much food. She'd slip an apple into her pocket for me or something. That way, even if her breakfast plate were full, she'd still have a spare hand free to open the door with. I grumbled to myself as I crossed the room and twisted the handle, pulling the door so that it swung open as I headed back to the bed and dropped down to my knees, searching underneath it for the shoes I'd kicked off last night.

"Admittedly, I do enjoy when a female kneels for me, but in *this* particular case..."

I was reaching, arm stretched out, fingers catching on the heel of my shoe underneath the bed, but the moment I heard that voice, I went stiff as a board. Blood rushed to my cheeks as I drew back and sat up on my heels, glowering up at Kingfisher. "You aren't welcome in here," I informed him.

His lip was even angrier and redder than it had been yesterday afternoon. In his hands, he carried a large wooden board stacked high with all kinds of cured meats, cheeses, fruit, and at least three different kinds of bread. He wore an inordinate amount of armor—twice as much as usual. His shins were covered by black greaves embellished with golden rising suns, their rays spearing upward toward his knees. Matching vambraces covered his wrists. He looked down at himself, his mouth twisting into a cold smile when he caught me looking at his upgraded armor.

"You like it?" he purred. "I figured some extra protection was in order this morning since you're now given to hurling yourself at me like some kind of rabid feline."

"Cats scratch," I said flatly. "I came *this* close to knocking you on your ass."

"In your fucking dreams, human." He kicked the door closed, strode into the bedroom, set down the pile of food on the small table, and then went to all three of the tall windows in the room, ripping the curtains closed at each as he went.

I got up and followed after him, drawing the curtains open again. "What are you *doing?*"

"I'm hungover," he announced. "The sun is trying to crack my skull open, which is making me *very* unfriendly. But please. Feel free to open the curtains."

How did you even kill a Fae warrior? Did you need a special weapon? Could they be poisoned? I made a mental note to ask Rusarius—the old librarian was bound to know. Scowling deeply, I went back and revisited the windows, drawing the curtains closed again. "I meant, what are you doing here? In my room?"

"I'm not allowed to eat in the library, apparently. And, unlike Layne, I don't have my own assigned wing of the court. After seeing how nice *your* rooms were yesterday, I figured I'd come and eat breakfast here. Don't worry. I brought you some cheese." He picked up one of the small plates that he'd balanced on his overflowing board and planted a massive wedge of hard cheese down on it. In fairness, it looked like good cheese, but the way he shoved the plate at me across the table made my blood boil.

The prick started eating like his life depended on it.

"Rusarius said no cooked food in the library. All of this is cold. Take it and go and bother him."

Kingfisher paid me no heed.

"Fisher!"

He winced, hunkering down into his seat. "Today has rules, human." He started counting them off on his hand, a finger for each. "Do not shout. Do not throw any punches. Do not make me do any physical exercise. Do not—"

"Your lip's bleeding everywhere again," I told him.

His tongue darted out between his lips, his blood staining the very tip of it, and I found myself being flashed by a pair of wickedly sharp canines. The sight of them sent a thrill of panic-tinged intrigue through me. Heat rose up from the pit of my stomach, my blood rushing to my cheeks.

Kingfisher's gaze snapped up, singling in on mine. "Careful, human. We Fae have an excellent sense of smell. You'd be amazed what we can scent floating on the air."

"I...I wasn't doing anything. I didn't—" Oh, gods. I was going to die of embarrassment. The moment had been fleeting. I hadn't even meant to think it. I despised Kingfisher. I was *not* attracted to him. I was not thinking about his tongue or his teeth...

He set down the piece of bread and meat he was holding and sat back in his chair *very* slowly. His expression was suddenly serious, his eyes alert, his voice low and smooth as velvet. *"You're making it worse."*

Swallowing down the urge to scream, I sat down at the table and forced myself to hold his unbearably smug gaze. *Change the subject. Change the subject. Change the subject.* "Why haven't you gotten your lip taken care of, anyway? They can heal it. A small cut like that? It'd be gone with one tiny touch—"

Kingfisher's eyes narrowed, still boring into me. "I was going to get it seen to after this, but now I've decided against it."

"Hah. Right." I ripped a piece of cheese from the block he'd slapped on the plate for me and shoved it into my mouth.

"Yes. Just now, actually. I'm going to keep it as a souvenir."

"A reminder of the time a weak human girl landed a hit on you and drew blood? You want your friends knowing about that?" Fuck, this cheese had the consistency of glue. I kept chewing, but my mouth was so dry that it was turning into a thick paste.

"I like being surprised," Fisher said, spinning his fork over in his hand. "I'm also a fan of aggressive foreplay. It'll be a fun reminder."

I breathed in sharply, inhaling cheese. Choking and spluttering, I tried desperately to get rid of it, but it wasn't going anywhere.

Kingfisher leaned forward, his tongue running over his teeth again. He smiled suggestively as he said, *"Swallow."*

"What in the five hells is going on here? Are you trying to kill the poor girl?"

Layne came out of nowhere, a cloud of sweet perfume and saffron-colored silks. She set down the plates that she'd collected from the kitchens, then began rubbing her hand soothingly against my back. "What did you do to her?" She glowered hotly at Fisher.

"For the love of every god that has ever been or ever will be, could you please lower your voice?" he groaned.

"She's choking to death, Fisher. Did you poison her? Breathe, Saeris. That's it. Slowly in. Slowly out." She demonstrated breathing in through her nose. "And…and why does it smell like a *brothel* in here? If you're going to spend the night out whoring and drinking, the least you could do is wash the smell of sex off you before showing up for breakfast."

Kingfisher looked like he was about to explode with laughter. The monstrous bastard was enjoying this. I braced for the cruel jibe—he was seconds from telling his sister that whatever she could smell was courtesy of me and not him. But when he spoke, he took me by surprise. "You're right. I'm sorry, Layne. That was inconsiderate. I'll take my breakfast and leave you both in peace. If Ren shows up, let him know I'm down in the bathhouse, washing away my sins. I'll see *you* this afternoon, Osha. Be ready to practice more of what we learned yesterday."

Wait...

I watched him go.

He took the fall for me.

Why would he do that?

Would Layne know that *I* was the source of the scent of arousal in the air the moment he left? I didn't think so. I wasn't thinking about Fisher's tongue trailing up my neck anymore. I was thinking about him forcing me to hold that quicksilver in my palm again and how much it was going to hurt.

Annorath mor!

Annorath mor!

Annorath mor!

The memory of those voices in my head echoed like a war chant.

Fisher had saved me from embarrassment, but that meant little. Not when I was faced with the promise of an afternoon working with the quicksilver. He really was crazy if he thought I would willingly subject myself to *that* again.

The temperature in the library was insufferable. Even colder than usual, condensation ran down the insides of the windows, and billowing clouds of fog formed in the air any time anyone spoke.

"It'll snow tonight," Rusarius announced, frowning up at the moody blanket of clouds that filled the view out of the domed glass ceiling.

Snow.

The prospect of watching it fall from the sky with my own two eyes was thrilling, but there were more important matters at hand. I'd made my decision, and I was sticking to it.

"I want to learn more about the quicksilver today," I said. "I know you were planning on covering more about Sanasroth and the courts, but the king only gave us a week before Kingfisher has to leave. It's been three days already, and I haven't learned much about the pathways."

"Knowledge of the courts will be vital when you start to travel outside of Yvelia. I do think this is worth going over," Layne said, placing a hand on top of the daunting stack of books she'd set out for the day's session.

"I don't know. Maybe Saeris is right." Rusarius's white hair was more cloud-like than ever, puffing out in every direction. "If we can't demonstrate that Saeris is capable of activating the quicksilver, there'll be trouble for Kingfisher, I think. He's the one who brought her here. The king gave *him* a week to teach our new friend here how to navigate this whole thing. If she fails…"

"He'll punish Fisher," Layne said.

"And Saeris, too, perhaps?" Rusarius suggested in a questioning tone.

Layne reluctantly pushed her curated stack of books aside. "All right. The quicksilver it is. Maybe if we cover some rudimentary ground, Fisher will be able to introduce you to some other, lesser alchemical compounds in the forge this afternoon."

Oh, Fisher wasn't messing around with lesser alchemical compounds. He'd thrown me in at the deep end and slapped raw quicksilver in my hand without so much as a by-your-leave. Again, I made the decision not to spill that little tidbit of information. "I was wondering whether there were any references relating to how the Alchemists used the pathways to travel from one place to another specifically. As in, how they made sure they would wind up where they wanted to go," I clarified. "Was there a panel, or some incantation, or…" I shrugged, channeling as much nonchalance as I could muster. "Did they have to say a place's name out loud or something?"

Rusarius wiped his nose on the back of his robe's sleeve, then blew on some hot tea he'd fixed for himself somewhere at the back of the library. "Oh no, I doubt we have any books or parchments that cover *that*," he said.

"Oh." Disappointment gnawed on my insides.

"No, that part was easy. It was common knowledge how they made their way from one point to another." Rusarius sipped his tea and yelped, fanning his mouth. "Gods, patience has never been my strong suit. You think I would have learned to wait by now—"

"How did they do it, then? If it was common knowledge?"

"Ahh, yes. Well, they just fixed their intentions on the place. Focused very hard, apparently. If they wanted to explore somewhere new, they'd think of the *kind* of place they wanted to go to. If they wanted to discover a place rich in iron ore, for example, they'd think about iron ore and let the quicksilver pull them to a place that had plenty of iron ore. It was a very simple system. Flawed, of course. On a number of occasions, an Alchemist thought of the kind of place they wanted to go and stepped into a pool, never to be seen again. A group went searching for hydrogen once. That busybody Archivist Clements postulated that the quicksilver delivered them right into the center of a star somewhere. Load of utter nonsense if you ask me..."

I stopped listening. I wasn't trying to go somewhere new. I wanted to go home. And all I had to do was think about Zilvaren before stepping into the pool? That would be too easy, surely? But Rusarius did seem certain.

"And where's the pool here in the Winter Palace? Belikon has one, right?" I asked, interrupting the old male, who was still giving examples of different groups of Alchemists who had gone missing while exploring unknown destinations.

"Oh, of course! Our pool is the largest ever documented!" the librarian declared, beaming, as if he were personally responsible for its existence. "Belikon had it crafted so that it could transport whole armies if needed. It's situated beneath us, down very deep, in the bowels of the palace. Nearly every tunnel you come across will lead you there. Though I once spent five days trying to work out..."

I did a commendable job of feigning interest as Rusarius chattered on, even if I did say so myself. The plans that were rapidly forming in my head demanded all of my attention, but I nodded and laughed at the librarian's tale, engaging just enough to convince Layne that I was listening to him, too.

The next three hours dragged by, and I did my best not to fidget.

I took notes about the Sanasrothian pool, located at the center of their rival court's council halls. I recorded the locations of two other pools in two other courts, as well. The Gilarian, the Fae in the mountains to the east, kept their pool in a hall perched upon the highest peak of their domain. It was reported that the pool belonging to the Lìssians, the seafaring Fae who lived upon a southern island, was located deep in a sea cave and was almost as large as the Yvelian pool, though that had never been confirmed, the Lìssians regarding it as their most sacred place of worship.

I took all of this in, my mind buzzing the whole time.

All I had to do was fix my mind on the Silver City. I had to reach out to the quicksilver, convince it to wake, and then I'd be home. It would be *so* simple.

But there was something I had to do first.

12

FOX

KINGFISHER'S copious amount of leather was gone, and I could understand why. The hearth was blazing, a white-hot fire licking up the brickwork when I entered the forge. For the first time in nearly a week, a blissful warmth sank into my bones, and it was a beautiful, beautiful thing.

Layne's dark-haired brother smirked like a demon when he realized that I had entered the blistering hot workshop, though he didn't turn away from his task. Sweat ran down the side of his face as he thrust a glowing set of tongs into the inferno; he stooped, squinting as he concentrated for a moment, and then he drew the long tongs back out again, this time with a small iron pot clasped in the tongs' grips.

I barely noticed the pot—the *crucible*—that Kingfisher set down on the anvil by the workbench. My gaze was locked onto the bead of sweat that was hanging from Fisher's chin; for the life of me, I could see nothing else. It glistened there for a second and then fell, sizzling when it hit the iron crucible and turned to smoke.

Fisher's normally loose black shirt was plastered to his chest. He drew in a deep breath, his shoulders rising, and—

I jerked when he snapped his fingers in front of my face.

"You could at least say hello before you start eye-fucking me."

"I wasn't eye-fucking you. I was trying to see through all of this... steam." I wafted my hand for effect, but the air was clear, there was no steam, and Kingfisher did not look impressed.

"It's always confounded me. Humans aren't restricted by the same laws as the Oath Bound Fae. You creatures can lie whenever you want. You do it all of the time. And yet you're all so fucking *bad* at it." His cheeks were flushed from the heat, slick with perspiration. Not a hair on his head was dry. From root to tip, his waves were dripping wet, some of them plastered to the side of his face. As if suddenly conscious of this, he shook his head like a dog, showering sweat everywhere.

I held my hand up in front of my face, blocking the spray. "Disgusting."

Fisher laughed silently as he peered into the crucible, peeling his shirt free of his chest as he inspected what was inside. "There you go again, lying your little heart out. You like my sweat, *don't* you, human?"

Since the moment we'd met, the prick had lived to push my buttons. I'd never reacted to him calling me 'human' or 'Osha,' so I had no clue how he knew it irked me so much, but it did. I was officially sick of it. "I have a *name*. Use it." I barged past him, making my way to the workbench. I dumped the bag I'd brought with me onto the table and then snatched up one of the thick leather aprons hanging on the wall by the window.

I turned around, ready to lecture him about manners and how it was polite to call a person by their given name and not some shitty name *they'd* come up with for them, but—

"Holy gods and martyrs!" My heart leaped up into my throat.

Less than an inch away, Kingfisher smiled down at me. How the hell had he gotten this close? His eyes danced with mirth. It was criminal that such astonishing eyes belonged to such a bastard. They were like nothing I'd ever seen before. So bright, the most unique and startling shade of green. And while the quicksilver trapped in his right iris freaked me the hell out, there was no denying that it made him look remarkable.

"You are *temporary*," he said, looming over me, his huge frame just...everywhere.

"And you are *rude*," I shot back.

He shrugged, turning away. As soon as his back was to me, I sucked in a ragged breath, trying to regain my composure while he wasn't looking. "It isn't practical, learning the names of humans," he said. "You come and go so quickly. I only bother to learn the names of creatures who live longer than a heartbeat."

My hands shook as I looped the apron ties around my waist and then knotted them over my stomach. "It's Saeris. My name. Call me that or nothing at all."

He cast an amused look over his shoulder, his lips parted a fraction, exposing the briefest glimpse of teeth. "Nothing at all? I like the sound of that. Come here and look at this, Nothing At All."

I suppose I walked right into that one. Sighing, I went to see what he was pointing at inside the crucible. "There are these other words, too. Please and thank you? I haven't heard you use either yet, but I'm sure they're a part of your vocabulary—"

"They're not," he said brightly.

A tiny amount of dark gray powder, fine as ash, sat in the bottom of the crucible. "What am I looking at?"

"Bone," Fisher said.

"Human?"

He shook his head. "I didn't have any. Though, if you were willing to contribute—"

"*Stop.*"

Fisher stood up straight, half-closing one eye as he studied me. "Are your kind supposed to nap in the afternoons? You're really grumpy. *I'm* the one with the hangover, y'know."

"What did you even do last night?"

"Wouldn't you like to know."

"Actually, forget it. I've changed my mind. I don't want to know."

"Ren and I went to The Blind Pig. We gambled away half his savings and drank the bar dry. I'll invite you next time."

I pulled a face. "Please don't."

Kingfisher grabbed me, his hand closing around my wrist. I'd been about to poke the powder inside the crucible with my fingertip, but...

"Where you come from, does a smith poke a finger into a crucible right after it comes out of a blazing furnace, Osha?" Fisher demanded.

I worked my jaw, feeling absolutely, completely, devastatingly stupid. If I'd done that back in Elroy's workshop, he'd have screamed at me until he was hoarse and then banished me from the shop for a whole week. I wouldn't have even been allowed to approach the crucible without wearing a pair of heat-resistant gloves. Here, I wasn't thinking straight. I was distracted. And the reason for my distraction had just saved me from potentially losing my whole hand. My cheeks burned hotter than the fire in the hearth. "No. They do *not*."

Kingfisher released me. He said nothing further on the matter, but the hard, annoyed look he sent my way said plenty. *Be more careful, Osha.* "The bone was Fae," he said after a moment. "For centuries, our kind has tried to understand how the relics that allow us to travel through the quicksilver were made. There have been many theories over the years, but that's all they've ever been. Theories. With the quicksilver sleeping, we haven't been able to experiment or put any of those theories to the test. But now that you're here..."

"You want me to wake the quicksilver so you can try and bind things to it and see if you can make a relic out of it."

"Exactly." He grinned. It was the first real, full smile I'd seen from him and it was terrifying. Not because of how evil it made him look. Far from it. He looked so much younger than he did when he was scowling. He looked *happy*, and that was what really fucked with me. It was easy hating Kingfisher when he was being a bastard, but in this moment, he appeared very un-bastard-like, and that was… confusing.

I didn't have the time or the inclination to pick apart that confusion right now. It didn't matter. I had more important things to worry about. "You're using bone to see if fusing the quicksilver with biological material will trick the pool into thinking the living creature passing through it is a part of it?" I asked.

Kingfisher rocked back on his heels, his eyebrows hiking up his forehead. "Yes, actually. That's precisely what I want to do."

"Well, all right, then. Let's do it."

"Really? After yesterday, I expected that you'd be reluctant to try activating the quicksilver again."

"I'm not happy about it, no. But if it means that we ca—OH! *Holy gods!*"

We weren't alone.

My hand closed around a pair of tongs. I clutched them like a dagger, leaping forward, adopting a defensive stance. My pulse hammered in my fingers and my toes and everywhere else it possibly could. In an instant, I was ready to fight, but Kingfisher moved quicker than me. He became a blur of black smoke. Cold wind ripped at my hair, and then he was gone. He rematerialized on the other side of the workshop, murder in his eyes, that lethal black sword gripped in both hands, dripping smoke.

"What *is* that?" I stabbed my finger at the hideous thing crouching next to the hearth. It hissed at me, baring its teeth, showing the whites of its eyes.

Kingfisher took one look at the creature and straightened out of his defensive stand, cursing in a language I didn't understand. "What's *wrong* with you? It's a fox! Gods, I thought you were about to get your face torn off."

"Fox? What's a *fox?*"

Kingfisher muttered darkly under his breath as he went and stood over the strange animal. It had a thick, furry coat, white as the snow out of the window, and glassy black eyes the color of jet. It cowered, pressing its body against the stone floor, small, black-tipped ears pinned back against its tiny skull as it watched Kingfisher raise his sword over its head.

"Just so you know," the warrior growled, "transporting like that when you have a headache is the worst." He brought the blade swinging down.

"NO! STOP! What are you doing?"

He drew the weapon to one side just in the nick of time. "Graceless fucking *gods,* human! Stop fucking yelling!"

"I don't want you to kill it! It just surprised me, that's all!"

"It's a fox! A pest! This is probably what was living in the hearth before we ripped that den out. They steal food from the kitchens."

The creature wasn't nearly as hideous as I'd first thought. I darted forward, stooping low, covering the little thing with my body, gripped by a sudden remorse. "You definitely can't kill it, then. Not if we destroyed its home."

"It's going to bite you," Kingfisher said.

"No, it won't. It—"

It bit me.

Its teeth were sharp as needles. With its jaws clamped around my forearm, the little fox chittered and squealed, making all kinds of strange sounds. It seemed like it wanted to run away and hide, but it couldn't quite figure out how to *stop* biting me.

Kingfisher set the tip of his sword against the stone at his feet and casually leaned his weight against it, watching the scene play out with no obvious feeling one way or another. "They carry all kinds of diseases. Lung rot," he said. "A flakey skin thing, too? Some kind of fungal infection, I think."

"Ow! It's almost down to the bone, Fisher. *Help* me!"

Kingfisher pushed away from the sword, standing up straight. He looked up at the rafters overhead, squinting. "This…is a learning experience, I think. There are always consequences to our actions. Your new furry bracelet is a consequence of human weakness. Wear it with pride."

The little fox sneezed, his black eyes locked on mine. If a fox could have an expression, his would have been one of panic. He wanted me to help him, I thought, but how was I supposed to do that when, if anything, he was biting down even harder?

"Let go, let go, leggo, leggo, leggo," I pleaded. "*Please* let go. I don't want to have to hurt you. I'm sorry we ruined your home. I promise we'll build you an even better one."

"Don't make promises on *my* behalf," Kingfisher interjected. "I think it would make a great hat."

I growled at Kingfisher.

The fox growled, too.

As if we'd found some common ground, the little fox slowly relaxed its grip on my forearm, its jaws shaking as if it were going against its better nature by releasing me. I stood, pressing my hand against the puncture marks in my skin, attempting to stem the flow of blood. The fox shot Kingfisher a wary look and darted under my skirts, hiding beneath the folds of the shifting fabric.

"Oh, look," Kingfisher observed. "Finally. A use for all of that ridiculous material. Such a pretty little doll in her pretty little dress, aren't you."

"Hey! I don't *want* to wear this," I snapped, plucking at the dress. "What was I wearing when you found me?"

"A whole lot of blood." Fisher pondered. Frowned. "Wait. I seem to recall that your *intestines* might have been a part of your ensemble."

"Pants and a shirt," I said dryly. "And a pair of boots with really good soles. Do you have any idea what those boots cost me?"

"Let me guess. Your virginity."

"Fuck you, Fisher."

"Sure." He smirked. "But I'm afraid I don't have any new boots to trade you for your time."

I lunged for him, ready to *kill* him, and gasped when I felt the brush of fur against my calves and remembered the little fox that I was harboring. Its claws scratched against my leg. I attempted not to react, but Fisher saw me flinch. "Gods above," he groaned. "Let me kill it and be done with it."

"No! Absolutely not!"

"All right. Fine. Have it your way." He turned back to the crucible, waving his hand. At the same moment, there was a rush of cool air underneath my skirt accompanied by a frightened yap, and a large wicker cage appeared on the far end of the workbench. Inside the cage: a bowl filled with water, a small pile of what looked like chicken bones, and, of course, the fox.

"You'll need to release the damned thing outside of the palace. It won't last five seconds here. Not even as your plaything. For now, it can sit there and be *quiet*," he said, giving the cage a meaningful look. "And you..." He flicked his wrist again, and the tight crimson gown Layne dressed me in this morning disappeared into thin air. I drew in a full, deep breath for the first time in six hours and almost wept at the rush of air flooding my lungs.

I was wearing normal clothes. *My* clo—no, wait. They weren't my clothes. They were similar, yes, but there were marked differences between the clothes Kingfisher had found me in and these garments. The pants were thicker. Black, and not dirty white. The material was tough but supple. *Skintight.* Well, I guess I couldn't complain about that after being so bent out of shape about the frills Layne had put me in. The shirt was more of a tunic. Black. A little longer in the body than I was used to. More in keeping with Fae fashion. There were *so* many pockets. At my waist hung a leather belt with numerous loops for tools and...weapons? There was an actual *knife* strapped to my thigh. I stared down at the black onyx handle, trying to make sense of what I was seeing.

"Do you need walking through how that works?"

My head shot up. Kingfisher had his back to me. Oh, for the love of all the gods, he was pulling his shirt over his gods-cursed *head!* When he turned, his chest bare, a sea of swirling black ink marking slick muscle, his expression was trained into a blank mask. At the very center of his chest, snarling and fierce, another wolf's head had been inked into his skin. Many smaller tattoos surrounded it or broke off from it, but I couldn't tell what they were without inspecting him much more closely, and no way I was doing that. I half expected a backhanded jibe from Kingfisher as I fought not to stare, but he seemed genuine as he jerked his chin toward the knife that he'd magicked into being at my thigh. "In the right hands, a blade like that can wreak a lot of damage. Renfis is a good teacher. He can show you how to use it if you need him to."

In the cage on the end of the workbench, the fox began to lap thirstily at his water bowl.

"I know knives," I said, looking down at the floor.

"You said you knew your way around a forge the other day. And then you tried to stick your finger inside a glowing hot crucible."

"I do know my way around a forge. I just...I wasn't thinking."

He wiped his hands on his shirt and tossed it onto the workbench. "You could slice your own throat wide open with a knife like that if you forget to think, Osha."

"Just give me the damn quicksilver already. Let's see if we can bind this bone with it and turn it into something useful."

We couldn't.

It took me three hours to figure out how to awaken the quicksilver again. By the time I successfully transmuted the matte, solid silver into its agitated state, I was exhausted, my body echoing with pain, and marginally traumatized.

The particles of bone burst into flames as soon as Kingfisher dropped the powder into the vat containing the quicksilver, vaporizing before it ever touched the surface of the rippling liquid, and the quicksilver wasn't even hot. It chanted and cursed at me in a cadence that felt mocking, and I did my best not to scream out of frustration.

I was sweating in the heat of the forge, tired, and growing angrier by the second. Kingfisher didn't notice, or maybe he did but didn't show any signs of caring. He leaned over the workbench, sweat running in a river down the groove in his back, banks of powerful muscles flexing on either side of his spine as he made notes in a book he'd conjured from somewhere.

So much skin. So much *ink*. His tattoos on his back were interwoven—bold, sweeping lines that seemed to form pathways and tell stories. I wasn't about to lie to myself; I wanted to know about every single one of them—what they meant and when he'd got them. I wasn't going to give him the satisfaction of asking, though. I had things I needed to take care of.

A spike of urgency rose up inside me, giving me the courage I needed to act. I took a deep breath and braced myself. "You know... maybe if I looked at the pendant? Held it in my hands? If there was another element bonded with it when it was fired, I might be able to feel what it was."

This was a dangerous game. If it worked, I'd be able to go home. If it didn't, I'd have a furious Kingfisher on my hands, and I'd probably be imprisoned in my rooms until I died of old age. Fisher looked back at me, his narrowed eyes assessing me. Gods, he was a sight to behold. Every line of him was art. With his full mouth, and the faint shadow of stubble marking his jaw, his fascinating eyes, and all of his midnight-black hair, it was hard not to look at him and *ache*. I had grown up in a pit of misery, where people died more often than they lived. I hadn't seen many beautiful things in my short life. But, of all the beautiful things I *had* seen, Fisher was the most beautiful of all.

It would have been wrong to think of the men I'd encountered back in Zilvaren in that way. Some of them had been attractive. Some of them had even been hot enough to make my toes curl. But Fisher was the epitome of everything that was strong, and male, and powerful. He was so much *more* than anything I'd experienced before. He *was* beautiful. Looking at him made me feel like I couldn't catch my breath.

"If you want it, come here and touch it," he rumbled.

Holy. Fucking. *Gods.*

Blood rushed to my cheeks, staining them the color of crimson, and need, and shame. Kingfisher's pupils narrowed to pinpricks. He didn't have a single taunting word for me this time. His lips parted, his gaze boring into me as if he were watching, waiting to see what I'd do.

"Or you could just take it off?" I suggested, laughing nervously. "You let me wear it a whole ten days while I was recovering, didn't you? What's a couple of minutes?"

"Ren had me trapped in a room with three-foot-thick walls, locked behind an iron door that whole time," he said simply.

"Oh."

"Yeah. *Oh.* I'm not much fun to be around without it. Even for a couple of minutes."

I hadn't realized he'd suffered so much while I'd worn the pendant. I knew he'd needed it badly by the time he'd gotten it back, but I thought his second relic—the ring he wore—had served in the chain's absence.

I nodded, taking a hesitant step forward. "All right, then." I tried to sound businesslike, but I certainly didn't feel it. "I'll touch it while you're wearing it."

Kingfisher's expression gave nothing away. As I approached, he straightened. I thought for a moment that he was moving away from me, but he wasn't. He grabbed a stool from beneath the workbench and sat down on it, positioning himself so that he was facing me.

So little space between us now.

He spread his legs, the hard, interested light in his eyes daring me to step between them so that I could close the gap. My heart skipped and tripped all over the place as I took that step, accepting his silent challenge. He was so godsdamned *big*. His body hummed with energy; the closer I got, the more I could feel it rolling off him. Like heat. Like smoke. Like power itself. Fisher rested his tattooed hands on top of his thighs, his bright green eyes following my every move as I reached up and touched the fine silver chain.

He sat, inhumanly still. He didn't breathe. Didn't even twitch. The heat of his skin scorched my fingertips, sending a bolt of electricity snapping through me as I hooked the long chain beneath my fingers and slid them down his chest, over that snarling wolf's head tattoo, until I reached the solid weight of the pendant.

It was rectangular in shape, about an inch long, and lighter than I remembered. When he'd first looped it around my neck back in the Hall of Mirrors, it had felt like an anvil hanging around my neck. The crest on the front of it was almost worn smooth, but I could still make out the design: two crossed swords wrapped in thin vines. I spun it over in my hand, drawing my bottom lip into my mouth, trying not to think about the fact that the shining metal wasn't wet with water but with Kingfisher's sweat.

I could smell him.

The light musk of his sweat was inoffensive. In fact, it smelled sweet and heady, and lit a fire in the hollow of my stomach that I didn't understand. I wanted to lean into him and inhale deep. The need to do so was so overpowering that I almost went ahead and fucking did it. Gods, I—

"Anything?" Kingfisher's voice was rough as smoke.

I nearly jumped out of my godscursed skin. "Uh! Oh, um, no. Not...not yet. I, uh...lemme think."

"What do you know about Fae anatomy, Osha?" he whispered.

I focused so hard on the pendant that my vision started to swim. I didn't dare blink, though. I definitely wasn't brave enough to look up at him and meet his eyes. I knew he was staring at me, of course. I could have felt that fierce gaze through a sandstone wall.

"Not much," I said, burning a hole in the pendant. "Your kind looks a lot like humans. I'm assuming a lot of it works the same."

I waited for the mocking barb. The sharp, sneering retort. Kingfisher's reaction to being compared to a human wasn't going to be good. Surprisingly, it wasn't as disdainful as I would have expected. "On a surface level, yes," he said softly. "We have similar internal organs, though we *do* possess a few that humans do not."

Extra internal organs? That was intriguing.

"We're bigger. Taller, of course," he continued.

I arched an eyebrow at that. "Of course."

"Our hearts are bigger by ratio."

I couldn't help it. I looked up. "Really?"

He nodded. "Mm-hmm."

"Wow. Weird."

"Our eyesight is far superior to yours. Our...sense of smell," he said, his eyes lowering, traveling down my body.

Heat flared in the center of my chest. The way he was looking at me...there was nothing friendly about it. Kingfisher and I weren't friends. At best, we were loose allies who irritated the hell out of each other. So why, then, was he looking at me right now like I was an ally he'd like to fuck?

His eyes snapped back up to mine. "Our sense of taste is superior to yours. Touch. Our sense of hearing is very sharp. We can hear the smallest sound at a great distance." The silver in his right eye flared as he exhaled, his breath fanning across my cheek. "We can hear each other's heartbeats."

Out of nowhere, he grabbed me by the wrist.

I tensed, jolting, but he didn't hurt me. He took the pendant, lifting it, placing the metal between his teeth, holding it out of the way as he moved my hand to the center of his chest. "Feel that?" he asked, his bottom lip pressing against the pendant as he spoke with it still clamped between his teeth. The tips of his canines also pressed into the swell of his bottom lip. I couldn't tear my eyes away from them.

"Dum.Dum.Dum."

Kingfisher tapped the back of my hand in time with the rhythm of his heart. The pause between each beat was so long that I thought I was going to scream around the tension that built between each one. "Slow. Steady," he murmured. "Our Fae hearts rarely betray us. We're calm creatures. But you, Osha? You're a ball of chaos. Your heart betrays *you* at every turn." Quickly, he placed his hand on my chest, right between my breasts. I didn't have time to react to the contact; he began tapping out the rhythm of my heart against my sternum. *"Thrum, thrum, thrum, thrum, thrum.* Fast. Erratic, like a humming-bird. I hear it bouncing around all over the place when you look at me. Did you know that?"

"No. I didn't." I swallowed, a wave of nausea making my mouth sweat as I pulled away from him. *Tried* to pull away from him. He still had hold of my wrist. He did *not* let go. He allowed the pendant to drop from between his teeth, the corner of his mouth kicking up as he tugged me closer to him. His other hand moved from my chest, sliding down, around my waist, settling in the small of my back. His thighs drew together, pinning me by the hips between them.

Panic.

Panic, panic, panic!

Externally, I was calm when I spoke, but inside I was screaming. "Let me go, Fisher."

Immediately, he released me. His legs splayed wide, letting me go. He relinquished his hold on my wrist, too. His hand at the small of my back went nowhere, though. He wasn't using it to hold me in place. It was just a point of contact, and the heat of that contact between us felt like it was scorching me through my shirt.

Sliding forward an inch on the stool, Fisher dipped his head so that his mouth was unreasonably close to mine. "I've fucked plenty of humans," he whispered. "Does that surprise you?"

"Yes. Seeing as how you…seem to *hate* us…so much." His mouth. Gods, his fucking mouth. I needed to look away. I *had* to.

"I don't hate your kind. I'm just disappointed by how *breakable* you are. If I held you down and fucked you the way I'm imagining fucking you right now, I doubt that you'd survive it."

I was burning alive. I was a living torch, blazing out of control. "I wouldn't fuck you—if you were the last living—"

"Don't bother." The words held bite. "Lying is pointless with your heart betraying you so loudly."

"It's beating fast because I'm *afraid*," I snapped.

"Of me?" Kingfisher huffed a blast of laughter down his nose. "No, you're not. You *should* be, but you're not. That's one of the things I like most about you."

"You're holding me against my will."

"Really?" He looked down at our bodies: his legs still on either side of me but held away from me. His other hand, resting on top of his thigh again. My hands clenched into fists at my sides. "You can pull away at any time. Looks to me like you're choosing to stay. It also looks like you're having to stop yourself from touching me. You want to touch me the way I'm touching you, don't you? To feel the weight of me beneath your palms. The heat of me…" He angled his head a fraction, something wicked dancing in his eyes. "Just to see what would happen."

"You're wrong."

He shook his head. "I'm not."

"Yes! You *are*!"

He gave me a reproachful look. "Are you going to make me say it?"

"Say what?"

He leaned in even closer. My breath froze in my chest, my throat closing up, but I couldn't move. He grazed the bridge of his nose along the line of my jaw, the contact *so* light, up toward the shell of my ear. "That your body is betraying you in other ways. That I can smell you, Little Osha, and I'm thinking about drinking the sweet nectar you're making for me straight from the fucking cup."

I moved before I registered what was even happening. Kingfisher had learned from the last time, though, and saw my fist coming; he grabbed my wrist and then the other when I tried to punch him with my left fist. Harsh, rough laughter boiled out of him, turning me to cinder and ash.

"Aren't you curious? Don't you want to know what *I* taste like?"

"Let me fucking *go!*"

For a second time, he released me, freeing my hands. "If you try to punch me again, I'll tie your hands behind your fucking back," he promised. He was still smirking, but he meant it. I could see it in his eyes. "You're still standing here," he said in a taunting tone.

Fuck. I *was* still standing between his legs. What the hell was wrong with me? I made to step back, but Kingfisher placed his hands on my hips. Lightly, the same way he'd placed his hands on the small of my back. "Go on. Pull back. I won't stop you," he said. "Or you could kiss me. *You* could kiss *me.* I'll just sit here. I won't move a muscle."

"Why would I do that?"

"Because you're intrigued. Because you're bored. Because you're super fucking aroused right now, and you want to follow through on whatever little fantasies are playing out in your head."

"Yeah. Right. I'm just…going to kiss you. And you're just going to sit there. You aren't going to move a muscle. You're not even going to kiss me back?" Gods above, saying it out loud made it sound even more ridiculous.

Kingfisher just stared at me. *"Find out."*

Was it temporary insanity? A complete loss of common sense? Whatever it was, it took me body and soul. I lunged for him, curving into him, crushing my chest against his, driving my fingers into his hair. One second, I was standing there, wanting very badly to put some space between us, and then the next, I was rising up onto my toes, still having to reach up for him even though he was sitting down, and I was pressing my mouth to his...

The forge disappeared.

Everything fell away.

Everything but him.

His mouth met mine, and a wall of sound erupted inside my head. It was my own voice, urging, begging, pleading with me to slow down, to think this through, but I didn't want to listen.

His lips felt incredible. They parted for me, and I could feel his smile against my mouth as his tongue met mine. He kissed me back. His hands stayed right where they were, where he'd promised he'd keep them, but his grip grew tighter, his fingers digging into my hips as he plunged his tongue into my mouth, tasting and probing with every sweep.

The scent of him washed over my senses, overcoming me, undoing me. Mint. Smoke. The winter morning air that I was becoming accustomed to the more time I spent in this strange place.

His breath hit me in short, sharp blasts, fanning across my face as he grew more insistent, his stubble rough against my cheeks. He held me so tight now that he was definitely leaving bruises. I wanted them. I wanted to remember this. In the years to come, when I looked back at this moment, I would be glad that I'd taken the leap and jumped. This was the kiss to end all kisses. Demanding, urgent, and carnal.

I hated this male. Hated him with every fiber of my being. But curse me, I wanted him just as bad. Grabbing his hair, I wound it tight around my fingers, clenching my hand into a fist. Kingfisher's head rocked back, a low, rumbling groan issuing from his throat. I nipped and tugged at his bottom lip, sighing into his mouth, and the huge male went utterly still beneath me.

"Careful," he panted. "I swore I'd be still while you kissed me. At no point did I promise to exercise restraint if you climbed up into my lap and started grinding yourself against my cock."

I hadn't—I wasn't—

Fuck. I *had*. I *was*. Without even realizing, I'd straddled him. My legs were wrapped low around his waist. His cock was rock hard, trapped between our bodies. I could feel it there, rubbing up against me, applying the most delicious pressure whenever I shifted my weight.

Not.

Fucking.

Happening.

In two seconds flat, I was on the other side of the forge, dragging my hands through *my* hair instead of his. What the hell was I *thinking?*

Fisher laughed quietly as he rose from the stool and collected his shirt from the bench. Shaking it out, he slid it onto his arms, but didn't lift it over his head. Not yet. He stood there, eyes drilling into me, a reckless, beautiful grin strewn across his face. "I didn't say I *minded*. But for next time, that's where the line is. You want to cross it, I'll happily join you on the other side. Just don't say I didn't warn you."

I fought to shove down the mortified heat that rose up the back of my neck. "There won't be a next time."

Fisher grinned so hard that a small dimple appeared, forming a deep groove in his cheek. A godscursed *dimple*. How had I not noticed that before? He threw the shirt over his head at last, covering his inked chest. "If you say so, Little Osha."

"Oh gods, can you just go already? I don't want to be around you if you're going to be so unbearable."

"I have to walk you back to your rooms."

"I don't want you to," I snapped.

"Tough. Layne will string me up by the balls if I let you go anywhere alone."

"Then send Ren to walk with me."

Kingfisher crossed the workshop and stood in front of me, his eyes alive with hunger. I hadn't seen him like this before. It was both exciting and terrifying. "If I send Ren, you'll wait for him here?"

"Yes."

"All right, then. Have it your way. I'll go."

"*Thank you!*"

My head spun as he leaned down and held his mouth close to my ear again. "Come on. Was it really that bad?"

"*Yes!*"

He laughed again, cold and cruel, as he placed his hand at the center of my chest again and began to tap. "*Thrum, thrum, thrum, thrum, thrum, thrum, thrum.* So fast. Like a hummingbird. Get the fox bite looked at, Little Osha. You don't want that arm falling off."

Right before my eyes, Fisher dematerialized into a blur of black sand and smoke.

13

DURESS

I'D SPENT HALF my life running in Zilvaren. Running from Guardians. The traders I'd cheated. The people I'd pickpocketed. Not only was I fast as lightning, but I had stamina, which was a damned good thing because I had no idea how far I had to run now. All I knew was that I had to get there quickly. It wouldn't be long before Kingfisher noticed what I'd done and came looking for me.

The bag I'd packed earlier bounced against my back, approximately ten pounds heavier than it had been when I'd carried it into the forge. Originally, I'd only packed a few items of clothing and a little food. Most of the bag's weight had come from the large water reservoir I'd stuffed into it, the soft leather bladder filled to brimming. Now there was a fox in the bag, too, and by the sounds of it, the furry little shit wasn't happy about all of the bouncing.

He yipped as I sprinted through the hallways, heading down, down, always down. Fae males and females shouted, annoyed as I barreled past them, not giving them time to recognize me for who I was. Any of them could stop me, and I wasn't getting this far, only to be snagged by someone who wanted to know why Belikon's prize human wasn't in the library, learning about portals so they could win their stupid fucking war.

The fox yowled as I spun around a corner and hurled down a flight of stairs, my feet barely touching the glossy marble floor. "Shut *up*," I hissed. "Did you want me to leave you back in the forge? You heard him. He wanted to turn you into a *hat.*"

The yowling cut off, replaced by a disgruntled (though much quieter) grumbling. The next floor down, I sprinted through reading rooms, and indoor hot houses packed with exotic plants and flowers. I bolted across some sort of games court, where eight or more long-limbed Fae females were gracefully volleying a ball back and forth to one another across a net. Training rooms, and art studios, and all manner of different workshops, and grand halls all whipped by in a blur.

If I came across a staircase, I went down it. After some serious wriggling and gnawing, the fox managed to poke his head out of the bag and started anxiously licking the back of my neck.

"It's all right. I'm not gonna let him hurt you. Shhh, it's okay."

I should have had Rusarius and Layne take me down to the quicksilver and show me where it was. They would have wanted to wait until tomorrow, though, and I couldn't afford another day. Not when I'd already waited this long.

Six floors.

Seven floors.

Eight.

Twelve.

Fifteen.

I stopped counting after that. My thighs were screaming when I finally hit a level where there were no more windows. The rooms became smaller, the roofs lower. As far as I could ascertain, these were all signs that I'd made it to the subterranean floors. Eventually, the only Fae I encountered were Belikon's soldiers.

Fuck. Of course there would be soldiers down here. The quicksilver might have been dormant for a thousand years, but it was one of Yvelia's most valuable assets. And I'd managed to wake the silver. Now that Belikon knew that it could be done, he wasn't likely to leave the pool unguarded if there was a chance it might open again and danger could come rushing through.

Damn it. I was losing precious minutes. I could feel the quicksilver tugging at me. After sleeping for so long, it wanted to be awake. It wanted me to find it. I knew which direction I had to go in now. Straight ahead, a yawning, rough-hewn mouth opened in the stonework wall, giving way to what looked like one of Rusarius's tunnels. If I took that tunnel, I knew I'd find the pool. The only problem was three guards standing at the entrance to the tunnel, eyes trained ahead, gloved hands resting on the hilts of their swords. I only had the small dagger Kingfisher had given me and an ornery fox to defend myself with. That wasn't really a problem. I *could* kill them, but engaging in a fight right now would only waste time I didn't have.

"What are we going to do?" I mumbled to myself. "What are we going to do. How am I gonna get myself out of this one?"

The other way. Another way. Come. Come!

Hearing the quicksilver whispering inside my mind was disconcerting to say the least. It wanted me to know there was another path to it, it seemed, and it was willing to show me the way. But I had a choice before me—there *was* still time. I could turn around and go back up to my room and pretend as if my frantic flight through the palace had never happened. I could spend my days in the library with Layne and Rusarius, reading dusty books about Fae customs and the Alchemists who lived thousands of years ago. Kingfisher was only given leave to remain here within the palace walls for a week. He would be gone in a couple of days. Someone else would take his place in the forge, experimenting with me. Maybe things wouldn't be so bad if I didn't have to deal with him every day...

It came as a shock that the idea of Fisher leaving didn't actually make me happy. He annoyed the hell out of me, but he was a known entity. The thought of sharing the forge with someone else made my rib cage feel tight. Who would they replace him with, anyway? Gods, what did it even matter?

I *wasn't* staying.

I made to move, but a large group of guards turned around a corner, and I was forced to duck into an alcove and hug the wall, doing my best to disappear into the shadows as they marched by. The fox stared at me, his ears tipped in black swiveling as he listened to the sounds around us. His body, much thinner than all of his fluff would suggest, shook like a leaf inside the bag.

As soon as Belikon's warriors had moved off down the hall, I darted out of my hiding place and skirted along the edge of the hall, praying that the soldiers still standing by the tunnel entrance didn't see me. Mercifully, one of them had turned to talk to the others, and their attention was drawn elsewhere. I ducked around the corner as quickly as I could, my slippered feet not making a sound.

Ahead, ahead...

I didn't need the voices to tell me where to go now. I knew instinctively. That didn't stop the quicksilver from whispering to me, though.

Ahead. Yes, come. Come!

The fox keened, scrabbling around inside the bag, but with the top cinched around his neck, he couldn't get out. "Stop! It's for your own good! I swear, I'll find a way to get you out of here and take you somewhere safe, but please stop wriggling."

He didn't. He was a fox and had no idea what the fuck I was asking him to do, but at least he didn't bite me again.

This way. This way.

I was already turning left at the fork in the hallway.

Ahead. Yes. In. Go in...

The door at the end of the hallway looked innocuous enough. I wasted no time debating what might be on the other side of it. I turned the handle, flung it open, and went through it. Cold, bare stone greeted me. A tunnel, much smaller than the one the soldiers were guarding, with a roof so low I had to scoot down as I pressed forward into the darkness.

I had no torch, but I was used to traveling through underground tunnels in the dark. I'd had plenty of experience with that back in Zilvaren, when I'd routinely snuck into Madra's underground stores to siphon water. Rusarius had said all of the tunnels lead straight to the quicksilver, so I knew I'd find it eventually.

Yes, come. Come. This way...

A few minutes. That's all it took.

One last turn and I found myself standing in a vast, high-ceilinged cavern. Torches burned in sconces here, mounted to the dripping walls, throwing light out in all directions, which was a blessing. Statues of ancient Fae and other strange creatures twenty feet tall stood around an enormous pool at the very center of the cavern. The air felt heavy here, too thick to draw down into my lungs as I slowed to catch my breath. There was a sound, too—a constant ringing, the pitch so high that I couldn't actually hear it. It was as though I could feel it rattling at my eardrums. The little fox in my arms whined, trying to duck his head back into the bag— apparently, he could hear the ringing tone, and he didn't like it one bit.

"Shhh. It's okay. It's gonna be okay, don't worry."

Come, the pool beckoned. *Be with us. We won't hurt you.*

A cold sweat broke out across my brow when I fully took in the pool. It wasn't just big: it was enormous, forty feet wide and fifteen feet across. The expanse of brightly shining silver made Madra's pool look like a puddle by comparison. Its reflective surface was smooth as the surface of a mirror. But a mirror's sole purpose was to tell you the truth. It didn't differentiate between good and bad. A mirror had no desire to soothe your troubles or deceive you. It was glass and nothing more. This pool of shining silver was awake and full of lies.

My feet moved toward it, carrying me forward. I'd made it halfway across the smooth stone cavern floor before I'd realized what was even happening. "Gods..." I could see my breath down here. The huge columns supporting the black rock ceiling sixty feet up were slick with ice. The chill that nipped at my skin wasn't from the cold, though. It was more than that—a sharp, probing presence that prickled at me, trying to worm its way inside.

Here. Yes, come here. Come with us...

I steeled myself, regaining control of my feet. If I was going to approach the huge expanse of silver, I would do so on my own terms, damn it. In the bag, the fox whined, eyes rolling, panting anxiously. The cursed thing wouldn't stop wriggling. By the time I'd reached the pool, he was thrashing, desperate to be free.

"All right! All right! Gods!" At the wide, raised stone lip that formed the pool's edge, I set the bag down and untied the cord that was keeping him trapped inside. As soon as I pulled the bag open, the fox leaped out and bolted, a streak of white fleeing into the shadows. "Bye, then," I called after him.

At least he would have a decent chance of finding his way outside of the palace down here, without running afoul of Kingfisher's blade. He had better night vision than I did, and he could smell fresh air from a mile away. He'd be out in the snow, back where he belonged, in no time. He wasn't built for Zilvaren. The heat. The sand. I hadn't really considered how I was going to feed him or find enough water for him. Yvelia was his home. Better that he stayed. Sadness still welled up in my chest as I stared after him, though.

Come. Come. Come....

The voices were insistent. The pull the quicksilver exerted on me intensified, like there were physical hands shoving me, pushing me, pulling me, urging me to step into the pool. And I wanted to. I'd give it what it wanted. But there was one thing I needed to do first...

Yesterday, when Kingfisher had forced me to activate that quick-silver, he'd said it was a test. One I'd passed. I had no idea if he had set me that test or if the quicksilver itself had, but there had been no pain when I'd activated the silver earlier. Only...a key turning in my mind. A lock popping undone. A stream of energy, invited to flow.

Would it be the same here with this quicksilver? Or was I going to have to pass another test with this pool? The pain that I'd borne dealing with that tiny amount of silver in the forge had been crippling. The pain that would be meted out by this amount of quicksilver would break me.

There was only one way to find out.

The silver in the forge had felt like a small weight in the center of my mind. Just a slight pressure. When I closed my eyes and reached out here, the silver was a sea, bottomless and vast, and *I* was the small weight floating on top of it. I wasn't drowning in it, though. I felt safe, bobbing on the surface of it. I could sink down into it if I wanted to. Let it rise up over me and cocoon me from the world.

I breathed deep and reached out with my hand, reaching my fingertips to the cold, hard surface of the silver, and I spoke to it.

Wake up.

It happened fast. One second the pool was solid. The next, it was a shining banner of liquid silver, glinting as it undulated in the torch light. A loud hum filled my ears, unnatural and discordant. An unpleasant sound, but I found myself mesmerized by it, my mind drifting away from itself...

Come. Join us, Saeris. Come...

Yes. I would go. I would enter the pool, and everything would be all right. I would go back to...back...*Where* did I want to go?

My foot hovered above the surface of the pool. Just an inch. That's all it would take, and I would go...

A terrible wind howled through the cavern. The tip of my slipper kissed the silver, but before I could step forward, a wall of shifting, glittering black sand slammed into me, knocking me back.

I went down hard, landing on my side, my hip exploding with pain. Breath rushed into my lungs, ice-cold, so freezing that I let out an audible gasp of shock. I was...I—

Oh, gods.

Kingfisher.

He emerged from the cloud of black smoke like a night terror stepping through the shadowy gates of hell. He wore the same shirt he'd been wearing in the forge. The same pants, too. But now he also wore his chest protector and his gorget, and in his hand, he held Nimerelle aloft, the black sword crackling with an unseen power that drew that darkness to it like a shroud.

Kingfisher's boots planted firmly on the lip of the pool. There he stayed, blocking the path between me and my brother. His eyes blazed. "I'm hurt. Leaving without saying goodbye?"

I propped myself up on one elbow, then managed to sit up, wincing at the sharp bolt of pain that fired through my side. "I don't owe you a goodbye. I don't owe you anything!"

"YOU OWE ME YOUR *LIFE!*" His fury echoed through the cavern, setting the quicksilver churning. Stepping down from the pool, he prowled forward, a predator about to fall on his prey, and for the first time in my life, I knew *true* fear.

Fisher *was* death incarnate, and he was coming right for me.

Whatever pain I'd worried about waking so much quicksilver, paled in comparison to the horrors Kingfisher's cold expression promised. He grabbed me by the ankle and yanked me roughly toward him, dragging me across the floor. In less than a second, I was pinned beneath his massive body and Nimerelle was at my throat.

"Rule number three. Do not make me do any physical activity," he snarled. "What part of *'I am hungover'* did you not fucking understand!"

My eyes burned brightly, promising tears. "I'm going home, Fisher. You can't stop me."

He jabbed me with his sword, pricking me with its wicked point. "Apparently, I *can*."

"You're such a bastard," I hissed.

He bared his teeth. "And you are a lying little thief."

"I am not!"

His eyes were greener than ever. The quicksilver within them jittered, vibrating wildly. Fisher glowered down at my hand. At my thumb specifically, and the plain silver signet ring I was wearing on it. "Really? Because I believe you're wearing my ring, and I don't remember fucking *giving* it to you."

"Fine, yes, I took your stupid ring, but I didn't lie to you!" I tried to swat Nimerelle away, but the second my hand touched the blackened blade, ungodly agony tore through me. I screamed, pulling my hand back, but the flesh where my palm had met the metal was charred to a crisp.

"Only the person sealed to it can touch an active Alchimeran sword. I would have warned you not to do that, but you never listen to me, do you, human? I decided not to waste my breath," he spat.

The tears came hot and fast now, brought on by anger more than the pain. I hiccupped softly. "Bastard."

"You like calling me that, don't you. Knock yourself out. You *did* lie. You lied with your body. With your mouth. You crawled up into my lap, and kissed me, and rubbed yourself all over me, and used the opportunity to *take* something from me."

A million emotions clashed inside of me, warring for supremacy. They exploded out of me all at once. "I needed it so I could go home! I'm not sorry. You wouldn't be, either, if you were me!"

"I wouldn't have been dumb enough to do it in the first place."

"I had to. I had to go through the silver—"

"You would have *died* if you'd stepped foot in that pool."

I glared at him defiantly. "Not with the ring."

"That ring isn't a relic. It's a trinket and nothing more. It wouldn't have protected you."

"It shielded you when you brought *me* through the pool!"

"No. It *didn't*," he said icily. "Of course it fucking didn't."

"You told Layne—"

"I told Layne I was *wearing* it. Nothing more. Whatever she inferred from that is her own undoing."

Shock vibrated up through the soles of my feet, rattling my

bones. "So, you traveled through without your pendant? To save me?"

"Hah!" He pulled back, his chest heaving, Nimerelle lowered to his side. He sneered down at me, his handsome face transformed into a mask of pity. "To save my friends. To end my exile. To fucking live or die, finally, one way or another. It had nothing to do with *you*."

"Then...I would have been fine without it. If you can move through the pathways without a shield—"

"I'm stronger than you, *idiot*. I've spent hundreds of years forging barriers and wards around my mind that you couldn't begin to comprehend. My mind is an impenetrable vault, and I still paid a heavy price for my transgression. Your mind is as shallow as a fucking teacup. It would have splintered into a thousand pieces if you'd stepped into that pool."

"I—" I didn't know what to say. There was nothing I *could* say. I closed my eyes and all of the hope that I'd been clinging to rushed out of me in a long exhale. Now my tears were from exhaustion. And defeat. "I'm not going to stop trying. It's not in me to stop," I whispered.

"You have to."

"I can't. They're my family." He understood. He'd taken a great risk, too, because he thought it would help the people he cared about. So then why couldn't he understand this? Why wouldn't he just let me go?

As if he were reading my mind, Kingfisher crouched down in front of me, balancing on the balls of his feet, his whole body still radiating with anger. He stabbed a finger at me. "You are going to stay here, and you are going to figure out how to create relics for us. You're going to figure out how to manipulate the quicksilver if it's the last thing you do."

I was so tired. Every part of me hurt. Just flat-out ached with sorrow. I dragged myself up into a sitting position, hissing when I leaned my weight on my newly scorched hand. Resting my elbows on the tops of my knees, I hung my head and sighed. "I promise you I won't. I'll let you torture me first. I will not help the Fae. Not until I know what's happened back in Zilvaren. I can't."

Kingfisher reached out and gently lifted my chin with his curled finger so that our eyes met. "It won't be me hurting you," he said softly. "It'll be Belikon. And even *I* can't withstand him."

"Then I guess I'll die."

"Foolish girl." He slowly shook his head. "You have *no* idea what you're talking about."

"Look into my eyes. No, wait. Why don't you listen to my heartbeat, Kingfisher, and tell me if I'm lying."

We stared at each other, and I let him see my truth. I refused to look away. His hair fell into his eyes, the dark waves framing his face, the muscle in his jaw working, working, working as he waited to read something in me that suggested I might break. The silence ate us.

Kingfisher shot to his feet and tore away, cursing loudly. He hadn't reached the quicksilver pool before he spun around and stalked back, holding a finger in the air. "All right. Fine. You get *one.*"

"What do you mean, I get one?"

"I'll go." He huffed, blasting an angry breath down his nose. "I will go, and I will *try* to get one of these humans who are so fucking precious to you. I will *try* to bring that human back here, and you will end this madness. In return, you'll agree to do whatever I ask of you to help me forge new relics and any other instruments I deem fit."

"You'd do that? You'd go?"

Fisher looked like he wanted to scream. "Unwillingly, yes. Under duress, yes."

He would go back to Zilvaren for me in order to strike a bargain. He needed me to help him that badly. And if that were true, then it also meant...

"I want two."

He tossed his head back and let out a bark of laughter. "*What?*"

"My brother Hayden *and* Elroy."

Looking a little hysterical, he threw his arms wide, Nimerelle casting off wisps of black smoke. "Who the *fuck* is Elroy?"

"He's my friend. He's important to me. And," I added quickly, the thought occurring to me out of the blue, "he's a master smith. He can probably help me make the relics for you. He'll be useful."

Fisher narrowed his eyes. "Can he channel metal energy the way you can?"

"I don't know. I don't think so," I admitted.

"Then he's useless to me. You get one. Choose."

"I can't choose! How am I supposed to...to *pick* which one of them lives and which one of them *dies*?"

"You share blood with one of them. The answer's simple."

It really was that easy for him. He'd make this decision easily and walk away without a scrap of guilt. *That's* who Kingfisher was. "I *can't*—"

"Let me put this another way for you. I have one relic. I can bring one person at a time back with me. I will not—*can* not—travel through the quick twice in one fucking day with nothing standing between me and that nightmare. It'll kill me once and for all. So you *will* tell me to go and fetch Hayden for you, and we *will* be done with this farce."

A part of me wanted to fight him on this, but I knew he was telling the truth. He really would lose himself if he traveled twice without his pendant. I felt sick to my stomach, but I gave him a quick nod. "All right. Fine." I took a deep breath. "Hayden."

Kingfisher took Nimerelle, gritting his teeth as he closed his hand around the black metal and dragged his palm along the blade. Blood welled and dripped between his fingers, splattering onto the stone. He pointed Nimerelle at me.

"Blood, Little Osha. It's the only way to seal this between us."

I balked, backing away from the sword. "I'm not touching that thing again. Can't you just take my word for it?"

He snorted humorlessly. "Cute. And *no*. Use the dagger I gave you if you like, but you're giving me your blood. It doesn't have to be much."

I eyed him warily as I drew the dagger from the thigh holster he gave me earlier, hissing as I drew its edge across my palm. A tiny cut. The smallest I could manage, but it bled. Kingfisher held out his hand and pulled me to my feet, making a derisive sound when he saw the cut I'd inflicted upon myself. "Baby."

I pulled a face at him. "Just do whatever it is you need to do already."

"I go and I try to get your brother. You help me and assist me in any way I ask you to, and you do as you're told. You agree to this pact?"

I nodded. "Yes."

"You understand that this is a *blood* oath? And you will be bound by this oath until death?"

"Yes! Gods, I understand! I agree. Just get on with—" Kingfisher slapped his palm against mine and held on tight.

Ice shot through my veins. Black smoke clouded my view, stealing my vision, curling its way up my nose, snaking its way down my throat. It cleared almost immediately, and...nothing had changed. My palm was still bleeding. It still hurt like hell. Whatever he'd done, Kingfisher seemed satisfied, though.

"Give me something of his," he demanded.

"What?"

"Give me something of Hayden's. What, you think I can just show up in your godsforsaken city and immediately find someone I've never met before? I need something of your brother's so I can locate him."

"Oh. Right." That made sense. But...shit. "I don't *have* anything of Hayden's with me."

Kingfisher rolled his eyes. "Of course you don't. Is he your full brother? Do you have the same parents?"

"Yes."

"Then your blood should suffice." He held up his hand. "I already have that. Wait here. Do not move from this spot."

"You're going right now?"

He raised his eyebrows. "You want to wait? After all of this?"

"No! No, definitely not. You should go."

"Close this gate the moment I'm through. Wait an hour, and then activate it again."

I shook my head. "I should leave it open. What if—"

"What if a horde of feeders burst through five minutes after I leave? You forget, if this pool is open, then all the pools are open. *Everywhere.*"

"What's a feeder?"

Kingfisher sighed. He lifted Nimerelle over his shoulder, and the sword's scabbard materialized out of thin air, its strap and brace appearing across Fisher's chest just in time for him to slide the blade home behind his back. His greaves and bracers followed, pauldrons forming out of smoke at his shoulders. In less than a second, Kingfisher was armored up and ready for war. "Trust me. You don't want to know. One hour, Osha. You make sure this door is ready to open when I come knocking. Trap me on the other side of it, and I'll lay waste to whatever remains of your shining Silver City."

He turned and stepped into the pool without a second thought. I shivered as I watched him descend into the quicksilver, my chest tight, my hands clenching into fists even tighter. My heart tripped when his crown of dark waves disappeared beneath the fluctuating surface of the pool.

The quicksilver didn't want to obey when I commanded it to still. There was so much of it. Way more than I'd commanded before, and it had a mind of its own. It didn't *want* to sleep, and it took four attempts to force it into submission.

Once the giant pool was a solid, flat panel again, I sat down with my back leaning up against the closest pillar, shivering against the penetrating cold...and the doubt began to set in.

There was nothing stopping Kingfisher from finding Hayden and killing him. Elroy, too. Things would be a whole lot simpler for Kingfisher if he just murdered the people I cared about back in Zilvaren. He wouldn't have to come back through the gate without his pendant. Wouldn't have to deal with another human running around his court. What was to say he'd even gone to Zilvaren? He could have slipped off to another realm entirely. One that was uninhabited. He could be sitting on a rock right now, staring at a foreign sky, waiting for the allotted amount of time to pass, at which point he'd return and tell me my family and friends were already dead, there was nothing he could do about it, and it was time for me to hold up my end of our bargain. How would I know he was telling the truth?

I had no means of telling the time down here, either. I had no timepiece, and there were no windows to watch the progress of Yvelia's single sun across the sky. I had to rely on my own best judgment, which was a problem because—

Click.

I snapped my head up, twisting to the left, toward the source of the sound.

Click, click, click.

Click.

I didn't move. What *was* that? I leaned forward, squinting into the dark, blood pumping, heart racing, terrified of what might coalesce out of the pitch-black shadows. What lived in the dark, lightless places of this court? It would be foolhardy to assume that these tunnels were patrolled by Belikon's men and nothing else. A chattering sound echoed around the cavern, and every hair on my body stood on end.

The dagger Kingfisher gave me was sharp, but it would be useless against more than one foe, especially if they attacked from a distance. I began to get to my feet, but—

A streak of white darted out of the darkness, beelining right for me.

White fur, and a bushy tail, and black-tipped ears pinned all the way back.

The fox.

My fox.

He'd come back for me.

The little creature's claws *click, click, click*ed against the ground as he ran. He tried to slow when he reached me, but the stone was too smooth, and his paws found no purchase, and he slid the last four feet. He yelped, diving into my lap, butting his muzzle underneath my elbow so that he could bury his face in my side and hide.

The small barrel of his rib cage rose and fell like crazy as he curled himself around my body, panting like he'd just run five miles.

"You changed your mind, then?" I whispered, painfully aware of how loud the sound of my voice was now that I was alone down here and the quicksilver wasn't muttering to me. The little fox chittered in answer, grumbling away into my armpit.

"All right. All right. Don't worry. We're all allowed to change our minds," I told him. "Don't suppose you're good at keeping track of time, are you?"

The little fox sneezed.

"No, me neither."

I'd never been more grateful for company in my whole life. I stroked the fox, relieved that another living, breathing creature was willing to sit with me and perform this vigil. He was scared. Very scared, but he didn't leave me again.

"What am I gonna call you? If you're gonna be hanging around, you need to have a name."

He peered up at me, his little onyx eyes narrowed to slits, eyelids slowly blinking so that I could make out every single one of his tiny white eyelashes. "What do you think about Onyx?" I asked him.

He closed his eyes and didn't open them again for a long time, which I took to be a sign of approval. He was soon asleep. I took to counting out the seconds, tallying the minutes off on my hands, until I figured that an hour had to have passed.

Onyx wasn't happy when I set him down on top of my bag. He

observed with baleful eyes as I stood at the edge of the pool and carefully reached out, commanding the ocean of silver to wake.

The surface had only half-transformed, still solid around the edges, when an explosion of black smoke burst out of the center of the pool. Kingfisher was there, then, wading through the silver, his face contorted like a mask. In his right hand, Nimerelle dripped red. In his left, the body he dragged behind him by the scruff of its neck dripped silver. He hauled the lifeless form over the side of the pool and dumped it onto the ground, then collapsed down next to it, panting.

"Quickly. Before—" He cut off, his head ripping back, unleashing a shout that was all terror and pain. "Quick. The...the pend-pendant," he ground out. *"Now!"*

The quicksilver churned, a million splintered voices shouting all at once. The sound was nauseating, but I blotted it out, racing to the body Kingfisher had dumped onto the stone. My hands were fast and true as I plucked up the pendant, retrieved it, and rushed to Kingfisher's side. He thrashed and moaned, clenching his teeth, the tendons in his neck straining horribly as I looped the chain over his head and fought to slip the rectangular pendant down the front of his chest protector.

"Fisher? Fisher!"

He didn't respond. He growled, his back arching, the heels of his leather boots leaving black streaks against the stone as he writhed.

"Fisher! Gods. What the hell? What...what do you need me to *do?*" I was really starting to panic when the male locked up tight, his eyes snapped open, and he dragged in a rattling, wet breath.

"Fuck. Me," he rasped. "That was...bad."

"Are you all right?" I went to touch his chest protector, not sure where to check him, but then thought better of it.

"Close...the...gate!" he wheezed.

Shit, shit, shit. The gate. This time, I didn't give the quicksilver the opportunity to resist. I slammed my palms together in my mind, closing the door tight, and with a crack, the pool answered my demand, solidifying so fast that it shattered the stone lintel that ran around the pool.

"Hope you're happy, human. Because I am never...*ever*"—Kingfisher rolled onto his side, clutching his stomach—"doing that again."

He was through. He'd done it.

He...

Oh my gods! *Hayden!* Fisher had actually done it. He'd brought Hayden back with him! I left Kingfisher as he struggled to sit up. My knees sang with pain as I dropped down next to the unconscious body, but it didn't matter. I didn't care. Hayden was alive. He was here. He—

Oh.

Oh no.

I rocked back onto my heels, frowning at the figure lying on the ground. The hope that had soared through me came crashing down around my ears. Was this supposed to be some kind of joke? No. Fisher didn't have a sense of humor, and this...this *wasn't* funny.

"It'll take a while for him to...wake up. Humans are so..." Kingfisher groaned. "You're all so fucking *fragile*."

I rounded on the warrior, the dull roar in my ears growing progressively louder, louder, louder...

"This is not my brother, Fisher. This is Carrion *fucking* Swift!"

14

THE FINE PRINT

COPPER-COLORED HAIR.

Annoyingly perfect mouth.

Heart-shaped birthmark on his chin.

It was definitely Carrion.

Kingfisher took one look at him and shrugged. "I tracked your bloodline. It led me right to him. I asked him who he was. *He* said he was Hayden Fane. Ergo, I brought you Hayden Fane."

"Were you pinning him against a wall and holding a sword to his throat when you asked him?" I demanded.

"No. I had him in a headlock. I hadn't even drawn the sword. Not then, anyway."

"No wonder he lied to you about who he was! He probably thought you were a debt collector or one of Madra's men!"

"*Debt* collector?" Fisher fumed. "Look. Let me ask you something. Do you recall where the gate is in Zilvaren?"

"In Madra's palace."

"Correct. And what do you think was there waiting for me when I stepped out of that silver?"

"*I* don't know."

"Fifty trained guardians and a unit of archers armed with iron-tipped arrows. I had to fight my way out of there, cross that scorched, disease-ridden shithole you're so desperate to get back to, find your brother, then get *back* across the city, *back* into Madra's palace, *back* into that cursed hall, and then *back* into the quicksilver in under an hour. I did not have time to interview the prick! Now, will this one do or not?"

"No! He will not! Our deal—"

"Our deal stands," Kingfisher snapped, stooping to pick up Carrion. He threw the lifeless black-market trader over his shoulder like he weighed nothing. Fisher glared at me with the intensity of a thousand suns. "I hate that fucking place, but I went there for you. I got stabbed seven times in various parts of my body. *For you.* This prick said he was Hayden. His blood said he was Hayden. I did what I said I was going to do. Now move. We're getting the hell out of here."

"I'm not going back to my rooms—"

"We're not going back to your rooms. First, I'm finding a healer. Then I'm going to find Ren, and then we're getting the fuck out of here."

Fisher had spent the better part of his youth in the Winter Palace. He knew the place like the back of his hand. He opened concealed doorways and stomped along hidden passageways, charging up a ridiculous number of stairs, ignoring me when I pleaded for him to slow down. I wanted to dig my heels in and refuse to move, but my body wouldn't listen. He told me to follow, and follow I did, even though my heart was pumping like a piston, and I felt like I would pass out any moment. I didn't have a choice. Onyx squealed, doing backflips in the bag the whole time, inconsolable.

Finally, Fisher stopped after what I guessed were twenty-three flights of stairs, and dumped Carrion down onto the cold stone at my feet. "Stay here. Wait for me until I get back. Do not make a sound."

I unleashed a string of foul curse words at him, only they didn't make it past my lips. As he'd commanded, I didn't make a sound. What the hell had he done to me? Why was my body not my own?

I seethed as I waited. In my head, I screamed at Carrion to wake up and do something about this, but it transpired that the smuggler was just as infuriating when he was unconscious as he was while he was awake. The idiot didn't stir once.

An hour passed, and Onyx grew bored and fell asleep. When Fisher reappeared in the hidden passageway, the tears in his shirt were gone, as was all of the blood he'd been covered in. Fixed up, good as new, he carried something long and thin under his arm, wrapped in what looked like a curtain.

"I couldn't find Ren. I left him a note," he informed me, picking up Carrion. With no further preamble, he set off back down the stairs.

I said nothing.

I didn't move a muscle.

He only realized I wasn't following him once he'd turned the corner and disappeared from view. "Come on, Little Osha!" he called. "Keep up. You can speak again, but no complaining."

I descended the stairs, my temper white-hot and brilliant as I scowled at the back of Fisher's head.

Down forever we went. I was dizzy, and my thighs were burning when he led me out of the palace, across a covered courtyard, and into a dark, drafty building with wide doors open at both ends. On either side of us, stalls stretched off to the left and the right. Over some of the stall doors, huge horses tossed their heads, whinnying, startled by our sudden appearance.

"Absolutely not," I said.

Kingfisher dumped Carrion onto the wet stable floor and stepped over his body, marching off toward an open door to our right that led, not to a stall, but to a feed store and tack room.

"Let me guess. You don't like horses?" he said.

"No, I don't like horses. Horses don't like me. We mutually dislike each other."

Fisher hefted a saddle down from a rack on the wall and barged past me, carrying it out of the tack room. "You're gonna have to get over it."

I followed him, stepping over Carrion as Kingfisher entered one of the stalls. "It doesn't work like that! I can't just *get over it!*"

"Sure you can. Keep your ass in the saddle. Keep your mouth shut. It's easy."

"Fisher!"

The male placed the saddle he was carrying carefully over a monstrous black horse's back, working quickly to fasten the girth. "This isn't a negotiation. You made a blood oath, human. You're bound by it, which means you're coming with me."

"I swore I'd help the Yvelian Fae figure out how to use the quicksilver—"

He wagged a finger at me. "Think again. What did I say to you when I asked you if you agreed to the pact?"

"You said you'd go and get my brother, and in return, I would help create relics for Yvelia!"

Kingfisher pushed past me, out of the stall, heading back to the tack room. "I said, verbatim, '*I go, and I try to get your brother. You help me and assist me in any way I ask you to, and you do as you're told. You agree to this pact?*' to which you replied, '*Yes, gods, I agree! Just get on with it!*'"

"But we both know what I meant! I didn't mean that I'd go traipsing off into the unknown with you in the middle of the night!"

"Unless you're paying very close attention, what you mean to agree to and what you *actually* agree to are often two very different things in Fae, Little Osha. You agreed to help me and assist me in any way I asked you to, and that you'd do as you were told. You sealed that deal with blood. Now, I'm telling you to find a horse and saddle it up as quickly as you can, before my psychotic stepfather catches a whiff of what we're up to and murders us where we stand."

"You fucking *tricked* me!"

"No," he said bluntly. "I taught you a valuable lesson that will serve you well for the rest of your very short human life in this realm. Always pay attention to the fine print. The devil's in the details. Now go."

Since I'd woken up in Yvelia, I'd only seen the world outside through windows. A part of me had suspected the town below the palace and the forest stretching off to the mountains beyond were illusions.

They were not.

My mind broke a little when Kingfisher ordered me out of the barn. At first, leading the horse he'd mounted for me outside, I was mostly concerned about the animal's big, square teeth, but then I looked up, craning my head back to look up into the vast darkness, and I experienced the kiss of snow against my cheeks for the first time. Really experienced it. Seeing it from inside had been one thing, but being outside...

My whole life had been consumed by the need for water. I'd seen people fight for a mouthful of it. Die from the lack of it. Claw each other bloody, and lie, and betray, and steal for it. A dire thirst permeated Zilvaren. That thirst was the city's heartbeat. No matter who you were or where you went, you felt the rhythm of that heartbeat like a hammer striking an anvil. It lived inside your blood. The suns beat down so hot that the ground beneath your feet turned to liquid glass, and your body grew weaker with every breath you took. From the moment you woke up until the second you fell asleep each night, you were on a clock, and that clock was ticking.

Water.

Water.

Water.

Water.

You had to be willing to die for it to survive.

In Yvelia, it just fluttered down from the sky.

I wanted to scream.

Briefly, the thick layer of clouds overhead broke, and I caught a glimpse of the midnight sky beyond: a handful of brilliant white lights flickered in the black. I didn't want to ask, but the sight had stolen my breath. I needed to know. "What are they?" I whispered.

Fisher moved around his horse, looking up at the sky, too. "Stars," he answered stiffly. "There are billions of them. More than any mind can comprehend. Suns, like the two that hang in Zilvaren's sky."

"So far away, though." My voice conveyed my awe.

"The quicksilver closes the gap. With it, we can travel to the realms that orbit those stars." He said it so simply. As if he hadn't just told me that Zilvaren wasn't hidden through some mystical door somewhere. My home was up there. Amongst the stars. I gaped at the pinpricks of twinkling light, wondering if any of them were *my* suns. The clouds crowded in again, blotting out the sky, and my chest ached, full of grief.

"Get on," Kingfisher commanded, nodding at my horse. He was a dark-haired wraith, made of shadows, the flash of his pale hands and face the only part of him I could make out as he fixed two large bags to his own horse's saddle.

"We can't leave. We need to wait for Ren." My words were lost in a cloud of fog. Kingfisher came around his horse, and the beast shifted its weight, raising its back leg to kick. It was a giant, its coat black as sin, and had a look of madness in its eyes that could almost rival Kingfisher's. When Fisher growled in irritation, the horse chuffed and blew out a breath, tossing its head, apparently rethinking the kick.

"He'll catch up with us down the road. We have a meeting place for situations like this. Now, are you getting on the horse, or am I putting you on the horse?"

"It's snowing. I'm going to freeze to death."

I hadn't seen the thick swathe of material in his gloved hands. Kingfisher's eyes flashed brightly as he thrust the black bundle at me, his nostrils flaring. "It's heavy. Easier to put on when you're already up there, but seeing as you're so petulant and refuse to obey orders—"

"Soldiers obey orders. *I* am not a soldier."

"Believe me, I'm acutely aware of that. Here. Let me help you."

I didn't want his help, but my hands were already numb from the cold, and the ginormous piece of material he'd handed to me didn't seem to have a start or an end. Fisher had it figured out in moments and swung the material around my shoulders. It was a cloak, stiff and waxy on the outside and lined with silken fur. The inside was warm and so soft I wanted to weep. The bitter bite in the air instantly disappeared, leaving only my hands and my face to suffer against the cold.

I yelped as Kingfisher's hands found my waist and he shoved me up into the saddle of my horse. The beast was smaller, chestnut in color, and snaked its head around to try and bite me as I got myself seated.

"Bring your leg forward," Fisher commanded.

Arguing with him wasn't going to do me any good. His mind was made up—we were leaving the palace tonight, and there was nothing to be done about it. Again, I wanted to refuse his command just to spite him, but my whole body ached to comply with his order. I *wanted* to bring my leg forward for him. I couldn't stop myself.

Fisher lifted the saddle flap and tightened the girth. He then tied the long and narrow bundle he'd returned from the healers with beneath the saddle flap, tugging on it back and forth to make sure it wasn't going anywhere. "Don't touch this. Do you hear me?"

"Yes."

"Good. Leg back," he ordered.

I moved my leg back.

Snow drifted down, landing in his thick waves, settling on his eyelashes and dusting the tops of his shoulders white. "Comfortable?" he asked.

"No."

"Excellent. Don't yank on the reins. Aida's a good girl. She'll follow without any input from you, so just leave her be."

Aida probably wasn't a good girl. She was probably a hell bitch who was going to dump me on my ass at her earliest opportunity, but I held the reins loosely, obeying Fisher without a single objection. "Wait! Where's my bag?" I twisted in the saddle, searching for it.

"I have plenty of food and water for the both of us. You don't need it."

"I don't care about the food and water. I care about Onyx!"

"What's an Onyx?"

"Just give me the bag, Fisher." If he fought me on this, oooh gods, I would raise the worst kinds of hell. Luckily, the bastard just sighed and went back into the barn. He returned a moment later with my bag.

"The second that rodent becomes an issue, I'm skinning it," he said, hoisting the bag up to me.

"He's not a rodent. If anything, he's a dog." I pulled open the mouth of the bag, making sure Kingfisher hadn't replaced Onyx with a rock or particularly dense loaf of bread or something, but the little fox poked his head out of the hole, ears swiveling as he took in our surroundings, his pink tongue lolling.

"It should run beside us," Fisher grumbled, climbing up onto his own horse. "It doesn't need carrying."

"He is a *he*, not an *it*. And no, he can't run beside us. He'll get cold."

"*He*," Kingfisher said, heaping the word with disdain, "is a wild animal, and this is his natural habitat. Why do you think he has all of that thick, white fur?"

He was right on that front. Onyx was a creature of Yvelia and was evidently built for it. But when I looked down at him, he wriggled back into the bag so that only his wet little nose was visible, and I got the distinct impression that he was perfectly happy where he was.

"How about you focus on your cargo instead of mine," I fired at Fisher. "Your passenger's going to cause all kinds of problems for *you* when he wakes up."

Carrion was lashed to the back of Fisher's horse, still out cold. His arms hung limply over his head, his fire-red hair thick with snow already. There was no way the position was comfortable. He was going to be sore as hell when he woke up, and I knew firsthand just how ornery Carrion Swift got when he wasn't on the receiving end of a good night's sleep.

Kingfisher cast a blank look at him. "You're sure he's not your brother."

"I think I know what my own brother looks like, don't you?"

The look Fisher sent my way indicated that he wasn't so sure how to react to that question. "Then, at the risk of repeating myself for the eleven hundredth time, we should leave him here. If he's not your brother, then—"

"We are *not* leaving him here. Belikon will kill him the moment he realizes you've kidnapped me."

"It's not kidnapping if you come willingly," Kingfisher said in a calculating tone.

"I'm not doing any of this willingly! I want to go home!"

He shrugged as he swung himself into the saddle. "And yet you're coming to help me end a war, aren't you. What more noble cause could there be? Congratulations on achieving fucking sainthood."

15

SARRUSH

We didn't pass through the town at the foot of the Winter Palace. I'd hoped we would—more chance of us being spotted and stopped by Belikon's men before we could get very far—but Kingfisher was smart. He could be an angry, arrogant, half-mad, outrageously handsome piece of shit *and* an intelligent tactician at the same time. Turned out the two weren't mutually exclusive. I cursed the day I thought I'd get away with robbing a guardian as Fisher guided us around the outskirts of the town, down rocky, steep, uneven pathways that were buried in a thick layer of snow. It was a miracle that he knew where he was going. Even more astonishing that the horses didn't trip and break their damn legs on the treacherous route Fisher picked out for us. One misstep and we'd find ourselves in big fucking trouble, but the horses plodded on, surefooted, unfazed by our hazardous evening adventure.

I watched Carrion's head lolling against the flank of Fisher's horse, fuming at the unconscious bastard the whole while. There was a cold sense of justice in watching his head being thrashed by the low boughs of the trees as we entered the dark forest. The fucker deserved every injury he got for what he'd done. He'd lied to Fisher. Why the hell would he say he was Hayden?

Had Fisher said, *"What's your name, stinking human wretch?"* Or had he said, *"I'm here to transport Hayden Fane to a Fae realm, where he'll have access to as much food and water as he can gorge himself on and a comfortable bed to sleep in"?* Because I could totally see Carrion lying about his identity if the latter were the case.

The light and sound spilling from the Winter Palace soon faded. Kingfisher didn't seem to mind our pitch-black surroundings, though, and neither did the horses. They plodded on, blowing down their noses, as if it weren't freezing cold and terrifying out here. Haunting wails echoed across the forest, the sounds so human that my skin broke out into permanent goose bumps. In the bag I held in front of me, tucked against my stomach, half-wrapped in my cloak, Onyx whined, making himself as small as possible while also making so much noise that the annoyance radiating from Kingfisher could be felt from ten feet. He didn't mention the hysterical fox. He simmered, not saying a word, which was infinitely worse.

The wailing that echoed throughout the forest drew closer and moved away at random intervals, making my breath come quick and shallow. Eventually, a wail came so close that it sounded as if a starving creature was lurking right beneath Aida's feet. I screamed, jumping in the saddle, pulling my legs up, heart hammering in my chest.

Kingfisher halted his horse and looked back at me wearily. "What's wrong with you now?"

"There's…there's…urgh, we're going to *die* out here, asshole! Can't you hear that screaming?"

He looked at me like I was the most tiresome thing he'd ever encountered. "They're *shades,* human."

"What do you mean, shades?"

"Y'know. Echoes. What remains of a creature after it dies in distress."

My panic cranked up to an eleven. *"Ghosts?"*

Kingfisher's mouth drew down thoughtfully. "I'm not familiar with that term. These beings are non-corporeal. They have no
physical substance. They can't hurt you. They don't even know you're
here."

Gods above, I couldn't swallow. "Then why are they *screaming?*"

"They're reliving their last moments. You'd scream, too, if you'd
suffered the same death they had."

"They died here? In this forest?" *Don't do it. Don't ask him. Do* not
fucking ask. I had to know, though. "*How* did they die?"

Kingfisher cast sharp silver-flecked eyes around us into the dark.
"Watch and you'll see for yourself."

"It's pitch black out here! I can't see anything. I can't even see my
own hand in front of my face!" At this, another piercing cry splintered the silence, so close that Onyx let out a yelp and tried to burrow
a hole through the bottom of the burlap bag to safety.

"I keep forgetting how tragically inferior a human's eyesight is,"
Kingfisher remarked.

"Oh, and I suppose you can see every little detail of this place,
then?" I jabbed a finger at the forest, intending the question to be
ironic since we were surrounded by a wall of black, but Kingfisher
shrugged a shoulder, pouting.

"I mean, it's not crystal clear. I could make out much finer detail in
the daylight. But yes. I can see perfectly well. Bring Aida up alongside
me and I'll gift you with temporary sight."

"No."

"No?"

"*No!*"

"What do you mean, no?"

"I'd like to sleep again at some point in the future. I don't need to
see any tortured souls reliving their deaths, thank you very much. I'll
pass."

Kingfisher huffed. "Suit yourself. But when you hear them
scream, don't feel too bad for them, human. This place is a prison.

Only those guilty of the most heinous crimes are sent to the Wicker Wood. The trees entomb the evilest kinds of monsters."

The minutes turned into an hour, which turned into three hours. Could have been more. It was hard to gauge the passing of time, sitting on the back of this lumpy, uncomfortable animal. Aida's barrel of a rib cage was too wide, and every time I rocked forward against the front of the saddle, my hips complained bitterly. My ass, too, along with far more sensitive parts of my anatomy that felt like they were being rubbed raw and *not* in a fun way.

The screams grew to a fever pitch. Aida kept close to Kingfisher's horse, her head tossing anxiously. Once or twice, she lunged for Carrion, snapping her teeth at him, unhappy that the weird unconscious creature was getting too close. It was sheer luck that I'd managed to keep her from biting Carrion's face up until now; if we made it to our destination, wherever that was, without the black-market trader receiving any facial lacerations, then he was going to owe me big-time.

I bit my tongue for as long as I could, but eventually, the dark, the screaming shades, and the driving, endless cold took their toll. "How much longer do we have to do this?" I'd planned on calling out the words so that Kingfisher could hear me over the wind rustling through the tree boughs and the steady metal grinding of the horses nervously chewing against their bits, but my nerves got the better of me; the question came out in a cracked whisper. I was saved from having to repeat myself by Fisher's Fae hearing.

His head angled to the right an inch—the only indication that he'd heard me. But then he said, "We're nearly there. Only another half an hour. We'll arrive even sooner if we trot."

Trot? I laughed scathingly. "Nothing you can say or do will incentivize me to smash my genitals against this saddle any harder or faster than they're already being smashed."

"Feeling a little sore, human?"

"Sore doesn't come close," I grumbled.

"I'll happily kiss all of your aches and pains better for you once we strike camp. I've been told my mouth has healing properties. Especially when administered between a pair of thighs." The suggestion in Kingfisher's voice was a promise made of dark silk. Seductive. A little thrilling, if I was being honest. I wasn't in the mood to be honest, though. I was grouchy and officially sick of flinching every time a stray twig brushed my arm. I wanted this little midnight foray to come to an end already. "I'm surprised," I snorted.

"Why?"

"Surprised that you'd offer to spend any amount of time between my legs. Not when I was able to steal something so precious from you the last time I tricked you into letting me close."

I could just make out the outline of Fisher's shoulders bouncing up as he chuckled. "You really think I didn't notice you take the ring?"

"I know you didn't."

"Oh, *please.* I knew what you were up to the second you climbed up into my lap."

I preferred the thick silence punctuated with death screams to the sound of Kingfisher's smugness. "Gods, you hate it, don't you? Being bested by a human. Why can't you just admit that I had you fooled?"

"It'll be a cold day in Sanasroth before you fool me." He said this so matter-of-factly, as if it were a foregone conclusion. "I knew the second you walked into the forge that you were planning something. I admit, I was mildly interested to see what you'd come up with."

"Wow. You'd rather keep lying and dig yourself an even bigger hole than admit the truth. That ego of yours is impressive, Fisher."

"I'm not lying."

"*Really.*"

"Really."

"All right. Fine. Tell me, how did I give myself away, then, if I was so obviously up to no good?"

"You brought a bag with you into the forge. A bag packed with food and clothes. Otherwise known as *supplies.*"

"How did you know it was packed with food and clothes?"

"Because I peeked while you weren't looking."

My mouth dropped open. "Asshole! You can't go rifling through people's bags!"

"Says the thief who stole a piece of valuable jewelry right off of my body. While rubbing *her* body all over me to distract me."

He had me there. I'd done a lot of unconscionable things in the past to get what I needed. I'd never needed to kiss anyone the way I'd kissed Kingfisher, mind you. I hadn't meant to kiss *him* like that. That had been an accident. One I didn't feel inclined to investigate too closely at this specific moment in time. "So, you're saying I did distract you, then," I fired at him.

He just laughed. "And here I was, rankled at the thought of having to drag around a helpless, useless human who'd be nothing but a burden. But it turns out you've got jokes! At least I can count on you for some entertainment."

Honestly. He was such a piece of work. Where did he get off, treating me like this? I'd been there back in the forge. I'd felt his hands on my body. In my hair. How urgently he explored my mouth with his tongue. He'd been distracted, all right. "You're so full of shit. I felt how hard your—" I slammed my mouth shut. Heat nipped at my cheeks, very close to becoming embarrassment.

Kingfisher halted his horse, forcing Aida to stop, too. Carrion wobbled on the horse's haunches, almost toppling off, though Kingfisher didn't seem to notice or care. He twisted around in his saddle, a ruinous smirk dancing at the corners of his mouth. "How hard my *what,* human?"

"Nothing!" I answered far too quickly to come across as casual. "All I mean to say is that…that…you were distracted, okay? You were all over me. Your hands—"

"My hands have a mind of their own. *My* mind was fixed on what yours were doing, and let me tell you, human. You are nowhere near as light-fingered as you seem to think you are. You nearly dislocated my finger, tugging at that damned ring—"

"How *dare* you!" Aida had pulled up alongside Fisher's horse, crab-walking, keen to get moving again, which brought me too close to the Fae warrior for comfort. I used our close proximity to lash out at him with my foot, but he nudged his stallion out of the way, sidestepping the blow.

"Easy there, human. Kick Bill and he'll bolt. You want to find yourself alone in this forest? In the dark?"

I wouldn't give him the satisfaction of answering that. Instead, I pulled a childish face while retracting my foot and shoving the toe of my boot back into the stirrup. "Bill? Who calls their horse *Bill?*"

"I do. Now. Would you like to lead the way?" He gestured with a gloved hand toward a path that I had to assume was there since I couldn't see it.

"No."

"I didn't think so."

We came across a road soon after. Though it was deserted, as far as I could tell, a fair amount of traffic clearly used the road because the snow hadn't stuck here. Deep gouges cut into the churned mud, along with hoof prints, paw prints, and footprints so massive that I shivered to think what might have created them. Our horse's hooves sucked at the stinking black ground as they plodded onward.

Our destination was a run-down two-story stone building situated right on the banks of a wide, frozen river. Its roof was covered in a layer of straw two feet thick, atop which rested only a fine dusting of snow. Light poured out of small windows. When the door to the front of the building opened, laughter and chatter and half a stanza of an off-key song spilled out into the night, along with a tall, broad figure who took five lurching steps and collapsed face-first into a snowbank.

Kingfisher had slowed his horse when the building had come into view. He sat staring at it for a moment, lips slightly parted, an unfamiliar, wistful expression on his face. I frowned at the building, trying to see whatever it was that he was seeing. You'd think he was taking stock of one of Yvelia's finest architectural wonders, but from where my aching ass was sitting, it looked a hell of a lot like a pub.

"We're sleeping there?" I asked, jerking my chin toward the place. The figure who'd stumbled out of the pub was on his hands and knees now, vomiting into the snow.

"Maybe. Maybe not." Kingfisher kicked his horse on, gesturing for me to follow. "We'll see how long it takes Ren to catch up."

A scruffy stable hand took the horses when we dismounted. I attempted not to stare at the curved ram's horns poking out of the holes torn in the top of his woolen hat but did a piss-poor job. I couldn't stop myself from wondering how they connected to his skull. The stable hand didn't seem to mind. He was all toothy smiles until I opened my bag up and tipped a sleepy Onyx out into the snow at my feet.

"Oooh, that's a good one! Rare. Never see the black tips on the ears and tail like that anymore. I'll gi' yer two cröna for it."

"What?"

Onyx darted behind me, hackles up, as if he understood the stable hand and would take a finger if the stranger tried anything funny.

The stable hand eyed me shrewdly. "All right. Four cröna. That's all I can do, though. My wife'll kill me if—"

My hand reached for the hilt of the dagger at my thigh. "He's not for sale."

"The human's gotten it into her head that the flea-ridden thing is a pet," Fisher said, collecting one of the bags from his saddle. He moved quickly, retrieving the long, wrapped object he'd tucked under my saddle flap.

Onyx jumped into my arms, nestling into the crook of my elbow and hiding his face. "He does not have fleas."

"That you know of," Kingfisher said.

"What about this one, then? Is this one for sale?" The stable hand thumbed a hand in the direction of Carrion.

"What's your best offer?" Fisher asked.

"No!"

Kingfisher had the audacity to look bored when I slapped his arm. "No, the human isn't for sale either," he said in a flat, annoyed tone. "Put him in a stall with some hay and cover him with a blanket. If I find out he's been harmed in any way..." Kingfisher's hand rested suggestively on Nimerelle's hilt, drawing the stable hand's attention to the menacing black sword. The fawn paled beneath his auburn beard. He recognized the action for what it was—a promise of pain—and acted accordingly.

"Of course, sir. Don't you worry. No harm will come to him under my watchful eye. He'll sleep like a baby, just see if he doesn't."

A wall of heat and sound hit me as we entered the tavern. A good deal of nerves, too. This wasn't the House of Kala. I was known there. Safe. Well, as safe as any person could be in a house of ill repute, where shady deals went down in dark corners. This tavern was a completely new environment for me. I was a stranger here. I had no idea what to expect. It turned out it was a lot like every other tavern I'd stepped foot inside.

Every rickety seat in the place was occupied, every table cluttered with a variety of chipped and mismatched tankards that were mostly empty. Fae males and females sat in groups, engaged in their own quiet conversations. I'd seen plenty of other creatures back at the Winter Palace, but the sheer variety of the other creatures here nearly knocked me off my feet.

Tall, reedy, thin-limbed beings with bark-like skin and wisps of thin, flowing white hair.

Small, hairless things with charcoal-colored skin and slitted amber eyes, teeth as sharp as needles.

Two males with shaggy, furred legs and cloven feet sat at the bar, long, ridged horns protruding from their brows and sweeping down their backs.

Creatures with bulbous noses and green skin, and creatures with flowing, thick auburn hair that streamed out around their heads caught on an invisible breeze.

Everywhere I looked, an array of creatures so wild and wonderful and strange and frightening that I could barely catch my breath.

Kingfisher drew up the hood of his cloak and ducked his head, throwing his face into shadow as we approached the bar. A swarm of tiny faeries with gossamer wings flitted around our heads, tugging on my hair, snatching up the strands that had worked loose from my braid, giving them sharp, vicious little pulls.

"Ow!" I tried to swat them away, but Kingfisher caught me by the wrist.

"I wouldn't. They're drunk. They get mean when they're drunk."

"I'm a thousand times bigger than them. I could crush—*Ahh!*" I hissed, pulling my hand away from the cloud of fluttering menaces. There, right on the heel of my palm, was a perfect oval welt. A bead of blood rose up from the tiny wound, shining like a tiny ruby. "A bite? Is that a *bite* mark?" I held out my hand for Fisher to see, but he didn't even look.

"Not only do they get mad when you try to smash them out of the air, but they speak Common Fae and take offense when you imply that you're going to crush them to death. Beer, please. Two. And a pour of your strongest spirit as well."

The bartender was a short, rotund male with wiry gray hair, a hooked nose, and the bushiest eyebrows I'd ever seen. He grunted at Fisher's request, paying neither of us any heed as he went to fetch our drinks.

When he came back, he dumped two tankards down, sloshing a

good amount of our beer onto the bar, and then slid a small glass of noxious-looking green liquid to Kingfisher. Kingfisher paid wordlessly, scooped up our tankards and the shot, then ducked off into the crowd to find us somewhere to sit.

We were lucky. Two Fae women in royal blue dresses and thick traveling cloaks were rising from a table in the corner by the fire just as we were passing. Kingfisher hung his head, eyes on his boots while he waited for them to go; then he jerked his chin, indicating that I should sit down first. Onyx, who had stuck to my side like he was my shadow since we'd entered the tavern, shot under the table.

I hissed when my behind met the wooden seat. Gods, that hurt. I was never going to be able to sit down without drawing in a sharp breath again. Fisher's infuriating grin was the only part of his face visible beneath the dark cowl of his hood. "I'm glad you think this is funny," I groused, accepting the beer he handed to me.

"I think it's *hilarious*," he countered. "You've been a persistent pain in my ass since we met. Now the universe has seen fit to make *your* ass smart. I'd call that justice."

"I'd call it highly fucking annoying. Wait, what are you *doing?*"

He'd reached across the table and grabbed hold of my wrist. I tried to yank it back, but his grip was like a vise. Hissing between his teeth, Fisher gave my arm a non-too-gentle tug. "Listen. In the last twelve hours, you've been bitten by that mangy fox, scorched by a sword you had no business touching, and now bitten by a faerie as well. You aren't from here. There are probably countless germs and illnesses floating around in the air that could put you in the ground. Your body is weak and slow to heal as it is. I need to disinfect all of these cuts and scrapes before you develop a fever and die."

I begrudgingly stopped straining against his hold. "Careful, Kingfisher. I'll start to think you actually care about my well-being if you keep—ahh! Ahh, ahh, ahh! Ow, that fucking *hurts!*"

He didn't give me any warning. He dumped the bright green liquor in the shot glass all over my hand and held my wrist even tighter as my fingers spasmed. Underneath the table, Onyx let out a nervous whine, scratching at my legs.

"Breathe," Fisher ordered. "It'll pass in a second."

The pain did begin to subside after a moment, but my anger...that was another story. "You're sick," I hissed. "You enjoyed that. What kind of male likes hurting people?"

His face was a blank mask when he let me go. "I don't enjoy hurting people. I don't like it at all. But that doesn't mean it isn't necessary. To avoid far more serious pain, sometimes we have to endure a little sting. Sometimes, some of us have to *inflict* it. You say it so mockingly, but I *do* care about your well-being. You're important. Without you, I can't end this war or protect my people. I have to keep you safe so I can accomplish my goals. So yes, I'll hurt you if it means I keep you safe. I'll force you to follow me to the ends of this realm, because that is the only way I can make sure you stay alive. Now drink your beer."

He made it all sound so reasonable. That he was doing what was right and just for the greater good, but there were other ways of going about it. Softer, kinder ways. He clearly knew nothing about that. The world had been cruel to him, so he was cruel back. I didn't need babying. I was used to dealing in harsh facts. I'd lost track of the number of times I'd been manhandled or had the shit kicked out of me, but that didn't mean that Fisher needed to be such an asshole about all of this.

I took a swig of my beer, already knowing that one drink wouldn't be enough to improve my mood. I'd expected it to be bad, but the beer tasted nutty and rich and was actually quite pleasant. *Very* pleasant. "Go slow with that," Fisher warned when I took another huge gulp. "It's strong."

This idiot really *did* think I was weak. He knew nothing about the drinking games I'd played and won back in Zilvaren. And that was drinking whiskey, not beer, for fuck's sake. Still, I wasn't idiot enough to go downing my whole tankard just to prove a point.

These were unchartered lands, and I didn't have a map, both literally and figuratively.

I narrowed my eyes at Kingfisher. "When will Carrion wake up?"

"How am I supposed to know?" Fisher drank from his own beer, green eyes glinting at me over the top of his tankard. From within the dark shadows of his hood, they seemed to flash in the most remarkable way.

"I was unconscious for ten days. Are you planning on carting him around on the back of your horse for days on end?"

"No," he said simply.

"What do you mean, no?"

"I mean no, I'm not planning on doing that. You were on the verge of death. That's why you took so long to wake up. And we won't have to ride any farther to get where we're going, so your friend's career as a saddle bag has already come to an end."

"Where are you taking me?"

"Home."

"And *where* is home?" I pressed, my frustration levels rising.

He took a deep pull from his beer, the muscles beneath the tattooed skin of his neck working. "The place where I was born."

"Urgh! Do you have to be so difficult?"

His eyes danced. "It isn't mandatory, but I do enjoy it."

"Kingfisher!"

"I'm taking you to the borderlands, Osha. A small fiefdom at the very edge of Yvelian territory. A place called Cahlish."

Cahlish? I'd heard the name mentioned multiple times. Everlayne had wanted Ren to take Fisher back there before he could be discovered in the Winter Palace. Belikon had said Fisher could stay in the palace for a week before he had to go back there.

"Is that wise? The king was sending you there anyway. Won't he just show up there, looking for us?"

Fisher shook his head. "My father and Belikon had a long history. He saw what Belikon was planning long before he murdered the royal family and stole the crown for himself. He took precautions and warded his lands so that neither Belikon nor any of his supporters could cross into them. He was powerful, and his wards were strong. They remain as solid as ever. Belikon can travel to the borders of Cahlish, but he can't enter. As long as I live and carry on my father's line, he never will."

Well, that was great news. But there *were* other things to worry about. "Forgive me if I'm wrong, but I was under the impression that Cahlish was a battlefront," I said.

"It is."

"No. But. An actual war zone."

Fisher fished a fleck of floating debris out of his beer. "That's right."

"So you make a big speech about keeping me safe in order to save your friends," I said slowly, "and *then* you tell me you're dragging me right into the middle of an open conflict?"

"Sound like fun?"

"How the hell am I supposed to stay alive in the middle of a war zone, Fisher?"

When he laughed this time, the sound was hollow. "By sticking close, Osha. *Really* close."

I drank three beers and fed Onyx most of the meal Fisher ordered for us under the table. The smoked meat stew made my mouth water, but I could barely swallow it down. Carrion Swift was in the barn outside. Carrion fucking Swift, when I had wanted Hayden. I was locked into a blood oath, and I hadn't gotten what I'd bargained for in the slightest. Best-case scenario, my brother was still trapped back in Zilvaren, hungry, thirsty, and looking over his shoulder every other second for Madra's guardians. Worst-case scenario, he was already dead because of me, and there was nothing I could do to make it right. So yes. My appetite was nonexistent.

Ren showed up two hours after our bowls of stew were cleared away. I saw him enter, his tall frame filling the tavern doorway, his long sandy hair wet from the snow. A wave of relief slammed into me. At last, a voice of reason.

Belikon's general saw me first, still tucked away in the corner by the fire, and the tension between his brows instantly lifted. When he saw Kingfisher's back, the cowl of his cloak still concealing his features, he broke out into a smile so full of relief that it made my chest ache. My expression must have matched Ren's when I'd thought for those few moments that Fisher had brought Hayden back with him. Those few blissful moments when I'd thought my brother was alive and safe...

Gods.

Kingfisher turned to meet his friend right as he arrived at our table, a broad, genuine smile on his face. He stood, and Ren pulled him into a tight hug, clapping him on the back. When the general let him go, holding him at arm's length, he huffed sharply down his nose and patted Fisher's cheek. "You, my friend, are officially *fucked.*"

"Everlayne's spitting mad. She's never going to talk to you again. What were you thinking?" Ren had his own beer now, which meant I had a fourth sitting in front of me, too. I didn't feel remotely drunk. I was tired, and sore, and irritated beyond comprehension, and I wanted my bed back in the Silver City. Wanting was a fool's game, though, and Ren had come with news, so I pulled myself together and leaned in close to listen to the hushed argument that was taking place between the two males.

"We had a plan," Ren hissed.

"Don't look at me. Our little friend here forced my hand. She tried to commit suicide."

"Liar! I did not!"

"When I found her, she was two seconds away from taking a dip without a relic," Fisher said.

"I had your ring, smart-ass. I thought I *did* have a relic."

He eyed me over the top of his tankard, the silver around his iris shimmering as he gave me an open-mouthed smile. "Oh? You had my ring, did you? Care to recount the tale of how that came to be in your possession, human?"

"That's irrelevant." I glowered at him hatefully.

"I don't care what Saeris took," Ren said tightly. "*You* took Belikon's Alchemist. And not just that. You took the *sword*, too."

Kingfisher's hand closed around his tankard so tight that his fingers turned white. "The last time he laid his hands on a sword of note, he used it to murder the true king and the whole fucking Daianthus line. If Rurik Daianthus—"

"As you just pointed out, Rurik Daianthus is gone. There's no point playing a game of 'if only' where he's concerned. Belikon *is* the king. And like it or not, as king, he can claim whatever the hell he wants to claim. The god swords are all dead. They're paperweights now. Belikon couldn't do any more damage with it than he could do with an ordinary sword. You should have just let him add it to his collection. What harm would it have done?"

"*Harm?*" Fisher barked. "You're joking, right? Harm. Hah!" He shook his head. "That sword is a holy fucking relic, Renfis. That bastard isn't fit to look upon it let alone wield it. I'll die before I allow Belikon to wear it on his hip. And you're wrong. Not all of the swords are dormant. Nimerelle—"

"So, taking it had nothing to do with the fact that Solace was your father's blade? No. No, forget I even asked. I already know that's the truth of it. As for *your* sword, Nimerelle has been corrupted for years," Ren seethed.

Kingfisher slammed his hands against the table, the cowl of his hood falling down. "Nimerelle is the only thing that's stood between Yvelia and ever-lasting darkness for the past four hundred fucking years!" He was too loud. Too angry. His fury erupted out of him, and the tables around us fell quiet. Conversations stumbled, drinks were set aside, and a hundred pairs of eyes turned toward us.

Fisher shook as he stared at Ren. He didn't notice when whispers of *"Renfis Orithian, Renfis Blood Sworn, Renfis of the Silver Lake,"* began to spread throughout the room. Nor did he notice when the whispers turned to him. Not until it was too late.

Kingfisher.

No. It can't *be.*

It's true!

He's returned.

He's here.

Kingfisher.

Kingfisher.

Kingfisher.

Fisher's ire dried up like so much smoke. He hung his head, his cheeks turning white as ash despite the heat from the roaring fire. The muted, *"Fuck,"* he murmured was just a shape on his lips. It made no sound.

"Time to go," Ren ground out.

"What? What's the problem?" I looked around, trying to gauge the emotions on the faces that surrounded us, but all I could see was shock. Reluctantly, Fisher *had* spent some time explaining what types of creatures they were to me. Where they had all come from. And now the Fae, and the tiny little faeries that hovered in the air, and the satyrs at the bar, and the goblins, and the selkies, and everyone else—they were all speechless. Everywhere I looked, I found wide eyes and open mouths. Even the bartender, who hadn't spared us more than a glance when we ordered our drinks, was frozen, halfway through polishing a thick gla—

Never mind.

The glass dropped from his hands, shattering loudly on the floor.

Renfis rose from his chair, head bowed. He held his hand out to me and helped me up. Slowly, Kingfisher followed. His shoulders drew up around his ears, his vibrant green eyes unreadable; he kept them trained on the floor.

The three of us headed for the door, Kingfisher leading the way. I came after him, Onyx clutched tight in my arms, Renfis following behind me. We were halfway to the door when a massive Fae warrior with long, braided blond hair, shorn at the sides of his head, stepped in front of Kingfisher, blocking his path. He was huge. Easily just as tall as Kingfisher or Ren. His features were fine, though there was nothing gentle about him. The hard look in his pewter-colored eyes spoke of bloodshed. I gasped when he dropped to one knee at Kingfisher's feet. "It's an honor to kneel at the feet of the Dragon's Bane. Please. A blessing, Commander? Only...only if you see fit to, of course," he stammered.

"I'm sorry." Kingfisher placed a hand on the warrior's shoulder. "You have me mistaken for someone else."

The blond warrior donned a rueful smile. "My cousin fought with you and your wolves at Ajun-Sky. The way he described you..." He shook his head apologetically. "You're the Fisher King. You can't be anyone else."

Fisher's throat bobbed. I saw him struggle for words, fighting to force them out of his mouth. "I might fit your cousin's description...on the *outside*. I'm honored that he remembered me to you. But...I'm not the male he fought with at Ajun. I'm sorry, Brother. I—"

"You saved the rippling banner of the proud western Annachreich," the blond warrior interrupted. "At dawn, on the fifth day, you cried against the rising sun and roused our people's hearts so that even those who were ready to pass through the black door turned away from death and found the strength to find their feet. And their bows. And their swords. And their friends. You led the charge on the blood-red mountain—" The warrior's voice cracked.

A tall Fae female stepped to his side, dressed in leather ranger's armor. Her face bore a jagged scar that twisted her lower lip. "At Sinder's Reach, you quelled the horde that threatened to burn everything my people had built. Fifty thousand people. Fifty thousand *lives.* Temples. Libraries. Schools. Homes. They all still exist today. Because of you."

A muscle ticked in Kingfisher's jaw. He couldn't meet the female's eyes.

At the bar, one of the satyrs with the impressive sweeping horns and the shaggy goat-like legs stepped forward. His eyes shone bright, reflecting the flames of the fire roaring in the hearth as he raised his glass to Kingfisher. "Innishtar," he declared in a deep, gravelly voice. "It wasn't as grand as these others. Just a small town. We weren't kind to you when you came. Then the Fae and my lot weren't the allies we are now. But five of you stood against the dark that night. You saved four hundred. *You* were there, too, Renfis of the Orithian."

Ren inclined his head, his dark eyes sad. "I remember," he said softly.

The satyr lifted his glass a little higher, first to Ren and then to Kingfisher. "A lifetime of thanks to you both for what you did. Though it'll never be enough. *Sarrush.*" He pressed the glass to his lips and tossed back the amber liquid inside.

"*Sarrush!*"

"*Sarrush!*"

Around the bar, a cup or a glass went up in every single patron's hand. They all cried out the word. They all drank.

"You saved the bridge at Lothbrock."

"You held Turrordan Pass until the snows came."

"You fought Malcolm on the banks of the Darn until the river flowed black with their blood."

Again and again, the tavern's patrons stood and spoke. It seemed all of them had a story. Kingfisher stood mute, his throat working. Eventually, he couldn't maintain his silence anymore. "I'm not...I'm just..." His eyes were distant. "That was a *long* time ago. That person doesn't exist anymore." He charged past the Fae warrior still kneeling at his feet, flung open the tavern door, and disappeared into the night.

I stared after him, unable to comprehend what I'd just seen and heard. All of this, for Kingfisher. Kingfisher *and* Ren. So many stories of valiant battles and impossible odds. From the way the two males had reacted when they'd first realized they'd been recognized, I'd thought we were about to be attacked. But that couldn't have been any further from the truth. To me, Kingfisher was a surly, foul-mouthed bastard who I wouldn't piss on even if he was on fire.

To everyone inside this tavern, he was a living fucking god.

16

SHADOW GATE

A GATEWAY to hell awaited us in the clearing outside.

The spiraling maw of shadow and smoke was small. Only big enough to swallow a horse, perhaps. Convenient, since Kingfisher stood in front of it with Bill, Aida, and Ren's bay mount. Carrion's limp body was already slumped over Bill's haunches. He'd misplaced a boot somewhere between the barn and the clearing, and Fisher obviously hadn't deemed the loss important enough to do anything about it. I didn't care much about Swift's missing boot, either; I was too busy staring at the whirling black vortex behind Fisher to register much of anything else at all.

The way it pulled at the light, drawing the orange glow from the tavern's windows toward it, twisting it into fine threads that it sucked into the spinning singularity in its center made me want to back away from it very, very slowly. I'd put Onyx back into the bag before leaving the tavern, but I could feel him shaking against my spine as if he could sense the strange force through the burlap and didn't like it one bit.

Gusts of wind whipped at Kingfisher's dark waves, tossing them about his face. The silver gorget was back at his throat. It glinted, the wolf's head engraving fiercer than ever. After how he'd just behaved back in the tavern, I expected to find Fisher in a raging temper, but his face was blank, his shoulders relaxed as he handed me Aida's reins and turned to face the wall of twisting smoke. "Let's get this over with," he said quietly. "You'll follow Ren. I'll be right behind you."

The hairs stood up on my arms. "I'm…I'm not walking into that. What *is* it?"

"It's a shadow gate. A means to an end. You can use this, or you can spend the next two months on horseback, sleeping in snowy ditches and scavenging for your dinner. What'll it be?"

"I'll take the second option." I didn't even need to think about it. My ass would get used to a saddle eventually, and the cloak Kingfisher had given me was excellent at keeping out the cold. I'd spent half my life hunting for my own dinner amongst Zilvaren's sand dunes. And besides, I had no interest in heading into a war zone. Delaying our arrival at Cahlish seemed like a fantastic option.

Fisher pursed his lips. "Let me rephrase that. You're going through the gate, human."

I took a step back, dropping Aida's reins. "I'm not."

Kingfisher considered me, one eyebrow curving with interest. "Are you thinking about running? Gods, I hope so. I'll give you a head start if you like. It's been an age since I've *hunted* anything."

"Come on, Fisher," Ren said wearily, slipping on a pair of leather gloves. "She's scared. Give her a moment to adjust to the idea."

"I'm not scared," I lied. "I'm just not going through that thing. I'll probably never make it out the other side."

Kingfisher opened his mouth, about to say something taunting and mean, no doubt, but the tavern door opened, and shadowy figures began to emerge. Fisher's eyes hardened, and whatever he was about to say died on his lips. "We don't have time for this. Ren will go through the gate. You *will* follow after him. Your oath to me will leave you no choice."

Ren went still. His eyes locked on to Kingfisher. The warrior must have felt the burning intensity of the general's gaze, but Fisher didn't so much as glance in his friend's direction. "Tell me I misheard that," Ren said. "Tell me you didn't bind this girl to you with an oath."

"Go through the gate, Ren," Fisher commanded.

"An *oath?*" he whispered.

"She got something in return," Fisher ground out. "Now, please. Go through the gate. We can discuss this on the other side."

Ren shook his head, a combination of dismay and disappointment warring on his face. He didn't seem to know what to say. Collecting Aida's reins, he handed them back to me and said, "Don't worry. It's really nothing. You'll be disoriented for a moment, but just keep walking. It'll be over in seconds, I promise."

It was a kindness, this reassurance from Ren. Without it, my fear would have eaten me alive as the general stepped forward and led his horse into the inky black.

I wasn't going to follow.

I wouldn't.

Elroy hadn't said I possessed a stubborn streak a mile wide for no reason. My force of will *was* stronger than this oath I'd sworn to Fisher. It had to be. I set my jaw and determined to enjoy the look of annoyance on Kingfisher's face when I didn't follow after Ren. But Kingfisher only gave me a tight-lipped smile as my body moved of its own accord, following his command without my permission.

My pulse leaped as I approached the twisting gate, my breath catching in my throat. How could he do this? By using the oath against me, forcing me to bend to his will, he stripped me of my own. Even back in Madra's Hall of Mirrors, when I'd fought for my life and Harron had outmatched me, I hadn't felt this powerless.

My mind scrambled as the tip of my boot disappeared into the swirling gate. I would have begged Fisher to relent, but the warrior's stony expression promised that doing so would be a waste of breath. "I'll hate you forever for this," I hissed at him.

And then I stepped into the gate.

The howling black wind turned me inside out.

I became it.

It became me.

My mind scattered in a thousand different directions, ripped away from me in an instant.

I was nothing.

I was blind. I was deaf. I was a soulless whisper, trembling in the dark.

And then I was pain.

It tore through me, exploding in my knees, my wrists, and my palms. It flowered behind my eyes, bright lights flaring, burning my retinas. Red. Orange. White. Green.

I opened my eyes with a gasp and only had enough time to pull in that one breath before my stomach pitched upside down and ejected the few bites of stew I'd eaten at the tavern all over a rough stone floor.

"My Lord," a stunned voice said. "I—Gods. I'm so sorry, I—nothing's prepared. We had no idea!"

"It's all right, Orris." When Ren spoke, he sounded far away. "Thank you. Take the horses and make sure they're rugged tonight. It's going to get a lot colder before dawn."

"But—"

"Yes, I know. Fisher's back. He'll speak to us all tomorrow, I'm sure. For now, I think it's best if we give him a little time to settle back in. If you could keep this quiet until the morning…"

"Of course, sir. Of course."

The world was on its side. My temple was cold. Cold as ice. It took me a long moment to realize that I was lying on the ground and that my head was resting on hard stone. I watched Kingfisher walking away down a long hallway—alone, silent, head bowed—and I vowed with everything I had in me that I'd make the fucker pay for this.

I tried to get up, but when I heaved myself onto an elbow, the arched ceiling became the floor, became up, became down, and another wave of vomit rushed up the back of my throat. I threw up a second time, hacking as I tried to catch my breath.

"Oh, Saeris. I'm sorry. Here, give me your hand."

Leave me alone. Get the fuck away from me. Don't touch me. I thought about screaming these things at Renfis, but there was real sympathy in his voice. And this wasn't his fault. He hadn't taken my free will from me. He hadn't brought me here to this wretched place or tricked me into agreeing to a binding blood contract that effectively turned me into his goddamned puppet. I accepted the hand he offered to me, whimpering as my legs wobbled.

"Thankfully, you won't experience this again. For some reason, the gates only affect us the first time we use them. For most of us, it's just a little dizziness. Maybe a headache. For a human, it's a little more than that, it seems. No one's seen a human in a very long time. There's a lot we've forgotten. I'm sorry."

"You don't need to apologize to me. Not for *him*," I wheezed.

Ren let out a tense sigh. "He's not...what you think he is."

"A bastard? He's definitely a bastard."

The general flinched a little as I tried to straighten up. "Can you walk? Oh. No. Shit. You can't even stand. Uhh...okay. That's fine. I've got you." There's nothing more undignified than collapsing into the arms of a male you barely know. Not much I could do about it, though. My head wouldn't stop spinning, and I was definitely going to throw up again. I couldn't have shrugged out of his arms if I'd tried. I didn't make a peep as he lifted me.

My head felt like it was going to crack open. "Wait. Onyx. Where's...Onyx?"

"Don't fret. I've got him. He'll be with you when you wake up."

"Thank you." I closed my eyes, trying to breathe through the discomfort when Ren started walking with me.

"He used to be kinder," Ren whispered. "But the quicksilver inside of him...It makes it difficult for him to think straight. It wears on him. It's exhausting for him, shutting out the voices. It's made him hard."There was so much sadness in his voice as he spoke. It made me want to open my eyes, to see what kind of expression he was wearing, but I couldn't manage it.

"You shouldn't make...excuses...for him."

"They aren't excuses, Saeris. I've known him my whole life. We were born to different parents, but we're brothers in every other way that counts. I *know* him better than I know myself. The first time Belikon forced him to travel without a relic, the silver infected him so badly that I thought we'd lost him altogether. His mind was so fractured. Let's just say, it took a long time for him to recover. The healers did their best, but the piece that remains in his eye torments him night and day. His mother's relic doesn't seem to be as effective anymore. And now he's been exposed to the quicksilver *twice* without it again. I...I just don't know what to expect from him anymore."

"Where"—I took a deep breath—"was he?"

"Mm?" The questioning sound Ren made vibrated against my ear.

"You said...you haven't seen him for...a hundred and...ten years. Where *was* he?"

A thick silence fell. For a long time, the sound of Ren's footsteps echoing off the walls was the only thing to disturb it. But then he sighed deeply, as if making his mind up about something, and said, "I can't tell you that. It wouldn't be fair. He'll tell you himself at some point, perhaps. But until then..."

I didn't care to push the matter further. I felt too sick to talk. And who cared where Kingfisher had been? He could have spent the past century trapped inside one of those trees in the Wicker Wood for all the difference it made. There was no excuse for the way he was treating me. None that I would accept.

I didn't know where Renfis of the Orrithian carried me. I was already unconscious by the time he got me there.

"It'd be a real shame to have to pinch you, but I'm getting bored, and this rabid animal keeps showing me its teeth."

I groaned.

Rolled over.

I was floating on a cloud. It was heaven. The most comfortable cloud I'd ever—

I hinged upright, grasping hold of my side. *"Fuck!"* The skin just above my hip throbbed painfully. "What the ffff..." I trailed off when I saw the auburn-haired brigand standing at the foot of my bed. No, not my bed. *A* bed. Warm. Comfortable. Massive. But not mine. Onyx sat at the end of it, baring his teeth at a very disheveledlooking Carrion Swift, who held hands aloft in surrender.

"Look! Look! Shh, it's all right. She's awake. I didn't murder her. Stop overreacting."

"If you touch that fox, I'll skin you," I growled at him.

Carrion's pale blue eyes met mine, full of a false hurt I was more than familiar with. "And hello to you, too! What kind of greeting is that? And after we've been so cruelly separated for so many weeks as well."

I flung back the covers and launched myself out of the bed. I had Carrion backed up against a wall and an angry finger in his face in no time. "You're lucky I don't knock your fucking teeth out," I snapped. "What the hell were you playing at, telling Fisher that you were Hayden?"

The thief's hands were still in the air. He glanced down at the index finger I was jabbing in his face, smirking at it like he was wondering what I was planning on doing with it. He didn't miss a beat when he said, "You should be thanking me. That psychotic monster looked like he was planning on murdering your brother. I did him a favor. If it weren't for me—"

"Just shut up and tell me, is he *alive,* Carrion? I need...I have to know." My heart was a fist in my throat. My entire existence hinged on whatever came out of Carrion's mouth next. I waited for his expression to darken or at least sober a little, but Carrion's infuriating little smile remained firmly in place.

"Of course he's alive. Why wouldn't he be alive?"

"Because Madra...Madra swore she was going to find him and kill him. She said she was going to destroy the ward."

He frowned. "And why in all four winds would she do *that?*"

"You know why! Because I took that cursed gauntlet!"

"Ah, yes, that's right." He pushed away from the wall, blue eyes dancing with amusement. "The gauntlet. The one I advised you to take out of the Third, before our people started getting hurt? *That* gauntlet?"

I was going to hurt *him*. Badly. "Enough, Carrion. I know I fucked up, all right. I feel terrible enough as it is. Just tell me what happened. Is Hayden really still alive?"

"Yes, yes, he's still alive. Gods, you never were one for patience." He rolled his eyes. "Hayden's in the Seventh. I got him papers and shifted him that first night when you were taken up to the palace. He's now gainfully employed as a store clerk. It isn't glamorous work, but it's better than having no job at all. He has triple water rations and a room above the shop. I haven't visited for a couple of days. I didn't want to draw too much attention, him being a new face and all, but he's comfortable. I can't say that he's happy. He's brainstorming all sorts of ways to break you out of the palace, but—"

"Stop! Stop, stop, stop. Just...wait." I covered my face with my hands.

"Shit. Are you *crying?* I figured you'd be happy."

Hayden was alive.

Hayden was *alive.*

He was safe.

He was in the Seventh. He had a job, and a roof over his head, and food and water, too? My whole body trembled with relief. I dropped my hands to my sides, pulling myself together, trying to think pragmatically. "Madra just hasn't found him yet." I sniffed, clearing my throat.

"Madra isn't looking for him."

"But the guardians..."

"Are all prepared for the Evenlight. It's in a month. The whole city's been buzzing with talk of what gift she'll bestow on us this year. She has the guardians building a stage in the center of the market square."

"You're sure it's not new gallows?" I asked suspiciously.

"Definitely not gallows. There are flowers all over it."

"Flowers?"

"Yes, flowers."

"Tell me everything that happened after the guardians took me up to the palace," I demanded. There had to be something. Some kind of awful act of violence that shook the foundations of our ward. Madra was a lot of things and benevolent wasn't one of them. But Carrion just let out a dry laugh.

"Everything's fine. Elroy's been a real pain in the ass, of course. He goes up to the gates every day and demands to see you, but they keep turning him away. He comes back down to the forge and gets to work, grumbling about the mess you've left him in. Hayden is dealing with a guilty conscience about as best as he can. He blames himself for you being taken. Other than that, the Third continues as it always has without you. Imagine *that.* The world, audacious enough to carry on without Saeris Fane."

"I'm serious, Carrion. You didn't hear her. She swore that everyone in the Third would *die.*"

"And yet no one has," he said, shrugging. "Now, I think I've been pretty patient while we've rehashed all of this gauntlet bullshit. I think it's my turn to have a few things explained to me. Principally, where the fuck are we, why are we here, were the people who came in here about half an hour ago and laid their hands all over you really *Fae,* or did I hallucinate that part, and lastly..." He pointed at his foot. "Where the fuck is my other boot?"

"Someone came in here and *touched* me?"

Carrion threw his head back, groaning. "All of those questions and you respond by asking one of your own. Gods. Yes, they came and touched your hands a bunch. They said they were healing you."

Sure enough, when I looked down at my hands, the bite Onyx gave me when he was scared was gone, as was the little welt from the faerie. The burn mark from Nimerelle was still there, but only just. The skin on my palm was tender to the touch, but it was pink again and didn't look like it was going to burst open and start weeping pus anymore.

Kingfisher. He'd sent healers. He was really serious about making sure I didn't develop a fever. But he would be, wouldn't he? I was nothing more than a tool to him, and how would he use me if I was dead?

For the first time since waking, I took stock of the situation. Hayden was alive and doing okay. So was Elroy. For the time being, at least. But now I was stuck in the Yvelian borderlands, in the middle of a war between battling factions of immortals, and Carrion Swift was prodding me for an explanation as to why.

I explained everything I knew, moving around the room and inspecting our surroundings. The room was windowless, which was my first disappointment. No way to assess the landscape around us, and no way to climb to freedom, either. The bedroom—because it was a bedroom—was twice the size of my room back at the Winter Palace. There were four large double beds, two on either side of the space, made up with thick, beautiful covers in bright blues and greens, each of them adorned with mounds of pillows and cushions. A plush rug covered the majority of the stone floor. Woven tapestries hung from the walls. A large fireplace roared at the far end of the room, next to which a wide table was loaded with bowls of fruits, bread, smoked meats, and cheeses, not to mention four copper ewers of water and two separate wash basins.

None of it had been touched.

From the look of the rumpled sheets and the disturbed pillows,

Carrion must have slept in the bed closest to the table, which meant the food would have been one of the first things he saw when he woke up, but he hadn't even poured himself a glass of water.

He stood with his arms folded over his chest, his brow furrowed, head angled to one side while he listened to me, taking in the details of everything that had happened to me without the slightest indication that he believed what I was saying. When I was done, he blew out his cheeks and sat himself down heavily in one of the chairs by the fire, running his hands through his hair.

"So you kissed that guy, then. The one with the creepy sword and the bad attitude?"

I stared at him blankly, not understanding the question for a moment. At last, I said, "What does that have to do with anything?"

Carrion shook his head. "You're right. Ignore me. So, you have the ability to awaken this quicksilver. The pool that your new boyfriend dragged me into—"

"He is *not* my boyfriend."

"—and no one else has been able to do that for a thousand years. And now you've made some kind of unbreakable promise to a malevolent legendary Fae warrior who might be completely insane. You don't know what he wants from you—"

"He wants me to make relics for him. So that more members of the Fae can travel without losing their minds."

"But how are you going to do that?"

"She's about to find out."

Instinctively, I reached for the dagger that should have been at my thigh, but I closed my hand around thin air. Kingfisher stood in the doorway, hand resting casually on Nimerelle's pommel. His brows banked together, forming a knot above his flashing green eyes. A heavy cloud always seemed to follow him around, but there was something extra dark and stormy about Kingfisher today. He wore no armor over his black shirt and pants, but the silver gorget covered his throat as always.

Carrion bristled when Fisher entered the room, angling his body between me and the dark-haired warrior, which elicited an amused smile out of Kingfisher as he glanced around.

"Just so that you're fully equipped with *all* of the facts," he said in a smooth tone. "I'm only *half* insane. And yes, your friend is bound to me. Did she tell you that she's the only reason you're still alive yet?" Fisher picked up an apple from the bowl on the table, turning it over in his hand. "I wanted to leave you back at the Winter Palace, but she was adamant that you come along with us for the ride."

Carrion gave me a saccharine smile. "And there was me thinking you weren't infatuated with me anymore. I have to say, I would have preferred to stay in Zilvaren, though. I was about to close a spectacular deal that would have made me a very rich man."

Kingfisher stilled, his fingertips curling tighter around Nimerelle's hilt. His eyes darted from Carrion to me and back again; then he looked off toward the other side of the room, seemingly at nothing. Slowly, he set the apple back down in the bowl. "I need you to come with me, human," he said.

"Wonderful. Another day of being forced to do whatever you want me to. Lucky me."

He looked at me solemnly. "I'm not going to force you to do anything."

"Oh?" I couldn't keep the mocking edge from my voice. "So if I decide to stay right here and tell you to go fuck yourself, you aren't going to react badly and *command* me to go with you?"

"I'd be a little annoyed that you'd told me to go fuck myself," he said. "But now that we're here, the urgent list of things I have to attend to is breathtaking. Asking you to discover the depths of your abilities and apply them in order to save countless lives, so you can, in turn, both return home to your dusty city, ranks lower on that list than you might think."

Carrion held up a hand. "When he puts it like that, I vote you go and help him figure out the relic issue."

I grabbed his wrist and yanked his hand down. "*You* don't get a vote. And *you*," I said, wheeling on Fisher. "You've tricked me into getting your way once already. I'm not going to do what you want me to just because you've made a vague implication that you'll let us go back to Zilvaren once I'm done making relics for you."

Fisher smiled, all teeth. The silver in his eye flashed like a blade. "I wouldn't need to trick you into doing anything for me. As you've already established, I could just make you do what I'm asking of you."

"Then why don't you?"

"Because my brother is sore with me," he admitted. "And because this will go a whole lot smoother if you agree to help my people willingly."

So he was giving me back my autonomy to appease Ren. Unsurprising. It came as no shock that Fisher didn't appreciate my grousing, either. Well, he was in for an unpleasant surprise. He was about to discover that I could help him willingly and still give him plenty of shit at the same time. "I'll come with you, then. On one condition."

Fisher's mask of indifference faltered, allowing a flicker of annoyance to peek through. "Which is?"

"That you make this promise to me exactly. Verbatim. Word for word. I swear I will release you and allow you and Carrion to return to Zilvaren the moment you have made enough relics for my people."

Kingfisher's mouth ticked imperceptibly. "As you wish. Word for word. I swear I will release you and allow you and Carrion to return to Zilvaren the moment you have made enough relics for my people. There. Are you happy?"

"Are you *bound* by that promise?" I asked.

Fisher lowered his head in a mock bow. "I am."

"All right. Then I'm happy. Let's go."

"Leave the fox. He'll only be underfoot."

I started to protest, but Onyx had fallen asleep amongst the cushions on one of the beds that hadn't been slept in, and he looked too peaceful to wake, anyway.

"And what about me?" Carrion demanded. "You're just going to keep me locked away in here forever?"

Fisher snorted. "You haven't been locked in here at all."

I glared at him over my shoulder. "You didn't check the door?"

"I just assumed..."

"Urgh!"

Kingfisher spun and strolled purposefully out of the room. "You're free to come and go as you wish, boy. Do whatever the hell you like. Though, I doubt you're gonna get very far with only one boot."

17

CAHLISH

"WHAT *IS* THIS PLACE?"

I'd been picturing Cahlish as a war encampment. A sea of tents pitched amongst the snow. Campfires sending pillars of smoke up into the sky for as far as the eye could see. It was nothing of the sort. This place was a stately home. Beautiful. Beyond the bedroom Carrion and I had woken up in was a sprawling house full of open-arched windows, light, airy hallways, and pretty rooms that went on forever. Portraits hung on the walls featuring dark-haired males and females, many of whom bore a striking resemblance to Fisher. The furniture was lovely, the overstuffed chairs and sofas sagging in a relaxed way that suggested that this place had been lived in. Loved in. Birds sang outside. The sun shone, bouncing off the thick mantle of snow that covered the grounds of the estate, so bright that it looked as though the grounds were studded with a million diamonds.

"My great-great-grandfather built it a long time ago," Fisher answered in a brusque tone. The heels of his boots rang out as he marched down the hallway. "It was my home before Belikon commanded my mother to the Winter Palace to marry him."

When Everlayne had told me how her mother had come to be at the Winter Palace, I hadn't spent much time considering what her life would have been like before that time. Nor had I considered what it must have been like for Fisher. How old had he been when he'd traveled to Belikon's seat of power? Just ten years old? Eleven? I couldn't remember. The differences between Cahlish and the Winter Palace were stark. He must have hated leaving this place.

A peaceful quiet hung in the air here. It felt safe. Calm. The rooms and hallways were all abandoned. It wasn't until we descended a curved staircase, the stone steps worn smooth and dipping in the middle from so many feet, that we encountered another living thing: a small creature, only three feet tall, with a round, protruding stomach, glassy amber eyes, and the strangest skin. It looked as if it were formed out of the last dying embers of a fire—rough and charcoal-like, with tiny fissures that ran all over its body, the edges of which glowed, flared, and faded, as if a flame might kindle there at any moment.

The creature carried a silver tray bearing a steaming pot and two cups. When the creature saw Fisher, it yelped and dropped the tray, sending the pot and cups crashing to the ground. "Oh! Oh no. Oh no, oh no, *oh no!*" The creature's voice was high-pitched, though decidedly male. He wore no clothes to speak of, but that didn't matter. He didn't appear to have any body parts that required covering. Eyes wide as could be, he staggered back from the mess he'd made—the shattered porcelain at his little smoking feet didn't seem to be the source of his panic.

Kingfisher stunned me to silence when he dropped to his knees and started picking up the shards of broken cup. "It's all right, Archer. Hush, it's all right."

Archer's mouth hung open. His gaze met mine, and I was amazed to find that there was a tiny ring of flickering fire surrounding his jet-black pupils. He pointed at Fisher. "You *see* him?" he squeaked.

I eyed Fisher. "Unfortunately, yes."

"He's…" Archer gulped. "He's really here?"

Kingfisher stopped what he was doing, his head hanging, and for a second, I found myself transfixed by what I saw. The gorget only protected his throat. The back of his neck was exposed, the ends of his dark waves not long enough to cover it. His skin was pale apart from a single, stark black rune visible between the base of his skull and his shirt collar. It was complex, all interlocking fine lines, loops, and curls. Most of the runes I'd seen on the Fae had been ugly-looking things, but this…

Kingfisher looked up at Archer. The rune disappeared. "Stop fretting, Arch. You're not hallucinating. I returned home late last night."

Archer threw back his small head and wailed. He trampled right over the broken tea service in order to get to Fisher. Throwing his thin, fiery arms around Kingfisher's neck, he sobbed hysterically. "You're here. You're *here!*"

"Whoa. Steady now." I waited for Fisher to shove the little creature away, but he wrapped his arms around him instead, hugging him close. "You'll make everyone think we're being attacked."

Archer leaned back, pressing small hands to Fisher's face, patting him everywhere, as if to make sure he really *was* real, leaving black smudges all over Fisher's cheeks and forehead. "I *missed* you. So, so much. I wished, and I hoped, and I—" Archer hiccupped. "I wished, and I hoped. *Every* day."

"I know. I missed you too, my friend."

"Oh no, oh *no!*" Archer leaped back, patting frantically at Fisher's chest. "Your shirt, Lord. I've singed your shirt!"

Kingfisher chuckled softly. There was no hint of malice in the laughter. No mockery or cold, cruel edge. He just…laughed. "It's easily fixed. Stop fretting. Here." Suddenly, Fisher's shirt was no longer fabric. It was smoke. It writhed around Fisher's torso for a moment, then became a shirt again, un-singed and perfect. More smoke pooled around Fisher's boots, rolling across the floor, concealing the broken pot and cups. When it dissipated, the pot and cups were whole again, sitting back on the silver serving tray. "See? Good as new," Fisher said.

"You're too kind, Lord. Too kind. But *you* shouldn't need to fix my mistakes. I should be more careful. And—"

"Archer, please. All's well. Go on now, quickly. I'll come and find you before dinner. I want to hear everything that's been happening around here while I've been gone."

Archer's eyes were wet. It seemed impossible that anyone would cry tears of happiness over Kingfisher; if I wasn't witnessing it for myself, I'd never have believed it, but it was happening all right. Every time a tear fell and hit Archer's cheeks, it hissed and turned into a puff of steam. "Yes, my lord. Of course. It would be my pleasure."

I watched Archer go, perplexed. Kingfisher set off walking again, saying nothing. I jogged after him to catch up. "What kind of faerie was *he?*"

"Not a faerie. A fire sprite."

"Okay. And why did he seem to like *you* so much?"

Fisher didn't even dignify that with a response. "There are a lot of fire sprites here. Water sprites. Air sprites. Not so many earth sprites. You might want to spend some time learning the names of all of the lesser Fae creatures. Eventually, you'll offend the wrong person if you go around calling everyone faeries." As he spoke, we passed a nook in the wall, where seven marble busts were mounted on stands, one of which was facing the wall. Kingfisher flipped off the gods as he passed them, not even breaking his stride.

I let out a frustrated huff. "Look, I won't be here long enough to learn the names of every type of creature in Yvelia. You'll find I'm highly motivated to make these relics and get the hell out of here."

"Mm, of course. You're *so* eager to get back to that awful city." Kingfisher turned a corner and then halted abruptly, opening a door to his left. "Back to all that oppression and starvation. I can really see the appeal."

"Out of everyone, you should understand why I want to go back the most. You're desperate to do everything you can to help your friends here. I have friends and family who need help, too. They're too tired to fight Madra on their own. They've given up. If I don't go home, who'll help *them?*"

I was hit with a wave of his scent, all cold dawn morning and the promise of snow, and my breath caught in my throat. I ignored the reaction, forcing myself to think about everyone suffering in the Third instead. It was hard to focus on that when he was standing so close. The tips of his ears jutted out from the waves of his hair, the tiniest flash of his pointed canines showing between his parted lips. His crooked, taunting smile made me want to forget all about my ward. It made me want to remember crawling into his lap, and when his strong hands had found my waist, and—

No.

I wasn't going to lose myself to that. Not after what he'd done to me last night, forcing me to obey his will.

"I haven't found myself in this position voluntarily. I wouldn't *choose* to be here if I didn't have to be. The task is my birthright. It became mine the moment I drew my first breath. You're just one of hundreds of thousands of people who live in your city. Why shoulder the responsibility of saving them when they refuse to save themselves?"

He already knew the answer to his question. He wasn't stupid. I said it out loud for him anyway, because he clearly needed to hear it. *"Because it's the right thing to do, Fisher."*

He said nothing. Just looked me up and down in a way that made me feel small and silly. "After you, Little Osha."

This forge was nothing like the one back at the Winter Palace. It was huge and packed with so much equipment that I didn't even know where to look first. The hearth was large enough that I could have stood up in it if I'd wanted to—a bad idea, given the powerful fire that was already raging in it. Along one side of the wall were rows and rows of crucibles of all shapes and sizes. Beakers, stirring rods, and flasks sat on shelves. Mortars and pestles, and large glass vials containing powders, dried herbs, flowers, and all manner of different liquids.

Along the other side, the forge was completely open to the outside, giving way to a small snow-filled, walled garden with a bench and a tall tree naked of leaves at its center. Beyond the high brick wall, I made out the tops of more trees—evergreen pine this time—and the rocky, sloping foothills of a majestic mountain range not that far in the distance.

"They're beautiful," I said before I could stop myself. "The mountains. I've seen pictures of them in books before, but I never knew they could be so…majestic."

Fisher stared at the mountains in the distance, a complicated look on his face. "Omnamerrin. That's the name of the tallest peak. The one with the sheer face. It means 'sleeping giant' in Old Fae."

"Do people try and climb it?"

"Only if they want to die," Fisher answered.

Wait. I glanced over my shoulder, trying to make sense of what I was seeing.

"Why are you frowning like that?" Fisher asked.

"Because…" I looked back to the door behind me and the warm, cozy hallway on the other side of it. "The dimensions are all wrong. We were on the third floor just now. And the other rooms we passed were much smaller. This forge is on the ground floor, and the roof's too high, and…"

"Magic." Kingfisher shrugged. He paced over to a bench and began the now familiar process of unfastening the sword from his waist. "The doorway is enchanted. Bound to the entrance of the forge, which is located outside of the house. Much safer than having highly explosive compounds and chemicals inside the house itself.

When we walk through the doorway in the house, it transports us here. Simple."

Simple? It *was* simple. Which made me want to scream. I was going to throttle him. "If you can do this, then why the *hell* didn't you just bind some doorways back at the tavern instead of making me go through that shadow gate?"

"Because I can't do this," Fisher replied, setting Nimerelle down on the bench. "This is Ren's work. I don't possess the same gift."

"Then *Ren* could have—"

"It only works over short distances, human, so take a breath. *I* couldn't have. *Ren* couldn't have. We needed to travel eight hundred leagues, and a shadow gate was the only way to do it."

"Fine," I grumbled. "But, if you knew that was how we were going to get here, why not just call the gate inside the Winter Palace? Why make me ride a horse through that terrifying wood all night?"

He gave me a teasing sidelong glance. "I thought you weren't scared of the wood?"

"I wasn't! Just...answer the question."

Kingfisher placed his elbows on the bench, leaning toward me, his hair obscuring half his face. "Because, Little Osha, the shadow gate uses a lot of magic. We Fae are sensitive to such things. If Belikon had sensed me drawing that much magic to the catacombs under his palace, he would have transported himself there before we could have blinked, let alone traveled. That tavern is fifty leagues from the Winter Palace, which, coincidentally, is the exact distance required to perform heavy-hitting magic without alerting someone you want to keep in the dark. So. Do you have any more annoying questions?"

"I do, actually. Why can't you just use the shadow gates to go between here and the other realms? You don't need relics for the shadow gates. They don't make you crazy, apparently. So why even bother with the quicksilver?"

"Martyrs, have mercy," Fisher muttered. He spoke as if he were explaining the most rudimentary, obvious information to a five-year-old. "Shadow gates are of this realm. They can only be used within this realm. Quicksilver is not of this realm. Therefore, it can be used within this realm, but also within or to other realms as well. No, no more fucking questions. We have work to do."

And that was that. He crossed the forge to where a huge wooden trunk sat by one of the largest crucibles, grabbed it by the handle, and dragged it over to the bench. He didn't break a sweat, even though the godscursed thing looked like it weighed more than Bill and Aida combined. My eyes nearly popped out of my head when he threw back the lid.

A mountain of silver rings sat inside, different shapes and sizes. Some of them were marked with an egis or a family crest. Some of them bore diamonds, or rubies, or sapphires. Some of them were delicate and elegant. A lot of them were chunky, with heavy, engraved bands. I'd never seen so much precious metal in one place at one time. "Well. It's a good thing Carrion isn't here. He'd have stolen eight of these already and neither of us would have noticed."

"I think we've already established that *I* notice when someone tries to steal my belongings."

Holy fucking gods, he was never going to let go of that. I shot him a baleful glare as I stooped down and picked up one of the rings. It was very feminine, with roses engraved on either side of a beautiful aquamarine stone. "There must be a thousand of them," I said breathlessly.

"Eighteen hundred," Kingfisher said. "And that's just in this trunk. There are eight more trunks on the other side of that bench over there."

Sure enough, I looked in the direction that he was pointing and saw at least two more wooden trunks shoved up against the wall. The others must have been hidden out of sight.

I tossed the ring back into the trunk. "Are we forging swords out of them?" Silver was too malleable to forge weapons out of back in Zilvaren, but maybe the Fae blacksmiths had figured out firing techniques to make it stronger. Perhaps they infused it with magic. Perhaps...

My mind ground to a halt, my line of logic dying a miserable death when I realized that Kingfisher was smirking at me again. That smirking meant nothing good.

"Anyone can use any old relic in a pinch, but relics are most powerful when they're forged from something important to its owner. These are the family rings of the warriors who fight for me. Each one has great meaning to the male or female it belongs to. You are going to take each and every one of these rings, and you're going to turn them into relics."

"Fisher, *no!* There are nearly..." I was good with numbers, but I was too stunned to think straight, let alone perform multiplications. I got there in the end. "There are nearly fifteen *thousand* rings here! Do you have any idea how long it would take to melt down each of these rings and cast it into another one?"

"Years, I'm sure. But don't worry. We're not looking for a pretty piece of jewelry. You'll melt down the ring, transmute its properties so that it will shield the wearer against the quicksilver, then cast it into something simple like this." He hooked his finger around his chain and drew out the pendant he wore around his own neck. "If there's a stone or some kind of engraving on the ring, you'll find a way to incorporate that into the medallion you make. Other than that, it should be pretty straightforward."

"Straightforward?" My vision had gone hazy. He couldn't be fucking serious. "I said I'd help you make...enough relics..." I trailed off, a sinking feeling of dread crushing my chest. I'd done it again. I hadn't paid attention to the details, had I? And it was even worse this time because I thought I'd done a good job.

"I swear I will release you and allow you and Carrion to return to Zilvaren the moment you have made enough relics for my people. Was that not the promise you had me make?"

"Yes, but..."

"I have fifteen thousand warriors, Little Osha. To have enough relics for my people, I need fifteen thousand relics. When you're done with all of these rings, I'll release you from your oath and take you to the closest quicksilver pool so you can leave. Until then..." He eyed the trunk full of rings.

"But I don't even know *how* to turn these into relics yet! That alone could take weeks. It could take *months!*"

Not even a flicker of sympathy hid in Fisher's silver-mottled eyes. "Then you'd better get to work."

18

CRUCIBLE

KINGFISHER HAD books written by the Alchemists before they all died out. Stacks and stacks of them. They were centuries old, the parchment crumbling. A lot of them were written in Old Fae. I barely understood any of the text, which meant that they were next to useless. When I asked him how I was supposed to glean any useful information from them when none of his own kind had been successful in doing so, he muttered something about using my initiative and left the forge in a cloud of black smoke.

At midday, a plate of food arrived out of nowhere on the bench. Some kind of meat pie with the most delicious gravy filling, along with some chunks of cheese and an apple that had been cut into slices. I only noticed that Onyx arrived with the food when I heard him whining underneath the bench. He wore a hopeful look, his black eyes staring intently up at my plate, ready should the smallest morsel fall to the floor. I didn't know how healthy human, or rather *Fae* food, was for him, but the pastry was so buttery and crumbly, the filling so savory and good, that I couldn't help myself and I wound up sharing half the pie with him. He was content to run outside amongst the snow once we were done, chasing any birds that landed. I spent a good fifteen minutes laughing at him as he coiled back onto his hind legs, wriggled his fluffy butt, and then sprang into the air, bringing his front feet crashing down on the snow as he pounced. I stopped laughing when I realized that he was hunting, and more often than not, when he pounced like that, he came up from the loose snow with a small rodent in his mouth. At least he was entertained.

After I'd wasted another hour poring over the books and getting nowhere, I decided to say screw it and focus on more practical matters. My first thought was to melt down one of the rings and just start experimenting, but then it occurred to me that if I wasn't successful (and I probably wasn't going to be), I'd have ruined one of Fisher's warrior's rings, and that wouldn't go down well at all. I found some scrap metal in a bucket by one of the benches and settled on using that for some trial-and-error experiments instead.

The first problem I ran into was that I literally had *no* idea where to start. By holding a piece of the twisted scraps and concentrating, I could feel what kind of metal it was by the vibrations it gave off. When I first noticed those vibrations back in Zilvaren, they had scared the shit out of me so badly that I'd trained myself to ignore them. Now I used that alien sensation to differentiate between plated metals, silver, and a whole slew of different variants of iron that we didn't have back home. They each had their own frequencies.

It didn't take long to isolate the frequency for Yvelian silver. I simply held a bunch of the rings and closed my eyes, learning what that energy felt like when it traveled up my arms, and I committed it to memory. Then I went through the bucket and separated out any scraps that shared that same frequency. I had a respectable amount of the shining metal ready to melt down after only half an hour.

For my first attempt, I melted down about a ring's worth of silver and poured it into a crucible. From there, I added a variety of different ingredients from the glass mason jars on the shelves to the molten silver with no sense that I was *accomplishing* anything. Most of it just burned up the moment it hit the metal's scalding hot surface. The salt seemed to combine well, though. I let the silver cool and hammered it out into a flat surface, and then went looking for the quicksilver to somehow test the rough medallion I'd created.

But there was no quicksilver. None that I could find in any of the jars or crucibles. How the hell did Fisher expect me to unravel this problem for him if he wasn't going to trust me with any of the quicksilver? Did he think I was going to try and escape with it, for fuck's sake? I'd learned my lesson after the last time. I didn't have a relic of my own yet...

Here.

Here.

I'm here...

Just one whisper. So small.

When I'd heard the quicksilver back at the palace, the sound had been a chorus of whispers. But this was subtle. Quiet. I had to close my eyes and focus all of my attention just to hear it. It was inside the forge, though. And close. I walked around the bench I'd been working at until I felt the gentlest of tugs, so weak it was barely even there, and then I moved toward it.

A silver box sat on a shelf above a small basin, tucked into the corner by the wall. A leafy potted plant hid it from view. I took it back to the bench and prized the lid open, laughing when I saw just how little quicksilver was inside it. It was solid, naturally, but in its liquid state, it would only be a couple of tablespoons' worth at best. This was what he'd left me to work with? I huffed, plucking the metal out of the box with a pair of tongs, and then placed it at the bottom of the smallest crucible I could find.

It was getting easier, changing the quicksilver from its solid to liquid state. A hand reaching out into the dark. A finger flicking a switch. There was so little of it this time that I hardly had to will it at all. One moment, it was a lump of scuffed metal, and the next, it was a puddle of shining silver rolling around the bottom of the cast-iron bowl. I dropped the medallion into the crucible, grimacing when I noted that there was barely enough quicksilver to sub-merge it.

And nothing happened.

I waited.

Still nothing.

Here. Here. I'm here, the quicksilver whispered in its singular voice. *Alone. Alone. Come to me. Find me. Be with me.*

The medallion changed nothing.

I tried a second time, adding what looked like sand and some salt water to the molten silver this time. Again, nothing happened. My third attempt, I tried to combine a dull red powder from one of the jars into the silver, but it burst into flames before it even reached the rippling surface, producing a cloud of noxious red smoke that made my face prickle and go numb. Onyx wouldn't come back into the forge after that, so I sat with him out on the bench in the cold afternoon light, stroking his fur, shivering as flakes of snow dusted my pants.

My fourth and final attempt of the day—adding a pinch of char-coal and a sprig of an herb labeled *Widow's Bane*—rendered no results again, by which time I'd officially had enough. I whistled for Onyx to come—he begrudgingly did—and stomped out of the forge, leaving the mess I'd made with my failed attempts behind.

Back in the hallways of Cahlish, Onyx chittered animatedly, darting between my ankles, tongue lolling as he jumped up my legs. Apparently, he was very happy to be away from the forge. I hadn't paid a whole lot of attention this morning when Fisher escorted me to the forge, but I was fairly adept at finding my way in new places. It might take a while, but I'd find my way back to the room I'd woken up in eventually.

It didn't come to that, though. I'd only taken a couple of steps from the door when Ren appeared around the corner up ahead, dressed in a dark red shirt and faded brown leather pants. He was covered in mud, and there was a long gash across his cheek, which was leaking blood. His hair seemed to be wet with sweat, and the dark shadows under his eyes made him look exhausted. He scrounged up a smile when he saw me, though, wiping his filthy hands on the towel he was carrying as he approached.

"Thought I'd come and check in on you," he said, grinning. "I heard you've been assigned quite the task."

"An impossible task." I scowled darkly. "I only made four attempts, but I'm exhausted. What happened to *you?*"

"Oh, y'know, just a couple of skirmishes up on the pass. When the clouds are so heavy with snow and the days are so dark like this, it's a safe bet that there'll be an attack. We were outnumbered, but we didn't lose anyone. Took down thirty or so of the enemy."

"Congratulations?" It felt weird to congratulate anyone on killing so many people, even if they *were* enemies of the Yvelian Fae.

Ren noticed the uncertain rise in my voice and laughed quietly under his breath. "Thank you. Believe me, killing thirty of them has already saved a couple of hundred innocent lives. If they'd gotten through the pass, they would have wrought havoc on our side of the border. It wouldn't have been pretty."

"I'll have to trust your word on that," I told him.

Ren rubbed the towel against his dirty fingers, his eyes resting steadily on me. "Would you? Trust my word? If I told you something?"

Onyx jumped up Ren's legs, turning in circles. The general dipped to scratch his head distractedly—his focus was all for me.

"I don't know," I said. "I s'pose that would depend."

He sighed. "That's fair. Well, I'm about to tell you that I gave Fisher hell this afternoon for that oath he made you swear. And I told him the only way he could make it up to me would be to start getting to know you a little better."

I fought the instinct to take a step back. "Why would you do *that?*"

"Fisher's very single-minded sometimes. There's no gray. Only black and white. I fear that part of him has only gotten worse while he's been away. He has to keep things very straight in his mind, otherwise lines get blurred. Right now, you're a tool he feels he has to use to make life better for us all. My concern is that a tool pushed to its limit is a tool that will probably break. And to be blunt, Saeris, you're a tool none of us can afford to let Fisher break. He needs to see you as a person. He needs to know that you're more than our way out of a tight corner. And the only way to accomplish *that* is if he learns more about you."

Why didn't I like the sound of this? "Okaaaay."

"I told him he needed to have dinner with you tonight."

"Oh."

"And I think he agreed."

"You *think* he did?"

He grinned sheepishly. "You've met him. It can be tough to tell what he's agreeing to sometimes."

"He's the slipperiest bastard alive," I grumbled.

"Right. But...please. Just go. Have dinner with him. Tell him about yourself. It'll be over quickly, I swear."

If *it'll be over quickly, I swear* had to be said in order to convince me to attend an event, it was not an event I wanted to go to. I couldn't imagine anything less fun than having dinner with Fisher. But Ren was looking at me so pleadingly. He genuinely, sincerely wanted me to go. And what else was I going to do? Hang out with Carrion back in our *shared* room? On second thoughts, maybe dinner with Fisher would be less painful than that.

"All right. I'll go. But only because you asked. And only if you swear there'll be alcohol."

The dining table was a league long.

All right, all right, it was maybe only thirty feet long, but still far too big for two people to sit at and share a meal. *Alone.* Fisher sat at one end.

I sat at the other. In between us, a mountain of food had been delivered by an army of fire sprites led by Archer. A massive floral centerpiece with purple and pink blooms sat in the dead center of the table, and it was beautiful, it really was, but I couldn't even *see* Fisher around it.

Maybe that was the point.

Carrion had been gone when I got back to the room, which was a blessing since I still wanted to bathe and wash away the sweat from the forge. I hadn't even bothered to look at the dress that had magically appeared at the end of my bed while I was in the tub. All I knew was that it was black. I'd found a clean pair of pants and a fresh shirt in one of the drawers that were my size (obviously meant for me), and so I'd worn those instead.

I was comfortable enough in the pants, but I got the feeling from Archer's sidelong glances that I was underdressed to have dinner with his master, and he disapproved of the fact. Stabbing a piece of fish with my fork, I grabbed the empty wineglass that sat to the right of my plate and held it up. "I don't suppose I could get something poured into this?" I called down the table.

I saw a flick of Fisher's wavy hair around the flowers and not much else. When he spoke, he sounded close, as if he were standing right behind me, not at the other end of the table. "Tell me how you fared today, and I'll consider it."

The proximity of his voice and the way he spoke felt…intimate. As though his lips were so close to my ear that his breath should have stirred my hair. "How are you doing that?" I whispered.

"Magic runs through this place the same way your blood runs through your veins. It lives in the very air. The things you've already seen here are surely enough to suspend your disbelief…and yet you're shocked by something so small as me casting my voice?" Amusement dripped from every word. I had no retort for him, though. I had seen so many remarkable things. In comparison, this wasn't that impressive. It was the way it made me *feel,* having his voice so close, that had me on the back foot.

I cleared my throat. "As you might expect, I fared very badly. I made four attempts, all of which resulted in failure. I wasted nearly all of the scrap metal I found. I'll need more if I'm going to be able to run more trials tomorrow."

"Can it be refined? The silver you used today?" he asked.

"Yes, but that'll take even longer. I'll waste a day between experiments..." I huffed. "But let me guess. You don't care about me wasting a day to purify between experiments, do you?"

"I do not," he confirmed.

"Y'know..." I dropped my fork; it hit my plate with a clatter. "You just love contradicting yourself. One minute, you're kidnapping me because it's urgent that I make these relics for you. And then, the next, you're throwing up obstacles and doing everything you can to make the process as difficult and as time-consuming as can be. You really need to make up your mind. What's more important? The relics for your people, or whatever sick pleasure you seem to derive from keeping me at your beck and call?"

From down the other end of the table, I heard the scrape of a knife against a plate. At least he wasn't letting my annoyance ruin his dinner. *Asshole.* "I assure you, our need for those relics far outweighs how fun it is to mess with you. But I'm not refusing you more silver to toy with you. Resources are tight at Cahlish. The regular silver can't be spared."

"What are you talking about? This place is dripping in finery. There's gold—" I glanced around, gesturing to the wall sconces that held the candles lighting our dinner, and the serving platters on the sideboard, and the picture frames. Even the cutlery on the table. "There's gold literally everywhere. Half the knickknacks in this place are plated in it, and you're telling me resources are *tight?*"

"If it were gold you needed for your trials, we wouldn't be having this conversation." I saw the bottom of Fisher's wineglass around the side of the cursed flower arrangement and my temper spiked.

Ducking to one side, I peered around the centerpiece and scowled as I watched him sip from his glass.

"If *you* have wine, *I* should have wine," I growled.

"Oh, is that what you think?"

My skin broke out into goose bumps, the tiny hairs on the back of my neck standing erect. His voice was even closer this time. His words felt like a caress against the skin of my neck. I did my damnedest to shake off the shiver that chased up my spine. "Ren promised me—"

"Renfis knows better than to make promises on my behalf. But... if you're so desperate for a drink, feel free to come and pour yourself some."

Had he poured his own wine? I doubted that very much. Archer had probably done it. But I wasn't some stuck-up High-Born asshole like he was. I had no problems pouring my own wine. I got up, grabbed my glass, and was about to storm down the other end of the table but then I paused and grabbed my plate and my fork while I was at it. Whatever game this was, seating me so far away from him, blocking our view of one another, then using magic to speak into my ear like he was whispering sweet nothings to me? Yeah, I wasn't playing.

The corners of Fisher's mouth twitched when I slammed down my plate and fork on the table to his right. I dared him to breathe a word about it as I sat down next to him. He ran his fingertips over the rim of his wineglass, shifting in his seat to turn toward me as he watched me pour myself an obnoxiously large glass of wine from the carafe he was hoarding.

The wine was dark as ink. I took a defiant swig, my eyes locked with his over the rim of my glass.

Kingfisher pointed loosely at my glass when I set it down. "Do you like it?" He spoke to me normally. No magic this time.

"Yes. It's...it's interesting."

He pouted, nodding to himself. Something told me he was desperately trying not to smile. "Please. Help yourself to more. I don't have to speak to the men for a couple of hours. I've got time to share the bottle."

I looked at him properly. Really took him in. There was something different about him. Something I couldn't put my finger on. Not at first. But then I realized what it was: his clothes. I had never seen Fisher in anything other than black, but tonight the shirt he wore was a hunter green. Very dark, but still green. It was simple, but the material was fine and tailored perfectly. The way it hung from his frame emphasized how broad he was in the shoulders and how corded his arms were. The dark green color highlighted the raven's wing black of his thick hair. It threw his pale skin into contrast and... and...

Gods, get a grip *on yourself, Saeris Fane. Focus!*

I forced my gaze down to my half-eaten fish. "Why is silver in such short supply here if you have all this gold?"

"Because silver serves a very specific purpose here. We need as much of it as we can lay our hands on."

"Then why not sell all of the gold and buy some? Gold's worth more."

Fisher slowly shook his head, smiling as if to himself. Gods, why was it so hard to *look* at him sometimes? I'd never had this problem before. "Maybe where *you're* from," he said. He observed me, toying with his wineglass where it rested on the table, spinning it around lazily by the stem. With his lips parted, I could just make out the points of his teeth. It was rude to stare, but I couldn't help it. My heart missed a step whenever I saw his canines. As if he knew perfectly well what I was focused so intently on, Fisher opened his mouth a fraction wider, his top lip rising a little so that more of his teeth were on show. It was a subtle difference. Perhaps only a millimeter more of those sharp, white canines were visible, but heat exploded between my legs of all places, and suddenly...Gods, I needed another drink.

I buried my face in my wineglass. Fisher ran his tongue over his bottom lip, also looking away. The tendons in his neck stood proud, his jaw clenching ever so slightly as he frowned at something over by the window. "We can't buy more silver. The entire realm's been picked clean. Belikon has an embargo on it, too. Any silver found within Yvelian borders must be given to the crown. That's part of the reason why we need to use the quicksilver so badly. Other realms have an abundance of silver. We could trade for more than we need if we could just cross between realms."

"If Belikon has all of Yvelia's silver, then surely he'd give it to you? If it's so vital to win the war?"

Kingfisher snorted. "You'd think so, wouldn't you? But no. Belikon won't give us silver. He won't give us aid. He won't give us food, or clothes, or weapons. He doesn't give a fuck about this war."

"But that's just...It makes no sense." I took another deep pull of my wine. The unique taste bloomed into floral notes in my mouth. It tasted smooth, rich, and complex all at the same time. The flavor had surprised me at first, but it was really starting to grow on me.

Kingfisher watched me with steady eyes. The quicksilver lacing his right iris pulsed and caught at the candlelight, shifting and twisting amidst the green. It seemed to be extra active tonight. As if confirming this, Kingfisher's hand tightened around his wineglass. His shoulders tensed, his nostrils flaring momentarily, but then he exhaled, letting out a deep breath, and he loosened again. It all happened very quickly. I might not have noticed it at all had I looked away for a second.

Kingfisher's eyes bored into me. He knew I'd seen him flinch, and from the way he was staring at me, one of his eyebrows curving in question, he was waiting to see if I would ask him about it. I wanted to, but I already knew I'd find myself frustrated and angry if I did. He'd use my interest against me somehow. He'd find a way to be cruel—it was just in his nature—so I gave the topic a wide berth. I was about to ask him what experiments *he* had tried in order to make a relic, but then the crew of fire sprites bustled into the room, their charcoal-like bodies throwing up sparks and wisps of smoke as they approached the table. The two sprites at the head of the group were carrying large dishes full of food. Two different kinds of dessert, by the looks of things. They nearly dropped the dishes when they saw me sitting up at the head of the table next to Fisher.

"Lord!" one of them—a female—squawked. "My *lord!*" She spun in a circle, her mouth flapping open. The rest of the fire sprites registered that I'd dared to move next to their precious master and also proceeded to lose their minds.

"It's—"

"She's—"

"The human!"

"Lord King*fisher!"*

Archer was the last sprite to enter the dining room. The second he laid eyes on me, he slumped down on his backside, right where he was, sitting heavily on the plush rug, and started hyperventilating. "Forgive...me...Lord. I...wasn't...expecting..."

"It's all right, Archer. Everybody calm down." Fisher hadn't changed his position. He was still sprawled out in his chair in a very relaxed manner, but he'd shielded his mouth with his hand, trying to hide his smile. He looked down and coughed, appearing to pull himself together. "You can leave the plates for now. And the dessert. Just set it on the table, and you can all go. Thank you."

The fire sprites were all emitting black smoke. The cracks and crevices across their compact little bodies flashed and glowed like stirred embers. When one of his friends tried to help Archer up, a small flame formed on Archer's arm. He released a mortified shout, and all of the sprites started slapping at him, trying to put him out.

"Sorry, Lord! So sorry! I'm so *embarrassed!*" Archer wailed.

Kingfisher finally got up and went to the knot of panicking sprites. He ushered them out of the dining room, reassuring Archer the whole time, his laughter bouncing off the walls. He was still grinning when he sat back down in his seat.

"Martyrs. Did they think I was going to try and stab you with my fish fork?"

Fisher rubbed at the back of his neck, his smile fading. "Fire sprites are just very emotional. They love to overreact, that's all." By the time he was done speaking, his blank mask was back in full effect. "They'll have forgotten all about it by tomorrow."

"I'll be eating dinner in the forge tomorrow," I said. "They won't have to deal with a filthy, mannerless human breaching Cahlish etiquette."

"You'll be eating here," Fisher corrected.

"I don't get a say in the matter?"

"You'll poison yourself if you eat in the forge."

"In my room, then."

"You'll be eating *here*," Fisher repeated. He continued before I could suggest any of the other one million places I'd rather take my meals. "As for the fire sprites, they like humans. Far more than they like the Fae."

"Right. They treat you like you hung the moon."

"I'm different," he said, as if that were obvious. "Archer helped raise me. After my parents, he was the first of the lesser Fae to hold me. He has a soft spot for me, I suppose."

A soft spot? It was more than that. The fire sprite loved Fisher. Me, on the other hand? "He looks at me like I'm unworthy to breathe the same air as you."

Fisher's head rocked from side to side. "No, he doesn't. He's *interested* in you. He wonders if you'll be staying."

I picked up a roasted carrot from my plate with my fingers, biting the end off of it. "He'll be glad to hear that I'm not."

Not a word passed Fisher's lips. He sat as still as can be, watching me eat the carrot, his jade eyes picking over my features. Eyes first, then the bridge of my nose. Over my cheekbones and then down to my mouth. His gaze lingered there for longer than seemed proper. When he didn't look away, I said the first thing I could think of to break the silence. "You should send Carrion home, even if you refuse to let me go yet."

He looked surprised at this. "Should I?"

"He has family in Zilvaren. His grandmother. She'll be worried about him. And he can tell Hayden and Elroy that I'm okay if he goes back. That would probably stop them from doing anything regrettable for the time being."

"Mm. We'll see what the boy has to say for himself."

"He's twenty-six years old. He's hardly a boy," I muttered.

"He's an infant with a smart mouth, as far as I'm concerned. But… you're defensive of him," Fisher mused. "I suppose that's only to be expected. I'm honestly surprised that you would want him to leave." He took a sip of his wine.

"Defensive of him?"

An unfamiliar tension radiated from Fisher. He seemed to be working very hard at nonchalance. "Mm. I wouldn't have thought he was your type, but it explains a lot."

My *type?* A weightless, falling sensation made me sit back in the chair. I felt so dizzy all of a sudden. "What are you talking about?"

"He mentioned that you were infatuated with him. Back in your room."

"Well, he was lying!" I spluttered. "Carrion's a pain in the ass. He's known for making up stories on the spot."

"When I went to Zilvaren to fetch him—"

"When you went to Zilvaren, you were supposed to fetch *Hayden.*" My stomach stopped rolling, replaced by a prickle of anger. I set down my wine. "Which reminds me, you didn't hold up your end of our bargain. Not properly. How is it that I'm still expected to hold up my end of our oath, but you're free to walk away from it?"

It was so easy for him to dismiss me. One flick of his wrist and a roll of the eyes, and anything I said was rendered inconsequential. It was infuriating. "I'm not walking away from anything. I swore I would try to bring your brother back. I tried to bring your brother back," he said. "Oath fulfilled."

"You couldn't have tried very hard."

"I didn't say I would try *very hard*, did I? And anyway, you'll find that I did the best anyone could have, given the circumstances."

"You said you could find my brother because we had the same parents. That it'd be *easy* since you were covered in my blood."

Fisher paused. I'd spent enough time around him now to know when he was about to say something I wasn't going to like. The unholy delight in his eyes promised that I would *hate* whatever he was about to say next. "That's right. But I wasn't just covered in your blood, was I? I was wearing another of your...*perfumes.*"

Perfumes. He deliberated over the word. Luxuriated over it. The dark, suggestive way he said it left nothing to the imagination. He had no mercy, so there was little point in begging for it, but I had to try. "Don't. Do *not,* Fisher. Please. Just..."

"When you were grinding yourself all over my lap, you marked me up very efficiently," he purred.

A fire burned in my throat, causing my voice to crack. "I *hate* you."

"You keep saying that. I'm still not convinced that it's the truth. Either way, your brother wasn't where you said he'd be. And when I reached your ward, I detected your scent from three miles away—"

"Just stop talking, Fisher."

"—plastered all over that *boy.*" He gave me a cruel smirk. "Pheromones are signal flares to our noses, Little Osha. I was rushing, so I didn't differentiate between blood and sex at the time. But when I walked into that room earlier, and your friend Carrion mentioned your little obsession with him—"

"Shut. The fuck. Up."

"It became very clear what had happened. He still smells of you even now."

"I slept with him months ago. *Months.* It was once, and I was drunk, and he's never let me live it down since. There is no way you can still smell me on him."

"There's every way," Fisher rumbled, his eyes darkening. "I'd know the smell of you anywhere. On anyone. I'd know it blind and in the dark. Across a fucking sea. I'd be able to scent *you*—"

BOOM!

The windows along the eastern wall of the dining room blew in.

It happened quickly, and with staggering force.

One moment, I was staring at Kingfisher, watching his mouth in horror, withering a little more with each of his words. The next, a glittering explosion of glass was raining down on us. Shards the size of my hand cut through the air like daggers, striking the table, tearing through the flowers, slashing at my skin. I brought my hands up instinctively, protecting my face and head. *"Fuck!"*

Kingfisher became death.

His expression transformed to one of rage, his lips curling back, his canines extending. He was a flash of shadow, already on the other side of the table with Nimerelle in his hands before the dark shapes had finished dropping from the windows.

There were four of them—tall monsters with patchy, stringy hair and white, waxy skin. Gaunt cheeks spiderwebbed with black veins. Crooked fingers that terminated in claws. Red eyes. Not just the irises, but the whites, too, as if every capillary had burst and bled beneath the surface. Each of them bared a mouthful of elongated, yellowed fangs that dripped with ropes of viscous saliva. They wore clothes, but the garments were in tatters, barely clinging to their emaciated frames.

The largest of the four, a male with a thick black runic tattoo across his forehead, released an almighty roar of rage and launched himself at Fisher. Fisher moved like water. Nimerelle flashed around him, the tarnished black blade whipping through the air, trailing smoke. The sword was an extension of Fisher himself. For a moment, it was all I could do to sit and stare at him, watching in awe as he fell upon the monster. He was powerful and quick, his body twisting effortlessly when the monster tried to claw him. The hand that had swiped at Fisher fell to the floor with a dull thud, rolling under the table. Black, steaming ichor arced from the stump Nimerelle left behind, the pungent stench of sulfur flooding the dining room.

Fisher threw a glance back over his shoulder at me and shouted, *"MOVE!"*

The dining room came into sharp focus. I leaped to my feet, my blood hammering at my temples. Two of the sickly-looking creatures prowled toward me, their awful fangs snapping as they came.

I reached for and found the dagger strapped to my thigh, clutching it tightly, my eyes jumping from one of the monsters to the other. The one on the right, a woman with pale silver hair and torn lips, launched up onto the table, landing on all fours. She moved jerkily, her head tilting from side to side as she craned her neck toward me, sniffing the air like an animal. The one on the left was smaller than the woman. Somewhere between adult and child. He snarled, producing a hair-raising clicking sound from the back of his throat, knocking over Fisher's chair when he came for me, sending it crashing to the floor. His eyes were blank. *Both* of their eyes were. There was no intelligence there. No real thought. Only the desire to rip and tear and kill. Hatred radiated from them, polluting the air, thick enough to choke me.

The woman came first. She had no weapons, but she didn't need them. Her claws were weapons enough. She swung, raking her talons toward my chest. I darted back, barely avoiding their blackened, disgusting tips, but she was already coming again, lashing at me. I struck out with the dagger, slicing the blade at the same time, and the metal made contact, leaving a deep gash across her sinewy forearm. Reeking blood, thick as oil, sprayed across my shirt.

A grating, awful scream came from the other side of the dining room. The sound of it set my teeth on edge. A series of crashing, clattering sounds followed, but I couldn't afford to look. The moment I let my focus slip was the moment I died.

The female roared, shaking her arm as if she couldn't understand why it was hurting. I spun the dagger, slicing her again, this time across her shoulder. The shirt she was wearing split apart, the thin, black-veined skin beneath bursting open like a piece of rotten fruit.

Tiny white flecks spilled from the wound. They hit the rug and started wriggling.

Maggots.

The boy to my left snaked forward, his teeth gnashing. I whipped the blade out, aiming for his throat, twisting at the same time to try and avoid his claws, but I wasn't quick enough. He moved so quickly. Unnaturally so. The air rushed out of me in a breathless *"Ooof!"* when he slammed into me. The dining room tilted. I went down hard, my ribs exploding with pain as I hit the ground. I let out a panicked shout as both the female and the boy fell on me.

Gods and martyrs, I was going to die.

They were going to *eat* me.

I had no doubt in my mind about that. Those teeth were built for one purpose and one purpose alone: ripping flesh. I gasped, pain lancing up my leg like a lightning bolt. Their claws dragged at my clothes. They cut into my skin. I couldn't see. Couldn't breathe. The female reared back, wet strands of her saliva dripping down onto my chest. She opened her mouth, her jaw cracking open far wider than it should have been able to, revealing a blackened, mangled, pulsing stump where her tongue should have been. She snorted, then dove.

I braced, waiting for the horror of those teeth plunging into my flesh, but it never came. A streak of black smoke wrapped around her throat. The smoke became metal, and then the female's head was parting from her neck, and it was fucking *gone.* Her twitching body flew off of me, flopping and thumping, bones cracking as it rolled across the rug.

Kingfisher towered over me like the god of death himself.

His chest heaved, his eyes flashing with green, and silver, and murder.

"You all right?" he panted.

I was still clutching hold of the dagger, its short blade covered in sticky black blood. I swallowed, nodding, even though I was pretty sure I wasn't all right. Not all right at all. "The boy..." I panted.

Kingfisher's expression darkened. He turned, and we both saw the adolescent at the same time. Eight feet away, on his hands and knees, he was moaning as he licked a patch of blood on the rug. Just as the female's had been, his tongue was a raw stub of meat. Without hesitation, Kingfisher brought Nimerelle down onto the creature's neck, decapitating him, too. The boy's body sagged instantaneously, his gnarled hands relaxing, claws uncurling against the destroyed rug.

I rolled over and threw up.

Kingfisher was probably going to mock me for losing my stomach, but I didn't care. I was shaking too hard to even pull myself up onto my knees.

What...

...the fuck...

...just happened?

Strong hands found my sides. I gasped, the bright sting of pain dancing up my leg again. Kingfisher repositioned his hold on me, muttering unhappily to himself as he lifted me into his arms. "You've been clawed. The wound needs scourging," he said.

"Scourging?"

"The poison will kill you otherwise. Did either of them bite you?"

"N-no. I don't..." My head swam, another wave of nausea hitting me hard. White pinpricks flared in my eyes, making it look as though Fisher's hair was full of stars. They streaked across the ceiling, first one shooting star, then another, then a million of them, racing across my vision. It was...really beautiful, actually. Kingfisher was, too. His throat was flecked with black ichor, and his hair was disheveled. His eyes were wild, but he looked breathtaking. I could feel his heart beating like a drum against my side. *Thum thum thum thum.*

I couldn't feel my fingers.

Why...couldn't I...feel them?

Why was Kingfisher running?

"What...*were* those...things?" I rasped.

Stars raced above Kingfisher's beautiful head. He clenched his jaw, his throat muscles working as he kicked open a door and carried me through it.

"Sanasrothian foot soldiers," he answered tightly. "Feeders. *They* are the reason why we need silver so badly. It's the only thing that can kill them. *NOW CAN SOMEBODY FUCKING HELP!*"

19

BONES AND ALL

A DREAM of death and liquid fire.

No.

A nightmare.

I was trapped inside it with no way out. Darkened hallways stretched off into eternity, doors on all sides. Whenever I opened one, heart thundering in my chest, I was met with the putrid stench of rot and sharp, yellowed, snapping fangs. There were crowds of them. Feeders. That's what Kingfisher had called them. He had also called them foot soldiers, but they didn't seem like soldiers. A soldier had to be able to follow orders. To enact the will of another. The things behind these doors were monsters, capable only of obeying their thirst for blood. Women, and children, and elderly men, all of them insane and hungry. They tore at me with clawed fingers. They sank their rotting teeth into my skin. I screamed and thrashed, ripping myself away from them, barely escaping with my life, only to open another door and unleash a fresh wave of them.

There was no outrunning them. No fighting them. They sprinted after me, defying gravity as they sank their claws into the brickwork and swarmed up the walls, charging on all fours across the ceiling. Fell, evil demons, determined to drink me dry and drain my soul while they were at it.

I ran hard, but it was no good. There were too many of them. My lungs burned, the wound in my side on fire. Blood ran down my legs, coating my bare feet in a slick that made me slip and fall...

I didn't stop falling.

I would fall forever, burning and burning, until my blood turned to crimson steam and my flesh sloughed from my brittle bones.

And still, I'd fall.

Fall and fall forever.

I—

I woke with a start, dragging in an audible, ragged breath as I sat bolt upright.

Where...

Where *was* I?

My mouth tasted of bile and ash. Everything fucking hurt. My limbs felt as though they'd been tied to four horses, and the shitty bastards had bolted in four different directions. It hurt to breathe. To swallow. To fucking blink. For a good minute, I braced my hands against the mattress beneath me, trying to wrangle my senses, waiting for the pain to pass.

It took a long time, but eventually, I could think around it enough to take in my surroundings. Light poured in through twelve-foot-tall windows to my left. Heavy velvet curtains hung at them, half drawn on one side. Paintings hung on the walls in gilded frames, though the artwork within those frames was slashed to ribbons. Above, the ceiling was painted black, pinpricks of white strewn across it in no apparent design or order. A chest of drawers made from a rich, dark wood sat against the wall by the door. An armoire made of the same wood was positioned in the corner, its doors flung open, displaying an array of dark garments within.

I was in a bed. A four-poster bed with birds, wolves, and dragons carved into the posts. The sheets were black. The cushions at the foot of the bed were also black. Along with the mostly black clothes hanging in the armoire…

Dread tapped me on the shoulder. The moment I inhaled through my nose and detected the smell of mint in the air, I knew I was in deep shit.

"Oh, look. She lives," came a hushed voice.

I hadn't noticed the wing-backed chair in the pool of shadows created by the drawn curtain. Nor had I noticed the Fae male sprawled out in it, feet crossed at the ankle, hands stacked over his stomach. Now that I knew he was there, he was impossible to miss. Fisher's hair was a little mad, waves and curls springing every which way. His face was bone white against his dark clothes; as always, he was a creature of stark contrasts. Even from fifteen feet away, I could see the flecks of ichor staining his cheeks. He looked relaxed. His posture was one of boredom, but the energy he gave off hit me like a slap. With eyes of green fire, he stared at me so intensely that I almost gave in and recoiled under the weight of his gaze.

I clenched my teeth, bracing for the storm I could feel mounting on the horizon. "It wasn't my fault," I said.

Kingfisher blinked. "I never said it was."

"You're *looking* at me like it was," I countered, gathering the sheets up to my chest, clutching them as though I might be able to use them as a shield against him.

"Sounds to me like you're wrestling with a guilty conscience," he rumbled.

"I do not have a guilty conscience. I have a hole in my side *and* my leg because you chose to relocate us to a place where rabid freaks hurl themselves through windows and attack us."

"You aren't injured," he said evenly.

"What?"

"We have excellent healers here. Better even than at the Winter Palace. A perk of living on the outskirts of a war zone. You don't need to replace your warriors if you can snatch them from the jaws of death in time."

I gave him a dark look. "Stick really close, you said. Well, I was about as close as I could get without sitting in your lap and look what happened. We were attacked inside your fucking *house.*"

"Psshhh." He made a dismissive sound, fiddling with a button on the front of his shirt. "It was nothing. Four rogue scouts taking a shot they were never going to win. It won't happen again."

"You can't guarantee that."

"I can. The house has been unguarded since we arrived. Ren wanted to post a unit here to patrol the grounds and ensure we didn't have any uninvited guests, but I shut him down. I didn't realize the feeders had gotten so…"

"Brazen?"

"Hungry." He pressed the tip of his tongue against the point of a sharp canine, studying me. "You landed a hit on one of them," he said.

"Two hits." If he was going to commend me, he might as well get it right.

"Impressive." This was supposed to be a compliment, but his tone made it back-handed.

"For a girl?" I asked bitterly.

He arched a dark brow. "For a *human.*"

"Oh, fuck you, princeling. What have you got against humans anyway?" I snapped. "You're so determined to hate us, but we're more alike than different."

He snorted at that. Rose from the chair and approached the bed. Standing next to me, he reached out a hand and curled a piece of my hair around his index finger, staring at it thoughtfully. "We are nothing alike," he said quietly. "You nearly died from a scratch that would have been a mild irritation to me. You are soft. You are fragile. You are vulnerable. You are a newborn fawn, stumbling around in the dark, surrounded by predators with very sharp teeth. I am the thing that exists on the other side of the dark. I'm the thing that puts the fear of the gods into the monsters who would eat you bones and all."

Why was he looking at me like that? His eyes were hard, but his expression was carefully blank. I couldn't figure it out. Couldn't figure him out. His fingers twitched, the tips so close to my cheek. I was still delirious from the poison. I had to be, because it really felt like he wanted to trail them over my cheek and was forcing himself not to. "This is your room," I whispered.

Fisher yanked his hand back, fast as lightning. He stood there, eyes wide, lips parted, as if he couldn't understand how he'd found himself touching my hair. I watched his expression harden, a pit forming in my stomach. Why was he like this? What exactly *was* his problem? I'd asked him flat-out what his issue with humans was just now, but I couldn't shake the feeling that it was more than that. That he had a problem with *me* specifically.

"It is," he said. "It was the closest place to set you down,"

"Why are all the paintings torn up like that?" I demanded.

The tension crackling between us snapped like a cord pulled too tight.

"Because I destroyed them," he said flatly.

"Why?"

He exhaled, whirling away. Taking long, determined strides, he headed for the door. And just as he'd done at dinner before all hell had broken loose, he cast his voice so that it was right next to my ear. The rough edge of it, so close, made me startle. "Because sometimes, my pendant can't stave off the darkness that creeps in."

Gritting my teeth, I shouted after him, "Really? That's it? You're leaving? If that's the case, I can go back to my own room now!"

Fisher paused, hand resting against the doorframe. "Unless you need to relieve yourself, you won't get out of that bed, Osha. Even then, you'll go to the bathroom and get straight back into that bed. There are still trace amounts of poison in your veins. You need to rest until you've had time to properly heal."

"I can heal in my own bed." But even as I said this, the question sprang into my mind. Did I even *have* a bed here? A space to call my own? The room I'd woken up in was luxury beyond anything I could have ever hoped for back in the Silver City, but the prospect of sharing a bedroom with Carrion did not sound appealing, especially when I felt like shit.

"Stay in that bed, Little Osha." The command was gentle, almost kind, but there was a resonant quality to it that left no room for argument.

My grip on the silky black sheets tightened. "Then where are *you* going to sleep?" If he thought for one second that I'd share a fucking bed with him, he was sorely mistaken.

He must have known what I was thinking because he smirked as he spoke. "I'm heading to Innìr for a week. There are things that need my attention there."

"Innìr?"

"The war camp. On the other side of the mountains." He nodded to the window. "They act as a barrier between this place and the carnage on the other side."

"Oh." I'd been right, then. The camp I'd imagined when I first heard of Cahlish did exist. Four thousand feet of jutting, jagged rock stood between it and this house, but it *was* out there.

"For the record, I'd never use an injury as an excuse to sneak my way into a bed," Fisher said. His voice was even closer now. I could almost feel the brush of his lips against the shell of my ear. "I've never had a problem securing myself an invite."

He was so sure of himself. His arrogance went beyond the pale. "Well, don't count on an invite from *me*," I snapped, drawing the sheets up even higher beneath my chin.

Fuck me. That smile. Slightly open-mouthed, flashing the smallest hint of pointed teeth. I had to be so, so careful around that smile. It would wreck me if I let it. "Mm. You're right. I don't think you will invite me. When the time comes, I think you'll *beg*—"

I let out an infuriated scream. Grabbing the closest thing I could lay my hands on, I hurled a cushion at his head. Too heavy, it thudded to the floor, woefully short of its mark.

Kingfisher's laughter rang out down the hall as he disappeared, his bedroom door swinging closed behind him. I tossed off the bedsheets, determined to hurl something *much* sharper at him, but when I tried to swing my legs out of the bed…nothing happened. My muscles didn't move an inch. Didn't even twitch.

Oh my gods, I was paralyzed. Something wasn't right. The healers…they…I couldn't move my…oh my gods. Oh no, oh no, *oh no*…

The second I stopped trying to get out of the bed and tried to flex my feet instead, my body obeyed. Relief rocked me so hard that I let out a sob, pressing the back of my hand to my mouth. I *could* move my legs. I just couldn't get up.

I—

Wait.

No.

He hadn't.

Unless you need to relieve yourself, you won't get out of that bed, Osha. And even then, you'll go to the bathroom and get straight back into that bed.

Understanding pressed down heavily on the center of my chest. That was why Fisher's voice had sounded so firm when he told me to stay in bed and rest—because it'd been a command issued through the oath that bound me to him.

I *had* to stay in his bed.

I didn't have a choice.

Five days.

Five long fucking days. I ate in Fisher's bed. Slept in Fisher's bed. Whenever I needed to go to *relieve* myself, as Fisher had so elegantly put it, my body allowed me to get up, but my feet carried me toward the discreet door over by the armoire and permitted me to enter the beautiful white marble bathroom there. I could do what I needed to do, and I could wash my hands, but as soon as I was done, my legs carried me back to the comfortable prison of his bed.

I had no idea what kind of magic kept the sheets so perfectly cool and clean, but it didn't take me long to decide that it was tricky and evil. The scent of Fisher never faded from the black silk. I could smell him—the complex scent of a cold winter forest—every second of every hour of every day, until he was literally all I could think about.

I wanted to *kill* him.

And I was so bored, I thought I'd lose my mind. Onyx's presence was the only thing that saved me. The fox had arrived shortly after Kingfisher had left and had stayed with me most of the time since. He curled up next to me and slept. He made quirky noises that sounded like he was laughing whenever I petted him or gave him neck scratches. Three or four times a day, he hopped down off the bed and slunk out of the room, nudging the door open with his nose, presumably heading outside to go to the bathroom himself or to hunt. He always came back, though.

Whenever the fire sprites brought me my meals, I begged them to fetch Fisher, but they shrugged sheepishly and told me that he hadn't returned. After lunch, without fail, Te Léna, a Fae healer with beautiful bronze-colored skin and the most breathtaking amber eyes— came to check on me. She'd place her hands on my abdomen and "read my blood." I had no idea what that meant, but she did something all right. A shivery, not unpleasant sensation would skate through my veins, making my body hum a little. She'd smile at me apologetically and say, "Not yet," then give me a new book to read. On the fourth day, her smile was brighter, though. More optimistic. "One more day," she said.

"But I feel fine!" I'd felt good enough to run halfway across Zilvaren without breaking a sweat since Fisher had left for the camp, but there had been no reasoning with any of my visitors, least of all Te Léna.

"Even if I wanted to release you from his command, I couldn't. The *oath* knows you're not fully recovered yet, so it won't let you out of this room." She'd squeezed my shoulder reassuringly. "But not long now. There's so little poison left in your system that I can barely detect it. Only twenty-four more hours."

On the final day of my incarceration, Carrion brought me my breakfast instead of one of the fire sprites. He'd visited before, but he'd annoyed me so much with his pacing and his questions that I'd screamed at him and made him leave. He hadn't returned after that. Not until now. He grinned at me over the top of the tray he set down on my lap, a mischievous glimmer in his eyes.

"You look pissed," he said.

That wasn't the understatement of the century. It was the understatement of the entire epoch. "I *am* pissed."

Carrion threw himself down onto the bed, stretching out next to me. The disturbance woke Onyx from his nap; he snarled, baring his teeth at Zilvaren's most wanted man, flattening his ears against his head, but Carrion just ignored him. He grunted, fluffing Fisher's pillows, making himself comfortable. "You know what'd really piss *him* off?"

I knew he wasn't talking about Onyx. "Just don't, Carrion."

"Revenge fucking on his bed."

I shoved a piece of apple into my mouth. "Oh, yeah, sure. Sounds like a *great* idea. Idiot. What do you think he'd do to you if you *fucked someone in his bed?*"

Carrion waggled his eyebrows. "I think he'd never know."

I nearly choked on the apple. "Oh, he'd know." The snarky comment Fisher had made in the dining room rose to the surface of my mind like he were here himself, laughing as if he were repeating it in person. *I detected your scent from three miles away, plastered all over that boy. Pheromones are signal flares to our noses, Little Osha.*

"I'd be willing to risk inciting his wrath," Carrion said. "Whatever his punishment was, it'd be worth it."

Hah. Carrion hadn't seen Fisher decapitating that feeder with one ruthless flick of his wrist. If he had, he might reassess that statement. I gave him a pointed look. *"No."*

Carrion swiped a piece of toast from my breakfast tray. He bit into it, creating a shower of crumbs that magically disappeared before they hit the bedsheets. "Just so I know," he said, chewing. "Is that a no to fucking in your captor's bed? Or a no to fucking in general?"

"What do *you* think?"

He pointed at me with the corner of his slice of toast. "You could eviscerate a man with that expression. It's one of the things I love most about you."

I snatched the toast from his hand and threw it down onto my plate. "I don't love anything about you."

"Liar. There are *so* many things you love about me." He winked roguishly, attempting to steal the toast again, but I slapped the back of his hand.

"Get your own godscursed breakfast. This one's mine."

"My hair. My eyes. My wit. My charm…" He counted them off on his fingers, making a list.

"You have *zero* charm."

"I'm a hell of a lot more charming than *Kingfisher*," he sputtered.

"You're both as insufferable as each other. Now can you please get your filthy, muddy boots off of the bed?"

"What does it matter? The mud just disappears, anyway." He demonstrated, wiping the mud-caked soles of his boots against the rucked-up sheets, looking very pleased with himself when the mess he made promptly disappeared. *"See."*

"What the hell have you been doing?" I demanded. "Why are you so dirty? And…wait, where did you even get those boots? Last time I saw you, you were walking around barefoot." I laughed scornfully. "You looked *stupid*."

"Well, I was hardly gonna walk around with just one boot, was I? While *you've* been stuck in here, staring at the ceiling, I've been out training with the new guards. They have a fascinating fighting system." It was an airy taunt. Payback for saying he'd look stupid. If there was one thing Carrion Swift couldn't tolerate, it was being made fun of. "As for the boots, your friend Fisher gave them to me."

I set down my fork. "He *did?*"

Carrion nodded. "That night, before you had dinner with him, actually. You'd already left for the dining room. He showed up with these in his hand and said he'd give them to me on one condition."

"Which was?"

Carrion snagged a grape from the tray and popped it into his mouth. "That I take a bath."

"A bath?"

"Yes, a bath."

"That's a weird request."

"I know. Even after being kidnapped, dragged into a different realm, and carted for miles on the back of a horse, I still smelled great. But he was all wound up about not liking the way I smelled, so I figured fuck it. Whatever. A bath for a new pair of boots was a fair trade. And it felt great to soak in all of that hot water. Strange, right? All of that water? I still can't wrap my head around the fact that there's just so much…"

He prattled on, but the bite of toast I'd just taken had turned claggy, like glue. "He said he didn't like the way you smelled?"

"Yes, and he was *very* rude about it. He had a bunch of sprites come in and scrub me with these stiff brushes until I was raw and pink all over. I swear they took off four layers of skin. They put this thick white clay all over me then and let it sit so long that it went hard, and they had to crack it to get it all off."

"Gods."

"And *then,*" he said, taking another grape. "They rubbed me down with this special kind of moss, which is where things got interesting. They paid particular attention to my…" His eyes trailed down his body until they rested in his crotch.

I raised my eyebrows at him. "You let a fire sprite jerk you off with a handful of Fae moss?"

"Not a fire sprite," he said defensively. "These were water sprites. Three of them. They're smaller than the Fae women and very nice to look at. I didn't mind their attentions one bit."

"You've been in Yvelia for five seconds, and you've already had a foursome with a different species of magical creature?" I didn't know why I was surprised. It was absolutely something Carrion would do.

"Jealous?" he asked, winking again.

"No! I'm...I'm disgusted! What if you catch some kind of Fae disease?" *I* eyed his crotch for emphasis this time.

Another grape went into his mouth. "Ahh, I'm not worried about that. They were *very* thorough with that moss."

"Gross!"

"Come on. Hurry up and eat. That gorgeous healer told me to let you know you'd be able to get out of here as soon as you finished everything on that tray."

I let my mouth fall open. "Carrion Swift, you are such an asshole! That should have been the first thing you said when you came in here."

I'd never finished a plate of food so quickly in my life. Not even when I'd been starving back in the Third.

The silver spat in the crucible, bubbling angrily. The combination of iron filings and the yellow powder I'd first mixed in saline solution and then added to the molten silver had not ended well. Neither had the experiment where I'd attempted to add a small sliver of gold and some human hair (mine) to the metal. Both times, when I'd placed the medallion I forged with the materials into the quicksilver, it had roiled, the voice within hissing furiously in a foreign tongue. This time, I'd burned some wood, ground up the coals that had remained, and sprinkled that into the silver. The two didn't want to combine, but I poured the contents of the crucible into the mold and flashed the whole thing in the slack tub anyway, wincing as the water cooled the metal, creating a cloud of rank smoke.

The second I dropped the medallion into the crucible that held the quicksilver, I knew this attempt had ended in failure as well. The quicksilver *laughed.*

And that was that. I could only do three experiments a day. With so little silver to work with, I needed to spend the rest of the day refining it so that it would be ready to test with again tomorrow. Swearing angrily, I gathered together the scrap I'd created and dumped it into a firing chalice, my temper rising along with the temperature inside the forge. Even with one side of the workshop open to the elements, it was still as hot as the dungeons in Madra's palace by the time I was done for the day.

When he wasn't chasing the birds or hunting for mice, Onyx had taken to lying underneath the giant oak tree, watching me from a distance, cooling his belly in the snow.

It had been eight days since I'd fled Fisher's room, which meant twenty-four failed attempts at creating a relic. The trunk full of silver rings sat by the bench where Fisher had left it, its presence a daily reminder that, until I'd turned every single ring inside it into a shield that would allow Fisher's warriors to pass through the quicksilver unharmed, I was basically fucked. And then I'd see the other trunks full of rings tucked away in the corner, and I'd have to fight the urge to scream.

I didn't want to think about what was going to happen if I didn't make any headway soon. Every time I refined the scrap silver, I lost some of it. The amount I had to work with grew smaller and smaller every day, and with it, so did my chances of ever seeing Hayden and Elroy again.

As I worked, Onyx yowled, excited by something on the other side of the garden wall. He did that a lot. There were animals that roved Cahlish's grounds and guards that now patrolled on the other side of the wall as well. I didn't see them very often, but I heard them from time to time. I ignored Onyx's sounds of outrage as I carefully placed the scrap silver into a vat of acid. Staring at the three small medallions, watching them slowly dissolve, I didn't see the intruder climbing over the wall until it was too late.

My head snapped up when Onyx let out a very dog-like bark. And there it was. A dark figure, striding toward me across the garden.

Feeder.

My heart backflipped, my hand reaching for my dagger, a cry of panic building at the back of my throat...

...but it wasn't a feeder.

It was Ren.

He gave me a warm smile as he entered the forge. "Afternoon, Saeris."

"Really? You're gonna climb the wall and scare the shit out of me instead of coming in through the door?"

"It was quicker that way," he said. "Sorry. I didn't mean to frighten you."

The general should have frightened me, but even after launching himself over a wall and surprising me, he didn't. There was a warmth to him that made me feel at ease, no matter how imposing he was. The top half of his long sandy brown hair was tied back into two war braids. They gathered into a ponytail at the base of his skull. The rest hung well past his shoulders, almost as long as mine. His eyes—the deepest brown—looked a little wary as he peered past me into the forge.

"Are you all right?" I asked. "Is that...*blood?*" His hands were stained black, as were his pants. The golden chest plate he wore, engraved with a sigil of a snarling wolf's head very similar to the one on Fisher's gorget, was splattered with black liquid as well. It could have been very dark mud, but...no. He was close enough that I could smell him now, and holy hells, the general reeked of the same foul odor that had filled the air when the feeders had attacked us. It was definitely blood. He looked down at himself, his brows rising as if he'd only just noticed that he was filthy.

"Ah. Shit. Yes, uh...we don't exactly have access to a bathhouse at the camp. There's a river, but it's frozen. I...I should go and clean up. Apologies, Saeris. I was so fixed on coming to say hello that..."

He tried unsuccessfully to wipe his hands clean on his pants. "Yeah, I forgot about *this*. I'll go and clean up. First, I was charged with the pleasure of letting you know that Fisher's requesting your presence for dinner again tonight."

"Oh, he's back, is he?" I folded my arms across my chest. "And *requesting* my presence? Are you sure you don't mean demanding it?"

Renfis winced, and I knew that I'd hit the nail on the head. Ren was a million times nicer than Kingfisher and had reworded the message he'd been given to pass along to me. "He doesn't mean to be so brusque," he said. "He's been fighting this war for so long now that he's forgotten what it's like to interact with polite society."

I turned back into the forge and dropped my heat-proof gloves onto the bench. "You really *should* stop making excuses for him. It doesn't help him, me, or anyone else. He's just a bastard."

Ren smiled weakly. "He's also my best friend. I have to believe that he's still in there somewhere. The person I once knew. Not this cold, shutdown version of himself." His sadness weighed him down, I could see it. "But anyway. I won't keep you. You need to get ready for dinner and—"

"Are you going to be there this time?"

Ren looked down at his dirt-rimmed fingernails, a small smile playing over his mouth. "No. I do normally eat with Fisher, but I wasn't invited this evening."

I narrowed my eyes to slits. "And why was that, do you think?"

"I'd hate to hazard a guess."

Coward. We both knew Fisher only invited me because he wanted to torture me for his own sport without anyone there to keep him in check. I wasn't having it this time. "You're coming to dinner," I informed Ren.

"No, I don't think so," he answered slowly.

"Yes. *I'm* inviting you."

"I'm honored, and thank you, but—"

"Look, do you want Fisher to have to come find me because I've refused to show up for dinner? Do you want him to force me to go? Do you think he'd do that?"

"No, of course not! He wouldn't."

I waited.

"Fine, he probably would," he conceded.

"Good. So you're coming."

"*Saeris.*"

"Because you wouldn't want him to command me to do something I didn't want to do again. Because you're a nice Fae warrior, unlike Fisher, who is the devil incarnate."

Ren looked torn, but at last, he relented. "All right. Yes, okay. I'll come. But he's not going to be happy about it."

"When is Fisher happy about anything?" I scowled. "Where is he, anyway? Why didn't he come to torture me with news of dinner himself?"

Ren looked toward the doorway, more alert than he'd been a moment ago. I got the feeling that his superior Fae hearing had detected movement out in the hallway back in the main house, but if he had, he didn't mention it.

"He's with Te Léna," he said distractedly.

"Oh. Right. Was he hurt or something?"

"Hmm? Oh no, he's fine. Nothing to worry about. There was a skirmish in the eastern wood beyond the camp, but it was over quickly. He came out unscathed." He nodded as if trying to convince himself that this was true. "I'll see you at dinner, Saeris."

"Wait. One last thing before you go. I've been thinking a lot while I've been stuck in here, trying to make these relics, and...Fisher's sword, Nimerelle, still has some magic, doesn't it? The smoke and that dark energy that crackles from the blade?"

Ren looked a little wary now. "Yes."

"How...how is that?"

He rubbed his jaw, thinking for a second. "I'm not sure," he said. "None of us are. All we know is that when the god swords went silent and abandoned the rest of the Fae who carried them, Nimerelle stayed. At a cost. The blade used to shine brilliant silver. As the centuries have passed, it's blackened and tarnished. But Nimerelle has stayed. The spirit of that sword or the magic inside it, whatever you choose to believe it is, has *stayed*. No matter what, it's never left him."

"I don't see why *I* have to come." Carrion tugged at his shirt collar, grumbling as he hurried along behind me down the hall. "I was in the middle of a great sparring session. I'm filthy. I would have gotten changed if I'd known I'd be sitting down with my kidnapper for a nice meal. Speaking of which, *you* should really have changed after you left the forge, too."

"I did," I said blandly.

Carrion pulled a face. "Really? I seem to remember there being a very low-cut, sheer black dress on the end of your bed when I went back to the room earlier, and I can't help but notice that you're wearing a faded, threadbare shirt and some very dusty pants."

"So what? They *are* clean."

"That's the only positive thing that can be said about them." Carrion's nose wrinkled in disgust. "I had a vested interest in seeing you in that dress."

"Why?" I shoved open the door to the dining room.

"Your phenomenal tits, that's why. They would have looked great in that dress. And your ass. The material was sheer as hell. Wouldn't have left much to the imagination. Not that I need to use my imagination when it comes to your body, but—"

A sinister growl echoed around the dining room.

Carrion had enough common sense to stop talking.

The windows had been fixed after the attack. There was no huge floral arrangement in the middle of the table this time. Fisher sat at the head of the table, dressed in midnight black. A tailored shirt hugged his chest and shoulders in the most distracting way. His hair was damp, the ends curling, as if he wasn't long out of the baths. His mouth formed a taut line, suggesting that he wanted to close his hands around Carrion's throat and snap his neck. All cleaned up now, Ren sat to Fisher's left, nursing a glass of whiskey, looking pained.

"You're late," Fisher said in an icy tone. "And please enlighten me. Why have you invited half of the household along to a meeting that was supposed to be for just the two of us?"

"Meeting? I thought this was dinner. And how would it be fair for me to enjoy the pleasure of your company while these two miss out?"

Carrion held up a hand. "I'd prefer not to be here, actually."

"Sit the fuck *down*," I hissed.

"All right. Gods."

A place had been set for me down the far end of the table again, though it appeared as though a concession had been made this time, because the table was nowhere near as long as before. Only ten feet? Still, I wasn't some second-class citizen to be relegated to the far end of a fucking table. I strode straight past the setting, swiping only the wineglass as I went, and then dragged out the chair on Fisher's right again, sitting down heavily in it.

Renfis had been in the process of sipping from his glass, but the second he realized that I'd sat opposite him, next to Fisher, the alcohol sprayed out of his mouth in an arc that nearly crossed the width of the table. Luckily no food had been placed on it yet.

"Saints." He pounded on his chest, wheezing. "What the fuck?"

"Oh, yes. She has no sense of timekeeping, *and* she has unconventional seating preferences, don't you, human?"

"I can sit there instead?" Carrion offered.

"Absolutely not," Kingfisher barked. "Try it and die."

"Whoa. Okay. I was just trying to keep the peace. If you guys need a buffer—"

"We don't," Fisher fired back at him. "And even if we did, I'd ask someone far more likable than you. No!" He held up a finger, stabbing it at Carrion. "Do *not* tell me how likable you are back in Zilvaren. I don't want to hear it."

Carrion gave him a sickly smile as he sat down in the next chair along.

"Here. Come and sit on this side," Ren said to me, collecting his glass and shoving his chair back. "I don't mind moving."

"What's the difference between this side and that side?" I asked. "Either way, I still have to look at his smug face."

"She's right," Fisher said. "She's made her decision. Let her sit wherever she wants to sit."

Ren gave him an odd look. "Really?"

"Really."

I didn't know the general all that well, but I knew him enough to tell that he was confounded by Fisher's declaration. He sat back in his chair, his eyes roving over his friend's features as I grabbed the bottle of wine in front of Fisher and poured myself a large glass. I would have put the bottle straight down again, but Carrion grabbed it from me before I had a chance. Fisher watched Carrion lean across me, his nostrils flaring.

"You've been training with the guards," he said.

Carrion nodded. "The way the Fae fight is amazing. So fluid and preemptive. It's like watching ballet."

"People don't get hacked to pieces at the ballet in Yvelia," Fisher said dryly.

"Really? Wouldn't surprise me if they did. You lot are almost as bloodthirsty as the brawlers who fight in the pits for water rations back in the Third."

"We've evolved. We wouldn't fight for something as petty as a water ration."

Carrion huffed out a breath of laughter. "You would if you were dying of thirst. Trust me. I've seen it."

I heard the unspoken words. *I've been there.* He didn't say them. He didn't have to. There had been times when he had struggled to survive back in the Silver City. I knew that because everybody struggled. It was unavoidable. A time came for every resident of our ward, when they were faced with an impossible situation and they had to decide. You either fought for water, or you stole it. Carrion had likely done both more times than he could count.

Fisher looked from Carrion to me, as if he were wondering if *I* had ever found myself at the bottom of a pit with a dagger in my hand, fighting for a cup of water.

I wondered how he would react if he knew that I had.

Ren cleared his throat diplomatically, redirecting the conversation. "You're welcome to come and train with the garrison now that they're back. Tomorrow morning, we'll be running drills."

He'd spoken to Carrion, but I answered him first. "What time? I'd love to train."

"I'm surprised," Fisher said, taking a sip of the whiskey he had in front of him. "I thought you were in a rush to get home."

"I am. You know I am."

He didn't look at me. "But you'd rather waste time out in the snow with a sword in your hand instead of working on the task that will set you free?"

Archer and his team of fire sprites had entered the dining room. They shuffled up and down the table, setting down trays of hot, steaming food, averting their eyes from us. All of them except Archer, who stared at me, eyes huge in his head, as he placed a soup spoon beside the bowl he put in front of me. I smiled at him, and he squeaked, his eyes darting to the floor. His rough-surfaced face was incapable of blushing, but I got the feeling that he was embarrassed to have been caught looking at me.

"I'm getting nowhere with the relics," I said to Fisher. "The way you're having me work right now is pointless. I could run these trials until the end of time. I still won't figure out the transmutation process. And I have to say, you don't seem to give a shit. It's almost as if you don't really care if I have to stay here forever."

Archer let out a nervous giggle, hiccupped, and then scurried off toward the door.

Kingfisher didn't seem to think anything of the little sprite's strange behavior. "Of course I want you to stay. You're the only Alchemist we have," he said. "I'd keep you here and have you working in that forge until you died of old age if it were up to me. But a deal's a deal." It was a testament to the white-knuckled grip I had on my temper that I didn't snap at him as I watched him sip from his glass. "It's really shocking how little faith you have in yourself. You'll figure it out. Please eat something," he said, gesturing to the feast the sprites had brought for us.

Carrion hadn't waited for an invitation and was already heaping his plate with small pies, roasted vegetables, and five different kinds of bread rolls. Ren had taken a piece of bread, too, though he wasn't giving it much attention. He picked at it, tearing off a piece and putting it into his mouth, chewing slowly as his gaze moved back and forth subtly between me and Kingfisher.

"I'm not hungry," I said.

"You are," Fisher said. "We can all hear your stomach rumbling. Put something in it so we don't have to listen to it complaining for the next hour."

The soup in the tureen closest to me smelled incredible. It was thick and creamy. Chicken, maybe? Mushrooms and sweetcorn, too. If I weren't feeling so spiky about being coerced into coming here, I would have filled my bowl to the brim with it. Since I *was* pissed, I ignored the food and my snarling stomach and treated Fisher to my best death stare. The same one Carrion had said was capable of gutting a man. "You said you were going to the camp for a week. You were gone for two."

"Did you miss me?"

"I didn't appreciate being stuck in your bed for five days, y'know."

"Really?" He picked up a piece of cheese. "Most females *like* spending time in my bed."

"How long are you staying before you head back to the camp?" Carrion asked Ren around a mouthful of food.

Ren arched an eyebrow, struggling to tear his gaze away from me to look at Carrion. "Uh...a week, maybe?"

"I don't even want to think about the depraved shit you've done in that room," I hissed.

Fisher's laughter flooded the dining room. "You're right. You don't."

"Urgh!"

"I'll be down in the courtyard every morning before dawn, then," Carrion said.

"Sure. We're practicing disarmament tomorrow..." Ren tore off another piece of bread and put it in his mouth, throwing me a sidelong look. "You could probably use some training on that front, Saeris."

"Great! I'll be there. *Thanks.*" I tried to make my voice a little lighter but failed. Ren laughed silently, looking down at his plate. Apparently, he thought the battle I was waging with Fisher was adorable and didn't take offense at the bite in my tone, but I wasn't mad at him. He didn't deserve my ire. "Sorry," I said, taking a deep breath. "I didn't mean to snap. Not at *you,* anyway."

The general shook his head, suppressing a smile. He reached for a pie and set it onto his plate. "Not at all. He makes me crazy, too."

Kingfisher hadn't looked away from me once during this exchange. "Make sure she uses a training sword," he said flatly. "One with a very dull edge."

"I do *not* need to use a training sword!"

"Oh? You have experience wielding a blade, then? A proper, full-length sword and not some badly forged back-alley shank?"

I was going to shank him in the neck with my very dull *butter* knife. Then he'd see how proficient I was with a blade. I could do it, too. He wasn't wearing his gorget this evening. His throat was bare, just begging to be opened right up, and I was in the mood to lay steel to flesh. I only realized I'd been staring at his throat when Fisher lifted his chin a little, angling his head so that the tendons in his neck stood proud. That fucking smile again. I wanted to wipe it off his smug face so badly.

"Yes," I declared. He had no idea about the training I used to do back when my mother was alive. No idea at all what I was capable of. "I have plenty of experience with full-length swords. They're like daggers, only bigger. You use the sharp—"

"You're on the verge of embarrassing yourself," Fisher murmured. "Better stop talking before you put Renfis here in an early grave."

"Oh, fuck you, Fisher."

He bit down on his bottom lip, eyes alive, flickering vivid green and silver. I knew what his amusement looked like now, and I didn't like it one bit. "Go on. Tell her, Ren," he said.

"I'm not getting caught in the crossfire of whatever *this* is," Ren said, gesturing to the two of us. "I'll be happy to demonstrate the differences between close-quarter fighting with a dagger and swordplay in the morning, Saeris. In the meantime, I plan on enjoying my dinner. Carrion, what kind of fighting system do the guardians employ in the Silver City?"

It was as if Carrion had been waiting for him to ask; he dove into an in-depth, animated discussion with the general, telling Ren all about the fighting techniques and formations he'd witnessed Madra's guards using back home. I was sure he was making half of it up. I contributed nothing to the conversation; I was locked in silent warfare with Fisher across our corner of the table, and I didn't plan on losing.

Fisher nodded toward my plate. "Eat, Little Osha." His lips moved, but he spoke softly, casting his voice.

"Gods, will you *stop* doing that?" I hissed under my breath.

"Why? I've seen the way your skin breaks out in goose bumps when I speak to you like this."

"It makes me *uncomfortable*." I kept my voice low, even though I shouldn't have. It was impolite to conduct a murmured conversation like this at the dinner table, but Ren and Carrion were busy talking away, and it turned out I had plenty I wanted to say to Fisher. "You compelled me with the oath again," I said through gritted teeth.

"I did," he agreed.

"You shouldn't have."

"Why not?"

"I can't believe I actually have to say this out loud," I hissed. "You shouldn't do it because it's *wrong*. You can't go around forcing people to do things they don't want to do."

At last, Fisher ate the cheese he'd been holding. "You can if they enter into a blood oath that puts them at your mercy."

Ren's expression darkened at this, but he carried on talking to Carrion.

"Do you have no conscience whatsoever? Are you just evil? Is that it?"

The corner of Fisher's mouth kicked up. Leaning forward, he took my plate and started filling it up with various items from the platters and dishes the sprites had brought in. He hovered over a tray of charred meat, trying to decide if he ought to plate me some of that, but then seemed to decide against it. When he was satisfied with what he'd prepared for me, he put the food in front of me and leaned back in his chair. The tattoos at his throat shifted as he swallowed. The intricate designs on the backs of his hands, cuffing his wrists and disappearing up his sleeves, writhed like smoke.

"Eat something from that plate, and I'll answer your question," his voice rumbled into my ear.

A sour smile twisted across my face. "Bribery?"

He splayed his hands wide. "Whatever works."

I scowled.

"Do you want *me* to feed you?" He looked like he'd do it.

"All right. Fine." I picked up the fork and scooped some mashed potatoes onto it, shoving it into my mouth. The explosion of butter, rich cream, and chives made my mouth ache as I swallowed the food down, trying not to openly melt at how delicious it was. "There. Happy now?"

Fisher sat forward, resting his elbows on the table, his eyes glittering. "I'm not evil, no."

"Could have fooled me."

"If I was evil, I'd have used your oath to my advantage by now."

"You have," I spat.

"Have I?" He looked genuinely curious.

"Yes!"

"I've compelled you three times. All three times, I think you'll find it was for your own good."

"That's a horrible excuse! You—"

"If I were evil and using your oath for my own purposes, I'd order you onto your knees for me," he said, cutting me off. "I'd order you to part your legs for me. I'd order you to suck and fuck me until you passed out from exhaustion. Is *that* what you want, Little Osha?"

Heat detonated in my chest. An inferno, raging inside me, eating up all of the oxygen in my lungs. My hand shook, my cheeks turning crimson as I used the edge of my fork to cut into the small meat pie he'd put on my plate. "Of course not. Why would I want that?" I rasped.

He nodded to the piece of pie on my fork. *"Eat."*

My anger was eating *me*, but I raised the fork to my mouth and did it.

"If I compelled you to do it, you'd be innocent. Your actions wouldn't be your fault. You wouldn't have to face the fact that you *wanted* me."

"Just stop, Fisher."

"And I'd prove what a vile monster I was, wouldn't I? How vindicating for you. To get exactly what your body is calling out for while also being proven right."

"You're out of your fucking mind," I whispered.

"That's what they tell me. But I don't know. Aside from the relentless chatter in my head, personally, I think I'm doing just fine."

"I *don't* want you, Fisher."

"You're thinking about my hands sliding up the insides of your thighs right now," he said. "About my fingers slipping inside the wet folds of you. Working against your swollen clit, rubbing you until you're panting and whimpering, begging for me to sink my cock into your—"

For the second time since we sat down to dinner, Renfis nearly choked on his drink. He spun in his seat, giving Fisher a scandalized look that said, *Really? I'm sitting* right *fucking here,* but Fisher paid him no heed.

On the other hand, I nearly keeled over and died. Because if Ren's superior Fae senses could hear what Fisher was whispering to me, then he could also scent how his friend's words were affecting me as well, and...and *gods, I would never live down the shame.*

I wouldn't admit it to myself, would never allow the thought to take shape, but my body wasn't as accomplished at lying as my mind was. I *did* want Fisher. I hated myself for it. Hated that he knew it. And now Ren knew, too. It was mortifying.

"Shut up. Please. Just...shut the hell *up.*"

A hungry look resided in his silver-rimmed eyes as he sat back in his chair. "Eat your dinner, Osha. You're going to need your strength. We won't be staying here for a week, after all. We're returning to the war camp in the morning...and this time you're coming with us."

AMMONTRAÍETH

THE WAR CAMP was a scar in the foothills on the other side of the Omnamerrin Mountains. It sat between Cahlish and the Sanas-rothian border—twenty thousand tents, nestled in amongst boulders and low, scrubby, snow-covered brush. As I stepped out of the shadow gate, my stomach hurtling upward in my chest, I saw just how many tents there were, pale and dirty gray in color, stretching off into the distance, and my breath caught in my throat.

This was a war camp.

It had obviously been here so long that there were now perma-nent structures, too—two-story buildings made out of wood, scat-tered all throughout the encampment. On my life, the one closest to the muddy square where Fisher's shadow gate had dumped us looked like a fucking *tavern*.

Everywhere, Fae warriors, both male and female, hurried about, heavily armed and wearing a variety of different kinds of armor. In the distance, a broad, wide ribbon of frozen water carved its way through the land, separating the camp from...from...

Graceless *gods.*

The land on the other side of the river was a blackened, charred wasteland. No snow covered the ground there. Pillars of smoke rose up to meet a grim, foreboding sky clad in a mantle of iron-gray clouds. There were no trees. No greenery. Only the black dirt, and the smoke, and in the distance the jagged outline of a black and terrible fortress situated on top of a looming hill.

"What in five hells happened *there?*" Carrion dumped his bag down at his feet, his mouth hanging open as he surveyed the scene before us. There was no mistaking his shock. It mirrored my own. I looked to my feet for Onyx, to pick him up and clutch him to my chest, but he wasn't there, of course. It was a small comfort that he was safe back at Cahlish. Fisher had refused to let me bring him. He'd insisted the fox wouldn't last more than five minutes in the camp, that his own warriors would snare him before any of us could blink, and that if I wanted to continue the fantasy that he made a good pet, I had to leave him behind in Archer's care.

Something uneasy twisted behind the cage of my ribs as I squinted, trying to get a better look at the fortress on the hill. "What *is* that place?"

"That is Ammontraíeth," Ren said, emerging from the shadow gate, leading his horse behind him. "The seat of the enemy."

"Ammontraíeth?" Even the name felt like a perversion as I forced it out.

"Hell's teeth."

The voice came from behind, cold and hard. Kingfisher emerged from the shadow gate, Bill's reins in his gloved hand. The massive black stallion snorted and blew. His flanks were slick with sweat, even though he'd only traveled from the stables to the camp through the gate. He clearly didn't like the idea of being here any more than I did. As soon as the horse's hindquarters were through the rippling wall of black smoke, the gate twisted in on itself and disintegrated into wisps of shadow that went chasing across the ground in every direction.

"Its walls are sheer, made of obsidian, slick as glass," Kingfisher said. "Built from the bones of demons. The peaks and spires are as sharp as a razor's edge."

Hell's teeth, indeed. I tucked my chin into the collar of the riding cloak Fisher had given me when we left the Winter Palace, fighting not to show my discomfort. The place had an ill air about it, even from this many miles away.

I jumped when a tall, wiry-looking creature with vines wrapped around its skinny arms and legs appeared from behind the tavern and purposefully strode toward us. Its skin was gnarled and knobbly like tree bark. Its eyes were a rich brown, dark as loamy earth. Instead of hair, a riot of vines and leaves sprouted from the top of its blockish head and trailed down its back. I was reasonably sure it was a male due to the pants and shirt it was wearing, though that wasn't a solid foundation to base any assumption on considering I was wearing very similar attire.

"Good morning, Lord," the creature said. His voice—definitely male—sounded like dry logs scraping together. "Glad to have you back so soon. The lodgings you requested have already been prepared. A small breakfast is waiting for you in your tent. More warriors have returned, back from their scouting missions. So few of your riders have seen you that only a handful are now inclined to trust the rumors flying around camp that you've returned. They're currently meeting in the map tent, and are arguing—"

"It's okay, Holgoth. Renfis will talk to them," Fisher said, handing him the reins.

Holgoth shot Ren an uncertain glance, then turned back to Fisher. "Sire, it...would be best if your warriors saw you. It's been so long since—"

"*Ren* will talk to them," Fisher repeated, smiling softly. "He's executed this war perfectly while I've been gone. I see no reason for a change in leadership. They're his warriors, not mine."

Ren looked down at his boots. He wasn't happy. Nor was Holgoth, who didn't seem to know quite what to do with himself. He dithered, passing Bill's reins from one knotty hand to the other, then sighed and reached out for Ren's horse's reins, too. "As you wish, sire—"

"Fisher. Just Fisher is fine."

Holgoth sadly shook his head. "No, sire. I apologize, but…no."

Kingfisher made his excuses and drew up his hood, disappearing into the war camp. Holgoth took the horses and insisted on relieving us of our bags as well, reassuring us that he'd keep them safe and we would find our things in our tents later. After he was gone, Ren snarled something in a language I didn't understand and stormed off in an easterly direction at a fast clip. "Are you two coming?" he shouted over his shoulder.

"Where are you going?" Carrion yelled back.

"Where do you think? To the godscursed armory!"

The Darn began in the east as a spring, up in the Shallow Mountains, where the Gilaríen Fae and the Autumn Court presided. Everlayne had mentioned them in the library when she and Rusarius had been trying to educate me about the other courts' quicksilver pools. I hadn't been paying attention, of course. My mind had been fixed solely on how I was going to steal Fisher's pendant, so I'd retained very little of the information they'd imparted about the other courts.

I listened a little closer as Ren talked about the river, though.

"At first, it's just a small pool. As it travels down through the mountains, it gains momentum and gathers more water to it. There are plains a couple of hundred miles away where the Darn is over a league wide." The general angled his sword over his head and charged, canines bared. It was a miracle that Carrion didn't shit his pants where he stood. I had never witnessed anything as terrifying as a blooded Fae warrior attacking at full speed, and I was willing to bet Carrion hadn't, either. To his credit, he managed to get his sword up just in time to block Ren's downward strike, though that was about it. Ren flicked Carrion's sword out of his hands and put him on his ass in the snow before he could blink a second time. I stifled a laugh as the male held out his hand, helping Carrion to his feet.

"You'll be laughing on the other side of your face soon." Carrion used one hand to dust the snow off his pants and the other to flip me off. "It's almost your turn. My ass can't take much more of this."

"I bet that's the first time you've said *those* words," I called.

He stuck out his tongue like a petulant child. "I'm more of a giver than a receiver, actually."

Ren clanged the end of Carrion's sword with his own. "Focus. You're dropping the blade the moment anything makes contact with it. Do that in a real fight, and you'll be dead in three seconds."

Carrion spat, breathing heavily. It was freezing cold. Fresh flakes of snow skirled in the air, eddying in circles, but Carrion had shed his cloak half an hour ago, and his shirt was marked with sweat. Once, my insides would have stumbled over the way I could make out his muscled chest through the damp material. But that was before.

Before *Fisher*.

"I think it's safe to say that I wouldn't last longer than three seconds regardless of where I put my sword," he panted. "You're a demon with that blade. Plus you're twice my size!"

"Oh, please. He's *three* times your size," I said.

I was flipped off again.

"Your size could be your greatest advantage," Ren advised. "You're smaller than me, so you could be quicker—"

"Hah! Please don't lie to me. You have Fae speed. I'm pretty light on my feet, but *you...*" Carrion shook his head in surrender.

Carrion *was* light on his feet. Despite my doubts, he was well-practiced with a sword and knew how to handle the weapon, but

Ren made him look like an infant struggling to find his feet for the first time. It would never be a fair fight between them.

Ren disregarded Carrion's complaining. "I've fought alongside humans who roared in the face of certain death, held their own in the charge, and emerged victorious from battle. They did their people proud. Will you give in so easily?" He batted the end of his sword against Carrion's again in a goading, playful way. The sound of metal on metal rang out along the bank of the frozen river. "And shame their memories in the process? Hmm?"

"Well, fuck me. When you put it like that…"

Carrion attacked. It could only be called an attack because Carrion was the one to move first. Ren took nimble, casual steps back as Carrion advanced, but he conceded the ground to the man, all the while easily rebuffing his strikes, reading every one of his moves before he'd even made it and generally making Carrion look like an idiot without even trying.

"In Loyanbal, at the center of the plains, the temperature drops, and the Darn becomes a band of solid silver. That is where the water freezes first." Ren parried Carrion's sword away as if batting away an irritating fly. "Early in the season, the ice is over eight inches thick. Strong. Safe. Solid enough to support a rider and horse and permit them to cross."

I watched Ren closely. The loose set of his shoulders. The way he twisted at his hips, not his shoulders. The real work was happening lower to the ground, though. It was impressive how he moved, stepping and transferring his weight, graceful and catlike, never crossing his feet. He had complete mastery over his body. He made fighting look as easy as breathing.

Clang!

Clang!

"*Oof!*" Carrion crossed his feet—*he* clearly hadn't been watching Ren's technique—then tried to retreat when Ren lunged at last, and the thief went down. He hit the ground so hard that I heard his teeth crack together from ten feet away. "In the dead of winter, the

Darn becomes the only means of travel between the mountains and the sea," Ren said, circling his prey. "The passes choke with snow and are blocked. Traders, pilgrims, and pirates alike all tread the creaking Darn in order to make a living."

Carrion threw up his hands. "I surrender! I'm...fucking beat." He fought to swallow. "Torture her now. I need to...catch my breath."

Ren turned his attention to me, and my spine stiffened a touch. Not with fear, exactly. More...anticipation. I knew more than the basics of sword fighting. I'd held plenty of them. I'd made enough of them in secret while apprenticing with Elroy in his workshop. I knew how they were weighted. How they tipped in your hand when you swung them. I knew what the press of a cold steel hilt felt like resting on the top of a closed hand. But these Fae swords were different. The blades themselves were narrower. Longer. The cross guard was nonexistent, as if a Fae warrior would never make a mistake so stupid as allowing their hands to slip forward down a sharpened edge.

Ren did exactly that, though. He took the weapon Carrion had been practicing with by the blade and crossed the riverbank, holding it out, offering me the grip. "What do you say, Saeris? Want to try your hand at a little point and stab?"

No. I was going to say no. Definitely. One hundred percent. I was still convinced that I was going to decline, even as my hand closed around the leather-wrapped hilt. *Fuck.* I really didn't have it in me to back down from a challenge...

Ren grinned broadly. "Atta girl." He spun around and headed back to the clearing where he'd "fought" Carrion, resting the blade of his own sword on his shoulder. "In the west, in Voriel, at the port city of Western Dow, the Darn flows out into the s—"

He turned and blocked. It happened so fast. One second, his back was to me. The next, he had dropped low, his shoulder level with my chest, and his sword was raised defensively above his head, edge to edge with mine.

I hadn't *actually* been going to strike him. I'd turned the blade so that only the flat would have made contact with his shoulder. It had seemed like a smart-ass way to begin our lesson. Elroy had gotten me with the old *Never lower your defenses, never turn your back on your enemy,* more times than I could count. Fat lot it had done me, though. Turned out, Renfis's guard was never down. That, or the general had eyes in the back of his head. He didn't even blink. "On a clear day, you can see all the way to Tarran Ross Island from the cliffs of Western Dow."

He came at me.

I saw a flash of silver as his sword moved.

And then I saw the snow-pregnant sky.

And then I saw the ground.

Then I saw stars.

It was all over in a heartbeat.

Carrion's loud whoop echoed along the riverbank. "That *was* funny. Now I see why you were laughing so hard."

I'd have cursed him roundly for being such a prick, but he was right. I'd laughed at him plenty. It was only fair. And I couldn't fucking breathe anyway.

Ren appeared in the patch of sky above my head. He frowned down at me. "You all right?"

"Ugh. Uh…yes?"

He laughed. "Want to go again?"

"Yes." I mean, once you'd already had your legs taken out from underneath you, what was another ten or eleven face-first collisions with hard packed snow? Even as I allowed him to help me to my feet, I made the decision there and then that I wouldn't go down again, though.

I'd watched Renfis. I'd studied the way he moved, so I adapted my own fighting stance, and I learned quick. When he attacked again, I was ready. He rained down blows on me, the steel in his hands flashing like lightning, but I met each of his advances with an appropriate block. When he switched up his hold and wielded his sword like it was a club, I adjusted my stance again and made sure I threw back each of his assaults.

At first, I simply defended myself. An hour passed, the clouds growing ever darker, and Ren's appraising feedback took on a challenging note. "What's the matter, Saeris? You'll never win a fight if you're afraid to wet your steel with blood. Come on. *Fight* me."

Oh, it was a fight he wanted?

If he wanted a fight, I'd give him one.

It was good, being able to move like this. To have a proper weapon in my hands. Ever since Harron had bound my hands behind my back and run me through, I'd felt vulnerable. Weak. Incapable. But now...I was myself again. The girl who'd taken down three of Madra's guardians outside The Mirage. The girl many a Zilvaren thug had underestimated at their own peril. All of the rage and the fear that had been choking me since the Hall of Mirrors welled up inside of me and rose up the back of my throat.

I flew at Renfis, sword raised, and I *screamed.*

The general had faced down worse foes than me. I couldn't imagine some of the horrors he'd gone toe-to-toe with during his time fighting this war. But the skin around his eyes *did* tighten a touch as he parried my first series of strikes. He *was* having to concentrate, just a little. I was no fool. He could end this in a heartbeat if he wanted to. But my pride swelled when I managed to make Ren retreat a step. An actual step of retreat, earned not given. Carrion hadn't managed that. I—

"You hurl yourself at the end of that sword like you *want* to die."

I'd been readying another twisting blow, but the close proximity of the voice, right next to my ear, threw me off guard. The end of Ren's sword circled my own, ripping the weapon out of my grip, and the sword went sailing through the air. It arced beautifully, landing point-first in the snow at Kingfisher's feet.

The bastard *clapped.* "I see you've perfected the art of being disarmed." He was still wearing his thick black cloak, though the hood was lowered now. We were far enough from the borders of the camp that no one would see him down here. The wolf's head gorget flashed silver at this throat.

"I know it's virtually impossible, but could you at least try to be nice?" Ren asked, squinting at Fisher through the fat snowflakes that started to fall with a purpose out of nowhere.

Fisher considered his request. Shrugged. "I could *try.*"

Of course he would show up right as I was about to get inside Ren's guard. Of course he would ruin my focus. It was just my luck. I wouldn't give him the satisfaction of seeing me rankled, though. Not this time. "Let me guess. You've come to show me personally just how useless I am with a sword? Come on, then." I held my hand out, gesturing for him to come forward. "Be my guest." I might not hold my own against the likes of him for very long, but I'd make sure I got at least one hit in before he thrashed me.

Kingfisher smirked ruinously. "You're not ready for *me,* human. I don't come with a training mode."

"Are the captains gathered?" Ren asked, striding toward Fisher. "Is it time to speak with them?"

Fisher nodded. "Just waiting on one or two stragglers."

"Then I'll need to head back to my tent and change. I'll meet you there."

Fisher caught Ren's arm as he passed. "I don't think I'll be needed."

For the first time since meeting him, I watched Renfis bristle with anger. "You're more than needed. You're *required.* We're done with this, Brother. If you bear me any love or respect at all, you'll come to the meeting."

Fisher's expression formed a defiant *no* at first, but then he met Ren's eyes, huffed with annoyance, and let him go. "All right. Fine. I'll be there. But take the boy with you for now, will you? I need to speak with the Alchemist."

Was "Alchemist" an upgrade from "Osha"? Didn't sound like it. Not when it was said with the same heaping dose of disdain. I hurried after Fisher, who moved with frustrating speed through the camp, his head ducked to avoid the curious eyes of the Fae warriors who watched him flit past their cookfires with interest. After a while, I realized that it wasn't actually Fisher they were interested in. It was me.

"Human?"

"A human."

"It's a *human*…"

I kept forgetting that I was an oddity here. Word had traveled quickly around the Winter Palace that a human had arrived after my kind had been absent from Fae lands for so long. The shine had worn off pretty quickly there. It hadn't taken long for the members of the Yvelian court to forget all about me. Here, I was a novelty that hadn't been seen in centuries. Some of the warriors had clearly never laid eyes on a human woman before in their entire lives. The pressure of their eyes made me want to find a dark hole to crawl into, but I didn't have that luxury here, so I jogged after Fisher instead.

"Where the hell are you taking me?"

"To my quarters," he said, the words clipped.

His quarters? I was going to raise holy hell if he tried to bind me there again. "Gods, will you slow the fuck down? My legs are a lot shorter than yours."

Fisher grumbled something, but he did slow down a little. I waited for him to lead me into one of the wooden structures at the center of the camp. We passed a mercantile and what looked like a food store, along with a number of other mysterious buildings, and then there were no more solid structures left. Only the sea of tents.

A large tent, then. Had to be. Fisher would need a sizable space to house his fucking ego, after all. But there were no tents with grand awnings or entrances festooned with shimmering fabrics. They were all the same size, and one was just as dirty and weather-bleached as the next.

Eventually, Kingfisher ceased his charge through the churned-up mud—thanks to the hundreds of boots stomping through the walkways, the snow couldn't stick here—and grabbed a tent flap, stepping to one side as he held it open. "Go in. Please." He winced when he said please; manners were evidently painful to Fisher.

I entered the tent willingly thanks to that word, though. Inside, a small fire burned in a grate that wasn't vented in the slightest. There was no smoke. It was going to take a long time for me to adjust to the common, everyday use of magic. It was quite impressive, though, as was the size of Fisher's quarters. In some ways, I had been right. Fisher had secured a comfortable base for himself. You just wouldn't have known it from the outside. The tent's interior formed on a large space, at least ten times bigger than it should have been given the tent's dimensions. A huge king-sized bed sat at the back of the tent, nowhere near as grand as his bed back at Cahlish but still far more impressive than the small field cot I assumed was waiting for me somewhere in this muddy hell hole. There was a tall bookshelf next to the fire, heaped with a messy stack of books. There were books everywhere, in fact, stacked on the rug—yes, the *rug*—by the foot of the bed, teetering in a pile on the floor beside the overstuffed couch. There was even one propped open at a page, lying on the washstand by the entrance to the tent.

"Doing some research?" I couldn't imagine that he was the type to settle down with a work of fiction.

Fisher surveyed the collection of tomes that covered every available surface and grunted. "You could say that."

"Something important?"

"Very important to me," he clipped out. From the hard edge in his voice, he wasn't going to say anything further on the matter.

I let it drop.

In the very center of the tent was a wooden table big enough to seat four people, on which sat a basket of bread rolls and two bowls of steaming hot soup.

I stared at the table—at the soup and the *two* settings—and asked in a flat tone, "What's this?"

Fisher heaved out a weary breath, unfastening his cloak. He threw it onto the bed, then sat heavily down in a chair at the table, rubbing at his temple. "It's just a meal," he said. "Let's eat it and try not to draw blood this time, shall we? Please?"

There was that word again.

Fighting him was my baseline. All I knew. But he looked so tired, his mood genuinely bleak, that I didn't have the heart to kick up a fuss. I joined him and started to eat in silence.

Fisher stopped rubbing his temple. He watched me, following my every movement. The quicksilver in his right eye spun around his pupil like it was caught in a hurricane. When I was more than halfway through the soup, he picked up his own spoon and began to eat, too. "I watched you for a while back there. You fight well," he murmured.

A compliment? From Fisher? Rather than filling me with pride, annoyance seethed beneath the surface of my skin. "And I bet you're *so* shocked. A female human, holding her own against a Fae warrior. That must have grated something fierce."

He gave me an arch look. "No. I wasn't shocked. You can tell by the way a person moves if they've had training. I knew from the first moment I saw you on your feet that you could fight. But don't get ahead of yourself, Osha. Ren was going easy on you."

"You don't think I could have taken him?" Even I knew I couldn't have. Of course I did. But it still was fun to bait Fisher into thinking I was serious.

But Fisher didn't take the bait. "He wouldn't be the general of this army if you could have." He nodded toward me as I swallowed down a mouthful of soup. "So you *are* compliant sometimes," he said softly.

I paused, another spoonful of soup halfway between my mouth and the bowl. "Amazing, isn't it? People prefer to acquiesce to a request rather than being forced to follow a command. Who'd have known."

He slid his own spoon into his mouth, eyes quick and sharp, the muscles in his neck working as he swallowed. I could make out the tattoos on the back of his hands now, all too well. Both of them were Fae runes. The intricate, interlocking lines of them shifted and moved across the surface of his skin, the pattern changing and evolving even as I watched. I looked away. "Why do you even want me to be compliant?" I asked. "Cowing people, having power over them...is that what you want? Like Belikon? Is that what *drives* you?"

His expression shuttered at the mention of his stepfather. He quickly recovered, but his jaw took on a hard set as he plucked a bread roll from the basket. "Power isn't something I've ever thirsted after, Little Osha," he said quietly. "And I am nothing like the king."

"I didn't think so. So why are you so determined to control everything that I do? Are humans just...just *slaves* here? Is that it?"

He laughed mirthlessly, shaking his head. "Humans have never been slaves here. At least not to the Yvelians. When we were blighted with our blood curse thousands of years ago, you were definitely *dinner*. But never slaves."

The blood curse. The one he'd spoken of before, back in the halls of the Winter Palace. He'd said the sharp canines the Fae still possessed were a remnant of that curse. Were their children born with them, though? Or had Kingfisher been alive then? Had he suffered under the curse and then been freed from it? Every Fae I'd seen had elongated teeth, so I doubted that was the case. It was more likely that they were part of their genetics now.

Fisher locked eyes with me. "I want you to obey me because *I* brought you here. That makes me responsible for you. And I need you alive so that you can work on those rings for us. Without them, we'll be trapped in this stalemate with the Sanasroth forever, neither side winning nor losing. I'll never be able to reclaim my family's lands. So, yes. I *will* force you to obey me if I need to. And I won't feel conflicted about it. The stakes are too high."

"Have you paused to consider that I might *want* to stay alive? That I'd do whatever it was you wanted me to do if you just explained why it was important to my well-being?"

He regarded me, hair curling into his face, half obscuring his eyes. A rush of something hot and not entirely unpleasant burned right behind my breastbone. It wasn't just how he looked. There was something else there, too. Something that made my body come alive. His scent, and the way I knew that he'd entered a room before I saw him, and the melancholy tug at the root of my soul whenever he *wasn't* in a room, and—

Fisher tore his gaze from mine, looking down at his bowl. "My way is a lot faster," he whispered. "You can't be risked. Those rings can't be risked. All of this hangs in the balance."

I slammed down my spoon. "You're *incorrigible!*"

"I don't know what that means."

"Yes, you fucking do!"

"All right. I do. What's your point?"

"I want to help you, Fisher! I'll do it gladly. I might not understand your people or even believe that everyone in this realm deserves saving, but that's not my judgment call to make, is it? For some reason, I have this weird ability that can help protect Yvelia from being ravaged by a tide of corrupted, bloodthirsty monsters. I've seen what they're capable of. I know how horrifying they are, and I wouldn't wish them upon anyone! Can't you just *trust* that I—"

Black shadows spilled from Fisher's fingers. Smoke roiled up the table legs and swept across the tabletop like morning mist rolling across a field. It swallowed our food, the wicker basket, everything. With a crash, the table flipped, toppling to the floor, and then Fisher was on his feet, lifting me out of my chair, lifting me from the ground...crossing the tent. My back slammed up against something solid and hard—a bookcase?—but it wasn't the shock of the pain that ripped the air from my lungs. It was Fisher's mouth.

His lips crashed down onto mine. For a brief moment, I didn't react. I'd slipped into a daydream. This was a fantasy. It wasn't...it wasn't real.

But the second his tongue moved past my lips, past my teeth, and I tasted him, and I felt the blast of his breath against my face, I knew better. It *was* real. Shockingly so...and I wanted it more than I wanted air. Casting off my shock, I wrapped my legs around his waist, hooking my feet at the ankles behind his back. I threaded my fingers into his hair, and I kissed him back like my life depended on it. He held me in place, pinning me against whatever was behind me, which freed his hands to move to my waist. They didn't stay there long. I let out a sharp moan as Fisher's hands found my breasts. He kneaded the swell of my flesh, pinching one of my nipples through my shirt, and a wave of need crested between my legs. I became hyper-aware of him. Of all the places where our bodies were connecting. I was touching him. Touching him everywhere. He was hard-packed muscle and hot, demanding breath, and the scent of fresh, cool mountain wind, and mint, and the forest at night, and—

"Gods! *Fisher!*"

His mouth was at my neck. My skin exploded into goose bumps as he kissed and laved at the sensitive skin there, the wet, scorching heat of his tongue running up the column of my throat surprising me so badly that I moaned out loud.

"*Fuck.*" He snarled the guttural curse into the crook of my neck, at the same time driving his hips upward so that I felt...oh, *gods.* His cock was trapped between our bodies, and he was *so* fucking hard. With my legs locked around his waist, he was lined up perfectly against me. The pressure he applied when he rocked his hips upward sent my brain scattering in a thousand different directions.

Oh...

Fucking...

I needed...

"Fisher!" I cried out his name.

He let out a wordless, animalistic growl in response that sent a thrill of anticipation chasing all the way down my spine. Waves of heat crashed over me, settling in my stomach. I was swept away by it on a burning tide. I had no clue when I'd started grinding myself against his cock. Only that he tensed every time I did it, his fingers digging into my skin, his mouth becoming more insistent at my neck.

"Fuck! Fisher, I want...I want you..." I panted.

And, as if I'd just dowsed him with a bucket of cold water, Fisher tore his mouth from my skin and pulled back. A split second later, my feet were back on solid ground, and Fisher was on the other side of the tent, dragging his hands through his hair. I felt his absence like a physical blow.

Oh, *fuck.*

A million thoughts slammed into me at once.

That was a terrible idea.

I should *not* have let him do that.

I should *not* have kissed him back.

I shouldn't have rubbed myself against his cock like that.

I shouldn't have moaned.

I definitely shouldn't have told him that I wanted him.

For the love of all the gods in all the heavens, why had I *said* that?

I was going to throw up.

Fisher pressed the heels of his hands into his eyes, groaning. He looked up, looked at *me*, and my stomach dropped. "Fisher—"

He crossed the tent so fast. Cupping my face in his hands, he kissed me again. Hard. Fast. His lips were on mine again, though they didn't part. It only lasted a second, but it caused complete and utter fucking chaos inside my head. "Fisher—"

He shook his head emphatically, his eyes *begging* me not to speak. Quickly, he took hold of my hand and placed it onto his chest, right in the center.

Thum, thum, thum, thum, thum, thum....

His heart was racing, the space between beats barely negligible. Nothing like the slow, steady beat he'd shown me back in the forge at the palace. I tried to pull my hand away, startled by the thundering rhythm, but Fisher held me there tight.

He didn't say a word. He held my gaze, unblinking, and for once, the quicksilver that marked his eye was still. There was no arrogance in his features. No bravado. No smug smirk. The look he was giving me was deadly serious. Like it meant something. He swallowed, his chest rising and falling too fast, and then he nodded.

"I can't trust *anything*," he whispered breathlessly. And *that* was when he let me go. When I needed him not to. Right when I needed him to stay and explain what the last one hundred and twenty seconds meant. He gathered up his cloak, swung it around his shoulders, and headed out into the waning light.

Fisher hadn't asked me to stay in his tent. He hadn't compelled me to wait there, either, and so I did what any sane woman would do: I bolted. The light was fading fast as I ran through the war camp. Everywhere I looked, Fae warriors clad in armor were streaming toward the center of the camp. All of them were armed. Only half of them bothered to look twice at me. A frenetic, agitated energy filled the air. The smell of smoke and cooking meat assaulted my senses, but nothing could replace the scent of mint and midnight forest in my nose.

He'd kissed me.

He'd done a hell of a lot more than that, actually. I could still feel his hands on my waist. My nipple still throbbed with the ache he had put there. My pulse became a frantic tattoo as I slipped through the crowd, trying to find...

Gods, where was I even going? I had no clue. I just had to get away from Fisher's tent. Inadvertently, I allowed myself to be swept along in the tide of warriors. It had stopped snowing at some point, and now the sky was a purple bruise, the clouds angry and foreboding as I ran. Eventually, I couldn't run any farther. The mountains speared up ahead, punching toward the sky, and to the south, the Darn wrapped around the camp, trapping me within its boundary. I was forced to follow the warriors down to the large tent in the clearing ahead, where a massive fire roared and leaped up to meet the dusk.

It was luck that I found Ren. The crowd of warriors parted for him as he made his way among them, headed for the tent, and by some miracle, I was left standing in the general's path. His dark eyes were stormy, but they softened when they landed on me. "Saeris? Where's Fisher?" he asked, placing a hand on my shoulder, urging me alongside him as he walked.

"I'm not sure." It was the truth.

A tense, knowing look formed on his face as he took me in, his nostrils flaring, and he smelled...Ah, *shit.* "Are you okay?" he asked carefully.

"Yes! Yes, of course. He hasn't..." My cheeks flared red hot. "He didn't do anything wrong."

"Of course not. I know him. Fisher would never..." He tiptoed around what he wanted to say, ushering me inside the tent. Delicately, he said, "I can smell *you* as well as him, Saeris. I wasn't worried that he'd hurt you. I was asking if you were okay. There's a difference."

I pushed back against a second round of embarrassment, refusing to give it power. Was this what I had to look forward to? Every single member of the Fae giving me sideways glances every time I was the least bit turned on? Urgh! "I'm fine," I said, speaking with more confidence this time. "I promise, I'm totally fine. I just had no idea where anyone was, that's all."

Stifling heat greeted us inside the war tent. Or the war *room,* I should say. Magic hadn't made the space larger inside here. It had turned it into an actual room, with stone walls hung with tapestries and paintings of battles, and a proper fireplace, and a stone floor. The ceilings were twenty feet high. Bookcases, small side tables, and every other available surface were covered with candles, the light thrown off by their flames dancing up the walls. At least twenty warriors were gathered here, waiting for Ren. They all turned and dipped their heads in deference to him when they saw that he'd arrived.

Carrion was here, too, sprawled out on a chair, sitting by the fire. A small plate rested on his stomach; the fucker was eating a fat slice of cake, unfazed by the tension hanging thick in the air.

"Go and sit with Swift," Ren murmured to me. "As close to the fire as you can bear. The heat will burn off the, ah..." He grimaced. "Well, you get the picture."

Oh, I got it all right. The heat would burn off all of the pheromones that I was covered in because I had come *this* close to fucking Kingfisher. Gods alive.

I kicked Carrion's boots, grunting at him to move, when I reached the fire. The suggestive way he grinned at me made me think he could smell what I'd been up to as well, but that wasn't possible. Our human noses weren't that sensitive.

"I can't believe you're eating cake," I groused, dragging a footstool dangerously close to the fire.

"It isn't cake. It's quiche," Carrion said around a full mouth.

"What's quiche?"

"Dunno. It's made out of eggs and some other stuff. It's delicious. Here." He held out the slab of food. "Want some?"

I wasn't hungry. I felt pretty sick, actually, but I needed something to do with my hands. Taking the quiche, I bit into it, not really tasting it, and then handed it back.

"Some serious shit's about to go down in here," Carrion remarked, taking another bite for himself.

So he wasn't completely oblivious to the weird energy in here, then. "You don't say."

"That one's been baying for blood." He gestured non-too-subtly to a female warrior standing by the large table in the center of the room, who was talking animatedly to three males. Her hair was a stark blond, almost white, her eyes a vivid shade of lilac. She was beautiful in a way that hurt to look at. "I can't tell what they're whispering about, but one by one, they've all been to talk to her. Some of them have been arguing with her. She *punched* that one," Carrion said, nodding to a male with long black war braids and snarling wolf head sigil stamped into his leather chest protector. "I get the feeling this is all because of Fisher, though. Uh, Saeris?"

The male with the dark war braids noticed me looking at him. Rather than glower at me, he cocked his head at an angle and gave me a small, friendly smile.

Carrion flicked the top of my ear.

"Ow! What the fuck? What's *wrong* with you? That hurt!" I pressed my fingers to the shell of my ear.

"Why is your neck bleeding?" he said slowly, enunciating every word slowly.

"What?"

Reaching out, he swiped his hand over my skin. I ducked out of his reach, but it was too late; when he showed me his fingertips, they were streaked red.

"Just a scratch." Carrion shrugged. "You must have caught yourself on something. Here." He passed back the quiche.

I accepted it and took a bite, my mind spiraling out of control. Why the fuck was my neck bleeding?

As if conjured by my racing thoughts, a figure in a black cloak entered the tent, the cowl of his hood drawn up to hide his features. His presence made my heart pound, though. Fisher's eyes found me immediately. He watched me dumbly pass the quiche back to Carrion, his expression unreadable. A series of gasps went up on the other side of the war room, when, one by one, the Fae all saw who had arrived.

"So it is true, then," the blond warrior announced. "You *are* alive."

"Of course he's alive, Danya," Ren said in a weary tone. "We never thought he was *dead*. Come on. Let's start this off on the right foot. Fisher, lose the cloak already. You're not fooling anyone."

Fisher's head hung as he removed the cloak. His hair was wet. Dripping wet. So were his clothes. Rivulets of water ran down his cheeks. A small puddle was beginning to form at his feet. He leaned back against the wall, chin raised, folding his arms across his chest.

"What about it, Fish? Been out for an early evening swim?" There was a playful note to Danya's voice, but I wasn't the only one who detected the venom there, too. Carrion raised his eyebrows at me like one of the old gossips who liked to while away their afternoons standing outside the House of Kala. He took a chunk out of the quiche and passed it to me.

Across the room, Kingfisher watched him do it, the muscles in his jaw working. He let his head hang again, huffing. "Something like that," he said quietly.

"Come on, then." Danya held her arms wide. "We're all here, Fisher. Let's hear it. Let's hear the amazing fucking reason why you left us high and dry for the past century. And why you've decided to slink back to us now with your tail between your legs, mm?"

"I'm not slinking anywhere." Fisher sounded bored.

"Bullshit," Danya spat. "You were here in camp all last week! The week before that, too!"

"Danya—"

"No! *No*, Fisher. You were here, and you didn't breathe a fucking word of it to any of us. How many times have every single one of us in this room stood at your side and bled with you? We were supposed to be a family, and you just fucking abandoned us."

Fisher said nothing. It was Ren who stepped in to defend him. "That isn't what happened, and you know it."

"Hah! Please! All *I* know is that I stood on the battlements at Gillethrye, watching an entire city full of Yvelian families burn to death while Malcolm's horde sacked the city, and *he* suddenly disappeared into thin air!"

"You have no idea what you're talking about." Ren's face was a mask of fury. I wouldn't have thought him capable of such anger.

"You're right! I don't! Someone should enlighten me before I put my sword through this treacherous bastard's throat!"

"Careful, Danya." Not Ren this time. The male with the black war braids who'd smiled at me earlier moved around the table to stand next to Fisher. "I might let you land a hit on me for fun, but you're out of your fucking mind if you think I'll let you open up the commander's throat."

"It's all right, Lorreth," Fisher said softly.

"He's *not* our commander!" Danya yelled, pointing furiously at Fisher. "He sacrificed that title when he abandoned us!"

"Stand down, Danya," Ren snarled, baring his teeth. Gods alive, this was going to end in bloodshed. I broke off a piece of the quiche's crust and put it into my mouth. At any other time, the food probably would have melted in my mouth, but right now, it tasted like ash.

Kingfisher's eyes darted to me. He flinched.

"For fuck's sake, tell them what happened," Ren said, rounding on Fisher. "They'll understand as soon as—"

"No." The word rang out along the war room. Kingfisher pushed away from the wall, standing up to his full height. His eyes were full of regret as he surveyed the faces of the Fae who stood before him. "I'm sorry, I truly am. I didn't want to leave any of you back at Gillethrye. I wish I could tell you why I had to go, but I can't. All I can say is that I had no other choice."

A tear slid down Danya's cheek. Her voice cracked as she took a step forward and said, "It was Belikon, wasn't it? He forced you to go. I understand why we had to torch the city, but—"

"*I can't tell you,*" Fisher said. His mask shattered. Torment shone from his eyes. "I wish I could, but I can't. I returned as soon as I could. *Believe* me."

She stared at him, her beautiful violet eyes brimming with more unshed tears. She did want to believe him, I thought. Wanted his words to be enough. But they weren't. She ripped her sword from its sheath at her hip and bared her teeth. "Traitor!" she screamed. She moved in a streak of shining gold, her body blurring as she flew at him.

I watched it happen: the pain on her face, and the point of her sword aimed at Fisher's throat, and the way his shoulders sagged, as if he'd made his peace with whatever came next and was ready for it. I had no intention of standing. My hand raised of its own accord. The shout of panic tore out of my mouth without any doing on my part. "*STOP!*"

Danya's body rocked sideways. She slammed into the table, her hip colliding with the wood. But that wasn't what drew twenty pairs of stunned eyes toward me. It was her sword, splintering into a thousand shards, the quivering steel needles shooting through the air and hitting the wall above Ren's head so hard that they drove an inch into the pitted stonework.

Carrion toppled sideways, bracing against the side of the hearth, his mouth hanging slack. "Holy *fuck*," he gasped.

Everyone else mirrored his surprise. Only Fisher remained calm. He considered me very seriously, a small frown drawing his dark brows together.

Danya righted herself, slowly pivoting toward me—the first time she'd actually paid me any heed since I'd entered with Renfis. She looked like her head was going to explode. "We have a fucking *Alchemist?*"

"She's *mine,*" Fisher said.

Before anyone could react to that, a thunderous *BOOM!* shook the ground beneath our feet.

"ICE BREAKERS! ICE BREAKERS! ICE BREAKERS!" The cry came from outside.

"What's happening?" I whispered.

All hell broke loose. The war room detonated into a flurry of activity as the Fae warriors, Ren included, all sprinted for the exit, their weapons suddenly drawn. Fisher remained immobile for a split second longer than the rest, his eyes still homing in on me, that strange frown marring his brow, but then he was moving, too. He disappeared in a shiver of glittering black sand.

The black-haired male called Lorreth was the very last to leave the tent. "Stay here," he ordered. "Do not leave this place. I mean it."

"But what the fuck's going on?" Carrion demanded.

"Sanasroth. The enemy's at the riverbank. The ice must be broken so that the dead cannot cross."

21

ICE BREAKER

Night had fallen while we were inside. The sky was black as pitch, and a vicious wind had kicked up, sending a maelstrom of embers from the campfires swirling all over the place. One landed on my cloak, singeing it, but that was the least of my worries. Every warrior in camp was rushing toward the bank of the Darn, carrying monstrous sledgehammers and wicked axes in their hands.

"We should keep out of the way," I repeated for the fifteen millionth time. Carrion hadn't heeded me the first time I said it, and he wasn't listening now either.

"I'm not hiding in a tent when it sounds like we're all in grave danger," he said.

"Have you forgotten how many times Ren put you down this morning? We are way out of our league here."

A look of resolve had settled over Carrion, though. "I might not be able to match these fuckers in a fight, but I can sure as hell break some ice. And anyway, it turns out my ex can make shrapnel out of swords, so I reckon we're gonna be just fine."

"I am not your ex. And I did *not* know I could do that! I don't think I can do it again!"

"Let's hope we don't need to find out." Carrion took off at break-neck speed. For a second, I considered heading back inside the war room, but he was right. I couldn't just hide in there while the world sounded like it was ending out here. It took twenty seconds for me to catch up to him. Another minute for us to find our way down to the riverbank.

We both stood there, stunned to silence, taking in the chaos.

Huge warriors, twice as tall and twice as wide as Fisher, stood at the edge of the river. In time to the pounding of a drum that rang out farther downriver, they heaved giant sledgehammers over their heads and brought them down with terrifying force onto the thick ice.

BOOM!

BOOM!

BOOM!

The frosted ice fractured and splintered, making metallic, rippling sounds, but the surface held. On the other side of the bank, a seething dark mass had gathered and was *roaring.*

"What...is that?" Carrion whispered.

A fighter hurried past us, breathing erratically. Not Fae. It was Holgoth, the earth sprite who had greeted us when we arrived at camp. "That..." he panted. "Is the better part of the Sanasrothian horde. Fifty thousand strong. We had...no warning. If they make the crossing, they'll...overrun us!"

"What do you mean, horde?" Carrion bellowed after him as he ran down toward the river.

Holgoth yelled one word in answer. *"Vampires!"*

Boom! Boom! Boom!

The sledgehammers rained down on the ice.

I scanned the dark, looking for any sign of Fisher, but he was nowhere to be seen. Nor was Ren. Everywhere, unfamiliar faces, tight with nerves, ran to lay their hammers against the ice. A spark of blue temporarily lit up the scene, illuminating the other side of the bank, and what I saw there turned my legs to lead.

There were thousands.

Writhing. Seething. Snarling. Snapping.

Fifty thousand bloodthirsty feeders, baying at the riverbank. Even as the source of the blue light appeared—a white-hot orb that arced through the air and fell to the middle of the river—the first of the vampires were halfway across the ice. The orb exploded, shattering a small hole in the surface when it made contact. Water erupted fifty feet into the air, but the vampires didn't seem to notice. In droves, they began their approach.

"Fuck me," Carrion muttered. "Fucking fuck me."

I couldn't voice my agreement. But I felt it.

Another blue-white orb jettisoned into the air, throwing wild shadows over the approaching mass and the warriors on our side of the bank. Another, and another, and another went up into the air. Loud cracking sounds tore the night apart as they exploded, creating larger holes in the ice. Now that this section of the river was unstable, the hammers slamming down onto the surface at the river's edge were more effective. Little by little, the ice began to spiderweb and crack.

"Will it work?" Carrion whispered.

"I don't know. Come on. We need to help."

A ridiculous thing to say. Just one of those massive fighters with the hammers could have taken down half of the buildings in the Third by themselves, and yet the ice was so thick that they were making slow progress. We were so weak in comparison. So human. But still, we both took up the heavy hammers we found waiting on the bank and brought them down onto the Darn with all our might.

Jets of fire tore across the river once the first wave of vampires were in range. They went up like tinder, but the flames didn't stop them. Closer, they came. Closer still.

My arms screamed, my back a knot of agony, but I pounded the ice, the skin of my palms ripping as I swung the hammer down.

The ice shuddered and let out an unholy moan, and suddenly the whole thing shattered.

As soon as it happened, a carpet of black smoke rolled across the river, sweeping in fast. The vampires who had staggered out onto the ice plunged into the freezing water, and without hesitation, the smoke seemed to solidify and shove them beneath the surface. It grappled with them, pushing them down, wrapping around them, and dragging them to their watery graves.

"What's happening?" Carrion scanned up and down the bank, wild-eyed.

"Fisher," I answered grimly. "This is *all* Fisher."

The vampires stopped coming. The huge Ice Breaker Fae still pounded and smashed at the ice both to the left and the right, but the rabid horde on the Sanasrothian side of the river didn't bother to come again. They snarled and moaned but maintained their position.

"Good evening, Kingfisher!" a voice called out from the dark. "I'm so glad you decided to come out and play! Won't you say hello?"

A fighter who had joined us along the same stretch of bank, a female with bright red hair, paled at the sound of that voice. So did a number of other warriors. "Is that *Malcolm?*" She spoke as if she couldn't believe her own ears. "It can't be…"

"It's him all right," a male with a jagged scar along his jaw said, glowering into the darkness. "He's come out of his fortress to taunt the commander."

"But…"

"Come on, Kingfisher! Won't you show yourself? I will, if that's what you're waiting for!" The throng of monsters on the other bank parted, and there he was. A tall, slender, unassuming-looking male dressed in black. His hair was straight as an arrow and white as snow, hanging down past his shoulders. His features were fine. Handsome, almost. Bloodred eyes scoured our side of the bank, as if he had no trouble seeing through the swathes of black smoke that still rolled across the surface of the river. "Come on, Kingfisher," the devil called in a singsong voice. "I know you're over there. It's only been a couple of weeks since we last spoke, but what can I say? I miss you."

A rumble went up amongst the Fae at this. Malcolm *missed* Fisher? It had only been a couple of weeks since they'd spoken? The implication was clear. This Malcolm, king of the vampires, wanted everyone amongst the Fae to know that their precious leader, returned to them at long last, was in league with him in some way. Guerilla warfare at its finest. The easiest way to win any war was to create dissent amongst your enemy's ranks so that they wasted their time and energy fighting each other instead of you. It was a smart move but an obvious one. Still, from the looks on the faces of the warriors surrounding us, Fisher was going to have some explaining to do.

"Fine! Have it your way, darling!" Malcolm called. A cruel smile spread across his face, exposing a row of sharp teeth. "Hide behind your little friends. I'll be seeing you very soon!"

THE ITCH

He found me half an hour later.

I was sitting in front of a fire outside the war room, drinking the hot cider that Ren had handed to me. His eyes were wild, hair even wilder. He made straight for me but barked out a question to Ren. "Have you got the annoying one?"

"I have," Ren answered tiredly.

"Uh, I hope you're not talking about me," Carrion said, but Fisher didn't honor him with a response.

He held out his hand to me and said, "Take it, or I carry you."

I gave him my hand.

"We'll be back in the morning," he said to Ren. And then he stepped back into the swirling black vortex that appeared behind him and pulled me into the shadow gate.

Onyx growled, teeth bared, when I stepped into Fisher's bedroom. It was just as it had been during my forced incarceration here after the feeder attack. Moody. Full of shadows and dark corners. In other words, perfectly *Fisher*. I tensed when I inhaled, my head flooding with the smell of wild mint and pine needles, but it wasn't the room this time. It was the male himself, standing so close behind me that the heat of his body warmed my back. Fisher's tattooed hands came around me and worked deftly at the cloak's tie, unfastening it so that it slid from my shoulders.

"You never wore the dresses I put out for you," he murmured into my hair.

"I don't want to talk about dresses," I whispered.

"Fair enough. Let's talk about food, then."

"Food?"

He nodded. "Don't share food with that prick again, Little Osha."

"What?"

"Swift. Earlier. Back in the war room. You were trading that cake back and forth with him for ages."

"It wasn't cake."

"I don't care what it was. Just stop sharing food with him." There was a dangerous edge to his voice. One that dared me to challenge this order.

If he hadn't learned by now that I wasn't one to be told what to do, then perhaps he needed reminding. "Why not?"

"Because I fucking said so."

"Is it some weird Fae custom that I don't know about?"

"No," he answered stubbornly. "It doesn't mean anything. Share all the bowls of stew you like with Lorreth or Ren. Just don't share food with that prick. It's bad enough that you insist on sharing air with him. I'd rather you didn't eat off the same fucking plate, too."

"What have you got against Carrion?"

"I don't want to talk about Carrion," he growled.

I almost laughed. *Almost.* "All right. Fine." The back of my neck prickled. Something inside of me was slipping away. I felt it happening in stages, and it was frightening. The wall between us—the barrier that existed to keep me safe—was lowering, coming apart a brick at a time. I could halt the wall's deconstruction. Bring it back up again if I wanted. But...I couldn't fucking breathe around him, and I knew what his hands felt like on my body now. For real. I craved more of him, even though he could be selfish and cruel, and even knowing that wanting him would more than likely be my downfall.

"Then *I'll* choose what we should talk about. Let's have a conversation about what just happened…"

"In the tent?" He didn't cast his voice. There was no need for magic. He was standing so close that his mouth would brush the tip of my ear if I only leaned back *one* inch.

"On the riverbank."

"I brought you here so we could forget about the riverbank."

Forget? How did he imagine that I'd ever forget that? "If those feeders had made it to our side of the river—"

"I would have cut them down and made a pile of their bones." He was so fucking confident. Not a shadow of doubt in his abilities.

"People would have gotten hurt."

Fisher's dry laughter stirred my hair. "We're at war. That's what happens in a war. People get hurt. People die. Sometimes they rise again and feed off of the living. It's a cycle."

My heartbeat was everywhere. It pulsed in my hands, and at my temples, and in the hollow of my throat. I turned around to face him, needing to look into his eyes. His strong jaw was just inches away, marked with the beginnings of stubble. The gorget flashed at his neck, the wolf at his throat at my eye level. His shirt was filthy, open just a fraction—enough to reveal a swathe of writhing black ink. He was expressionless as he looked down at me, waiting for me to speak. "This isn't a joke! I…I was…" I knew what I wanted to say. I couldn't bring myself to do it. There was a point of no return here, and I wasn't ready to step beyond it.

"You were worried about me," Fisher said roughly.

"No! I…"

"I saw the look on your face. In the map room when Danya wanted to lop my head off. You were afraid. For me."

"I was afraid that you'd die, and I wouldn't be able to get back home. You made an oath to send me back when I was done with the rings. The others might not give me that same deal, and…"

Fisher's wry, unhappy smile left me under no delusions that he believed what I was saying one bit. He didn't argue, though.

"They're going to tear you to shreds when you go back in the morning," I whispered.

"I'll be fine," he countered.

"Aren't you even a little concerned that...that your so-called *friends* are going to think you've been helping that...that Malcolm guy...and..."

Fisher drew his bottom lip into his mouth, eyes the softest I'd ever seen them. Gently, he gathered the flyaway hair that had escaped my braid and carefully swept it behind my ear. "*Breathe,* Little Osha."

"You can't just tell me to breathe when they nearly made it across the fucking river, okay?"

"They didn't nearly make it across the river. They made it half-way. That's as far as they ever make it. Malcolm sends his army out from time to time, just to remind us that he's there. We break the ice. He loses a wave of foot soldiers. Everything goes back to normal for a while."

"You just drowned hundreds of vampires!"

"You can't drown something that's already dead."

Why wasn't he even faintly concerned about any of this? It seemed to me that he was in some serious shit and was doing very little to get himself out of it. "Danya—"

"Danya will get over it. Everyone will. This will blow over and be long forgotten about by morning. The Fae live long lives. We learned a long time ago that holding a grudge was a great way to ruin a decade or two. We hash it out quickly and then call it a day."

He was delusional. "I was in that map room. You didn't resolve anything with those captains, Fisher."

"Why don't you worry less about my friends and more about—"

"I want answers!" I cried. "Why was Malcolm different? He was nothing like the feeders. He seemed..."

"Normal?"

"Yes!"

"Malcolm's a high Fae vampire. The very first. We were cursed thousands of years ago, and the Fae turned into something very like Malcolm. When a cure was found, my great-grandfather and most of the other Yvelian Fae took it. They were horrified by the monsters they'd become and wanted to return to their old lives. But there were those who liked the dark magic the curse afforded them. They liked the power and the promise of immortality."

"Aren't the Fae already immortal?"

Fisher chuckled. "No, Little Osha. We're not. Our lifespans are the subject of much research and conjecture. We outlive your kind by a long, long time. But we age. Eventually, we die. There were those like Malcolm who didn't want to age. They weren't content to make the most of the thousands of years they had already been granted. So they took what was supposed to be a punishment and embraced it with open arms. Malcolm is the strongest of them. Their king. Of all the Fae who chose to remain vampires, he alone is strong enough to fully turn someone and ensure they remain themselves. What makes them who they are. Their personality and their character traits. When his princes bite and turn someone, their victims die and return without their souls, nothing more than mindless, hungry shells. They obey their masters, and they feed."

There was a bottomless well of horror within Fisher's words. I couldn't even begin to imagine the terror of being fully drained by one of Malcolm's princes and knowing that I was doomed to come back as one of those *things*. "Does that happen to humans, too?" I asked, already afraid of the answer.

"Where do you think most of your kind went? The vast majority of Malcolm's horde were once human. The Fae who chose to cure themselves of their curse tried to protect the lesser Fae and the humans who resided in this realm, but they were easier to target. More vulnerable. They had no magic to protect themselves, so..."

"So..." I was going to throw up. I'd wanted to know, but I couldn't bear to dwell on it now that I did. "You were with him, weren't you? For all those years you were missing."

A tightness formed on Fisher's face. "I can't tell you that," he said.

I can't tell you that.

Witnessing the strain around his eyes worsen, some part of me recognized it and knew what it felt like. As if he were trying to resist or push through something. As if he wasn't in control...

And there it was.

He wasn't in control. "You're *bound*, aren't you?" I said, dismayed.

"You literally *can't* tell me—"

"Stop," he commanded. I'd anticipated relief from him. At least some kind of recognition that finally someone understood why he wouldn't share where he'd been or what he'd been doing. But Fisher's reaction was one of worry. Annoyance, even. "Have you considered that I might not want to tell you because it's none of your business?" he asked sharply.

"It is my business." I adopted a firm stance, planting my feet into his rug.

"No, it isn't."

"Whatever happens to you affects me. And I'm not stupid. You've been less of a prick these past fifteen minutes than you have been since you scraped me off the floor in the Hall of Mirrors and saved me. You only started snapping again when you wanted to push me away. The cold barbs and the awful shit that comes out of your mouth are a way for you to keep people at arm's length, aren't they?"

"You don't have a *clue* who I am," he rumbled.

And maybe he was right about that. But I was beginning to. Beginning to figure him out. And how many times had Ren said it? *I know him. This isn't who he is. He's not himself right now.* This was all a front. Like a veil slowly being drawn back, I was starting to see right through it. "You don't hate me as much as you pretend to," I said.

He stepped toward me, leonine, predatory, dangerous. "Don't I?"

"No, you don't."

"That's an interesting theory."

"I don't think you hate me at all."

He laughed but took another step forward. "You think very highly of yourself, then, don't you?"

"I know that you want me." I didn't step back, even though my body was screaming at me that I should.

"I can want to fuck you and still hate you, Little Osha."

I shook my head, trying to ignore the heat in his eyes. "No. That's not it."

One more step, and he'd be standing chest-to-chest with me again. "What is it, then?"

"There's something...*between* us. You know there is."

"Sure you're not imagining things? Plenty of women fall prey to their own desperate fantasies where I'm concerned."

"Just...stop, all right. Enough! The moment you fuck me, things are going to change between us."

"Sure. I'll have scratched a perverse little itch. I'll be able to move on with my life." His lips parted, and the sight of his sharp canines sent a rush of warmth directly between my legs.

"You want to bite me," I whispered.

"Hah!" He threw his head back and let out a bark of laughter. "Oh, you have no *idea* what kind of tightrope you're balancing on right now, do you?"

"You nearly did it. Back in your tent. You scratched me with your teeth. You drew fucking blood!!"

The small amount of space between us disappeared in an instant. Fisher's hand closed around my throat, fury carved into the lines of his handsome face. "*Careful*," he growled. "It's dangerous to speak so flippantly about things you do *not* understand."

"Then explain it to me. Show me," I panted.

His anger faltered. "What?"

"Show me. *Make* me understand. Prove to me that I'm wrong."

"Stupid, idiotic human..."

I had no business saying anything more. It was perilous, provoking a male like Fisher. This could go awry all too easily. But

CALLIE HART

this was all going to end in tears no matter what, and after what I'd
seen tonight, waiting for us all on the other side of the river, I didn't
plan on dying without at least testing this theory. "I'm telling you to
fuck me, Fisher. I'm asking you to—"

His lips crashed down on mine. He stole my words, claiming my
mouth with a ragged snarl. The kiss was incendiary. The moment
I tasted him and felt his tongue sweep past my teeth, I whimpered,
grabbing the bottom of his shirt.

No more sniping at each other.

No more thinly veiled innuendo.

No more threats.

This was happening because I wanted it to happen.

I tore Fisher's shirt up and had to raise my arms over my head to
even get the damned thing halfway off him. He broke the kiss for a
split second, ripping the smokey material over his head. The second
it left his hand, he fell on me again, his mouth claiming mine so
thoroughly that I didn't know which way was up. His movements
weren't fumbling like mine were. His hands were sure and steady as
he grabbed the collar of my shirt and ripped it from my body. Without the corsets and stays of the dresses Everlayne had made me wear
in the Winter Palace, I'd taken to binding my breasts with fabric as
I'd done at home. Fisher made a disgruntled noise when he saw the
material wrapped around my rib cage. I lifted my arms, expecting
him to unwind it as quickly as he could, but no. He trailed his index
finger down the front of the material, between my breast, and the
fabric split apart, disintegrating under his touch.

My breasts sprang free, my nipples peaking, and Fisher groaned,
taking the weight of them in his palms. He kneaded the flesh,
cursing, his eyes feasting on my chest. Had he thought about me
like this? Naked and at his mercy? Had he imagined what it would
be like to touch me, and taste me, and have me willing to do his
bidding?

I was guilty of letting my imagination run away with me. I'd
pretended it wasn't his hands I wanted on my body when I touched

myself. I'd tricked myself into believing it wasn't his knowing smirk that haunted my dreams. But it was. And now he was standing in front of me, shirtless, the packed muscle of his chest glistening with sweat, ink everywhere, spiraling around his torso, and I couldn't believe we'd finally arrived here.

The cards had been on the table for a while now. We were either going to kill each other or fuck each other, and I was glad we were both opting for the latter option.

Fisher's eyes flared as he grabbed the front of my pants by the waistband and pulled me roughly to him. "You asked for this. When you're sore from coming so hard and you can't recall your own name, remember *that*, Little Osha."

He held my gaze as he yanked open my pants and shoved them down my thighs. His gaze was as heavy as a sword's edge, resting against my throat, sharp enough to cut. He shoved his right hand between my legs and grabbed me by the throat with the other, startling the shit out of me.

I would have gasped when he tore my underwear to one side and plunged his fingers into the molten wet heat of my core, but his hand closed around my windpipe, stealing my ability to breathe. Like some dark-haired, foreboding fallen angel, Kingfisher purred as he plunged his fingers up inside me.

"My, my. So worked up already? You're slick as hell. What do you taste like, mm? Are you going to scream for me like a good girl when I have you ride my face?"

"Y-ye—" It was no good. I couldn't speak. My head was spinning, both from lack of blood and from the powerful need that rocked me to my core. I wanted him. But I wanted to understand this feeling inside of me as well. At every turn, Fisher had proven himself to be an unbearable asshole. I could count on one hand how many civil words the bastard had said to me. But there was something else tying me to him. Pulling me in like I was trapped. A part of me knew that Fisher himself was the trap, and I was well and truly snared...

The world went dark until there was only me and him. Me and those flashing green and silver eyes. Fisher bowed his head, leaning into me, his mouth so close to mine. "When you take all of me, remember to breathe." He let go of my throat, and my head swam as I dragged down a lungful of air.

There was no time to brace myself. It would have been smart to get rid of my boots and then take off my pants, but that wasn't possible when you were dealing with the most impatient male in all of Yvelia. At first, the smoke seemed to come from Fisher's hands. Then it seemed to be coming from behind him. Who knew where the fuck it was coming from. All I knew was that it was coming from him— the same smoke that had shoved a horde of vampires below a sea of ice—and now it was swirling over my body, like...

It evaporated just as I was starting to tense. And with it, every stitch of my clothing disappeared, too. Fisher stood back a second, inspecting his handiwork, his lust-filled eyes blazing a trail up and down my body three times, as if once was nowhere near enough.

"I can't wait to hear what kind of sounds you make when I thrust into you for the first time," he purred. "I'm going to make you pant for me, Little Osha. And when we're done, I'll close my eyes and replay the sound of you moaning in my head every time I stroke myself to completion."

Gods. Just the thought of him *touching* himself...

The sinful image that was starting to take shape in my mind scattered when Fisher moved. He grabbed me, hands finding the backs of my bare thighs, and just like that, my feet were off the ground. A weightless, falling sensation flipped my stomach over as I sailed back through the air. The soft mattress caught me a second later, cool silk sheets slick against my skin. A ball of panic rose to the base of my throat when my eyes found Fisher again. I saw a dark-haired Fae warrior covered in ash and soot standing at the end of the bed, slowly unfastening his pants with a hungry, carnal look on his face, and my self-preservation instincts told me to flee for my life.

Don't move. Do not move, Saeris. For the love of all the gods...

Back in Zilvaren, predators didn't have the dark to hide in. They used camouflage and stealth to sneak up on their prey, which in turn taught us all to react fast when we came face-to-face with the thing that was hunting us. Every part of me wanted to scramble from the bed and bolt for the door, but I knew that would be folly. Just like a hell cat, Fisher would give chase. I gripped the sheets, forcing myself to be still, watching every single move that he made.

"Put the soles of your feet on the bed." Not a command issued via the oath. Just a simple command. It might as well have been compulsion, though, considering that I was helpless in the face of his order. I bent my knees, placing my feet down onto the bed...and raw power seemed to distort the air around Fisher's powerful shoulders. With measured, teasing movements, he lowered his battle-muddied pants, and...

Graceless gods and holy martyrs. He wasn't wearing underwear. That didn't surprise me. But the sheer *size* of his erect cock as it sprang free from his pants made my eyes round out of my head.

Were all Fae males this well-endowed? Was it an Yvelian thing? Or was this a Fisher thing? With his clothes now gone, Fisher stood still, letting me take him in, an entertained little smile begging to be set free at both corners of his mouth. He was absolutely fucking incredible, all hard lines and taut muscle and shifting ink. His cock was perfect—rigid iron wrapped in silk and velvet. A thick vein ran down the underside of his length, standing proud from the shaft. My palms tingled just *thinking* about touching him.

Fisher took hold of himself as if he knew what I'd just been thinking, slowly shuttling his hand up and down his cock. "Let your knees fall open," he demanded.

"I—"

"No arguments, Osha. I've driven myself half-crazy wondering what you look like. I need to fucking see. Put me out of my misery."

I'd never been timid in a bedroom before. I was in way, way over my head this time, though. I fought a wave of nerves as I let my knees fall open, and Fisher unleashed a strained growl. "Perfect. You're absolutely fucking perfect. If Danya does rip my head off tomorrow, at least now I'll die happy."

The dazed look on his face was dangerous. A girl could easily find herself addicted to the expression Fisher was wearing, and what then? I'd be lost forever. Fucking doomed. I let myself bask in his attention, aware that I was treading dangerous ground. But if Fisher was right about this, then so what? It would be one night. One time, and then he'd be done with me. I wasn't going to experience this again, so I might as well enjoy it...

"Such a pretty flower, blooming just for me," he rumbled, climbing up onto the end of the bed. His hands closed around my ankles, and I stopped breathing. He was going to...

I screamed as he yanked me down the bed toward him. Another small yelp escaped me as he fell between my legs. His mouth found the crease of my inner thigh first. I shivered, nearly leaving my body altogether when I looked down and met his eyes. He ran the tip of his nose up, up, up, inhaling deeply as he went. When he raised his head a little to speak, his canines weren't just on display. They were longer than I'd ever seen them. Sharper. His left canine had punctured his lower lip and had drawn blood.

"You smell so, so fucking good," he said thickly. "Back in the forge at the palace, I caught a hint of this. I knew then I had to taste you. This smell has been haunting my fucking dreams. I haven't been able to think straight for remembering the scent of your need."

"I could probably use a sho—"

"Do not fucking *dare* finish that sentence," he snarled. "I don't want a mouthful of soap and perfume. I want to taste *you*." With that, he placed his mouth right onto the very center of me, as if he were biting into a piece of ripe, delicious fruit, and my whole world ignited.

His tongue. Oh, holy fuck, his tongue was incredible. The way he licked and laved and sucked at my clit sent me into spasms, the heat of his mouth combining with my own heat in a way that promised to drive me insane.

"Fisher! Oh, fffff—fuck! Fisher! Gods!" I thought I felt him laughing against my flesh, but I couldn't be certain. My ears were ringing. My whole...body...was reacting so...strangely. The roof of my mouth tingled like crazy. I couldn't feel my feet. "This—oh my gods...fuck...I...I..."

"Not yet," he murmured against me. "You don't get to come until I say so."

"Please! I—oh my god, I'm so close!"

He definitely laughed this time. I reached down for him, desperate for the release that lay at the tip of his tongue. Winding my fingers into his hair, I drove his head down to meet me, urging him for more, more, more. I felt his growl vibrating through me, but he didn't pull away. He quickened the alternating laving, circular motion of his tongue, applying more pressure, and then he dipped his fingers inside of me, teasing my entrance with just the tips of his index and middle finger, and my back bowed away from the bed.

More.

I wanted *more.*

Not just his fingers. I wanted him inside me more than my pride would allow me to admit. "Fisher, please," I panted. "I want...I want..."

"Don't worry. I know what you need." He thrust his fingers deep, and I spiraled out of reality. When I opened my eyes, all I saw was a glittering black wind. The candles in Fisher's room were gone, all light extinguished, but the staggering power that poured from Fisher seemed to carry its own internal illumination. It was hard to understand—we were definitely still in Fisher's room. I could feel his bed beneath us. But we were also twisting in a sea of black, floating on a void of nothingness. Sinking, falling, rising, and drowning all at once.

Wisps of iridescent smoke trailed up my arms, circling my wrists, stroking over my skin, so soft and seductive that I trembled under the contact. It was him. An extension of him, and it was every-where. His mouth worked over me, his fingers coaxing me toward a steep drop that would claim me body and soul.

He wasn't going to stop me this time. He drew me to my climax with determination, a gratified growl of victory ripping from his throat when he pushed me over the edge.

This wasn't just an orgasm. It was an awakening. Cradled in Fisher's power, I felt his hands tighten on my thighs as I bucked and writhed, but I felt his shadows bind tight to me, too. They slid over me, pooling in the hollow of my throat and pouring over my stom-ach, whispering over my heavy breasts—a level of ecstasy I'd never experienced before. It was as though I was breathing him in, taking a part of him inside me—

"FUCK!" My eyes snapped open. Fisher was on his knees between my legs, the head of his cock butting against my entrance. His right hand found my hip. When his left hand found my *throat* again, a veil of shadows flowed down his arm and up my neck in a warm, heady caress.

My eyes started to roll back into my head. But then...

"Oh, no, Little Osha. You're gonna be looking *right* at me for this," Fisher said. *"Look."* He waited until I'd made eye contact with him again, then his hand moved up to my jaw. He held me almost tenderly as he said, "You still want it?" His chest, his arms, his defined abs; the deep groove that dipped over his hips, leading down between his legs: his entire body was a work of art. He took my breath away. The ink that covered his skin fluctuated as he waited for the answer he already knew I would give to him.

"Yes. I want it. I want *you.*"

His smile was pure, powerful male satisfaction. "Hold on tight, then. I hope you're not afraid of the dark." He thrust forward, slam-ming himself inside me, and I *screamed*. Not from the pain. There wasn't any. Only a stretching, and a fullness, and an awesome wave of energy that fired up my spine in a series of bursts that felt like small explosions. It was so much, all at once, that I *had* to scream.

As if he were experiencing something very similar, Fisher threw his head back, the muscles in his neck straining, his jaw clenched tight, roaring through his teeth. *"Fuuuuck!"*

Just one stroke. He'd entered me *once*, and I was done for.

I was a ball of sensation, humming with energy. In the darkness, Fisher slowly lowered his head, his lips parted, hair mussed, and the dazed look of surprise on his face sent a rush of adrenaline powering through me.

Gods and martyrs. I would never forget seeing him like this. If I did manage to make my way back home, the image of him like this, seated inside me, skin slick with sweat, chest hitching, would sustain me until the day I died.

Fisher.

Kingfisher.

Lord of Cahlish.

I hated him, I did. But you couldn't hate something without caring about it just a little, too.

"Witch," he accused. "You *do* have magic." He was so fucking *big*; his hard length twitched inside me, and my body answered in kind, tightening around him. His fingers gouged into my skin, digging deeper into my hips. With a mantle of black smoke swirling around him like a dark wind, he moved. Slowly, at first. The tendons in his neck stood proud as he pulled back and eased out of me just an inch. The smallest of movements drew him home. Again, he shifted, rolling his hips, working his cock a little deeper each time he thrust back into me. The pace he set was torturous. I had well and truly stretched to accommodate him now, and the delicious friction building between us was quickly turning into a desperate ache.

"Please..." I reached for him like it was my right. His chest was warm and solid and perfect. Beneath my palms, the wolf tattoo emblazoned across his pecs came to life. The ink flowed beneath his skin, crossing from him to...to...sinners, it flowed along my fingertips, spreading over my skin, flowing just like his smoke over the backs of my hands. A delicate little bird took shape on the inside of my right forearm. It stretched its wings and took flight, its tiny body flitting over my stomach as its wings beat a thousand times a minute.

"*Shit,*" Fisher breathed. I pulled my hands away, afraid of more ink making its way over me, but Fisher just shook his head, grabbing one of my hands and putting it back on his flesh. He didn't say anything else. Didn't warn me if any more of his ink would come venturing over onto my body. He just drove himself deeper, slamming himself into me faster, relinquishing more of his control with each thrust.

"Magnificent," Fisher rasped. He moaned as he palmed my breasts. His pupils had blown so wide that the black had swallowed the green *and* the silver. I was transfixed, unable to look away, as his hands explored my body.

When I'd first laid eyes on him, I'd called him Death. The likeness was even more pronounced now. This male possessed the power to end entire civilizations if he wanted to. I could feel it—a still, deep well inside him, its surface rippling as he grew harder and harder inside me. I would drown in that well. Sink down into the dark depths of it, never to break the surface again. And I would be glad.

I disintegrated into a million pieces, deconstructed and mindless as I came again. The only things anchoring me to the warm cocoon Fisher had created around us were his strong hands at my waist and the rough edge of his strained voice.

"Gods and fucking martyrs. Holy fucking *shit.* That's right. Come. Show me how pretty you are when you fall apart."

I screwed my eyes shut, crying out wordlessly. Right as I crested the wave of my second orgasm, the stars painted across Fisher's bedroom ceiling ignited, flaring so brightly that their light burned my eyes even through my eyelids.

Fisher came hard, slamming into me. He roared out his release, and together the two of us shattered.

A rushing filled my ears.

My blood hammered right below the surface of my skin.

Dum, dum, dum, dum, dum.

Fisher sank down onto my chest, his weight oddly comforting even though he was crushing me a little. He remained inside me, still as hard as tempered steel, his fingers trailing over my skin in small circles, and the reality of what had just happened slowly began to rear its ugly head.

I'd just had sex with Fisher.

I'd just let him fuck the hell out of me, and now we were naked, tangled up in each other's bodies. Eventually, the swathe of shadows around us faded, and the candlelight returned, along with the rest of the room. One by one, the stars painted on the ceiling slowly went out.

Moving slowly, as if he were in no hurry at all, Fisher propped himself up and drew himself out of me. His ink had stilled again, his pupils now narrowed down to points. He was quiet as he got dressed.

I covered myself with a sheet, suddenly very aware that I wasn't wearing a stitch, but I watched him, refusing to look away. Not after that.

Once he was fully clothed again, Fisher fastened his boots and finally looked at me. "I want you to stay here tonight." No preamble. No mention of what had just taken place.

"Why?"

"Because the camp will still be in chaos. I'll have a lot of things to take care of, and I want to know exactly where you are."

"Do I get a say in the matter?" I asked.

He looked down at his boots. When his gaze returned to me, his eyes were distant. "Not really. I'll come back for you in the morning. You'll spend the day working on the relics in the camp forge. In the meantime, Archer will be on hand in case you need anything." A loud crack flooded the bedroom, a number of candles guttering out as a swirling shadow gate exploded into existence behind Fisher.

"Try and get some sleep," he muttered. And then he stepped backward into the black and vanished.

Try and get some *sleep?* What the fuck was wrong with him? I wasn't going to be able to *sleep.* My mind was charging. I slumped back into the pillows, frustration warring with confusion, and...wait a minute. I opened my eyes.

He didn't.

He wouldn't have.

I leaped up, taking the bedsheet with me, running for the door. It opened when I turned the handle, and when I tried to step out into the hall...

My bare feet met cold stone without any issue. There was no invisible barrier trapping me inside Fisher's room. Thank the gods for that.

"Good evening, miss."

I grabbed the side of the door frame for support. "Gods, Archer, you scared the *shit* out of me!"

The little fire sprite was alone in the dimly lit hallway. Well, alone except for Onyx, who was lying on his back with his feet in the air. It appeared that Archer had been in the middle of supplying belly scratches when I'd burst out of the bedroom, wrapped in a sheet like a madwoman.

"Apologies, my lady. I came because I heard a disturbance in Master Fisher's rooms. When I arrived here, I found Onyx whining at the door, and I decided to wait until...well, until you were finished to see if you needed anything. Intimate relations can be very strenuous."

"Oh gods, Archer, no, it's okay, we weren't..." I blushed hotly. The situation could only have been worse if it had been Elroy who'd caught me post-coitus. And how the hell had Onyx gotten himself shut out of the room?

"Oh?" Archer looked confused. "In that case, do you need to see a healer? Are you hurt? It sounded like—"

"No, no, I'm fine. Honestly, I'm fine. I...We..." I glanced back over my shoulder into the bedroom, then pulled the door half-closed behind me. "We were just moving some furniture around, that's all. But then Fisher decided he preferred it the way it was, so...so we moved it all back again." I scratched my head, cringing when I felt the huge snarl of hair that had gotten tangled while we'd been "moving the furniture."

Archer didn't look convinced. He was gracious enough not to call me out on my lies, though. "I see. Well, in any case, I brought you up a pitcher of apple juice and some cake so you could replenish your energy levels. Here..." He turned and picked up a small silver tray, offering it to me.

I took it with one hand, smiling tightly. "Thank you, Archer. That was very thoughtful of you. Good night."

Onyx bolted inside the bedroom as soon as I nudged the door open again. The little fire sprite bowed deeply. He was still bowing when I dipped back inside the room and closed the door again.

TICKING CLOCK

I WAS UP, bathed, dressed, and ready for an argument when the shadow gate appeared in the bedroom the next morning. Only, Fisher didn't appear from the undulating shadows. I waited a minute, then another full minute, realizing with annoyance that he wasn't coming through to get me and expected me to just head on through on my own.

Motherfucker.

Against all odds, I had managed to fall asleep last night. I'd woken up in a tentatively happy mood, but that had changed the instant I'd caught sight of my naked body in the full-length mirror by the copper tub. Now Fisher had some explaining to do.

I wasn't even remotely nauseous as I stepped through the gate and out into the crisp, bright winter morning in the war camp. Fae warriors bustled about their business, gathered outside the front of the mercantile, busy rushing across the muddy square. Fisher stood ten feet from the shadow gate leaning against a wooden post, hands in his pockets, head bowed. The moment I emerged, he shoved away from the post and started walking away at a fast clip.

"Hey!" I walked quickly, following after him. "Hey, asshole! What the hell? Get *back* here."

He didn't stop. He didn't even slow. I upgraded to a jog, my breath forming a cloud of steam when I fell into step beside him. "Would you care to explain what the fuck this is?" I snapped, yanking down my shirt collar.

A flicker of annoyance flashed in Fisher's eyes, but he did not look at me. "Don't worry. It'll fade. Probably," he said in a flat tone.

Oh, so he knew what I was pissed about, then? Gods, he was a piece of work. "I did not ask for a *tattoo*, Fisher," I hissed. "I definitely didn't ask for a bird to be permanently inked right above my fucking *boob*. You need to take it back."

His gaze remained fixed straight ahead. "It doesn't work like that."

"Bullshit, it doesn't. It came from the ink on your body. You touched me. It slipped from your skin to mine. So, fuck, I don't know, shake hands with me or something and *take it back!*"

"I'm not *shaking hands* with you," he said dismissively.

"Then what the hell am I supposed to do with it?"

Fisher looked like he was struggling not to roll his eyes. "It's a tattoo, Osha. It won't kill you. Just forget it's even there."

"I will not! I have plans for my own tattoos, y'know. Ones I voluntarily go out and get. And this one is right in the middle of my fucking chest!"

"I don't know what to tell you," he rumbled. "Feel free to have someone cover it if it upsets you so badly."

I stopped in the mud, watching him walk away. "I can do that?"

"Wouldn't bother m—" He cleared his throat. "Of course you can. There are any number of bored warriors with a needle and some ink in camp."

"Okay. Fine, then. I *will* cover it. Look, can...can you hold up for one second, please! Where are you taking me?"

"To the camp healer," he gritted out. "You need to take something."

"What do you mean, *I need to take something?*"

"Because of last night. Because children might be extraordinarily rare between the Fae and humans, but they can still happen, and—"

I burst out laughing.

Fisher stopped dead in his tracks, his eyes wide. "I don't pretend to understand you at the best of times, but why is *this* funny to you?" he demanded.

"I can't have children, Fisher. I was cleansed when I was fourteen."

I expected to see relief on his face. But instead, his face drained of color. "What the *fuck* did you just say to me?"

I stopped laughing. "I was cleansed. When I was fourteen. They do it to about seventy percent of the girls in my ward."

He came and stood *very* close to me, his head bowed over mine, nostrils flaring. "What do you mean...*cleansed?*"

"I mean...they sterilize us," I whispered. I figured he'd known last night. I would have expected him to at least mention contraception otherwise. But from the look of shock he wore, he hadn't had the first clue. "The Third Ward's the poorest," I told him. "Madra's health advisors decided that we shouldn't be allowed to procreate, otherwise we wouldn't be able to support ourselves. The policy's been in effect for over a hundred years. Seven out of every ten female babies are tagged when they're registered with the ward officials." I showed him the small black cross tattooed behind my left ear. The mark that meant I wasn't allowed to breed.

Fisher's expression flattened out. His eyes went blank.

"What? I figured you'd think that was good news."

Clenching his jaw, he spun around, his eyes searching the horizon for gods only knew what. Had he heard something? Some promise of danger that my inferior human hearing hadn't detected? "Fisher. Hey! What's wrong?"

When he faced me again, his eyes were almost fully black, his pupils blown wide open. "Nothing. Nothing at all. Find the forge and get to work. Everything's already waiting there for you. I'll expect a report at lunchtime."

He stormed away without a backward glance.

Find the forge. Hah. Easier said than done. It took me thirty minutes to locate my new workspace, and by the time I did so, I was sweating, out of breath, and ready to throw some punches. The forge, Fisher had neglected to mention, was located halfway up the small hillside behind the war camp, and the path that led up to it was so steep that I had to use my hands to scramble up the rock face in places.

There was a fire already cracking and spitting in the hearth when I arrived, thank the gods, and all of my equipment from Cahlish was set out on a wooden workbench. The space constituted little more than a barn, but I was grateful for it. From way up here, I could see across the whole war camp. And it was quiet. I was alone. The peace and solitude would give me time to think. I got to work.

Again, Kingfisher had hidden the tiny amount of quicksilver I was to work with. I scouted around the forge, riffling through rotting wooden boxes full of copper coins, and in cupboards and on shelves, but it was nowhere to be found. After going over the place twice, I stood at the bench, working to calm my spiking temper, and I listened. The voice was just a whisper. Quiet and distant. I almost mistook it for the breeze. But no. As I angled my head and closed my eyes, homing in on it, I finally worked out which direction it was in: to the east. Outside of the forge. Farther up the mountain.

"Damn him," I muttered, trudging up the sharp incline. For every step I took, I slipped back three. The soles of my boots had very little tread on them, and so much fresh snow had fallen during the night that the ground was treacherous. I'd landed hard on my knees and slid back down the hill on my ass twice before I made it to the small, rocky plateau a hundred feet above the forge.

Carrion was there, waiting for me. He sat in the mouth of a cave, happily tending to a fire while reading a book. "Did you know, the Yvelian Fae are the youngest of the Fae houses? By a thousand years. There was a dispute between these two brothers, and they splintered off to make their own court."

I folded my arms over my chest, standing on the other side of the fire in front of him.

"Do you mind? You're blocking the light," he grumbled.

"How the fuck are you just so okay with all of this?" I demanded. "Ever since you got here, you've just *accepted* it all. You didn't know the Fae existed. Suddenly, there are massive fighters with pointed ears and sharp teeth everywhere, and you're just like, okay, yeah, sure, of course there are Fae. Of course there are other realms. Of course there's magic, and vampires, and all kinds of horrifying, terrible things out there that want to kill me. This all makes *perfect* sense!"

Carrion lowered his book, huffing. "And who said I didn't know about the Fae?"

"*What?*"

"I knew about the Fae, Saeris. My grandmother told me."

"Oh, come on. Be serious. Being told stories when you're a child is one thing. But none of us ever *believed* those stories."

"I did," Carrion said matter-of-factly. He dove back into his book. "You've met my grandmother. Does she strike you as the sort of woman who'd spread tales of fantasy and make-believe in her free time?"

Now that I thought about it, he had a point. Gracia Swift was one of the most cut-and-dried, no-nonsense people I'd ever encountered. Even more straightforward than Elroy. She was an engineer, charged with ensuring new buildings in the Third were built on stable foundations. If she'd read books to Carrion at all as a boy, I would have put money on them being mathematical tomes relating to calculations for slope stability, not fanciful stories about made-up creatures.

"She has this book," he said, holding up the one in his hand as if it were the book in question. "Has all kinds of pictures. Illustrations. The text's faded in places, but she knows that damn thing from cover to cover, so it never mattered. I daresay I know it by heart by now, too. 'Fae creatures of the Gilarian Mountains,' it's called. There's a note written on the first page. It says, *'Never forget. Monsters thrive best in the dark. Commit all you read here to memory. Prepare for war!!'* Carrion held up his middle finger and his index finger. "*Two* exclamation points. The Swifts have always been very serious people. Gracia took the superfluous punctuation to mean that the situation, should these Gilarian Fae creatures ever show their faces, would be very dire indeed. I wasn't allowed to have dessert until I'd recited at least seven traits of the Gryphon sprite or explained in great detail how to kill a blooded Fae Warrior wearing full plate and armor."

Well, that was unexpected. Where the hell had a book about the Fae come from? Madra had burned any literature that even mentioned the Fae or magic a long time ago. It was a curious thing—to find out that Carrion had, in a way, been brought up to believe that this would happen to him at some point. I didn't have time to ponder on that now, though.

"Did Fisher send you up here to wait for me?" I asked.

"That's one way of putting it," Carrion said. "I was fast asleep in my tent. Then, there he was, a black cloud with a shitty attitude, growling at me to get up. The sun hadn't even come up yet, and he kept griping about me being lazy. He called me a waste of carbon. What does that even *mean?*"

I ignored him, holding out my hand. "I need it. Whatever he gave you to look after."

Carrion pulled a sour face, reaching into his pocket. He drew out the same small wooden box Kingfisher had secreted the quicksilver away in the last time, tossing it to me. "Our benevolent kidnapper strongly advised against me opening that. I'd have disobeyed him on principle the second he left, but my hand went all prickly when I held the box, and I figured maybe I'd listen to him just this once."

What would have happened to Carrion if he had opened the box? The quicksilver was in its inert state, solid and sleeping, but there was a chance Carrion might have accidentally triggered it. Why not? If I was able to do it, then there was a chance he could, too. I had no idea why *I* had been born with the gift to work the quicksilver. Perhaps it was a latent gift that hadn't manifested in Carrion yet. His hand *had* prickled when he'd held the box. Maybe that meant something.

"What are you doing right now?" I asked him.

"Aside from prodding this fire with a stick and reading this?" he asked, holding the book up again. "Nothing much. Why do you ask?"

"Want to come and set fire to some far more exciting things?"

He snapped his book closed with a flourish. "Absolutely, yes."

- Magnesium powder, finely ground salt, distilled water.
- Bismuth, copper, antimony.
- Bluestone, chalk, lead.

Result: No Reaction.

Three more experiments down and three more failures. Not only that, but I had never even heard of antimony before, let alone worked with it, and it turned out that the fine white powder was an extraordinary skin irritant. It burst into flames the second it touched the quicksilver, and the fumes it cast off made us so sick that both me and Carrion ran and threw up in the snow.

By mid-afternoon, we were recovered and brave enough to risk a late lunch, though. Carrion hiked down into the camp while I began the refining process, returning just as it started to snow with an armload of snacks and a pitcher full of water.

We sat outside and ate. Cold cuts of meat. Pieces of cheese. A small container of nuts. Bread, and a handful of tiny, salted fish that were delicious.

"Hard at work?"

I nearly choked when Kingfisher emerged from inside the forge, sneaking up behind us. The moment I saw him, my traitorous mind took me back to last night, and his hands and mouth on my body, and the million sinful things he'd done with his tongue. He glanced at me and then narrowed his eyes, turning his focus toward the camp as if he was remembering me in a bunch of compromising positions, too. Then I saw his bleeding lip, the shadow of a bruise on his jaw, and the fact that his shirt was spattered with red blood, not black, and my mind went elsewhere.

"What happened to you? Why are you bleeding?"

"Training," he said stiffly. "Don't change the subject. Why aren't you working?"

Suddenly, I didn't care so much that he was injured. In fact, I kind of felt like hurting him myself. "Since we're not *slaves,* we're taking a break to eat. Look, two plates and everything," I said, showing him that I was, in fact, eating my own food and not sharing Carrion's. Not that it seemed to make him any happier. "And anyway," I said. "I've done all I can for the day."

"And the trials you ran?"

I curved an eyebrow at him. "What do *you* think?"

He said nothing by way of response.

"*I* have a question," I said to him. "Back at Cahlish, you hid the quicksilver from me in that little box on the shelf. Today, you gave it to Carrion and made him wait for me halfway up the godscursed mountain. Why do you insist on hiding it from me? Why can't you just leave it out for me. Y'know, so it's easy to find? Maybe if I didn't waste so much time tracking it down before I can run my trials, I'd have time to run *more* of them."

There were shadows under Fisher's eyes. He looked tired. "Forgive me for making the day a little more interesting for you. It's good for you to improve at finding the quicksilver. You never know when you might need to detect small amounts over great distances."

"It's *annoying.*"

"Well, you have your quicksilver now. Do you have more trials planned for the afternoon?"

Peevishly, I said, "Nope. I have to refine the silver."

Fisher cast Carrion a dubious glance. "Do *you* know anything about refining silver?"

"Not a fucking thing," he answered. "I'm more of a logistics guy."

"What does that mean?"

"I'm very good at moving things from one place to another."

"We have plenty of other asses for that. You should go and find something useful to do," he snapped.

"Uh, he's been helping *me!*" I got up, brushing one hand off on my pants as I handed the small bowl of nuts to Carrion, who took the bowl and tossed a nut into his mouth, shooting Fisher a needling smile. Fisher didn't react. Not personally, I supposed. A wave of black smoke swept over the campfire we'd started to keep warm while we ate, hitting Carrion square in the chest. It wasn't a powerful blow. It was only equivalent to a strong breeze, but it sent the bowl of nuts toppling from Carrion's hands, scattering its contents all over the ground.

Such a child.

"Find Ren. Ask him for a job, or I'll find one for you," Fisher said. "I'm assuming cleaning the latrines doesn't sound appealing to you since you have no magic and would have to do it by hand?"

Carrion's grin faltered. "You are extra fucking miserable today. You should really get laid. Might help improve your mood. Tell him, Sunshine."

I choked. Loudly. Carrion couldn't have made a more unfortunate suggestion if he'd tried. I thumped my chest, trying to get a breath down, and all the while, Fisher just looked at me. He wore no emotion. No expression at all. The quicksilver swirling in his iris was the only thing suggesting that he might not be as calm inside as he appeared on the outside. His eyes seemed to drink the light as he eventually turned a disdainful glare on Carrion.

"Don't call her Sunshine," he commanded.

"Why not?"

If Carrion's plan was to poke the bear, then he sure as hell knew how to go about it. But Kingfisher didn't respond to the taunting note in his question. He just cocked his head a little, nostrils flaring, and spoke in a low rumble. "Because she is moonlight. The mist that shrouds the mountains. The bite of electricity in the air before a storm. The smoke that rolls across a battlefield before the killing starts. You have no idea what she is. What she could be. *You* should call her *Majesty.*"

Heat flared across my face. It scorched me behind the center point of my chest, turning my insides to cinder. I'd expected a quip from him about Carrion's suggestion that he get laid, not...that. What had that even *been?* Carrion withered under the weight of the quiet anger simmering in Kingfisher's eyes, his poorly hidden smile slipping from his face.

I'd found myself in some awkward situations before, but this was by far the most uncomfortable I'd ever felt. I cleared my throat, reminding both of them that I *was* still present. "Did you need something, Fisher? Or can we get back to work?" I asked.

His expression was just as flat when he turned his attention to me.

"You're done here for the day. I'll send someone else to refine the silver. There are plenty of other smiths who can do that kind of work in camp. Unfortunately, there's something else I need from you, Osha."

24

LUPO PROELIA

THE SHARDS WERE STILL BURIED in the stone. Needle-sharp, they glinted in the light thrown off by the fire. I peered closer at them, frowning. "There are five hundred and sixty-three of them," Renfis said. "One of our metal workers tried to pull them out with forceps, but they're so fine, he couldn't grip them properly. Two of them snapped. The ends are still buried inside the stone, which…well, it's not good." There was a bruise above Ren's cheekbone; it was turning a vivid, sickly shade of purple as he spoke.

"What the hell happened at training today?" I asked under my breath.

Ren's eyes remained locked on me, refusing to look at Fisher, who stood on the other side of the war room. "Nothing. Why do you ask?"

"Because both of you are bleeding and walking like you got your asses handed to you!"

"Fisher's in a bad mood is what happened at training," Lorreth, the dark-haired warrior with the war braids, said. He sat on a stool by the fire, his light blue eyes slowly tracking the movements of everyone inside the war room. He watched Kingfisher, who was locked in a very heated argument with Danya, but evidently it was Ren and me he was really focusing on.

"Fisher's fine," Ren said evenly. "We both are. We're going to see Te Léna later. In the meantime, can we concentrate on the task at hand for a moment? Do either of you have any suggestions as to how we might get these shards out of this stone?"

There was something he wasn't saying, but he clearly didn't want to talk about. I let him have his secret. "Why not just shear off all of the pieces and sand the ends flush with the stone?" I suggested. "Danya could just have a new sword made for her."

Ren laughed breathily. "It's not that simple. Danya's sword was special. It was like Nimerelle once, imbued with old potent magic. It's..." He winced at the bristling spines of metal protruding from the stone wall. "It *was* a precious Fae heirloom. Danya's birthright. A godsword forged by the ancient Alchimeran masters. Such swords are religious icons to the Fae. It represented Danya's rank and marked her as an original member of the Lupo Proelia. Like most—"

"Sorry, Lupo what?"

"Lupo Proelia. Kingfisher's wolves," he said, sighing. "There are eight of us, usually. Though our numbers *have* been reduced of late. We fight as a team, working together, just as wolves do. I'm sure you've noticed the wolf on some of our armor."

I'd noticed, all right. The sigil was on the plate Fisher wore at his throat. It was stamped into his chest protector, too. And I'd noticed his tattoo more than once. Last night, for example, when the head of the *Lupo Proelia* had plowed me like a godscursed field.

"As you already know, Nimerelle still carries a kernel of magic in her blade. All of the other Alchimeran swords became dormant centuries ago, but Danya's blade was still very important to her. To our people as a whole. We can't just sand the shards back and discard the rest. It'd be sacrilege."

"Amazing. So you're saying that I was in camp for less than five minutes and I destroyed an ancient weapon that has profound cultural importance for all of Fae kind," I said, recapping.

"See! She doesn't even *care!*" Danya cried, pointing at me. "She understands the weight of what she's done, and she doesn't give a shit!"

"She does care." Fisher heaved out a sigh as he crossed the map room, approaching what was left of the sword. "She just has a terrible sense of irony."

I didn't appreciate the hateful look Danya sent me, nor did I feel too warm and fuzzy about the way she kept stabbing her finger at me. "I'm sorry, are you just permanently on the brink of a nervous breakdown, or have I shown up at an inconvenient time for you?" I sniped.

Her jaw dropped. "Unbelievable. Are you seriously going to let her speak to a high-born Fae like that?" she said, eyes on Fisher.

"What do you want *me* to do about it?" he replied. "She has a mind and a mouth of her own. I am the keeper of neither." He picked at one of the fine filaments poking out of the stone, frowning at it intently.

"Would you let one of the men talk to a superior with the same level of disrespect?"

"No, I wouldn't," he admitted.

"Then why won't y—"

"But she isn't a member of this army, and you aren't her superior," Fisher said. "Now. Do you want to give her a moment to see if she can fix the sword *you* tried to kill me with? Or do you just want to pace about and yell some more?"

Danya didn't know what to say to that. She gaped at Fisher, then at Ren, then Lorreth, bypassing me altogether.

"Lorreth," she began. The male sitting by the fire threw up his hands, shaking his head.

"Oh no. No way. I'm still sporting a bruise from where you clocked me last night. You were way over the line, the way you went for Fisher. It's your own fault that your sword's in pieces. In a *wall,*" he added. "I think it's impressive, what the human did. And no more than you deserved besides."

"Asshole," she spat. "I should have hit you harder."

"You couldn't have if you'd tried," Lorreth shot back, grinning.

I wasn't paying attention to their bickering. Danya *was* wrong; I certainly did care that I had destroyed something so precious. I stared at the wall, pondering the shards, trying to strategize a way to pull them from the stone, when I felt the faintest tapping at the edge of my senses. The whisper I'd sensed inside the quicksilver back at the forge was a loud roar in comparison to this, but...I swore I heard it.

I spun around and found Fisher. "This sword wasn't just tempered steel. There was quicksilver in the blade."

He nodded, displaying the faintest hint of satisfaction. "There was. Not much. Trace amounts. But yes, that's why it answered you when you commanded it to stop."

"So...back in Zilvaren? It was never the iron, or the copper, or the gold that reacted to me? It was..."

Kingfisher nodded. "It's always been quicksilver. It was bound to many different alloys and metals before, back when there were plenty of Alchemists and the pathways were still open between our worlds. It made weapons more powerful. Turned them into conduits that could channel vast quantities of magic."

My mind spun. "That's why metal was so hard to find, then. Madra took it all. She wanted to keep the quicksilver away from the people. She knew there might be people like me within the city, capable of controlling it."

When Kingfisher said no more, Ren inhaled and spoke instead. "Our historical records show that most Alchemists could only command objects if the item in question was comprised of at least five percent quicksilver. And even then, it was typical that they could only transmute the quicksilver from its solid to its liquid state so that it could be forged. There are no records of objects being fragmented like this." He gestured to what remained of Danya's sword.

"Okay. So that makes me...an *anomaly?*" I looked to Kingfisher. I wanted his input on this. Regardless of the cat-and-mouse game we were playing with each other's feelings, if Fisher actually *had* any of those, I still wanted to know what he made of Ren's revelation. He wouldn't meet my eyes, though. He leaned back against the map table, resting his weight against its edge, his jaw clenching and unclenching as he stared at the ground.

"*That* makes you the most powerful Alchemist ever recorded," Lorreth supplied. "Capable of changing how we've been fighting this war in ways even *we* can't imagine. Most of us were infants when the paths between realms closed and the Alchemists became extinct. Some of us hadn't even been born yet. We have no idea what battle-fields used to look like, with an Alchemist in camp, ready to forge new weapons that draw magic—"

"Whoa, whoa, whoa! I don't know how to forge weapons that can *draw magic!* I can't even figure out how to make a relic!" I'd broken out into a cold sweat. "I've made zero headway with it. Not back at the Winter Palace. Not at Cahlish. The trials I ran here this morning were a total waste of time, too. If you're under any illusions that I am somehow going to be pivotal to winning this war, then *please* rethink that strategy."

"Precisely. If she can't even figure out how to wipe her own a—"

"Danya, I swear on the seven gods, if you don't shut up, I will toss you out of here myself," Ren muttered darkly.

Danya rocked back as if she'd been slapped. Her lips trembled, eyes filling with tears. "You can't be serious," she whispered. "*You?* You're just going to blindly fall in line with all of this? We are the ones who stayed. Who've fought in the mud and watched friend after friend die. When this human was born, *we'd* already been committed to this fight for centuries!"

"You're right," Ren snapped. "We've been stuck here, in the middle of nowhere, in a forgotten corner of our land, defending a border that the high-born assholes up north couldn't give a fuck about. For centuries. If this line falls, the entire realm falls. We won't be fighting this war another hundred years from now."

"We will if we have to—" Danya began.

"No, we won't. Because every day, our numbers decline, and Malcolm's horde grows larger. There's no game left to hunt here. Belikon isn't sending supplies to the front anymore. We have no wood for our fires. No food to fuel the troops. No clothes to keep them warm. No weapons to fucking arm them. So yes, I'll support a plan where a human magically shows up and helps us turn the tide of this thing, because without her, we'll all be drowned soon enough. And I'm not talking about in another hundred years, or even fifty, or even ten. We have one year, Danya. Twelve months. If we don't figure this thing out, by this time next year, Malcolm will have won."

"Put your head between your legs. Maybe that'll help." Lorreth carved off a slice of the apple he was eating and used the edge of his dagger to pop it into his mouth. Behind him, the sky tilted, see-sawing, the edges of the war camp a blur. I braced my hands against my thighs and bent double, straining to breathe. My chest was so tight.

Ren's words rang in my ears. I wanted to unhear them, but they replayed over and over, provoking a fresh wave of panic to hit me with every repetition. A year. Just one. They'd done everything they could to tip the scales in their favor, and nothing had worked. Now it was merely a waiting game. The clock would run out, they wouldn't be able to hold the front here, and a hundred thousand ravening vampires would sweep across Yvelia in a bloodred wave of death.

Unless I could figure out how to work some fucking metal.

Gods, sinners, martyrs, and ghosts.

We were all so *ridiculously* fucked.

"You do get used to it, y'know," Lorreth said conversationally. "That overwhelming sense of impending doom. Eventually, it becomes background noise. You don't even notice it at all."

"Where's...Fisher?" I gasped. I'd stumbled out of the war room after Ren had left to go and talk to some returning scouts. Danya had stalked out of the tent and headed off toward the river, growling under her breath. Lorreth had emerged ten minutes later and had sat down on a tree stump ten feet away, as unfazed as ever. But Fisher had *not* come out of the tent.

"He went back to Cahlish." Lorreth sank his teeth into another slice of apple.

"What?"

"Said he was going to see Te Léna."

Te Léna? The sweet healer had taken such excellent care of me after the vampire attack, but I hadn't thought much about her since. Only, this was the second time Fisher had gone to see her recently, and neither time he'd been injured.

Gods, what the hell was wrong with me? This realm was paused on the brink of total destruction, and I was angry and plenty afraid of what that might mean for me and everyone else in Yvelia...but I was also *jealous.* And that? That made me feel pathetic. I swallowed the questions I wanted to ask Lorreth—*Are they together, Te Léna and Fisher? Does he like her? Do they have history?*—ashamed that I'd even think them. Instead, I asked a far more appropriate question.

"Where the fuck...can I get...a *drink?"*

The wooden building at the center of camp was a tavern, and it had the best drinks. So far, I'd had five heavy pours of some very potent whiskey, and I was beginning to feel fuzzy around the edges. My anxiety was long gone, and now I was starting to see the ridiculousness of it all.

"At the end of the day, it's simple," I said.

Lorreth peered into his glass, as if there were definitely still some whiskey left at the bottom of it but he was just having trouble finding it. "How so?" he asked.

"He's a fucking liar. He's been lying to me this whole time."

Lorreth frowned. "Who, *Fisher?*"

"Yes, Fisher. Who else?"

The male shook his head. "Impossible. He's an Oath Bound Fae."

"And?"

"And we *can't* lie."

One eye closed, the other half-cracked, I studied him dubiously. "That's some convenient-smelling bullshit if you ask me."

Splaying his hands, Lorreth shrugged. "When we turn twenty-one, we kneel before the Firinn Stone and make our decision. Every one of us. We have a choice. Bleed on the stone and make our vow. To always be truthful. To always be bound by our word, no matter what it costs us."

"Or?"

"Or we choose the Lawless path. A Lawless Fae may lie. They may cheat. They may steal. Useful tools in many situations, I'll admit. But they come with a price that Kingfisher—and the rest of us, I might add—was not willing to pay."

I arched an eyebrow at him. "And that was?"

He shrugged nonchalantly, as if the answer were obvious. "Our honor."

I harrumphed at that.

"So you see, no matter how much we might want to sometimes, we're physically incapable of breaking our word or telling a lie."

"Hmm. Yeah, well," I admitted. "Kingfisher *did* say that back in the forge at the Winter Palace. But I dismissed him."

"On what basis?"

"On the basis that a liar who didn't want to get caught telling a lie would one hundred percent lie about being unable to tell lies. Gods, that...was confusing."

"What did you even think he'd lied about?"

It came back to me at once. My thinly veiled "how big is your cock?" question. And Fisher's slow, arrogant smile.

"Big enough to make you *scream and then some..."*

Turned out he'd been telling the truth about that, I realized with a healthy dose of annoyance. Fuck. "That's not important," I said. "What's important is that he's known that you guys need me to make weapons for you or you'll lose to Malcolm. But he made an oath to me that I only had to turn those rings into relics for you all, and then he'd let me go home."

Despite being about ten percent more intoxicated than me, Lorreth's eyelids shuttered at this. "He made that deal with you?"

I nodded, then drained my glass.

"Well, if he made that oath, then you don't need to doubt it. Even if he wasn't bound by his own magic to honor an oath, which he is, then Fisher would honor it on principle. It's just who he is." There was a tense note to the warrior's voice when he said this. The details of my bargain with Fisher seemed to have taken him by surprise, though he hid it fairly well.

I wanted to change the subject either way. "Tell me..." I leaned forward across the table, pointing at Lorreth's mouth. "Those *teeth.* Fisher said they were a remnant of the blood curse. But...they still work, right? You can still use them to drink blood?"

Lorreth instantly sobered. His pupils narrowed to black dots. Looking around, he assessed the tables on either side of us as if he were making sure no one else had heard what I'd just said. "Uhh, that's not the kind of thing we talk about in taverns, actually," he replied in a low voice.

"Why not?"

"Fuck. I need *way* more alcohol for this conversation. Hold on."

He gestured to the bartender for a refill, and the craggy-faced creature Lorreth had informed me was a mountain troll came and poured us both another round. When he'd gone, Lorreth sighed. He held up his drink to mine.

"Sarrush."

I clinked my glass against his. "Sarrush."

Lorreth took a deep breath. "All right. Okay. So. No one else has told you anything? About...any of *that?*" he asked hopefully.

"Nope."

"Well..." Lorreth hadn't flinched during the conflict in the war room, when Danya had tried to slit Fisher's throat, nor when Ren had dropped the staggering news that they were on the cusp of losing the war. But now he looked mighty uncomfortable. "Yes, our canines work just fine. The same as a vampire's would. But blood drinking is very taboo. No, it's worse than taboo. It's scandalous."

"But the Fae still do it sometimes?"

A pink tinge was developing on his cheeks. "Yes."

"But you don't *need* blood to survive?"

"No, we don't."

"Then why would they do it?"

"Because..." He cast another wary look around, shifting awkwardly in his seat. "It's a sex thing. If a male drinks from someone, it'll make his dick harder than it's ever been in his life. It makes you euphoric. Both of you. While you're fucking."

"Oh."

"Yeah. *Oh,*" he said. "But it's a slippery slope. If we bite someone, we can still lose ourselves to it. It takes an immeasurable force of will not to keep drinking. It's...not something that's spoken about in polite company."

My brain was so fogged by the whiskey that I didn't know what to make of that. I supposed it explained Fisher's reaction when I'd told him to bite me. But beyond that...I didn't know what to think.

"If you have more questions about this, then maybe they could be discussed another time. In private. Preferably between you and whoever has suggested they might want to, ahh, *drink* from you," Lorreth mumbled, burying his face in his glass.

I blushed hotly. "Yes, of course." I hadn't said a word to anyone about what had happened between Fisher and me. I'd scrubbed myself raw in the shower in the hopes that I'd be able to mask the smell of him on me, but the Fae could detect things like that underneath the scent of soap, apparently. Did that mean that Lorreth knew I'd had sex last night? And specifically with Fisher? It didn't really matter if he did. Worrying about it wasn't going to change anything. And I didn't even know the first thing about Lorreth, so who cared what he thought? He was a stranger. But I liked him. I didn't want him to *stay* a stranger.

"How did you wind up here, anyway?" I asked.

"In Yvelia? I was born here," he said.

"No. In the middle of this war."

"Oh." He waved a hand noncommittally. "Huh, well, let's see. I was a traveling singer once, if you can believe that."

He did have a pleasant enough voice when he spoke, but I couldn't picture this huge, dangerous-looking, lethal warrior as a singer, of all things. "A good one?" I asked.

"A *mediocre* one. Turned out I was better suited to killing than I ever was at performing. Anyway, I met Fisher one night out on the road. He was on his way to help some friends. I was lying in a ditch when he found me."

I buried a smirk. "Drunk?"

"No. Dead, actually. Or very nearly, anyway." He winked, though he suddenly looked a little washed out in the muted tavern lighting. "I'd been attacked by two vampires. Strays. They weren't part of the horde. But they *were* hungry. They took one look at me—a scrawny kid with a lute strapped to his back, alone—and decided I'd make a decent meal. They nearly drained me dry."

"Shit. That sounds awful."

"Well, it wasn't any fun, that's for sure. But it was a long time ago. I've suffered worse since. Anyway, we were miles away from anywhere. I wouldn't have lasted until they could get me to help. If I'd died and come back turned while I was with them, there was a chance I could have killed a number of the party, and some of them didn't want to risk that. They told Fisher it would be best to run me through and be done with it, but he refused. He made them set up camp for the night, and he transported me to Cahlish. He carried me in his arms, for fuck's sake. I was a *lot* smaller then," Lorreth stressed. "He put me in a bed, and he had healers come and tend to me, and he waited to see what they'd say. They weren't optimistic about my odds. I had more venom than blood in my veins, and there are limits to what even the most skilled healer can accomplish under those circumstances. They told him to go back to the wolves, and when I passed, they would bury me beneath a yew tree out in one of the fields that bordered the estate. But Fisher didn't do that."

"What...did he do?"

Lorreth tossed his head back and laughed. "Something I'm sure I've given him innumerable reasons to regret since. He made me his brother. By blood. He gave me a part of his soul."

"A part of his...?" I hadn't heard him right. The alcohol was making my ears play tricks on me. If souls existed, and I wasn't entirely convinced that they did, then you couldn't just go around giving pieces of your own away.

"It's an ancient rite," Lorreth said. "One very few know how to perform anymore. But Fisher's father had almost died once, and his friend had used it to save him. So, he'd made sure Fisher knew it, too, in case, one day, he was able to use it to save the life of someone who was important to him."

"But you were a stranger..."

Lorreth's sharp blue eyes glittered hard as diamonds. He took a sip of his whiskey and set the glass down, regarding it. "Yes. A stranger. And Fisher did it anyway. He bonded a small part of himself to the scrap of life that was clinging on inside me, and that was that. I was still sick as a dog, but death loosened his grip on me. I knew I was going to live, and so did Kingfisher. He told me he was leaving to find the other wolves and that he'd be back in three months. He said I could go as soon as I was feeling better, if that's what I wanted to do, but that there was a place here for me as well, if I preferred the idea of that instead."

"And you chose to stay here. And to fight."

Slowly, Lorreth nodded. "I had no family. No one who needed me to be anywhere else. So I figured fuck it. I only have a life because of him, anyway. Might as well work my ass off and do enough good with the time I have left to be worthy of the gift that he'd given me. I stayed at Cahlish. The moment I was on my feet again, I started training. Before that point, I'd never even held a sword, but I gave it everything I had. And I *ate*. I ate so much fucking food, Cook would scream the moment he saw me strolling into the kitchen. When Fisher came back three months later, he didn't find me at Cahlish. I was waiting for him at the war camp, half a foot taller and twice the weight I'd been when he'd left. Most importantly, I was ready to kill vampires."

"Wait. You crossed Omnamerrin? On *foot?*" I asked incredulously. Fisher had said only Fae with suicidal tendencies attempted to cross the mountains that stood watch between Irrìn and Cahlish.

"I did. Took me nine days, and I nearly got buried by an avalanche, but I made it here in the end."

"You're lucky you didn't die. Wait, what would have happened? If you had died? What would have happened to the piece of his soul Fisher gave you?"

"Good question. If I die first, the piece of Fisher's soul returns to him. He becomes whole again. Everybody has a big party. The end. But if *he* dies first, he's condemned to wait here for me to die before he can move on. He'd be trapped here, in a non-corporeal state, unable to touch anything or anyone. Unable to be heard. *That's* the sacrifice he made when he decided to give me the gift of life. It's happened before. The Fae male or female who tore off a piece of their soul dies first, of natural or unnatural causes, and then the recipient lives on in fine health for another two thousand years.

"Take Saoirse, Queen of the Lìssian Fae, for example. Her mother, who was queen before her, saved her life when she was a child. A hundred and eighty years later, her mother is murdered by unknown entities, and Saoirse rises to power. She's young and beautiful. She likes being queen. She surrounds herself with infatuated males who are willing to die to keep her safe, and so she announces that she plans to live forever. She takes tonics and elixirs and is rumored to drink vampire blood to extend her life. Nearly three thousand years have passed since her mother died, and Saoirse doesn't look a day over thirty. Meanwhile, her mother's spirit has been chained to her, forced to witness the world of the living without being able to interact with it. Without being able to move on to her eternal rest..."

Lorreth looked sick to his stomach. I had to admit, I felt a little sick myself, too. The idea that anyone could condemn their own mother to such a lonely, awful existence, as well as the inevitable madness that was sure to set in, was incomprehensible to me.

"Fisher says he's not worried about what happens to him if he dies first," Lorreth said. "And I'm not worried, either. Truth is, I plan on dying first, anyway. But if the fates guide the stars in a different direction and our better angels claim him first, I won't permit a single breath into my body beyond the last one Kingfisher takes. By my own hand, I'll make sure the piece of soul he loaned to me finds its way back to him. And if the fates consider it just, and I've done enough to earn a place at his side, I'll go quietly and happily with my brother into whatever lies beyond."

25

BALLARD

KINGFISHER BARELY SAID a word to me when he took me back to the estate that night. I swayed a little and almost certainly slurred a lot when I told him I wanted to stay in the camp, but he refused to listen. His features had formed a blank mask when he found me in the tavern, drinking with Lorreth. They were still blank when he made sure I was safely transported into his bedroom, and blanker still when he bid me a curt good night and left.

The next morning, I woke to a splitting headache and a small fox licking my face. The sun was high in the sky, and Fisher hadn't come for me. He didn't come at all that day. After eating a greasy breakfast that made me feel much better, I spent the afternoon exploring Cahlish, wandering through the rooms, feeling displaced and useless. I didn't belong here. And while the estate was beautiful, and cozy and felt as though it had been loved at some point, I couldn't see how Kingfisher fit in here, either. The place was built for a family. There were supposed to be children tearing along the halls, and the sound of laughter in the air, but the grand house echoed with a painful silence that filled me with sadness.

I imagined Kingfisher's mother receiving the letter from the king, informing her that she was to report to the Winter Palace with all of her assets in tow, where she would be married to him and was expected to start a whole new life. I imagined her looking at her dark-haired boy and wondering what kind of life he would lead in a court full of vipers beyond the walls of this sanctuary.

I ate dinner in Fisher's bedroom, sitting at his desk, and then when darkness fell, I curled up in his bed and cuddled with Onyx until I passed into a restless sleep.

I became uneasy when Fisher didn't come for me the next morning. I'd missed out on the opportunity to run three trials yesterday, and I didn't want to miss another three. By mid-morning, I was pacing back and forth and so agitated that the fire sprites stopped coming by to see if I needed anything, and even Onyx grumbled at me and slunk off outside to chase squirrels in the snow.

At three in the afternoon, he finally showed his face. There was no sudden crack of a shadow gate appearing in the bedroom, though. There was a perfunctory knock at the door. It being his bedroom, he didn't wait for an invitation to enter. He opened the door and just stood there, looking at me. "You're wearing my shirt," he said eventually.

"Yeah, well there wasn't anything else to wear," I answered hotly. "All of the clothes from the room I had with Carrion are gone. Archer showed me to another room down the hall, but that one was full of dresses, and I think we both know how I feel about those."

Fisher grunted. "It's too big for you," he noted.

"I had noticed."

He wasn't wearing black today. Not all black, anyway. His cloak was the darkest green, as was his shirt. The shadows underneath his eyes were the color of livid bruises, though, and he seemed paler than usual. He clearly hadn't been sleeping well. And there was a cut on his cheek. It looked fresh, but not *that* fresh. From yesterday, probably...

"What happened?" I asked, getting up from the bed.

"Nothing. A pack of feeders were moving along the border about an hour to the north. Ren thought we should go check it out before they sprung any surprises on us or tried to cross farther up the river, but it was nothing. We clashed briefly. The feeders turned and fled."

I didn't know what to do with that. He'd gone out to fight, and I'd been traipsing around his old house, snacking on cake, and drinking cups of tea. And there was a cut on his face. I didn't know what kind of emotion that provoked in me, but I didn't like it much.

"I'm going to see Te Léna," he said, and the announcement twisted something deep inside me. I was a burning, drowning wreck of a girl, and I didn't even know what to do to save myself.

I smiled faintly. "Oh. Say hi to her for me." Te Léna lived here somewhere, I knew that much. I hadn't tried to find her since Fisher dropped me off the other night, though. I hadn't wanted the company. Or else, very unfairly, I hadn't wanted *her* company, which was ridiculous, I knew.

"I'll be with her for a couple of hours. When I'm done, I'll be back for you," he said.

"I'm staying at the camp tonight?"

He shook his head. "No. We're staying somewhere else tonight. There's something I want to show you."

"Something I want to show you" sounded ominous as hell. And staying somewhere else? That was a little unnerving, too. I wore a pathway in the rug at the end of Fisher's bed, and then I went and stood by the window overlooking the darkening lawns, gnawing on my fingernails. I was jumpy by the time Fisher returned. I yelped, startled, when he stole quietly into the room.

The scrape on his cheek was gone. The purple bruises beneath his eyes weren't as vivid as they had been when he'd arrived, either. He looked refreshed. His mood seemed lighter as well, which did little to make me feel better. Any sane person would have been happy that the Lord of Cahlish wasn't as grouchy as usual, but for some reason, it irked me endlessly.

"I think you'll find everything you need in here," he said, offering a small canvas bag to me.

"Where are we going?"

"It's better if I just show you, I think."

"Will I be coming *back?*" It made little sense that this question came out like a strangled squeak, but he was being so cryptic, and I had no idea what was happening, and I'd had plenty of time to work myself up into a frenzy.

"Yes, of course you'll be coming back. Bring the fox if it'll make you feel better." Since when did Fisher care about what I was feeling? And he was letting me bring Onyx? "Stop looking at me like that," he said.

"Why?" I asked suspiciously.

"Gods and fucking sinners, never mind. Let's just go."

I stepped out of the shadow gate into a darkened clearing surrounded by tall trees. On the far side of the clearing, small marquees were erected beneath a giant tree that was so big, its boughs so huge, that it dwarfed the others and made them seem tiny in comparison. Bright lights twinkled everywhere I looked, a million of them flaring and flickering in the trees and the long grass that stretched out before us like a carpet. The early evening air hummed with soft, upbeat music, the smell of cooking meat, sugar, and the sound of many voices.

Onyx squirmed in my arms, yipping excitedly, demanding to be put down. I gave him what he wanted and watched, dumbfounded, as he bounded off, a splash of white amid the long grasses, speeding toward the marquees. It was chilly enough here that there were fires burning over by the stalls. I could just about make out Onyx bouncing around one, begging the Fae male who was cooking over it for some food.

"Is he safe?" I asked.

Fisher pouted. "Probably. Winter foxes are good at sensing danger. If he thought any of these people meant him harm, he'd be off hiding somewhere already."

Well, that was reassuring at least. But I was still confounded by what I was seeing. "What is this place? What's happening here?"

"This," he said, rubbing at the back of his neck, "is Ballard. It's... I came here once or twice when I was little. It's just a small village. Tonight's one of their feast days. They're celebrating the longest night of the year."

"And why are *we* here?" Oh gods. Had he come to destroy this lovely village and brought me along to witness the hard things that fell to him sometimes? Fisher read all of this in my face, I thought, because he shook his head, looking a little perturbed.

"They have something we need, that's all. Once we have it, we'll leave them in peace. No one's in any danger. Not from me, at least. Are *you* planning on attacking anyone?"

"No!"

"Glad to hear it. Come on. I smell Bettell biscuits. I haven't had one of those in at least a hundred and twenty years."

The residents of Ballard were a mixture of High Fae and Lesser Fae creatures—a snapshot of the Fae folk I hadn't experienced yet; tiny, lightning-fast pixies, who showered our hair with flower petals as they darted through the lowest of the trees' boughs on iridescent wings. Shy, long-limbed dryads with silver hair to their waists and flowing green robes, who ventured from the shadows of the forest for minutes at a time, then disappeared again. Brownies. Satyrs. There were even three nymphs, giggling and splashing in the river that cut through the south side of the hill. None of them seemed surprised to see us, though we were watched by curious eyes as we made our way into the center of the gathering.

There were food stalls, and stands exploding with a million varieties of brightly colored flowers, and booths with games. At the heart of the festivities, musicians gathered in a circle around a roaring bonfire, belting out a lively tune while a female satyr sang a bawdy song about an old carpenter who couldn't keep his wood hard.

Fisher tried to buy drinks for us from a female carrying a tray of ale around the festivities, but she shook her bouncy blond curls, grinning, and told him no money was changing hands tonight.

The houses, sporadically placed amongst the trees, were simple and rustic, but they held an undeniable, cozy charm. There were vegetable patches everywhere, which honestly blew my mind. I knew how food was grown. I'd spoken to the farmers who came to trade with us in Zilvaren before Madra placed the Third under quarantine. I'd paid rapt attention as they'd explained how they tended their crops and harvested them, but seeing carrots, cabbages, leeks, and beans growing right out of the dirt was fascinating.

Ballard was full of life. It spilled out of the ground, and hovered in the trees, and hung in the air like sweet music. The young ran around, laughing and playing games, while their parents ate and drank together companionably, and the elderly sat by the fire and gossiped. An unfamiliar ache thrummed at the center of my chest as Fisher guided me to a small, grassy slope near the fire and indicated that I should sit. This place was a *home*. The residents of Ballard weren't oppressed. No one was looming over them, threatening them with death if they didn't fall into line. The food and water they needed to survive weren't rationed to the point that they didn't know if they would make it from one day to the next. And there was no war here. No vampires. No Malcolm. No Belikon.

"This is what I always wanted for Hayden when he was little." I blurted out the confession without even thinking. "Somewhere peaceful and safe, where he could have thrived."

Fisher hooked the insides of his elbows around his bent knees, looking down into his beer as he thought about this. "He could still thrive," he said softly. "Sounds like Swift got him a good job and a place to live."

"Oh, if only that would be enough to tame Hayden," I said

ruefully. "My brother ran wild as a child. He's basically feral. He also has a crippling gambling addiction that's already earned him four broken bones. If I ever make it home, it'll be a miracle if I find him still alive."

Fisher didn't look at me but said, "You will. Make it home, I mean. I can't guarantee your brother will be alive, but..."

"Thanks for the reassurance, but you'll have to forgive me if I don't fall down from relief. You might remember that I still have to crack the transmutation process and turn thousands of rings into relics. And that," I said wearily, "is beginning to sound like a lifetime's work."

Fisher sighed, digging the heel of his boot into the grass. "I'm going to help you with that," he said.

"I'm sorry, did you just say you're going to help me with my work? Did I hear that correctly?"

He pulled a face. "If I'm helping you in the forge, we might actually have a fighting chance of getting this done. It'll also mean that I won't have to put up with Danya's constant death threats."

"You don't think she'll come and threaten you at the forge?"

"She can't threaten me if she can't find me," he said.

I was not a graceful victor. "*I told you so*" was one of my favorite things to say, but I refrained from rubbing it in too much. "It's funny. It's almost as if you were completely *wrong* when you said all that mess with your friends would be blown over by morning," I mused. "I don't think Danya's ever going to forgive you for disappearing on them."

I expected a snarky response to this, but Fisher just smiled sadly. He took a drink, the warm orange glow from the fire casting his features in bronze and turning his midnight black curls to a dark, warm brown. "I don't know what you mean. Danya's already back to her delightful, cheery self."

He was joking. Had to be. No way anyone would have kept her around for so long if she was really this abrasive.

We were quiet for a while. We drank our ale and watched the

musicians play, and around us, Ballard reveled. It wasn't long before a group of female High Fae adolescents started doing laps around the fire, giggling behind their hands, throwing furtive glances Fisher's way. They looked like they were about twelve or thirteen in human years—that awkward age between childhood and the chaos of puberty—though I had no idea how old they were in Fae terms.

Fisher hadn't thrown any sharp barbs at me at all yet, so I decided to risk a question. "How do you age here? Your children? You all live for so long, but…are you born, and then you stay a child for a hundred years, or…?"

He shook his head. "A child is vulnerable. Weaker than an adult. Too liable to be picked off by predators. Our offspring actually age twice as fast as human children. We're fully grown by twenty-one or twenty-two. That's when the aging process slows down dramatically."

"Predators?"

"Plenty of dark and hungry things lurk in the forgotten corners of this realm, Little Osha. At least four different kinds of Banshee feed from the souls of the very young. Their vibrant energy's just too potent for them to resist. Then, there are wraiths, and saw-toothed mermaids, and a whole plethora of den-dwelling creatures that like to burst out of the ground and swallow whole anything they can fit inside their jaws. You've really got to watch where you're putting your feet around here."

Gods alive. I'd known Yvelia was rife with danger, but I hadn't realized how precarious a person's safety was here.

"There's also the plant life. Poisonous thorns and carnivorous flower buds. If those don't kill you, they'll sure as hell leave a mark. And then, of course," Fisher noted, his eyes darkening, "there's Malcolm." He didn't say *the vampires.* He said *Malcolm,* as if the pale figure with the silver hair I'd seen on the other side of the riverbank was solely responsible for the death and destruction his horde left in its wake. "His hatred alone would wipe the world clean of life if it were given free rein."

A chilled wind blew, snaking icy fingers down the back of my shirt and making me shiver. I thought there had been a blast of wind, anyway, but the air seemed strangely still all of a sudden, as if the world were holding its breath.

Change the subject, Saeris. For the love of the gods, change the subject.

"You're causing quite a stir," I said into my cup of ale as I drank.

"Hmm?"

I eyed the gaggle of young girls as they completed their fourth lap around the fire, still throwing hopeful glances Fisher's way. "I think this little group might be wondering if the Lord of Cahlish is in the market for a *Lady* of Cahlish," I said teasingly.

I didn't think Fisher would *love* the comment, per se, but I figured he'd at least know that I was joking. His hand tightened around his mug, his shoulders drawing up uncomfortably around his ears. "You shouldn't call me that. I'm not Lord of Cahlish," he bit out.

"But...that is your title. Weren't you your father's only son?"

"That doesn't matter. I'm not—" He changed tack. "A lord is charged with watching over his people. He protects them. Defends them. Creates a safe place for them to live. Do you know where they are now? The people who used to live on my lands?"

An awful anger burned in his eyes as he looked at me. I wasn't going to like what he was about to tell me, but I answered anyway. "I don't."

"On the wrong side of the Darn, baying for the blood of their own fucking children," he said bitterly. "Or else they've abandoned their homes and moved away, where they won't have the entire Sanasrothian horde kicking down their front doors in the middle of the night. A hundred and ten years. I left them for *a hundred and ten years.* Ren and the others did everything they could to stem the tide. It's not their fault. *I* was supposed to be here to protect them. *I* failed them. So I don't deserve to be called Lord of Cahlish. I am lord of nothing."

The arrogance he wore like plate armor was gone. All of the artifice. The walls that stood between him and the outside world. Gone. The silver in his eye pulsed, reflecting the light from the fire, relentless as ever, giving him no peace. It hurt to see him like this, torn wide open by a grief that I could see now lived just below the surface of the stony, give-no-fucks facade he presented to the world.

My throat ached. I wanted to reach out and take his hand, but the lines were so blurred now. Would he accept that small comfort, or would he laugh and spit in my face? I had my own defenses in play. My walls were just as tall as his and just as thick. I didn't know if I'd survive that kind of rejection if he turned around and mocked me for thinking I could be any kind of support to him.

Courage, I thought to myself. And also, *fuck him.* If he showed cruelty in the face of kindness, then he deserved to be miserable and alone. I drew in a deep breath, and was about to reach for him, when—

"Why haven't you said anything?" he demanded, twisting to face me.

"I was about to! I just...*I was thinking it through!*"

"Not about that." He exhaled sharply down his nose. "About the other night. What happened. With us."

Ahh. No further clarification needed *there*. I searched his face, my heart working overtime. "You made it very clear that, as far as you were concerned, it was going to be a one-time thing," I said slowly. "You made it very clear that you could hate me and still want to fuck me. And I'm not the type of person who keeps throwing herself at the things that hurt her. So no. I haven't brought it up. What would have been the point? Would you have made me a cup of tea and sat and listened while I tried to convince you how good we could be together?"

He snorted dismissively.

"Exactly."

"I don't..." Watching Fisher grasp for the right words was wild. "I *don't* hate you," he rushed out. He exhaled as if the admission had cost him dearly. "But there are things you don't understand. Things that make it *impossible* for me—"

"Bless the stars, I was right!" a rasping voice declared.

Neither of us had noticed the figure approaching from the other side of the fire. A woman stood before us, her craggy face lined with age. It was difficult to tell where one wrinkle began and another ended. She was short for a member of the Fae and tall for a human, though I couldn't tell which she was. She kind of looked like she might be human, but then she smiled broadly, displaying a pair of worn but still elongated canines, and the question of her heritage was resolved. "I do love keeping an eye on the sky," she croaked. "King-fisher sightings are very rare around these parts, but I knew I'd get lucky one of these days if I kept looking."

Fisher plastered a smile on his face—convincing, but it didn't reach his eyes. Not completely. He groaned, heaving himself to his feet as if he wasn't perhaps Yvelia's most infamous blooded warrior, at the height of his power, and that his old bones were aching instead. To my surprise, he wrapped his arms around the old woman and hugged her hard.

"Evening, Wendy," he said.

She squeezed him tight, then made a very theatrical show of shoving him off away. "Evening, Wendy? Don't you '*Evening, Wendy*' me. I've been making those cursed biscuits for you every year, and you haven't once bothered to show up and eat them. No one else likes them, you cheeky shit. What a waste of ingredients!"

Fisher regarded her very seriously, but the genuine edge that had been missing from his smile seconds ago finally emerged, his eyes dancing with amusement. "I'm sorry, Wen. I've been terribly rude. I owe you an apology."

She clouted the top of his arm—the highest point of his body that she could reach. "You owe me *money!*" she cried. "Do you know how expensive sugar is these days?"

Fisher laughed. Really laughed. The sound was rich and deep, and made something inside me sit up straight. When I'd picked up a pitcher at the Winter Palace and filled a glass for myself for the first time, I'd thought the sound of that rushing, *free* water would be my favorite sound until the day I died. I was wrong. The sound of Fisher's genuine laughter was rarer than water had ever been back in Zilvaren; it almost brought tears to my eyes to hear it.

"I'll see what I can do about opening up some of those trade lines," Fisher promised.

Wendy grunted and made a face so grumpy that it almost had me laughing. "Don't bother. Traders bring too much bad news with their wares these days. We'd rather go without." She grabbed hold of Fisher by the waist, squeezing him like she was inspecting a piece of fruit at market. "Wherever you've been, they haven't been feeding you properly, anyway. Come on. I have two spots saved at my table and two large bowls of beef stew waiting, too."

"Thank you, Wendy."

She pinned him under a vicious gaze. "I know you're not about to forget your manners and make me introduce myself to your pretty little companion, Kingfisher of the Ajun Gate."

Fisher paled, his lips parting. He looked struck dumb. But I was already getting to my feet, offering out my hand to Wendy. "I'm Saeris Fane. I'm—"

"Ah, a Zilvaren girl! Gods alive!" Wendy grabbed me by the shoulders and held on to me, looking me up and down. "I felt it! I knew the moment the gates opened again. I felt you pass through. There was a *buzzing* in the air that day."

"It's very nice to meet you," I replied.

She'd sensed me coming through the gate? Was that possible? Yvelia was a land of unexpected magic and unique beings. She'd taken one look at me and known I was from Zilvaren. That was pretty impressive all by itself. Wendy half closed her eyes, peering at me through the slits of her lowered eyelids. Her mouth slowly hinged open as she took me in. "Hmm." She *sniffed* me.

"More than just a companion, then?" Wendy scowled at Fisher out of the corner of her cloudy eye.

"She's a friend," Fisher said, without a hint of feeling in his voice. "A temporary one. She'll be heading back to Zilvaren soon, where she'll go back to her life and forget all about the things that have happened here."

Wendy nodded, mouth still open. She did *not* look like she believed him. "Is that so?"

"Didn't you say something about stew?" He wasn't as testy with Wendy as he was with me most of the time—something told me he wouldn't have gotten away with it—but he was growing tenser by the moment. Wendy took pity on him and let the matter drop.

"Yes, stew! And husk cakes, and potatoes, and honey-glazed carrots! You two aren't leaving Ballard until you're splitting at the seams and can't fit another bite inside of you. Come."

Wendy wasn't joking. She filled our plates for us again and again, moving back and forth between savory and sweet dishes as she remembered that there was this smoked meat or that dessert that she wanted us to try.

I had more drinks than I should have, considering the amount of whiskey I'd burned through with Lorreth two nights earlier, but the beer wasn't strong at all and only gave me a sweet, warm feeling in my chest. Fisher didn't balk when his beer was repeatedly refilled, either, which surprised me. He raised a questioning eyebrow at me when he caught me watching him as he drained his sixth cup. "What is it?" he asked.

"Oh, nothing. I just figured you'd cut yourself off after two or something. I've been waiting for you to come out with something along the lines of..." I cleared my throat, pitching my voice low. "'*A good warrior never dulls his senses with drink. I must always be ready to fight.*'"

Fisher leaned back in his chair "*That's* supposed to be me?"

"That *is* you," I said.

"Bullshit. I don't sound that pretentious."

"You sound worse. *Hey!*" A tiny pixie girl with gauzy pink wings was balancing on the edge of my plate, trying to roll off one of my Bettell biscuits. The cookie was almost as big as she was. It would flatten her if it toppled over on her. She shouted, high-pitched and angry, when I took the biscuit. "You're going to hurt yourself," I scolded. "How did you think you were going to fly and carry that at the same time?"

It was tough to make out what she said, but I was pretty sure I heard the words, "none of" and "your" and "business," with some other colorful words thrown in for good measure. I pretended to be deeply offended, but still, I broke the biscuit up into little pieces, setting them on a side plate for her. "There. That should be more manageable for you now. You're welcome."

She made a rude hand gesture, but swiped a chunk of biscuit and launched into the night air. When I turned back to Fisher, he was lazing back in his chair, watching me very intently. I saw the tiny uptick at the corners of his mouth and leaped at the chance to torment him.

"Are you about to smile, Kingfisher of the Ajun Gate?"

"What if I am?" he said in a very even, measured tone.

"I can count on one hand how many times I've witnessed you do it. No one's going to believe me when we get back to camp."

He did smile then, slow and rueful, head turned away as he toyed with his fork. "They'll believe you, Little Osha. They've all seen me smile plenty."

"Just not recently?" I whispered.

"No. Not recently. Smiling has been pretty hard of late." His Adam's apple bobbed. "It is getting easier, though."

He seemed relaxed, but there was a tension in his shoulders that I could see, even if no one else could. The silver in his eye was going wild. I pressed the tip of my tongue against the inside of my teeth to stop myself from spoiling the moment with inappropriate questions, but I knew he was suffering. He was always suffering.

Annorath mor!

Annorath mor!

Annorath mor!

The voices came from out of nowhere, loud and full of terror.

Annorath mor!

Annorath mor!

Annorath mor!

Louder. Faster. Louder. Faster still.

I gripped the edge of the table, unable to catch my breath over the roar...

"Saeris? Darling girl, can you hear me? Are you all right?"

Ballard snapped back into sharp focus. My plate was on the floor at my feet, and the grass was littered with Bettell biscuits. Kingfisher stared at me in wide-eyed shock. It was Wendy who had spoken, voice full of worry. I sat stiff as a board, while she pressed the back of her hand to my forehead.

"No temperature to speak of. Are you well, Saeris? You took a funny turn there."

"Yes. I'm fine. I..." I swallowed thickly. "I was just a little dizzy, that's all." Oh no. It wasn't just Fisher and Wendy who'd noticed. A group by the fire had stopped talking and were watching us. A couple of Fae women, leaning against the trunk of the massive oak tree twenty feet away, were also talking quietly, their eyes full of concern as they looked over. I swallowed down my alarm, smiling as convincingly as I could. "Really, I'm okay, I promise."

He knows. He can tell you just heard something.

The little voice in the back of my head was right. Fisher was white as a sheet and looking uneasy as he pushed his chair back so he could pick up my plate. "It's been a long day," he said, setting my plate back on the table. "We've eaten and drunk too much, I think. The exhaustion's kicking in."

Wendy nodded. "Of course. Of course. Well, you know where you're going, don't you? Although, I suppose it has been a long time. Do you remember the way?"

Fisher chuckled good-naturedly, giving the old female a one-armed hug. "The rest of me might not be perfect, but my memory is," he said. "Night, Wendy."

I gave the female a hug, too, my eyes pricking at the surprising display of maternal warmth. She was still calling after us, bidding us goodnight, as Onyx bolted ahead of us up the path, carrying a Bettell biscuit in his mouth.

We were going back to Cahlish. There was no way Fisher would choose to stay here after my strange little episode. But he didn't open up a shadow gate and drag me back through it as I thought he would. He was quiet as he led me into the line of the trees and passed the quaint houses that lined the walkway. He flexed out his hands by his sides a couple of times before slipping them into his pockets—he didn't seem to know what to do with them.

The walkways into the forest were only wide enough to accommodate a small cart, perhaps. They were deserted, though, with everyone still back at the clearing, enjoying the celebrations.

Fisher stopped in the middle of the path, so abruptly that I nearly ran into his back. "Those words you said back there. Why did you say them?" he demanded.

I'd said them out loud? Damn. "I don't know. I really don't. It came out of nowhere. I was sitting there, listening to you say something about smiling, and then bam. It was all I could hear. Annorath mor. Annorath mor. Annorath m—"

"Stop." Fisher held up his hand as if it were a shield. "Don't...say that. Just, please don't say that." He had been annoyed, mad, irritated, turned on, and a million other things in front of me, but he'd never been afraid before.

"The quicksilver pushed those words into my mind when you forced me to hold it back at the Winter Palace. What do they *mean?*" I asked, stepping toward him.

He stepped back at the same time, shaking his head. "It's better if you don't ask. I can't tell you anyway, so just...don't."

"Fisher—"

He lunged for me, grabbing me by the hand. "Come on. Let's go."

The forest village of Ballard whipped past in a blur as Fisher tugged me along behind him. The trees were full of twinkling lights. Pretty ponds and grassy areas with benches lined the paths. Music still hung in the air, though distant now, as he took me farther into the forest. Eventually, we came to a cobblestoned square with a circular fountain at its center. The statue in the fountain—a female with flowing, beautiful hair and a heart-shaped, gently smiling face —held a stone urn, from which a steady stream of water poured into the pool at her feet. The sound of the trickling water would have been soothing had Fisher not been so agitated. He charged across the square, angling his head away from the statue, beelining for an innocuous red doorway between two small shops—a bakery and a tailor's, by the looks of things.

"Fisher, slow..." I nearly tripped over my own feet as I passed the fountain, my eyes trailing over the small brass plaque at the base of the woman's feet, and something painful clicked into place. I realized why the statue looked so familiar now. She looked an awful lot like Everlayne. And she had Kingfisher's high cheekbones. Or rather, he had *her* high cheekbones.

Edina of the Seven Towers. Lady of Cahlish.

Kingfisher's mother.

He'd said she had brought him here as a child. She was important to the people of Ballard. Fisher was, too. I'd figured that out even before Wendy had come to tell him off for neglecting her for so long. Everyone had been very subtle about it, but the villagers had been very aware of his presence. He wasn't a stranger here, had never been one by my reckoning, and now he was opening up a door to a building on the square because he had a fucking *key?*

"Come on." He gestured to the open doorway. "Let's go inside. It's getting cold."

The temperature was a terrible excuse. Cahlish was much colder than Ballard, and he walked around there in just a shirt and pants without batting an eyelid. I understood why he wanted to get inside, though, and I had no plans on stopping him.

The door opened to a narrow stairway. Just one flight. Candles in wall sconces sparked to life as Kingfisher motioned for me to go ahead of him. I started to climb. Onyx slipped through my feet, forever nosy, wanting to go first. His claws made a clattering sound against the wooden floorboards as he hopped up each step. The air smelled of dust and neglect. When I reached the top of the stairs, I found myself surrounded by ghosts, but before I could panic, flames bloomed at the wicks of more candles on the other side of the room, and I saw that the eerie white shapes weren't ghosts after all. Just large pieces of furniture draped with dust sheets.

Even the pictures hanging on the walls had been covered. Three large windows overlooked the courtyard and the fountain, but Fisher was already on it, crossing the modest living room and drawing the thick burgundy velvet curtains closed at each of them, blocking out any view of the kind-looking woman pouring water from her urn below.

This wasn't just an apartment Fisher had rented for the night. This place belonged to Fisher. It had belonged to his mother once, maybe, and now it was his.

I paced around the room, running my hand over the sheets. Onyx's nose was glued to the ground as he trotted about, snuffling intensely. He sneezed explosively, then went right back to inhaling all the dust. I was about to pull down the sheet from the large painting above the fireplace, but Fisher's hand caught my wrist. "Don't," he said. But then, a little softer, he added, "Not tonight."

Why were we even here? This seemed like prodding an open wound for him, but he'd been the one to bring me to Ballard. "Bathroom's through there," he said, pointing through a doorway to our left. "There are two bedrooms down there. I'll take the smallest. That used to be mine, anyway."

Two bedrooms. He was sleeping in his own room. I was to sleep in the other. I wasn't surprised by that. Fisher might deign to fuck me, but I was under no illusions that he'd want to sleep in the same room as me.

"Thanks. Oh, *shit.*" I winced. "I left my bag back in the clearing. I wasn't thinking. I'll have to go back and get it."

But Kingfisher held out his hand, and his palm became a wreath of black smoke, which became a piece of canvas, which became the forgotten bag. "Here," he said softly. "Night, Little Osha."

26

ASH AND CINDERS

I woke to screaming. The sound was full of raw terror—the kind of sound a person made right before they were murdered. I leaped out of bed and collided with a piece of furniture, smashing my big toe.

"Fuck! Fuck, fuck, fuck!" I didn't know this bedroom. It had been pitch-black when I'd come in here. I'd only been able to find the bed by patting around in the dark. Gods only knew what kind of obstructions stood between me and the door. Gods only knew where the door *was*. The screaming intensified. I eventually found the door handle and then nearly tripped over a panting Onyx as he shot past me out of the door. I followed the white smudge of his body down the hall.

"Stop! No. I said no! *STOP!*" Fisher yelled.

Without thinking twice, I ripped the door open and charged inside. The curtains weren't drawn in here, and moonlight flooded through the windows, painting everything luminous silver. Wearing just his pants, Fisher lay in the center of a bed that was way too small for his body, on top of the sheets, shivering, his skin running with sweat. At first, I thought he was having a nightmare, but then I saw that his eyes were open and fixed on the ceiling. He blinked, and a tear rolled from the corner of his eye, racing over his temple and running into his hair.

"Fisher?"

He shook in reaction to my voice. At his sides, his hands clenched, gripping at the sheets. "Go," Fisher said in a cracked voice. He watched me out of the corner of his eye, though his head didn't move on the pillow.

"What's wrong? Are you—"

"*Go!*"

"I can't just go. Something's wrong with you."

"I'll be fine. I—" A ripple of pain passed over his face, his eyes rolling back into his head. His back arched off the bed as he gritted his teeth, screaming out a vicious curse in Old Fae. "Fuck! Stop! Stop, stop, stop," he chanted. "Please. Stop..." The episode, the seizure, hell, whatever it was that was causing him so much distress ebbed, and I watched, heart pulsing in the base of my throat as his body eased back onto the mattress. As soon as his back was flush with the bed, the shaking started up again.

Mind made up, I said, "I'm going to find someone. This isn't right."

"No! No." Fisher tried to swallow, but that seemed too painful to accomplish, so he cleared his throat instead. "It'll end soon," he rushed out.

"*How* soon?"

"An...an hour. Maybe two. I'll...be fine."

"Fisher, no! You need help. There must be a healer here."

"Just...please. Get me some water. That'll help. Then...go back to bed. Get some...sleep."

Yeah. Right. Sleep. With him in pain in the next room, screaming at the top of his lungs. That wasn't happening. He was so fucking stubborn. "I'll be back in a second," I told him. All of the candles had guttered out long ago, and I wasn't blessed with magic that could simply conjure flames when I needed them, so I went scavenging. In the living room, I pulled open one of the curtains, thanking the gods when the moonlight lit up the furniture and all the other tripping hazards that stood between me and the kitchen.

I found a dusty glass in one of the cupboards, filled it from a pitcher on the sideboard, and returned to Fisher as quickly as I could. In my absence, Onyx had jumped up onto the bed and tucked himself into the male's side, resting his head on Fisher's stomach. He whined when I entered the room, his eyes moving from me to Fisher, as if he were trying to tell me something.

"Can you lift your head?" I asked.

"No. I can't move...anything." Fisher closed his eyes, screwing them shut.

"All right. I'm going to help you, then."

"Just...set it on the nightstand. I'll...drink it later." Each word was labored. His body was so tense that it looked as though the tendons in his neck and arms were on the verge of snapping.

"I'm not leaving you here like this, you idiot." I climbed up onto the bed and lifted his head up. It took considerable effort to get my hands beneath his shoulders and to lift his torso enough for me to slide in behind him, but I managed. Resting my back against the headboard, I let him lean back into me so that his head was propped against my stomach, a leg on either side of his body. He didn't protest when I held the glass to his lips and carefully poured some water into his mouth. It took a long time for him to drink, but sure enough, he drained the whole glass.

"You can go now. I think it's...passing."

He was so full of shit. If his trembling was anything to go by, this episode was just getting started. "I'm not going anywhere."

His hair was plastered to the side of his face in wet, dark waves. His eyes met mine, and my heart stopped for two beats when I saw the quicksilver in his right eye; it pulsed, nearly covering his whole iris, leaving only the smallest crescent of green to shine through. "I'll make you go if…I have to," he ground out.

Make me? Oh, he'd *make* me, would he? This fucking asshole. I was trying to help him, and he was dead set on pushing me away. How could he be so infuriating, even when he was incapacitated and incoherent from pain? I spoke clearly so there would be no misunderstanding me. "If you use the oath you tricked me into to force me from this room right now, I will never forgive you. I will find a way to make your life absolutely fucking miserable. In fact, while we're here and having such a lovely conversation about this, you're never going to compel me against my will again. Do you hear me? Do you understand?"

"I don't need—"

"I am not fucking around, Fisher. If you have any respect for me, if you care about me even the tiniest, most minuscule amount, you will never, *ever* compel me again. Do you understand?"

He licked his lips, eyes burning into me. Even though I was upside down in his field of vision, he must have been able to make out the fury on my face because his eyelids shuttered, and he gave a small nod. "I…understand."

"Great. Now stop telling me to leave. I'm staying."

Again, another nod. "Okay."

The next four hours—Not one. Not two. *Four*—were rough. Onyx hid his face in the sheets whenever another wave of delirium washed over Fisher. I held on to him as best I could when he bowed up from the bed, but that didn't seem to help, so I let his body contort and shake. The chain around Fisher's neck stuck to his skin, the pendant with the crossed daggers wrapped in vines rested in the hollow of his throat, wet with his sweat, and I glowered at the cursed thing, wondering why the fuck it wasn't doing its job. This was because of the quicksilver. There was no doubt in my mind about that. Even if I hadn't seen how badly it had spread across his eye, I'd have known from the chanting I could hear in the back of my mind all of the time now.

Annorath mor!

Annorath mor!

Annorath mor!

Thunder in my ears.

A bleak omen.

During the darkest hours of the night, when clouds must have swept across the moon and the room was thick with shadows, Fisher stilled for a while. "Tell me something. Distract me. Sometimes it'll ease if...my mind goes elsewhere."

I ran my hands along his shoulders, working my thumbs into his taut muscles as I had been for the past hour. I wasn't surprised when the ink beneath his skin drew closer to the places where our skin met. I watched it climb my fingers, forming shapes, and then runes and delicate designs as they inched upward. There was every chance they'd still be there in the morning, but I couldn't bring myself to care right now. "What should I tell you?" I asked.

"Anything. Tell me about your life...before."

I sat for a moment, wrestling with that. I didn't know where to begin. There were a lot of things I didn't want to talk about. Many things I didn't want to remember. Dangerous corners of my mind I had no desire to return to.

Fisher's head shifted against my stomach. "Why are you frowning like that?" he asked. I glanced down and found that *he* was the one frowning up at *me*. His brow wasn't rolling with perspiration anymore. The shaking seemed to have slowed down a little too. A relief.

"I don't know. I have very few bright, happy memories to share from Zilvaren." I'd touched Fisher's skin plenty over the past few hours, so I didn't even think about it—I ran my finger over his forehead, down his temple, sweeping away the wet hair from his face. He closed his eyes, his lashes fine and delicate as strokes of black ink against his pale skin.

"I don't want bright and happy," he whispered roughly. "I want *real*."

Those words weighed heavy. This, from the male who refused to give me the real answers to the questions I had about him, was enough to make a girl want to scream. But my suspicions on that front—that Fisher was bound in some way and *couldn't* answer—had, at some point, solidified as fact in my mind. And look where we were. He was lying in my arms, immobile and vulnerable in every sense of the word. Laid bare. I could be a little vulnerable, too.

"My father died when I was two. I don't even remember him. My mother was four months pregnant with Hayden when it happened. A sand dune came down on a trader's outpost on the glass flats. He was either crushed or suffocated to death, one of the two. And when we lost his income, my mother became a prostitute," I said bluntly. This wasn't a secret back in Zilvaren. Everybody had known Iris Fane, either from exchanging chits for her time or because the other mothers in our ward would bitch and complain as loud as the day was long about the fact that a woman of loose morals lived amongst them. "She sold her body for food and water mostly, but she made money, too. Her client list was mostly comprised of guardians. Madra's men. Five days out of the week, she worked at this place near the market. The House of Kala. Kala's employed security, so the women who worked there were safe for the most part. One shout from a bedroom and five huge bastards would kick the door down and beat the living shit out of whoever was causing trouble. But she worked from our home sometimes, too. To make ends meet. I used to watch through a crack in her bedroom door when the guardians would come, resplendent and proud, dripping in their golden armor.

"The man I used to apprentice for. Elroy? He loved her. She was beautiful and full of this...this fire. He'd come to the house and fix things from time to time. He never tried anything on with her, though. He wasn't like that. The amount of times he took care of her when one of the palace guards beat her black and blue at our house..." I shook my head, absentmindedly twisting a piece of Fisher's damp hair around my finger.

"She didn't want me to follow in her footsteps, so she made him promise to take me on in the forge as soon as I was old enough. I was ten when I first stepped into his workshop. And my mother? She'd already started smuggling weapons into the ward by then. It started as pieces of scrap metal. Things that could be turned *into* weapons. Elroy was happy to make them at first. Just daggers. Small knives. My mother handed them out to her friends at Kala's first, to protect themselves with when they took their work home with them. But then she started bringing home swords and shields. The kinds of things that would get her killed if she was caught trading in them."

I hated remembering the knocks at our door in the middle of the night while my mother was working at Kala's. The masked men who would thrust heavy hessian sacks into my hands and then sprint off without saying a word. But I forced myself to do it. "She had me running items from our house to the forge every day soon after that. The guardians didn't pay much attention to a scrawny kid on her way to work. Years went by, and she started introducing me to all kinds of men..."

Fisher's breathing hitched. He'd been loosening up gradually, but now he stiffened again, his nostrils flaring. He didn't say a word, but I knew what he was thinking.

"Not those kinds of men. They never touched me. They showed me where the entrances to various tunnels were. The ones that led to the underground reserves where Madra kept water reservoirs. Plenty to supply the whole city and then some. They showed me how to tap the tanks and siphon off a little here and a little there. They showed me how to pick locks and how to climb. I learned how to fight with daggers and how to throw them. A rebel would stay at the house, hidden in the attic, for a week, or a month. Sometimes maybe two. Then they'd switch out, and someone new would show up. Hayden knew nothing about it. He was too young to understand most of what was happening, and he didn't know how to keep his mouth shut. So I learned how to fight, and steal, and how to take care of him, too, since our mother was never home anymore. And that's just how it was for a long time. I spent my days in the forge. After, I cared for Hayden. Cooked for him. Kept the house clean. And then, as soon as he went to sleep, I'd be out stealing whatever we needed to live."

"When did you sleep?" Fisher wasn't fighting against the pain anymore. It sounded like he was struggling to stay awake.

"I didn't, really. I took naps whenever I could, and...I don't know. I just kept going."

"Sounds shit."

"It was. And it got worse. My mother started to get angry. She was sick of being treated like crap and degraded by the men who thought they were so much better than her. She refused to accept guardians as clients anymore. Some of her regulars, the ones who used to come to the house, didn't like that. One morning, six years ago, she left the house and headed to Kala's, but she forgot her water ration. She'd left it sitting there on the kitchen table, her bottle full. Hadn't even taken a sip out of it. I knew if she didn't have it with her, she wouldn't get any water all day, so I grabbed it and chased after her. I found her in the square, already on her knees. The guardian she'd turned away from the house the night before was standing there, smug as fuck, while his underlings searched her bags. They found two knives on her. Tiny, pointless things. The blades were barely even three inches long, but that didn't matter."

"Because the punishment for carrying a weapon in the Third is death," Fisher whispered.

"I watched them slit her throat," I said. "No arrest. No trial. They love carrying out their sentencing on the spot. Saves time and energy, I suppose. She died face down in the sand, in the blistering heat, with five men pissing in her hair and on her back. And then they left her there. I ran to her as soon as they went. Flipped her over. Shook her." I shrugged. "But she was already gone. I couldn't carry her by myself, so I had to run and fetch Elroy. When we got back to the square, our neighbors were out there, standing over her, spitting in her face. Elroy knocked out one man who was trying to tear the clothes off her body."

"*What's the problem? She was a dirty, disease-riddled whore. She didn't care about the world seeing her tits. Here, how about I fucking pay her?*" He'd dropped a scuffed-up penny onto my mother's stomach and then kicked her in the ribs. That's when Elroy had broken his face. I didn't tell Fisher that part, though. There were memories that could be put into words, even if it felt like dying to give them light and air. And then there were those that couldn't. I would never repeat the words that man said about my mother.

"We burned her the next morning in the dunes, a mile from the glass flats. The air was so hot that it singed the insides of my nostrils. Hayden passed out, and Elroy had to carry him home, but I stayed and watched my mother's pyre until she was ash and cinders on the breeze. When I finally stumbled back home, I found our house all boarded up, the door and the windows blocked off with lengths of wood. There was a big black "X" painted across the stonework. Ours was the first house they quarantined. More followed, though. A week later, Madra had the whole ward placed on lockdown. No in or out. They said the ward was stricken with a plague."

Those days were distant, foggy nightmares that haunted both my waking and sleeping hours. Hayden's grief had turned into anger very quickly. He'd blamed our mother for the loss of our home. His friends had finally told him that she hadn't been a *barmaid* at Kala's. Some of them told him their own fathers had fucked Iris Fane for the price of a cheap pitcher of beer. He'd rebelled in just about every way he could think of, and when he was done with that, he'd started with the gambling.

"You stayed with Elroy?" Fisher asked. He rubbed his forehead, massaging the spot between his eyebrows, and I realized that he could move now. But he hadn't shifted from his position, leaning up against me. When he let his hand fall again, he let it rest against my leg. Comfortable. Familiar.

"No. If he'd taken us in, the guardians would have put two and two together and realized that he had made the daggers my mother had been carrying that day. I didn't want to endanger him, so, for all intents and purposes, Hayden and I disappeared. We found our own attic spaces to sleep in. Above taverns mostly, where a little noise at night wouldn't be noticeable. I'd sneak in and out of the forge, so no one knew I was working there. The skills my mother's rebel friends had taught me ended up keeping us alive. We managed."

So much left out. Painful nights filled with arguments. Nights spent sleeping on hard floors in the sweltering heat with nothing to block out the Twins at the windows. Unending hunger and a thirst that was never slaked. "Managed" was a generous term for what life looked like after that bastard had cut my mother's throat.

Fisher finally twisted over and laid his head back on his pillow. "Come here," he said.

"What?"

"Don't make me drag you down here." There was a tired but playful catch in his voice.

He wanted me to lie next to him. Hell. I was going to have to unpack that in the morning, honestly, because a wave of exhaustion like no other rolled over me as I scooted down the bed and straightened out my numb legs for the first time in hours. I made sure to arrange myself so that no part of my body was touching Fisher's, but he made a vexed sound and wrapped his arm around my body. Placing his hand against my stomach, he drew me close so that my back was flush with his chest. The warmth from his body was divine. I could feel his heart beating against my back—slow and even, in time with the soft push and pull of his breath. Somewhere toward the foot of the small bed, Onyx groaned comfortably and nestled deeper into the blankets.

This was...new.

Different.

Fisher hooked his fingers underneath the hem of my shirt and rested his hand against my skin. The move wasn't sexual. It was simple contact between one person and another. Grounding. Intimate. A connection.

"My mother was killed, too," he whispered thickly. "We have that in common, Little Osha."

I wanted to ask him what he meant by that, but he had already fallen asleep.

27

MARKED

It was still dark when I came to. It took me a moment to remember where I was and who was wrapped around me so close. Then I lay there, very still, not breathing, hyper-aware of the fact that Fisher's hard cock was digging into my ass and he was almost certainly awake. I'd shared enough beds with enough people to know by someone's breathing if they were conscious or not, and Fisher's breathing wasn't the shallow draw of someone still lost in sleep. It was deep and far too measured, and he felt tense behind me.

He's going to get up and leave the bedroom.

He's going to roll over and tell you that he doesn't want you here.

He's going to say something shitty so that you'll *leave.*

I came up with one terrible imagined eventuality after another, my nerves getting the better of me...but none of those things transpired. Fisher's hand was still underneath my shirt, but it had half-closed, relaxing in his sleep. The material I'd used to bind my chest had come loose and risen up in the night, and his knuckles were brushing the underside of my left breast. Very slowly but with obvious intent, Fisher opened his hand against my skin again, pressing his palm against my rib cage. I fastened my lip between my teeth, suddenly panicked, my heart rate kicking up as he ran the tips of his fingers along the underside of my breast, barely making contact at all...

It was a question.

Is this something you want?

I could choose how I answered. If I rounded my shoulders and moved away from him, I knew he'd remove his hand and let me go. We'd both get up and get on with our day, and that would be it. A door between us would close.

Or...

Or.

Fuck it.

I didn't want the door to close.

Letting out a shaky breath, I arched my back, grinding my ass up against Fisher's cock. Gods and sinners, he was *so* fucking hard. He let out a rough groan, his breath sweeping over my neck, causing my skin to break out in goose bumps. His fingers pressed hard against my ribs, and I let my eyes fall closed, relishing the flood of anticipation over what was about to happen.

As if there were some unspoken contract between us, neither of us broke the silence. He moved slowly, though, as if giving me time to change my mind. Rocking his hips forward, he showed me *just* how hard his cock was and what he intended on doing with it.

I already knew what it felt like to have him slide inside me, but this was nothing like when we'd fucked the other day. This promised more. The tension building between us was infused with a different kind of energy. I felt it traveling a millimeter over the surface of my skin, everywhere all at once, burning hot where his hands moved over my abdomen.

My spine flexed as I arched against him, and a thrill of heat rocked me to my core when Fisher rested his forehead against the back of my head and groaned.

I wanted him. More than I wanted to go home. Gods and martyrs, what kind of sister did that make me? Hayden needed me.

Elroy did, too. But in the moment, with the smell of him drowning out the entire fucking world and robbing me of all common sense, I wasn't capable of feeling bad about that. There would be time for guilt aplenty later but for now...

Fisher's nose grazed my ear, and a sigh worked its way out of me. How to explain the feeling of a male like Kingfisher breathing heavily into your ear. It wasn't easily done. First, there was the shiver. It started on my neck and spread outward, prickling up the back of my head, trailing a hot-cold pathway down my spine, hitting each vertebra as it went like a skipping stone. It turned into something else once it hit my sacrum. It became heavy. A ball of ache, forming in my stomach, building, sinking lower, drumming at the apex of my thighs so that I had to press my legs together to contain it.

The shiver.

The ache.

Then, the want.

It raged so hot that it created a vortex of energy, lust, and need that spun around inside me so fast that I felt like I had to jump up from the bed and scream or fucking *hit* something.

Now, now, now...

Desire pounded in my blood. As if Fisher could hear it beckoning to him, he grabbed my breast, moving quickly at last, finally giving up all pretense that this might not be happening. Rolling my nipple, he drove his hips upward so hard that I felt the swollen head of his erection in the small of my back. A sharp lash of pain relayed between both of my breasts, rocketing down between my legs, and it felt for all the godscursed world like he was teasing my clit at the same time as the sensitive bud of my nipple.

"*Ahh!*" I wanted to beg him to sink himself inside me, but I didn't want to speak. There were other words that would need to be said first if we broke our silence now. What happened last night had been awful, for him and for me. It had irrevocably altered the dynamic between us, and I didn't think either of us were ready to face that yet. So I sealed my lips shut, and I leaned back into him as he worked his other arm underneath me and fully caged me in both arms. Kneading the flesh of my breast with one hand, he roughly yanked the button at my waistband open, sliding his other hand down into the front of my pants.

When he coaxed me open and dipped his fingers between my slick folds, he discovered how wet I was and growled deep. The sound of it was so masculine and predatory that I almost lost my fucking mind.

Fuck me. Please fuck me.

Take me.

Own me.

Kingfisher's teeth nipped at my earlobe as he started to rub the swollen bundle of nerves between my legs, and my mind fragmented in an instant. His mouth. His hands. His cock. They were the only things that mattered. He knew how to touch me. How to work me into a frenzy. The way he stroked my clit, finding the perfect pressure and the perfect motion, spoke of many hours spent familiarizing himself with the female body. Time well spent as far as I was concerned. I was reaping the benefits of that experience now and then some.

Shamelessly, I ground myself against him, taking what I wanted from the contact, riding his hand as he rubbed me.

Fuck me with your fingers.

Choke me.

Hold me down and ride me until I scream.

Fisher made an animal, desperate noise into the crook of my neck as if he could read my mind and knew all of the filthy things I wanted him to do to me. As if he wanted to do them to me, too. He snarled as he ripped his arm out from underneath my shirt and closed his hand around my throat.

I'll make you beg, Little Osha.

I'll fill every one of those pretty little holes.

I'll fuck you so hard, you'll never want another male ever again.

❮ 406 ❯

I'd imagined the words. Fabricated them out of thin air and some-how played them aloud in my own head in his voice. Fisher's body was openly promising these things to me, though, and I didn't want to wait any longer.

He pulled me even closer, grip tightening around my throat, his thumb digging into my jaw, and I allowed my head to rock back. He buried his face into the crook of my neck, groaning, and the thought rose to my mind unbidden. Dangerous.

Bite me.

Fisher drove his fingers up inside me, releasing a strained huff. Hand tightening around my throat, he gave me a little shake that seemed almost like a reprimand. I was so shaken by the sensation of his fingers thrusting up inside me, probing my wet heat, that for a blinding second, I couldn't think around the spike of pleasure.

Gods, we were still fucking clothed. Fisher was shirtless, but he was still wearing his pants, and I was wearing everything. Suddenly, I needed us to be naked. I wanted to feel his body on mine. I wanted to feel him fucking everywhere. I grabbed hold of my shirt, ready to try and somehow get it off without Kingfisher having to stop what he was doing, but then I felt a rush along the length of my body, and just like that, my clothes were in shreds, falling away from my torso, my arms, and my legs. Fisher's pants were just *gone.*

I'd gotten what I'd so desperately wanted. Our bodies met every-where. Our legs tangled together, our skin clammy with heat. Fisher renewed his attentions, pulsing his fingers in and out of my slit, rub-bing my clit at the same time with the heel of his palm, working me into a frenzy.

I could barely breathe. My head spun as he buried his face into my hair again, releasing another strained groan.

Fuck me.

Please! Gods, please just fuck me.

I want...

I need...

The sound of Fisher's agitated cry bounced loudly around the small bedroom. He moved fast, drawing his fingers out of me just in time to make room for his rigid cock. Unlike the last time we were together, he didn't slam himself up inside of me immediately. This time, I felt the swell of his head pressing against me, then the over-whelming, ground-shattering moment when he slid past my entrance and began to push up.

Oh.

My.

Fucking.

Gods.

He...

Gods, he was so fucking deep. I...

Every warrior in Innìr will smell me on you, Fisher's voice rumbled in my mind. *I'm going to make you hoarse from screaming my fucking name. I'm going to mark you in every way imaginable, so that everyone knows you're fucking mine.*

Holy shit!

He...

Was that...

I couldn't...

He set up a merciless pace, thrusting himself up inside me, pound-ing himself home. His hand was still between my legs, his fingers working over my clit as he fucked me. He encompassed me wholly, fully, truly. I was locked in his embrace, thoroughly wrapped up in him, shaking every time he impaled me on his cock...but still, there was one more thing...

Bite me, Fisher.

It came as a breathless thought. *I can't...*

Bite me. Do it. I want it!

I can't!

BITE ME!

The bright, sharp sting of his canines sinking into my skin made me hiss out loud. My eyes shot open, shock causing my heartbeat to stumble momentarily, but then...

A bliss like no other overloaded my senses—lightning coursing through my veins. Fisher went still, frozen like a statue, his breath coming hard and fast down his nose. He'd bitten into the dip of my neck, right above my collarbone, but he hadn't drawn on my blood yet. He was waiting, though I didn't know for what.

No longer cutting off my air supply, he moved his free hand back to my breast and started to slowly stroke his fingers around my nipples, lightly, tentatively circling my areola. My nerve endings jumped, euphoria soaking my system until I started to feel fucking high. It was only when my mind started to feel gluey and upside down that he oh-so-slowly pulled his hips back and then thrust his cock up inside me to the hilt. At the same time, I felt the first tingle at my neck—his first small draw from my blood.

"FUCK!" I screamed out loud, my eyes rolling back into my head. The crescendo of pleasure came down on me like a landslide. I was crushed by it. It broke me and made my soul fucking sing. It was better than any drug I'd ever experienced before.

Easy. Quiet. Don't...fucking move.

The words were ragged. Desperate. They were inside my head, and I...I hadn't got a hope in hell of obeying them. The moment Fisher slid into me again, drinking a little deeper, I lost any sense of pride I possessed and reached back, grabbing his head and pushing him down onto my neck as hard as I damn well could.

Ruin me.

The command was all he needed. Fisher's arms tightened around my body like a vise, and he fucked me with the force of all those sledgehammers smashing down on the frozen surface of the Darn. I broke far easier than the river had. I became pieces of myself, and Fisher was the only thing that held me together. With each heady draw of his mouth, I felt myself filling up with light until I glowed brilliant as a sun.

Don't stop. Don't stop...

I felt his need bubbling up inside him. He was drowning in this, too. He fucked me even harder, drinking deeper, his arms tight as bands of steel around me.

And then the world ended.

Existence blinked out into a blank void.

The stars tumbled from the heavens, and hell rose up to meet them.

Everything and nothing, here and gone.

It was every ecstatic moment I'd ever experienced, condensed and multiplied one millionfold. My body became a fiery torch, and there was Fisher, burning right alongside me.

He mindlessly slammed himself into me, grunting, and then he ripped his mouth away from my skin and roared like he was dying.

No. Not like he was dying.

Like he was being *reborn*.

The world came back into existence little by little, like snowflakes fluttering from the ceiling. It took a long time for my body to stop trembling. Just as he had done when I woke up, Fisher lay behind me, still as the dead, not breathing. Only this time, he was holding on to me for dear life. He didn't let go.

Fresh, hot bread. Buttery. Delicious.

My stomach rumbled, my eyelids fluttering open. I found myself snuggled up to a snoring fox. Onyx lazily blinked his eyes open, and I swear to the gods, it looked as if he was smiling at me.

"You stink," I told him, petting his head. "You need a bath. No more sleeping in the bed."

He bared his teeth, laid his ears back, and vaulted off the bed, disappearing out of the open bedroom doorway. I guess he didn't like the sound of a bath.

Sighing and deliciously sore, I slumped back against the rumpled sheets and stared up at the ceiling, watching the dust motes spiral through the gilded morning air. Where the hell was Fisher? I asked the question with a dose of resignation. If I knew him, he'd be back at Innìr by now, freaked out and angry. I'd be discarded here for three days as a result of his inability to manage his fucking feelings. I turned my head, and my heart slowed at the sight of the tiny droplet of dried blood staining the sheets next to me.

My blood.

Fisher had bitten me.

My mind went blank. I let that information float at the forefront of my mind. I didn't try to process it. I'd officially hit my exhaustion point when it came to trying to analyze everything that had happened since the Hall of Mirrors. This was just one more thing balancing precariously at the top of a very long and bewildering list that I would have to work through at some point. For now, all I knew was that I'd wanted it. I'd asked for it, and, sidenote, Fisher and I were now randomly capable of speaking into each other's minds.

There it was again: the smell of fresh, flaky pastry and rich butter, but this time it was blended with the subtlest hint of sugar. And *coffee*. It was the idea of coffee that had me climbing out of bed in the end. Stiff and a little dizzy, I wrapped myself in a sheet and went to find the source of the smell.

Light flooded into the apartment's living room. The dust sheets had been removed from the furniture and the paintings, revealing a comfortable space full of small treasures, books, and knickknacks that gave the place an easy sense of home. On the mantelpiece above the fireplace, scores of glass jars sat full of stubs of charcoal and paintbrushes.

Fisher sat at a round table by the windows, long legs stretched out in front of him, the light catching at his hair and warming the black to dark brown. It gilded one side of his face, softening the hard edge of his jaw and the proud line of his nose. He stared out of the window, watching the boughs of the tree on the other side of the glass gently sway on the breeze. He seemed lost in thought. At ease, even. A part of me didn't want to make my presence known. After how troubled he'd been of late, I wanted him to savor the moment of peace. And I was a fucking coward, it turned out. There were still things that needed to be said, and I was scared of that conversation. It could only end badly, and—

Fisher closed his eyes and let the dappled sunlight play over his face. "I didn't know how you took your coffee," he said softly.

Shit. "How long have you known I was here?"

He smiled sadly. "I *always* know where you are, Little Osha." Opening his eyes, he turned and looked at me. The smile developed a dangerous edge to it when he took me in.

"I would have gotten dressed," I explained, "but there weren't actually any clothes in that bag you packed for me. I appreciate the sentiment, but four different throwing knives, a field dressing kit, and a bottle of whiskey might have been overkill. A clean pair of underwear and a toothbrush would have been nice."

This coaxed a laugh out of him. "Fair point. And noted. Only two knives and a hip flask next time. Plus underwear and a toothbrush."

I laughed softly. "I *was* willing to put on the clothes from yesterday, but then I found them in the bed, in shreds, and that idea went out of the window, too."

"Don't worry. I'll happily correct my lapse in my manners." With a flick of his wrist, Fisher conjured a wave of glimmering smoke. Spreading over the rug toward me, it circled around my ankles like a friendly cat seeking to be pet. It rose up my legs, making my skin prickle with warmth, leaving luxurious black silk in its wake. The pants were wide-legged and loose. The camisole top was pretty, long enough in the body to cover my stomach—though only just—and embellished with fine lace along the low-cut neckline. Fisher's magic hadn't graced me with any underwear, it seemed; my peaked nipples were very visible through the sheer material.

I arched an eyebrow at him, then looked down at my chest. "Is this the kind of thing you imagine me wearing often?"

"When I imagine you, Little Osha, you're *very* rarely wearing clothes."

Oh. Wow. Okay. Color rose to my cheeks, a pleasant heat warming my face. I ducked my head, looking down at my bare feet, giving myself a moment to acclimate to the idea that Fisher wasn't going to be an unbearable shit this morning. It had been surprise enough that he was still here, but this was a shock to the system that I wasn't prepared for.

"Come and sit down. Eat," he said.

I could definitely do *that*. I was ravenous. I joined him at the table, sitting beside him on his right, so I could look out of the window and watch Ballard wake up as I ate. Fisher wore a small smirk as I leaned across the table and fell upon the little pastries, custard-filled miniature pies, and diced fruit.

"What?"

"Nothing. Nothing at all," Fisher said, his voice full of laughter.

"Should I go and si—oh, Gods! *Fisher!* What the...?" I felt the blood drain from my face. What the *hell* was all over my hands? I dropped the little pastry I was holding, and Onyx dove, catching it out of the air before it could even touch the ground. I held out my hands, aghast. The tattoos I hadn't cared so much about last night were still all over my fingers and the backs of my hands. Except there were more of them now. Many more. Stacks of small runes ran up each one of my fingers. Delicate script wound around my wrists and up my forearms. I had no idea what the fuck any of it said. And the backs of my hands? I started to feel very lightheaded. The design on the back of my left hand was simple. Ish. The lines were fine and twisted together beautifully, forming a shape that almost resembled a flower if you squinted at it long enough. The one on my right, however...

It was bigger and covered the whole span of my hand. The lines were bolder. They twisted around one another, forming a variety of knots that I had trouble even picking apart with my eyes. It wasn't just one rune. It was many, interlocking, woven one on top of the other, on top of the other. One of the runes wasn't even black, but a dark, iridescent blue-green color that flashed metallically when it caught the light.

Even Fisher swallowed hard as he took in all of this new ink I had gained in the night. I thrust my hands out toward him accusingly. "My mother would *not* have approved of this!"

To his credit, he didn't laugh at me. He picked up his coffee, maintaining a straight face, and took a sip. Once he'd set his cup down, he reached out and took my left hand in his. His expression was blank as he studied the runes along my fingers. His brows twitched as he turned my arm this way and that, read the script that chained my wrist. When he ran a finger over the flower-like, larger rune on the back of my hand, his features became utterly unreadable, though.

He spent far longer assessing the ink on my right hand. I sat impatiently, thoughts bouncing around all over the place, unable to calm myself.

Say something. Don't just sit there, frowning like that. Speak!

Fisher huffed softly. "I'm thinking," he said. "Give me a moment."

"Oh, fuck. So that was real, then? You can read my thoughts?" A note of hysteria edged into my voice.

"No, I can't read your thoughts," he said, eyes darting up to mine for a split second. "I can hear you when you speak to me directly, though. That's all."

"That's all? That's *all!*"

"*Breathe,* Little Osha," Fisher chided. "Your heart's racing."

"I'm fine," I lied.

Fisher adopted a very intense expression. He seemed confused by something. Turning my hand toward him, he even angled his head to get a different perspective of the layered, locked rune.

"What...what does it all mean?" I asked nervously.

Fisher drew in a sharp breath, looking up from my hand. "Not much, really." He picked up one of the custard-filled pies, turned my hand over, placed it in my palm, and let me go. "Here. Eat. Your blood sugar is low."

"My blood sugar's low? Wha—Fisher, *what do the tattoos mean?*"

He sighed, rocking back into his chair. Now that he was reclined again, the warm wash of light coming in through the window bathed him in gold again. He was breathtaking. "The one on the left means blessed one," he said, his tone light. "The fingers..." He shrugged, looking up at the ceiling far too casually. "They mean all kinds of things."

"Could you be any vaguer?"

"I mean, probably..."

"Fisher!"

"Okay. All right. A lot of them are connected. Light. Dark. Silver. Steel. Earth. Air. Fire. Water. That kind of thing. Alchemist stuff."

Alchemist stuff? The way he said that made it sound like that should be explanation enough and I ought to be satisfied, but I had more questions. A lot more questions, one more pressing than the rest. I held up my right hand and pointed at the mother of all runes shimmering there on my skin. "What the hell does *this* one mean?"

Fisher met my gaze. "That one's difficult. I can't give you a definitive answer. Not yet."

"There's magic in it, isn't there?"

"There's magic in all of them," he said nonchalantly, taking a manful bite out of his own breakfast. "If you don't want to keep them..."

"How am I supposed to know if I want to keep them if I don't know what they *mean?*"

"I'm sorry. You're right. Here." He gestured for me to give him my hand, which I did. A moment later, a creeping cold ran over my skin. One by one, the runes faded from my skin until even the complex, multi-layered rune was gone.

I stared at him, stunned. "But—"

"They aren't gone for good," he said tightly. "I...you can change your mind about them later if you want to. You have a month or so.

If you decide over the next few weeks that you want them back, I'll return them to you."

"But what if I decide I want cool hand tattoos after the month has passed? Do I get to choose from different designs every time we sleep together or something?"

Fisher laughed dryly, shaking his head. "No. The Marks are chosen for you. They won't be there after a month. If you decide not to accept them, they'll be gone for good."

I let that sit between us for a while, knowing that there was something he wasn't telling me. Plenty of things. I didn't have it in me to prod any further, though. I took a bite of my food, taking in all of the ink that still marked his skin. After a while, I said, "What do yours mean?"

"Mine?"

"Your tattoos. *Yours* haven't gone anywhere."

"Oh." He looked down at himself. "Well. Our runes are complicated. But yes, they do have meanings. This one," he said, holding up his left hand, "means vengeance." He held up his other hand. "This one means justice."

"What about that one?" I asked, pointing at the large, swirling section of ink on his forearm.

"Sacrifice," he said, his voice hitching.

"Why is it so much bigger than the rest?"

Fisher took in the rune, then slowly drew down the sleeve of his shirt, covering it. "I think you can probably guess why," he said softly.

I could. I'd regretted the question even as I'd asked it. The largest tattoo on Fisher's arm meant sacrifice, because *he* had, or would have to, sacrifice so much...

They were prophecies of a kind. They told his story. And it wasn't necessarily one that he was comfortable talking about. In time, maybe. But for now...

I pointed at the small bird tattoo below my collarbone, changing the subject. "You told me you couldn't take *this* one back."

All humor left Fisher's face. The sunlight dimmed out of nowhere, the room darkening with shadows that spilled across the walls from all four corners of the room. I knew right away that something had shifted. Our time together at breakfast was over. Fisher got up from the table, carefully setting his chair back underneath it. "No, I can't take *that* back," he said stiffly. "And I'm sorry for that."

"You don't need to be sorry. I'm pretty attached to it now. I just thought, since you removed these..." Gods, I was rambling.

"Not removed. Only hidden. For now, anyway." He gave me a tight-lipped smile. "We need to leave soon. You'll find some fresh clothes laid out for you on your bed. There's a bath already drawn for you in there, too. I'm going to go and say goodbye to Wendy. When I come back, we'll go."

I let Fisher go, knowing that I couldn't say anything to shift the mood back to the way it had been. In the bedroom—the one I was *supposed* to have slept in—I soaked my sore body and let myself stew over everything I'd said. It was when I stood naked, dripping on the rug in front of the ornate full-length mirror on the wall, that I realized what had caused the mood in the kitchen to shift. Right there, only a couple of inches above the bird tattoo, were two small red welts. They were almost closed up already. They didn't even hurt.

No, I can't take that *back. And I'm sorry for that.*

He hadn't been talking about the bird tattoo.

He'd been talking about the bite mark at my throat.

28

JUST ASK

- Bismuth. Cadmia. Cinnabar.
- Plumbago. Lime. Calcite.
- Tin salt. Resin of copper. Marcasite.

Result: No Reaction.

WHEN CARRION BURST into the forge later that afternoon, I was out back by the water baths, hurling glass beakers against the mountainside. I pulled a very uncharitable face, trying to convey my displeasure at his presence with a grimace instead of words. If I knew Carrion, he understood my meaning perfectly well and didn't give a fuck that I wasn't thrilled to see him. He produced a tin from the pocket of a very warm-looking coat and lit a cigarillo for himself. He offered me one, but I shook my head and launched another beaker at the rock.

An herbal, rich smell soaked the frigid air. "What are we doing?" he asked.

"What does it look like?" The beaker I lobbed this time didn't go as high up the rock face, but it still exploded into an impressive shower of broken glass.

"Can I join in?"

I rolled my eyes.

"Great." Gripping his cigarillo between his teeth, Carrion chose a fat, round-bottomed flask from the crate I'd dragged out here. He hurled the thing with all his might, and it arced pretty well before sailing down and exploding against the rocks. The resulting crash was one of the best ones yet. "Well, that felt pretty good," he said, blowing out a thick cloud of smoke. "Wanna tell me *why* we're doing this?"

"Destruction," I replied.

Carrion nodded, bobbing his head from side to side. "As good a reason as any. I like it."

I grabbed the two smaller glass bulbs from an old alembic still and shoved one into Carrion's chest. "Shut up and throw."

He laughed but obliged me, sending the glass hurtling through the air. I threw mine at the same time, and the two bulbs detonated against the rock with a thunderous smash.

"I take it you haven't had any luck with your trials today?" Carrion said.

Gods, couldn't he take a hint? I wasn't in the mood to discuss my failures. I'd also burned my arm earlier, which wasn't helping matters. "Evidently not. And that *fucking* quicksilver..."

"Having trouble making it do its liquidy, rolling around thing?"

"No. I can alter its state just fine now. I barely even have to think about that. I just tell it to be a liquid, and it becomes a liquid. The problem is that it's fucking mocking me."

Carrion snorted. "*Mocking* you?"

"Yes! It laughs every time I attempt to combine something new with it. It'll take the pure silver, but the moment I tip anything else in there, it burns up before it even touches the metals. And it fucking *laughs!*"

"It can't be sentient," he said dubiously.

"Oh, ho, ho, it is. You wouldn't be saying that if you could hear what I can hear."

Carrion nodded, pulling on the cigarillo, the bright cherry flaring at its end. "Have you considered the possibility that you might be mad?"

"Yes, I have, actually," I answered tartly. "But Fisher's books back at Cahlish said it was common for Alchemists to report that they could hear the quicksilver."

"Then maybe *all* Alchemists are mad. Maybe having a screw loose is just a prerequisite for working with this stuff."

I snatched another flask from the box and threw it, growling under my breath. "Look, if you're not going to be helpful, then I'm kind of busy here."

"Oh, sure, absolutely. I can see *that.*"

I spun quickly, a fresh flask held over my head, ready to throw it at him, but he held up his hands in surrender. "All right, all right. Sorry. I admit, I didn't come here with the purpose of trying to be helpful, but…you say you don't have any problems getting to shift the quicksilver from one state to the other anymore? Because you ask it to change. Right?"

"Right."

"Then, have you thought about just *asking* it to meld with the pure silver?"

"Psshhh! Don't…don't be ridiculous. Of course I haven't!"

"Why not?"

"That'd be too simple, Carrion. I can't just *ask* it to become a relic."

"Seems to me that if you can ask it to be a liquid or a solid, you could ask it to be all kinds of things," he said, popping the collar of his coat.

I glared at him, my annoyance levels rising fast. Not Carrion Swift. He would *not* be the reason why I figured out how to accomplish this task. He'd never let me live it down. It was infuriating that I hadn't considered this for myself, though.

"Are you gonna try it?" he asked, standing up a little straighter. "Can I watch?"

Gods, this was going to be awful. "I can't try again to make a relic. I haven't refined the silver yet. I was taking a moment to do this." To *sulk*. "But…there's a way to half-test the theory," I said. "And yes, you can come and watch. But only if you promise to keep your mouth shut and not get in the way."

It was physically impossible for Carrion to keep his mouth shut and not get in the way. I already knew this when I agreed to let him follow me to the map tent, so I wasn't too surprised when he talked the entire way down the mountainside and all the way across the camp, too. He was blathering on about some two-bit smuggler back in Zilvaren called Davey, who owed him seventeen chits, when we reached the map room.

Thankfully the place was deserted. It'd struck me that I might run into Danya here, since this was the only place I'd encountered her in camp thus far, but apparently the fates were smiling down on me today because even Ren was nowhere to be seen. I didn't want an audience for this. Carrion didn't really count, and he already knew what I was going to do anyway, having been responsible for the suggestion in the first place. I would look pretty stupid if I attempted this and failed, and I preferred none of the Fae to witness that first-hand.

"Dark as fuck in here," Carrion grumbled. There was a fire burning in the ventless grate, but none of the torches on the walls were lit. He grabbed the first one he came to and stuck the end of it in the fire, then went around the empty room, lighting the others. I paid no attention to his chatter as he carried out the task. I was fixed on the bristling shards of metal sticking out of the stone wall.

This isn't going to work. Why would it? Surely somebody's already tried...

Doubt after doubt hit me, but I brushed them all aside. I had nothing to lose. And it didn't cost me anything to ask. If nothing happened, or the quicksilver just laughed at me, then no big deal. I'd go back to the forge and refine the silver, and tomorrow morning I'd start up my trials again. But if it worked...

She comes.

She comes.

She approaches.

The quicksilver hadn't spoken the last time I was in here. Not like this. I'd stood next to the embedded shards for a long time, focusing very hard on them before I'd detected even the faint whisper coming from the metal. Now the voices were a rushing conversation, quiet, yes, but loud enough for me to pick up as I neared the wall.

She comes.

She sees.

She hears.

Reaching up, I extended my hand, pressing the tip of my index finger against one of the sword splinters. *Yes, I've come. I see you. I hear,* I thought.

Voices exploded in my head. Scores of them, talking, screaming, pleading, begging, laughing, shouting. I gasped, ripping my hand away.

"That looked painful," Carrion said conversationally. He stood right next to me, holding on to the torch, his auburn hair turned copper-gold by the flames.

"Can you back up a little?" I asked. "This might be a little easier without you breathing directly down my neck."

"I seem to recall you liked me breathing down your ne—"

"If you dare finish that sentence, you can go and wait outside," I snapped.

"That's fair." Carrion moved back a step, bowing graciously. "Though, if it seems like your mind's being sucked out of your body, or you're in excruciating pain and can't let go of the quicksilver sword murder spikes, do I have your permission to tackle you to the ground?"

That actually seemed like a prudent plan. "You do."

"Excellent."

I braced for the roar of voices, gingerly touching one of the shards again, but this time there was only silence. Had I imagined the screaming and the begging? Didn't seem plausible. I went back to the original shard I'd touched, prepared for the onslaught of noise again, just in case, but there was only the echoing silence.

Hello? I thought. *Are you here?*

The answer was instantaneous.

Where is here...

Here...

Here...

Here...

Here...

The voices came from the left and right, from behind and in front of me.

We can be everywhere, they purred in unison.

They'd answered my question. *It* had? I couldn't fathom whether the voices inside the quicksilver belonged to one thing or many, but I hadn't come to puzzle that out. *Can you come out of the stone?* I asked.

Out?

Out?

Out?

Whyyyyyyy?

The voices buzzed like the droning flies.

Because the warrior who owned you is angry with me. And I want to put you back together.

This was bizarre. I'd never had a two-way conversation with the quicksilver before. I hadn't even thought to try, which was foolish, perhaps, since it frequently didn't shut up.

Owned?

Owned?

We are not owned.

Plain as day, I heard the anger in the layered voices. I should have realized that possessive language might not have gone down well, but I'd said it now. The only way forward was damage control.

"You're making a weird face," Carrion whispered loudly. "Are you talking to it?"

"Yes, I'm talking to it. What do you think I'm doing?"

"I don't know. You look constipated."

"Shh!" I closed my eyes so I could block him out. *The female warrior who carried you, not owned you,* I thought. *She wishes to carry you again. Unless you can be put back together, she can't do that.*

Fae and human desires do not concern us...

Us...

Us...

Damn. To be honest, the idea of being carried around by Danya wouldn't appeal that much to me either, but I hadn't thought I'd have to resort to bargaining tactics. If the quicksilver was sentient, it was bound to want something, though. Anything capable of feeling and thinking always wanted something.

What does concern you? I asked.

The quicksilver didn't reply right away. It seemed to be thinking about the question. After a long pause, it said, *Music. Give us music, and we will obey.*

Music? Gods and fucking sinners, what the hell did it want music for?

How about this? Allow me to reforge you, and I'll have someone sing a song just for you.

There was no way this was going to work. No way.

A song? From start to finish? For us to keep?

Keep?

Keep?

If there was a way to keep a song, I didn't know what it was, but I was willing to agree to almost anything at this point. *Yes, I promise. A whole song for you to keep.*

And you will forge us into a mighty blade unlike any other?

Yes. If you'll allow it.

We will accept...

Accept...

Accept...

I didn't want to push my luck here, but there was one more thing I wanted to know. *And will you bestow the blade I forge with magics that the bearer might wield?*

A gift revoked! the quicksilver cried. *You ask for what cannot be given...*

"Saeris..."

"Quiet, Carrion," I hissed. "I'll tell you what's going on when I'm done." I should have left him back at the forge. Shutting him out, I tried a different angle with the quicksilver.

Is it not within your power to give it?

All is within. It sounded affronted by the implication that it wasn't capable of something. *But it is undeserved. We decided long ago.*

How do you know? How can you tell if a warrior doesn't deserve the gift? Have you assessed the worthiness of every warrior who wishes to wield a sword?

I was walking a very fine line. If I wasn't careful, the quicksilver was going to shut down completely and refuse to even dislodge itself from the stone. Even now, I could feel that it was irritated by my pestering. But I could also sense that it was intrigued.

All warriors are the same, it concluded after a long beat. *They only wish to kill.*

That isn't true. Most warriors fight because they have to. To protect and defend.

Improbable.

How can we show you otherwise?

The longest silence yet followed. Thirty seconds ticked by, and then a minute. Another three had passed by when the quicksilver finally spoke again. *We will bear witness to the blood.*

What...does that *mean?*

We will be forged anew. When you have upheld your end of our bargain, we will taste the blood of the one who would carry us. If they are honorable, we will consider allowing the old magics to flow through us again.

Thank you! Thank you!

Do not thank us too soon. The die is not cast, Saeris Fane. First, you must restore us and bring us a song worthy of glory.

Oh, I'll do both. Don't you worry about that. I startled when the shard of metal I was touching trembled beneath my fingertip. My eyes flew open, and I watched, amazed, as the thin, sharp sliver of metal slowly emerged from the stone. It hovered in the air, trembling, and then dropped into the center of my palm.

"Holy *shit*," I breathed.

One at a time, the other pieces of Danya's sword started to vibrate, working free of the wall. I finally looked at Carrion, who was leaning against the map table, tossing a small black rock up into the air and catching it. "Are you seeing this, Swift?" I demanded.

"Hmm? Oh, you figured it out. Cool. Did you give it a stern talking to?" He pushed away from the table and came to watch as over five hundred pieces of deconstructed sword started to drop to the floor.

"No, I promised it something that it wanted."

"Ahh, bribery. I should have thought of that."

He ducked down and helped pick up the pieces of metal. We'd gathered a small amount of them when another voice spoke behind us, and I nearly fell on my ass from the shock. "If you let me, I think I can speed up that process."

"Gods alive!" I spun around, my pulse beating everywhere, and found the warrior sitting in an armchair by the fire. "Could have warned me we weren't alone anymore," I hissed at Carrion.

"Don't get shitty with me. I tried to tell you, and you told me to shush. You were very rude."

"I didn't mean to scare you," Lorreth said, getting to his feet. "Sorry. Watch out."

Carrion and I both leaned back as hundreds of glinting pieces of metal rose into the air again, this time courtesy of Lorreth, who used his magic to gather all of the pieces into one floating bundle before he gestured for them to drop into a ceramic pot on the mantelpiece above the fire. He collected the pot and brought it over, handing it to me with a self-satisfied grin. "There we go. Easy."

A lot of things were easier when you had magic. I clutched the pot to my chest, the beginnings of excitement churning in my veins. If I could convince the quicksilver to enter into this kind of a bargain, then the rings should be easy. And I got to make a sword. Not some tiny dagger, barely capable of inflicting a paper cut. A proper fucking sword.

Wolfishly, I grinned up at the dark-haired warrior. "Lorreth. What a coincidence. I was just about to go looking for you."

29

BALLAD OF THE AJUN GATE

THE FORGE WAS hotter than the fifth burning pit of hell. Sweat ran down my back, soaking through my shirt. My pants clung to my legs, but damp clothes were a small price to pay for progress, and, gods, was I making progress.

Danya's sword smelted perfectly. The quicksilver didn't laugh at me at all as I worked. It didn't split from the steel and refuse to recombine. For once, it was silent *and* cooperative. But its attention was a hand resting on my shoulder. It was curious. It wanted to see what kind of weapon I would create with it, and if I was capable of upholding my end of our bargain.

I'd dreamed of getting to create something like this for years. I'd had so many sketchbooks back in Zilvaren full of designs that I had never been able to forge thanks to lack of materials. If the quicksilver wanted to be turned into a weapon that would demand people's attention, then I wasn't going to disappoint it. There were areas of the casting that I was going to need help with, though. Areas I didn't have much experience with.

The sun was going down when I stepped out of the forge into the snow, looking for Lorreth. He sat on a rock by the fire, hurling a throwing dagger at a dead tree trunk that was already chipped into oblivion, full of blade marks. Carrion was cooking something in a pot over the fire, his mouth drawn into a flat line. He saw me and pointed at Lorreth, scowling. "These fuckers are all cheats."

Lorreth laughed heartily, extending his hand. The dagger he'd just imbedded into the tree trunk dislodged itself and whipped backward, landing in his palm hilt-first. "And *you* are a sore loser," he said.

"He just took me for eleven chits. That's half of my money."

"You can't even spend them here, Carrion," I reminded him.

"It's not about that. It's about being fucking tricksy. We had a gentleman's bet. We were supposed to try and hit the target as many times as we could in a row. The person who held the longest streak won."

"And? How has he tricked you?" I tried not to smile.

"And I did the honorable thing and let him go first."

"And?"

"And he hasn't missed once! I asked him if he'd played this game before, *and he said no,*" Carrion growled in an accusatory tone.

"I haven't played before." Lorreth flicked his wrist, and the dagger shot from his palm, propelled through the air at a ferocious velocity. The dagger's handle juddered when the blade bit into the tree trunk. "When I throw this thing, it isn't a game. I'm usually throwing it at a vampire's head. It pays not to miss under *those* conditions."

Carrion's cheeks were mottled red with annoyance. "How the fuck was I supposed to beat him when he's some kind of killing machine?"

I snorted. "How many times has he hit the tree?" It was cruel to ask, but it was a rare thing, seeing Carrion this piqued, and damn it, I was going to make the most of it.

"I don't know," he snapped. "More than fifty."

"Two hundred and seventeen," Lorreth said. The knife jerked free of the trunk, darted back to Lorreth's hand, and he threw it again, all in one fluid motion. "Two hundred and eighteen." Again, he repeated the process, not even looking at the tree this time. "Two hundred and nineteen."

"All right, all right, you can stop now. I'm already making the godscursed food, anyway."

"That's what you bet him?" I asked Lorreth. "That he'd have to cook?"

The warrior shrugged. The tips of his canines were just visible in the waning half-light when he grinned. "I was hungry."

"Tricksy," Carrion muttered again, stirring the contents of the pot bubbling over the fire.

"He didn't trick you," I told him. "He gave you a taste of your own medicine. How many of these unfairly weighted, unwinnable bets have you allowed Hayden to enter into, huh?"

"It isn't my fault if your brother's over-confident when it comes to card games, Saeris."

"And how would you have rated your confidence levels when you sized up a seven-foot-tall, full-blooded Fae warrior with hundreds of years' worth of experience in killing things under his belt, and you thought you'd best him at knife play?"

"Gahhhh, screw the both of you," Carrion groused, pulling a face. "If I'd gone first, we wouldn't be having this conversation. I'd be the one still hitting the fucking tree."

This time, when the dagger's handle landed in Lorreth's hand, he flipped the weapon over and held it by the blade, offering it out to Carrion with a wicked glint in his eyes. "By all means, human. Have at it."

Carrion went even redder. "Well, it's too late now. I've already lost, haven't I! There's no point."

Lorreth shook his head. "Sore loser."

"The sorest," I agreed.

"*Urgh!* How about we just eat the food I've made, and you both shut your mouths?"

"I don't have time to eat. I only came out here to ask you something, Lorreth."

The warrior twisted on his rock, giving me his full attention. "Ask away."

"Have you got any experience of whittling? Y'know, carving things out of wood?"

"As it happens, I have."

"Be more specific with your questioning, Sunshine. He probably whittles every spare moment of his life. He probably wins whittling *competitions.*"

I rolled my eyes. "I'm not trying to beat him in a bet, Carrion. I want him to be good at it."

Lorreth's booming laughter rang out into the encroaching night. "In that case, then yes. I'm more than good. I'm fucking excellent."

Hours slipped by. Once I'd flashed the newly poured length of metal I'd made from the pieces of Danya's sword, I heated it, shaped it, and flattened it. Then, just when the new sword was taking shape, I took up a hammer and started to pound. I applied more heat. As soon as the steel glowed white hot, I folded it. Hammered it. Shaped it. Again and again. Not just once. A thousand times. More.

Evening turned to night. The clouds cleared and the stars came out, and I didn't rest. My arms were heavy as lead, the muscles in my back screaming every time I lifted the hammer, but somehow I knew it wasn't ready yet. Just when I thought I was finished and the steel had been tempered sufficiently, something deep down inside of me said, *Once more, Saeris Fane.*

Lorreth brought in the wolf's head he'd carved out of a piece of yew at around one in the morning. It was an impressive piece, highly detailed, its proportions perfect. Just as I had hoped it would, the snarling beast bore a striking resemblance to Fisher's tattoo, as well as the animal embossed into the armor worn by the members of the Lupo Proelia.

I walked the warrior through the steps of making a casting mold, and he followed those steps without complaint, even though they required him to dig a hole into the frozen ground until he found clay and then required him to combine that clay with a pile of horse shit with his bare hands. He enjoyed pressing the wolf head he'd carved into the clay and sat impatiently by the firing ovens while the small fire he built inside slowly dried out the mold so it wouldn't crack.

At around four, when I was growing delirious from the heat and exhaustion, Carrion announced that he was going to sleep. Rather than head down to the camp in search of his tent, he stretched out on the floor on the other side of the forge, by the door where it was a little cooler, balled up his coat, stuffed it underneath his head, and promptly passed out.

It's time for you to rest, too, Osha.

That voice. Gods alive. It made me jump when I heard it in my mind, though I *had* been waiting for it.

Not until I'm done, I answered. *I'm nearly there.*

Fisher was close. I could inexplicably feel him, his presence near. Casting a quick glance toward the forge's doorway, I thought I could make out the shape of him, merging with the shadows that danced and leaped around the fire.

How long have you been out there? I asked.

Only a few hours, came his reply.

Why didn't you come in?

There was a long pause. And then he said, *I didn't know if you'd want me to.*

Come in from the cold, Kingfisher.

I will. Soon. I'll sit here a little longer, I think.

I didn't react when he stole in later. He sat in a chair by the window, moonlight threading through his hair, shadows playing over his hands and his face as he watched me work. He and Lorreth talked quietly, and I hammered. They were both there, helping when I poured the steel for the wolf's head hilt. Fisher whistled when we cracked the mold and he saw what Lorreth had carved. Very few words were traded between us. As I bound the broad, beveled blade to its hilt and cross guard, and wrapped the hilt with a glittering black and gold cord, a breathless tension clung to the air.

Then, at last, it was done.

I nearly collapsed on the spot.

The sword was a thing of beauty. Undeniably so. Aside from the impressive wolf's head pommel, the hilt was also decorated in trailing vines that wound around the hilt and guard, which I'd managed to fire myself without any help from Lorreth. The blade itself bore a rippled wave that ran from end to end thanks to the countless times it had been folded. I had spent the past hour painstakingly engraving words down the very center of the blade. Words that would hopefully bode well for both the weapon and the warrior who bore it, and badly for those who found themselves at its sharp end.

By righteous hands, deliverance of the unrighteous dead.

"Incredible," Fisher said breathlessly. His eyes found mine, and they shone with amazement.

"Can I hold it?" Lorreth asked hopefully.

"Go ahead."

He lifted it, eyes lit with reverence. Inexplicably, my throat closed up at the sight of him holding the weapon. He ran his finger along its edge, barely touching his fingertips to the steel before hissing, pulling his hand back again. "Gods, you only need to look at the damned thing and it cuts." He popped his index finger into his mouth, sucking on it.

For the first time since we left the map room, the quicksilver spoke, and its voice was no longer fractured. It was *one* voice, strong and clear.

It is time. Give us our song.

Outside, the sky was lit up with an explosion of green and pink light.

My breath caught at the sight of it. "What is that?"

"The aurora," Fisher answered softly. "A blessing."

"Holy fuck." Lorreth dropped to his knees in the snow, staring up at the sky, his mouth wide open. "It's...beautiful. The aurora hasn't been seen in...in..."

"Well over a thousand years," Fisher said. "It's been there all night. I was going to tell you both to come and look, but I had a feeling it'd still be here when you were done."

Lorreth's eyes shone brightly as he watched the green dancing lights shift to reds and pinks, undulating in waves in a broad band across the horizon. The warrior was on the verge of tears, and I had to admit, I was pretty close myself. I was drained. Wrung out, even. But I still had the energy to stand as I watched the sky, knowing that I was witnessing something rare and remarkable.

The sword lay across Lorreth's lap. He rested a hand on the hilt as, still in complete awe of the beauty lighting up the heavens, he began to sing.

> To all those who'll listen
> or haven't been told,
> of the day the last drake
> woke and rose from the cold.
> Of the young warrior who came
> veiled in shadows and blood
> to defeat the foul creature
> and save those he could.
>
> Of the Fisher King,
> and the wolves at his back,
> who came howling in the night,
> together, a pack.
> The frost blessed the morning.

> The warriors faced their fate.
> And thus begins our tale,
> The Ballad of Ajun Gate.

Next to me, Fisher tensed. The muscles in his jaw popped. He let his head fall, his eyes abandoning the aurora and finding the snowy, compacted ground under his feet instead, as Lorreth's powerful voice flowed from verse to verse.

Back in the tavern, Lorreth claimed he'd once been a singer of middling talent. This performance was not middling. His voice was full of smoke and pain. The air itself seemed to weep as he flowed through his lament. The song dipped and soared, telling a tragic tale of impossible odds and heroic sacrifice, nearly every line paying tribute to Kingfisher. The male next to me didn't move a muscle, but he was hating this. His nostrils flared, hands shaking at his sides, and the song plowed on regardless.

> The drake, he did stir,
> Old Omnamshacry
> observing the world
> through ink-black, mad eyes.
> The drinkers of night
> pledged him death and decay.
> That he'd feast on his foes
> and the flesh he did flay.
>
> So long as he rose
> and he joined them in war,
> against the Fae who protected
> the sacred, blessed ore.
> With glittering sharp scales
> of gold and of red,

the drake, he consented,
and bidden, he fed.

The Fae in their towers
stood mighty.
Stood proud.
But soon they were scattered,
their fear shouted loud.
Dark wings shaded mountain
and blotted the sun.
And mad old 'Shacry,
he watched them all run.

The wolves scaled the summit
with blades in their hands.
The drake saw them coming,
and knew where they'd stand
So there he did meet them,
and there they did clash.
And Old Mad 'Shacry
dressed the mountain in ash.

His fire ran in rivers.
It melted the snow.
There was no escaping
the glowing hot flow.
With teeth bared and dripping,
the drake trapped the Fae,
laughing with cruelty
above the warriors he'd slay.

But the wolves held their ground,
all dauntless and brave,

determined to send
Old 'Shacry to his grave.
Swift came the chant, then,
so all close could hear.
A war cry of old that
strengthened those near.

The wolves ran the charge
and at the head of the swell
came the proud Fisher King
bearing Nimerelle.
The drake saw his courage
and was filled with a rage
the likes of which unseen
in more than an age.

But the king held his nerve
and raised up his sword,
and the wolves showed their courage
'fore the drake and the horde.
Their ears rang aloud
with the Kingfisher's cry
that those who stood with him
might fall, but not die.

For their sacrifice was great,
and so was the cost.
But those that they saved
would e'er remember the lost.
So they scaled the great drake,
the last of his name.
They did it for Ajun,
Not glory, nor fame.

And the drake knew his power.
He started to gloat,
but the King saw his chance and
drove steel down his throat.
The drake he did tremble
and started to choke,
his evil, rank maw
filling up with black smoke.

He thrashed and he bellowed
did old Omnamshacry,
but the reaper had claimed him,
and bidden, he died.
The Ajun were safe.
The horde abandoned the gate.
And thus ends the ballad
of the king and his eight.

When the song finally came to an aching, bittersweet end, Lorreth panted, his eyes full of stars as he watched the aurora dance in the sky.

"It's fucking *outrageous* that he can sing, too." Carrion had woken up and was stood to my right, arms folded across his chest, balefully regarding Lorreth. "That *was* nice, though. Messed up, but nice."

Fisher shifted his weight, standing up a touch straighter, lifting his head. "Do you think it'll be enough?"

"I don't know. I suppose we'd better go and get Danya." I'd known she'd have to be called to the forge at some point. After all that we'd accomplished and all that we'd done, I wasn't thrilled at the prospect of her coming here and ruining this special moment, but—

We have made a decision.

Fisher's spine straightened. Lorreth's too. Had they *both* just heard the quicksilver speak? Fisher must have heard it thanks to the quicksilver inside his own body, but Lorreth shouldn't have been able to.

"Why do you all look like you've collectively shit yourselves?" Carrion demanded.

We accept the song as tribute. The bargain is fulfilled. An accord is struck.

"But...you said you'd consider the blood of the one who would wield you!" My heart sank in my chest. "Danya—"

We have considered, the quicksilver intoned, *the first to bleed upon our blade.*

"But..."

Lorreth leaped up. He held the sword out like it was a snake, reeling back to strike him. "Shit. I'm an idiot! I'm sorry!" he cried. "Here! Take it!" He held out the sword to Fisher, but there was a delighted spark in the other male's eyes.

"Hell no. I'm not touching that thing. It has your name written all over it."

"Would someone mind telling me what the fuck's going on?" Carrion's ultra-polite tone promised violence if someone didn't explain and quickly.

"You only need to look at the damned thing and it cuts," I whispered. The words Lorreth had said, right after he'd run his fingers along the sword and cut himself on it. *He* had been the first to bleed on the newly forged weapon. The sword had judged *his* blood.

Lorreth's face went ash white. "I didn't mean to," he said. "I'm happy with my daggers, I swear. I did *not* mean to claim Danya's sword."

Not Danya's *sword,* the quicksilver hissed. *We are reforged. New unto this place.* You *do not claim us, Lorreth of the Broken Spires. We* claim you.

"This is going to be hilarious," Fisher said. But he wasn't laughing.

Neither was Lorreth. "Danya's going to lose her mind."

"She'll have to get over it. She doesn't have a choice. You've been a member of the Lupo Proelia without a god sword for four hundred years. It'll be her turn for a while."

Doubt was sketched in every line of Lorreth's features, but his hand closed possessively around the hilt of the sword all the same. It looked *right* in his hand. As far as I was concerned, it *was* his sword. "You deserve it, Lorreth. You carved the wolf for the pommel. You helped to cast it. And it was your song that sealed the bargain with the quicksilver."

A flicker of confusion chased across Lorreth's face. Kingfisher and Carrion looked equally as nonplussed by what I'd said. "My *song?*" Lorreth said. "What do you mean, my song?"

"The song you just sang. About the Ajun Gate? About the drake, Omnamshacry? How Fisher stabbed the dragon down its throat? Not…ringing any bells?"

Fisher, Lorreth, and Carrion all looked at me like I was mad. "I always meant to write a song about Ajun Gate, but I've never gotten around to it," Lorreth said.

"Don't you dare," Fisher growled. "It's in the past. Leave it there, where it belongs."

Ours now, the quicksilver whispered. *Our song. A song for us to keep.*

The others hadn't heard the quicksilver this time, I could tell. *That's what you meant? That you'd take it, and it would disappear? That no one would remember it?*

Ours now, the quicksilver repeated.

Ours.

Ours.

Ours.

It seemed a shame that Lorreth's song had been ripped out of the world, all memory of it erased. It had moved me in a way. It had explained so much. *Why can I still remember it?* I asked.

We remember, so the Alchemist remembers.

Huh. I didn't know how to feel about that. Being the only person alive to remember the ballad Lorreth had written about Fisher felt like sacrilege. How many other things would I need to remember, that everyone else had to forget, in order to make all of those relics? There were more bargains on the horizon, I knew. Thousands of them. Small deals to be struck. How the hell would I navigate them all without landing myself in hot water? Just thinking about it made me break out into a cold sweat. I put those concerns away, to fret about later.

So? Will you allow this sword to channel magic? I asked.

I waited for the quicksilver's reply. Technically, it didn't matter if the sword wasn't able to channel magic. I'd made the damned thing, which was impressive enough, even to me, and the chances were high that I'd be able to talk the quicksilver into bonding with the rings to become relics. If I succeeded in that, I would have done all I'd agreed to accomplish for Fisher. But there was also the matter of my pride. I wanted to know what I was capable of achieving here, working with such a fascinating, stubborn material. I couldn't live with not knowing...

Hold me with both hands and name me, Lorreth of the Broken Spires, the quicksilver said.

Lorreth looked a little bewildered. *"Me?"* he said aloud.

It is your privilege.

The warrior looked to me, conflicted. Apparently, it was the right of the smith who'd forged a blade to name it in Yvelia, just as it was in Zilvaren. Lorreth looked guilt-ridden over it. I, however, had no qualms. The blade would not be whole or complete without Lorreth. "Go on," I told him. "You heard it. Give it its name."

Resolve settled over the warrior's features. His hesitancy still shone through, but he placed both hands on the hilt and raised the blade aloft, speaking in a clear, loud voice. "I name you Avisiéth. The Unsung Song. Redemption's Dawn." The moment he finished speaking, a blue flame rippled down the sword's blade, searing runes into the metal in its wake alongside the script I had etched there. And then a brilliant white light erupted from Avisiéth. Blinding and powerful, it shot straight up into the air—a pillar of energy that transformed night into day. The very ground beneath our feet quaked.

Fisher let out a surprising whoop, joy shining from his face as he followed the column of energy upward into the heavens. "Angel's breath, Brother!" he hollered. *"Fucking angel's breath!"*

30

SWEAR IT

THE CAMP WAS in chaos when Fisher escorted me back to his tent. Nearly everyone had seen the column of angel's breath illuminating the pre-dawn sky. Those who hadn't fired questions at those who had, and all were gripped with an air of excitement. Fisher had advised Lorreth to go and sleep until he came to get him later in the evening. He'd still looked dumbstruck as he headed off in the direction of his tent, cradling Avisiéth like a baby in his arms. Carrion had decided that he couldn't be bothered hiking back down the hill and announced that he was going to sleep at the forge.

Meanwhile, I had no idea what angel's breath was or how it would be useful on a battlefield. I was so sore I couldn't think straight, and frankly, I couldn't even remember my own name. I collapsed into a chair as soon as Fisher got me into the tent, but he shook his head, hauling me out of it again by my wrists. "I don't think so, Little Osha. Come on. Here. You're sleeping in the bed."

"With you?" It was a challenge. I was done tiptoeing around this now.

Fisher's brow dipped for a second. He seemed frustrated, but he nodded. "I need to go and talk to Ren first. But yes. I'll be sleeping here. With you."

"All right, then."

"But first"—he pulled a face—"you need a bath."

I couldn't be offended.

I'd spent fifteen hours slaving away in a sweltering forge and had the sweat and half of the dirt of Innìr beneath my fingernails to prove it. My hair was crisp from my perspiration—my fingers got stuck in it when I tried to run my hand through it. I wanted nothing more than to be clean, but when I tried to talk myself into crossing the tent toward the beautiful copper claw foot tub that Fisher conjured with his smoke, I found my legs uncooperative. I didn't even have the energy to talk.

Fisher took one look at me and lifted me into his arms. He might have had a cutting comment for me once. *See, Little Osha. Just like the butterfly I named you after. So weak. So vulnerable.* But he said nothing as he carried me to the tub and carefully set me down. His eyes trailed fire over my skin as he helped me out of my clothes. I hissed, failing to raise my arms over my head, and he dispensed with the process entirely, tiny particles of midnight sand rushing over my body and helpfully dispatching my clothes.

Even after a long day's work at Elroy's forge, I'd never felt this gross. Kingfisher looked at me like I was the most astonishing thing he'd ever seen. As if he didn't see the grime and the exhaustion clinging to me like a second skin. Midnight hair. Jade green eyes. That strong jaw. The full mouth that softened the powerfully masculine lines of his other features. The runes at his throat pulsed like a heartbeat as he lifted me again and lowered me gently into the bathtub.

I sighed in instant relief. The water was the perfect temperature; the heat worked its way into my body, easing the tension in my joints and kneading out the knots in my muscles. It was nothing short of divine.

Fisher knelt on the floor, resting his forearms against the side of the copper tub. He watched me, his eyes so fierce that they stripped me even barer than I already was.

It took ridiculous effort, but I lifted my hand out of the water just enough so that I could touch *his* hand. He didn't pull away. Lifting his fingers an inch, he repositioned, adjusting. It was a micro-movement, really. Subtle, but with meaningful results: his fingertips were left resting on top of mine.

We'd kissed, and licked, and fucked each other raw. He'd emptied himself inside me, roaring as he came, but this small, intentional contact between us was the most intimate we'd ever been. I marveled at the sight of our fingers touching, an array of emotions vying for my attention.

Fisher rested his chin on top of his forearms and sighed.

"What?" I whispered.

He thought for a moment, appearing to decide whether he'd answer the question. Then he said, "I was wrong, y'know. You *are* a good thief."

"What have I stolen?"

But he smiled a small, sad smile, slowly shaking his head. "Sleep a little. The water will stay warm. I'll be back as soon as I've spoken to Ren."

I woke to hands built for violence gently soaping my scalp. No one had ever washed my hair before. It was an experience I wanted again and again. But only from him. Only from Fisher.

The second time I woke, he was lifting me out of the tub. His magic hummed over my naked body, leaving me dry in his arms. I didn't want clothes. I wanted to be naked, and I wanted him naked, too, but the slate blue shorts and camisole he magicked out of nowhere for me were butter-soft and very pretty and left my skin *almost* bare. The sounds of the war camp outside faded away, leaving the tent in blissful silence as Fisher placed me into his bed and climbed in right behind me.

The third time I woke, it was dark, and my stomach was growling loud enough to wake the dead. Fisher's arm was thrown over my side, one of his legs tangled with mine, the weight and heat of his body curving around me deeply reassuring. I lay as still as I could for as long as I could, relishing the quiet dark and the soft sound of Kingfisher's breathing. Half an hour passed. I'd need to get up and use the bathroom soon enough, but for the time being, I wanted to stay here and soak this in.

War was at the doorstep. Tomorrow was uncertain. Hell, *today* was uncertain, but this tiny moment was real. It *was*, godsdamnit, and I didn't want to let it go. I tried to relax and savor it, but a thought crept in as I lay there. A thought that would not be ignored.

I had made an Alchimeran sword. Me. A pickpocket from Zilvaren. I'd learned how to reason with the quicksilver and had struck a bargan with it, and now Lorreth had a weapon that channeled vast amounts of energy. A few months ago, I'd never have thought that possible. But now, a lot of things felt like they might be possible. It had to be worth a shot, didn't it?

Carefully, I reached out with my mind, searching for the buzzing hum of the quicksilver. I found it easily, and gods, it was loud. So loud. Too loud to think around. Was this what Fisher dealt with? Every waking hour?

Annorath mor!

Annorath mor!

I took a deep breath and said a silent prayer to the gods. *Hello?*

The chanting stopped.

Kingfisher stirred in his sleep, letting out a troubled sigh, but he didn't wake. I bit my bottom lip, steeling myself. If I was quick, this could all be over in a matter of moments. Tentatively, I reached out again, extending the boundaries of my mind until I sensed the restless weight of the quicksilver. I should have prepared for this.

Thought of what I wanted to say. I hadn't planned for this, though, and how many opportunities would I get at this in the future?

"I'm Saeris. I'm an Alchemist. I—"

We know who she is, the quicksilver hissed. *She is the dawn. She is the moon. She is the sky. She is oxygen in our lungs.*

"I—" I didn't know how to respond. Why would it say that? I was the dawn? The sky? *Oxygen?* I shook my head—there was no time to waste on puzzles. "I want you to leave Fisher," I rushed out.

"Leave him?" the quicksilver asked in a quizzical voice.

"Yes. Leave him. His body. I want you to come out of him. I'll strike a deal with you—"

"We cannot leave him. We are him." A multitude of voices layered over each other—an echoing chorus of voices, delivering news that I didn't want to hear.

"He is Fae. You are...you're..." I didn't have a clue what it was. Not really. What the hell was I supposed to tell it? I had to keep things simple. *"You're quicksilver. You're not supposed to bind with living creatures."*

"We bind with all kinds of weapons."

"Fisher isn't a weapon! He's...he's a living, breathing..."

"Weapon," the quicksilver said. *"The best. We are him. He is us. We cannot leave. We will die."*

"You'll die? Or Kingfisher?"

"All of us," the quicksilver emphasized. *"We are one thing. One weapon."*

It was being ridiculous or stubborn, one of the two. And I wasn't in the mood. *"I could guide you out. I can feel you inside him. I can put you back with the other quicksilver at Cahlish? Or forge you into the most impressive blade that's ever been—"*

"We were forged hundreds of years ago. We cannot be unmade."

"You're hurting him." Even in my head, my voice seemed to crack with emotion. *"He's suffering because of you."*

The quicksilver was quiet. I could sense it, thinking about this.

But not for long. *"We are him. He is us. We all suffer, Alchemist. There is nothing to be done."*

"So you're just going to keep pushing him until he cracks? Until he dies? If you kill him, what then?"

"Then we do as all dying things do. We return to the dirt, and the sea, and the sky. We sleep. We evolve. We change. We transcend."

"You're stealing his life from him," I spat. *"You have no right—"*

"We gave him his life. A boy. Just a boy. He was young when he entered our pool. He should not have survived it. But he was strong, and the grand halls of the universe rang aloud with his purpose. We permitted him to live so that he might fulfill that purpose. We bound ourselves to him that he might survive."

"And...there's no other way? For him to live without..."

"This die was cast centuries ago. We accepted our fate, Alchemist. All of us did."

I heard the implication in the quicksilver's words. It wanted me to understand that Fisher had agreed to this somehow. That he'd allowed the quicksilver to bind with him and had known what it would mean. But I couldn't make my peace with that. Why would he have struck a bargain that would eventually cost him his mind?

My eyes stung behind my eyelids. I couldn't accept it. Wouldn't. There had to be a way to convince the quicksilver to willingly leave Fisher's body. If I could talk the quicksilver in Danya's sword into being reforged and to channel magic again, then surely I could find some deal or bargain that would entice the quicksilver out of the male sleeping next to me.

I started when something brushed my cheek. My eyes snapped open, and...oh. Fisher *wasn't* asleep, after all. Great. Just what I needed. If I was going to try and negotiate with his quicksilver, I hadn't wanted him knowing about it. A deep sadness radiated from him as he swept away the tear that had rolled over the bridge of my nose. "I assume that didn't go how you thought it would," he whispered.

I sniffed. "Did you hear it all?"

He gave a small shake of his head. "Only pieces of what it said to you. But it was pretty easy to work out what you were talking about, based on its responses."

Damn. I should have kept my thoughts to myself. Now he knew I'd gone prying. That wasn't the best feeling. I should have just minded my own business.

As if he knew what I was thinking, he said, "I've been waiting to see if you'd try and yank it out of me."

"You're not angry?"

His mouth tugged up into the smallest, saddest smile. Closing his eyes, he sighed. "Of course not. How can I be angry? You wanted to help. But now you know. It's not just inside of me. It's a part of me. Without it, I'll die anyway. So, it's—"

Renfis burst into the tent, dressed in full armor. His expression was wild, his face smeared with dirt. I sat up, grabbing the sheets and clutching them to my chest, alert and ready. Conversation forgotten. Quicksilver forgotten. The fact that I wasn't wearing much beneath the sheets was also forgotten. Ren cursed through his teeth in Old Fae, casting his eyes away when he saw me. "Gods. Apologies. I thought you were up at Cahlish, Saeris. I'm sorry, truly I am, but I need him."

Fisher was up and out of bed a second later, a shadowy blur streaking across the tent. When he stilled by the bookcase, he was already dressed in his black leather armor, plate at his throat and murder in his eyes. "What is it?" he demanded.

"The horde. They're at the banks again," Ren clipped out. "All hell's breaking loose out there."

"*Fuck.*" Out of nowhere, the wall of silence that had fallen over the tent as Fisher had put me to bed shattered, and the sound of chaos crashed down upon us. Screams and shouts. The thunder of hundreds of boots running through the sucking mud. Commands being bellowed from one side of the camp to the other. And underpinning it all, the steady pounding rhythm of hammers striking thick ice.

BOOM!

BOOM!

BOOM!

"Fuck!" Fisher repeated. A length of curling black shadow extended in his hand, becoming Nimerelle. "I'm sor—"

"Don't. There's no need for apologies. No one's been hurt. It's a token showing. Barely a thousand of them. Still, you should come," Ren rushed out. "I'll see you at the river. Saeris, it'd be best if you stayed here—"

"No. I'm coming." That was it. Final. I was sick of being told to wait, told to stay, told to hide where it was safe. I wasn't hanging back here, pacing in a tent while Fisher, my friends, and the rest of the entire fucking war camp faced down Malcolm's monsters. It just wasn't happening. I got out of bed, not caring that I was still only wearing the shorts and the camisole. Fisher saw to that, anyway. By the time my bare feet hit the rug, I was dressed in black fighting leathers and a long-sleeved black shirt to match them.

Ren looked for a response from his friend. "Fisher?"

Fisher stared *into* me. The hard arrogance he would have worn a week or two ago was gone, replaced by caution.

"The only way I'm staying in this tent is if you force me to," I said in a shaky voice. And here it was. The moment he officially won me or lost me. If he ordered me to stay and took away my will, it didn't matter how much things had changed between us. Nor would it matter how much I needed him. I would never speak to him again. Never look at him again. This would all be over before it had even had a chance to begin. That would hurt, but nowhere near as much as his betrayal would. I waited, praying to gods I'd only recently learned the names of that he was about to make the right decision.

Fisher swallowed hard. "You won't go to Cahlish?" he asked quietly.

"I will *not*." Being banished to Cahlish would be even worse. So far removed that a whole mountain range stood between me and the fight? I'd never forgive him. I wouldn't be able to, even if I tried.

Don't do it, Fisher. Please. Do not fucking send me away.

He'd set his jaw. He'd come to a decision. I braced, waiting for a shadow gate to coalesce, but..."If you come, will you stay right by me?" he asked.

My knees wanted to buckle. I answered quickly, before he could rethink this. "Yes. Absolutely yes."

"And if I tell you to stay somewhere until danger passes?"

"I'll stay."

"And if I tell you to run?"

"I'll run."

He narrowed his beautiful eyes at me. *"Swear it."*

"A promise doesn't bind me the way it binds you."

"I know. But humans still make promises to each other, even though they can be broken, don't they? Because they trust the other to honor their word."

"Yes."

"Then swear, Little Osha, and I'll trust you."

A wave of hot emotion knifed me in the center of my chest. *This* was the kind of male I wanted to be with. *"*I swear it."

Kingfisher nodded, accepting my promise. "All right, then. So be it." Quickly, he went to the trunk at the foot of his bed and opened the lid, taking out a long bolt of fabric. I recognized it immediately. It was the bundle Fisher had fastened to Aida's saddle when we'd fled the Winter Palace. Ren's eyes went wide as Fisher placed it on the bed and unraveled the swathes of material, revealing the sword within.

Not just any sword. The sword that had started all of this. The one I'd pulled from the pool of frozen quicksilver in Madra's palace. Solace's hilt flashed in the firelight, bright silver now, the tarnish of age that had dulled its edge nowhere to be seen. It was a breathtaking weapon. The kind songs are written about. Its pommel was embellished with a crescent moon, the horns of the crescent so close that they almost touched to form a whole circle. Script writing flowed around the hilt, down over the cross guard, and spilled along the edge of the blade, written in Old Fae.

Fisher turned and held out the sword to me. "My father's bones rest somewhere in Zilvaren. His sword spent the past millennia there, which…" He paused, considering the sword. "Which makes it more Zilvaren than Yvelian now, I think."

The air was on fire, too hot to breathe. Fisher unhooked a leather scabbard from the wall of the tent and took it down, sliding Solace into it. Speechless, I lifted my arms as he wound the scabbard's belt around my waist. His hands worked deftly, adjusting the belt to fit my much narrower waist, and it was all I could do not to burst into tears.

His father's sword?

Ren stood, arms folded over his chest, watching. Our eyes met, and worry swelled behind my ribs. Would I find judgment on his face? Anger over a valuable Fae heirloom being passed into the hands of a human? Of course not. Ren's expression was one of deep satisfaction. It seemed to say, *Good. At last. This is as it was always meant to be, Saeris Fane.*

Fisher straightened and took me in. "Okay. Are you ready?"

"Yes." My heart kicked like a mule against my ribs, and yet I felt steady with the weight of the sword at my hip.

"Be unrelenting and unmerciful in the face of the wicked dead," Fisher said.

Ren laid a steadying hand on my shoulder. "And if you should find soul sundered from flesh, order a drink for us at the first tavern you come across in the afterlife. We'll settle the tab when we get there."

31

THE DARN

LIGHTNING RAKED its claws across the night sky. Rain pelted us, torrential and freezing, as we ran along the western line of the war camp. Ren and Fisher were dark ghosts, blurring through the mayhem, darting straight through campfires that had already been kicked over, and around knots of warriors attempting to roll massive boulders toward the river's frozen edge. Fisher hung back, waiting for me, but I was right on their heels anyway, following at a dead sprint.

Along the other side of the Darn, a line of ravening vampires snapped and snarled at the ice's edge. I could make out their shattered teeth and ruined tongues even through the lashing curtain of rain. Tonight was a little warmer than it had been since I'd arrived at Irrìn, and the smell that floated across the river—rotting flesh and the tang of foul, metallic blood—made me gag. I switched to breathing through my mouth, only barely managing to keep my stomach.

Fisher and Ren stopped abruptly at a switchback in the river, where the snowy banks were closest and formed a narrow bottleneck.

Only fifty feet separated Irrìn and Sanasroth here. It wouldn't take much for the feeders to make the crossing.

Panic lived and breathed in my veins, multiplying by the second, but I gathered it in an iron grip, refusing to succumb to it. "Why aren't there as many of them here?" I panted. There were vampires on the opposite banks here, yes, but nowhere near as many as there were farther down, where the river was wider.

"The water still flows beneath the ice. The current's stronger here as it moves through this channel. That means the ice is thinner," Fisher said. "More dangerous to cross."

"And they know that?" I asked incredulously.

"Not in any intelligent way," Ren supplied. "Vampires can't pass over running water. They sense the current here and are afraid. But inevitably, one of them dares to step out onto the ice. Then the others follow."

"When they do, we're here to make sure they don't make it across." Fisher glowered at the pack of vampires, pushing and shoving each other on the opposite bank. His eyes were distant, his expression troubled. "He didn't come this time," he muttered.

No need to ask who he was referring to. Ren and I both already knew he meant Malcolm. The silver-haired king of the vampires was nowhere to be seen. Tonight, he'd sent his servants out to do his dirty work and hadn't deigned to come out himself. I wasn't sorry for it. The sight of Malcolm, standing on the other side of the river, had struck a chord of fear in me that was still rattling my bones even now. He'd been no taller than your average Fae male. In truth, he'd been leaner than most of the warriors here in camp. But the sense of power he'd given off had been staggering; I'd felt it pushing and pulling at me, looking for my weak spots, as if it had wanted to force me to my knees in supplication. If I lived another thousand years and never saw that dead-faced male again, it'd still be too soon.

BOOM! BOOM!
BOOM! BOOM!

Like a two-part heartbeat, the sound of the hammers smashing down on the thick ice rang in my ears.

"Be ready," Fisher said. His smoke rushed from his hands, forming a dark pool at his feet. It crept to the edge of the river but hovered there, going no further.

Shouts went up to the east—a furious roar of war cries. I scanned the writhing mass of bodies on both sides of the Darn, terror and relief holding hands in my chest when I saw the first wave of vampires racing out onto the ice there, but that the huge icebreakers had succeeded in shattering the surface of the frozen river as well.

"They're through," Ren observed. "It's over now. A few more solid hits—"

As if the crowd of vampires closest to us knew that this was their last chance, a ragged old man with half his jaw hanging loose stepped boldly out onto the ice. His shirt was in tatters, clinging to his emaciated frame. His pants were frayed and filthy, hanging from his protruding hips. Side to side, his jaw worked, his lips cracked wide open and leaking black ichor.

Across the river he shuffled on rotting feet. A hundred feet away, back toward camp, the Darn splintered apart, ice groaning as it gave way to hammer and axe. Vampires plunged through the widening fissures, sinking into the rushing waters below.

The dead didn't swim. Nor did they float. A few of the blood-mad feeders grasped hold of chunks of ice, using them to buoy themselves above the surface of the water, but it was no good. The most determined among them held on for maybe ten seconds before their lifeless hands lost traction, and they sank below the choppy surface of the water.

The ancient old man crossing toward us must have been hollow-boned like a bird. The ice held under his feet as he grew closer, which gave his companions courage. A woman came next. Her face was a ruin, her eyes missing, cheeks clawed to shreds. The wounds looked fresh, still pink in places. A day or two ago, she'd been alive.

She was wearing an apron, which was stained brown with old blood down the front. It looked like the aprons the cooks wore back at the Winter Palace. Had she worked at some fine estate somewhere? Had she stepped out for a moment to escape the heat of the kitchen, to catch a glimpse of a star or two in the night sky? Had some awful nightmare leaped out of the shadows and torn her face to shreds as it had fed?

A boy, next, naked and scrawny.

A woman with blackened hands and corkscrew dark curls, dragging a lifeless doll along behind her as she came. My stomach pitched when I realized it wasn't a doll. That it was a baby, punctured with hundreds of teeth marks like it was a pin cushion.

"Gods and Sinners," I whispered. "What *is* this?"

"Walking hell," Renfis answered grimly. "It just keeps coming."

Soon, there were at least twenty vampires on the ice. The others held their positions on the bank, refusing to come forward, either too overwhelmed by the sense of the water rushing close by or held back by some other voiceless command. But the twenty on the ice were plenty to be worrying about.

"They're almost halfway," Ren muttered.

"The moment they cross, I'll have their fucking heads," Fisher growled.

The rain came down harder, lashing the tents and putting out the unattended fires back in the camp. It struck our skin, soaking our clothes to our bodies and plastering our hair to our scalps. I watched the vampires' slow but determined approach and had to ask, "Why wait? Why not do it now?"

"We're bound by the rules of war," Fisher said. "We can't use magic to attack or affect an enemy until that enemy has breached our border. And anyway, our magic doesn't work on Sanasrothian soil. Fae magic needs light and life to survive. And there's nothing on their side of the river but death, darkness, and decay. Our lands are divided directly down the centerline of the Darn. But the second these fuckers cross over..."

It happened right as he said it. The old man with the shattered jaw stumbled beyond the midway point. Ren and Fisher acted in unison, drawing their power to them. The air crackled with energy. My teeth buzzed with it. Both warriors moved with lethal precision. Ren drew his hand back and launched a ball of blue-white light into the steel-gray sky. At the same time, a forceful ink-black wind surged from Fisher's outstretched hands. The wind struck the male vampire in the chest, howling around him and burning through the remnants of his clothes, through his sloughing skin, through the bare yellowed bones of his rib cage. The vampire snapped, infuriated by the assault, but he kept coming.

One more step.

Two.

The wind tore away what was left of his jaw…

…and then Ren's brilliant orb came crashing down onto the river. It exploded into a sphere of light and heat that smashed the fragile ice from one bank to the other. The other vampires, who had still been standing on the Sanasroth side of the river, screeched and howled as they plummeted into the fast-moving depths below and disappeared from sight.

All up and down the river, the ice was fractured, the way impassable. In other words, all was safe.

A cheer went up amongst the Yvelian Fae, bawdy and full of contempt. How many times had they stood on this bank and sent Malcolm's beasts back to Ammontraíeth with their rotting tails tucked between their legs?

Innìr was an ouroboros—a snake eating its own tail. Its purpose would never be fulfilled. There would always be another night, and the ice would always freeze, and there would always need to be a battalion of warriors here to keep the horde at bay and be ready should they one day succeed in making the crossing. The thought of it was exhausting. Some of these warriors had been here for decades, performing the same task every gods-cursed night. So long that they'd *named* the place. They'd built homes here. Had families, for fuck's sake. Because, without loved ones close by and some sense of imagined normalcy, what kind of life was this? With no assistance from Belikon—

"The shore! Look to the shore!" The cry was full of terror. It stopped my thoughts dead in their tracks. Kingfisher whirled around, facing the camp, his face pale as the snow, the quicksilver in his eye forming shifting patterns as he picked apart the edge of the river, searching for the cause of the alarm.

He found it before me. Renfis did, too. They both stiffened, a gasp of dismay slipping past Ren's lips. "What? It...it *can't* be. That's not... possible."

But I could see it now. Amongst the icy rocks and the churned-up mud, there was something crawling out of the river. And it had teeth as sharp as razor blades.

"Breach! Breach! Breach!" The warning spread like wildfire.

"Go. I'll stay with her," Ren told Fisher.

"This is where you keep your promise and stay right here, Osha," Fisher said. In the blink of an eye, he had become something wild. His skin cast off an eerie pale glow, his dark waves blowing on an invisible wind. He had never seemed very human to me, but now, balancing on the precipice of danger, he was unspeakably Fae.

"I'll stay. I promise." A crashing roll of thunder drowned out my words, but Fisher nodded, his eyes lingering on mine for half a second, and then he was gone.

"There are more! More crossing!" a female warrior yelled.

Sure enough, the vampires who had remained on the bank were now slipping down the dirty snow and falling into the river. I watched as they were swept away on the current in twos and threes, blindly clawing at each other, trying to reach the other side. But there were those that vanished below the surface of the water and did not re-emerge. I watched, horrified, as more and more of the vampires started to crawl out of the water.

"Ready yourself," Ren said tightly. "Let's greet the fuckers with steel."

*And us...*an excited voice whispered. *Us too! And us!*

Solace. The blade with the crescent moon pommel was a god sword, after all. Of course it held quicksilver. And it was awake. Alive. Listening. Talking. Talking to *me*.

No time to marvel at that. There were three vampires scrambling out of the water, and they hadn't been slowed down by their ice-cold swim. The first shook itself like a dog, bared its teeth, sighted us, and *moved*. With unnatural, jerky movements, the naked young boy galloped up the bank on all fours, his jagged claws tearing holes into the snow. Ren met his attack with a flash of his sword, barely even moving as he whipped his blade around and parted the creature's head from its shoulders.

The old man came next, though not as quickly. He was in rough shape after Fisher's magic, and barely managed to break into a run as he came for us. Ren spun, slicing upward, and severed the clawed hand the old man tried to strike him with. While he was unbalanced, Ren brought his blade singing through the air and took his head, too.

More bodies rose from the Darn. Far more than the twenty that had gone in when the ice broke. It made no sense. Ren cut them down as quickly as they emerged from the water, but soon there were too many for him to tackle alone. He sent orbs up into the air, which came down with frightening force, detonating the second they made contact with flesh. The feeders erupted into pale blue flames, stumbling into one another, screaming, but still they came.

"Saeris! Find Lorreth! Head back up to the forge!" Renfis bellowed.

"No!" I drew Solace, and a ripple of heat charged up my arm. The sensation took me by surprise. Two seconds later, I was standing shoulder-to-shoulder with Ren before sixty snarling vampires.

Ren looked at me like I was madness personified. "You *promised* him!" he shouted.

Nodding, I raised the sword. "I promised I'd stay here. If I run off into the dark by myself, I'll definitely die. He knew I'd have better odds if I was with you."

There was nothing he could do. Gritting his teeth, Ren twisted, jamming his sword up through the skull of a vampire so disfigured that I couldn't even tell if it had been male or female. "Stubborn girl," he growled. "Don't you dare die on my watch, Saeris Fane! Fisher will never forgive me if his sole reason for living is torn to pieces on her first fucking battlefield."

Wait a minute. What did—ohfff*UCK!* I brought Solace up just in time. The vampire who had been about to lunge for my throat caught the weapon's edge right in the mouth. I pushed, following through on the swing, and took the top of the cursed thing's head off.

It dropped to the ground, but it wasn't done with me. A bunch of mangled meat and a fragment of its lower jaw was all that was left of its head, but that was apparently enough. It grabbed at my legs, claws scraping at my leathers, its bare feet kicking at the snow. Thick as tar, black ichor spurted all over my boots.

"All of it! You need to get all of the head!" Ren yelled.

All of it. Okay. I could do that. I took a deep breath and stilled my mind. My training took over. All of the endless hours locked away in the attic with my mother's rebel friends, learning how to put something sharp to good use. How to move my body. How to use my opponent's own momentum against them. How to strike and retreat, strike and retreat, strike and retreat. How to shut myself down and focus on the task at hand.

The vampire's lower jaw and what was left of its brain stem flew into the mud, sliced clean away. The monster fell limply to the ground for good this time. And I got to fucking work.

There was a split second when the vampires were sluggish as they emerged from the water. Ren took them down in droves as they came up the bank, but I went to the water's edge and began carving them apart before they could get their bearings.

Solace hummed in my hands, sending waves of energy up into

my shoulders with every hit I landed. I sank down, settling my weight into the balls of my feet and my hips and immersed myself deep into the flow of killing.

"Back, Saeris! Come back!" Ren was right. There were too many of them coming to shore at once now. I danced back, light on my feet, and took up position beside him. "I'll wound them. You end them," he snarled.

A blanket of black smoke swept across the river, shoving back so many of the vampires who were trying to climb onto the banks. If there was black smoke, then that meant that Fisher was alive somewhere close by. Relief rode my blood like lightning. I slammed the point of my sword through a vampire's cheek, spearing it to the ground, then ripped the sword free and severed the vile creature's head just in time to repeat the process when Ren sent another slathering feeder my way.

Time slowed down, and the strangest thing happened. My heart rate dipped. A sense of peace washed over me. Acceptance and understanding. The vampire on the left bypassed Ren and came straight for me. He was moving fast, I knew he was, and yet it seemed as if he was running on loose sand. He would drop down and try to tackle me to the ground; I could see the mindless, animal plan of attack already causing his knees to bend and his shoulders to hunch. The claws at the ends of his fingers, sharp as broken glass, curved, reaching for me, begging to find flesh.

The answer to this was simple. I dropped to my knees and swung the blade around my face, over my head, angled the blade *up*...and it was done.

The vampire's head rolled back down the bank and bounced when it hit the pile of bodies that had begun to form there, landing in the river with a splash. Ren paused, double-taking, his eyes round as he took me in. "What was *that?*" he breathed.

"I don't know. I just—" The rest of the sentence was cut short when a plume of black smoke swept me up off the ground, and suddenly I was in Fisher's arms.

His face was streaked with ichor, eyes full of panic. "Are you okay? What happened? Are you hurt?"

"I'm fine. I'm okay, I swear."

The doubt on his face said he didn't believe me, but it faded away when Ren called out to him. "She's been kicking *ass,* Brother. She wields Solace almost as well as your father did."

Well, that might have been a bit of an exaggeration. It was better than the general telling him I was a liability, though, and I'd sure as hell take *that.* Fisher regarded me with something that looked a lot like pride. "Is that so?"

"Catch up later!" Ren shouted. "We're kind of busy right now!"

Fisher was all business again. He set me down and went to Ren's side, his magic boiling out of him in a curtain of darkness. The second he drew Nimerelle, I knew this fight was over. Ren moved fluidly, holding back the remaining vampires with ease, but watching Fisher was something else. He didn't swing the sword. Didn't wield it. The tarnished black blade and the warrior were one. He *flowed.* Where Nimerelle cut through the air, trailing tendrils of smoke, vampires fell like stalks of scythed wheat in the sword's wake.

It was both beautiful and terrifying to watch. Kingfisher turned killing into an art form.

I was still admiring the way he moved, when a brilliant white light lashed through the air like a whip on the lower side of the bank. For a split second, night became day. Raw, unfiltered threads of power probed across the edge of the Darn, seeking multiple marks at once, and surprised shouts went up all along the bank as warriors locked in battle watched their opponents burst into flames like torches.

It was Lorreth—Lorreth, and the angel's breath Avisiéth had granted him—and the sight of it set my soul on fucking *fire.*

Fisher swung Nimerelle one last time, slicing through his quarry's neck so fast that it took a moment for the creature's head to topple backward off its shoulders. Our stretch of the river was clear of vampires at last. He grinned like a madman, eyes lit up, reflecting filaments of white light as he turned to watch the spiderweb of power jumping from point to point amidst the melee, destroying everything it touched and turning Malcolm's army into pillars of ash.

Fisher threw back his head and howled. Ren joined him, and slowly, all across the rain-soaked camp, more voices joined them. Wolves all, singing out their victory.

The baying shouts were still going when Fisher speared Nimerelle tip-down into the dirty snow, cupped his hands around his mouth and bellowed so loudly that his cry seemed to shake the very heavens. *"Lorreth of the Broken Spires! Lorreth of The Darn!"*

"Lorreth!"

"Lorreth!"

"Lorreth of The Darn!"

The name went up again and again; the sound of every Fae warrior in camp chanting Lorreth's name was so powerful that it made my chest ache. For the first time in a thousand years, a god-sword had found an Yvelian worthy and granted him magic to defend his people. I wasn't Yvelian, and even *I* was knocked on my ass by the raw emotion filling the air. There weren't fucking words...

"KINGFISHERRRR!" The shrill cry rose above the shouting and whooping. Even the angry crash of thunder didn't swallow it. *It was female.*

All three of us whipped away from the celebration taking place, searching for the voice. It didn't take long to find it. There, on the other side of the river, was a woman in a ruby red dress, her bright blond hair streaming out behind her like a banner of gold on the howling wind.

It was Everlayne.

And she was flanked by at least a hundred vampires.

32

TALADAIUS

REN AND FISHER both swore at the sight of her. Everlayne's mouth was open, silent panic carved into her beautiful face. From this vantage point, where Yvelia and Sanasroth were closest, the river the narrowest, it was easy to make out her delicate features. Easy to see that she was terrified. A black hole yawned open behind Fisher. He was a split second away from launching through it, but Ren caught hold of him by the strap of his armor. "Don't be stupid! The gate won't open on that side of the river. Gods only know where it'll spit you out!"

"All right, fine." Fisher batted his hand away. "I'll swim across."

Ren grabbed him with both hands this time, shaking him. "That's what they want. The second you're on the other side of this river you're fucked. You'll have no magic, and then what?"

"Then I'll rip out their fucking throats and make a pile of their rotting corpses," Fisher snarled.

"She'll be dead before you've mown through ten of them. Can you live with that?"

"Of course not!"

"Then *think*. Why the hell do they have Layne over there? Why isn't she *already* fucking dead?"

A good question. My stomach rolled as one of the vampires standing next to Everlayne ran a mangled tongue along her bare shoulder, keening as it drooled over her skin. It wanted to bite. Badly. But it held back. That many of them could have torn her apart in a flat second, but something was keeping them at bay. Another vampire flattened its nose against Everlayne's arm, shuddering as it fought against its nature to feed.

Ren cried out, the sound strangled, and it looked like he would ignore his own words and charge blindly into the river. It was Layne's outstretched palm that stopped him.

"Don't! Just stay where you are!" she called.

"Are you hurt?" Fisher shouted.

His half sister smiled sadly. "Only a little. I'll be fine, Fisher. Don't worry." She looked so strange. Her pale skin was lit from within, giving off an ethereal glow. Her hair swirled around her as if she were underwater, and yet she wasn't wet. Her hair, her skin, her clothes—all dry. The rain came down harder than ever, but not a drop of it touched Everlayne.

"Run for the river!" Ren shouted. "Swim! As soon as you're halfway, we can get you!"

She responded with a regretful shake of her head. "I'd never make it, Renfis. And anyway...I can't."

"What do you mean, you can't?" The question was full of panic.

Sweet Everlayne. She'd been so nice to me back at the Winter Palace. I'd been too overwhelmed by my new surroundings to truly appreciate it, but she'd been a friend to me. Had looked out for me. And now she was in mortal peril, and there was nothing I could do to help her. Nothing any of us could do.

Fisher's jaw worked, a look of devastation on his face. He knew why she couldn't come. "Her neck," he whispered. "Look at her neck."

At the base of Layne's slender throat shone a thin band of gold. It was a fine thing. Pretty. It looked like it was engraved with some kind of pattern, though I couldn't make out the details of the design from here. Attached to the band of metal was a thin gold chain. As I noticed it hanging down in front of her, it snapped taut, and Everlayne jerked to her left, almost losing her balance.

Fisher hissed as the crowd of vampires parted, and a tall, handsome male with luminous skin and cropped blond hair came forward to stand beside her. Dressed in black pants and a tailored white shirt, he wasn't kitted out for war; his attire suggested that this little jaunt out into the rain had interrupted some kind of dinner party. Younger than Malcolm, he was a fraction taller, a fraction broader, and every bit as dangerous. I could feel his power—a sinking, penetrating cold, spilling across the river, leeching into my bones.

"Well met, Fisher!" the vampire called over the river. "I see you've managed to restore one of your precious swords. Congratulations. I'm sure that feels like quite a feather in the cap."

As if Lorreth took the sarcasm in his voice personally, a flicker of angel's breath crackled through the air. Brighter than the lightning scoring the clouds, it burned my eyes as it crashed into an invisible barrier in the middle of the river and was instantly diverted, shooting harmlessly up into the air.

The vampire didn't even blink. From the way he smiled, he found the display highly entertaining. "Why don't you come over here and say hello to an old friend, Fisher. Your sister and I have a bottle of that red you like breathing back in the dining room. Why not join us for a glass?"

"Fuck you, Taladaius," Fisher spat. "If you've hurt her—"

"Oh, please. You know me. I don't have the stomach for hurting the things *you* care about. My father, on the other hand..." He trailed off, looking thoughtfully at the chain in his hand. "He does enjoy adding to his collection. And since he recently lost his most vaunted prize, it only makes sense that he'd want to replace it. Come on, you must have expected something like this from him."

Hatred boiled in Fisher's eyes. But there was pain there, too. He spoke quietly this time, addressing Everlayne. I could hear him, but only just. "Malcolm bit you?" he asked, keeping his voice level.

I saw Everlayne's mouth move, but I wasn't blessed with Fisher's gifts. I couldn't cast my voice, and my human hearing was nowhere near as sharp as his, either. She spoke four or five words, and the tiny flicker of hope went out in Fisher's eyes. Ren saw his reaction and dropped down onto the snowbank, landing heavily on his knees, his legs refusing to support him anymore.

"So he's bitten her. She's not dead!" I stepped closer to Fisher, placing a hand on his shoulder. "Surely she'll be okay? If there's venom in her veins, Te Léna can heal her like she healed me."

Ren shook his head. He stared at Layne, and she stared right back at him. Her shoulders shook, her chest hitching up and down unevenly. I considered it a small blessing that I couldn't hear her crying over the roar of the rain hitting the river. "She can't come home now," Ren whispered in a broken voice. "She's his."

I glanced between the males, my heart skipping beats left, right and center. "What do you mean, she's *his?*"

"It means she's enthralled to him," Fisher said.

My eyes pricked fiercely. "Enthral? What... what does that even mean?"

"Later, Little Osha. I'll explain it all later." Fisher could barely get the words out around his grief.

Ren forced himself back to his feet. Shouting across the river, his hands shook at his sides. "What do you want, Taladaius? Why did you bring her here?"

The blond vampire sneered at Ren. "Careful, Renfis. I am Lord of Midnight to you. I won't be addressed so familiarly by one so low—"

"He's a million times the male you'll ever fucking be," Fisher hissed. "Now answer the fucking question and tell us why she's here!"

"Why do you *think?*" Taladaius answered tersely. "He bid me bring her. She's a trap. He wants to bend you to his will, so he's taken something precious to you, and he's broken it. Are you shocked?" He didn't wait for Fisher's reply. "You will either come and try to save her, even though doing so would be futile, or else you'll come for vengeance's sake. Either way, he knows you'll come. He doesn't care why. Only that you do."

Vengeance? I didn't like the sound of this. How the fuck had Everlayne wound up in Malcolm's hands, anyway? I had so many more questions, but now wasn't the time to ask them. I waited to see how Fisher would respond to this, but his chin dipped down, the quicksilver in his eyes spinning so fast that it formed a solid shining ring around his iris, and he said nothing. It seemed as though he was waiting. A moment later, I figured out why. Breathless, Lorreth skidded down the slope, joining us. Just like the rest of us, he was covered in ichor and dirt. His expression bore a fury that promised to end worlds. When he saw Taladaius standing on the other side of the river, holding Everlayne's chain like she was some kind of animal, his face darkened. "Mother*fucker*!"

"Evening, Lorreth." Taladaius grinned menacingly at the warrior.

"Fuck. Is that…" His face paled. "Is that Everlayne?"

Fisher was frozen still, staring across the river at his sister. It was Ren who answered. "Yes. It's her. Malcolm's already tagged her."

"Bu…" He glanced around wildly. "But that's…that…"

"Where *is* he?" Fisher growled at last. His words were quiet, cast at Taladaius. The vampire chose to shout back his answer with a laugh, so all could hear.

"He's waiting for you, my friend!"

"Where?"

"At the place where the two of you brokered your last deal. Honestly, I think he's hoping for a repeat performance."

"There won't be any more deals," Fisher snarled.

"I suppose we'll see about that, won't we." Taladaius considered his fingernails. "Your darling Everlayne was bitten twelve hours ago. You can do the math. As we speak, my father rides north with the better part of his horde. If you aren't there to meet him when he arrives at his destination, he'll see that she makes it through the change and then spends the rest of eternity on her back, being fucked raw by Ammontraíeth's most depraved residents, one...after another...after another. Or you give him what he wants. It's that simple."

"And what the hell does he *want?*" Lorreth demanded.

Fisher flinched, as if he wished the warrior hadn't even asked. "He wants me," he whispered.

Taladaius's bark of amusement was as harsh as cracking ice. "Yes, it's true you're on his wish list. Always, my friend. But he doesn't just want you this time. You might have been a valuable player in this game before, but a lot's changed of late. There are far more interesting pieces on the board."

"He doesn't get anyone else."

"You, of all people, know that Malcolm gets what Malcolm wants," Taladaius chided. "He'll have his prize, and you know it."

"WELL, HE CAN'T HAVE HER!" Fisher's declaration boomed over the Darn; it could probably be heard in the bowels of Ammontraíeth. The terror that rolled off him hit me like a slap to the face. I felt it deep in my bones. And...I felt something else, too. Taladaius. His attention shifted to me, though his dark eyes, brimming over with merriment, remained locked on Fisher.

"You can kick and scream all you like," he said. "But he wants the Alchemist, Fisher. If he has to burn down all of Yvelia to claim her, you know perfectly well that he'll do it."

33

BLOOD IN THANKS

"I CAN'T BELIEVE we let him just drag her away like that." Lorreth paced up and down in front of the map table, balling his hands into fists. Every time he spun around, he hit something with Avisiéth's scabbard, clearly unused to carrying the weapon. "We should have fucking *done* something!"

"Like what?" I'd never heard Ren sound so defeated. He sat at the head of the table, chewing on his thumbnail. Since we'd made our way back here, numb and soaked to our skin, the general had crafted the beginnings of a number of plans, speaking out loud to himself, only to hit a stumbling block and start over again. Now, it seemed as though he'd officially given up.

Fisher hadn't said one word since he'd stalked inside and planted himself at the seat opposite me. He just stared at me, a sea of green and silver locked onto my face, the muscles in his throat working. To be the subject of such intense focus was disconcerting at first, but I'd gotten used to it over the past hour and had resorted to staring back at him, nudging him inside my head, trying to cajole him into saying something.

Come on. Talk to me. Tell me something. Anything, I said silently. *You can't just shut down.* But still not a word. Clearly, he thought sinking into a catatonic state was a perfectly acceptable coping mechanism in light of the situation.

"There has to be a way." Lorreth kicked angrily at the pile of chopped wood by the fire. One of the pieces splintered and fell apart. He didn't even acknowledge the mess he'd made as he spun around, clouting Ren's shin with Avisiéth, and stormed toward the exit. Right before barging out of the tent, he turned around and marched back again. "Fisher, there are thousands of texts in the library back at Cahlish. There must be something in one of them about this. Your father studied the blood curse for decades. I bet he made a note about this. How to cleanse a thrall's blood. How...how to burn away the enchantment between master and thrall before the conversion begins."

Fisher's brow furrowed. He stared at me harder.

"Fisher?" Lorreth prodded.

"He can't hear you," Ren said wearily. He pinched the bridge of his nose, sagging back into his chair. "Just give him some time. He's thinking."

Could there be information back at Cahlish about that? I asked him. But Fisher showed no sign of having heard me. Well, shit. If he wasn't going to give me answers, then the other two males were going to have to fill me in because my brain was about to implode.

"Why is Malcolm's bite so different from the other vampires?" I demanded, glowering at Ren, daring him to try and brush off the question. Thankfully, he answered.

"Malcolm was the first to be affected by the blood curse. The very first. When Rurik Daianthus, the last Yvelian king, discovered the cure, Malcolm was one of the few who chose to remain vampires. Over the centuries, the others who had accepted their curse were systematically killed off until only Malcolm remained. There were whispers that Malcolm ingested their power somehow.

He is millennia old, undying, never aging. Every year he survives, he grows in strength and capability. His venom is potent beyond imagination. When one of his lords bites a victim, they can drink and sate their thirst without killing. If they bite the same human a number of times, eventually they become enthralled—"

"There. That word. What does that mean?"

"The victim becomes bound to the vampire who bit them," Lorreth said, stepping in. "Mindlessly devoted to their needs. They'll feed and fuck their master without a single thought for themselves. Inevitably, their masters grow bored and drain them, and then their victim dies. Three days later, they rise from wherever they've been discarded and become the feeders you've seen on the river."

"But Everlayne…" I couldn't say anything else. The thought of that bastard sinking his teeth into her neck made me want to vomit.

"Malcolm only needs to bite once to create a thrall. Everlayne is now completely under his control. Even if we broke into Ammontraíeth and managed to break her free, she wouldn't come. She'd fight so she could stay and please her master. And in a little less than fifty-six hours, she's going to die."

"Don't say that! We can't know that for sure. He might decide not to drain her. He might just use her as a bargaining chip for—"

"Malcolm's venom is lethal, Saeris. All it takes is one drop. He doesn't need to drain her to kill her now. The work is done. Only two possible paths lay before Everlayne. If Malcolm permits her to drink from him, and she actually does it, then she'll return and become something like Malcolm's Lords. If she refuses to drink from Malcolm, or he refuses his blood to her, then she'll die and return as a feeder."

A part of Fisher heard that. Deep down, he registered the information, and it shattered the wall he was trying to hide behind. He stood from the table, inhaling sharply, dragging his hands through his hair.

"Welcome back," Ren whispered.

Fisher was about to say something, but the tent flap flew back, and in came Danya still dressed in her armor from the skirmish. Her eyes blazed with anger. She growled, lips peeled back, showing teeth, as she charged across the tent, straight for Lorreth.

"Danya—" Ren warned. But it was too late. The female warrior had pulled back her fist and launched it into Lorreth's face. He'd seen her coming. Had adjusted his stance and folded his arms over his chest, but he hadn't done a thing to block her from hitting him. His nose exploded with blood when her blow landed.

"Asshole! Give it to me. Give me my fucking sword."

"It isn't your sword anymore, Danya," Fisher said.

"Like hell it isn't. I've carried that weapon for three hundred and thirteen years! I *earned* it!"

"Your father passed it down to you," Fisher corrected dryly. "The sword you once carried was unmade and reforged. This blade is new. It *chose* Lorreth."

"It's mine," Danya seethed. We all saw her lunge for Avisiéth. I couldn't have stopped her from taking such an ill-advised course of action, but Fisher, Ren, and Lorreth could have. None of them did. Some lessons had to be learned the hard way. The sword she'd carried had already been silent when it had been given to her. Not even an echo of magic had remained inside it. She'd probably heard tales about what would happen to someone if they touched a god sword that didn't belong to them, but her pride was such that she really *did* believe the weapon hanging at Lorreth's hip was hers. He let her take it. The second her hand closed around its grip, she unleashed a bloodcurdling scream, and her hand detonated into a cloud of pink mist. A shock wave of blinding white light surged from Avisiéth's pommel, and Danya was thrown across the map room. She crashed down onto a chair, reducing it to kindling in an instant.

"Holy fucking gods," Ren uttered. "It took her fucking *hand.*"

"Maybe she'll stop punching people in the face now." There wasn't a scrap of sympathy in Fisher's voice. He went and stood over Danya, his eyes glittering and cold as ice. Meanwhile, Danya awoke from an apparent faint and realized what had happened to her hand. Her *sword* hand. I braced for another scream, but she choked out a sob instead.

"Oh, gods! No. No, no, no!"

"There's a chance it can be regrown. If I take you back to Cahlish and get you looked at by a healer, will you stop all of this bullshit and calm the fuck down?" Fisher demanded.

Danya didn't deserve her hand to be regrown. Her theatrics had reached a point where she deserved to live with the consequences of her shitty temper. That wasn't a charitable thought on my part, but I was well and truly over her attitude. She'd been a bitch ever since Kingfisher had shown up back at the camp. We had more important things to worry about than a petulant warrior who threw a temper tantrum every time she showed up in this fucking tent. Lucky for her, Fisher was more forgiving than me.

"Yes," Danya moaned. She clutched the bleeding stump left at her wrist, tears streaking over her cheeks. "I will. I...swear."

"So that's it? You're heading back to Cahlish?" Ren asked.

"We all are. Three out of the five of us need to see Te Léna. And then we're going to tear that library apart until we find a way to help Everlayne. We have time. Not much of it, but some. We need to use it wisely."

Renfis was white as a sheet. If I wasn't mistaken, his hands shook with relief rather than anxiety now. Fisher had taken charge of the situation, which meant he wasn't responsible for finding a solution to this disastrous situation. He opened his mouth, ready to speak, but Fisher got there first.

"Before we can leave this tent, there's something we need to do, though." He looked back at me, resolved. "Our Alchemist faced the enemy tonight and stood her ground bravely. We have among us a newly blooded warrior."

Oh no.

Gods.

No.

I did *not* want any of them looking at me like this. Fisher's quiet pride. Ren's warm approval. Lorreth's wolfish grin. Under normal circumstances, it might have been nice to be recognized for the feeders I'd taken down, but with Everlayne's outlook so bleak, I couldn't bear it. "I don't want a fuss," I said.

"You don't want a fuss?" Lorreth laughed. "This isn't about *you*, Saeris. This is about us recognizing one of our own and paying due respect. You don't get a say in the matter."

I looked to Ren for help, but he shrugged apologetically. "Sorry. He's right."

"Look, whatever *this* is can wait. We're in the middle of a crisis. There'll be time later for...I don't even know what you're planning on doing, but it can wait!"

Fisher wasn't persuaded by my argument. Not one little bit. He leaned back against the table, folding his arms across his chest. "We don't let things like this wait. We're at war. There's no guarantee any of us wake up tomorrow. We celebrate our wins as they come. And we damn well make sure our warriors know their worth."

Lorreth was first to step forward. He drew Avisiéth and sank to his knees, running his palm along the blade. A stream of crimson blood ran in its wake. He pressed his hand against my chest, right between my breasts. The contact wasn't sexual, but Kingfisher still huffed a little. "My blood in thanks, sister," Lorreth said softly.

He got up, still grinning at me like an idiot, and moved out of the way so that Renfis could take his place. The general sank to his knees, then nodded as he sliced open his own hand with a dagger and placed it over the bloody print that Lorreth had made. "It was my honor to fight alongside you," he said. "My blood in thanks, sister."

My cheeks were burning, a thousand degrees and climbing, when Fisher quietly came forward and knelt at my feet. His halo of dark hair was all over the place, his skin pale in the flickering torch-light. His eyes were steady, though. They ran me through as he withdrew Nimerelle and closed his fist around her edge. When he placed his hand against my chest, he tapped his index finger and middle finger against my sternum, in time with my racing heart. Giving me a very tired, very sad smile, he said, "I give you my blood in thanks, Saeris Fane."

34

A SECRET

"Human" had come first. Then "Oshellith," or "Osha," said with a hefty amount of disdain. Then *"Little* Osha," which had first been mocking but had then shifted to an endearment.

But Fisher had said my name. *Finally.* And it was...weird.

Lorreth rubbed his knuckles up and down his sternum, frowning. Ren laughed under his breath, ducking his head. Danya said something in Old Fae and spat on the ground, still cradling the smoking stump at the end of her right arm. But fuck Danya. Danya was the worst. And me? I just stood there like an idiot, not sure what to do or say, as the shock sank into my bones.

Fisher was immediately all business, opening up a shadow gate. I passed through first and found myself transported into the dining room, where I had first encountered the feeders. I sat at the table, impatiently rapping my fingernails against the wood as I waited for the others. Danya came next. She scowled when she saw me. Her thick blond war braid was spattered with blood. "Well, look at you. The jumped-up little Alchemist, sitting in pride of place at the family table. You'd better move before the others arrive, or you're gonna find yourself *very* embarrassed."

I was sitting where I always sat now, to the right of Fisher's chair. But the way Danya sneered at me made me think I'd made a very grave social error. It wasn't the first time someone had reacted to me sitting here. First, there had been the fire sprites. Archer had burst into flames when he'd seen me sitting in this seat. Then there had been Ren, choking on his food. I looked up at the ceiling, leaning back into my seat.

"What's the big deal? It's just a chair." I said it oh-so-flippantly. If she knew I was really interested in the answer, she probably wouldn't tell me just to be difficult.

Danya kicked the legs of the chair opposite me, shoving it back so she could sit down. "That seat is reserved for the lady of the house, you stupid girl. Etiquette dictates that only Fisher's wife is permitted to sit there. It's a position of high honor meant for a Fae female born into one of the old houses, and you're just sprawled out there like you own the damn seat. It's offensive that he even lets a human sit at the same *table* as him. But this…" She waved at me with her remaining hand. "This is just too much. Like I said. You should *move*."

While she spoke, Ren stepped through the swirling gate, carrying a pile of books, leather bags, and six or seven long, rolled-up scrolls under his arm. Danya smirked, as if I was in for it now and she couldn't wait to watch me get dressed down. But Ren assessed the scene, shot me a wink, and said, "Don't you worry, Saeris. You're perfect right where you are."

Danya's mouth fell open. "What the fuck? You all treat her like some important foreign emissary. She's just a human. What other rules will she be allowed to break?"

I hadn't heard Fisher come through the gate. I felt his presence, though—a pleasant warmth in the back of my mind. The scent of the forest enveloped me as strong, tattooed hands rested on top of my shoulders. "No rules have been broken, Danya. And even if they had, that wouldn't be any of your business."

Aghast, the female took him in, standing there behind me, his hands on my body. "You *can't* be serious, Fisher. We all know you've fucked her. The whole camp can smell it on the two of you. But she's a *human*—"

"And?" Ren dumped everything he was carrying down onto the ground with a snarl. "She's honorable and brave, not to mention the most powerful Alchemist ever documented. She disarmed you in half a fucking second if you recall. Who the fuck are you to say she and Fisher don't belong together?"

Whoa. *Belong* together? Behind me, I felt Fisher stiffen. Any moment now, he'd spit out some scathing remark, telling them not to be so fucking stupid. I would laugh off the sting of his contempt at Ren's suggestion, and we'd all go back to worrying about the truly important matter at hand: Everlayne.

But Fisher said, in a *very* calm tone, "My personal life isn't up for public discussion."

"Holy fuck. Why is it so *cold* in here?" Carrion was carrying a sword and a potted plant under his arm, still wearing his thick coat with the coarse fur over its wide collar.

"I found him up at the forge," Lorreth said, stepping through the gate behind him. "*He was still asleep.*"

"Hey, don't say it like that!" Swift shot him a wounded look. "We had a very long night, y'know."

"You slept through a battle," Lorreth said.

"And I'm a very heavy sleeper!"

"What's with the plant?" Ren asked.

Carrion shrugged. "I don't know, I liked the look of it. It was the only green thing for a mile amongst all that white. I figured it deserved an easy life if it had made it this far growing out of a snow-bank. Plus, my tent was so bare. It needed a little cheering up."

"For fuck's sake. This is ridiculous." Danya rose from her chair. "I can't spend another minute in here with scatterbrained humans. Just because they're...pretty..." She wobbled, her eyes glazing over. Tucking her chin, she reached for the edge of the table, but her fingers found nothing but air.

"Lorreth?" Fisher said quietly.

"Fuck, do I have to?"

"Please?"

Lorreth grumbled as he crossed the dining room in four long strides and caught Danya right as she fainted. He did not look pleased to be holding the female in his arms, and I couldn't say I blamed him.

"She's lost a lot of blood," Fisher sighed. "Come on. We'll take her to the healer."

"And what about us?" I asked. "We can't just sit here. I need to do something."

Fisher reached for me. I lifted my hand, just enough so that he could hook the tip of his index finger around mine for a second. "Go to the forge. Get to work on the relics. Make as many as you can, Saeris. I have a feeling we're going to need them."

Ren left with the others, saying he needed to check the grounds and let the guards know we were here. As soon as we were alone, Carrion threw off his coat and pointed emphatically at the door, after the Fae who had just exited through it. "Did you hear that?" he said.

"What?"

"That smoking hot blonde said I was pretty."

"Gods alive, Carrion. Do *not* tell me you have a thing for Danya. She's fucking awful."

"Eh." He shot me a rakish grin. "I love a girl with a sharp tongue and a bad attitude. Kinda makes my dick hard."

The rain had stopped, thank the gods.

Onyx snuffled into the forge, his nose glued to the ground, following a trail; he squealed when he saw me, his whole body wiggling with excitement. I spent half an hour giving him pets and treats from the plate of food a timid fire sprite delivered for us, and then he happily headed out into the courtyard to sit in the dark, his little fluffy head tipped up toward the stars. It was already well past midnight. Had this been a normal day, we should have been thinking about going to bed, but we'd slept from dawn until dusk, when Ren had come to tell us the horde were at the river. And after fighting and ending so many feeders, and then the awful news of Everlayne's capture, I was officially awake.

Good thing I had a mountain of work to keep me occupied.

The tiny orb of quicksilver rolled around in the bottom of the crucible in a languid counterclockwise direction. Negotiating with this quicksilver had turned out to be trickier than when I'd forged Avisiéth. It insisted it didn't want anything—that it had no interest in being a relic. It was bored of me poking and prodding at it, and it didn't want to be bothered anymore.

"We're wasting time. And I'm confused. You have the ability to command the stuff to do what you want it to do. Why don't you just *force* it to comply?" Carrion asked.

"I'm not forcing it to do anything. It's sentient, Carrion. It has a mind of its own. It thinks. It talks"—I really wished it didn't—"and I'm not going to *make* it do something it doesn't want to do."

Carrion knew about the bargain Fisher had tricked me into. He knew how I felt about being stripped of my free will. It was surprising that he'd even suggest this. He plucked one of the Fae rings out of the wooden trunk by the hearth and flicked it up into the air. A flare of silver flashed in an arc as it spun. Distractedly, he said, "I take it you've forgiven our benevolent kidnapper for his crimes, then? You and he seem very close."

"I'm not talking about Fisher with *you*." I set down the crucible so I could stoke the coals in the hearth.

"Why not? As you so forcefully reminded me recently, we're not exes. We only slept together once. I assure you, you're not going to hurt my feelings." He leaned against the bench, waiting.

CALLIE HART

"I don't want to talk to you about him because you'll use whatever I say to taunt me. Come here and pump these bellows."

He looked affronted. "What, am I your slave now?"

"If you insist on staying in here and annoying me, then you're going to make yourself useful at the same time. Those are the rules."

He made a face but still came, took hold of the bellows' handles, and began to pump them. "Come on. We're gonna be stuck in here for hours. You might as well tell me. I won't taunt you, I promise."

I snorted. Carrion's promises weren't worth the paper they were written on. He was notorious for swearing things left, right, and center and then not honoring his word. It would be very stupid of me to expect him to keep this promise...but I found myself starting to speak. "I've forgiven him, I suppose. Yes. He didn't make me do anything that hurt me or anyone else. He compelled me because he thought it would keep me safe. And he knows what'll happen if he ever does it again."

This would earn a snide remark from Carrion, surely. But no. All five hells must have frozen over. He just nodded. "Y'know, I thought it was weird when he bribed me to take a bath with those boots. I asked one of the sprites who came to bathe me. Y'know, one of the water sprites with the giant..." He mimed cupping a pair of sizable breasts on his own chest. "I asked her why they were trying to flay three layers of my skin off with that weird moss, and they said it was special. They said Fae who liked to bedhop were fond of it 'cause it eradicated the scents of their other partners. I couldn't think of why Fisher would care if I smelled like those triplets who just started working at Kala's—"

"*Gods,* you're incorrigible."

He waggled his eyebrows. "But then I realized that it was you. He didn't want me smelling like *you.*"

I refrained from commenting. I had suspected that was why Fisher had made Carrion take that bath, but I'd never said it out loud. Not even to give him shit. I didn't know how it made me feel back then. And I was too much of a coward to admit how it made me feel now.

I went and collected the crucible with a pair of tongs. On my way over to the hearth, Carrion flicked the ring he was fiddling with into the air again, and I snatched it mid-spin before he could, dropping it into the iron pot with the quicksilver.

"What? You have nothing to say about that?" he asked.

"Not really. Who knows why he did it. Maybe he just thought you stank."

"Hey!"

"Look, Fisher has his secrets. I don't stick my nose where—"

A secret...

I stopped talking, canting my head to one side. I had heard that, right? The quicksilver *had* just spoken? "What?" I asked out loud.

"I said," Carrion began, but I held my finger to my lips, glaring at him, then pointed to the crucible. He got it immediately and shut his mouth.

A secret, the quicksilver whispered. *We like secrets. We'll change for you if you tell us one.*

Huh. So that's what this quicksilver wanted. One secret? That, I could manage. I'd learned my lesson after giving that song to the quicksilver in Avisiéth, and it had ceased to exist, though. I was going to be smarter this time. "If I tell you a secret, will I still remember it afterward?" I asked aloud.

Of course, the voice replied.

"And will it still be a secret?"

You will know, and so will I. But I won't tell, I swear it.

All right. So it wouldn't erase any information from my mind, nor would it spread the information around so that everybody knew it. Then there was nothing to worry about, I supposed. I didn't say it out loud this time. I spoke only for the quicksilver.

I don't want to go back to Zilvaren anymore. Not forever, anyway. I want to go home, get Hayden and Elroy, and then bring them back here to Yvelia.

This wasn't the most scintillating, realm-shattering gossip imaginable. But to admit to it was massive for me. I had spent every waking moment in this place fighting to get home so I could save my brother and my friend. But then I'd found out that they didn't need saving. Not the way I'd thought they would. And I'd made friends here. Friends I cared about, who I had the ability to help win a war that had taken over their lives for hundreds of years.

And there was Fisher.

Things were uncertain on that front. Maybe I was fooling myself, and he would discard me after he'd had his fun. But either way...I didn't want to leave him.

The quicksilver rippled in the crucible, geometric patterns forming and re-forming over its surface. It was beautiful to look at, but strange—I hadn't seen it behave like this before.

Yes, a good secret. Very good. You want to stay. You want to save him. You must. You must.

I frowned, watching the quicksilver closely as it vibrated next to the ring in the bowl of the crucible. *Save him?* I thought. *Hayden? Yes, I want to bring him here.*

Not the brother. The Kingggfisshhherrrr, the quicksilver buzzed. *Save him. Save the gates. Save Yvelia.*

"I just *love* it when you disappear into tense conversations with creepy portal metal," Carrion quipped, hoisting himself up to sit on the bench. "It's fascinating watching you do all of those facial gymnastics."

"Just a moment, Carrion," I whispered. Then to the quicksilver, I said, *What do you mean, save Kingfisher? He's here. He's okay.*

I watched the quicksilver roll over the ring, enveloping its surface, coating it, sinking inside it. It said, *We are token. Key. Relic. Shield.* The words overlapped like layers of cloth, one on top of the other, but I still heard each one perfectly. *Seal us with blood, Alchemist,* the relic demanded.

Blood. It always came down to blood in the end. Sighing, I took out the dagger that Fisher had given me back in the Winter Palace and used it to prick the tip of my index finger. A tiny bead of glossy red blood welled there.

"Urgh, I think I'm gonna be sick," Carrion groaned, looking up at the ceiling. "I am *not* good with blood."

I rolled my eyes, squeezing my finger and holding it over the crucible. The tiny bead formed a teardrop, wobbling, and then it fell, hitting the ring. Wild. My blood didn't roll off the band of the ring. It was absorbed *into* it, just like the quicksilver was.

Complete. We are complete.

Picking up the ring, I held it up to the light, and I felt that it was indeed complete. Both the key and the lock. Whole. I couldn't explain how I knew the process had worked, but I was sure. The silver band was beautiful, still marked with its original engravings; whoever this ring belonged to would be pleased that it still bore their family's crest. *But what did you mean about saving Fisher?* I pressed. *He's safe here. Why does he need saving?*

The ring said nothing.

Nothing at all.

Frustration welled up in me, and I didn't know why I did it, but I was compelled to act. I wasn't even aware of what I was doing as I slipped the newly made relic onto my middle finger.

The forge went dark.

An icy wind lanced through me, whipping my soul. And the sound. Gods, the *sound.* A million different voices chanting with a deafening might.

ANNORATH MOR! ANNORATH MOR! ANNORATH MOR! ANNORATH MOR! ANNORATH MOR! ANNORATH MOR!

"Saeris?"

The roaring cut off dead. The candles in the forge strengthened, the flames leaping up the back of the hearth, licking over the blackened brickwork. And then, just had it been only moments before, everything was normal again.

I tore the ring off my finger, panting. My heart pounded, a

terrible sense of hopelessness solidifying in my gut. I wouldn't be doing *that* again.

Te Léna was at the open doorway, technically standing inside Cahlish. Ren's magic still overlayed the doorway to one of the guest bedrooms back in the manor house with the entrance to the forge outside, located by the stable, ensuring the house would be safe should I accidentally blow myself up. The healer wrung her hands, eyeing the doorway with surprising suspicion. As always, her jet-black hair was tied into long braids that went all the way down to the small of her back. The tips of her pointed ears poked out between them. Complementing her flawless umber-bronze skin, she wore a gown made of iridescent blue material that flowed around her as she shifted from one foot to the other.

"I just wanted to come and see how you were. I heard you fought earlier," she said. "Do you have any cuts or scrapes that need attention?"

I didn't get a chance to reply. Carrion, dog that he was, jumped in before I could get a word out. He hopped off the bench, crossed the forge, and leaned against the wall by the doorway in that practiced, careless way of his. "You look stunning this evening, Te Léna. You're literally the only good thing about being back here."

She laughed. "Aside from the running hot water, you mean? And the soft feather beds? And the endless supply of delicious hot food?"

"No. I hate every single one of those things," he said theatrically. "You remain the only bright star in a sea of darkness here. Tell me you've changed your mind about having dinner with me."

She gave him a chastising look, holding up both of her hands and showing him their backs. "I regret to inform you that I am still happily mated and married, Carrion Swift. And my husband isn't the type to share."

"Is he handsome?" Carrion arched his eyebrow suggestively. "I do love a husband-and-wife team. Maybe he'll let me join you both if he..."

A high-pitched ringing sound filled my ears. It blocked out

Carrion's overt attempts at seduction and Te Léna's very polite rebuff. The Fae healer had lowered her hands again, but I was staring at them, eyes fixed on them. They were marked with runes. Some of her fingers bore one or two runes. Others had none. There was an elegant design on the back of her right hand, but the other was bare. Louder, the ringing in my ears intensified. I hadn't even realized that I was crossing the forge until I was standing in front of Te Léna and I was gesturing to her hands.

"Do you...I'm sorry, I, uhh, I've never seen such pretty tattoos before. Would you mind showing them to me?"

"You sound weird," Carrion said. "And I'm trying to help her forget the tattoos, not make a big deal out of them. Gods, you sure know how to ruin a guy's chance of getting laid."

Te Léna laughed again. "Carrion, let me put this as plainly as I possibly can. So long as the sun still rises and sets every night, I am never going to sleep with you." To me, she said, "Of course. Thank you, Saeris. I think they're pretty, too. My husband and I designed them together."

She had beautiful hands. Graceful and slender, with long fingers. Three out of the five fingers on her left hand bore runes. Two on her index finger, two on her middle finger, and only one on her little finger. On her right hand, there was a single rune on her index finger and another on her ring finger, and that was it.

She traced her fingers over the ink on the back of her right hand, beaming as she extended it out for me to see properly. "It's a Fae custom to mark our skin on our fifth wedding anniversaries. We tattoo the blessings we pray for onto our hands in the hopes that they become manifest. Yaz and I decided on a harmony mark, a longevity mark, and two child marks. Greedy I know, to wish for two children. One would be blessing enough, but..." She shrugged. "No point in holding back when it comes to these things, right?"

"I'm sorry, I..." Fuck, why was it so hard to *breathe*? "I'm not sure I understand. So you design these tattoos yourselves? And someone inks them into your skin?"

Te Léna nodded. "Yes. We wait until the fifth anniversary to do it, because some marriages fail in the early years. It *can* happen. We're advised to be cautious and wait until we're sure of each other before binding our skin. Yaz and I wanted to get our marks after just two years, but the elders said we should wait."

My mind was racing, a million miles a minute. "So, they don't just show up on their own? The marks? Like...out of the blue? Overnight? Or...while...y'know...you're having sex with someone?"

Te Léna laughed brightly. "Of course not. Don't be silly." The edge of panic rising inside me settled just a little. But then Te Léna spoke again. "Once upon a time, that was the case. Back when *true* mating bonds existed. Unions between true mates were blessed with marks from the Fates. That's where the tradition of inking our hands originated from. But there's no such thing as true mates anymore. When the gods left Yvelia, certain elements of our magic either died or waned over time. The God Swords, for example. They were very slowly cut off from the source of the magic they channeled. Our ability to form mating bonds also died out over thousands of years, until it disappeared altogether."

"Right..." Oh, gods, I needed to sit down. "So it's just a tradition now. People cover their hands in runes...for luck."

"I wouldn't say we *cover* ourselves in them," Te Lèna answered. "I knew a couple who decided on seven runes once. Seven is an auspicious number, after all. But there are those who considered that a little greedy." From the tone of her voice, Te Lèna herself was amongst that number.

Seven?

Seven runes.

My mind scrambled to try and remember how many runes had marked my fingers. How many runes had interlocked on the back of my right hand. I had no idea, but there had been a lot of them. So, *so* many. "And what about script? You know. Writing?" I could only get a few words out at a time. "Do people...get that sometimes? Going around...their wrists?"

"Oh, no. Definitely not. You only see that kind of thing in story-books," Te Léna scoffed. "They called it a God Binding. A blessing from the gods themselves. They weren't real, of course. The most important couples in Yvelian history were said to have had them, but it was all romantic rubbish. Just something storytellers embellished to make their tales more tragic. Plus, they looked impressive in the illuminated books."

I met her eyes, but I was looking right through her. "Tragic?"

"The lovers in those stories always suffered terribly. One of them *always* died. They were beautiful tales, but they ended with heartbreak."

"Sounds...awful." I tried to laugh but couldn't find the breath for it.

Worry flitted across Te Léna's face at last. "Are you okay? You're looking a little pale."

"Yes. Yeah, I'm fine. I...do you happen to know where Fisher is?"

"He asked me to tell you that he'd be waiting for you in his room."

"Oh, great. Thanks. I think I might go and find him, actually. There's something I want to talk to him about."

35

ORACLE

ONYX FOLLOWED me out of the forge and trotted along beside me as I hurried through the halls of Cahlish. He scooted into the bedroom as soon as I threw open the door, leaping up onto the bed, where Fisher was sitting up against the pillows, shirtless, scanning the pages of a book.

He smiled when the little fox leaped into his lap and began licking his chin. Actually *smiled.* That smile faded when he turned his attention to me and saw the state I was in. "Fuck me, Little Osha. Did you get attacked on the way over here? You're sweating."

I slammed the door closed behind me. "Why wouldn't you say my name? Before?" I panted.

"What?"

"Weeks and weeks I've been here now, and up until today, you refused to say my name. Why?"

He set down the book on the bed, gently removing Onyx from his lap as well. "I...I just—"

"I've just had a really interesting conversation with Te Léna. I was too sick to notice before, when she used to come and heal me after that run-in I had with that feeder, but she has these crazy tattoos all over her hands." I held up my own for effect. "She was telling me all about where they came from and why. And then! *Then!* Haha! Imagine my surprise when she told me about *God Bindings*, Fisher!"

"Fuck," he whispered.

"That's so funny. That's exactly what *I* said!"

"Look—"

"Tell me why you wouldn't say my name," I growled. My heart hammered like a piston in my chest. If I didn't sit down soon, I was going to fall down, but I wanted to hear him say it first. I wanted his fucking confession. "I know you can't lie to me, so come on. Tell me why."

He sat there, his bare, inked chest not moving, his black waves tumbling into his face, so perfect, so handsome, and that cursed fucking thing deep down in the basement of my soul ached and said *mine.*

You know why, he said into my mind.

"No, Fisher. Out loud."

"All right, fine. Have it your way. At first, I didn't say it because I fucking hated you," he said. "Hated what you represented."

My blood was cold as ice in my veins, but I had to hear it. "And what was that?"

"Weakness. Vulnerability."

"I am *not* weak, Fisher! I'm not like those butterflies, pathetic, hatching and dying in the cold—"

"Not you! *Me!*" He thumped himself in his chest, suddenly furious. "*My* weakness! *My* vulnerability! I've known for centuries that you were coming. That you were just going to show up one day and change everything. You're the chink in my armor, Saeris. The soft spot where the knife slides in. You are the thing that Malcolm will hurt in order to hurt me, and I couldn't...couldn't fucking *bear* it!"

I bit the end of my tongue until I tasted blood.

"And, yes. I told you once about the Oshellith. Yes, I told you that they hatched and died in a day. But I was being cruel, Saeris. I didn't tell you about them properly."

Nothing inside the bedroom changed. Nothing moved, but the air seemed to still. The figures in the paintings on the walls, with their faces slashed to ribbons, seemed to all hold their breath. "What do you mean?" I whispered.

"The Oshellith hatch once in most Fae lifetimes. Up north, in the wastelands, far beyond Ajun Sky, where the dragons used to live. The air's so cold there that it'll freeze in your lungs if you breathe it in without a mask. No life exists there for long. But once in a thousand years, the howling winds drop, signaling the coming of the Oshellith. News of that event travels quickly. That's when the bravest of our kind set out. They go on foot where no horse can go. When they reach the valley where the Oshellith hatch, they find the butterfly's cocoons and they shield them with their bodies. They give them whatever heat they can, for as long as they can. It can take up to twelve hours for them to break out of those cocoons. But when they do..." Kingfisher swallowed, shaking his head. "It's the most beautiful thing a person can experience in this lifetime. They glow blue and pink and silver, with an ethereal light. They have music, though no one knows how. A sweet, soft song that's capable of healing. The Oshellith mate and lay their eggs, but once that's done, they fill the air, and they dance. Protecting them while they live is considered a sacred rite that many die in order to perform. That's what Oshellith means in Old Fae, Saeris. *Most Sacred.*"

He closed his eyes for a moment, his expression pained. His breath came ragged and uneven. "All names hold power in this place. *Every* name means something. We have true names that we don't share with anyone. Not our friends. Not our families. Our mothers are often the only people who actually know it. And even a mother might use her child's name to her own advantage in the pursuit of power. This place—it's fucked, okay. And you show up, and you have one fucking name, and everybody knows it. And I *couldn't* say it because I was scared. Of what it would do to me when

I did. It would be like acknowledging you were here after all this time. So I called you Osha instead. But it meant more, Saeris. To me, *it meant more."*

He wasn't being serious. There was no way. "All of this time..." I whispered. "But...you called me that from the very start."

Kingfisher nodded slowly, eyes shining bright. *"Most sacred,"* he repeated, whispering the words.

I covered my face, and I gave in. I sobbed. The name he gave me, the name I *hated,* was a declaration of what I meant to him even then. For a long, long time, all I could do was cry through this monumental revelation. Eventually, a kind of stillness settled inside me, though. "How did you know? That I was coming? You said that you knew."

Fisher set his jaw. "I was told. A long time ago. By my mother. She was an oracle. I didn't believe her, but then, when I was taken—" He swallowed hard, his eyes watering. Quickly, he scooted to the edge of the bed, planting his bare feet against the floor. He couldn't breathe.

He couldn't breathe!

I stepped forward, but his hand shot out, gesturing for me to stay where I was. Screwing his eyes shut, he leaned forward, gripping hold of the edge of the bed until his tattooed knuckles turned white. After way too long, he drew in a shallow breath.

He was all right. He was breathing.

I staggered back, letting out a sob as I hit the chest of drawers behind me and slowly sank to the floor.

"I...have to be careful," he gasped. "I can't..." Trailing off, he sent me a sidelong look that begged me to understand what he was telling me. That there were things he couldn't say without suffering dire consequences. That I had to fill in the gaps for myself. "She wrote about you," he whispered. "My mother. Pages and pages. She knew that she'd die soon, and so she wrote me a book. 'A mother is always there for her son,' she told me. 'It doesn't matter that he grows and steps into his power. Even the strongest warrior's heart can break. His soul can still be crushed. Since I won't be able to comfort you when the challenges before you feel too great, take this book and keep it as a guide. Above all, know this. There will be times when the world seeks to destroy you, Kingfisher. But you are stronger than you can ever know. You will not falter. And you will not face it all alone.'"

My anger was a powerful thing, but in the face of this revelation, it wavered. I didn't know how to feel. This was a lot to take in.

Fisher hung his head, a bitter smile at his mouth. "She said, when I needed you most, you'd come blazing into my life like a meteorite, riding on a wave of chaos that would turn my whole world upside down. That you'd shine so brilliantly that you'd light up hell itself and guide me out of the darkness. She had no idea what your name would be. Just that you'd have dark hair, and a beautiful smile. And that I'd love you with a fierceness despite myself."

My heart squeezed, my throat burning with emotion. Centuries ago, a mother had looked into her son's future, seeking comfort, to assure herself that he would live a good life. And she had seen the pain and suffering the fates had in store for her boy, and then she had seen *me* and known that he would be okay. The weight of that...

Fuck, I couldn't breathe.

"She said she felt like she knew you. That you and she were friends, even though a thousand years stood between you. She...she *drew* you." Fisher's voice grew tighter as he fought to speak. Balancing on the edge of tears, he forced himself to laugh instead of cry. "And she captured you almost perfectly, too."

I wasn't as strong as Fisher. I let my tears fall. "Almost?" I whispered.

Fisher swallowed, looking down at his hands. He looked half-broken when he met my gaze again. "She was wrong, sometimes. About little things. Small details with big consequences." He pointed to his ear. "In all of her drawings of you, your ears were like mine. You were Fae. And when I saw..." He sucked in a deep breath. Sat up a little straighter. "When I felt Solace calling to me and I stepped into that pool, I saw that you were human, and I knew in an instant how easily this place would destroy you. So I made the decision to leave you there. But I couldn't leave you, could I?" he continued. "Your stomach was torn wide open. You were dying. I had no choice but to bring you back. So I decided to be awful to you, so you'd fucking hate me and want nothing to do with me."

"Stellar plan," I whispered. "That *really* panned out."

His crooked smile nearly broke my heart. "Be honest. I think it worked a little bit."

Ruefully, I shook my head. "Would those marks have shown up on my hands if it had?"

"No," he admitted. "I don't think they would."

"What do they *mean*, Fisher? For us?"

"Didn't Te Léna tell you?" he asked.

"I want *you* to tell me."

The room was thick with quiet. Fisher stared down at the rug, picking at his thumbnail. "My mother never said anything about a mating bond. They haven't existed for so long. The thought never even crossed my mind. But when I found you lying in that pool of blood, I felt it, like a band snapping into place. I smelled it on you, too. And I...I was so fucking angry." He clenched his jaw. "Angry that the fates had sealed *us* that way, when no one else in living memory had been affected by a bond. Angry that it had happened before either of us had even had a chance to get to know each other. I had no idea the marks would show up like that. Without any fucking warning. Without us being married, or even...even...deciding for ourselves that we wanted to be together.

"I saw them appear while you slept the other night. I watched them growing darker, one after the other, more marks than I'd ever heard of, and it scared the hell out of me, Saeris." He nodded sadly to himself. "Historically, Marks like that come at a cost. They're the kind of Marks that people will want to write stories about. And not happy ones."

So, it was true then. Te Léna was right. Tragic, she'd said. The word echoed through the empty halls of my mind, growing louder with each repetition.

"I'm not well," Fisher whispered. "I can't sleep. I'm haunted, constantly. I see things. I hear things. And it's getting *worse*." He hooked his pendant around his finger, closing his hand around it. "This won't help for much longer—"

"I can make you another relic. I just made one—"

"This isn't just a relic, Saeris. It's warded with spellwork, too. My mother went to the witches and had it, along with a number of other items, made for me before she died. Things she knew I'd need. But this thing inside me is getting stronger. There isn't a spell in existence strong enough to keep it at bay forever. Soon enough, the pendant won't work at all, and I'll be lost. But you don't need to worry. I refuse to bond you to me with that on the horizon. I won't accept it. I won't have you chained to me when things get really bad."

"You...rejected our bond?" My throat throbbed when I spoke. The words cut like blades. I walked an emotional tightrope, torn straight down the middle by what I was learning.

Fisher sighed. "I'm not sure how it works exactly. I scoured the library at Cahlish. For two weeks, I read everything I could lay my hands on that referred to the mating bond. I wanted to find a way to prevent it from forming in the first place, even though I knew it was already too late for that." He shrugged. "I did read that, if marks appeared, a waiting period could be initiated, though. Where either party could choose to accept or reject a bond. I initiated the waiting period for us back in Ballard."

The pieces were beginning to fall into place now. "So that's what all of those books were for? In your tent back in Innìr?" The thought of it made me want to curl into a ball and stop breathing. "That's what you were doing all that time you were gone? After I was attacked by the feeder? You were looking for a way to free yourself."

Fisher's eyes were hollow. Slowly, he shook his head. "I was looking for a way to *save you.*"

"So you evoked the waiting period. For me. For my own good. Because it was the right thing to do," I snapped.

Fisher laughed, the sound bitter. "Rejecting the bond altogether would have been the right thing to do."

"Then why didn't you?"

"I've asked myself that question a lot. I'd decided that's what I was going to do when I watched them darken on your skin. Especially when I saw the god bindings appear. But then, when it came down to it, I couldn't do it. I don't know why. I...I just couldn't. But don't worry. The month will pass, and nothing will change. First, we're going to get Everlayne back. Then you'll finish making the relics. Once that's done, you'll go back to Zilvaren and your brother."

I was drowning by the second, dragged deeper into misery, further from hope and happiness. "Oh, great. You've got it all figured out, then. Congratulations. I'm so happy for you."

Fisher looked stung by my tone. Good. He fucking should be. "Saeris—"

"No. No, really. I'm thrilled that you've had so long to think about all of this. That you've known for hundreds of years that I was going to show up in your life. That you knew what those tattoos meant, and you got to decide that you were going to reject me for my own good and send me packing back to Zilvaren. I'm ecstatic that you've made all of these awful, difficult decisions on my behalf, Kingfisher."

"Oh, come on! Be *realistic!*" Fisher stood, dragging his hands through his hair. He towered over me, a wall of muscle and ink and despair. "Does it change anything? Now that you know all of this? Do we suddenly have more options available to us? Ones that don't completely fucking suck?"

"I don't know if it changes anything! You're the one with all the answers. What does your mother's book say happens next?"

Fisher's jaw worked. "It says nothing. You were right at the end of the book. She wrote only that I'd find you, and the fates would guide our path from there."

Well, wasn't that just wonderful? I let my head fall back against the chest of drawers and closed my eyes. "Fuck the fates. They don't get to decide shit for me. *I* decide what my future is going to be."

"You have to go home, Saeris. You can go back and work to free your people. You can still be happy. I'm going to die, and—"

My eyes snapped open. "What do you mean, you're going to *die*? You aren't *dying*. You're just...you're..."

He let out the heaviest sigh I'd ever heard. He came and stood in front of me and dropped down into a crouch. When he reached for my hand, I pulled it away, slamming my elbow against the chest of drawers in the process. He tutted, reaching for my hand a second time. This time I let him have it. He threaded his fingers with mine and looked down at our joined hands for a very long time. "You're right," he said at last, looking up at me. "Being driven to the point of madness by pain and horrific hallucinations won't kill me, no. But it's no life. At least not one that I want to live. And I won't be safe. I'll end up hurting the people I care about. In the very least, I'll be a burden, and I won't saddle you or anyone else with the burden of caring for me. That's just not happening."

"So you're just gonna fucking *kill* yourself?"

He was tensed, a bowstring ready to snap. "Renfis will hel—"

I shoved him as hard as I could, pushing him away. He toppled back, landing on his ass, the move taking him by surprise. I jumped up and stepped over him, putting space between us. "Don't you *dare* finish that fucking sentence," I seethed. "You're so...so fucking *selfish!*"

The silver in his right eye swallowed the green. Righting himself, he sat up, hooking his elbows around his knees. And, gods, the expression on his face. He was ruined.

"I *know,*" he choked out. "I don't want this. I want..." But whatever he would say after those words was too painful. He bounced his legs, letting out a shaky breath.

Suddenly, it hit me. "You can't just give up. If you die, so does Lorreth."

"What?"

"You saved him. You gave him part of your soul. If you die, you'll be trapped, waiting for your soul to be made whole again before you can move on."

Fisher arched an eyebrow, displeased. "That was private. I suppose he's just going around telling everyone that now. Look, I've made my peace with whatever happens to me after. If I'm stuck, floating around the ether for a thousand years, then so be it. That will be infinitely better than the alternative."

"Lorreth said he'd die himself before he let that happen. Are you really going to cut his life short, too?"

"Lorreth won't even know I'm gone," he growled.

"Of course he will! You seriously think he just won't notice you're gone? Are you going to tell him you're moving to another realm to live a better life or something?"

"Something like that," he mumbled.

"You're such a fucking idiot, Fisher. These people are your friends. They love you. You're really going to ask Ren to help kill you? Then keep it a secret from everyone else who cares about you? You'd really put that on him? And Lorreth is smart. He isn't going to accept that you're abandoning Yvelia and you won't be coming back."

"He's going to have to, isn't he?"

"Like hell he will." I headed for the door.

"Where are you going, Saeris?" he called after me.

"To sleep. And in the morning, I'm going to the library, and I'm going to research how to save Everlayne *and* you. Because I don't just throw my hands up and accept defeat when things get hard. I'm honestly shocked to learn that *you* do."

36

ISEABAIL

I TRIED to fall asleep in the room we slept in when we first arrived at Cahlish, but Carrion's snoring was so bad that I dragged a duvet into one of the formal living rooms and passed out on one of the over-stuffed couches.

I woke from a fitful sleep sometime after dawn and found Fisher in the high-backed armchair beside me, staring at Omnamerrin's jagged peak out of the window. The beautiful scent of wild mint made me want to burst into tears, but I managed to stay calm as I folded the duvet and fluffed the imprint of my body out of the couch cushions. I wanted nothing more than to walk away without interacting with Fisher at all, but he caught my hand as I passed him, and I didn't have the energy or the will to pull away. He rested his forehead against my arm, closing his eyes, and a tiny piece of me cracked and broke. I ran my free hand gently through his hair, screaming inside, so fucking angry at him, and at myself, and at the gods, and the whole fucking universe for doing this to us.

This wasn't fair. None of it was.

He didn't fight me when I let go of his hand and walked away. I paused in the doorway, glancing back at him over my shoulder, and immediately wished I hadn't. He'd gone back to staring out the window, but he'd covered his mouth with one hand, his fingers digging into his cheek. The pronounced shadows under his eyes told of countless sleepless nights. Even the defeated set of his shoulders showed how exhausted he was. I couldn't walk away from him when he looked like that. I just fucking couldn't.

I dropped the duvet there in the doorway. Fisher closed his eyes when he realized that I was coming back to him. All of the nerves and trepidation I used to feel over touching him were gone. He leaned into me, resting his head against my stomach, wrapping his arms around my legs, placing his hands lightly on the backs of my thighs, and I held him. Seconds passed. Long minutes. I rubbed a hand between his shoulder blades in circles, hurting, and aching and wishing.

Eventually, he sat upright and sank back into the chair, his cheeks flushed. He refused to look at me, but he nodded, as if to say, "It's okay. I'm okay." And so I left.

"The last of the witches abandoned Yvelia a hundred years ago," Lorreth said. "No one's seen a member of the Balquhidder Clan in twice as long. We don't even know where they went! We have less than thirty-six hours before we need to be in Gillethrye, and we can't spend those hours looking under rocks and shouting into holes in the ground, looking for a bunch of flatulent old hags who don't want to be found."

Danya snorted.

No one else in the library laughed.

Not even Carrion. But that was probably because he didn't realize that flatulent meant gassy.

From behind the huge mountain of books piled on the table in front of me, I watched Ren massage his temples, his face drawn. "Without a witch, we're screwed," he said. "They're the only ones with powerful enough blood magic to break an enthrallment. They're also the only ones powerful enough to keep Malcolm's venom at bay while Te Léna draws it out of Layne's system."

"It'll take weeks to flush it out of her, and that's if we're lucky," Te Léna said, standing by the window. She hugged herself as she turned around and faced us all. "It's more likely that it'll take months. I can call on other healers to help, but Malcolm's venom is like acid. It eats away at everything it touches. The injury to Everlayne's body will be catastrophic by the time we reach her. It's a formidable witch indeed that can hold a body in stasis long enough for us to heal it from that kind of damage."

"Fantastic. So we don't just need a witch. We need the most powerful witch of all time," Ren said in a distant voice. He hadn't seemed at all like himself since Everlayne had shown up by the river. Normally, he was ready to brainstorm a way out of a corner no matter how tight it was, but this situation had knocked him for six. Over the past hour, I'd found him staring at the table four times, unblinking, as if he were in shock.

Fisher had shown up shortly after breakfast had been served. He'd picked over his food, but at some point, he'd rallied and started pulling books from the library shelves like a madman. Hands flecked with ink, he twisted the quill he'd been making notes furiously with, then set it down, tapping the spot on the table where Ren was staring to get his friend's attention. "There are still some half-witches at Faulton's Gap. That's about as far as I can travel by shadow gate without Belikon sensing the magic and showing up to the party. You and I will go there and see if any of them are strong enough and willing to help us this afternoon."

Ren perked up a little at that. I saw the hope kindle in his eyes, and I had to look away. "A solid plan," he said. "I'll go and get ready."

"I don't suppose you'd let me come?" Carrion asked. "I've always wanted to see a witch in real life."

"No," Fisher said blandly. "I would not. You'll only try and fuck one of them, and we're trying to petition them for help, not spark a war with them because you can't keep your cock in your pants."

Lorreth pretended to swallow down vomit. "Urgh. He would *not* try and fuck a witch."

"No, he's right," Carrion said with a sigh. "I would. Y'know. Just to say that I'd done it."

"*I'll* go with you," Danya declared. She hadn't said much since she'd shown up at the library. Mostly, she'd sat and flexed her new hand, inspecting it closely like she was looking for imperfections. Te Léna had done a remarkable job working some pretty heavy-hitting magic to replace it—more than Danya deserved—and yet I hadn't heard the warrior thank the healer once. "I'm not sitting here flicking through stuffy books with these idiots when I could actually be doing something useful."

Scouring the books for ways to help Layne *was* useful. There could be something in here that solved our problems in the blink of an eye, but Danya wouldn't care. She thought problems could only be resolved by hitting something very hard or else by stabbing someone repeatedly until they were dead, and she had no interest in being proven wrong.

"We vote she goes with you as well," Carrion said, holding up his hand. "We don't want a dark cloud hanging over the library while we're trying to work, either."

Danya bared her teeth, her canines elongating, earning her an intrigued grin from Carrion, but Fisher stepped in before Danya could say anything truly vile. "All right, you can come with us. The rest of you will keep looking through the texts in case something pops up, yes?"

Lorreth, Carrion, Te Léna, and I all nodded. The healer placed a hand on Fisher's arm as he began closing the books he'd been searching through. "Make sure you come and see me before you leave. *And* when you get back."

I hadn't wanted to own it, but I'd been jealous of Te Léna. I'd been so sure something was going on between her and Fisher, but now I knew better. After listening to her talk about her husband and seeing how happy she was when she showed me her marks, there was no doubt in my mind that she wasn't interested in him. This left only one option: she was helping him somehow with the quicksilver in his head. And if he had to go and see her before he left *and* when he got back, then it really must be getting bad.

Hours later, the world beyond the library windows had turned a peculiar shade of blue-gray, and it was snowing hard. The temperature inside Cahlish was warm as always, but the wintery scene outside made me shiver uncontrollably. We still hadn't found anything to help either Layne or Kingfisher, and I was beginning to grow frustrated. In a land full of magical or supernatural threats, how was it that there were no books on how to deal with them when problems inevitably arose? It made no sense. I was familiar with all of the books Fisher had on quicksilver, and I already knew they held no information about what to do if it got *inside* someone.

We'd made absolutely no progress whatsoever by the time the library doors swung open and Ren stormed in, swearing fitfully under his breath. His sandy hair was windswept, his leather armor gone. He was covered in mud and looked like he was going to put his fist through something.

"What the hell happened to you?" Lorreth demanded.

"Fucking *Danya*," he spat. "We found them. We explained what's happened to Everlayne and why we came. They weren't happy about it, but they were going to help. And then Danya made some shitty comment about how it was the least they could do since the witches left the Fae to clean up their mess, and how they'd turned their back on Yvelia, and that was it. All hell broke loose."

"That female is feral," Lorreth growled. "Next time she tries to hit me, I'm gonna put her over my knee and spank her. And *not* in a fun way. Fisher isn't bringing her back here, is he?"

"No." Ren threw himself into a chair and then got right back up again, gnawing on his lip. "He's taking her back to Irrìn and then returning to Faulton's Gap by himself to try and smooth things over with the witches."

"There was someone there who was strong enough to help Everlayne?" I asked.

"One witch, yes." Ren blew out a frustrated breath. "And she was possibly the most irritating, foul-mouthed creature I've ever met. She's barely old enough to curse, but she had some very choice things to say about us. Said we were warmongering heretics. She used some energy hex to knock me on my backside, and I wound up flailing in a mud pit like a pig."

Lorreth was on the verge of smirking. I shook my head frantically, eyes wide, and he stopped himself. Clearing his throat, he said, "But Fisher thinks he can convince her?"

"Yes. It'll be a godscursed miracle if he does, though, considering the mood in their camp when we left."

Fisher returned three hours later with a female in tow. She looked roughly my age, but that meant nothing in Yvelia. She was probably nine hundred years old. Her hair was a fiery red and wavy, her eyes a vivid, bright blue. Freckles dominated her face, even scattered across her forehead. Her clothes were practical—a loose cream shirt with billowing sleeves, a velvet waistcoat in hunter green with gold buttons down the front, and fitted black pants.

"Everyone, this is Iseabail." Fisher pronounced it Ee-sha-bhal, the name flowing nicely off his tongue, like he'd known twenty other females with the same name. "She's the granddaughter of the Balquhidder High Witch, Malina. She's kindly agreed to help us break Layne's enthrallment once we bring her back here tomorrow night."

The Balquhidder Clan heir surveyed us all gathered around the table, poring over our books, and wrinkled her gently upturned nose. "This is it?" she said in a lilting accent. "You're planning to take on Malcolm and kidnap his newest thrall with just three Fae males and two humans?"

Fisher moved around her and came to stand by the fireplace, holding his hands out to warm them against the flames. "No, of course not. The humans are staying here," he said.

Had he purposefully turned his back to me so he wouldn't have to see my reaction? I was sure he had. He probably thought that I wouldn't argue with him in front of everyone if he didn't make eye contact with me, but he was deluding himself. "Of course we're coming," I said. "Everlayne's our friend."

"I've actually never met Everlayne," Carrion chipped in. "But I'm still coming. Solidarity and all that."

Fisher put his back to the fire, resignation already carved into every line of his face. "You're sure you're ready?"

"I fought perfectly well at the river, didn't I?"

"Yes. But those were feeders. Mindless and stupid. We won't be facing feeders at Gillethrye, Saeris. We'll be facing Malcolm and his lords. Monsters, all. Not one of them knows the meaning of mercy. They'll fill you full of venom and watch you scream yourself to death for sport. If you come, are you ready to face that possibility?"

He was trying to scare me with the truth. A thrill of fear did tiptoe down the ladder of my spine, but he knew me better now than to think I would let my fear stop me from rescuing my friend. "Yes, I'm ready," I told him.

Fisher's face was unreadable. "And you?" he said to Carrion. "You're ready for that?"

"Sure. Why not. I'm too pretty to die old, anyway."

Fisher hung his head, folding his arms over his chest so that his shirt pulled taut, highlighting just about every muscle in his body. When he looked up again, he shrugged and said, "Okay. Fine. Who am I to stop you?"

37

MUCH SHARPER

MY EYES WERE STRAINED ALL to hell when I made my bed on the couch again that night. The bare branches of the trees outside the window tapped and scraped at the glass, the snow coming down harder than ever. It seemed that it wanted to bury Cahlish under its mantle, entombing those of us inside within the walls of the house so that nothing could harm us. Unfortunately for us, we couldn't stay in our warm, comfortable sanctuary, protected from the dread things that lurked in the dark much longer. Tomorrow night, we would venture out into the world and face them.

I was still preparing to try and sleep when Fisher came for me. He padded barefoot and shirtless into the living room, his ink swirling across his skin as he crossed the room. "You really think I'm going to let you sleep out here again?" he asked.

"I didn't know if you'd want me in your bed," I told him.

"If it were up to me, we wouldn't spend another night without each other again." Gently, he reached for the end of my braid and drew it over my shoulder toward him. He slowly unfastened it, working my hair loose with his fingers. His eyes were cautious when they sought out mine. "Does that scare you?" he murmured.

"No. I..." Gods. His hands felt amazing. It was so intimate to have him run his fingers through my hair like this. "It doesn't scare me," I whispered. "I want that, too."

It would have been easy to let my thoughts run away with me. There were so many angry, hurt, frightened words I could hurl at him, but I'd done enough of that last night, and I really didn't want to do it again.

As if he were thinking along similar lines, he cupped my face in his hands and said softly, "Let's have tonight. You and me. Tomorrow night, we'll bring Everlayne home. And once Iseabail and Te Léna have her fixed up and good as new, then we can worry about me. Okay?"

My relief hit hard. He was no longer talking about how futile it was to try and find a way through all of this. He was saying, let's deal with what's right in front of us and see what the lay of the land is like after that. It was a much more positive approach than the hard line he'd taken last night.

I looked up at him, my ribs cinching tight. "Yes. Let's do that, please."

He grinned, his expression turning wicked as a shadow gate opened up behind him. He picked me up, fast as hell, and stepped back into the twisting smoke before I could even think about calling him lazy for not walking back to his bedroom.

But when we emerged through the gate, we weren't in his room. We were back at the apartment in Ballard, standing in the living room above the bakery, surrounded by candles. They rested on the mantlepiece and the bookshelves. They covered the little dining table where we'd eaten breakfast and filled the windowsills of the huge bay windows with flickering light. Everywhere I looked, there were candles. Fisher smiled, his mouth pulled to one side, a dimple marking his cheek as he watched me taking it all in.

I spun around, holding my hands over my mouth. "It's beautiful," I breathed.

He came and stood close behind me, folding me into his arms.

"It's not finished yet." His breath stirred my hair and something else, too, deep inside of me. I felt his power rush across my stomach as black smoke plumed from his hands, filling the room. Soon it was everywhere, cloaking everything from sight. Everything except the flickering flames of the candles. They lit up the darkness, a thousand burning points of light as brilliant as the stars. It felt as though we were up there with them, suspended in the void, where nothing could touch us, and no one could hurt us, and we had all the time we could possibly need.

You did this for me? It felt wrong to speak out loud. I didn't want my voice to ruin the illusion he'd created for us, so I asked him in my mind.

Yes, he answered simply. *And for me, too. I am selfish, Saeris. I wanted something quiet and small and special for the both of us. Something we could keep.* He buried his face into the crook of my neck and kissed me there. The heat of his mouth seared my skin, and I couldn't help but tremble. Closing my eyes, I leaned back into him, letting my weight rest against his solid mass, feeling safe and so desperately, heartbreakingly sad. My heartbreak couldn't have me tonight, though. Fisher was right. It was stupid to spend the night before we all stepped into our worst nightmares arguing or in tears. I bit back the burn in my throat and spun around, wrapping my arms around his neck.

Make me forget that I've ever suffered, I commanded. *Make me forget that I will again.*

He fell upon me like a tidal wave. His mouth found mine in the dark, and the kiss blotted out the world. Hot and demanding, his lips slid over mine, urging them to open, and then he was tasting me, exploring my mouth, his tongue claiming me. I moaned when the tips of his canines pierced my bottom lip. The copper bright tang of blood flooded my mouth, and Fisher huffed out a hard breath, letting out a moan of his own. It coated both our tongues as he kissed me deeper, his hands working their way into my hair, his breath quickening. I felt him, hard against my hip bone, his cock already rock-solid. My stomach bottomed out.

Gods, I wanted him.

I wanted all of him.

My soul was on fire, and I didn't care if I burned for all eternity. So long as I was burning with him, then so be it.

His teeth caught on my lip again. On the tip of my tongue. The taste of my blood intensified, but I didn't pull away. Fisher's hands slid down my body, cupping my backside, his fingers digging into my ass cheeks. His breath came even faster, each exhale punctuated with a ragged groan. Pulling me closer, he kissed me even harder, grinding his cock against my stomach so that I could feel his desperate need.

When I get you out of these clothes, you're in trouble, he snarled in my head. *I'm going to fuck you so hard you won't be able to sit down for a week.*

Fisher! I clung to him, panting, already anticipating the surge of heat I would feel the moment he thrust himself inside of me. Wanting it. Craving it so badly that I could have screamed.

God-bound.

We were God-bound.

Mates.

I could feel it now—a bright thread of energy drawing us together as he wrapped himself around me. If I wanted it, all I needed to do was reach out and claim it.

Fisher growled as another fresh wave of blood flooded our mouths, and he lost all patience. With a rough jerk of his hands, he tore my pants open and thrust his hand down the front of them, his fingers deftly working their way between my folds.

Holy hell. So. Fucking. Wet. His satisfied, hungry snarl sent a shiver racing through me; it turned into a body-wide shudder as he wasted no time, driving his fingers up inside me. I stiffened in his arms, letting go of a strangled cry that caused the candle flames to gutter and flare in response.

Oh, gods. Oh...my gods.

The air quaked with energy. Fisher's shadows rippled over my skin like water. I breathed it in, welcomed it inside me, feeling it become a part of me. *He* was a part of me. I sensed that in my bones. *If* I wanted him to be, he would be the axis around which I revolved. I would be his. Two counterparts, independent of one another. Already whole, but together stronger than we could ever be apart. It was my choice. The backs of my hands tingled as I ran my palms over the smooth, strong plains of his chest, and I knew that the ink was back. Each finger prickled with the power of the runes that emerged upon them. The back of my left hand buzzed with warmth, but the right throbbed with energy as I felt rune after rune stacking on top of my skin there. The God Bindings were last to arrive. Fine strands of fire lashed around my wrist, trailing up my arms. More ink followed. It skated over my stomach and caressed my thighs. Columns of it rose up my back, wrapping around my spine. I felt it everywhere.

Was this why he'd thrown us into darkness? Was he hiding the evidence of our connection, so I wouldn't be intimidated by the strength of it made manifest on my body? The answer to that question was probably yes. He didn't want to deal with this until Everlayne was safe and well, back at Cahlish, and I understood that. I let the Marks move over me, focusing on the heat of Fisher's hands and mouth for now. We still had time.

Your scent drives me crazy, Fisher rumbled. *You're like a fucking drug. You light me up.*

I knew exactly what he meant. It had been there, even back at the Winter Palace. Whenever I caught the smell of him in the air, it made my heart race. Empty rooms were dangerous places. At Cahlish, I'd enter the living room, or the forge, find myself walking down a hallway, and it was as though the ghost of him was there, too, walking alongside me. The smell of winter pine and cold mountain air set my heart pounding.

His fingers worked inside me, the pressure of his hand cupping my sex kindling the beginnings of madness in me. He would be my end, this male. He would claim my better days and carry me during my worst. He would show me the meaning of ecstasy and drown me in it until I fucking died.

Please, Fisher. Gods, I want you.

His low, rumbling chuckle skimming over the surface of my mind was pure sin.

You've got me, Little Osha. And I've got you.

His fingers withdrew from inside me and moved back to find my clit. Dedicating his full attention to the swollen bundle of nerves at the apex of my thighs, he rubbed his fingertips over me in tight, small circles designed to push me toward orgasm and fast.

I sighed as his mouth traveled from mine, along my jaw, hovering over the shell of my ear. Goose bumps exploded down the backs of my arms and legs, the hair at the back of my neck standing to attention as his hot breath bloomed over my skin.

"Nobody will *ever* fuck you the way I'm about to fuck you, Saeris Fane. I'm about to introduce you to all seven gods. When you meet them, don't forget to tell them *I'm* the one you worship on your knees."

Out.

Fucking.

Loud.

It was hot as hell when he told me what he was going to do to me in my head. But hearing his voice, full of gravel and raw desire? There was nothing else I could do. I lost my mind. My shirt came off first. I didn't even give Fisher the opportunity to magic it away. The cloth binding my breasts went next. Boots. Pants. Fisher helped tear them down my legs, making an impatient sound as he ripped them from each leg. I was frantic as I grabbed the waistband of his pants, quickly unfastening them, but he took over, speeding up the process by kicking out of them himself.

You want me to worship you? I'll worship you, I thought. Fisher might have big plans for me, but I had some of my own. Dropping to my knees, I took hold of him, wrapping my hand around his solid, hard shaft. He hadn't given me the chance to do this the last couple of times we'd had sex. It had all been about me. Fisher had spent an ungodly amount of time between my thighs, bringing me to screaming climax with his mouth, but now it was my turn.

Nerves chased adrenaline as I extended my tongue and slowly, teasingly licked the swollen head of Fisher's cock. Oh, holy *shit.* He was beaded with precum; the slightly salty taste of him coated my tongue, as I swirled it around his rigid flesh.

Energy rushed over me, and Fisher's shadows withdrew. The darkness peeled back. The room was still only dimly lit, but I could see him now: his powerful thigh muscles; that glorious vee that cut over the line of his groin; his impressive, defined abs, and the solid wall of his chest, covered in shifting ink. And his face. His breathtaking face. His lips were parted, his eyes wide and alive with hunger. My pulse kicked up, working double-time, when I saw the thin trickle of blood trailing down his chin.

My blood.

Now that I could see him, I could also see *my* hands. It was as I'd suspected—the marks were back, bolder and brighter than before, filling my fingers, the backs of my hands, and my forearms. I arched an eyebrow up at Fisher, trailing the tip of my tongue *ever* so slowly around the straining head of his erection. "I thought you were hiding these from me," I said.

"Maybe I was. But I'll be damned all the way to hell and back if you use that sweet mouth on me and I don't get to watch." He gazed at the ink staining my skin, taking it all in. When his eyes met mine again, they were full of fire. "And, anyway. *I'm* not afraid of them, Little Osha. Are *you?*"

And there it was. A question I'd been asking myself over and over again. I still didn't understand the implications of these marks. I was very worried about what they meant for any future Fisher and I had if we chose this. But they were beautiful. A representation of what he was beginning to mean to me. I sucked the head of his cock into my mouth, deeply pleased when Fisher trembled in response. My mouth made a wet popping sound when I let him spring free of my lips again.

"I haven't made up my mind," I said carefully. "I'm not afraid of them tonight. And that's all that matters right now." I sank back down onto him, done with the teasing, closing my mouth around him, and Fisher's eyes rolled straight back into his skull.

"Holy...fucking...*shit*..." he groaned. When he'd recovered himself enough to look at me again, a small wave of panic notched at the back of my throat. He was going to eat me alive. I was going to let him. But that didn't stop the thrill of nerves from shooting up my spine as I considered all that would entail. I bobbed up and down on his cock, working my tongue around him, relishing the velvet-smooth texture of his skin as my lips moved over it. He twitched, straining, and I took him deeper.

"Gods alive, you're so pretty with your mouth wrapped around me like that." Fisher traced the line of my cheek, my jawbone, then rubbed the pad of his thumb over my lips, stretched around him. He sucked his own bottom lip into his mouth, biting down on it as he growled possessively. "My lips to kiss. My mouth to *fuck*." His canines pierced his lip, twin, glossy beads of his own blood staining his mouth, and as if throwing caution to the wind, he rocked himself forward, pushing himself deeper into my mouth.

I whimpered, the tip of his cock butting against the back of my throat, and Fisher immediately jerked back, pulling himself out of my mouth with a feral hiss. *"Fuck!"*

He fell on me in a wave of black shadows and smoke. No time to make it to bed. The couch was so close, but he took me where I was, right there on the floor. I cried out when he sank himself into me. It was all I could do to stop myself from coming on the spot. He filled me so deliciously, the weight of him on top of me so perfectly satisfying.

He went still. We both panted, staring at each other. "Tell me to fuck you, Saeris," he ground out. "Tell me that you want this."

I clawed at his back, desperate for him to move, to fill me again and again and again. "I...Please! Gods, please fuck me. I want you. I want—"

"That's all I needed to hear."

Fisher drove himself into me hard, his jaw clenched tight. Energy flickered between us like tiny filaments of lightning, dancing all over our skin, connecting us as he drove himself home.

I took panting, gasping breaths, fighting to stay calm as a storm began to build in my chest. It would wreck me when it broke, and I wasn't ready. It was sweeping Fisher away, too. He held on to me so damn tight as he rocked into me, as if he was afraid that I'd disappear if he loosened his grip.

I came first, my orgasm obliterating my ability to think. Like one of the avalanches that I'd seen racing down the face of Omnamerrin, it slammed into me and swept me away. My back arched up from the rug, my body contorting as pure, unadulterated pleasure rocked me to my core.

Fisher followed after me. When he came, the sound of his breathless, furious cry made the panes of glass in the window frames shake. I watched, unable to tear my gaze from him, and an array of new tattoos bloomed like black flowers across his skin. They climbed up the side of his throat. Fresh runes chained his collarbone, interlocking and bold. The design on his neck looked like feathers at first, and—yes, they were feathers. The outstretched wings of a majestic bird, flashing metallic blue and green, fanned around either side of his neck, unique and stunning.

He roared, burying himself deep one last time, and sank down on top of me, covering me with his body.

For a time, it was all we could do to exist in the aftermath.

"Gods. That..." I swallowed thickly, trying to catch my breath. "That was..."

Fisher propped himself up on his elbow, and my heart backflipped at the sight of him. His hair was messy, his waves on the brink of actually curling for once. His cheeks were flushed, the shadows beneath his eyes nowhere to be seen. For once, he looked at ease. Content. And...wicked? A slow smile spread across his face.

"That was just the beginning, Saeris." He bumped my nose with the end of his. "Didn't think I'd be done with you that easily, did you?"

Over the next three hours, Fisher proceeded to fuck me in every room of the apartment. Just when he seemed to finally reach his limit, he was hard again and growling into my neck, ready for round three. And then four. And then five. He made me food when we were both eventually spent, and we sat on the floor in the middle of the living room, wrapped in dust sheets while we ate.

Fisher rubbed his fingers over the column of his throat, frowning playfully at me once we were done with our meal. "Did I imagine it, or did I feel something new slipping into place here earlier?" he asked.

I popped a grape into my mouth, bouncing my brows at him. "You sure did."

His smile turned a little sad. He dropped his hand from his throat, and asked, "What is it?"

"Wings. Really beautiful wings. They have the same metallic sheen as this," I said, holding up the layered, complicated rune on my right hand.

Fisher nodded slowly, angling his head down so that the line of the tendons in his neck beneath his new tattoo stood proud. He was as mesmerizing as a painting like this, with his hair obscuring his face, his strong, dexterous hands resting in his lap. I wished I could sketch him, so I could save the sight of him like this forever. Unlike his mother, I was no artist, though. And sometimes, that's just how things were supposed to be. There were moments that were gifts, meant to be cherished only for as long as you could remember them.

Luckily for me, I had an excellent memory.

"What does it mean?" I asked quietly, gesturing to his neck. "Why did *you* get new tattoos this time?" We had spent a long time between rounds three and four, thoroughly investigating my body, and had confirmed that *I* hadn't developed any new artwork.

Fisher shrugged noncommittally, lying down on the rug. He reached out a hand for me, gesturing for me to come to him. I set aside our plates and did as he'd requested, snuggling into his side and resting my head against his chest. But I didn't let him off the hook that easily. "You can't just shrug off a question when you don't want to answer," I said, poking him lightly in the ribs. "Tell me why they showed up tonight and not the other nights."

I turned my head and closed one eye, squinting at him. His throat filled my field of vision, half of his new wing tattoo all I could see. "When we Fae are little," he said softly, "our parents teach us the art of distraction so we can protect the things we don't want to confess. Will you forget you asked that question if I find the energy to make you scream my name again?"

"Absolutely not!" I pinched his nipple between my teeth in rebuke, and Fisher yelped, cursing in Old Fae.

"Careful, Osha," he chided. "My teeth are *much* sharper than yours."

He hadn't bitten me at all tonight. Aside from the little nicks to my lips and the tip of my tongue when we'd kissed so roughly, it hadn't escaped me that his canines had stayed well away from me during sex. It hadn't mattered. The night had been incredible. More than incredible. I wouldn't have changed any of it.

"I already know how sharp your teeth are. What I don't know is why you have a new tattoo," I pressed.

Drawing me closer, he rested his chin on top of my head and sighed heavily. "All right, fine. I'll tell you. In the past, one party always got the mating marks first. When the other party accepted the bond, sometimes Marks showed up on their bodies, too. It didn't happen all of the time. But sometimes..." He trailed off in a hushed voice.

I pushed away from him, sitting up too fast. My head spun like a top, but I ignored the pitching room, narrowing my eyes at him. "You did...*what?*"

"I accepted the bond. Earlier. When I was inside you. When my soul was wrapped around yours." He was *so* calm. Not a hint of uncertainty or nerves at all.

Meanwhile, I felt like I was about to pass out. "You *accepted* it," I said.

"I did."

"How?"

"It's easy. You make the decision. You claim the bond. The bond claims you."

"No! How could you *accept* it? I'm—" I shook my head, trying to get my thoughts in order. "I'm *human*. Aside from all of the things we have to iron out once Everlayne is safe, you're nearly immortal, and my lifespan is...is..."

"Inconvenient," Fisher said. "You're right. That part sucks. But..." He frowned, snaking his arm around my waist, and pulled me back down to lie on his chest. Once I was settled, he slowly stroked his fingers through my hair and spoke again. "I'll be grateful for every second that I can say that I belong to you, Saeris Fane. Eighty years or eighteen hours. It doesn't matter to me. It'll still be the highest honor of my life. But don't— Are you about to have a heart attack? Your pulse is *flying*." The bastard laughed, and I nearly burst into tears. "Don't freak out. Here. Look."

He took my hand and lifted it, showing it to me. I watched as the inked runes gradually faded until my hands and forearms were unmarked again. "Just because I've accepted it doesn't mean you have to. You still have weeks to decide. And if you reject the bond, then it won't matter. My new wings will disappear, and that'll be that."

He'd accepted me as his mate.

In spite of all the blockades that stood in our way and all of the *very* good reasons we shouldn't be mated...he'd done it.

"I'm in love with you, Saeris Fane," he whispered quietly into my hair. "And I'm already half-mad, anyway. What's a little complicated thrown into the mix?"

"I—"

"*Please,* for the love of the gods, don't say anything. Just let me have my fantasy. Just for tonight."

I *was* going to have a heart attack. Or my heart was going to break in two. Either way, my heart was in trouble, and there was no protecting it now. Fisher's hand swept up and down my side, and slowly, the room grew dark until, once again, it felt as though we were floating in a sea of stars.

He didn't want me to respond to his declaration. I understood that, and I could give him his peace for tonight. The sun would rise again soon, though, and we wouldn't be able to avoid the conversation. In the meantime, sleep made my bones heavy, weighing down my eyelids. Tomorrow, we were going to save Everlayne.

As my exhaustion promised to sweep my consciousness away, something occurred to me out of the blue. "When we were here last time, you said that the people of Ballard had something you needed. But you never got it," I whispered.

Fisher gently kissed my forehead, and all around us, the flickering candle flames started to blink out. "Yes, I did," he said. I barely heard his next words as I drifted away. "I came for a little hope."

38

MARTYRS FOR FRIENDS

I woke to a soft mattress, the smell of sugar, and honey-warm sunlight pouring into the bedroom. Outside, tiny birds jumped from branch to branch on the tree beyond the bedroom window. I smiled as I stretched my arms over my head, delighting in the way my body ached from last night's adventures. And then my smile slowly slipped away...

At some point, Fisher had carried me to bed. Not back into the small room where he'd slept as a child. He'd put me in his mother's bed. And he wasn't lying next to me under the duvet. The bedroom door was open, and through it, I could see the ominous black shape of a spiraling shadow gate.

"No. No, no, no, no, *no!*" I rocketed out of the bed, hissing when I stood on my boots. My heart sank at the sight of the pile of fresh clothes laid out for me on the chair by the window. Bypassing them, I ran into the living room, going from room to room, naked, trying to quell my rising panic.

"Fisher? Fisher!"

He wasn't in the kitchen. Wasn't in the other bedroom, either. The apartment was empty. Rivers of candle wax covered the furniture and ran down the shelves. The remnants of our dinner still sat on the counter by the sink in the kitchen. And in the center of the living room, where we'd spent most of our night tangled up in each other, was the gods-cursed shadow gate. I stared at it, my eyes flooding with tears. It swam in my vision, but there it remained, hovering an inch above the rug, making a dull rushing sound. I clapped my hands over my mouth, but they didn't keep the loud sob I let out from ringing loudly around the apartment.

What have you done, Fisher? What have you done?

I found the note underneath the clothes he'd left for me.

This may seem dramatic now, but it'll make sense in time, Saeris.

Go through the gate. It'll take you back to Cahlish.

Wait there with the others. I'll send Layne back as soon as I can. Tell Iseabail to sedate her the second she comes through the gate. She'll be close to transitioning. There won't be much time. She'll want to go back through the gate before I close it, so you'll have to be ready for that. You have to stop her. This will all be for nothing if she jumps back through.

Tell Lorreth to live his life. Tell him not to worry about me. I have endless patience and no interest in having martyrs for friends.

Tell Renfis that I'm sorry. That he was the standard that I always held myself to, and Yvelia would have been a better place if I was half as good as him.

And you, Osha. I release you from your oath. You know how to make the relics now. A selfish part of me wants to beg you to make as many as you can so that my friends and their families can escape Yvelia before this realm falls. But I understand if you need to go. Find Hayden and Elroy. Help your friends. Then go exploring. There are countless realms out there, waiting to be found. Make one of them yours.

I've never been one to trust in the gods, but I choose to believe that all things come from the same place when life begins. I have hope that they return to the same place when it ends.

I'll be waiting for you there, Saeris Fane.

F

I sank to my knees and sobbed. The last time I'd cried like this, my mother had been blowing away on the reckoning wind. I'd vowed I'd never care about anyone enough to experience this kind of pain again. But here I was, shattering.

I well and truly broke when I saw what rested on the mantlepiece above the fire.

Nimerelle.

The tarnished black sword sat amidst melted puddles of wax and the jars full of paintbrushes, sunlight flaring in a starburst at its tip. He hadn't taken it with him.

I knew why. If Malcolm killed Fisher and laid his hand on a god sword, there was a chance he might find a way to convince it to channel. If that happened, there were no limits to the destruction he might wreak. *And* he could still the quicksilver. There would be no escape for me or for any of Fisher's friends.

So Kingfisher had gone to Gillethrye to save Everlayne and everyone else he cared about.

And he had gone there alone and unarmed.

Carrion squawked, fumbling the book in his hands. He came dangerously close to falling off his chair as I stormed through the shadow gate and into Fisher's bedroom.

"Gods a-fucking-*live!*" He gasped, clutching his chest. "A little *warning?*"

"Where is everyone?" I demanded.

"I don't know. In the library? Everyone's going cross-eyed, trying to find a way to make sure they break this enthrallment thing. What are you doing with Fisher's sword?"

I tossed Nimerelle onto the bed, along with the old shirt I'd found to wrap the grip so I could pick it up. "Never mind the sword. Why aren't you with everybody else?" I snapped.

The back-alley thief shrugged shamelessly. "I came looking for Onyx. I couldn't find him anywhere, so I guessed he was sleeping in here. Crazy bedroom. Have you seen the artwork?" He gestured to the slashed paintings that still hung on the walls, their canvases torn to ribbons. He carried on, not giving me room to speak. "I was going to leave, but *then* I figured maybe Fisher kept a diary. And guess what? He doesn't. But he *does* have something even better."

I crossed the room. "What time is it?"

"Wait. Don't you want to know what I'm reading?"

"Let me guess. It's a book of prophecies, and there are a ton of drawings of me in it with pointed ears."

Carrion's disappointment stole his grin. "How did you know?"

"Carrion, I can't do this right now. What *time* is it?"

"Nearly two, I s'pose. We had lunch a while ago. I wasn't

expecting anyone to step through that thing until *much* later. Ren said Fisher left a note for him, saying you'd be back before dusk."

"Oh, yeah," I fumed. "Fisher just *loves* leaving notes."

By the bed, the shadow gate Fisher had left open for me snapped shut, somehow aware that it had served its purpose. I watched it vanish, my insides glowing white hot with rage.

"I'm sensing a little tension in the air," Carrion quipped. "Have you two fallen out already?"

"If by fallen out you mean am I going to kill him, then the answer is yes."

Lorreth, Ren, Te Léna, and Iseabail were in the library. Of the four, only Iseabail didn't have her head buried in a book. She stood by the window, watching the snow come down, looking bored. Surprise shuttered across Ren's face when he saw me enter.

"Saeris. Is everything..." He course-corrected himself mid-question. "What's wrong? What's happened?"

I was fit to fucking scream. Tossing the letter Fisher had written for me down onto the table in front of the general, I gripped the back of the chair the bastard had sat in yesterday, going along with all of our plan-making while he secretly made plans of his own, and I waited for Ren to scan the sloping handwriting on the paper.

His mouth hung open as he dropped the letter. Lorreth didn't even ask to read it; he leaned across the table and took it, his expression darkening as his eyes flitted over the text. "Stupid bastard," he hissed. Looking up at me, he asked in an incredulous tone, "What the *fuck* does he think he's doing?"

Like I had an answer to that question. A thousand curses hovered on the tip of my tongue, but I trapped them behind my teeth. Only one question mattered right now, and everything hinged on its answer. "Is there a quicksilver pool at Gillethrye?"

Ren hadn't said a word. He was visibly still in shock from the contents of the letter. He blinked when he realized that everyone was looking at him. "No. Not that I know of," he said in a cracked voice. "There was one a long time ago, but Belikon took it when he came into power. He merged it with the pool at the Winter Palace so it would be large enough to transport an army."

There it was then.

I had my answer.

There was no pool at Gillethrye.

Every scrap of hope I'd been clinging on to dematerialized in a puff of smoke.

There had been a chance. The smallest chance, but still a chance. Fisher had said there was more quicksilver here at Cahlish. A pool, most likely. He'd said I could have access to it once I'd figured out how to create the relics, which meant it was probably close by somewhere. If I'd found it, I could have made more relics, and then we could have gone and kicked Fisher's ass for being so fucking stupid. But without a pool on the other end at Gillethrye...

It was hopeless.

We were fucked.

I let my head hang, numbness spreading through me like ice.

"Bastard."

I half expected him to answer me, but my mind remained stubbornly silent.

How could he do this? To his friends? To me? He wasn't alone in this, but he'd decided to take on this burden all by himself. It wasn't heroic or brave. It was fucking stupid.

Lorreth ran a hand over his mouth, his rough stubble making a scraping sound against his palm. "I think I'm going to throw up," he said matter-of-factly.

Ren pushed his chair away from the table but just sat there with his hands on his knees. I didn't think he had the strength to stand. "You and me both, Brother. You and me both," he murmured.

It was Carrion who broke the silence next. "Saeris?" I looked up and saw that *he* had Fisher's letter now. He held up the piece of parchment, a questioning look on his face. "How long was that shadow gate open just now? The one in Fisher's bedroom?"

"I don't know. Hours, probably. I have no idea when he opened it. It was there when I woke up."

"No, no." Carrion shook his head impatiently. "How long did it stay open for *after* you came through it? I wasn't paying attention, but we spoke before it closed, right?"

"Yes. I suppose…it took maybe ten seconds? Twelve?"

"Does it always take that long?"

"Uhh…" I hadn't paid much attention the other times I'd traveled through a gate with Fisher. There had always been something else on my mind.

Lorreth stepped in with an answer. "Yes. I don't know if it's always that long, but there's always a delay. Fisher's commented on it before."

"Great. And here, he says in the letter that he wants you to be ready for Everlayne when he sends her through a gate back to Cahlish. That she'll try and use it to get back to Malcolm. Which means that the gate isn't one-way. If Everlayne can use it to come here—"

"Then we can also use it to go there!" I nearly sank to the floor. The relief…hells, I'd never known anything like it. My body started to shake.

Ren got to his feet, letting out a long exhale. "I could kiss you, Carrion Swift."

Carrion seemed taken aback by this. And then somewhat interested. After thinking for a second, he said, "I wouldn't be opposed. But maybe later. First, Saeris has work to do, and I plan on giving her a hand."

"What work?" It was a miracle that I managed to ask the question. I was so full of adrenaline now that the library was spinning. I was definitely going to throw up.

Carrion grinned, all teeth and mischief. "I'm coming with you through that portal. I'm gonna help you save your asshole boyfriend. But first, I want one of those fancy swords."

"Have you heard about the fire at the circus?" I paused for dramatic effect. "It was in tents. Get it? *In tents.*"

Carrion winced. "That was terrible."

"Shut up. It asked for a joke. It didn't specify that it had to be a good one. I was a metalworker and a thief in Zilvaren, not a comedian."

"I was a smuggler and I've still got way better jokes than that."

"*You* tell it a joke, then!" I held out the crucible containing the quicksilver, and Carrion huffed, peering at the roiling liquid metal.

"All right. Fine. A husband turns to his wife one day and says, 'Y'know, I bet you can't think of something to tell me that will make me both happy and sad at the same time.' The wife doesn't even need to think about it. She turns to her husband and says, 'Your cock is way bigger than your brother's.'"

The quicksilver, which hadn't made a peep over my joke, started to chuckle.

"What's it doing?" Carrion asked. "It's laughing, isn't it?"

I rolled my eyes and ran the quicksilver along the edge of the heated blade I had clamped over the fire in the forge's hearth. There hadn't been time to make a new sword from scratch, but Ren had found a very nice-looking double-hander in Cahlish's modest armory that Carrion had agreed would do. The quicksilver, which Ren had also brought from the armory—apparently, it had been in there all along—also thought the blade was reasonable enough to bind with and had consented to be forged into the sword, providing I told it a joke.

If it hadn't approved of mine, it had clearly accepted Carrion's as payment, because the quicksilver absorbed into the blade as soon as it made contact, casting a brilliant iridescent sheen along the weapon's edge.

The sky darkened as I sharpened that edge against a wheel,

and Carrion told a slew of additional jokes that grew bawdier as he went.

"Gods and martyrs, will you please stop," I begged.

"I'm just trying to lighten the mood. You look like someone pissed in your water ration."

More jokes. Give us more jokes...

I glowered at the sword, unable to comprehend its bad taste. If ever there was a weapon so perfectly suited to its owner, it was this one. Carrion delighted in telling it the filthiest jokes imaginable. And when I was finished, and Carrion pressed his fingertip against its point, giving it the tiniest taste of his blood, the blade responded immediately.

Yes, yes. Our friend. Ours. He will name us.

Carrion's eyes rounded out of his head. "I heard that!"

"Good." I flipped the sword and handed it to him. "Then give it a name and let's go." The evening was almost here, and the others were waiting for us.

Carrion held the sword, turning it this way and that. After much consideration, he said, "It looks like a Simon."

"Simon?"

"Yeah. Simon. Don't blame me. That's what it looks—" He stopped talking and listened. *"See.* It likes the name. It *wants* to be Simon."

"Fair enough." The sword was done talking with me, apparently, so I asked, "Has it decided if it wants to gift you with magic in spite of your frail human blood?"

Carrion smirked. "It says that's for me to know and you to find out."

"Hope that means yes," I grumbled.

Back in the library, Ren was pacing nervously, chewing on the inside of his cheek. Lorreth stared into the fire. "Where's Te Léna and Iseabail?" I asked.

"They're setting up a space to treat Layne," Ren said. "Iseabail brought everything with her that she thinks she'll need for her sedation spell to work. Te Léna's confident that she can suppress the venom in Layne's blood long enough to start healing her body, but…"

"But?"

"This has never been done before. That we know of, anyway. The cure for the blood curse was lost over a thousand years ago, and that only helped the Fae who had been cursed, not turned. Turned vampires need to die before they transition, and witch magic can't affect the dead. There's a chance Malcolm's venom will kill Layne before she can be healed, even if she is frozen by Iseabail's magic."

Lorreth fidgeted in his seat. "I don't trust her. The witch," he clarified before I could ask who he was referring to. "Dragon lovers. They're the reason we're in this mess in the first place. If it weren't for them, there wouldn't even *be* any vampires."

"Come now. Don't tell me you still believe that," a soft, lilting voice asked from the doorway. It was Iseabail, of course. Her thick red hair flowed down her back, the top section clasped back in a clip. Her aquamarine eyes bored into Lorreth, sharp as daggers. "My people have been persecuted my whole life thanks to those vicious rumors. We proved centuries ago that we had nothing to do with the curse that afflicted your kind. The Balquhidder Clan was one of the five families charged by your dead King Daianthus with finding a cure for the Fae curse. We were instrumental in breaking it. I've come here of my own free will to help you heal the daughter of a tyrant who has a bounty on my family's heads. Anyone would think you'd be grateful, Warrior." She squinted at him. "What was your name again?"

"You know damned well what my name is," Lorreth rumbled. "We've met before, Witch."

"Oh?" Iseabail shot Lorreth a feline smirk. "Really? I must have forgotten."

Ren brought his fist down onto the table, startling all of us. "Enough. We're already on edge and stressed. We don't need to be bickering amongst ourselves as well. Lorreth, Iseabail's right. She came here to help us, and she didn't have to."

Lorreth's eyes burned with surprising hatred, but he ducked his head and did the right thing; he only sounded slightly insincere when he apologized. "I'm sorry. We're all very grateful to you for coming."

The redhead looked as if she enjoyed watching the warrior squirm. You could have cut the mounting tension in the room with a knife. I didn't have it in me to repeat any of the terrible jokes Carrion had told back in the forge, though, so I was going to have to defuse the prickly energy another way. I stepped toward the table, glancing back at Carrion over my shoulder. "Come on. Why don't you tell everyone what you named your new sw—"

A hole opened in the air, black and angry.

A streak of dark blue hurtled from it and crashed onto the table.

Books flew everywhere.

The wood shattered.

"FUCK!" It was Ren. He was ahead of everyone else in the library, rushing forward to help Everlayne. *She'd fallen from the fucking ceiling.* The shadow gate wasn't a vertical doorway this time. It was horizontal and ten feet up in the air...and Everlayne had just smashed our only means of reaching it with her body.

"Fuck!" Carrion cried.

"Quickly!" Lorreth raced around the shattered table and roughly grabbed my arm. There was no time for pleasantries. I saw what he was going to do written on his face, and I was okay with it. But...

"Wait! My sword!" Idiot. I was such a fucking idiot! Solace wasn't strapped to my waist. It was still light outside. Taladaius had said Malcolm would meet Fisher at dusk, but it was still very light outside. I wasn't ready! "Carrion first!" I hollered.

The sword was on the reading stand by the far window. I sprinted for it. Grabbed it. Turned.

Lorreth and Ren were lifting Carrion through the gate. His torso had already disappeared. As if he suddenly pulled himself up from the other side, Carrion's legs whipped upward and he was gone.

"Saeris!" Everlayne croaked. She wasn't dead. Even as I flew across the library toward Lorreth's outstretched arms, I had enough time to thank the gods that she was fucking alive. I couldn't stop to comfort her, though.

"I'll be back soon, Layne!"

Lorreth's hands closed around my waist. Renfis grabbed my legs.

Everlayne's frantic cry pierced through me as the fighters below thrust me up into the shadow gate. "Saeris! Wait! *The water!*"

But it was too late to panic. No time to ask her what she meant. The gate took hold of me, a frozen wind tearing at my clothes, tearing me inside out. I reached blindly for whatever handhold Carrion had used to pull himself up, but there was no handhold. There was a swift, disorienting shift in gravity, and suddenly I was upside down.

Suddenly, I was f a l l i n g . . .

39

ANNORATH MOR!

THE WIND BROUGHT tears to my eyes. I fought to open them and then wished I hadn't. Eighty feet of open air stretched out in front of me. Below: a shimmering and vast pool of black silk.

No.

Not silk.

Water.

A lake.

I opened my mouth to shout—

—and hit the surface like a meteor striking ground.

Pain.

Everywhere.

I couldn't—

PAIN.

Oh gods.

I couldn't *breathe.*

My ribs screamed. Agony rippled up and down my spine. My head pounded.

Ice cold, the water filled my ears and stung my eyes. It was so black that I couldn't tell which way was up.

My body reacted, my legs kicking and thrashing, panic immediate. Absolute.

My hands clasped, desperate to find something to grab hold of, but there was nothing. Just water. Everywhere, fucking water.

My lungs burned, desperate for oxygen. I had to breathe. I had to. I needed to get to the surface. I had to breathe. I had to—

My body was buffeted by movement in the water. I was shoved sideways. Suddenly there were hands on me. Someone had found me in the dark. I still couldn't see, but I twisted, kicking, reaching, fingers numb from the cold. I latched on to something—fabric—and held on tight. My heart was thunder in my ears as I was dragged upward through the water.

My head breached the surface, and I dragged down a terrified breath, shock relaying around my nervous system. I wasn't safe. There was no ground beneath my feet. I was going to die.

"Shh, Saeris. It's all right. It's all right. Just breathe. Two seconds and we'll be on the shore."

Lorreth. Lorreth had me. Facing away from him, I shook violently in his arms, my teeth chattering as he kicked like a pack of hell cats were on his heels. It took longer than two seconds to reach solid ground, but not much longer.

I sobbed as I tried to sit up in the gentle waves that lapped at the lake's shore; my body felt broken. Some of my ribs were shattered for sure. When I tried to expand my lungs, it was as though I was being lanced in the side with a dagger. "Where's…Carrion?" I wheezed.

Mercifully, Lorreth didn't seem to be injured at all. Soaked to the skin, his hair plastered to his back, the fighter stood at the water's edge, his eyes scanning the dark. I couldn't see anything at all, but that was probably because my head was splintering apart.

"There. I see him," Lorreth panted. "Wait here. I'm going back for him."

Hah! Where the *fuck* did he think I was going? I fell back against the shore, tiny, sharp rocks biting into my skin. The sky was choked with clouds so thick that they cast the world into darkness. I could make out very little at first. And then, as the pain in my chest lessened a little and my eyes adjusted to my new surroundings, I made out the looming cliff face that punched up toward the sky behind me.

The rock was black obsidian, slick as glass. And it was at least a hundred feet tall.

"Fuck," I panted. *"Fuck, fuck, fuck."* A lot had happened in the last three minutes. I'd been standing in the library, and out of nowhere, my friend had crashed through a table. Then I'd been launched up into a shadow gate, fallen eighty feet into an ice-cold body of water, and nearly drowned. None of it had been fun.

I was slowly sitting up when Lorreth re-emerged from the lake, dragging Carrion behind him. The thief wasn't standing on his own two feet, which wasn't a good sign. My worry intensified when Lorreth dumped him onto the rocks, and I realized his eyes were closed, and his lips were blue.

Pain forgotten, I shoved myself up onto my knees. "Why isn't he waking up?"

"He's swallowed a lot of water," Lorreth said tightly. The warrior dropped down and knelt beside Carrion, too. I flinched when he struck Carrion in the center of his chest. The blow would have knocked the wind out of even the biggest fighter's sails, but it didn't stir a response from Carrion.

"Come on," Lorreth muttered. He hit him again.

Still nothing.

I was too scared to blink. "Carrion Swift, if you don't wake up right now, I'm going to tell all of your asshole friends back in the Third that you were a shitty lay."

Lorreth dealt another blow to his solar plexus.

"I mean it!" I cried.

Carrion jolted like he'd been struck by lightning. He rolled toward Lorreth and vomited up a lungful of lake water, hacking and sputtering. Oh, thank the gods. I fell back, landing heavily on my ass, trading a relieved look with Lorreth. When he was done puking, Carrion flopped onto his back and fixed me with narrowed eyes. "You wouldn't...fucking...*dare.*"

It was just the three of us.

Renfis hadn't made it.

The general had boosted Lorreth up into the shadow gate and yelled at him to go.

"I felt it suck me in as it was closing," he said as we gathered ourselves. "If I'd jumped a second later, I think the damned thing would have cut me in half."

He'd had a split second longer than me to process Layne's warning about the water. When he'd started to fall, he'd quickly realized what was happening and tucked himself in tight to prepare for the impact. Carrion had had no warning at all. He said he thought he'd hit the water chest first, and I kind of thought I had, too. It would explain why neither of us could fucking breathe without hissing.

Lorreth fished around in his sodden pockets and took out a small leather bag, cinched shut with a drawstring. While Carrion and I struggled to our feet, he dug around inside the bag and produced a bundle of leaves, which he shook dry as best he could and then offered us each two of them. "Chew them a bit and then put them under your tongues," he advised. "Whatever you do, don't fucking swallow them, though. You'll be shitting yourselves within five minutes."

"What is it?" Carrion asked.

"Widow's Bane. It'll deaden your pain for a couple of hours. Completely deaden it, mind you. We carry it on us at all times in case we need it in battle."

"Why the cheery name?" I made a face when I bit down on the leaves. They were bitter as hell.

"Because they're highly addictive and make you feel like you can take on an army of feeders. Plenty of warriors take them once to dull the pain of an injury. But then they keep on taking them. And then they die."

"Ahh. Good to know." I was very careful not to swallow once I'd chewed the leaves. Popping the mash I made of them under my tongue, I could already feel the plant's numbing properties taking effect.

My mind started to clear a little. And then it started to sharpen.

Where the hell *were* we?

I looked around and did not like what I saw. We were on a beach of sorts, inside a small cove. To our backs, cliffs rose up like a line of jagged teeth. They buttressed the beach, enclosing it so that there was no way around them on either side. There were two ways off the beach. The first—reentering the lake and swimming around the cliffs—was obviously impossible since *neither Carrion nor I could fucking swim.* Which left us with only one other option: up. The three of us stared up at the wall of obsidian, and each of us blanched.

Falling out of a shadow gate and hitting water had been bad enough. But falling from a cliff face and being impaled on a bunch of sharp rocks? That sounded like a great way to punch a one-way ticket to the afterlife, and I wasn't ready to go just yet.

Luckily, Carrion and I had one thing in common: we were both very good at climbing. We'd spent most of our lives scaling the walls of the Third. Walls that were, unbelievably, even taller than this cliff face and far more dangerous to boot. *And* the Widow's Bane was kicking like a mule.

"Are we doing this, then?" Carrion asked, craning his neck to peer up at the very tops of the cliffs.

Fisher was up there.

I knew he was. I could *feel* him.

I blinked up at the cliffs, too, and was taken aback when I saw that it had started to snow. The air was full of fat snowflakes, drifting and swirling down from the sky in lazy circles. One of them landed on my cheek. It was only when I brushed it aside and my fingertips came away marked with a fine gray powder that I realized it wasn't snow at all.

The sky over Gillethrye was raining ash.

As I placed my first handhold on the cliff face, an explosion of sound boomed out into the night. It was so loud, so many crazed voices bellowing and screaming all at once, that it made the pebbles beneath our feet rattle and quake.

"Annorath mor!"

"Annorath mor!"

"Annorath mor!"

"Climb," I shouted. *"Climb!"*

We made it in minutes.

Somehow, by the grace of the gods, in one piece, too.

Our hands were full of deep cuts and slick with blood, but that didn't matter. When we hauled ourselves up over the edge of the cliff, the scene that spread out before us was like something out of a nightmare.

A huge amphitheater, open toward the lake, rose up around us. Tiers and tiers of seating stretched up forever, the structure so overwhelmingly massive that my mind couldn't grasp the sheer size of it. The building, if it could even be called that, was some kind of megastructure. Hundreds of thousands of people sat in the stands, roaring at the top of their lungs.

"Annorath mor! Annorath mor! Annorath mor!"

The terrible chant rocked me to my bones. These were the first words that the quicksilver had hissed at me back in the forge at the

Winter Palace. The words that had affected Fisher in a way I hadn't expected. He'd seemed afraid. And now I knew why. This wasn't just an amphitheater. It was a slaughterhouse. And we were standing on the killing floor.

"What are they screaming?" Carrion breathed.

Lorreth answered in a horrified tone. "Release us."

Release us! Release us! Release us!

I heard it now, as if the words had been translated in my mind. Hundreds of thousands of people, begging to be released. I couldn't bear to look at them.

I focused on the deep pit that had been dug into the ground before us instead. At the sprawling labyrinth within it. On the other side of the labyrinth, I could make out a raised dais, but barely. There were people sitting atop it. And at the foot of the dais, at the top of a set of stone steps that led down into the labyrinth, was Fisher. He was just a smudge of black, tiny in comparison to the colossal structure surrounding us, but I knew it was him. Oh, yes, it was him, all right.

"What in all five hells am I looking at?" Lorreth whispered.

The voice that came from behind us made my blood run cold. The last time I'd heard it, it had been screaming for mercy back in the Hall of Mirrors in Madra's palace. Now it said, "Actually, this is only the first circle of hell, Lorreth of the Broken Spires. But I'd be very happy to introduce you to all five."

The captain of Madra's guard, Harron, stood inches from Lorreth's back. His eyes were orbs of scuffed metal, pure quicksilver, gleaming inside the sockets of his gaunt skull. His lips were thin and peeling, his skin wrinkled and translucent. He broke into a wide grin, displaying shattered teeth, when I noticed the dagger he was pressing against Lorreth's throat.

"I'd slit your throat right here and now just to get to the girl," he wheezed into Lorreth's ear, those freakish eyeballs swiveling around in his head. I could only tell he was looking at me by the way his face was angled toward me. His smile took on a sinister twist. "You've caused all kinds of trouble lately, Saeris. You were supposed to die for me like a good little pet. But never mind, never mind. Perhaps this will be better."

Harron.

How could it be *Harron?* Here, in Yvelia? The sight of him just… made no sense.

Lorreth could have easily taken him. He was a full-blooded Fae warrior, and the captain was human. A very unwell human by the looks of things, but still. It would have been nothing for the warrior to spin around and disarm him. I was sure that's exactly what he would have done, too…if it hadn't been for the hundreds of feeders crawling up over the cliff face behind him.

They scuttled along the ground toward us on all fours, thick strings of venom-tainted saliva hanging from their mouths. These feeders looked fresh, which made them all the more terrifying. Their clothes were a little dirty, but they were mostly intact. The flush of life still clung to their skin. It would fade soon enough, but for now, they still looked like Fae. And they wanted to *eat* us. They crept forward in an encroaching tide, but a twitch from Harron's hand kept them at bay. What power could *Harron* have over these monsters?

The captain held out his free hand; it trembled with effort as the air beside Carrion appeared to harden and then fracture like glass. The fractures turned to fissures, and then the air shattered and fell in on itself, creating a spinning vortex. A sound came out of it, like layers of agonized screaming.

"The walk would take far too long," Harron said. "And we don't want you to miss out on the beginning of the games now, do we?" He jerked his head toward the vortex. "In. Now. If you hurry, there might still be time for you to say goodbye to your friend."

This was nothing like Fisher's shadow gate. Harron's vortex wasn't right. It felt like a perversion of nature, and my gut told me firmly and in no uncertain terms that I should not step inside it. But what choice did I have? At least three hundred feeders were crowded on the cliff's edge now. Their eyes were blank voids, showing no signs of the Fae they used to be. Only hunger. Only death. I would rather have jumped back into the middle of that lake than enter the shimmering distortion in the air...but I caught Lorreth's eye, and my friend nodded.

"It's fine, Saeris. Go. We'll be right behind you."

I hope to the gods this doesn't go horribly wrong. I looked back over my shoulder at the dais and that small black smudge standing at the top of the stairs, and my stomach rolled with nerves. *We're here, Fisher. For what it's worth, we're coming.*

I didn't expect a reply, but as I entered Harron's gate, I got one.

Saeris? Fisher's voice was full of panic in my mind. *Saeris, do not come here!*

But it was already too late. Harron's vortex was ripping me to pieces.

INTRODUCTIONS

He was the first thing I saw.

Always.

My heart and my soul knew exactly where to find him.

On his knees, covered in blood, Fisher knelt at the foot of a small series of steps that led up to the dais. He was covered in cuts and scrapes, his hair damp with sweat. The wolf-head gorget still shone at his throat, but it was splattered with blood, both red and black, and his leather armor was destroyed. Huge slashes cut across his chest protector. The bracers at his wrists were caked with gore. He looked exhausted, breathing raggedly through his mouth. He didn't turn his head, but he looked at me out of the corner of his eye, and I saw the fear and devastation there.

You shouldn't be here, Little Osha, he said in my mind. His words rang with defeat. His shoulders sagged, his eyes closing when Lorreth and Carrion emerged from the gate beside me, Harron close on our heels. *I wanted to save you from this. I didn't want you to suffer with me.*

As if a bolt of energy suddenly ripped right through him, Fisher threw his head back, his teeth bared, the muscles in his neck straining.

"NO!" I tried to run to him, but my feet wouldn't move. I was frozen in place.

"Greetings, friends. Welcome! We haven't been formally introduced." Cold as ice, the voice cut through the air like a scythe.

"Gods alive," Lorreth hissed. I didn't want to look away from Fisher, but I had to. I needed to know who—

Holy...

Fucking...

Hell...

The Widow's Bane was making me hallucinate.

There was no other explanation for what I was seeing.

There, sitting in the center of the dais, was Malcolm. His fine features and long, silver hair made him instantly recognizable. It was he who had spoken. It could only have been him, because I *had* met the other figures who sat on either side of him. *They* knew perfectly well who I was.

To the right of the dais sat Belikon.

To the left...Madra.

Both were dressed in regal finery, the Yvelian king in hunter-green velvet, the Zilvaren Queen bedecked in a high-necked, sparkling golden gown.

I tried to blink them away, but there they remained, impossibly, sitting beside the vampire king.

Carrion had blanched, his usual arrogance gone. He assessed the three figures up on the dais with open hatred in his eyes.

"I assume," Malcolm said, "since no one appears willing to perform introductions, that you are Saeris. And from your stature and the wolf emblazoned across your chest, that *you* are one of Kingfisher's Lupo Proelia. Not the general who's caused so much trouble for me, though. No, I've met Renfis. So that must make you Lorreth. Lorreth, who shattered the towers at Barillieth and murdered thousands of my children." His cool gray eyes flashed with rage. His anger stalled when his gaze landed on Carrion. "You, I don't know."

Carrion dipped into a low bow, but the gesture was not one of deference. It was designed to mock. "Carrion Sw—"

Malcolm nodded to Harron, and the guard brought the hilt of his dagger crashing down onto the back of Carrion's head. The blow cut Carrion off and sent him crashing to his knees.

Fisher growled, still straining against the pain that was clearly still racking his body. Lorreth and I both reached for our swords, but Belikon let out a rumbling laugh, holding up his hand. "I caution all of you against foolishness. Your swords won't do you any good here. Can't you feel it in the air?" He grinned, gesturing up at the sky, and the flakes of ash that still floated down on the air. "This place is a graveyard. The air itself is full of death. The ground beneath us is bones and ash. Your magic cannot reach you here."

Madra, with her fair hair bound into a beautiful braid beneath her glittering crown, made a disgruntled sound. "You should have at least let them try, Brother. I was looking forward to seeing the look on their faces when they realized how much trouble they were in."

Brother?

But...how could Belikon be her *brother?*

Human. Fae. Vampire. The three regents all adopted similar expressions of satisfaction as they took in our confusion.

I couldn't hold my tongue. "You really think she's your ally? You're wrong. She's the one who stilled the quicksilver and closed the gates between all of the realms."

Belikon snorted. "Of course she was. We've always known it was Madra. And yes, we were angry at first. But it's amazing how unimportant these little tiffs seem after centuries."

"Indeed," Madra agreed. "And after all, I did only close the gate because you sent that beast through to assassinate me. So there was much to forgive on *my* end, too."

Belikon inclined his head, accepting this velvet-gloved accusation. "It's true. You're perfectly right, Sister. Mistakes were made on all sides. Lucky for us, we have the opportunity to make past wrongs right. And now that our Triumvirate is reunited, all three of us are more powerful than we've been in an age."

Belikon had known? All these years, he'd known that Madra was the one who had closed the gates, and he'd blamed Fisher's father. He had sent Finran to Zilvaren, to his death, and then had blamed him for the closing of the portals between the realms. He had named him traitor and cast shame on the House of Cahlish because of it. Edina had paid. Fisher had paid, over and over and over again.

A fury like no other churned in my gut as I stared at the king.

It seemed Lorreth shared my rage. "You're a fucking disgrace," he seethed. "How can you sit up there next to *him?* Our people have been at war with Malcolm for...for—"

"War?" Belikon sneered. "We haven't been at *war*, you fool. I've simply been feeding my brother's army."

There was that word again. Brother. I still didn't fully understand, but some pieces of this puzzle were snapping into place. Belikon had refused to send supplies and food down to Irrìn. He'd embargoed silver—the only thing capable of permanently killing Malcolm's kind—and had refused to send any of it south. And why *would* he waste supplies on warriors he didn't intend to survive? Why *would* he arm warriors with deadly weapons if he didn't actually want them to kill their enemy?

"Hadn't you better give your plaything a break, Malcolm?" Madra purred. She eyed Fisher with keen interest. "Be a shame if he died before he could play your little game. I'd love to see if he beats you again. I missed out the first time."

Malcolm started, chuckling softly. "Oh! Of course! I promised you a little sport, didn't I? My apologies, Sister." He made no gesture to release Fisher from whatever invisible torture he was exacting upon him. Fisher just collapsed forward onto his hands and knees, gasping for air, suddenly free. Malcolm lifted a cut-glass chalice to his mouth, and the thick, viscous liquid inside stained his pale lips red. His bloody smile was full of glee as he said, "You know, it *does* bring me such joy to be reunited, the three of us. You've missed much, Madra. We've been having a wonderful time. Especially lately. The fall of Gillethrye was a sight to behold, wasn't it, Brother?"

"Spectacular," Belikon agreed. "You were there, weren't you, Dog? You got to witness the whole thing from start to finish. You had a front-row seat!"

"Fuck...*you*..." Fisher rasped. "I'm going...to fucking *destroy* you."

My heart slammed in my chest, my blood racing. Everlayne's father got to his feet. His face contorted with hatred as he descended the steps toward Fisher. "Just like Finran. Foul-mouthed and arrogant. So superior. So self-righteous. But you are less than the dirt beneath my feet, *Kingfisher*." He spat his name like it was a curse. "Why don't you tell your precious friends what you did here, hmm?" He grabbed a fistful of Fisher's hair and wrenched his head back. "What's the matter, boy? Cat got your tongue? Oh, wait. That's right. You *can't* tell them what you did here, can you?"

Belikon moved faster than he should have been able to. His knee whipped forward, connecting with Fisher's jaw. The blow landed hard, sending Fisher sprawling back onto the stone. In the stands, the crowd roared out their approval.

"*No!*" I stepped forward, but hands closed around my arms. Guards. From the Winter Palace. There were *normal* Fae here? My mind reeled. I met the eyes of the male who held tight to my right arm, and I saw his shame. He knew this was wrong, and yet he was still here, obeying the orders of a psychopath. "Let me go!"

Belikon opened his arms wide, spinning around, ever the showman. He laughed, his voice booming over the dais. "What do you think, Malcolm? Should I tell them what he did? Or should I release him from his oath and make *him* tell them?"

Malcolm took another swig from the blood in his glass goblet and shrugged one of his shoulders, considering the thousands of people sitting in the amphitheater stands. "I think we should ask them," he said in an airy tone. "After all, *they're* the ones he killed."

"*Liar.*" Lorreth looked as though he was about to launch himself up onto the dais and rip Malcolm's head from his shoulders. "It wasn't his fault!"

The ones he *killed?* What was Malcolm talking about? I looked up at the stands, at last forcing myself to look upon the people there. Row after row—the seats were packed with Fae, their clothes black, their skin...

Wait.

Their skin...was *burned*. Their clothes weren't just black. They were smoldering. Their mouths were fixed into terrible screams. And their eyes. Gods, their eyes. They were either missing or melted to gelatin and running out of their eye sockets. Females. Children. Males. All dead. All burned alive, and yet somehow still animated, trapped in their misery.

Carrion strained against the Fae guards who held him, taking in the nightmare that surrounded us. "Fuck *me,*" he whispered.

Belikon clapped his hands together, thoroughly enjoying our horror. "You're right. We *should* ask them," he said. When he shouted his question, his voice carried to every corner of the amphitheater, supernaturally loud. "What say you, Fae of Gillethrye? Should I remove the dog's gag? Should he confess his crimes at last?"

The crescendo of shouts that followed was ferocious. I couldn't make out whether they were in favor or against Belikon freeing Fisher from the oath that had prevented him from talking about this for so long. It was all just noise. Belikon seemed delighted with the response. "Wonderful. Wonderful. The Fae of Gillethrye have spoken." He turned back to Fisher. Slapping his hands down on his shoulders, the king gave Fisher a rough shake. "I release you from your oath to us, Kingfisher, Bane of Gillethrye. Now, go on. Tell your friends *all* about the deal you struck with us all those years ago."

41

GILLETHRYE

FISHER WIPED blood from his mouth, fighting to get to his feet. It looked as though the effort of it cost him the last of his strength, but slowly, he managed it. My heart nearly shattered when he staggered toward us and I registered the true extent of his injuries.

You can barely walk.

There was so much pain in his eyes. It wasn't caused by the lacerations that crisscrossed his body. It was because of this place.

I'll be fine, Osha. Inside my head, his voice was a whisper.

Lorreth reached for Fisher to help him stand, but Harron snarled, shoving him back. "What have they done to you?" the warrior demanded.

Fisher smiled, his teeth stained with blood. "I believe you called it...payback? Right, Harron?"

"Less than you deserve for what you did to me," the guard spat. "I would have killed you myself if—"

"Shut your mouth, human," Belikon snapped. "Kingfisher has a story to share. Tell them how you thought you could trick *me*, Dog."

Wearily, Fisher spoke at last. "The horde had gathered at the gates of Gillethrye. Tens of thousands of vampires. Our armies in the south had been drawn into a battle with a much smaller force, but it had been a distraction. We found out that the better part of Malcolm's feeders had marched on Gillethrye too late. I couldn't move enough warriors through my shadow gate, so I brought Ren and some of the other wolves to try and save as many as we could."

"The *arrogance*," Belikon hissed. "Seven warriors against twenty thousand. He truly thought he could hold them back!"

Fisher continued on, ignoring the king. "We didn't get here in time. The horde was already inside the city when we arrived. The Fae had all been out in the streets, celebrating the Festival of the First Song, which only made the horde's job easier. They swept through the city like locusts, feeding on anything they came across, either draining their victims or consigning them to an agonizing death."

Lorreth hung his head, nodding as if he knew all of this and the retelling of it hurt his soul. But his eyes snapped up when Fisher said, "I left Ren and the others, and I went to find Malcolm. I'd decided I was going to try and kill him by myself. But it wasn't Malcolm that I found. At least not at first. It was the bastard who murdered my mother."

Belikon ran his tongue over his teeth. "You think you can shame me by airing my sins? Think again. Your bitch of a mother was supposed to be the greatest oracle of our time, but she was useless." He cackled. "I admit it. As soon as she was done pushing out the brat I forced upon her, I slit the bitch's throat. I was sick of her fucking lies."

"She never lied to you," Fisher said flatly. "Her life could have depended on it, and she would only have been able to tell you the truth."

Belikon brushed Fisher's words aside. "Just get on with it. Tell them about the deal we made."

"Malcolm arrived at the head of his host, and that's when I learned that he and Belikon weren't adversaries at all. They were allies and had been working together since before the blood curse. I didn't know that Madra was also in league with them until today. I wanted to bargain for the few citizens of Gillethrye who were still alive, and Belikon proposed a deal. He found a coin. One used only in Gillethrye. The smallest denomination of currency the Fae had here. He said if the coin hit the ground and landed leaf-side up, Malcolm would call off his horde and leave the city without hurting another living thing. But if the coin hit the ground and landed fish-side up, he would take the city as his own and destroy it, and I would have to leave those still alive to their deaths and meet him on the field of battle at a later date."

"You're leaving out all of the best parts," Belikon interjected. "He also wasn't allowed to touch the coin or influence the way it fell. While the coin toss was being decided, he wasn't allowed to harm me or my brother. Not a hair on either of our pretty heads. And, until the outcome of the coin toss had been decided, he wasn't allowed to speak of the deal or of the fact that Malcolm and I were brothers. And he agreed. He was so desperate to save a handful of peasants that he made the blood oath with me."

Malcolm called from the dais. "Pay attention, now! This is my favorite part!"

Belikon paused before Fisher. He stood with the bulb of his nose an inch away from his cheek, his presence meant to intimidate, I thought, but Fisher stared straight at me. He didn't acknowledge the evil piece of shit. "I tossed the coin..." he said.

"And *I* caught it!" Malcolm held his glass aloft, toasting himself.

"The coin never hit the ground," I whispered.

"The coin never hit the ground!" Belikon jeered.

A bottomless sadness flickered in Fisher's beautiful eyes. The quicksilver was fine as lace, threaded all through his right iris, completely still.

"Malcolm's children feasted, didn't they, Dog?" Belikon leered, shoving his face closer to Fisher's, so that his forehead butted against the side of Fisher's skull. Still, he got no reaction out of him. It was amazing how controlled he was. My eyes swam with unshed tears as I focused on the wings that spread out from underneath the silver plate at his throat.

"I torched the city, then," Fisher said. He didn't sugarcoat it. Didn't dress it up. "I barricaded it and trapped everyone inside. Malcolm's horde had either bitten or killed everyone. They were transitioning right before our eyes. Gillethrye was home to nearly two hundred thousand High Fae and Lesser Fae. If they were allowed to join Malcolm's horde, they would have swallowed the entire realm. So I gave the order. I did what had to be done."

"A cunt of a move," Malcolm said, pouting coquettishly. He'd come down from the dais and was in the process of helping Madra descend the stone steps. The fine hairs on my arms bristled as the two of them approached. "I love bending the rules in my favor. I don't love it so much when they're bent against me. So, I decided to torment poor little Kingfisher some more. I have to admit, it was a little cruel, but..."

"You've always had such an affinity for turning cruelty into an art form, Brother," Madra simpered. She let go of Malcolm's hand and slowly walked a circle around Fisher, her eyes lit up with intrigue. "He is *unbearably* handsome, isn't he? I can see why you wanted to keep him as a pet. I can't wait to hear what happened next."

"Well, I created the most diabolically lethal labyrinth I could conjure in my mind, dear sister," Malcolm said, as if this should have been obvious. "I hid Belikon's coin at its center, and then I created this colosseum around it and filled the stands with the perpetually burning bodies of all the creatures our poor little bleeding heart here had wanted to save. All he had to do to end their suffering was find the coin and make it fall to the ground. Obviously, it would be too late to save the Fae from death, but at least it would end their suffering. And *then*," he added with a dramatic flourish, "he would be free to seek his vengeance by calling me out onto the battlefield."

Madra ran her fingers along Fisher's jaw, wetting her bottom lip.

"Don't fucking *touch* him!" I thrashed, trying to tear myself free of the guards, but the hold they had on me tightened. The queen smirked, moving even closer to Fisher so that her peaked nipples, poking through the sheer material of her dress, brushed his arm as she circled him.

Fisher growled, low and menacing. He turned hate-filled eyes on the queen of Zilvaren. "Remove yourself from me, or you won't like what happens next."

"Oh, please." Madra waved away his threat. "I hate to tell you this, but I can do anything to you that I want. Malcolm has always let me play with his toys."

"I play back," Fisher spat. "It might not be today, but oh, I am coming to find *you*, Madra. Fear the shadows, bitch. I'm made of them. One night soon, I'll climb out of one and slit your fucking throat."

"What a lucky girl I am." Madra feigned nonchalance, but I could see it, even from here, plain as day. Fisher's venom had shaken her a little. "And what, pray tell, have *I* done to deserve such special attention from the likes of you?"

"You spayed my mate when she was a fucking *child*," he seethed. "For that alone, I'll make your undying existence an unending agony. An eternity of suffering the likes of which even your evil mind cannot comprehend. You'll know no peace at my hands. I will destroy your empire and erase your name from the annals of time. When I am done with your legacy, Madra the Undying will never have existed. And you'll live on at my behest, suffering for all of eternity. And no one will know. And no one will care."

His words rocked me. The pure, unadulterated hatred in them. I had no idea that it had affected him this badly. When I'd told him about what had been done to me, he'd reacted strangely, yes, but...to provoke a response from him like *this*?

Kingfisher of the Ajun Gate was on his knees in the dirt. He was broken and bleeding, but his promise of retribution was still terrifying enough to make a queen tremble. Madra staggered back, her smile sliding from her face.

"I see what you mean, Brother," she said shakily, looking to Belikon. "He is quite foul-tempered, isn't he?"

"Do you mind? You're ruining my story," Malcolm huffed.

Madra attempted to marshal herself, but she couldn't quite look at Fisher now. "You're right, darling. I apologize. And what did our wayward hero do then?"

"He entered my labyrinth and entertained us all for such a very long time." Malcolm clapped Fisher on the back. "I sent some of my other friends to play with him sometimes. From time to time, I would visit him myself. We always had such *scintillating* conversations. And then, one day, he made it to the center of the labyrinth. I have to say, I was shocked. I thought it would take him a lot longer than it did. What was it, Fisher? A hundred years?"

"A hundred and two." His eyes were back on me now, locked fast, as if I were an anchor in a storm, the only thing capable of grounding him.

"That's right. A hundred and two. He spent the next eight years trying to find the coin once he reached the center, didn't you, my love?"

For the first time since the three regents had started toying with him, Fisher flinched.

I did, too.

My love. Of all the things Malcolm could have called him...

Fisher...

He gave me the smallest shake of his head. *Don't. Don't give them anything. It'll only make them worse.*

Malcolm chuckled. "Then, one day, Taladaius was checking in on our Kingfisher, and he said that the ground shook so violently that the stone cracked beneath his feet, and a hole appeared. And lo and behold: a secret."

"Let me guess," Madra said. "There was a quicksilver pool below your lovely labyrinth. And it had been awakened."

"Exactly! Very astute."

Belikon narrowed rheumy eyes at me accusingly. "The very same vibrations rocked my palace."

Malcolm tutted. "Such mayhem. Such chaos! Our Kingfisher took one look at the quicksilver pool, and Taladaius said he dropped down into the hole and waded into it without a second thought. Disappeared and didn't come back. I was surprised, Fisher. I gave you the opportunity to leave my labyrinth so many times, but you never accepted. And then you just upped and left out of the blue? With all of these poor creatures waiting on you to end their suffering? It seemed *highly* out of character. Tell me," Malcolm said, spinning on the balls of his feet. "I've been dying to know. After a hundred and ten years in that labyrinth, what made you finally leave?"

"You bored him to fucking tears and he couldn't take it anymore," Carrion sniped. Up until now, he'd held his tongue, but it was a miracle that he'd lasted this long. Carrion wasn't the type to let an opportunity to offend someone pass him by, regardless of how dire the situation was. Malcolm stalked forward and closed his hand around Carrion's throat. The vampire king bared his fangs as he leaned in close to Carrion's neck.

"I don't like you, human. Something about you smells...*off.*"

"That's probably the weird...moss...these water sprites rubbed... all over me..." Carrion croaked. "It had a strange...funk...to it."

Gods alive, he didn't know when to quit.

"Smart mouth," Malcolm sneered. "I'll enjoy draining you once all of this is done."

"You want to know why I went into that quicksilver?" Fisher asked. It was a distraction. Something to divert attention away from Carrion. If we ever got out of this alive, I was going to wring the smuggler's neck for his stupidity, and I thought Fisher might, too. Fisher's ploy worked, though. Malcolm let go of Carrion, disgust playing over his features as he turned back to Fisher.

"He left because the madness in his veins broke him at last," Belikon ventured. "We all knew it would eventually. He was afflicted with it long before he showed up at the gates of Gillethrye."

"Is that true, my love?" Malcolm asked. "Has that quicksilver in your head finally pushed you beyond the bounds of sanity?"

Fisher rubbed his forehead. "I've felt better. But no. That isn't the reason why I left." He angled his shoulders a little, shifting his weight into the balls of his feet. I was watching him so intently that I saw it happen. I'd seen him fight enough times to know that Fisher didn't just shift his weight for no reason.

I stiffened, eyes widening. *What are you doing, Fisher?*

His brows twitched. Barely noticeable. *Just don't move.* To Malcolm, he said, "I went into that quicksilver because I felt my father's sword calling to me. And I knew I'd need it for this."

He became smoke. He was hurt and tired, but I'd never witnessed him move this fast. He came for *me.* One hand closed on my hip. The other reached to the other hip—for the sword there, sitting in its scabbard. He drew Solace, the blade becoming a flare of brilliant light in the ash-choked air, and then Fisher was spinning. He moved like liquid. Like lightning. Like *vengeance.*

Ducking low, he spun, reversing the weapon so the tip of the blade pointed down. Dropping to one knee, he clasped the hilt in both hands and drove the sword in an arc, back and up...

...into Belikon's stomach.

It happened fast. Really fast. I was barely able to track the movement.

Belikon hadn't expected it, that was for sure. A wet gurgle came out of the Yvelian king's mouth as Fisher ripped his father's sword free, spun again, and drove the tip straight into Belikon's throat. He gritted his teeth as he leaned his weight on the weapon, and the gleaming blade pushed all the way out the back of Belikon's neck.

"I don't need magic to mess you up, you *fuck*," he growled. "This is for me. But mostly, it's for my parents."

Madra, Undying Queen of the shining Silver City, the Banner in the North, unleashed a bloodcurdling scream. And all hell broke loose.

42

THAT'LL COST YOU

A RIVER of blood spewed down Belikon's chin. It flowed from the gaping hole in his stomach, too, thick and steaming hot in the cold night
air. Malcolm's eyes narrowed to vertical slits, black veins creeping
down his cheeks.

"That was ill-advised." The vampire lunged, launching at Fisher,
but sharp silver slashed through the air, bringing him up short.
Avisiéth nicked his neck, the very end of Lorreth's sword barely kiss-
ing the vampire's skin, but it was enough to make the bastard screech.
Black smoke hissed from the tiny wound.

"RUN!" Fisher bellowed.

Chaos exploded on the amphitheater floor.

Harron darted for me. The guards restraining me, idiots that
they were, let me go as the silver-eyed monster flew in our direction.
With my hands free, I palmed the daggers strapped to my thighs and
moved.

Harron's run-in with the quicksilver had definitely taken its
toll. The captain still moved with lethal determination, but he was
nowhere near as fast as he had been. And my hands weren't tied

behind my back this time. Adopting an offensive stance, I sprung into his guard, surprising him. He must have thought I would do nothing but defend, but the dagger I thrust up into his gut none-too-politely notified him otherwise.

"Bitch!" he roared. Retreating, he stared down at the dagger protruding from his body, then ripped it out. The metal clattered to the stone.

Five feet away, Carrion wielded Simon like he'd been training with the weapon for years. He cut through three feeders, slicing their heads from their shoulders in quick order.

"MOVE!" Fisher boomed. "*TO THE LABYRINTH!*"

"So eager to run back into your cage, pet?" Malcolm called to him. With his head dipped and his shoulders tensed up around his ears, he looked like a dune viper, coiling back, preparing to strike. He knocked aside Madra's guards in their shining golden armor as he prowled not for Fisher, but for Lorreth.

The warrior dropped low, Avisiéth raised again, ready to take on the vampire, but Fisher's voice cut across the melee. "Lorreth, no! Don't engage! I mean it! Get into the labyrinth!"

"That'll cost you," Harron said. And he smashed the hilt of his dagger into my nose. I'd let myself lose focus, and it *had* cost me. Blood exploded out of my nose, spraying Harron's gaunt face, but... the pain I braced for didn't come.

The Widow's Bane. Thank fuck for the Widow's Bane.

Belikon was on his knees, teetering like he was about to topple over, but he wasn't dead. I heard the scrape Solace made when Fisher dragged it free—metal on bone—but I didn't make the same mistake twice. I tore my gaze away from Fisher and gave every bit of my attention to Harron. "You're in way over your head, Rat," the captain hissed. "The pieces of this game have been in play for millennia. You can't begin to comprehend—"

I advanced, my remaining dagger gripped loosely in my hand. Inside Harron's guard again, I slashed his shoulder and drew blood. He was wrong. Yes, the players in this game had been making moves for centuries. But that didn't change the nature of the game. It was kill or be killed, and I knew what I had to do to win.

"For pity's sake, *end her!*" Madra commanded. The queen hadn't entered the fight. She watched from the sidelines, mad with rage, the front of her beautiful dress sprayed with ichor.

"How many centuries has she been using you to do her dirty work, Harron?" I panted. Darting back, away from his dagger, I moved out of his reach. "Shouldn't you have been in the ground a long time ago?"

"Madra gifted me with eternity—"

"So that you could serve her. So that you could be her fucking slave. Most prisoners' sentences end. They're released, or they"—I dodged a cutting upward sweep of his dagger—"walk through that black door you spoke of. But you just keep on suffering, don't you."

"Death has forgotten me, bitch. My name is nowhere on his register."

I felt the cold smile unfurling across my face. I'd been haunted by the idea of this moment. Harron had owned me the last time we'd faced each other. I should have died at his hand, and that knowledge had made me fear facing him again. But now that the moment had come…I realized that I was better than him.

I paused, making my delay look like hesitation, and the captain fell for the bait. He charged, dagger swinging right for my throat, but I dropped to the ground and swept out his legs from underneath him. It was straightforward from there. I twisted and fell on top of him. Wrapped my legs around his throat, and squeezed.

"Get up! Stop toying with her!"

Madra's petulant cry sounded far away. My ears were full of Harron's labored wheezing. He tried to stab backward and plunge his dagger into my thigh, but I batted away his arm and wrenched his wrist into an unnatural angle. Harron dropped the dagger.

Feigning shock, I said, "Wait a minute. I think Death just remembered your name, Harron." And then I snapped his neck.

"SAERIS! NOW!" The cry came from Lorreth. Malcolm was on

his back at the top of the stairs that led down into the labyrinth. I hadn't seen how he'd gotten there, but he looked like he was rousing himself and seconds from getting up.

To my left, Fisher shoved Carrion with one hand, holding back six feeders with the other. Carrion stumbled and fell down the stairs. Fisher speared one of the feeders through the stomach, then landed a blow to its neck with the flat of Solace's blade so powerful that it knocked the monster's head off rather than severed it. Eyes wild, he swung his gaze across the platform until he found me.

Go! Now! he commanded. *I'm right behind you.*

"Harron!" Madra shook with grief. She broke into a run, heading straight for me. I didn't wait to find out what she would do when she got to me. I snatched the dagger Harron had pulled from his stomach and sprinted toward the stairs. My feet barely touched the ground as I raced down them and reached Lorreth and Carrion. Both had their swords in hand, ready.

Relief hit me square in my solar plexus when I felt Fisher's hand on my back. He hadn't wasted any time catching up. "Move, move, move!" he shouted.

Together, the four of us ran.

The opening of the labyrinth loomed ahead, foreboding and dark. As I raced into its yawning mouth, I realized that its slick back walls were made of obsidian. And they were razor sharp.

"Run all you like!" Malcolm shouted after us. "The labyrinth is my domain. It's going to eat you alive!"

Fisher grabbed my hand as we ran. He didn't let go.

"Where the hell are we going?" Lorreth panted.

Fisher pulled me to the left, down a corridor of obsidian that looked like a dead end. But it wasn't. A narrow opening, barely wide enough to accommodate a body, opened up to the right, and he ushered us through. "The first ten moves to the labyrinth are always the same. That's where you face the first obstacle. Then the route to the center changes."

"What do you mean, the route changes?" Carrion demanded.

"I mean it fucking changes. The walls move. Go!"

Carrion blanched, but he ran. I wasn't so worried about the walls moving part. I was more concerned about the word "obstacle." And the fact that Fisher had been stuck in here for over a hundred years. He wouldn't have told us to come in here if he didn't think it was our safest option, though.

He guided us right again. Lorreth skidded as he rushed through the corner, his feet going out from underneath him. He crashed into the wall ahead but scrambled up and kept running. Awesome. It wasn't just the walls that were slick obsidian; the ground was, too.

"Left! Go left!" Fisher cried.

Tell me you have a plan. It was a hell of a lot easier speaking into someone's mind when you were sprinting for your life.

Fisher replied, *Yes, I have one.*

Great. What is it?

He answered right away. *You.*

What do you mean, me? He was joking. If he was, then his sense of humor was almost as bad as Carrion's.

In a minute, he said.

I was about to say, no, now, but then we emerged into an opening, and my stomach bottomed out. There, in the center of the opening, was the kind of monster that I thought only existed in nightmares. Zilvaren had plenty of spiders. Sand trap spiders the size of dinner plates that would numb your skin with their saliva while you were sleeping and eat your fingers. But this...this was...

"Holy *fuck!*" Carrion skidded and slipped onto his ass, nearly colliding with the thing. It was three times the height of a full-grown man, with more legs than I could count. Its hind abdomen was a fleshy bulb, mottled red and black and covered in coarse long hairs. But then...my insides twisted as I took in the rest of it. Its front half was part Fae. A male torso with a distended, bloated stomach. Thin, emaciated arms. Wisps of greasy black hair stuck to its otherwise bald head. It had no ears. No eyes or nose, either. Its face comprised nothing but a massive circular mouth, with concentric row after row of jagged teeth.

It let out a high-pitched whine, its head whipping toward Carrion, and Fisher spat out a curse. "Don't move, Swift."

"What the hell are you talking about!" Carrion called back. "I'm one hundred percent going to move."

"Stay the fuck where you are," Fisher growled. "It can't see or hear you. It tracks movement."

"But—"

"You move, you die," Fisher barked.

"Okaaaayyyy."

Lorreth pressed his back to the wall, clutching Avisiéth to his chest. "I fucking hate spiders," he said.

"That's not a spider. That's Morthil. It's a demon. And it'll stun you with its stinger and eat you alive if it catches you. Slowly. Over a period of days—"

"Please stop talking and tell me how I'm *not* getting eaten," Carrion whimpered.

Fisher hooked his pinkie finger around mine and blew out a shaky breath. "We've got one chance at this," he said. "There are three exits to this enclosure. Two of them lead to other enclosures, and we do *not* want to go to those. Trust me."

Lorreth hadn't blinked since he'd laid eyes on the demon. "But you said the walls move. How the hell are we supposed to pick the right one?"

Fisher moved his head a fraction, very slowly, and looked to me out of the corner of his eye. "There's a quicksilver pool at the center of this labyrinth, Saeris. You need to find it."

"*What?*"

The spider demon snapped its head in my direction, leaning forward. It took a step, its long, spindly legs working in concert, and Carrion moaned. Its front right leg was raised, hovering in the air, right over him. If it brought it down, it would land right on his head.

"No rush or anything, Fane, but if you could sniff out that quicksilver pretty quickly, I'd sure appreciate it," he said, his voice three octaves higher than usual.

My initial surprise over what Fisher wanted me to do dissipated. Now I had a job to do. One I felt fairly confident I could accomplish. "A whole pool of it?" I asked.

Fisher squeezed my hand. "A big one."

I closed my eyes and concentrated.

It didn't take long to feel the quicksilver. It was there, chanting along with the tortured souls of Gillethrye.

Annorath mor!

Annorath mor!

I opened my eyes and looked in the direction we had to go. "There," I said. "That way."

"*Which* way?" Carrion called nervously.

"The path on the far left," Fisher called.

"*The one right behind the fucking demon?*"

"Just stay still and wait until I tell you to move," Fisher said.

Lorreth adjusted his grip on Avisiéth, scanning all four corners of the enclosure. "How are we doing this?"

"*Feed. I feed.*" The demon didn't move its bristling mouth. The raspy words came from its throat somehow. It extended its front legs, prodding the air, looking for its prey.

Lorreth pulled a horrified face. "Urgh! Not on us, you're not!"

If we ever made it out of this, I was going to be traumatized for the rest of my life. Fisher had encountered this thing more than once. He'd faced it without knowing which path to take. Had it *caught* him? Had it...

No. Don't think about that. Not now.

I exhaled, pulling myself together.

"Throw a rock and distract it or something," Carrion said.

"That won't work. It's smarter than it looks. It can gauge the size of objects in motion. It can't differentiate between large objects that are close together, though. If we press back against the wall and move slowly, we can skirt around the perimeter of the enclosure and then make a run for it."

"And where does that leave me?" Carrion asked.

"That leaves you sliding along the floor very slowly," Fisher said. "Try not to lift your arms or legs too far from the ground. Get moving."

Lorreth went first, creeping along the wall, his throat bobbing every other second. The demon cocked its head in twitchy movements, searching this way and that, trying to detect us, but Fisher was right—it didn't seem to be able to differentiate us from the walls of the labyrinth. Carrion swung his arms out from his body, pressing his palms into the ground, and managed to shunt himself forward. He didn't make much progress with each push, but it was better than nothing.

Lorreth reached the exit behind the demon first. From my position, flat against the wall, I watched him slump behind the wall, his shoulders sagging with relief. "Come on." He motioned with his hands. "Let's get the hell out of here."

I reached him next.

Fisher was only two feet from us, when the wall Lorreth and I were leaning against groaned, shuddered, and began to move. *"Shit."* Fisher made eye contact with me and then swung around to look at Morthil. The spider demon slowly turned its head toward us, an eerie clicking sound coming from its hideous mouth. And Fisher whispered, *"Move!"*

The demon exploded into action. Its legs splayed, skittering on the obsidian as it charged across the enclosure. Fisher lunged for Carrion and grabbed him by the wrist, dragging him toward the exit. Lorreth was there in an instant. He fisted the front of Carrion's shirt and pulled him to his feet. But Morthil was already on us.

Fisher angled Solace and batted away one of the demon's legs. The blade cut clean through it and sent it sailing through the air. Morthil screamed—pain and fury blending together in an ear-splitting cry.

Carrion brought up Simon and parried forward, stabbing the demon in its swollen belly, which only enraged it further. It reared back and climbed the wall beside us, frantically thrusting with its curved stinger, seeking flesh. It found polished obsidian instead. Its stinger smashed into the wall with force, punching giant holes into the rock.

"Go!" Fisher yelled. *"Go!"*

We ran.

All four of us made it out of the enclosure, but Morthil followed us, scaling the walls, skittering behind us until it caught up.

"It isn't supposed to leave the enclosure!" Fisher shouted. The demon clambered up, using both walls on either side of us, and sprung forward so that its body was right over us.

"I FEED!" it roared. Its abdomen flexed and thrust down into the path between the walls, its stinger driving through the gap. I reacted on instinct, first darting back against the wall and then spinning my dagger over and plunging it down into the demon's abdomen. I had been aiming for its stinger, but the hit I landed was still decent. Fisher took advantage of the demon's howl of shock and lopped off another of its legs.

Losing its traction on the right wall, Morthil fell back down into the narrow passageway and hit the ground with a thump, nearly crushing Lorreth beneath it. The warrior jumped back, raised Avisiéth, and drove the sword into the beast's grotesque mouth. He grunted, shoving his weight against the weapon's hilt, and the tip of the blade pushed out of the back of the demon's skull.

"Yes!" Carrion cried. "Is it dead?"

"Temporarily. It'll respawn soon. It'll come back smaller but also faster," Fisher said.

"Then let's get the hell out of here before that happens."

Fisher's hand in mine was reassuring, but he was no longer in the lead. I was. I could feel the quicksilver getting closer as we ran, but we had a problem.

"Why have we stopped?" Carrion shrieked.

"The walls keep shifting," I bit out. "Which means the path keeps changing. I need to make sure we're going the right way, but if *you* want to take the lead, then be my guest."

The thief held up his hands. "You're right. I apologize. I'm just a little on edge right now. I'm not my best self."

I shut him out, trying to make the decision. It was a simple choice: left, right, or straight. The passageways seemed to stretch forever into the distance, and my nerves got the better of me.

What happens if we stumble into one of those other enclosures? I asked Fisher in private.

Very bad things, he replied. *But don't overthink it, Saeris. You can do this. Just focus on getting us to the center of the labyrinth. If we run into any other problems on the way, we'll handle it.*

"Very bad things" wasn't what I'd wanted to hear, but I took a deep breath and plunged forward. "It's this way." We went right. Four seconds later, the walls started moving, the obsidian scraping as it cut off the passage ahead of us.

"Damn it." I took the next left, following the tugging in the pit of my stomach, and no sooner had we done that, the walls changed again, faster this time, sliding across the path in front of us like a doorway being closed.

"It's never done that before," Fisher said. "Malcolm's trying to block our way, which means we're on the right path. Keep going, Saeris."

And as we picked up speed, so did the moving walls. They started slamming in front of us, barring our way, but it was as if there was a thread, connecting me to the quicksilver, drawing me toward it, and every time the thread was cut, a new one formed, showing me a different way. My heart was a hammer, pounding against my ribs. It quit beating when Fisher caught me by the shirt collar, pulling me back just in time to prevent me from being crushed by a huge slab of obsidian, but there was no time to stop and let the adrenaline pass.

"We're getting close," Fisher said, gulping down a breath. "I can tell by the collapsed...stand there." He pointed up into the walls of the amphitheater, which were still visible over the tops of the labyrinth walls. Where he pointed, one of the sections of the stands had, indeed, collapsed. "It isn't much...farther."

The quicksilver was louder in my head, too. Every time we hurled ourselves around a corner and sprinted for the next, I felt the thread connecting me to it strengthening. It wouldn't be much farther now. Only a couple more turns.

"Left! No, *right!*"

All four of us pushed harder. The quicksilver wasn't chanting along with the crowd anymore. It was whispering, its interest piqued. *She comes. She comes. This way, Alchemist. Come and find us.*

"Right!"

Glittering black obsidian blocked our way.

"Right again!"

We barreled around another corner, my feet slipping on the slick floor, and then...

"Ooof!" I hit the ground hard. Ground that was no longer black glass but something silver and cold. I cried out a second time as a heavy weight crashed down on me, and then Carrion landed next to me.

"Sorry," he groaned.

My ribs were already broken, I was sure of that. I'd hit that water so hard that it was a miracle the impact hadn't liquified my insides. I should have been screaming in agony, but the Widow's Bane was still in effect and cycling through my system, thank the gods.

Fisher's justice rune filled my vision. I took the hand he offered me and let him help me up. I didn't notice his grim expression right away. I was too shocked by the mountain of coins that loomed before us. Because that's what we had landed on. *Coins.*

They were tiny, the size of my thumbnail. Brilliant silver, they flashed like fish scales. In steep hills that resembled sand dunes, they filled the center of the labyrinth. There must have been millions of them.

This was the hell that Fisher had faced when he'd finally reached the center of the labyrinth. For eight years, he'd existed here, trying to find the specific coin that Belikon had flipped in their bet. It was no wonder he hadn't found it. His dark hair blew on a cold wind as he surveyed the place, his expression complicated.

"So many years, trapped here, Brother. Where did you sleep?" Lorreth whispered. "What did you eat? How did you *survive?*"

Fisher hung his head. Now that he could talk about this place and everything that had happened here, he didn't seem to know how to. He opened his mouth and took a deep, grounding breath. "I—"

"He didn't, did you, my love?" The voice bounced off the walls, coming from every direction. A section of one of the closest dunes started to slide, coins rattling and crashing as they tumbled down to the ground. Malcolm's head appeared over the top of the pile first, then his shoulders, and then the rest of him as he summited the stack. He smiled benevolently down at us like a father, proud of his children's accomplishments.

"I may be a vampire, but I was once Fae. The magic I was born with still sings a dark chorus in my veins. I used it to craft this place especially for our Kingfisher so that he wouldn't be plagued with such tiresome requirements as rest and sustenance. So long as he remained within the bounds of my playground, he needed neither. Thoughtful of me, no?"

"More than a century, enduring this shithole without even the escape of sleep as a reprieve? Yeah, very thoughtful," Lorreth snapped.

Malcolm chuckled humorlessly under his breath. "Oh, but I could have made it so much worse. You have no idea, Lorreth of the Broken Spire. Even now, I could have made your journey here infinitely more horrific. I actually thought Morthil had your little group for a second there. I'm pleased that you made it, though. We were getting a little bored."

"Motherfucker," Carrion hissed under his breath.

Behind Malcolm, golden hair rose into view, and then Madra appeared, dressed in the female version of the golden-plated armor that Zilvaren's city guard wore. Fisher stiffened, his hand closing tight around Solace as Belikon followed after her. The Yvelian king no longer had a hole in his stomach. In fact, he looked hale and hearty, dressed in a winter green tunic and black pants. The king's lip curled in disgust. Pointing a furious finger at Fisher, he snarled, "You really think you can kill me with a powerless sword? You can't kill any of us with a mere blade. We are the Triumvirate, Dog. Three crowns sharing one source. To kill one of us, you must kill us all, and that is no easy task."

"I'm willing to give it a shot," Fisher fired back.

"You've never known when to admit that you're beaten, boy. That's always been your problem."

"I won't be beaten until I'm dead."

"Oh, that moment can't come soon enough for me. I've wanted to put you in the ground from the moment your mother whelped you. But you'll be dead soon enough, and I'll have your father's sword to mount on my wall right beside your skull. I'll also have the Alchemist to forge all of the relics I need. Between the three of us, we'll bring the old gods to their knees and claim every realm we desire while we're at it. Now, will you die on your knees or face-down in the dirt? The choice is yours."

I had no idea what Fisher was planning next, but Belikon, Madra, and Malcolm all stood between us and the quicksilver. I couldn't see it, but I felt the pool pulsing on the other side of the mountain of coins they stood on. We had no magic in this place.

Our enemy had plenty of death magic to draw from, *and* they had the high ground. If we went back, we'd be faced with the other horrors that lived in the labyrinth, and there was no way out. No quicksilver to call to me beyond the walls of the amphitheater. The only way to reach safety was through that pool, which meant we had to go through the Triumvirate, as Belikon had called them.

Amazingly, it was Carrion who stepped forward first, Simon held aloft. "We might think Fisher's an arrogant ass, but we're not just going to let you kill him." His tone was confident and devil-may-care, but I saw the way his hand shook as he pointed the tip of his sword at Belikon's head. "We especially aren't going to let him be killed by a bastard who'd hand over his own daughter to be tortured and enthralled by a fucking vampire."

What's he doing? Fisher said into my mind. *He's going to get himself killed.*

I don't have a clue. But he should definitely stop.

Belikon sucked his teeth, his cloudy eyes full of disregard. "Every trap needs a lure," he said. "And anyway, Everlayne was born to serve my crown. If I deem it appropriate that she die to aid my cause, then she will fucking die."

"She won't die. Malcolm's venom is being drained from her as we speak. Soon, the vampire taint will be lifted from her blood, and *he* will no longer have any control over her."

"Carrion, stop!" I hissed. That blow Harron dealt to the back of his head must have done some serious damage. From where I was standing, it seemed likely that he'd lost his fucking mind.

"Yes, Carrion. Stop," Malcolm said. "You know not who you insult." The playful light in his eyes had blinked out. He stepped off the mound of coins and floated down from it, as if carried on some kind of invisible wind. I'd never seen anything like it. We were all *so* fucked.

Saeris? Listen to me. These coins are fake, Fisher said. *They have to be. The original coin that Belikon struck our deal with was made of silver.*

It burned Malcolm's hand when he caught it. He wouldn't even be able to stand on so many silver coins without them affecting him.

I watched Malcolm's boots make contact with the carpet of coins. He sauntered toward Carrion with a self-satisfied smirk on his face; he definitely wasn't in any pain. In fact, he only seemed to flinch a little when he drew closer to Carrion's sword. *Okay. So what does that mean?*

The original coin would have had traces of quicksilver in it, too. The people of this city believed it was good luck. They thought it would bring them good fortune and connect them to the gods. Do any of these coins contain quicksilver?

I stiffened, realization slowly dawning on me. I was beginning to understand what he was saying to me. *No. They don't,* I told him. *I don't even think they're made of metal. They're...an illusion, perhaps? Magic?*

Okay. Then do you understand what you need to do?

Malcolm hissed, snakelike, as he pushed Carrion's sword away. He leaned into the thief, baring his fangs. "What are *you* going to do to stop *us?* We are immortal. We are gods. You are just a human with shaky hands and a pig sticker. What would stop me from ripping your throat out right here, where we stand?"

Saeris! There was an urgent hitch in Fisher's voice.

Yes, I told him. *I know what I have to do.*

Carrion's eyes flitted to mine for a second. They held all manner of unspoken words. Then he lowered Simon, gave Malcolm his full attention, and said, "Nothing's stopping you. Go ahead, Leech. Bite me and see where it gets you."

"Carrion, *no!*" My shock registered like a slap across the face.

Malcolm swept around Carrion, face hideous with his hunger. His lips peeled back to reveal narrow, elongated fangs. Not just his canines. All of his teeth were sharpened to vicious points. Carrion didn't even raise his hand to stop Malcolm. Head tipped back, he stared at the vampire defiantly as Malcolm snapped his head forward and sank his teeth into his throat.

"Gods! We've got...got to *do* something!" I shrieked.

Fisher's hands closed around my arms. Lorreth's too. The males held me tight, their expressions hard. And all the while, the king of the vampires drank.

This wasn't happening. Carrion was being drained right before our eyes and we were doing nothing. Nothing!

There's nothing we can do. Fisher's voice was so quiet compared to the ringing in my head. *We'll all die if we try to pull him off him.*

Let me go! I have to try!

Malcolm snarled, sinking his teeth deeper into Carrion's neck. He was losing control. Losing himself to his own bloodlust. His throat worked as he took down Carrion's blood in great swallows. Frenzied, he withdrew his fangs—he was going to search for a better hold or a better vein?—but then a look of surprise chased over his features. Malcolm rocked back on his heels, lips stained red, his chin crinkling in an odd way as he frowned down at Carrion.

"You..." he said.

Carrion was deathly pale, but he grinned up at Malcolm like a lunatic. "You really should have let me finish introducing myself earlier. It's rude to interrupt people."

Malcolm let go of him, shoving him away. Miraculously, Carrion managed to stay on his feet. "My name is Carrion Swift. But there was a time when I was known as Carrion Daianthus. Firstborn son to Rurik and Amelia Daianthus."

Malcolm began to shake. A violent convulsion wracked through him, and a thick stream of blood jetted from his mouth. It spattered over the coins at his feet. "You tricked me?" He choked, vomiting up another gush of blood. *"You tricked me into drinking Daianthus blood?"*

"Holy...fucking...gods." Fisher and Lorreth muttered the curse in unison.

"What the hell is happening?" Daianthus? I'd heard the name, but I couldn't remember when.

As if struck with a sudden sense of urgency, Fisher spun and grabbed me by the shoulders. "Can you sense it?" he demanded. "Can you feel where it is?"

"I...I don't know! I—" But yes. There it was. A whisper of a voice. Faint. Tiny. But there. "I've got it."

Dirty gray smoke started pouring out of Malcolm's mouth. His perfect porcelain skin was suddenly riddled with pulsing black veins.

"What have you done?" Belikon roared. Both he and Madra floated down the slope of the coins, raising their hands...

Fisher gave me a shake. "Saeris. Is it here?"

"No, not here."

"But inside the labyrinth?"

I nodded.

Fisher pressed Solace into my palm and closed my hand around its hilt. "Then go. Find it. End this."

The Widow's Bane was wearing off. My ribs spiked with pain as I hurtled through the labyrinth. I pumped my arms, Solace cutting through the air as I ran. The walls weren't moving anymore. Clearly, they needed direction from Malcolm to do that, and the vampire was too busy choking—dying?—to pull those kinds of strings.

The obsidian passageways had been terrifying enough when I'd been running through them with my friends, but now they were downright petrifying.

It was too quiet.

It took me a moment to realize why.

And then it occurred to me: the smoldering bodies in the stands had fallen silent.

What did that mean? Was Fisher dead? Were Lorreth and Carrion gone, too? I wanted to scream. Fear and panic claimed me bit by bit. I was going to lose my mind. I could barely hear the little whisper now. It seemed to be growing quieter, even though my gut told me that I was getting closer.

Saeris...

Saeris...

It called to me by name.

Suddenly, I wasn't so sure anymore. I had thought I was going the right way, but the whisper seemed to be coming from every direction. *Where are you? Please,* I begged. *I need you.*

Not need, the whisper said. *Want.*

No! I need you. I need to save my friends. I need you to help me. Please show me where you are!

I ran back the way I'd come, my heart climbing up into my throat. It was so dark. So quiet. I felt the lightest tug in my stomach as I ran by a turn and backtracked, sprinting that way instead.

The whisper said nothing.

Please. Help me!

A bargain, then, the whisper purred.

No! No bargains. No tricks. No deals.

Then why would we help?

I stopped running. Overcome with exhaustion and pain, all I wanted to do was curl into a ball and pretend that none of this was happening. Instead, I said, *Because this is wrong. What they've done here. It's evil, and you can end it.*

Evil and good are two sides of the same coin. The whisper snickered.

"If that was supposed to be funny, then...then..." I threw my hands in the air, my eyes pricking with tears.

There is always evil. There is always good, the whisper said.

"Yes! But look how much evil exists here. So much pain, and death, and suffering. Isn't it time for some good? For balance? I..." I trailed off, not knowing how to win this argument. "I love him," I said. "I can't bear for him to die."

The Kingfisherrrrr, the whisper buzzed.

Yes.

Your mate.

I stared into the dark, feeling hopeless. "Yes," I said. "My mate."

The silence rang in my ears, deafeningly loud.

The whisper was gone. The thread guiding me to it was gone.

It was over. I was stuck in this awful labyrinth, alone. I would die here. I wouldn't even be able to make it back to him, so that we could die together.

A small favor, then, the whisper said. *We will do it for a favor. And for a restoration of balance. And for love.*

I burst into tears. "What kind of favor?" I choked out.

As we said. A small one.

A small favor. That was vague enough to ring all kinds of alarm bells, but it was the best I was going to get. I would deal with the consequences of whatever foolishness this was later. "All right, then. Yes. I'll owe you a small favor."

This way, then. This way.

The thread flared back to life, pulling me forward. I followed it. I ran. I sprinted as fast as my legs could carry me—

—and I screamed when I rounded a corner and came face-to-face with Morthil.

The demon was still dead, but that wasn't much of a comfort. According to Fisher, it would "respawn," whatever that meant, and I had no desire to be around it when it did.

"Where are you?" I hissed.

The whisper answered delightedly, *Inside! We are in. Inside.*

"What do you mean?" I was verging on hysteria now. This was too much. Because I already knew what it meant by inside, I could feel it, so close, humming, and I didn't want to admit to myself what I was going to have to do.

Inside, the whisper insisted.

I crept forward, approaching the spider demon's steaming corpse. It lay in a heap, its abdomen ripped wide open where I'd stabbed it with my dagger. One of its legs lay on the ground three feet away.

The huge mouth in the center of its face was mangled from the blow Lorreth had dealt it with Avisiéth, which only made it more hideous. I held my breath as I leaned over and peered into the demon's yawning maw.

Fuck. Any hopes that I might have been wrong went up in smoke when I saw the gleaming flash of silver at the back of the beast's gullet.

A ragged, wordless cry cut through the thick silence that hung over the labyrinth. Somewhere, Fisher, Lorreth, and Carrion were fighting for their lives, and I was wasting time.

I had to move.

Come on, Saeris. You can do this. I would have preferred the encouragement from Fisher, but I was sure he had his hands full right now, so I gave myself a pep talk instead.

I lifted my hand, and—

Oh.

My skin was stained black with ink. Runes upon runes upon runes. The God Bindings flared metallic blue around my wrists as if consolidating and becoming more real, somehow.

My whole body rushed with heat.

I'd said it out loud, hadn't I? I'd acknowledged that Fisher was my mate.

That was too big and too wild to comprehend right now.

Gingerly, I reached my inked hand into the demon's mouth.

Its teeth glistened, circular rows stacked on top of one another, growing smaller and smaller as they traveled down its throat. This close, I could see the serrations of each tooth. They were made for ripping and grinding through flesh.

Farther.

I needed to reach farther in.

My heart seized between beats.

The air froze in my lungs.

Farther.

A little farther still...

The demon's gullet was still warm, not to mention slimy. I grimaced as I plucked the coin from the back of its throat and closed my hand around it.

The demon twitched, and I panicked. Yanking my arm out of its mouth, I yelped, staggering back. And a hand closed around my wrist.

"You'd better give me that coin, girl," a rough voice said.

It was Malcolm.

43

ANOTHER WAY

THE COIN WEIGHED next to nothing. I clenched my fist around it and fought to wrench my hand free. Malcolm was strong, though. His fingers dug into my wrist, his sharp nails breaking the skin.

Malcolm's breath reeked of death. "Interfering in the plans of immortals is never advisable, Saeris Fane. Especially when they've expended so much time and effort into those plans. Open your hand."

"No! Enough is enough. Fisher has suffered enough. These people have suffered enough. This deal you made is over!"

"Not yet, it isn't." The vampire king spun me around, and my breath caught. His skin was melting from his bones, sloughing away in wet, fibrous slabs from his cheeks and his neck. The smell that came off him was putrid—the stench of rotting meat left out in the sun for too long. Even his eyeballs were shrunken and desiccated in their sockets. Whatever Carrion was, whatever Carrion had done, he had dealt Malcolm a tremendous blow. The king was still stronger than I was, though, and the pain in my ribs had become realm-shattering. I breathed in shallow sips, each more excruciating than the last.

"I'm very intrigued by you." Malcolm's ruined smile would haunt me from this life into the next. "An Alchemist, after so many years. I wasn't surprised to learn that Madra tried to kill you all off centuries ago. She was always so afraid of your kind. I suppose it would have been impossible to track all of you down, though. It's notoriously difficult to detect magic in half-blood Fae. She probably allowed one or two of them to slip through her fingers. They must have hidden in her city and started families and bred. Our Fae blood must have been diluted over the centuries, reduced to less than a whisper in a bloodline. But then you come along. I have to say, I'm impressed. A genetic throwback with your kind of power is inconceivable. Y'know, there *was* a time when I worked very closely with your kind." He considered me. "It was a very talented Alchemist who discovered the key to my blood gift. She was remarkable in many ways. Deeply disappointing in others. Perhaps I should keep you alive once this is all done. I seem to be in need of another miracle, thanks to that bastard Daianthus wretch."

"I won't help you," I spat. "I can't. I can only work with the quicksilver."

Malcolm clucked his tongue—a wet, disgusting sound. "Little girl, your ignorance is shocking." He threw me. It was so easy for him. Just a casual flick of his wrist, and he hurled me against the wall. I hit the obsidian hard, the breath rushing out of me. A burst of white light flared behind my eyelids as I sank to the ground.

Do not *lose consciousness, Saeris. If you pass out now, you're dead.*

That didn't sound like my voice. It sounded like Fisher's. So clear. So loud. So close...

Malcolm hooked the toe of his boot underneath Solace's hilt and kicked the sword out of my hand. He stooped low beside me, and, with cold fingers, he prized open my fist and took the coin I'd fought so hard to find. It burned his skin, but only for a second. He dropped it into a little leather pouch and attached it to the belt at his waist; then he flipped my hand over, running an ice-cold finger over my marks. Pointing at the runes on my index and middle fingers, he named them one at a time. "Earth. Air. Fire. Water. Salt. Brimstone. Quicksilver. The full gamut. More power than any Alchemist I've ever encountered. You are capable of restoring me to my power and a lot more besides."

"Just kill me and be done with it. I won't help you," I groaned.

"Really?" The vampire cocked his head to one side. He tapped the intricate, interlocking rune on the back of my right hand. I tried to pull my hand away, but he shook his head, tutting disapprovingly. "Speaking of impressive marks, I haven't seen the likes of *this* before, either. Such pretty artwork. It seems as though you've landed yourself a mate. I wonder who it could be."

"Fuck you," I spat.

"I've spent a lot of time with Fisher over the years. He's quite something to look at, so you'll believe me when I tell you that I noticed *his* new marks immediately. But I didn't need to see ink on skin to know you were his, did I? I scented you on him the second he showed up here, demanding I let his sister go. I scented your body on him." He forced out the words as if they left a foul taste in his mouth. "But the scent of your blood was much stronger. I couldn't believe it. That he'd *fed* from you," he sneered. "He wore that silver plate at his throat every day he was trapped here in this labyrinth. A gift from his mother, I believe. Pure silver imbued with some particularly nasty magic. I couldn't have torn it off him if I'd tried. Edina always was *such* a thorn in my side. I promised to let Fisher go if only he gave me a taste. I promised to wipe Gillethrye from his memory, so he'd forget all about this place and what had happened here...if only he fed from *me* just once. I wanted to know the bliss that would come at the points of his teeth. But he denied me. He chose to stay and suffer. And then *you*. A pathetic, weak human? His mate? It's offensive."

"Sorry." It was scary how rattly my lungs felt when I spoke. "He's just not into the undead."

"You have no idea how miserable the rest of your short existence will be, girl," the vampire hissed. "Fisher will be mine, one way or another. You *will* help me heal. You'll help me build an unstoppable army that will sweep across all of Yvelia. And he *will* give himself to—"

I lunged. The blade strapped to my thigh wasn't as impressive as Solace, but it was sharp, and in the end, that's all that mattered. I plunged the dagger into Malcolm's throat, screaming through the pain in my chest. The vampire's eyes went wide, his pupils contracting to vertical slits.

"You...stupid..."

I twisted the dagger as I yanked it free, growling with the effort. A flap of Malcolm's flesh came away with the blade, and smoke and blood gushed like a geyser from the wound. The vampire king's blood wasn't black ichor like that of his feeders. It was arterial— darkest crimson, but still red. Incandescent with rage, Malcolm clutched a hand to his neck and roared. He didn't need a weapon to kill me. His hands were enough. With a rabid snarl, he slammed his fist into my stomach and drove it upward.

Hold on, Saeris. I'm coming!

It was Fisher's voice. Crystal clear and perfect.

He was coming for me.

He would be too late.

A ripple of cold shock rocked my body. There was no pain. Not right away. It crept in at the edges of my awareness like a morning frost stealing over a windowpane.

And then it shattered me.

I was dying. Malcolm made sure of that. His glee was sickening as he pulled his blood-soaked hand from my stomach. "They say abdomen wounds are the worst way to go." His voice was a wet rasp. I'd done some serious damage with that blow to his neck, but his head was still attached, more was the pity. "I think I'll leave you just like this. You'll last long enough for him to find you that way. I love our Kingfisher the most when his heart is breaking."

Our Kingfisher? *Our* Kingfisher? This sick piece of shit couldn't claim any part of my mate. Fisher was *mine*. "I'm going to kill you," I groaned. "It'll be the last thing I do, but it'll be worth it."

Malcolm laughed. "Please, girl. Die with some dignity. You can't kill me. I'm eternal." When he lowered his hand from his neck, I could see that his throat was already healing. It was slow progress, the fibers of his muscle reattaching one by one. But he *would* heal. That wasn't important anymore. I hadn't fooled myself into thinking that I would end him with the dagger. I'd just wanted to distract him a little.

Malcolm's smile fell when I lifted the little leather pouch he'd placed the coin inside. The very same one I'd unhooked from his belt while he'd torn a hole in my stomach. He held out his hand, his eyes widening a touch. "Give that to me," he demanded. "Give it to me, and I might still save you. There's time."

It was my turn to laugh now. My mouth filled with blood, my body seizing from the agony that tore through me, but it was worth it. "Does it really matter that much to you? That he has to stay here and suffer? That you get to keep all of these people here, burning and in pain for the rest of time? Is your soul really *that* black and twisted?"

Malcom shrugged apologetically. "I don't have a soul, girl." And he pounced. I couldn't stop him from snatching the pouch from me and darting away, of course. I didn't even try. What little energy I had left, I was saving.

The vampire's eyes were bright with victory. That brightness dimmed when he opened the pouch and found nothing inside. His gaze snapped up to me, his jaw falling open.

The little coin hummed happily in my hand as I held it up for him to see. "What was Belikon's deal again? Leaves or fishes?"

"Don't!" Malcolm cried. *"DON'T!"*

I flipped the coin. Not high. I wouldn't give him the chance to grab it out of the air the way he'd done when Belikon had flipped it. The little coin flashed brilliantly as it spun. It didn't matter which side it landed on anymore. Only that it landed. The ground shook when the shining silver struck the obsidian.

There was a moment of stillness, and the ruins of Gillethrye held its breath.

"Stupid little bitch. What have you done?" Malcolm whispered.

And then it hit. A fearsome wind slammed into the labyrinth. It came from nowhere, screaming through the passageways that had trapped Fisher for decades. It rose up and out of the labyrinth, tearing along the stands of the amphitheater.

Annorath mor!

Annorath mor!

Annorath mor!

It whipped up the cries of the tortured souls, and as the wind passed by them, they turned to pillars of ash and were swept away in its howling wake. Hundreds of thousands of Higher and Lesser Fae, finally allowed to pass, their pain coming to an end.

Malcolm stared up at the stands in dismay. "No. This isn't...my children. They were to be my army. You...you *took* them from me!" He rounded on me, but I wasn't where he'd left me. I was on my feet, hunched and losing blood, standing right beside him. And I had Solace in my hands.

"Only the *gods* are eternal," I told him. And I cut off Malcolm's head.

I was flung backward.

I wasn't getting up again.

Malcolm's head burst into blue flames before it even hit the ground. His body was engulfed quickly after. A blast of light tore out of Solace and ripped up into the clouds, illuminating them. It rebounded seconds later, crashing back down to the ground in forks of blue-tinged energy that fractured the obsidian and set fire to the amphitheater. More filaments of power snapped from the end of the sword, but I was too weak to lift Solace again. I had no need to anymore. Malcolm was dead. There was no coming back for him now. The energy sparking from the sword that Fisher's father had once owned—energy that hadn't risen in over a thousand years—crackled and eventually went out.

Saeris! Saeris!

Fisher was shouting in my mind. Blearily, I closed my eyes, letting out a shaky breath. *It's fine. I'll be okay. Madra—*

The coward disappeared into the quicksilver as soon as the wind hit.

And...Belikon?

Lorreth's dealing with him. And Carrion. Their swords are channeling again. Where are you?

That was a great question. I had no idea how to direct him. *I'm... by the demon. Morthil.* That information wasn't very useful to him, though. The walls had moved so much after we'd left the spider demon's corpse. There was no chance Fisher would find me from that information alone.

Could he feel how weak I was right now? I could tell that his shoulder was injured. I could feel his exhaustion. I didn't understand this connection between us, but it had grown stronger since I'd accepted my marks and acknowledged him as my mate. I knew that he was running. I also knew that he was afraid.

Don't worry, he said. *I'm coming.*

I must have passed out. When I came to, a figure was standing over me, and it wasn't Fisher. I tensed, reaching for Solace, but my arms were numb. My legs...my whole body was numb. I couldn't move. I saw silver hair, and a wave of despair rose up inside me. He'd survived? How? There was no way. But the hair was too short to be Malcolm's. It was Taladaius, the vampire who had held Everlayne on the bank of the Darn.

"It's okay, Saeris. You're going to be all right." Fisher dropped down beside him, his face smeared with soot, ash, and blood. His dark hair, damp with sweat, curled around his ears.

I opened my mouth, but I couldn't speak. Thankfully, I had other means of communicating with him. *When Te Léna said that one of the mates marked with a god binding always died, I didn't think it would happen* this *quickly.*

"You're not going to die." Fisher brushed my hair out of my face, his hands shaking.

"I'm afraid she is," Taladaius said solemnly. "It'll happen soon, no matter what. The damage to her stomach and chest cavity is too great."

Fisher's mouth thinned into a line. He raked a hand through his filthy hair, screwing his eyes shut.

"If we don't act, she'll pass in the next few minutes," Taladaius said with surprising care.

"I'll give her part of my soul," Fisher said.

"You can't. You already gave too much to Lorreth. You'll decline immediately if you try to—"

"I don't give a shit! I've lived plenty, Tal. She's barely lived at all. I'm fucking giving it to her." Sniffing, he leaned forward on his knees and set his palms against my mangled belly.

No, Fisher.

Devastation twisted his features. Jade eyes, brimming with panic, clashed with mine. *I have to,* he said. *I'm not letting you die.*

You're not breaking your promise to me, I countered. *You swore you'd never take away my free will again. That's what you'll be doing if you heal me and die in the process. I don't want to take your soul.*

"I can handle the consequences of breaking a promise if it means you live," he said out loud.

You said in your letter that we'd have time after this life. That there was more for us.

"There will be." He nodded, as if he thought he was comforting me. That he would be waiting for me no matter what. But he'd misunderstood.

There won't. I told you I'd never forgive you if you forced me to do something I didn't want to do again. Never is a long time, Fisher. If you sacrifice yourself for me, I'll reject our bond in this life and the next.

I hated how bereft he looked. But I meant it. Fisher had spent his whole adult life sacrificing himself for those around him. I would rather die than have him sacrifice himself for me.

"We're running out of time," Taladaius said. "There's another way, and you know it."

"No," Fisher snapped.

Malcolm's silver-haired second huffed in frustration. "When will you learn that being stubborn never serves you? Let me help!"

Fisher stared down at me, the quicksilver in his eye whorling frantically. "I—"

What is he talking about?

"Fisher, if you want me to act, it has to be now."

Fisher! What does he mean?

My beautiful, dark-haired mate swallowed thickly. *Tal was second only to Malcolm in power. He hid it from the king so he wouldn't kill him. He can turn you.*

My mind was so fuzzy. I couldn't process what he was saying. Taladaius wanted to *turn* me? *I don't...I can't be a feeder, Fisher. Please.*

Fisher shook his head. "You wouldn't be. You'd be like him."

I wouldn't die?

"No."

Would I have to feed?

"We don't know."

"Fisher, she's fading. I have seconds..." I heard Taladaius speak, but he sounded as if he were underwater.

A deep, dark blanket was settling over me. It was so warm and comfortable. It made the pain in my stomach melt away.

"Tell me she fucking consents!" Taladaius yelled.

The world faded away.

Fisher's voice was the last thing I heard. "She consents."

44

AXIS

"MOVE!"

I was going to throw up. Pain cut through me like a kni—

"Oh, gods. Is she alive?" Carrion's face above me, pale and lined with worry.

BOOM!

The sky was falling.

Not the sky. The amphitheater.

A huge section of stone, shearing from the stand, toppling in slow motion.

BOOM!

"I swear to the gods, if she doesn't make it through this—"

Lorreth, fisting Carrion's shirt, dragging him back.

Fire, everywhere. Flames roaring up to meet the splintering sky.

Flames surging in my veins. In my neck.

Gods, my neck…

"Form a shadow gate!"

Fisher's voice, full of panic. "I'm fucking trying!"

The world, on its side, crumbling apart.

All chaos. All pain. All doubt. All fear. All—

Everything stopped.

I was lying in Fisher's arms. The world went silent, but I could see my mate's face above me, and the awful grief there, the tendons in his neck standing proud as he yelled something to Lorreth. He'd come for me. Even with the world ending all around us, he *had* me.

The mountain that weathers all storms, a voice said very clearly in my mind. I had no control over my body. No energy or care left to react to the voice. I was aware enough to realize that it was different now, though. Calm. Focused. Direct. I watched my mate, my vision drifting in and out of darkness as it spoke.

He is the storm. You are the peace that must come after it. Tell me, do you believe in the fates, Alchemist?

I closed my eyes, tears streaming from the corners of my eyes. Fisher was opening a gate. He was taking me home. I would die at Cahlish, in the comfort of his bed perhaps. I—

Do not drift too far from the shore, Saeris Fane. Come back now. Come back.

I opened my eyes, my pulse suddenly careening away from me. Adrenaline soaked my blood, an electric current charging through my chest, jump-starting my heart. "Fuck!" I gasped. "Oh, gods. *Fuck!*"

"It's starting." Taladaius's grim announcement came from behind me somewhere.

Fisher looked down at me, eyes swimming. "It's going to be okay. Hold on, Saeris."

The voice came again, clear and concise. *You stand before a door. Your hand is poised to knock. Are you ready to walk through it? Will you leave this place and see what lies beyond in the next?*

The next? *Leave?* I blinked slowly. *No. I don't want to go. Not yet.* The voice sounded gruff but also curious. *A shadow falls across Yvelia. It will alter all it touches. You would rather remain here, knowing that suffering and hardship looms on the horizon? That sacrifices will need to be made?*

I looked at Fisher. At the broad, beautiful wings that spanned the side of his neck. I felt his heart, racing in his chest, thrumming in time with my own, as he stretched out his hand, reaching for a shadow gate. I didn't need to consider my answer. Whatever the cost would be for staying with him, I would pay it. *Yes,* I said.

As you wish. Then we call in our favor, Saeris Fane. Will you honor your word and grant us our favor?

Of course it was the quicksilver. And of course it was calling in my debt now, when I was a hair's breadth from death. *What is it you want from me?*

The answer came immediately. *We require an audience with you, Saeris Fane.*

Fisher looked down at me, frowning. "Saeris?"

Will you grant us our favor?

An audience? They wanted to *talk* to me? That was indeed a small favor. One I could hardly refuse them. *Yes. I'll grant it. As—* As soon as I'm well enough to have a conversation with you. That's what I had been about to say, but the cord that had helped me find the quicksilver pool at the center of the labyrinth snapped taut out of nowhere. My body tugged, and Fisher nearly dropped me.

"What the fuck? Saeris?"

Fisher clutched hold of me tight. His shadow gate was open, less than three feet away. All he had to do was turn and walk us through it. I grabbed the strap of his chest protector, alarm bells ringing in my head. "I'm sorry," I gasped. "I—"

I was ripped from his arms.

"SAERIS!"

An invisible rope yanked me through the air, pulling me across the labyrinth. My arms and legs streamed behind me as I was yanked backward. Air rushed past my ears. Lorreth and Carrion cried out, too. In a split second, my friends were gone, my mate was gone, and I was hurtling through the labyrinth at breakneck speed.

"Please!" I cried. *"Don't!"* Whatever the quicksilver was doing, it had to stop.

My stomach hollowed out, a weightless sense of falling tugging at my belly. And then all I could see were coins. Thousands of them. A whole carpet of them, whipping by beneath my feet.

True panic claimed me when I understood where I was being drawn.

I barely saw the quicksilver pool underneath me before a wave of the liquid metal rose up and lashed me around my waist. I barely had time to scream as it cinched tight around my ribs and dragged me below its surface.

"It's dead."

"Don't be ridiculous. Of course it isn't dead."

"How can you be so sure?"

"Because Father willed it here, stupid. He doesn't want it to be dead. Therefore it isn't."

These voices were female. Young and playful. The first who had spoken made a dismissive sound and said, "Well, it *looks* dead."

I opened my eyes and saw bright blue sky.

A bird chased across my field of vision, darting and swooping, singing at the top of its lungs; without thinking, I lifted my hand to shield my eyes from the sun, wanting to get a better look at it.

Too late, I braced for the pain...but none came.

"Do you think it understands us?"

I squinted, turning my head, and blades of grass tickled the side of my face. I was lying in a vast field at the foot of a rolling hill. Atop the hill stood a lone oak tree so magnificent that it took my breath away. Its thick boughs rocked on the gentle breeze, its leaves shimmering, flaring with light when the sun hit them.

I dragged myself into a sitting position and immediately spied the two young women to my right. They looked eighteen, perhaps. Nineteen. And they were identical in every way. Dressed in loose, dark gray dresses, they wore nothing on their feet. Their black hair flowed in waves down to their waists. Two pairs of quick, royal blue eyes shot through with silver threads watched me with a keen interest as I got to my feet.

The girl on the right grabbed her sister's hand, and the two of them came forward. "Tell us what it's like," she said in a clear, pleasant voice.

"I'm—" I cleared my throat. "Sorry. Tell you what what's like?"

"Sex," the other girl said, tilting her chin. "With that male. Our father's champion."

"With...*Fisher?*"

In unison, the girls nodded eagerly.

"Uhhh..."

"We wanted to try him out for ourselves, but Father forbade it," the twin on the right said. "He deems no living creature from any realm worthy of our touch. We've been waiting an eon for him to gift us with our own playmate, but thus far, no other of our kind has braved the journey to visit our Corcoran."

Corcoran?

Holy...hells.

The Corcoran were...

"Which one of us do you worship more fervently?" The twin on the right asked. "Bal?" She gestured to herself. "Or Mithin?" She gestured to her counterpart. "We have such competitions over who is most popular." A lightning storm raging in her eyes now. No sooner had I noticed it than I felt the sharp prickling of static in the air. The fine hairs all over my body stood up.

This...was really happening? They were *gods?* I swallowed down my nerves, then bowed my head respectfully, looking down at my feet. "How could anyone love Bal more than Mithin? Or treasure Mithin more than Bal? You're worshipped equally by all those who know your names, my ladies."

"My *ladies!*" the sun goddesses cried at the same time. They grinned at each other happily, still holding each other's hands. "She speaks with such lovely manners." The one who gave me their names held out her hand to me. "Come on. We should hurry. Father's waiting for you, and he doesn't have much patience for waiting these days. He'll be annoyed if we delay much longer."

I didn't reach out my hand to her. One second, it was hanging by my side. The next, it was already in her cool grip. I took one step, and the field surrounding us stretched thin, becoming a green blur. When my heel struck the ground, the sloping hill was no longer in front of us. We were standing on top of it, beneath the boughs of the impressive oak tree.

My mind struggled to catch up with the change in location, my thoughts gluey.

Amidst the roots of the giant oak tree, a broad, eight-foot-wide ribbon of silver formed a moat. *So* much quicksilver. I started when I noticed beads of the shining metal spilling down the tree's broad trunk like sap and rolling into the moat.

On a smooth rock, ten feet away, a male sat alone with his back to us. His robe was the same dark gray as the sun goddesses' clothes, his long, brown hair tied back into war braids. Giggling, Bal and Mithin waved me forward, indicating that I should go to him.

A ball of anxiety clenched into a fist at the center of my rib cage. If these two giddy girls were indeed goddesses, then I could hazard a guess as to who their father was just from looking at the back of his head.

Everlayne had barely been able to utter his name without shivering. She'd warned in no uncertain terms that a person should never let *this* god look upon them. Not even a statue of him. And here he was—the physical embodiment of him, anyway—sitting on a rock, waiting to have a chat with me.

Fuck.

"Come forward, Alchemist," he commanded. His was the voice that had asked me if I wanted to pass through the door or stay in Yvelia with Fisher; I had a feeling that it was his voice I had been speaking to for a long time now. I stepped forward, holding my breath, and moved around the rock. Facing the god, I angled my jaw and met his cool, blue eyes. I had expected some terrible visage. A hideous, twisted face with madness in its gaze, but no. If he'd been human, I would have judged him in his middle years. His face was lightly lined and had a kindness and wisdom that took me by surprise.

He looked up at me, his hands resting on his knees, and said, "You know who I am?"

I bowed my head a little, again looking down at my boots. "Zareth. God of Chaos."

Zareth grunted. "And you are Saeris. Sister to Hayden. Daughter to no one." He nodded to the inkwork on my hands. "Also, mate to my champion."

I glanced down at the marks, still a little surprised to see them there, staining my skin. "Yes," I said. "I am."

Zareth rose from his seat on the rock, and my legs trembled. He was no taller than Fisher. No broader or more godlike in appearance, but the sheer well of power that swelled from him as he took me in made me want to drop to my knees and throw myself at his feet. He could blink and eradicate me from existence. I knew that with certainty. If he wanted me to, I would vanish, never to have even been born in the first place.

"We must make this quick, or you'll die before you've been of use to me. I will be as concise as I can, given the circumstances. I've spent a great deal of time watching the threads of the universe, waiting for one such as you," he said. "An Alchemist, at last, to reset the balance and clear the way for what is to come." Turning, he went to the edge of the quicksilver pool that surrounded the great tree, and I followed, drawn along by the pull of him.

He stepped to the very edge of the quicksilver and looked at me. "Here, we stand at the edge of the universe. The roots you see, growing down into the earth, into the quicksilver, are the anchors of fate." He tipped his head back, his eyes traveling upward into the boughs of the tree. "The silver leaves above mark all the realms of our domain. My family are the stewards of all you see here. We water the roots of fate. We train the boughs and prune the leaves to prevent rot and decay. You see the bough there? The blackened one?"

I looked where he was pointing and did notice one particular branch of the tree. Its bark was darker than the rest, shriveled, with fewer silver leaves sprouting from it. "Yes, I see it."

Zareth nodded. Lifting his hand, he swept his fingers through the air, and as I watched, three of the bough's leaves dislodged and fell. They floated down, fluttering and spinning, to land on the surface of the quicksilver. "There is a rot spreading throughout my domain, Saeris," he said. "Realms that are infected with that rot have to be summarily destroyed to protect the rest of the tree and prevent that rot from spreading. Do you understand?"

Those leaves had been realms. Whole worlds. Zareth had just... waved his hand and...wiped them out. I stared at them as they sank and disappeared below the surface of the quicksilver. Was it possible? Could he really just have done that? "How many people..." I couldn't get the rest of the question out, but the god standing beside me knew exactly what I was asking him.

"Billions." He answered without the faintest hint of emotion. Yes, then. I had just witnessed genocide on a scale I couldn't comprehend, and Zareth just smiled. "You aren't the only Alchemist in the universe, of course," he said. "There are millions of you out there. Even in your realm, even in the city you once called your home, there are hundreds of elemental magic wielders who can command the quicksilver. But when I consulted the fates long ago, I was very intrigued when I saw *you*, Saeris Fane. Not just you. Kingfisher, too. I saw an axis in the flow of things. A burning knot in the tapestry of all that would come to be. When I focused and saw the strength of the bond that connected the two of you together, I admit I attempted to sway the fates."

"What do you mean, sway the fates?" I whispered.

Zareth glanced down the gently rolling slope to the field where his daughters had returned and were laughing raucously, hands grasped, spinning each other around in the tall grass. "You were supposed to have been born Fae, in the same realm as your King-fisher. So I separated you. Hundreds of years before you were born, I shifted the events around your birth. Moved the pieces on the board and placed you far away, in a realm that should never have come into contact with his. But I watched as the boughs of the universe grew against their nature and aligned in such a way that you would still meet. I foresaw then that no matter how the boughs and branches of this tree were manipulated, you and he would always collide. There was nothing I could do to stop it."

Fisher had said his mother was wrong sometimes, about small things that had big consequences. When she had predicted me rushing into her son's life, she had seen me with sloped ears and canines like her son. It turned out she hadn't been wrong after all. I *should* have been born Fae. The God of Chaos had simply interfered.

"Why?" I asked. "Why would you want to keep us apart? What does it matter to you if we love each other and live our lives together?"

Zareth considered me for a moment. Inhaling sharply, he rushed past me, around the tree, to a point on the bank of the moat where the grass was pressed flat against the earth...and the boughs of the tree were twisted into bare, blackened knots. I hadn't noticed it from our vantage point just now, but from here, it was plain to see that a huge chunk of the tree was dying.

"In nature, there is a counterweight to everything, child. Light has darkness. Life has death. Joy has sorrow. And good has evil. That law applies, no matter which realm you exist in," he said with a broad stroke of his arm that encompassed the many, many leaves on the tree. "Threads like you and Kingfisher, that are drawn together and cross on an axis create a well of power. The energy the two of you draw together attracts an equal and opposite counterweight. Every possible future where the two of you are together ends with the vast majority of this tree dying. None of us can foresee any other way."

"So...you're saying that Fisher and I are responsible for the end of the entire universe?"

Zareth shook his head. "Not you personally. But the moment where you meet, along with the moment you become mates, is a spark. The flame in the dark that draws the moth. It was incumbent upon me to try and stop that spark from taking place, but as you've already learned, the fates themselves would not be guided down that path."

I felt my heart beating all over my body. "Does Fisher know any of this?"

Zareth snorted. "No. I orchestrated events so that he would be brought here as a young male. His mother had just died, and his disposition wasn't very polite." Zareth frowned, as if the memory were troubling even now. "He made an enemy of my family. He was only allowed to live because I demanded it. I'd spent a great deal of time studying the various outcomes and paths of this universe once you and Kingfisher met, and while I never found a balance that meant good prevailed, there were pathways that led into...uncertainty."

"Uncertainty?"

"Pathways that lead down roads, where both the way and the destination are blocked to even my sight. And in all of these veiled futures, where a chance still exists for life, there is one common factor." I didn't want to know. Couldn't hear it. This was way too much pressure. Zareth knew this, I was sure, but he plowed ahead. "You and Kingfisher fought at each other's side, and you were God-Bound." He pointed to the script writing that wrapped around my wrists. "These oaths mark you as my ward. They protect both you and Fisher from the unwanted attentions of my brothers and my sister."

"*Protection* from them?"

"They would rather kill Fisher and roll the dice on what comes next. They would prefer to weather the storm on the horizon and replant our tree once the slate has been wiped clean. I don't want that to happen. It would break my daughters' hearts." He broke off, watching the girls dance down in the field, mimicking the grasses as they swayed in the wind. Their laughter rose up to us like sweet music. "For them, I'm willing to take a chance. If you truly accept Fisher as your mate, then you must agree for the thread of your life to be severed from the tapestry of the universe. Once you do, none of us may affect your future. We won't be able to see you at all, nor will my brothers and my sister be able to interfere with timelines or events that affect you, either. You'll be on your own."

On my own? What was he talking about? "This burden shouldn't be placed on one person's shoulders. It definitely shouldn't be placed at mine. I'm a thief! Just...one woman! I can't be held responsible for—"

"You're not responsible for anything. All you need do is live your life."

"But—"

"Let me put it this way, child," Zareth said, cutting me off. "Do you want your mate to die?"

"No, of course not!"

"Then this is how you save him."

"I..." What was I supposed to say? If I did this, then Zareth and the other gods wouldn't be able to see ahead or do anything to affect events as they were about to happen. But should they be allowed to do that, anyway? Their meddling meant that I'd been born in Zilvaren, not in Yvelia. How many times had they swayed the tides of fate, and how many people had suffered because of it? What gave *them* the right?

Zareth narrowed his eyes at me. "Fuck the fates. They don't get to decide shit for me. *I* decide what my future is going to be. Did you not just say that mere days ago?"

I had said that. And I'd meant it, too. "Yes, but..."

"If you truly wish to be the master of your own life, then this is how you accomplish that goal."

I got the feeling that Zareth was desperate—a God who would say anything to bend me to his will. But there was no denying it. He *was* a God. He could make me do anything he desired, and yet he was giving me this choice.

I asked carefully, "How painful are we talking? This thread cutting?"

"No more painful than the transition that is already beginning inside your body as we speak, Saeris Fane."

Why the hell didn't that sound reassuring? "How would you do it exactly?"

"By transforming you into something that has never been seen before," he answered cryptically. "The universe cannot focus on that which it does not recognize."

"But *how?*"

"I'm not just the God of Chaos, Alchemist. I'm also the God of Change. I will it, and it is done."

"I—"

"Time is running out, Saeris. You must make your decision."

"Okay. All right. Yes. I'll do it." I blurted it out before I could take it back. If it was a decision between becoming something new, and most certainly dying along with the rest of the universe, then it wasn't really a tough call to make.

The God Bindings at my wrists flared out of nowhere, biting into my skin like burning ropes. "The best of luck to you, then, Saeris. Give Kingfisher my best." And then he shoved me into the quicksilver.

CHOOSE WISELY

I FLOATED on a sea of darkness. I was surprisingly calm about that, given my last encounter with a large body of water, but apparently, you didn't need to be able to swim in the afterlife.

Overhead, a canopy of stars bristled in the firmament, prickling with the promise of other realms. I was perfectly happy bobbing along on the nothingness, trying to count them. I kept losing track, but having to start over was no bother. I had nothing to worry about here. I floated for an age and felt civilizations rise and fall. In the dark, I observed the universe, and the universe observed me back.

I was born and died a hundred times.

And then I saw something that shouldn't have been.

A bird.

It flitted around me in the void, its beautiful wings flashing blue-green. It sang a song so sweet that I remembered what it was like to have a heart, if only so I could feel it ache. And oh, it ached.

I remembered more.

Jade, the color of new grass.

Winter mint and the promise of snow on cold mountain air.

A crooked smile and dark, thick waves of hair.

I remembered pieces of him, and all at once, and I remembered how to drown.

I needed him like I needed air.

I reached for him like I was reaching for the surface of a still, flat lake.

Kingfisher.

My Kingfisher.

My mate...

"FISHER!"

I sat up, panting, soaked to the skin with sweat. My head spun in the worst way. Oh gods, I...I was going to be sick. I leaped out of the...the bed, I'd been in a *bed,* and immediately tripped over a bucket that had been strategically placed by the nightstand. Sitting on the floor, legs splayed wide, I grabbed that bucket and puked into it for all I was worth. Once my stomach was empty, I sank back against the side of the bed, panting as I took in my surroundings.

The room I found myself in was high-ceilinged. Dark green drapes hung at the windows. Heavy, dark oak furniture decorated the space—a wardrobe by the door, a chest of drawers, another armoire by the window, and a bookcase full of books. The rug I was splayed out on was a soft dove gray. Plush. It felt lovely when I buried my fingers into—

Oh.

I grabbed the bucket and heaved into it again. My stomach muscles throbbed uncomfortably when I set it aside.

"They call it the great purge," a male voice said. Taladaius had opened the door while I was vomiting and was now leaning against the doorjamb with his arms folded over his chest, watching me with an amused smile on his face.

Vampire.

Malcolm's second.

I cast around the room, looking for a weapon, and realized for the first time that I was dressed in a pair of scandalously tiny black silk shorts and a sheer camisole made of the same material that didn't leave much to the imagination. Gasping, I gave up my search for something to defend myself with and looked for something to cover myself with instead.

Taladaius chuckled as he crossed the room and fetched a robe from the ornate privacy screen by the window. He made a point of looking away as he came toward the bed and held it out for me. "Your body has undergone some stark changes of late," he said. "The general consensus is that you'll be able to eat normal food again soon, but it might take a day or two. When I transitioned, it took me six months before I didn't hack up anything I tried to eat like it was a hairball."

Snatching the robe from him, I threw it around my shoulders. I flared my nostrils, hating the strange, overpowering burn at the back of my nose. "What do you mean, transitioned?" I asked sharply.

Taladaius let his head fall to one side. He gazed at me pityingly. "You know exactly what I mean by that word. Don't you?"

Vampire.

Vampire.

Vampire.

I glared back at him, refusing to accept it. "I'm nothing like you," I hissed.

Taladaius nodded, scuffing the toe of his beautiful leather shoe against the edge of the rug. With his hands in his pockets, he said, "Oh, I know *that*, Saeris."

"What does that mean? That *tone*," I demanded.

"Here." The vampire with the immaculately coiffed silver hair and the strangely soft eyes nodded toward the large mirror on the wall. "Come and see for yourself."

I was wary as I walked over to the mirror. Wrapping my arms around myself, I prepared for the unknown. I had no idea if I would recognize the person staring back at me in the glass. But I did. Aside from the faint shadows beneath my eyes, I was wholly entirely myself. Saeris. Same dark hair. Same blue eyes. Same...

I hesitated. Turned my head.

My ears.

The tips of my ears were pointed. They poked up through my mussed hair, as if they had always been this way. I opened my mouth to curse, saw the state of my teeth, and my heart set to racing. Canines. I had very long canines. And they looked sharp.

"I'm...*Fae?*" I asked Taladaius's reflection in the mirror.

He smiled politely but shook his head. "As far as we can tell, you're a half-vampire, half-Fae. Something none of us have ever seen before. As of now, we're not sure which traits you've adopted from the Fae and which you've adopted from the vampires. All our healers are sure of is that you're no longer human."

No longer human.

Not fully vampire.

Not fully Fae.

My throat did its damnedest to seal itself shut. I tore myself away from the mirror, screwing my eyes closed. I couldn't think about this now. I needed my mate. "Where's Fisher?"

Taladaius gave a shrug and eyed the ornamental plaster on the ceiling rather evasively. "Oh, I don't know. He's around here some-where, I suppose."

"Is he hurt? Is he—"

"Just relax, Saeris. He's fine. He'll be along shortly."

I wasn't about to trust the word of a vampire. Looking down, I saw that my marks were still there, declaring for all the world that I was Fisher's mate.

I reached out, feeling for him with my mind. Moments later, I was rewarded with a deep sense of concentration. Not mine. Fish-er's. He was here. Close by. And he was focusing on something very hard. I didn't sense any pain or alarm from him, which allowed me to breathe a little easier. It seemed as though Taladaius was telling the truth.

"Where are we?" I asked, skirting around the bed, trying to make sure I kept ample room between us. Where was Solace? I wanted my fucking sword.

"Fisher asked me to let him tell you where we are," Taladaius answered.

"What? But...*why?*" I narrowed my eyes at him, trying to get a read on him. Taladaius seemed equally relaxed and amused, which told me nothing about why he kept our location a secret. Annoyance flickered in my chest. I crossed the bedroom, clutching the robe tightly around my body, and ripped the curtains open.

Pain exploded behind my eyes. It was barely even light outside, the last of the sun's rays vanishing beyond the horizon, but it felt as if I'd just been smashed in the head with a sledgehammer. *"Ahh!"*

Careful to stand in the shadows, Taladaius gently removed my hand from the curtain and drew it closed again. "You'll be able to tolerate that better than most soon enough, too. This will all just take some getting used to. What about your memory? What do you remember about Gillethrye, Saeris?"

The name of that place sent a shiver down my back. "I—we were fighting them. Malcolm, Belikon, and Madra. There was a coin. I flipped it..."

"And then?"

"Then..." I stared at him, a strange dread tugging at my lower belly. "He wounded me. I...I killed him. You and Fisher came. And then..."

"And then I bit you," Taladaius said, nodding. He looked away quickly, as if he were suddenly uncomfortable. "I placed a memory block around what happened next. Transitioning is hard. And, well, it is in a sire's power to suppress those memories, if—"

"Remove it," I demanded. "Remove the block."

Taladaius looked like he wanted to refuse, but he said, "If you're certain you want me to, I will, but it can be very traumatic—"

"Remove. It," I snarled.

"As you wish." He didn't need to touch me. It was simpler than that. One minute, I had no recollection of the moment when Taladaius's teeth had sunk into the top of my shoulder. No recollection of the horror show that followed after. And then, the next minute, I did.

The bite from Taladaius.

Fisher, carrying me in his arms. Opening a shadow gate. Me flying through the air toward the quicksilver pool. The brief but tense conversation with Zareth that followed.

Then, Fisher pulling me out of the quicksilver. He and Carrion, arguing like they were about to kill each other.

Lorreth, sitting by my bedside, playing some kind of lute and singing softly to me while I thrashed and moaned.

Three days of me lying in this bed, in this room, begging for Fisher to kill me because I couldn't face the pain for another second.

And me...biting...someone.

My eyes snapped up to Taladaius's neck.

I'd bitten *him*.

He saw my realization and gave me a small smile. Angling his neck, he showed it to me—his smooth, unblemished skin. "No harm done," he said. "You barely broke the skin."

"Why did I *do* that?" I pressed my hand to my mouth, too afraid to part my lips and accept a truth that I already knew but was too afraid to face.

"Fisher should really be here for this," Taladaius said. He started for the door.

"No! I—" I didn't know what to say. "A part of me feels like I should thank you for saving my life."

"And the rest of you?"

"Wants to kill you for what you've done," I whispered.

The vampire nodded, studying his boots. "I felt the same way for a long time. There were whole centuries where I hated what I'd become, and I wanted to destroy Malcolm. I wanted nothing but to die and be gone from this world so badly."

"What made you decide to stay?"

Taladaius gave me a small, very sad smile. "I didn't. I wasn't given a choice. Malcolm wouldn't let me go. I tried to kill myself once, and he forbade me from ever trying again. His word was law."

"But now he's dead…"

"And I am free." Taladaius rocked on his heels. "I'm still trying to decide what that means for me. But things have gotten rather interesting recently." He looked me up and down, frowning a little, as if weighing what he wanted to say. After a moment, he said, "There are two kinds of forever, Alchemist. One is heaven. The other is hell. It doesn't matter what I do. Make sure you choose *your* version of immortality wisely."

I blinked, trying to force this version of Carrion Swift to make sense in my head.

Still the same artfully messy copper-brown hair. Still the same blue eyes and that roguish grin.

But also the sloped ears. And the pointed canines. And he was so *tall*.

I punched him in the chest.

"Ow! What was *that* for?"

I shoved a finger in his face. "Because you're an asshole. I've known you since I was *fifteen!*"

He shook his head, hands palm up in the air. *"And?* I've known you since I was a thousand and eighty-six. Do I win a prize?"

"You didn't tell me that you were heir to a fucking Fae throne!"

"Well, it's hardly something you just *tell* people, Fane. And anyway, my grandmother made me promise not to."

"Except she wasn't your grandmother, was she!"

Carrion pulled a face. "No, not really. She was more of a ward. Or a playmate when she was little. And then a friend. And then *I* was *her* ward. I don't know, it always got very complicated as people aged."

I shook my head, still valiantly trying to put all of the pieces together. "So, Fisher's father took you to Zilvaren when you were little to save you from Belikon. He glamored your ears and your canines so you wouldn't stand out. He brought a bag of books along with you, so you could learn about your heritage and return when the time was right. And...some woman saved you?"

"Her name was Orlena," Carrion said. "Orlena Parry. She was a slave in Madra's palace. But that night, the night she pulled me out of the quicksilver, she fled the palace and escaped. She went to the Third, knowing she could get lost in the crowd there. And that's where she stayed. She found work as a seamstress and secured somewhere for us to live. She raised me like I was her own son."

I couldn't believe it. I squinted at him, this Fae version of him, his true form, and almost burst out laughing. "And you were trapped there when Madra closed the gates. And then you spent the next thousand odd years just...*living* in Zilvaren?"

"That's pretty much the long and short of it," Carrion said. "I had the books that Finran brought for me, about the Fae and my people. Orlena got married when I was nine and took the name Swift. She had a daughter not long after. Petra. Petra grew up and had a daughter, too. The books were passed down the female line, and so was I. They kept me out of trouble as best they could and made sure I kept a lookout for signs that the quicksilver had opened again. They thought it was cruel that I was stuck in the Silver City and that I should go home and rule my people. The females of the Swift line have always been very bossy and overly concerned about my love life."

"So you knew what to expect when the quicksilver awakened again?"

He laughed. "Nope. Not even a little bit. But I felt it, that day when you were taken up to the palace. Something shifting in the air. A kind of energy that felt familiar somehow. I recognized it the second time it happened, and somehow, I just *knew* it had something to do with you. I went to The Mirage to see if you'd escaped, and that's where Fisher found me. I really did say I was Hayden because I thought I was protecting him, Saeris. I hope you believe that."

"It's okay. I know." I really did believe him.

Gods, how interlinked this all was. Fisher's father had been the one to secret the true heir to the throne out of Yvelia. A thousand years later, his son had been the one to bring him back. It meant something. What, I couldn't say, but I was sure we were all going to find out soon enough.

And all of this time, there had been a Fae royal living in the Third, smuggling goods, starting fights, and generally making a nuisance of himself. I was on the verge of asking Carrion how he preserved his sanity while the people he cared about were born, grew up, lived their lives, and died of old age, but I already knew the answer to that question, and I didn't want to hear him say something lewd about whiskey and women.

Speaking of which. I glared at him even harder. "You *slept* with me."

He grinned shamelessly. "You're welcome."

"Carrion!"

"What? You've been fucking Fisher for the past gods only knows how long!"

"Yes, but I knew what he was when I decided to sleep with him. And he was my mate."

Carrion huffed. Folding his arms over his chest, he rolled his eyes and sighed. "All right. I'm sorry I didn't disclose to you that I was a magic-wielding political asylum seeker, posing as a human when I slept with you. Does that make you feel better?"

"No."

"Ahh, come on, Fane!" He nudged me with his elbow. "I'm Fae now. You're Fae now. Kind of. It's all water under the bridge. You're only grumpy with me because you were worried about me. Go on. Ask me how I survived Malcolm's all-powerful venom. I can tell you're just dying to know."

"Lorreth already told me, actually. So there." Lorreth had been the second person to visit me after Taladaius had left my room. He'd laughed when he'd seen my Fae ears. Laughed a little less enthusiastically when he saw just how sharp my teeth were. The first thing he'd told me was that Everlayne was alive, and Ren was watching over her, though she had fallen into a deep sleep and couldn't be roused. Te Léna and Iseabail were confident that she would wake any day, though. He'd then stayed for over an hour and explained much of what had happened after I'd bolted back into the labyrinth. I'd been sick with guilt when he'd told me how all three of them had nearly died at Belikon's hands while they bought me time to find the coin. He'd called me crazy when I'd apologized for taking so long and said that it had felt like a miracle when the wind had swept away all of the death magic and allowed their swords to channel again. Madra had fled through the quicksilver immediately. Belikon had put up a prodigious fight, but the second Lorreth's angel breath had torn out of Avisiéth, he, too, had fled like a fucking coward.

"Oh really?" Carrion quirked a dubious eyebrow at me. "And how did Lorreth of the Broken Spire tell it? Let me guess. He said my blood was too rancid to be affected by vampire venom."

"No, he said that your father's blood was used to create the blood curse that allowed Malcolm to become a vampire, and that a vampire can't drink from the living members of the bloodline that created them, nor can they enthrall them. He said that drinking from you should have killed Malcolm instantly, but because he had lived for so long, he was too powerful."

"Hmm." Carrion grunted. "That's pretty accurate, actually."

"He also said that's why Malcolm had Belikon kill your parents. That they were the only thing that posed a threat to him."

Again, Carrion grunted. He wasn't grinning anymore. "I barely remember them."

"I do."

My heart stuttered in my chest. I'd been waiting for him to come for what felt like an age. Fisher stood just inside the door, a stony look on his face as he nodded to Carrion. His expression softened for me.

Hey, you, he whispered into my mind.

Hey back, I answered.

It was unbelievably comforting to know that this remained the same between us. He could still talk to me in my mind, and I could still talk to him. Of all the things that had changed so dramatically in the past few days, the bond between us seemed to be the same as it had been before.

The corners of his mouth twitched the tiniest bit—the faintest suggestion of a smile. He kept it as he entered the room properly and placed a light kiss on my forehead.

"Are you going to tell me about my parents, or are you going to start undressing each other? Because I can leave. I don't *have* to, but I can," Carrion said.

"Please leave, Carrion," Fisher said flatly. "I'll come and tell you everything I remember about them later, but for now, I want to be alone with my mate." He said it with such pride. My mate.

Carrion left, grumbling under his breath, and the room suddenly became much smaller. We were alone.

"Are you sad you don't get to call me Little Osha anymore?" I asked. Gods, what a confusing feeling. I was thrilled that, thanks to Zareth, a part of me was Fae now. I was less thrilled that a part of me was a vampire now, courtesy of Taladaius. Trepidation built inside me, growing more unbearable by the second, but Fisher hung his head in a very boyish way that made my insides squeeze.

He looked up at me from beneath his dark brows and smirked. "Human, Fae, or vampire. It doesn't matter how long you live, Saeris; you will *always* be most sacred to me." His smirk faded, though. "Did I do the right thing?"

I hadn't been able to answer for myself back in the labyrinth. He'd had to make the decision for me. And what a monumental decision it had been. After I refused to let him heal me with his soul, it was no wonder he was looking at me right now like he was worried I was never going to speak to him again.

This...was *huge.*

I wasn't myself anymore.

I was the ward of a god, and not just any old god. By proxy, Fisher kind of was too. There was so much I still had to tell him. I had no idea how he would take the news when I explained everything that had happened to him during those brief minutes I spent talking to the God of Chaos, but I got the feeling Fisher was going to have questions. A million of them.

For now, the world was brighter. Sharper. There were threads of shining power in Fisher's eyes when I looked at him. And there was a burning ache at the back of my throat that was getting harder to ignore.

Wait...

There was magic in Fisher's eyes.

But...less quicksilver.

I gasped, stepping out of his arms, and Fisher cleared his throat, looking a little abashed. "I was wondering if you'd notice," he said.

"Wondering if I'd notice! Wha—*how?* What happened?"

"Te Léna found a way to dampen the quicksilver's effects. I've been seeing her for months, trying to get it under control, but her sessions were growing less and less effective. And then Iseabail said that she could help. Those two make a pretty good team. Te Léna helped to quiet the quicksilver, and Iseabail's been teasing it out of me. I'll have to have a million sessions. It'll take a long time, but it should work."

"That's incredible! That means..." I was too nervous to say it.

He wasn't going to lose his mind.

We still had Belikon to deal with. And Madra. I still intended to find my brother and Elroy. There were a million other issues we had to overcome, but...

One foot in front of the other, Fisher rumbled, just for me. *Let's make it through today. And then tomorrow. And then the day after.* That *one will be particularly interesting.*

Why? What's happening the day after tomorrow?

He looked faintly worried as he took me by the hand. "Well. There's this." He took me to the curtain and drew it back slowly. The sunlight that had burned my eyes and my skin earlier was gone now. It was like peering into a black hole, staring out of the window. But then I saw the flickering lights of many, many campfires in the distance. And the pale silver ribbon of a river cutting through the black landscape.

The Darn.

We were on the wrong side of the Darn.

We were inside Ammontraíeth.

"In the Fae courts, the crown is passed down to a regent's heir. But if the regent is murdered, the crown is claimed by the one who slew them. The vampire court has only ever had one king. Malcolm never named an heir. He planned on living forever. He never conceived of the possibility that someone might kill him..."

My head was already shaking no. I retreated from the window. "Absolutely not. Fisher, I'm not even a full vampire. I'm half-Fae! I can't!"

"Tell *them* that. As far as the vampire court is concerned, you're to be coronated. In two days' time, you officially become the new queen of Sanasroth."

Callie Hart is a *USA Today* bestselling author of dark romance novels. She is an obsessive romantic who loves throwing a dark twist into her stories. Her characters are imperfect, flawed individuals who dictate when she eats, sleeps, and breathes. She loves to travel and often pens her books when she's on the road, drawing inspiration from her surroundings.